THE SPELL OF THE CONQUISTADOR . . .

Something moved in the shadows. "I've been looking for you, Marina," said the voice of Cortés.

Startled, I turned to face him. He was wearing an open-collared blouse of a soft, thin material that rippled like water when he moved. I hated him.

"Do you need me to translate for you?" I asked in a dull voice.

"Good Lord, no!" He laughed roughly, then took a deep breath. "I only wanted to tell you . . ." He stopped, frustrated.

"Oh the devil with it!" he exploded, and suddenly his arms were pulling me hard against him.

I could only cling to him, feeling the impact of that long, brutal kiss as I had never felt anything in my life . . .

MISTRESS OF THE MORNING STAR

A glorious pageant of tragic destinies—and triumphant love!

Acknowledgments

This book is dedicated to the many individuals who helped to make its completion possible. First and foremost is my husband, Guy, without whose support, patience and help I could never have finished this work. I also wish to thank the many friends and family members whose interest and encouragement kept me moving ahead. I am especially grateful to Dr. Jack A. Nelson for his professional advice and the loan of some precious books, and to Diane Subashe for typing the final manuscript.

I would be remiss if I did not acknowledge at least a few of the authors and historians whose work enabled me to obtain the information I needed: H. H. Bancroft, probably my most consistent source; W. H. Prescott; Salvador de Madariaga; Bernal Diaz, who was almost a tangible presence during the writing of this book; Jacques Soustelle, George C. Vaillant and Victor Von Hagen for their books about the Aztecs; and the Mexican historian, Fredrico Gómez Orozco. I would also like to thank the staff of the *Instituto de Investigaciones Históricas* of the University of Mexico for their assistance.

Elizabeth Lane

MISTRESS OF THE MORNING STAR

ELIZABETH LANE

A JOVE BOOK

First Jove edition published September 1980

10 9 8 7 6 5 4 3 2 1

Printed in the United States of America

Jove books are published by Jove Publications, Inc., 200 Madison Avenue, New York, NY 10016

Acknowledgments

This book is dedicated to the many individuals who helped to make its completion possible. First and foremost is my husband, Guy, without whose support, patience and help I could never have finished this work. I also wish to thank the many friends and family members whose interest and encouragement kept me moving ahead. I am especially grateful to Dr. Jack A. Nelson for his professional advice and the loan of some precious books, and to Diane Subashe for typing the final manuscript.

I would be remiss if I did not acknowledge at least a few of the authors and historians whose work enabled me to obtain the information I needed: H. H. Bancroft, probably my most consistent source; W. H. Prescott; Salvador de Madariaga; Bernal Diaz, who was almost a tangible presence during the writing of this book; Jacques Soustelle, George C. Vaillant and Victor Von Hagen for their books about the Aztecs; and the Mexican historian, Fredrico Gómez Orozco. I would also like to thank the staff of the *Instituto de Investigaciones Históricas* of the University of Mexico for their assistance.

Elizabeth Lane

Contents

The Characters

* These persons actually lived and an effort has been made to portray them and their roles in history as truthfully as possible on the basis of available information. In some cases, however, this information is so scanty that a generous amount of my own imagination has gone into the creation of their personalities.

** The historical counterparts of these characters existed. Actual names and personal details are not known.

*** These characters are fictional.

THE PEOPLE OF OLUTA

TENEPAL* Chief of the town of Oluta
MALINALLI (MARINA)* His daughter
CIMATL* His wife and Malinalli's mother
ATOTOTL** Their slave woman
MIAHUAXITL** Atototl's daughter
ITZCOATL** Tenepal's slave and Malinalli's tutor
COZCAQUAUHTLI*** Aztec priest of Huitzilopochtli and official representative of the Aztec emperor in Oluta
Two slave traders from Xicalango**

THE PEOPLE OF TABASCO

TABASCO* Ruling chief of the Mayan province of Tabasco
CHILAM** Chief of the town of Centla
IXEL*** Chilam's wife
TONAXEL (ANTONIA)*** Chilam's young slave and intended concubine
POTOP*** One of Chilam's slaves
NACONTOC*** A young boy purchased as a slave by Tabasco
MELCHOR* A captured Mayan used by the Spaniards as an interpreter

THE AZTECS

MOCTEZUMA II* *Uei tlatoani*, emperor of the Aztecs
TLACOTZIN* The *ciuacoatl*, supreme judge of the empire
CUITLAHUAC* Moctezuma's brother, ruler of Iztapalapan
CACAMA* Ruler of Texcoco, son of Moctezuma's sister and Nezhuapilli, late ruler of Texcoco
IXTLILXOCHITL* Cacama's brother
MAZATL** Sister of Cacama and Ixtlilxochitl
CUAUHTEMOC* Moctezuma's nephew
ASUPACACI* Moctezuma's legitimate son and heir
TECUICHPO* Moctezuma's only legitimate daughter
DOÑA ANA* and DOÑA INÉS* Moctezuma's daughters by his concubines
FRANCISCA* A slave girl
THE POCHTECA** A wealthy Aztec trader
QUAUHTLATOA*** The *pochteca*'s son
SANCHA*** A little girl taken as a prisoner of war

THE CEMPOALLANS (TOTONACS)

CHICOMACATL* Ruler of Cempoalla
DOÑA CATALINA* Chicomacatl's niece
DOÑA FRANCISCA* A Totonac princess
TEUCH* A Totonac chief

THE TLAXCALANS

MAXIXCATZIN* } Two of the four rulers of
XICOTENCATL THE ELDER* } Tlaxcala
XICOTENCATL THE YOUNGER* The Tlaxcalan military commander
DOÑA LUISA* Daughter of Xicotencatl the Elder
DOÑA ELVIRA* Niece of Maxixcatzin
CHICHIMECATL* A military leader
CALMECAHUA* A military leader

THE SPANIARDS

HERNÁN CORTÉS* Commander

The Captains

PEDRO DE ALVARADO*
GONZALO DE SANDOVAL*
JUAN VELÁSQUEZ DE LEÓN*
JUAN DE ESCALANTE
ALONZO DE ÁVILA*
ANDRÉS DE TAPIA*
FRANCISCO DE LUGO*
CRISTOBAL DE OLID*
ALONZO HERNÁNDEZ PUERTOCARRERO*
DIEGO DE ORDAZ*

The Soldiers

BERNAL DIAZ DEL CASTILLO*
JUAN JARAMILLO*
MORLA*
LARES, the Good Horseman*
LARES, the Blacksmith*
ORTIZ, the Musician*
JERONIMO DE AGUILAR*
The translator
BOTELLO, the Astrologer*
TRUJILLO, the Seaman*
FERNANDO ESTRADA***
PERO FARFÁN*
BERNARDINO DE CORIA*
MARTÍN LÓPEZ, the Shipbuilder*

FRAY BARTOLOME DE OLMEDO* } The priests
PADRE JUAN DIAZ* }
ORTEGUILLA* The youngest page
CRISTOBAL DE GUZMAN* Cortés's chamberlain
MARÍA DE ESTRADA* A Spanish lady from Cuba
DIEGO VELÁSQUEZ* Governor of Cuba
PANFILO DE NARVAEZ* Leader of Velasquez's expedition to capture Cortés
CATALINA JUÁREZ DE CORTÉS* Wife of Hernán Cortés
VIOLANTE RODRÍGUEZ* Catalina's Spanish maid
SALAZAR* AND CHIRIÑO* Two agents of the King of Spain
MARTÍN CORTÉS* Son of Hernán Cortés and Marina
MARÍA* Daughter of Marina

DEITIES

AYOPECHCATL The goddess of childbirth (Nahuatl)
CHAC The rain god (Mayan)
COATLIQUE Mother of Huitzilopochtli (Aztec)
HUITZILOPOCHTLI The sun god (Aztec)
IXBUNIC Protectress of women in childbirth (Mayan)
IXTACCIHUATL Popocatepetl's wife; the White Woman (Aztec)

POPOCATEPETL Volcano-god (Aztec)

QUETZALCOATL (Nahuatl) or KUKULKAN (Aztec) The Plumed Serpent; god of the east wind, wisdom, knowledge, culture

TEMAZCALTECI Patroness of midwives (Aztec)

TEXCATLIPOCA Lord of the Underworld (Aztec)

TLALOC The rain god (Aztec)

TLAZOTEOTL The Eater of Sins (Nahuatl)

XIPE TOTEC The Flayed One; god of spring (Aztec)

XOCHIPILLI The Prince of Flowers; god of spring (Nahuatl)

A MAP OF AZTEC MEXICO

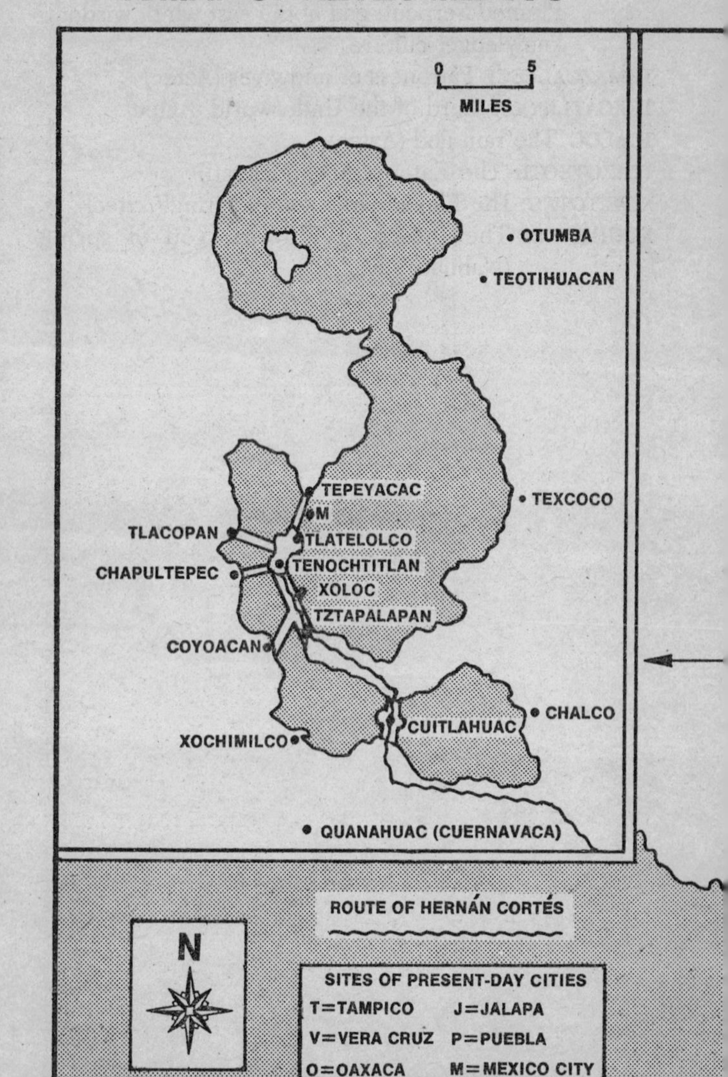

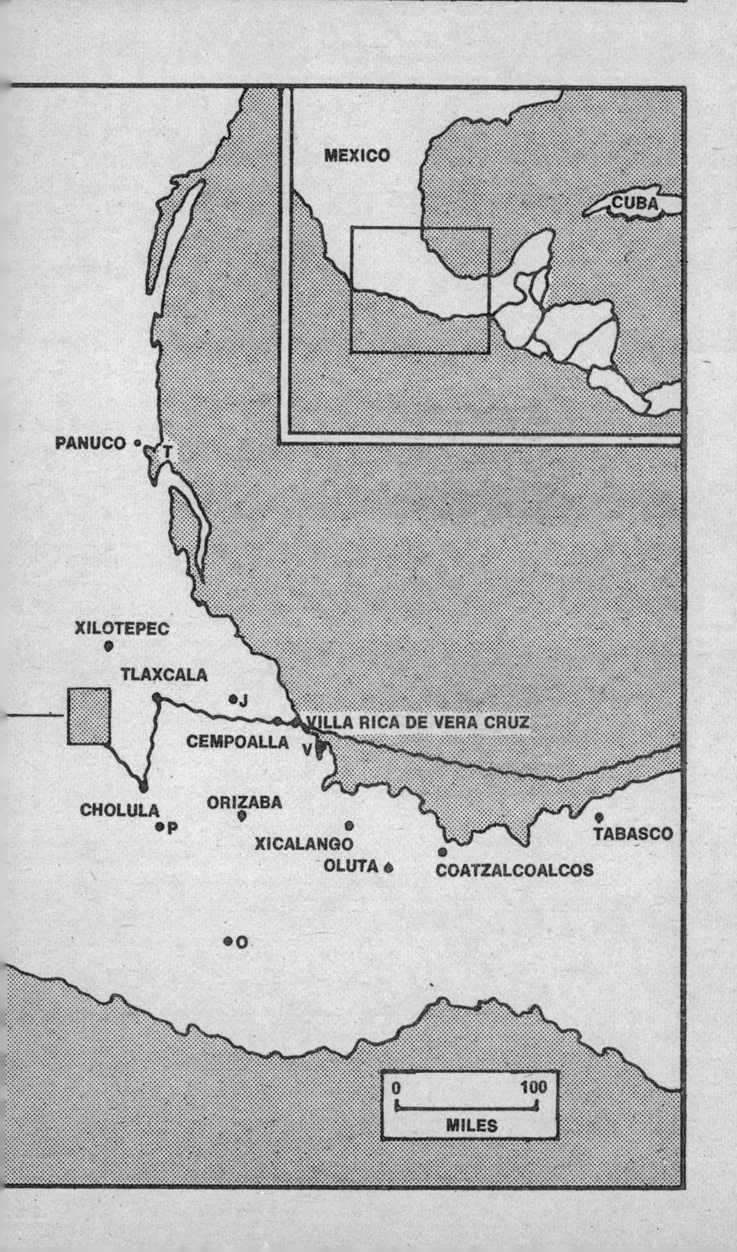
MEXICO
CUBA
PANUCO
T
XILOTEPEC
TLAXCALA
J
VILLA RICA DE VERA CRUZ
CEMPOALLA
V
CHOLULA
P
ORIZABA
XICALANGO
OLUTA
COATZALCOALCOS
TABASCO
O
0
100
MILES

Mexico—13 August 1528

My dearest María,

Today, as only a three-year-old can, you pushed my patience to its raw end. The issue was a dress, a silly piece of cloth. Sancha and I had made you an Indian costume to wear for the festival honoring the seventh anniversary of the fall of the Aztec empire, but you refused to put it on.

"I won't be an Indian!" you announced, and that was that. No threat, no bribe, not even my tears could move you. You went to the festival in your blue lace dress, a young Spanish lady from head to toe.

I always realized the time would come when you would choose between your father's world and mine, and I have even known what that choice would inevitably be. But I never expected it to come so soon.

Tonight I tiptoed out of your room, my eyes wet once more from the sight of you sleeping there so peacefully, so innocently. I walked out into the garden, trembling as I stared at the lilies, wondering when you would hear that first whisper, that first taunt. Wondering whether, when you knew, you would be ashamed of me.

You're bound to hear those whispers as you grow older, most likely from unkind lips. You'll hear what they call me: La Malinche, the traitoress, Cortés's whore. They're not pretty names. They've hurt me. They'll hurt you too, unless I can build a wall of truth around you to keep out the lies. Yet you must come to know that I am what I am: Doña Marina, the woman who walked with Hernán Cortés over the crushed bones of Tenochtitlan on that terrible day when the old gods of my people took flight forever.

How can I tell you? And when? You are so young, my daughter, so short of the understanding you will need. And already I feel the press of eternity upon me. I sense that by the time you are old enough to hear my story I may not be with you to tell it.

The best midwives in Mexico have examined me. All of them say the same thing: "Señora, you should not have taken the risk of having another child!" But your father has always wanted a son. You need a brother or a sister. If I must end my life, what better, braver way could there be than in the natural culmination of the love that flows between your father and me?

Your father worries. He agonizes so over the danger in which this very love has placed me. My gravest concern is that if I die he will take the burden of guilt upon himself, as he often does. Reach out to him, my little one. Comfort him in any small way you can or that burden will crush him.

I count the months ahead. There's so little time left. This very night I must begin with all haste to preserve my story for you, that you might learn to value your full heritage. I cannot bear the thought of your growing up without having known your grandfather, a Nahua chieftain as valiant as any knight who ever walked the streets of Spain, or your grandmother, a lovely, tragic woman. I want you to know the truth about me and to understand—for in years to come you'll need this understanding—that I was never the betrayer of my people.

You are a child of two worlds. Spanish and Indian blood flows in your veins, each as fine and noble as the other. It is only right that you be equally proud of both.

Yet I understand your choice. Your father's world surrounds us. My world, at least the world of my childhood, has disappeared. What you see of it now is no more than its pathetic remains. The power, the pride, the colossal savagery that was Mexico before Spanish civilization devastated its length and breadth has crumbled to dust and blown away on the east wind.

Permit me, daughter of mine, to bring it back for you. Come with me now. See it through my eyes. Hear it through my ears. Live with me through the first links in a chain of happenings that led me from a pampered childhood as the only daughter of a Nahua chieftain to bondage in the land of the Mayas. Feel, if you can, what my own heart felt the day when I stood on the beach at Tabasco and caught my first glimpse of the men we called the White Gods. And try to understand that I was no better able to resist the power of a man like Hernán Cortés than were all the armies of the land of my childhood, a land that fought valiantly to protect its great heritage, but was perhaps already doomed by divisiveness and by the ferocity it unleashed against its own people.

Chapter One

Oluta—1507

As you get older, María, you'll hear the horror tales of the Aztecs and their passion for human sacrifice—how the emperor Ahuitzotl had twenty thousand hearts ripped out on the altar to celebrate the completion of the huge pyramid-temple on the very site where the cathedral now stands; how no day could begin without fresh blood to feed the Aztec sun god, Huitzilopochtli, in his journey across the sky. Believe them, my daughter. These things and worse were true.

My father, Tenepal, was the *tlatoani*, or chief, of Oluta, and had long been opposed to the Aztecs and their human sacrifices. In spite of his unimposing appearance, he was respected by his subjects. From the young children on up, all had heard the story of how a younger Tenepal, with the ferocity of a jaguar, had led his warriors against the forces of the Aztec emperor, Ahuitzotl, who had decided it was time to bring Oluta under his rule. My father's wife and younger son were carried away, along with many others, to be sacrificed on the bloody altars of Tenochtitlan, and the elder of his two sons was killed in the fighting. Tenepal himself, gravely wounded, was carried from the battlefield by night and hidden in a cellar where his followers kept a deathwatch over him. He made a surprising recovery and went on to govern his people under the chafe of Aztec dominion; to marry the beautiful Cimatl, young daughter of the ruling family of nearby Xaltipan; and, in his old age, to become my father. He also became increasingly outspoken in his hatred of human sacrifice, a practice that showed no abatement under Ahuitzotl's successor, Moctezuma.

I remember passing with my father in front of the Aztec temple of Huitzilopochtli, which stood at the entrance to the marketplace. The temple steps and altar reeked of human blood, and the wisp of black smoke rising from the *teocalli* at its summit mingled with the odor of burning human hearts and stung my nostrils. Shaking his head in disgust, my father muttered, "Who fed the sun before these Aztec vultures came to Oluta?"

And I, child that I was, could only parrot what I'd been taught by the Aztec priests at the temple school: "If he's not fed human blood, the sun god will not have strength to rise. Tlaloc, the rain god, must have gifts of human hearts or he won't send rain. And in order for spring to come, we must give to Xipe Totec, the Flayed One, gifts of—"

"I know!" my father sputtered under his breath. "Before Ahuitzotl took Oluta we worshipped gentle gods—Quetzalcoatl . . . Xochipilli, the Prince of Flowers . . . Tlazoteotl, the Eater of Sins. Kind gods! We gave them flowers, butterflies, an occasional turkey at the most, and they were satisfied!"

He stopped and watched the thin column of black smoke rise into the sky over the pyramid of Huitzilopochtli, then looked sternly down at me. "I'm taking you out of the temple school, Malinalli," he said. "We'll find a teacher who'll educate you at home."

It was only a few days later that he found such a teacher, when we happened to be in a far corner of the market where slaves were sold. The slaves, perhaps a dozen of them, stood in a dejected row Some were well-dressed and unfettered. Others, mostly young men, slumped into the wooden collars around their necks, hostility in their eyes.

"Tenepaltzin, my lord! How can I serve you?" The voice of the slave dealer was as oily as his appearance. His long hair was elaborately coiffed in an imitation of the Aztec *calpixque* who came to town every few months to collect the tribute for Moctezuma. Around his neck he wore a broad collar of hammered gold. His abundant flesh hung in loose, quivering folds over the top of his loincloth, and even in the coolness of early morning he was glittering with perspiration. A tiny, naked boy stood beside him, wielding a fly-whisk made of reeds.

"Perhaps your wife needs a girl to care for her clothing and dress her hair." He turned to the line of slaves and pulled roughly forward a girl of thirteen or fourteen with huge, frightened eyes. She was wearing a simple cotton *huipilli*, well made but soiled. Her hair was unbraided and tangled.

"She's from Xaltipan, your wife's town. What do you think, eh? The girl's healthy and well formed. In no time she'll be a beautiful woman." His eyes gleamed suggestively.

My father shook his head. "You know my wife. Cimatl likes old women to wait on her. She wouldn't want a girl this age." He spoke the truth. Even at my young age I sensed that my mother would stand for no competition with her own beauty.

The little eyes of the slave dealer almost disappeared in the folds of his fat face as he gave a rueful smile. "Ah, yes, I'd almost forgotten what Cimatl said when I tried to get you to buy that pretty seventeen-year-old from Xochitlan. Ay! My ears stung for a month! You should have bought her anyway, Tenepal, just to show your wife that you were master."

My father sighed. "I can't function without peace in my house. Whatever the price of that peace, I'll pay it."

The slave dealer, motioning the girl back to her place, glanced down the row of slaves and singled out a tall young man with a wooden collar around his neck. "Now here's a fine specimen for you. Handsome as a god. Just before you came by I was talking with the priest," he said, referring to Cozcaquauhtli, Moctezuma's representative in Oluta. "He mentioned that something special would be needed for the New Year ceremony. This fellow is being sold for the third time, so he can be bought for sacrifice."

"I don't buy sacrifices," my father growled. "If Cozcaquauhtli wants a slave for his altar, let *him* do the buying." He studied the young man, who was of above-average height, finely proportioned though slender, with proud, classic features, lustrous deep-set eyes, flawless teeth, and thick, shining hair cut square at the shoulders. "The third time, you say? What's wrong with him? He looks intelligent enough."

"I won't lie to you, my lord. He's as lazy as he is handsome. He was here sold twice because neither of his masters could get him to work." He shrugged, his heavy flesh rolling with the gesture. "But that should make no difference to the gods."

The young man had been bending forward as far as the long pole attached to his collar would let him. "Great lord," he begged, "won't you let me speak for myself?"

"You have no right to speak," the slave dealer rumbled. "But perhaps if the *tlatoani* has the time and wants to hear you . . ."

My father nodded.

"You think I was born to this?" The slave s eyes were melancholy. "My name is Itzcoatl, from Tochtepec and of noble birth." His fine voice breaking, he told of how his father had died when he was sixteen, and how he'd been sold by an uncle to pay his debts. "They put me to work in the *milpas* and made me carry loads that almost broke my back. They'd have killed me if I'd let them. Great one, I'm well educated. I can write letters, keep accounts, sing, recite poetry, play the flute . . . the *teponatzli* . . ." He swallowed a sob. "Is it my fault my masters didn't put me to proper use?" He fell to his knees and gazed up imploringly at my father, his eyes brimming. "Buy me! I can keep your accounts, teach your children music, history, poetry. I can entertain your guests with my singing. You'll never be sorry." His hands clutched at my father's legs. "I don't want to be sacrificed!"

My father stepped backward at his touch. "Stand on your feet. I like dignity in a man, even in a slave. You say you can keep accounts?" The young man nodded. "I have a storehouse full of tribute for Moctezuma. Keeping track of what goes into it is nothing but a trial for me. If you can do it accurately you'll be worth any price I have to pay for you." He restrained Itzcoatl from falling at his feet again. "When you're not working in the tribute house you can tutor my daughter." He turned to the slave dealer. "What are you asking for him?"

"Very little, my lord," the slave dealer answered quickly, rubbing his chin. "Only four bundles of cotton cloth."

"I believe the customary price for a slave who is being sold the third time is two bundles of cloth," my father said. "I'll have them delivered to you before midday. When you have the cloth, set this fellow free from his collar and kindly direct him to my house."

"He'll run away. You'll never see the rascal again!"

"The man promised to serve me. If he's not to be trusted, better he make his disappearance at once." My father fixed his gaze on Itzcoatl. The slave was trembling with joy and would have kissed his new master's dusty sandals if the rigid wooden collar hadn't prevented it.

"I won't run away, my lord," he breathed. "You can trust me with your life!"

I didn't enjoy the time I was forced to spend with Itzcoatl. Not only did I miss my friends at the temple school, but Izcoatl had turned out to be vain and unpleasant and was a stern taskmaster. When my attention wandered he would beat my hands with a thorny stick or take me to the kitchen and force me to inhale the smoke of burning chili peppers. My parents looked upon such punishments as a necessary part of my education. Most children were disciplined in the same manner. Since I had never been treated harshly by my father,

I was resentful. To please my father, however, I studied hard, spending day after tedious day memorizing the history and poetry that Itzcoatl taught me.

My mother, Cimatl, would often come into the room during the lessons and sit with her loom, listening as Itzcoatl recited and I repeated the lines after him. She was so lovely, with flowers from the garden braided into her hair, long gold earrings dangling on either side of her graceful neck, her face agleam with *axin*, a cosmetic that gave the skin a pale yellowish glow. She wove all her own clothing and her *huipillis* were trimmed with exquisite embroidery.

Sometimes when the lesson was finished, Itzcoatl would reach for his *teponatzli*, a small, two-toned wooden drum that he played with round-tipped beaters. As he sang in a high, clear voice, tapping out the rhythm of the song, his eyes would rest on my mother, caressing her from the top of her flower-crowned head to her little sandaled feet. She would lower her gaze modestly, glancing up at him from time to time through her long lashes. These were uncomfortable moments for me. I was always relieved when a slave would call to my mother or when my father would arrive to take Itzcoatl to the tribute house, where the rich goods demanded by Moctezuma were stored.

In spite of my father's constant reminders that the payment of tribute to the Aztecs was a burden to our people, I liked visiting the tribute house almost as much as I enjoyed strolling through the market. It was dark inside, and cool. Only the light from the doorway and from the torches on the walls illuminated the mountainous stacks of cotton bales and sacks of beans, corn and feathers. Spotted hides of ocelot and jaguar, tanned with urine and giving off a musky scent, were piled higher than I could reach. Carriers trotted in with bundles on their backs, pausing while Itzcoatl jotted down the contents. As part of my training for future leadership I was allowed to unroll the long scroll of *amatl* paper and read from the tribute list.

"Two thousand quills filled with liquid amber," I would read in a singsong voice. "Four hundred tortoise shells, two thousand bags of *chocolatl* beans, forty bags of parrot feathers, twelve hundred bundles of cotton, two hundred live turkeys, two hundred bags of cochineal, the skins of forty jaguars, twenty pumas and twenty ocelots, one hundred sixty jars of honey, four hundred baskets of maize, two jade necklaces . . ."

The joy I took in working with my father on those occasions

was suddenly dispelled one day with the arrival of Cozcaquauhtli, high priest of Huitzilopochtli and Moctezuma's personal representative in Oluta. Without announcing himself he glided through the entrance, a tall man whose name, meaning "vulture," fitted him aptly. His face and body were cadaverous from constant fasting. His earlobes, hands and feet were a mass of scars in various stages of healing from daily bloodletting. Cozcaquauhtli was known throughout the Aztec world for his piety. It was even said that he thrust maguey spines through his penis, but I wasn't sure I believed it.

His waist-length hair was matted and caked with sacrificial blood, as was the loose-fitting black robe he wore. He towered over my stocky father as he spoke. "I see that the young princess reads well, even though you've taken her out of school."

"She learns faster at home," my father said with a shrug.

"Not that it's my affair," said the priest, "but as the future *tlatoani* and as a vassal of Moctezuma, shouldn't she be learning about our gods? I suspect she's not being adequately instructed in your house."

"Your gods turn my stomach," my father said, "and I have the right to educate my daughter as I see fit. Is that the only reason you've come?"

"Indeed not," the priest snapped. As always, when confronted by my father, Cozcaquauhtli's patience was in short supply. "I came to talk to you about the binding of the sheaf. Don't you realize it's only fifteen days away?" He reached into the folds of his bloodstained robe and drew out a roll of *amatl* paper, straightening it with a flourish. "This letter, my friend, was brought to me by special runner from Tenochtitlan. It's from the *ciuacoatl* himself."

The *ciuacoatl* was the supreme judge of the Aztec empire, second in authority only to the emperor. I listened with interest as Cozcaquauhtli read the letter, which requested that the major towns outside the valley of Mexico hold their own ceremonies of the lighting of the new fires. Each town was to duplicate the rites at Tenochtitlan with its own special sacrifice.

"I should have known that none of your rituals would be complete without a sacrifice," my father said sourly. "But we've only had ten years to get used to your ways and I don't know anything about your sheaf-tying ceremony or the lighting of new fires."

"Your daughter knows," the priest said. "She learned it in school. Tell him, Malinalli."

I glanced at my father for approval. "The binding of the sheaf," I recited in a small voice, well aware that he wouldn't be pleased by what he heard, "takes place at the end of every fifty-two-year calendar cycle. The old priest tells us that if the gods choose to put an end to our world they will do so at this time." I looked up, hoping I'd said enough.

"Tell your father how the world will end, Malinalli." The priest nudged my ribs with a bony finger, making me cringe.

"The stars will stop moving." Mechanically, I repeated the words of the old priest who had been my teacher. "The sun won't return to the sky and the night will stay forever. All the pregnant women will turn into *tzitzimitles*, who will fall on the people and devour them. After that the fire will come down from the sky and from the inside of the earth, consuming all the world and leaving nothing but ashes."

"That's enough, Malinalli," my father said disgustedly.

Cozcaquauhtli took up the instruction, his voice hoarse with conviction. With the arrival of the *nemontemi*, the five empty days that came at the end of the year and belonged to no month, the people were to throw all their household utensils—the *metatls*, the cooking pots, the *cumals*, the dishes, even the old household gods—into the river. The bare houses, he continued, were to be swept clean and all fires extinguished. "No fire," he warned my father, "not even the smallest torch, is to be left burning for the entire five days and nights." On the last night of the year, all the people except the pregnant women were to assemble in the square before the great temple. The astrologers would watch the heavens, especially the *mamalhoaztli*, the seven little stars that cluster together near the three bright ones, for when these stars passed the middle of the sky the astrologers would know that the world was to continue for another fifty-two years.

"And the sacrifice?" my father asked.

"I was coming to that," said the priest, brushing away the flies that had settled on a spot of fresh blood on his sleeve. "When the astrologers signal that the stars are still moving, the priests will lay the chosen one on the altar." I trembled, for I knew that next they would plunge an obsidian dagger into the sacrificial victim's chest and rip out his heart as an offering to the gods. The first fire of the new calendar cycle would be ignited by the high priest in the wound from which the heart was removed. As the fire grew, it would be fed first the heart, then the entire body of the victim. "The flames of the sacred fire will be carried to every house, lighting the new torches and hearths in even the poorest huts." Cozcaquauhtli's eyes gleamed. "It's of the greatest importance that the man chosen for sacrifice be worthy of the privilege."

"You can call it a privilege," my father said. "I'd call it something else."

The priest ignored him. "A man noble of character, fierce in battle. A man whose death will please the gods . . ." Something in his voice made me feel cold. "I want you to choose him, Tenepal."

My father paused only momentarily before replying. "You get your victims from the cages every day. You know the prisoners better than I do. If one is braver or nobler than the others, how should I know? Why don't you choose one yourself?"

"Because you're *tlatoani* and it's high time you took an active part in our rituals. Why, in some cities, the *tlatoani* even performs the sacrifice." The priest brushed away the flies that had tangled themselves in his long, blood-matted hair. "Out of consideration for your feelings, Tenepal, I haven't asked you to do that. But Moctezuma looks to his priests to tell him who's loyal. I wouldn't want to have to put you in an uncomfortable position."

"I'm a busy man," my father said. "I'll look over the prisoners if I have time, but don't go into one of your famous fasts while you're waiting for me to choose a victim for you. You might starve to death."

The priest's neck twitched convulsively as he glared at my father. "One more thing," he said tightly. "In another thirty days the *calpixque* will be here to collect the tribute. It's to be ready, along with enough *tlamemes* to carry it back to Tenochtitlan."

"It will be. Most of it's here already." My father's eyes narrowed slyly as he gazed at the stacks of tribute goods and gave a sigh of mock weariness. "It's been so much work, collecting and counting it, it's discouraging to think that if the world comes to an end all that effort will have been for nothing."

"You forget yourself at times, Tenepal. The old emperor let you continue here as *tlatoani* because he respected your courage, but Ahuitzotl's dead and Moctezuma has no use for troublemakers. If word gets back to him that you speak out against sacrifice and that you begrudge him the small tribute he asks in return for your wretched lives—"

"Small tribute!" My father spat on the dusty flagstones. "It's tribute that keeps Oluta in poverty! And I'd say it to Moctezuma's face if he were here!"

"Tenepal, you're a fool! One day you'll forget to pull in your tongue and Moctezuma will cut it off!" The priest whirled angrily, stalking out of the tribute house and back through the market toward the pyramid of Huitzilopochtli.

My father flicked his eyes about the tribute house. "Thirty days!" he exclaimed, gruff with irritation. "Itzcoatl, tell me again how much we lack."

"Eight hundred bundles of cotton, ten bags of feathers and the two jade necklaces, my lord."

"A curse on the tribute! And on Moctezuma! They think Oluta's nothing but a treasure chest without a bottom. Two jade necklaces, when even one's worth enough to keep a man and his family for ten years! And where am I going to get them?" He was pacing, his sandals shuffling against the flagstones with the odd meter of his limping gait. "The jade in our market is so poor that the *calpixque* reject it on sight and take the whole matter as a personal insult. And I don't need to tell you, Itzcoatl, the kinds of things they'll do to us if we come up short . . ."

I'd heard his tirades before but this one was even more vehement than usual. I watched him in silence, suddenly—and unaccountably—afraid for him. "Our people go hungry!" he raged. "They go ragged just so Moctezuma and his parasites can have a fresh change of clothing every day. Our sons die on his altars. Our daughters are carried off to become concubines and prostitutes in Tenochtitlan! He leaves us bloodless! And the gods, wherever they are, do nothing!" Worried, I glanced around to see if anyone was listening. Only Itzcoatl stood beside us in the flickering torchlight, eyes lowered, face impassive as my father muttered, "Right now, if I could die with my *maquahuitl* buried in Moctezuma's neck I'd die a happy man." He stopped speaking, his venom spent for the moment, and let the tension drain out of his body in one long breath. I slipped my hand into his and he gave me a sad smile.

"My lord," Itzcoatl spoke up, "there's a new dealer in jade in the market. There's a chance he may have the quality we need. With your permission, I'd like to go and see."

"Go," my father said. "If he has anything worth looking at,

come back and get me. I'll be busy here until dark." He turned away and became absorbed in counting jaguar pelts. Out of the corner of my eye, I saw Itzcoatl walking swiftly away, not toward the jade sellers' stalls but in the direction the high priest had taken.

I would never forget that ominous third night of the *nemontemi.* Not one flame cast its glow in the thick, heavy darkness, for every fire in the empire of Moctezuma had been extinguished. The people huddled on their sleeping mats, restless and wakeful, as even familiar night sounds set their hearts to pounding with fear. Only the little fireflies paid no heed to the emperor's decree. In joyful defiance they flitted through the night, flickering unexpectedly in many a dark corner or soaring so high that their tiny lights blended with those of the cold, distant stars.

The shuffle of sandals on the stones of the street outside startled me into alertness. It was not the distinct steps of one person I heard, but the muffled tread of several pairs of feet. They stopped at the door and a voice called, "Tenepal, my lord! We must speak with you!"

I heard my father's footsteps as he went to the entrance of the house and pulled aside the heavy cloth curtain that covered the doorway. Jumping up, I ran softly to his side. By the light of the thin moon I could make out his disheveled hair and jutting nose. Then I caught my breath as I saw the tall figure standing outside. Even in silhouette, no one in Oluta could mistake the gaunt, wild-haired form of Cozcaquauhtli.

"You're to come with us, Tenepal," he said coldly. "I have a letter from Moctezuma himself, authorizing me to take you prisoner in his name."

"May I ask why?" my father said calmly.

"Because you're an enemy to the *uei tlatoani,* and as such you're liable to arrest. You've spoken out openly against him and against our gods. You've spoken against the payment of tribute to which he is entitled."

"If that's all, why didn't you arrest me years ago? My feelings toward the emperor are well known. I've said nothing new."

"I'm not finished," said the priest. "We have it on good authority that you're plotting against Moctezuma's life. Do you deny it?"

"Certainly I deny it! I'm not fool enough to attempt the impossible."

"Then if you deny plotting to kill the *uei tlatoani*, can you also deny ever expressing the desire to murder him?"

So that was it. My father gave a disgusted snort. "I won't lie, even to you, Cozcaquauhtli. There've been times when I've wished I could kill him, but a wish and a plan are two different things. Anyone who interprets a fanciful desire as a plan is either stupid or lying!" His voice was emotionless but his hand had tightened around mine.

"Tenepal, what is it?" My mother had awakened and come into the room. She gasped as she recognized the high priest.

"This man says he has reason to arrest me," my father said quietly. "Suppose I refuse to go? What then?"

Cozcaquauhtli stepped away from the entrance to reveal four Aztec soldiers standing behind him, each armed with an obsidian-edged *maquahuitl* that could sever a man's neck with one blow. "Should you resist, my lord Tenepal, these men will have no mercy on your household."

At this, my mother seized me and, clutching me in her arms, retreated into a corner.

"You're every bit as much a monster as you look," my father said. "Very well, I've no choice but to go with you, but prepare yourself for a fight, priest. My people are loyal to me."

"Your people are so many rabbits!" Cozcaquauhtli snapped. "They'll run wherever they're driven. If you expect them to rise up and set you free, you'll be disappointed, Tenepal."

The high priest motioned to the soldiers, who quickly moved through the doorway and surrounded my father. "I've had my fill of this man's speaking," he said icily. "Take him away!" With a flourish of his bloodstained robe, he had wheeled around to follow the soldiers and their prisoner when I tore loose from my mother's arms and rushed to attack him, scratching and clawing at his legs in fury.

"You beast!" I shrieked. "You monster! You can't take my father!" I'd fallen to the floor and was pounding his feet with my fists. With as little loss of dignity as possible, Cozcaquauhtli disengaged himself and limped out of the door and down the street after the soldiers, blood streaming down the back of one leg where I'd sunk my teeth into his calf.

It came as a shock to the people of Oluta when the high priest announced from the steps of the pyramid that the *tlatoani* had chosen to offer his own life in the ceremony of the lighting of new fires. For the most part, however, it was hailed as a noble gesture. People who had been apprehensive about the coming of the new year now breathed more freely. Surely, they said, the sacrifice of such a courageous, honest and intelligent man as Tenepal would please the gods and insure a prosperous future.

There were those who asked questions, of course. If the *tlatoani* was offering his life willingly, why was he being held in a bamboo cage behind the temple? And why was a soldier stationed in the street outside Tenepal's house, permitting no one to enter or leave except the slave Itzcoatl, who was still occupied with counting the tribute for Moctezuma? But there were few who dared ask these questions, and their voices were no more than whispers.

For the most part, the people of Oluta accepted their *tlatoani's* impending death as they accepted droughts, hunger, disease, poverty and the sacrifice of their children. Everyone died sooner or later, and sacrifice was the most honorable of deaths. My father would be assured a place in the Kingdom of the Sun. Who could wish for more?

The priest had been correct after all in his assessment of my father's subjects.

The big drum atop the pyramid of Huitzilopochtli palpitated with the two-thump cadence of a heartbeat, telling the people that the final moments of their fifty-two-year calendar cycle had arrived. The people obeyed the call of the throbbing tones, leaving their houses and pouring into the pitch-black streets. They moved haltingly through the darkness toward the square, where the paraphernalia of the market had been cleared away to make room for the crowd that was to come for the ceremony. Young men, old men, women and children groped their way through the blackness. Only the pregnant women were missing. They had been shut securely into their houses as a precaution against their turning into the voracious *tzitzimitles*. The men carried unlit torches of pitch-pine to convey the new fire to their hearths in the event that the gods allowed the stars to continue their movement through the sky. Each person carried a sharp maguey thorn with which to draw blood from his earlobes if the fire was rekindled.

I stood beside my mother on a decorated platform near the steps of the pyramid. Though I felt weak and my eyes were rimmed with red, I shed no tears. I had promised my father that I would conduct myself as a *tlatoani*.

The night before, I had stolen out of the house, bribed the guard of the prison compound with a little piece of jade, and slipped through the darkness to sit beside my father as he squatted alone in his bamboo cage. "Look at this!" I'd fumbled in my sash and triumphantly pulled out an ornamental dagger that had come from among his ceremonial gear. "Cut the lashings on your cage! You can escape!"

"My little cub!" He reached through the bars and clasped my shoulder. "What's my life worth if I buy it at the cost of others? What do you think Moctezuma would do to our people if I ran away?" Awkwardly, he tried to pull me close to him. "Do you think being *tlatoani* only means living in a fine house, wearing a plumed headdress and having people bow to you?" He shook his head. "It carries a heavy burden, Malinalli. The *tlatoani* must always put the welfare of his people before his own."

I cried then—hot, stinging tears that trickled down my cheeks and over my father's hands. "Spend your tears now," he whispered. "Tomorrow night you'll be *tlatoani* and the people must not see you weep. Be brave. Set an example for them with your courage."

"I'll try, Father." My voice was choking.

"Now go, my precious one, before you break my heart."

But I only sobbed all the harder and clung so tightly to the bars of the cage that my wet fingers gleamed white in the starlight. It was nearly dawn before the guard came and led me away.

Now, in the square, the soldiers were clearing a path for the procession that was making its way through the throng toward the steps of the temple. Cozcaquauhtli came first, wearing a clean robe and the elaborate headdress of the god Huitzilopochtli, whom he served. In his hand he carried two pieces of dry wood, a spindle and a plank, which would ignite the new fire on his victim's breast. He was followed by other high-ranking priests, each dressed as a god: dark-visaged Tezcatlipoca, lord of the Underworld; Tlaloc, grim god of rain and water; Xipe Totec, god of spring, dressed in the flayed skin of that morning's sacrifice, and the green-plumed Quetzalcoatl. My father came next, walking slowly with his head held high. He was so heavily painted and covered with red plumes, representing fire, that except for his distinctive limp even I would have failed to recognize him. He was followed by the lesser priests, simply dressed in clean robes, along with the astrologers and an old man known as the Master of the Heavens, who would know whether the stars had passed the midpoint of the sky.

The column snaked its way through the crowded square, circled the pyramid once and began to make its way up the long flight of steps. They passed the platform where I stood. My eyes followed my father's plumed figure upward through the darkness until he disappeared into the *teocalli* with the others. Only the Master of the Heavens remained outside, staring intently at the starry sky.

Below, the people waited in fearful silence. Families huddled together, awaiting the pronouncement of hope or doom. All eyes were on the *mamalhoaztli*, the cluster of seven tiny stars that glittered directly overhead. Each watcher tried to determine whether the stars were passing the meridian of the sky, but only the Master of the Heavens could tell them for certain. They strained their eyes for a glimpse of some sign from the old man, their fear and expectancy muting all sound and seeming to slow time to a halt.

I heard the distant hoot of an owl and the thudding of my own heart against my ears as I waited for the sight of the flame that would tell us all that the priest had torn out my father's heart. I began to pray that the gods would choose to end the world instead.

Suddenly, from the doorway of the *teocalli*, there was a faint flicker of light. The light flared and grew stronger. A sound like the roaring of the sea rose from the multitude in the square. Soon a priest appeared at the top of the steps with a flaming brazier in his hand, followed by the lesser priests, who thrust pine torches into the fire. All the men and women pierced their earlobes with thorns, sprinkling blood in the direction of the new fire. With their torches blazing, the young priests hurried down the steps, stopping to give light to those who pressed around them. Before long every torch in the square was aflame, lighting up the joyful faces of the people, the temples with their idols, the tribute house, the streets and the homes. On the platform near the temple steps, the light illuminated the pale face of my mother, who trembled as the blood dripped from her earlobes and stained her white *huipilli*. Standing beside her, I stared ahead with an emotionless face. My dry eyes flashed with life only when I glanced down at the golden headdress of the *tlatoani*, with its trailing green plumes, which I cradled tenderly in my arms.

Chapter Two

Oluta—1512–1516

My mother had been chosen to act as *tlatoani* until I came of the proper age. She was a master of the arts of clothmaking, running a household and making herself beautiful, but she was ill-prepared to manage the complicated affairs of Oluta. After several costly mistakes she became increasingly dependent on Itzcoatl for assistance and advice. It was only a matter of time before everyone in the town knew that while I was hereditary *tlatoani* and my mother was acting *tlatoani*, it was the sharpeyed, efficient Itzcoatl who truly ruled Oluta.

With Itzcoatl's new-found authority came an assertiveness that rapidly became arrogance. I recall the time when I went to the market alone, something not permitted, and he punished me by ordering me to my room. I refused, haughtily reminding him, "You are only a slave!"

"All that will soon change," he said coldly. And indeed it did, for soon afterwards he married my mother. Although it was proper for a widow to marry a member of her dead husband's family, all of my father's male relatives had lost their lives in battle except for one old man who had no teeth and could no longer hold his water. This left my mother free to wed anyone she chose, and she chose Itzcoatl.

Even before their marriage my mother had come to depend more and more upon the handsome slave. His influence crept into every aspect of her life. Not only the ruling of Oluta, but the management of our household, the treatment of the other slaves, my own training and discipline, even the selection of her clothes and jewelry came under his dominion.

"Itzcoatl, sometimes I feel as though you were the master and I were your slave," I heard her say to him once, and she laughed like a young girl as she said it. My sober, dutiful mother had changed remarkably from the days when my father was alive. She twined flowers in her hair and sang every day as she sat at her loom. When Itzcoatl was near, her laughter filled the house.

Every important person in the province came to their wedding. They gave a sumptuous feast with turkey, dog, pheasant, beans, yams, agave worms in chili sauce, three different kinds of tamales, and frothy *chocolatl*, the drink of the gods, whipped with wooden beaters and sweetened with honey. My mother and Itzcoatl sat together on a reed mat before the hearth while an old woman tied the corners of their cloaks together and the ceremony was completed.

As I wandered among the feasting, laughing guests, dodging tottering old men and women who reeked of *octli*—for only the very old were allowed to get drunk—I had never felt so alone. I sought refuge with my friend Miahuaxitl, the daughter of my mother's slave, old Atototl. I went into the kitchen where Miahuaxitl was helping her mother make fresh *tlaxcalli*, took my friend's hand, and led her out of the house and up the street to the edge of the forest. Angrily, silently, I kept on walking, deeper and deeper into the dark green labyrinth of twisted trees, ferns, hanging vines and unearthly noises. By the time I finally gave in to Miahuaxitl's tearful pleas and turned around to go back, we were lost. We spent the next several hours wandering in circles or huddling together in the blackness, trembling at the distant hunting call of a jaguar. Toward dawn, the torch-carrying searchers finally found us. They brought us back to confront my pale-faced mother, the hysterical Atototl, and the livid Itzcoatl, whose wedding night had been ruined by my disappearance. I was beaten with a thorny branch by my new stepfather and forbidden to leave the house for a month.

Marriage agreed with my mother, at least in the beginning. She grew plump and gentle, humming as she walked about the house like a great purring cat. Listening to the sounds that came from their room at night, I sensed that there was something between her and Itzcoatl that had been missing when she was married to my father. Her attitude toward Tenepal, I realized, had been only that of a dutiful wife. It had taken the handsome, poetic Itzcoatl to ignite the fires of passion within her. It was not many months before her belly was round with child. In spite of her good health the pregnancy was clouded with anxiety. The deaths of the infants whose births had followed my own were well remembered. When her confinement came the members of our household walked softly and spoke guardedly, preparing themselves for another sickly yellow baby who would live no more than a day or two. But to everyone's delight, my mother brought forth a beautiful, red, squalling son. She put him to her breast and he nursed ravenously, like a young puma, while Atototl loudly declared how fortunate it was that the curse that had sickened the other babies had died with my father.

They named him Xochipilli, the prince of flowers. From the moment of his birth he became the darling of the house. I loved to carry him about in my arms, singing little songs to him as he gazed up at me with solemn, long-lashed eyes. Later, when he grew bigger, I would tie him to my back with a long shawl and skip about the house, bouncing up and down to make him giggle.

If I adored my little brother, my mother was obsessed with him. When Xochipilli took his first, toddling steps, my mother and Itzcoatl gave a feast in his honor. When he began to utter his first babyish words, my mother was spellbound with delight, laughing and mimicking his pronunciation. The joy of having a healthy and beautiful son completely overwhelmed my mother. She spent hours in the garden with him, putting flowers in his hair and rocking him in her arms, giving him her breast whenever he whimpered. When he slept she would steal up to him and put her hand on his little body to make sure he was breathing. At night she kept him next to her on her mat, with one arm curled protectively around him. So absorbed was she in her baby that she even began to neglect her own appearance, going with uncombed hair and rumpled clothing. The baby filled her life, excluding even me. Sometimes I felt as though I'd ceased to exist for my mother. Except for the hours I spent at the temple school—for Itzcoatl had long since tired of teaching me himself—I spent most of my time in the kitchen with Atototl and Miahuaxitl, or else I would wander alone along the edge of the forest like some half-wild creature.

I was growing tall now, like my mother. Beneath my loose-hanging *huipilli* I could see the softly curving outline of my breasts. When I walked through the market I could feel the eyes of the soldiers and young men watching me.

On the day that I became a woman, the first person to hear the news was not my mother but Miahuaxitl. Glancing forlornly down at her own bone-thin frame, she listened wistfully as I described the change that had come over my body. Miahuaxitl had never been a healthy child and had been increasingly unwell over the past year. Womanhood was out of reach for her and we both knew it. Impulsively, I threw my arms around her and we wept together.

Itzcoatl had never shown any affection for me, but his behavior suddenly took on a bewildering change. Now, especially when my mother was present, he began to smother me with attention. When he spoke to me, it was with the soft, caressing tones he'd once used to speak to my mother. He would stand so near me that I could feel his warm breath on my neck. Sometimes he would even put his arm around my shoulders or waist as he praised the beauty that had flowered with the coming of my womanhood.

At these times I would look at my mother. Her mouth would be smiling but her eyes would be seething with ill-hidden jealousy. She no longer took pride in her appearance. The birth of Xochipilli and her total preoccupation with his care had left her sloppy and unkempt. Itzcoatl's resulting loss of interest had brought out the shrew in her.

Naturally I was repelled by Itzcoatl's affection. His touch gave me the same sensation I'd have had if a poisonous snake, hissing sweetly, had coiled itself around my arm. But I was confused and helpless. Was Itzcoatl trying to win me to his power by such flattery? He might only have been trying to arouse my mother's jealousy. But then again, he might have been thinking of assuring his continued authority by taking me as a second wife or concubine. Sometimes when I came into the house from school or from the market I would overhear him arguing with my mother, his voice insistent as he said, "Cimatl, if you're my wife, you'll do it. Think of our son!" Her only answer was sobbing. As soon as the two of them knew that I'd entered the house their voices would lapse into silence.

I spent some sleepless nights wondering what was in my stepfather's mind. The time was growing near when I would be old enough to assume my duties as *tlatoani*, and I knew that Itzcoatl would not give up his power happily when that day arrived. Little Xochipilli, as the son of a former slave and a woman from another town, had no hereditary rights in Oluta. While I lived, my father's title and possessions could not be his.

At a time when I desperately needed an ally, my mother had become my enemy. I thought of confiding my fears in Atototl, but remembering the old woman's indiscreet tongue, I'd decided against it. Only Miahuaxitl could be trusted. Only

Miahuaxitl loved and understood me, but now even that solace was to be denied me.

So many crossroads in my life have been marked by death. After my father's sacrifice, the next death to touch me was that of my friend Miahuaxitl. Atototl was already an old woman when she conceived Miahuaxitl, and her birth was looked upon as something of a miracle. But Miahuaxitl was a sickly child and was only twelve or thirteen when she began to grow thin and tired. By the time she was fifteen, the flesh had melted from her bones and she could eat nothing except *atolli*, the thin porridge made from ground maize. Toward the end, she could eat nothing at all, and so her death came as no surprise. And yet I remember the day she died as one of the most terrifying in my life, for it not only brought the death of my friend but wrested me from all that was familiar and safe and threw me into a frighteningly alien world.

I recall being awakened at dawn by Atototl's shrieking, and I knew at once that Miahuaxitl was dead. I jumped up from my mat and ran to the little room the old woman and her daughter shared. I found Atototl kneeling on the floor beside Miahuaxitl's body, rocking with the force of her grief-stricken wailing. Near the body were several small idols of clay, and charms of feathers, plants and bones, left there in vain by the medicine man.

My mother hurried in with Itzcoatl, both of them still rubbing their eyes. They stood in the doorway and surveyed the scene in silence: the pale, stiff body of the dead girl; the noisily mourning old slave; and I, weeping softly beside my friend's mat.

Itzcoatl, his eyes hard, looked at my mother. "It's time," he said. "It must be today, Cimatl."

My mother's face went pale. She turned and walked swiftly out into the garden, followed by Itzcoatl.

I had heard Itzcoatl's words, but I was so absorbed in the tragedy that I didn't try to fathom their meaning until it was too late. The air reeked of death and vibrated with Atototl's groans. I gazed at my friend's lifeless face, the eyes slightly open, the mouth oddly twisted. A fly settled on Miahuaxitl's lower lip. Suddenly the room began to spin and I began to gag. Not wanting to go into the garden where my mother and Itzcoatl were, and knowing that I would be sick if I stayed in that death-filled room, I staggered to the front door of the house and out into the still-deserted street.

The freshness of the dawn air made me feel better. I began to walk. The stars were still visible in the sky and the drums and conches had not yet sounded from the temple, so no one was moving about in the streets. I walked on, past the faceless, whitewashed houses, breathing deeply the smell of damp earth mixed with the odors of urine, flowers, smoke from the banked cooking fires, and stale maize. I reached the end of the street, where the *milpas* were green with the new spring corn. A warbler sang from a thicket and another answered from the nearby forest. Life was everywhere and Miahuaxitl was dead.

The frog calls fell into silence as I walked along the edge of the *milpas*. There was nothing ahead of me but the forest, dark, mysterious and inviting. At its edge, I sank down on a large, moss-carpeted tree root and put my face in my hands.

With my father's death years before and now with Miahauxitl's, I had lost the two people who were closest to me. I had never felt the same nearness to my mother. She must have loved me, but I'd always sensed a thread of rivalry in our relationship, especially after her remarriage.

I sat there for some time, lost in mourning, when I was startled by the wail of conches and the pounding of the drum from the square. The town was awakening and soon the streets would be teeming with people. If I didn't hurry back to the house, those who saw me would wonder what their young *tlatoani* was doing outside in the early morning with her face unwashed and her hair and clothes still rumpled from sleep.

I jumped up and began to run through the empty streets, wincing as my bare feet struck the stones. I reached the house and slipped quietly through the entrance, hoping no one had missed me.

Itzcoatl was waiting, his face dark. "Where have you been? Your mother and I have looked everywhere for you! How can you leave when Atototl is so upset?"

"I'll go to her at once—" I was genuinely sorry for having left the old woman.

"No, not now," he snarled. "You're going to your room. You can expect to stay there the rest of the day. You can sit on your mat and think of how thoughtless you've been!" All traces of his pretended liking for me had disappeared. "You're never to leave this house again without my permission," he snapped, shoving me roughly into my room and lowering the cloth over the doorway.

I sat on my mat, my face against my raised knees, frightened, bewildered and hungry. Where was my mother? The beam of sunlight that shone through the small, high window moved from one end of the wall to the other. I tried to make the time pass by sleeping, but my bowstring-taut nerves would not let me rest. What had he meant, I tortured myself wondering, when he had looked at Miahuaxitl's dead body that morning and announced, "It must be today"?

All day I listened to the sound of Itzcoatl's footsteps outside my room as he paced back and forth like a sentry.

Night fell at last. I sat in the darkness, listening to the footsteps in the street outside as they became fewer and fewer and finally died away altogether. Silence stole over the town and I waited, remembering the dark night when the high priest had brought the soldiers to take my father away. There was no doubt in my mind that Itzcoatl had betrayed him.

My heart started to pound when I heard footsteps again, sinister and secretive, coming up to the house and entering through the front door. Suddenly the curtained doorway of my room was thrust aside and the light of a pitch-pine torch momentarily blinded me. I was seized roughly by unfamiliar hands that twisted my arms until pain drove the fight out of me. A cloth was tied over my eyes, and my wrists were bound behind my back with rough maguey rope. Then I was dragged into the hall, where I recognized Itzcoatl's voice.

"Pay me what you promised me for her. As you can see, she's well worth the price. After that, I never want to see your faces again."

"Don't worry. By morning we'll be long gone from here." The growling voice that answered was unfamiliar. "Can't we leave the old one? She'll only slow us down. We won't get enough for her to make it worth our trouble."

"That was part of our agreement," Itzcoatl hissed. "She can't stay here. She knows too much and she has a loose tongue. If she dies on the trail—" he paused, sucking in his breath— "so much the better for us all."

I panicked as I realized that I was being sold and that Atototl was being sold along with me. "Mother!" I screamed.

"Bind her mouth," Itzcoatl commanded. "Take them away!"

I staggered as rough hands stuffed a wad of dry cotton into my mouth and wrapped a strip of smelly rag around the lower part of my face. A muffled groan told me that Atototl, also blindfolded, bound and gagged, was standing next to me. I bumped against her shoulder as the two of us were pushed through the front doorway. Then I felt the cool stones of the street under my bare feet.

"Come along, old woman. Hurry, my pretty one. "The deep voice chuckled good-naturedly. "When we're far enough into the jungle that you can't find your way back home again we'll uncover your eyes and you'll have easier going. Until then, you'll just have to let Ozomatli and me guide you." He gave a rasping laugh as we stumbled along. "I know you can hardly wait to see me. You won't be disappointed, for I'm very handsome. But don't let yourself fall in love with me—oh no! If you do, you'll die of a broken heart when I sell you in Xicalango!"

I felt damp earth under my toes and heard the singing of frogs, which died away in silence as we passed. I knew that we were walking along the edge of the *milpas* where I had once walked with Miahuaxitl. Soon my feet touched the wet leaves and moss of the forest floor. I was leaving my town, my mother, my little brother, perhaps never to return. Tears soaked my blindfold.

Dawn broke over the jungle—not with the fanfare of conch and drum, but with the squabbling of parrots and the chattering of monkeys who celebrated the graying sky with rejoicing. Another night of snakes and sharp-fanged predators was over.

It was no longer necessary for us to have our arms bound or our eyes covered, but we stayed close to our captors in spite of our freedom. To run off into the jungle without food or weapons would have been suicidal. Ozomatli, a hulk of a man with vacant eyes and no tongue, led our little procession along the narrow trail. He was followed by myself, Atototl and the man with the deep voice, who had turned out to be squat, powerfully built and incredibly ugly. The men carried spears tipped with obsidian. Ozomatli, who must have been a slave, balanced a heavy bundle of provisions on his back, supported by a deerskin strap across his forehead, while the man with the deep voice carried his wealth in a leather bag slung around his neck and under one arm.

The jungle was beautiful, in its savage way. Morning light filtered down through layers of trees, casting feathery patterns on the moss-covered ground. The branches were festooned with vines and strands of hanging moss. Delicate ferns and orchids grew from little hollows in the bark, and flame-colored birds flitted overhead, scolding as we passed. From time to time a snake or a large iguana, green as jade, would slither out of our path.

I could hear Atototl behind me, gasping for breath in an effort to keep pace with the others. I hadn't eaten since the night before Miahuaxitl's death, and now I was faint from hunger. It was a relief when we came to a little clearing and the man with the deep voice announced that we would stop to rest and eat.

Ozomatli lowered the bundle from his back, pulled out some maize cakes wrapped in a cloth and tossed them to us. We seized them hungrily and sat down on a log to eat. Then he carefully unwrapped some freshly cooked pheasant and turtle eggs for his master and more maize cakes for himself.

I had never been really hungry before in my life. The maize cakes were stale but they were satisfying, filling me with new strength. As we ate I moved closer to Atototl. "Are you all right, Grandmother?" I whispered, using a term of affection I would never have uttered when I was her mistress. Misfortune had brought equality.

"Yes, only tired, little one. Ay, look at your feet! They're bleeding." She bent over and dabbed at my toes with the edge of her *huipilli*. "That dog Itzcoatl didn't even let you put on a pair of sandals. Here, take mine. My feet are old and tough."

I thanked her for her kindness but I couldn't bring myself to take them. We ate in silence for a time; both of us were ravenous. I concentrated furiously on my hunger and my smarting feet, trying to drown the thought that kept surfacing in my mind. It was an ugly thought, which I denied to myself a hundred times before I finally found the courage to voice it.

"Atototl?"

"Yes, Malinalli?" Her old eyes looked out at me from their woebegone depths. I almost hoped she would lie to me.

"Atototl, did my mother know . . ." I struggled with the words. "Was she with Itzcoatl in this?"

The old woman was silent, but the shifting lines in her face revealed the struggle being waged inside her. After a long time she nodded and answered bitterly, "Hiding the truth from you now would serve nothing. I heard them talking yesterday morning, while you were gone. I tried to warn you, but Itzcoatl got to you first and shut you in your room. Cimatl caught me trying to slip out of the house to get help and she tied me up in the kitchen until the slave dealers came."

Atototl's voice began to waver. "She slapped my face and tied me up and sold me, the one who had cared for her since she was a baby!"

"Don't cry." I patted her shoulder helplessly, fighting down the sickness that was flooding up into my throat. "Our people won't let their *tlatoani* be sold. When they find out I'm gone they'll come looking for us."

Atototl bowed her head in despair. "No, child, they won't come. This morning your death is being announced from the steps of the temple. The body of my Miahuaxitl has been wrapped with cloth and will be burned as your own. No one will miss the daughter of a slave or her old mother."

I wanted very much to weep. Tears would have dissolved the cold knot that was strangling my heart. But no tears came. Dry-eyed, I faced the truth. Itzcoatl and my mother had planned this together. They had been waiting like vultures, waiting for months perhaps, for Miahuaxitl to die so that they could sell me and claim her body as mine. When I put my hand to my face, my fingers were like ice.

Chapter Three

1516

Compared to the orderly, well-stocked market in Oluta, the market at Xicalango was a poor one. Vendors squatted next to their wares in random patterns, newcomers settling wherever there was an empty space. Customers stepped gingerly among piles of rubbish. Next to a cage full of live turkeys, an old woman toasted *tlaxcalli* on a flat *cumal*. Nearby, two dogs fought over a piece of dried venison that had fallen from a rack. A man covered with sores accepted a handful of cocoa nibs from a woman in payment for the stewed chili peppers, tomatoes and iguana meat he ladled into one of the pottery bowls set on the ground in front of him. On the lower steps of a temple, a pretty, pregnant young woman sold bags of copal incense for burning in ceremonial braziers.

Exhausted and footsore from the long trek through the jungle, I stood beside Atototl in one corner of the market. The deep-voiced slave trader had ordered me to wash and comb my hair and he had given me a clean *huipilli* to wear, but he had not considered Atototl worth the bother. The old woman, dirty and bedraggled, was so tired that she leaned against my shoulder to keep from falling down. There were no other slaves for sale that day, and passersby eyed the two of us curiously. One fat and sweating man inquired about my price, but when the slave trader replied he turned and strolled away, shaking his head.

"I'm in no hurry to sell you, princess," the slaver said to me with a wink. "You're worth enough to keep me living like a *tlatoani* for half a year, and sooner or later someone will come along who is willing to pay my price for you." He cast his eyes about the bustling market. "Ha! Over there! That fellow in the red plumes has the look of a *pochteca*, a fine, fat trader from Tenochtitlan. We're in luck. He's coming this way."

The man approaching us was somewhat past forty, short, muscular and splendidly clad in a helmet spouting scarlet plumes. An embroidered *tilmatli* or cloak, was knotted over one shoulder. A golden mass of chains hung around a neck that was as thick as a boar's.

"What price, my friend, for this little *chalchihuitl*?"

"Price!" the slaver exclaimed. "You can gaze upon such beauty and talk of price? Are you less than a man? Look at her! This jewel is beyond price!" He shuffled his feet and cleared his throat. "I'm a man of business, and if we must be so petty as to discuss her worth . . ." He shrugged. "So it must be."

The *pochteca* examined me critically. I gagged as his rough, salty fingers forced my mouth open for a look at my teeth, but I'd seen enough of the treatment of slaves to know that I'd be beaten for resisting.

"Is the girl a virgin?"

"A virgin? By the four hundred rabbits, you have the gall to ask? She's as pure as a bud."

"For the price you're asking, my friend, I've a right to demand proof."

The slaver spread his hands in acquiesence. "Every market employs a woman for that sort of thing, but you'll have to be the one to pay her."

A few inquiries produced an old crone with a bent back who cackled as she led me, trembling, to a tiny hut and shoved me with surprising strength through the low door and onto a mat.

"Just lie back, child," the old woman chattered, bending low. "So they want proof, do they? Well, men always do. Then, after the first time, there's no more to prove!" She tittered at her own cleverness. "Now I'll just lift your skirt— Ay! In the name of Tlazoteotl, open your legs or I'll go out and get your master to help me! If you're like this with me, how will you be with a man?"

As the leathery old hands probed my body, I bit my lip to keep from crying out, more from indignation than from pain. To think that the daughter of a *tlatoani* should be subjected to this obscenity! I tasted my own blood on the edge of my tongue.

"There," the woman grunted approvingly. "So they've got their proof and I'll get my twenty bags of *chocolatl*. Now see, my pretty one, was it worth such a fuss?"

I was hot-faced with humiliation when she led me out into the sunlight and gave the two men a nod.

"So you doubted my word, and now you must pay to learn what you should already have known!" The slaver chuckled in anticipation of the price he would get. "You see, I always tell the truth. She's a fitting prize for Moctezuma himself."

"That," replied the *pochteca*, "is just what I've been thinking, but buying her now would be trouble for me. You see, I'm not going directly back to Tenochtitlan from here. I'm bound for Tabasco to trade for *chocolatl* and feathers. She'll have to be fed and guarded for at least a month before I can see my way to sell her. For the extra trouble, I think you should give me a better price."

"A better price! Away with you! Someone else will buy her."

"Not in this town," said the *pochteca*, "and not at your price."

The haggling continued, the slave trader stubbornly extolling my beauty, virtue, intelligence and noble birth, and the *pochteca* arguing that the price was too high to pay even for a daughter of Moctezuma himself.

I scarcely listened to them, for my mind was racing with new hope. The *pochteca* was going to Tabasco, which lay far to the southeast in the land of the Mayas. After leaving Oluta, my captors and I had traveled northwest to reach Xicalango. It was logical, then, that to reach Tabasco from Xicalango, the *pochteca* would travel back along the way I had come with the slave trader. His route should take me near Oluta, where I could make my escape. As I recalled Itzcoatl's betrayal of my father and how Itzcoatl and my mother had plotted to use Miahuaxitl's death in order to sell me into slavery and continue as rulers of Oluta, my bitterness was relieved only by the thought that the people of Oluta loved me as they'd loved my father. Once they knew what had been done to me, Itzcoatl and Cimatl would pay dearly for their treachery . . .

The price had been agreed upon—a compromise between the highest the *pochteca* was willing to pay and the lowest the slaver was willing to accept. The *pochteca* motioned to a servant who hovered nearby. "Fetch Quauhtlatoa," he barked, and the servant scuttled off to do his bidding. "My son always carries our jewels," he explained proudly. "When he gets here, you'll see why."

I had not forgotten Atototl. "Noble lord," I said in my

sweetest voice, "won't you buy my companion? She's strong and skilled in cooking and caring for children."

The *pochteca* gave Atototl a disgusted glance. "Buy her! She's so weak that another day on the trail would kill her. I've no use for an old woman."

The *pochteca's* son had arrived, a massive young buck of about twenty. The merchant carefully counted the dazzling gems as he placed them in the slave dealer's outstretched hands. The son gazed at me with open admiration. He was even more muscular than his father and a full head taller. A lock of hair was bound high on the crown of his head in the manner of the Aztec nobles. He carried himself haughtily, conscious of his classic face, his splendid, arrogant body.

"Come along." The *pochteca* motioned to me. "I've business to finish here, but Quauhtlatoa will escort you to our camp." His expression softened a little. "Don't be afraid. As my most valuable acquisition you'll be treated with care."

I clung tenaciously to the old slave woman. "I won't leave her," I announced. "You'll not take me without Atototl."

A stinging slap across my face from the *pochteca's* powerful hand almost knocked me senseless.

"Forgive her manners," the slave dealer said, giving me a sympathetic look. "She's a princess, accustomed to giving orders, not taking them. She has much to learn, and you'll no doubt teach her." He placed a hand on Atototl's stooped back. "Don't fear for your friend, princess. I'll sell the old woman to some kind family. The *pochteca* is right when he says she'd die on the trail if she went with you."

Quauhtlatoa took my arm firmly, his hand hot against my cold flesh. Reluctantly, I walked along beside him. "Goodbye, Grandmother," I called to Atototl as I was led away, my cheek still burning from the slap. "Someday I'll find you again."

The old woman fluttered her hand in a feeble salute.

When I was able to collect my thoughts, I realized that the best course of action was to cooperate with my captors. If I could lull them into thinking I was contented, I would not be so closely watched, and when the time came, my escape would be easier.

The caravan trotted along the narrow forest paths at a brisk pace. The *pochteca* and his son, the guards who were armed with *maquahuitls*, the long train of *tlamemes* who carried the *pochteca's* goods in big bundles on their backs, and even the scraggly women who went along to prepare the meals—all were hardened to the trail. But as the coddled child of a *tlatoani*, I had never been accustomed to strenuous physical activity, and for the first few days my body throbbed with the effort of keeping up with the others. My legs ached and my feet developed such painful blisters from the new sandals I'd been given that I had to take them off and walk barefoot. At night, when the others sat chatting around the fire and smoking *tabac*, I would unroll my sleeping mat and collapse into oblivion.

The only person who spoke to me was Quauhtlatoa, and then only when he taunted me as he walked behind me on the trail. "Hurry, Princess Malinalli, or we'll have to put you in a net and let two *tlamemes* carry you between them on a pole. What a fetching sight you'd be!"

I wouldn't answer him. All my strength went into putting one foot ahead of the other as fast as I could. The only thing that kept me trudging on was the knowledge that the caravan was moving ever closer to Oluta. Here and there I would recognize the distant curve of a hill or a stream I'd crossed on my way to Xicalango with the slaver.

When we passed a village or town, the *pochteca* would usually stop long enough to investigate the marketplace for trading possibilities. His hawklike eyes would note every detail of the fortifications of the town, the evidence of arms, the apparent strength of its defending forces, and the potential for tribute, and all of this would later be reported to Moctezuma. The *pochteca* occupied a unique position in the intricate hierarchy of the Aztec empire. Only they were free to travel through any territory, friendly or hostile; trade, even among enemies, was essential to all. That they also functioned as spies was well known but tolerated by those who had developed a taste for goods made in Tenochtitlan.

Because I'd shown no inclination to run away, I was allowed some freedom, which was as I had hoped. The *pochteca* let me visit the towns with him, wandering through the streets and the markets, always closely guarded by Quauhtlatoa. Although the merchant's son was pleasant, there was something in his eyes when he looked at me that aroused my distrust. He was handsome enough, in a sleek, pumalike way, but his touch—and he touched me often—brought back chilling memories of Itzcoatl.

"My father's going to offer you to Moctezuma. He says you'll make him a rich man," Quauhtlatoa remarked one day as we strolled through the streets of a dirty little town. "Last night I asked him to give you to me instead." He paused, hoping for at least a flicker of a reaction from me. I gave him none. "But the old man's got a piece of jade for a heart. He says he's invested too much in you to keep you for his own son. What do you think of that, Malinalli?" He took a deep, painful breath. "If you said that you preferred me to an emperor . . ."

"A slave has no preferences," I said cautiously. "She goes where she's taken."

"Moctezuma has at least a hundred fifty concubines," Quauhtlatoa said. "Unless you become one of his favorites, you won't spend much time with him. Now if you belonged to me, you'd be my only concubine. I'd need no others to satisfy me." He took my arm and steered me between the ramshackle stalls, away from the center of the market. "I wish I could ask you to be my wife, but, curse the ill fortune, my father's arranged for me to marry a girl from Tenochtitlan. Skinny as a vulture and twice as ugly! I'll have to get drunk on *octli* before I take her to the sleeping mat, but her father's a man of rank. He's pleased to be getting such a handsome husband for his homely daughter, and my father's happy because his son is marrying into the nobility." His voice was melancholy now, but I felt no sympathy for this arrogant young man. "So you see, I'm almost as much a slave as you are. I too must go where I'm sent."

We'd turned a corner and found ourselves alone in the cool shade of a narrow street lined by whitewashed walls. Suddenly his grip on my arm tightened and he whirled me around to face him. His arms, strong and unyielding as two tree trunks, jerked me close. His hand moved downward, pressing me inward against his body. I fought rising waves of panic and revulsion, telling myself to use this moment . . .

"Malinalli!" he gasped, "I've got to have you! Now . . . tonight. Don't you feel something too," he breathed, "when I touch you like this . . . ?"

I groped for an answer. Telling him the truth would close one of my most promising avenues of escape. Still, if I lied, if I told him I returned his desire, it could lead me into new depths of captivity from which I could never break free.

"What difference do my feelings make?" I chose my words carefully. "Your father will sell me to Moctezuma and we'll never see each other again. There's nothing we can do as long as I'm not free."

His grip on me relaxed a little. "No, you're wrong," he whispered. "I have a plan. My father will be furious, but there'll be nothing he can do."

"Tell me about it." I tried to mask my nervousness with a smile.

He leaned close to my ear. "It would be unthinkable to offer Moctezuma a girl who was not a virgin," he said.

My control snapped and I drew back from him, the meaning of his words all too clear. "I'm the daughter of a *tlatoani*!" I exploded. "You expect to take me like a common *auianime*, like one of the women who follows the warriors?"

"Malinalli," he retorted coldly, dropping his arms from my shoulders, "you may have been the noblest princess in the land, but now you're a slave. You're the property of my father, and what is his is mine. I have the right to take you whenever I choose."

His voice was hard. I regretted having let my pride overcome my common sense. The chance that he would help me escape to Oluta was fading before my eyes.

"It's just that I've always expected to have a marriage ceremony, to be honored as a man's wife," I said, trying to catch at the lost thread before it disappeared. I took his big hand in mine. "Return me to my people, Quauhtlatoa. Then I'll be yours. We'll rule Oluta together."

Quauhtlatoa snorted. "I know Oluta. Compared to Tenochtitlan, it's a turkey-pen. My father controls the wealth of ten Olutas, my future father-in-law the wealth of forty." He waited, fuming, while a group of naked boys roughhoused their way past us in the narrow street. "No, Malinalli, it's you, not your filthy little town I want. I'll have you whether you want me or not, no matter what my father intends to do with you. I always get my way with him in the end."

Angry and disappointed, I pulled away from him and walked back toward the crowded market.

In the days that followed, I avoided being alone, staying always with the coarse, bedraggled cooking women, going for water with them and sleeping among them. Quauhtlatoa could not come near enough to say a word to me that they wouldn't have overheard.

The familiarity of the land through which we were now passing lifted my dejection and brought me more hope and determination. My eyes caressed the contours of distant hills I had known. After an absence of forty days, I was nearing home at last, determined to escape my captors and claim what was rightfully mine.

"We'll camp here," the *pochteca* announced, thumping the forest floor with his staff. "I plan to spend a day in Oluta trading for *chocolatl.*" He looked at me as I helped the women unload the cooking pots, my heart thudding against my ribs. "You won't be coming with me this time, little princess. You're to remain here with the other women. Quauhtlatoa, stay with her. See that she's closely guarded."

"As you wish, my father," Quauhtlatoa murmured. "We can't afford to let such a treasure get lost." He sauntered to my side and draped an arm around my shoulders.

As the *pochteca* and a contingent of *tlamemes* and guards filed off through the forest toward Oluta, I busied myself grinding maize, shoving the rounded stone furiously against the *metatl* in an effort to release my nervousness and disappointment. Quauhtlatoa lounged against a tree, watching me with half-closed eyes, the way a snake watches a bird. I prayed that he would soon tire of tending me so closely. When his attention lapsed, I would slip away. I'd take a circuitous route to Oluta and, entering the town with a shawl over my face, take refuge with the priests of Quetzalcoatl. They'd been loyal to my father and they would hide and protect me from Itzcoatl until word could be passed among the people that I had returned.

When I assumed power, I would have Itzcoatl's head chopped off with a *maquahuitl* in the center of the marketplace, and I would sell my mother into slavery as I myself had been sold. Xochipilli, my little half-brother, was too young to be anything but innocent. I would keep him with me and raise him as a prince, but I would forbid him ever to speak the name of our mother . . .

The day wore on. When Quauhtlatoa could not watch me himself, he ordered one of the guards to do so. As I watched the lengthening shadows I grew more and more frantic, praying for a chance to escape before the *pochteca* returned and ordered the caravan to move on, cutting off my escape.

As I tended the cooking fire, where the carcass of a freshly killed deer roasted on a stick over the sizzling coals, I looked around, grasping for a way to distract Quauhtlatoa's attention long enough to reach the forest and disappear. My eyes passed over the *pochteca*'s trade goods, tied in bundles stacked shoulder-high not far away. There were bales of cotton, bags of feathers and copal, bundles of embroidered skirts and cloaks . . . I glanced down at the red-hot coals near my feet and almost laughed with anticipation.

Casually, I picked up the smallest of the empty cooking pots. Turning my back to Quauhtlatoa, I pretended to stir the fire while I swiftly scooped a few glowing coals into the little pot.

Quauhtlatoa yawned as he leaned back against a tree. "What a delightful day it's been," he remarked, "with nothing to do except follow you about the camp. I half expected you to make things more interesting by trying to run away."

I sampled the beans from one of the cooking pots. "With you watching me all the time, I couldn't have run away if I'd wanted to." I pulled a face. "Ugh! These beans need salt." I pretended an unsuccessful search for the salt and then rose to get some from his father's bundles, but he started away from the tree to accompany me. "Oh, stay where you are," I said with unfeigned impatience. "You'll be able to see me the whole time." Holding my breath as he leaned back against the tree, I picked up the pot with the hot coals inside, walked over to the piled-up bundles and went around behind the stack. Quauhtlatoa could see my head—but not my hands, as they deftly opened a bag of feathers and dropped the coals inside.

"I couldn't find it," I complained, returning to the fire with the empty pot. As always, he watched me intently, but there was no suspicion in his eyes. I glanced around where the utensils were scattered near the fire. "There it is," I muttered just loud enough for him to hear me. Taking the bag of salt, I measured a little into my palm and slowly stirred it into the beans.

I crouched by the cooking pots, every muscle tensed for flight the moment the fire in the *pochteca's* goods was discovered. Nearby, a woman was cooking maize cakes on a *cumal*, while another appeared from the edge of the forest with a jar of water on her head. Two *tlamemes*, grateful for the day of rest, strolled past the fire toward the stacked bundles.

The acrid smell of burning feathers made my nostrils flare. Surely someone else would soon notice it. A wisp of smoke rose from the place where I had dumped the coals. Suddenly flames spouted up from among the bundles and bags. The eyes of the two *tlamemes* opened wide in horror as they ran, shouting the alarm to the camp. Quauhtlatoa leaped to his feet, seized a water jar and sprinted toward the blaze to save his father's property as the camp erupted into a melee of running, shouting figures.

Quite as a shadow, I rose and moved toward the forest. As soon as I was hidden from the view of the camp, I broke into flight, dodging trees, leaping roots and ducking under the hanging vines. I lost all sense of direction but there was no time to care. I was free. I only wanted to get as far from captivity as my legs would carry me. I could hide in the forest until the *pochteca* had given up looking for me. Then, somehow, I would find my way to Oluta. I ran like a rabbit, startling parrots into screeching flurries of movement and sending lizards scurrying out of my path.

My breath was coming in gasps and my sides throbbed. I paused to rest against a tree, head hanging down. It was only then that I heard the dull thud of footsteps on the forest floor and the swish of the leaves as something brushed swiftly past them. Someone was after me! Terror gave me new strength and I plunged on, thorns tearing at my hair, my footing unsure on the wet moss under my feet. Behind me, moving closer, came the sound of footfalls.

I came to a stream and stopped in confusion. It looked too wide to leap, but crossing on the slippery stones would slow me down, enabling my pursuer to catch me. Deciding to attempt the leap, I gathered up my narrow skirt and stepped back to gain a running start. At that instant, Quauhtlatoa's strong arms closed around me. His momentum carried us both to the ground, his chest smothering my face. I struggled wildly, biting, clawing like a trapped ocelot. The heaviness of his body pressed down on me. Suddenly his hands pulled away my skirt and I felt his hot, bare flesh against mine. Overhead, trees and sky whirled into a blue-green blur. From somewhere I heard an animal voice screaming out, again and again, and only gradually did I realize that the voice was my own.

When it was over, Quauhtlatoa carried my limp body back to the camp.

The *pochteca* paced back and forth, striking the trees angrily with his staff, eyes bloodshot with anger. His tall son cowered before his fury.

"You stupid, ungrateful fool!" he raged. "I paid a fortune for this girl and by one wanton act you've reduced her worth to a tiny part of what she cost me. With the profits from her sale, I could have bought you twenty concubines if you'd wanted them. Now she's ruined! I could beat you to death with my bare hands!"

Quauhtlatoa had known that his father would be angry, but he had in no way anticipated the magnitude of his fury. He pressed his face to the earth in submission while I slumped exhausted on the mat where he had dropped me.

"When I told you that I wanted Malinalli for myself, you wouldn't give her to me," he whined. "Now you may as well let me have her. Her beauty will enrich our household as much as anything your jewels might have bought." He looked up with a puppyish expression, confident of getting his own way.

Purple veins stood out on the *pochteca's* forehead. "Is this how I've raised you?" he sputtered. "You think you can betray your own father and then be rewarded for your disobedience? Well, whatever it is I've failed to teach you, you'll learn it now. Tomorrow morning I'm sending eighty of the *tlamemes* back to Tenochtitlan with part of my goods. You're going with them. When you arrive in the capital, you're to go directly to our house and remain there until I return to arrange for your marriage. You'll never see this girl again!"

Quauhtlatoa opened his mouth to protest, but one searing glance from his father was enough to silence him.

Next, the *pochteca* turned on me. "And you, little princess, deserve to die for all the trouble you've caused! Not only did your escape incite my son to do something that's rendered you worthless, but the fire you set ruined two bags of feathers and a bale of cotton before the *tlamemes* and the women were able to put it out. Tell me, is there any reason I shouldn't order a guard to lop off your head here and now?"

Scratched, bruised and humiliated, I gazed up at the man who owned me. Death, I thought, would have been pleasant compared to what I'd already suffered. I'd be released from my misery and Quauhtlatoa would be haunted forever by the sight of my headless body, the body he had dared to violate, lying there on the ground in a pool of blood. I wanted to spit in the *pochteca's* scowling face, to defy him. My father had given his life for his people. Now I'd be giving up mine. But for what a reason—for mere cowardice and spite . . .

Suddenly I knew that I must not let death end my fight. I wanted to live at any cost, to battle for my freedom, for vengeance and for the right to be *tlatoani* as my father had been.

Rising to my feet, I met the *pochteca*'s eyes fearlessly. When I spoke, my voice was clear and steady. "My lord, you have two reasons to spare me," I announced. "First of all, I have studied Aztec law and I know that it's forbidden for a master to take the life of a slave. Second, it's still possible for you to recover what you paid for me." Knowing I had gained his full attention, I gave him my most devastating smile. "Do you throw away a drum just because it has been played? The masters of the *teponatzli* say that the beauty of its tone increases with age and use. Somewhere you'll find a man who realizes that the same is true of a woman, and he'll pay a good price for me." I paused to glance at Quauhtlatoa, who squatted on his heels nearby, sulking like a child. "And as for punishment, my lord, I assure you that your son has already punished me enough to atone for anything I might have done."

The *pochteca's* scowl deepened and he peered at me intently. Abruptly, he threw back his head and roared with laughter. "Well said!" he exclaimed. "By the gods, I'm almost tempted to keep you for myself! That would teach that hot-blooded young whelp of mine!" He chuckled at my efforts to hide my repugnance. "No, I'm a practical man. I'll take you with me to Tabasco and perhaps along the way I can sell you to some rich *tlatoani*. But you must be disciplined first." He clapped his hands to summon a husky slave with a strip of leather coiled over his shoulder. "Give her twenty blows," he said, "but very carefully. We don't want to mar that skin."

The *pochteca's* caravan wound its way toward Tabasco, in the direction of the rising sun. By now my muscles had become as firm as a deer's, and I kept an effortless pace with the sturdy *tlamemes* and their master. Something in my spirit had changed as well. I felt the serenity of one who has seen her worst fears come to pass and found that life, after all, continues. Relieved of the presence of Quauhtlatoa, who had returned to Tenochtitlan as his father had ordered, I settled into the routine of marching, eating, marching and sleeping with the resignation that settles over a caged animal after a time in captivity.

One day, I vowed, I would find a way to return to Oluta and take my vengeance. For the present, my goal was survival: to remain strong in body and mind and to keep that mind unenslaved.

Days blended into weeks until I lost track of time. The very air had taken on a new heaviness. The jungle about us grew so lushly that it closed off the sunlight and we walked in semidarkness along its bare floor. Once we passed the ruins of a deserted city, almost buried by the thick green blanket. Above it rose a dilapidated pyramid, taller and more delicately constructed than anything I had seen in the kingdom of the Aztecs, with a comblike facade rising from the roof of the *teocalli*. Remembering drawings of such pyramids shown me by my father, I realized that we had penetrated the land of the Mayas.

When our caravan stopped in villages to trade, I was fascinated by the people I saw. For the most part, they were stockier than the Aztecs, with prominent noses sloping down from high, incredibly flat foreheads. I was mystified until I noticed that the babies on the backs of the women had boards tightly bound to the fronts of their little heads to flatten them to the desired shape.

The men flocked around me, muttering in their strange language, but they drifted away when the *pochteca* quoted my price to them in his halting Mayan.

In the slave market of one town, the *pochteca* purchased a fawn-eyed boy of fifteen, with hair that fell almost to his waist. "This lad is for Tabasco, the *tlatoani* for whom the place we're going is named," the trader explained to me. "Tabasco's an old acquaintance of mine, an odd sort. He married out of duty to his tribe, but since the day his wife gave him an heir, I'll wager he hasn't looked at a woman. No, young fellows like this one are Tabasco's meat, and he'll pay me well for finding him."

I gazed at the young boy with pity. He looked back and smiled timidly at me. He could not understand the *pochteca's* words and was unaware of his fate.

"Don't get the wrong impression of Tabasco," the *pochteca* continued. "He's as fearless as a wild boar in battle, and respected in peace for his wisdom. It's just that when it comes to partners, he has his own taste." He shrugged his broad shoulders. "He won't be buying you, of course, but the city of Tabasco and the towns around it are wealthy. There are men there who might be willing and able to pay my price for you." He studied me with narrowed eyes. "What a pity your mother didn't flatten your forehead. The Mayas consider that a mark of beauty, you know."

I judged the city of Tabasco to be two or three times as large as Oluta. It rested like a pearl in a setting of emerald *milpas* and *chocolatl* trees, with pyramids rising here and there among lime-washed houses with roofs of palm thatch. The streets were swept clean and filled with colorfully dressed people: women in multihued *huipillis* with baskets and jars on their heads and flat-browed babies tied to their backs; warriors in plumed helmets and jaguar-skin cloaks; wealthy merchants with rings in their noses and plugs of turquoise or jade set into their pierced lower lips and earlobes. Naked children capered in the sun. Farmers and craftsmen strained under loads of vegetables, clay pots, straw mats and baskets.

The market itself was an exuberant blend of colors, sounds and smells. Not even in Oluta had I seen such a variety of foods for sale. Tabasco's proximity to the sea made it possible to buy not only fish but crabs, clams, eels, octopus and an assortment of dried seaweed. Huge green turtles, their back flippers tied together with string, blinked piteously in the harsh sunlight as their leathery-shelled eggs were sold nearby. There were piles of salt and breathtaking collections of seashells.

I walked beside the *pochteca* and the young boy, shaking with apprehension. Would I be sold here, to live among these alien people with their unfamiliar customs and language? I let my eyes climb the steps of the temple that rose above the square, wondering what new gods stood in the ornately carved *teocalli* at its summit. My father had told me that the Mayas practiced human sacrifice, and I wondered if they shared the Aztec custom of feasting on sacrificial flesh. As a stranger with no family to protect me, I might be chosen as a victim. The thought made me almost faint from dread.

"Tabasco!" The *pochteca* hailed two men in plumed headdresses who were coming toward us. The more richly dressed of the two raised his arm in salute as he drew near. He was a thickset man, fleshy and red-faced, with a jade plug set into his full lower lip and his arms covered with gold bracelets. Brilliant green quetzal plumes cascaded from his pearl-encrusted helmet. He moved slowly, with a kind of rolling majesty, but his little dark eyes, deeply set in the folds of his face, darted about like a lizard's, taking in everything about him.

He clapped the *pochteca* on the shoulders in greeting, questioning him, perhaps, about the journey. I strained my ears to catch a few words of the new language that flowed from his lips, but I could understand nothing. The *pochteca* stepped to one side to reveal the trembling boy who cowered behind him. Tabasco's ruddy face lit up with pleasure. He proceeded to examine the boy closely, fingering his hair, inspecting his eyes and teeth. Turning away in disgust, I met the startling golden eyes of the second man.

He was considerably taller than the typical Mayan, and his body, revealed where his cloak was flung back over one shoulder, showed no trace of fat. I estimated his age at forty-five at least, for his face was lined. A jagged white scar ran from temple to chin, narrowly missing one eye. White heron plumes drooped from his helmet, brushing his narrow shoulders and falling down his back. He studied me forthrightly, his expression unchanging and unreadable. I lowered my eyes to the ground. My face grew warm.

The *pochteca* and Tabasco had reached a speedy agreement on the price of the boy. Now the *pochteca* turned his attention to me. The second man, in a low, expressionless voice, asked a few sparsely worded questions, which the *pochteca* answered with a flow of stumbling words and expansive gestures. He was doubtless recounting my history and, to protect his integrity as a trader, most likely explaining that I'd met with a slight "accident" on the trail. This seemed to make no difference to the man, for he opened a leather pouch and drew out the largest, most exquisitely carved *chalchihuitl* that I had ever seen. The *pochteca* swallowed twice. He took the jade stone, which was one of the most precious substances in trade, and examined it for flaws. Finding none, he bowed low, indicating to the man with words and gestures that I was his.

"Good fortune to you, princess," he said to me in Nahuatl. "You've just been purchased for a handsome price by Chilam, lord of Centla. You'll like Centla. It's a pleasant little town just over that ridge there." He pointed with a thick finger. "Chilam is rich and held in high regard by everyone who knows him. I couldn't wish you a happier fate." He chuckled. "You should thank the gods and me as well!"

I felt no gratitude, but only humiliation at having once more been sold like a sack of *chocolatl* beans or a turkey. Worse, the heron-eyed Chilam was old enough to be my father, and I couldn't understand a word of his speech. As two of Chilam's servants led me away, I didn't even look back at the *pochteca*, who was busy admiring his newly acquired *chalchihuitl*.

The two servants, small, quiet men clad only in white loincloths, led me through the streets of Tabasco and out onto a narrow path leading through the *milpas* and away from the city. One trotting ahead of me and one behind, they wound their way over a low, wooded ridge from which at last I saw the town of Centla, white as dried coral in the sunlight. Beyond the town, the land sloped gently down to the edge of the turquoise sea. Even in my unreceptive frame of mind, I had to admit that it was beautiful. I would be forced to live there until I could carry out a plan to return to Oluta. How long that would take I did not know, but I knew that I had to be patient, gathering my strength for the opportunity when it came.

We made our way down the ridge, through the fields and into the town, where we entered a spacious house surrounded by a high wall. I was ushered past a sour-faced woman in a yellow *huipilli* who sat in the garden shade with the ends of her loom tied around her back. As we passed, she dropped her shuttle and glared at me.

The two servants took me to a small, cool room with no windows. One of them watched me while the other brought a jar of water, a length of clean cloth for washing, a fresh, white *huipilli* edged in blue, a blue skirt, and a comb carved from tortoise shell. With signs, they indicated that I was to wash and change my clothing. Then they withdrew, lowering the embroidered cloth that covered the doorway.

As my eyes grew accustomed to the room's semidarkness, I saw that there was a sleeping mat in one corner and a low table nearby with a calabash full of fresh fruit on it. I removed my dusty clothing and began to wash myself.

There was no need for me to speculate about my fate. I'd been purchased as a concubine and it would only be a matter of time before I would hear footsteps outside the room and see the lean figure of Chilam stepping through the entrance. I thought of trying to escape, but because I was alone and did not know the countryside, escape would likely mean death. For now, my best chance of survival lay in doing as I was bid, in quiet, patient waiting.

I wound the length of skirt material around my hips, tied it with my sash and slipped the clean *huipilli* over my head. Then I sat down on the mat, my face against my raised knees, to wait.

Chapter Four

Tabasco—8 June 1518

I remember that there were four of them, growing like trees out of the distant horizon of the foam-flecked ocean. Four lofty towers hung with what appeared to be billowing white wings. I had come to the beach to gather turtle eggs that morning, and I dropped my basket in the sand to stare at them as they came nearer, their tops swaying with the rhythm of the waves. Now my astonished eyes could see that the base of each tower rose from a boat that was as big as any house in Tabasco.

I'd heard rumors of such things. Only a few days before, as I served the evening meal to my master, Chilam, lord of Centla, I'd listened incredulously to the story told by his guest, a runner from Champoton—a story of pale-skinned beings with beards who'd come to Champoton in such boats.

"Our people aren't cowards, you know," the runner said. He was a youth, fourteen perhaps, and obviously awed by what he had seen. "We were waiting for them when they came ashore. And we fought them. At least we tried. Spears and arrows against thunder and lightning!" He shivered. The strangers, with their fire-spitting metal sticks, had scattered his people like quail. The people of Champoton had snatched up their families and fled the town to hide in the jungle.

Chilam's heron-yellow eyes had narrowed. "You could be drunk or lying," he said, scooping up black beans with the edge of a flat maize cake, "but you don't look it." He shifted on his haunches as he squatted beside the straw mat on which the dishes had been placed. Suddenly he exclaimed softly. "Remember the legend of the bearded god, Kukulkan? Skin as white as a lily petal, they say . . ."

I remembered. I'd heard from childhood the story of the white god who had sailed away toward the rising sun with a promise to return one day.

"I was waiting for you to say that, my lord." The young runner sampled a chunk of roasted iguana meat. "But they couldn't be gods. Our arrows killed three of them before we ran. A warrior threw a rock at their leader that knocked out two of his teeth. Their skins may have been white, but their blood was as red as ours."

Chilam grunted and rubbed his long jaw. He was not a talkative man and he took his time in pondering what he'd heard. The runner finished his meal, spent the night at our house, and left early the next morning to carry his message to the towns on up the coast. As I went about my work, grinding corn on the *metatl* with the heavy, round grinding stone, patting out *tlaxcalli*, the leathery maize cakes that we call *tortillas* now, carrying water from the well in a pottery jar on my head, or combing the hair of Chilam's wife, Ixel, my thoughts had returned again and again to the white strangers.

Now, before my unbelieving eyes, the boats were coming, drawing majestically toward the mouth of the river that flowed past the city of Tabasco. My nails dug into the flesh of my palms. I almost expected to feel the ground tremble and hear music coming out of the sky, but of course nothing of the sort happened. I strained my eyes, but the boats were too far away for me to see whether there were gods standing on their decks.

I realized that it was my duty to run back to Centla and alert Chilam, for it was possible that no one else had seen the boats. With one last glance at the marvelous apparition I turned and started back through the trees. Three strides . . . four . . . five . . .

I collapsed against a withered stump, exhausted and out of breath. The immensity of my rounded body bulging out under my *huipilli* mocked my effort. Chilam's unborn child kicked hard, protesting the sudden activity. If only I hadn't come to the beach alone . . .

"Malinalli! You scare me, going off like this when your time's so near!" It was Tonaxel, Chilam's newest slave, slipping breathlessly through the tangle of the forest. She was fifteen years old, beautiful as a pearl from the sea, and so sweetly innocent that Chilam had decided to wait until her sixteenth birthday to take her as his second concubine. She put her hand to her mouth as she looked out through the trees and saw the boats.

I was still gasping for breath. "Run to Centla . . ." I panted. "Tell Chilam that the white gods are coming!"

Speechless with terror, Tonaxel bounded off through the trees like a doe. I followed her path, moving carefully with my precious burden. By the time I reached the maize fields surrounding the bone-white town of Centla, I could hear the boom of the big wooden drum from the steps of the pyramid of Kukulkan. Tonaxel had carried her message swiftly. I could imagine the farmers, fishermen and craftsmen dropping their work to hurry to the square. In my mind I could picture them painting their faces red and black as Chilam, resplendent in his battle headdress of white heron plumes, directed the passing out of shields, spears, bows and arrows from the town arsenal.

My sides ached from the long walk. Under the loose-fitting *huipilli* my chest heaved painfully, for the growing child pressed upward against my lungs, making it impossible to breathe deeply. Chilam had warned me not to go to the beach that morning, and I should have listened. It was only that I couldn't bear to stay in the house with the sullen Ixel, whose eyes burned with jealousy each time she looked at my body. Ixel, Chilam's only legal wife, was a handsome woman, but her barrenness had pickled her spirit. She made no effort to hide her resentment toward me, reminding Chilam persistently that the child of a Nahua woman was not fit to inherit the office of a Mayan ruler. It would be interesting, I reflected, to see how she'd deal with little Tonaxel, who was not only Mayan but the daughter of a neighboring chief by one of his slaves.

The clods of the maize field, where corn grew shoulder-high, were like boulders. Since I had trouble seeing my own feet, I stumbled frequently, twisting my ankles and scraping my knees. Now, from the nearby city of Tabasco, came the sound of another drum. So Tonaxel's message had been carried there already! Fat Tabasco himself, the senior chieftain of the province, would be gathering his forces and they would no doubt merge with those of Centla before confronting the invaders.

Perspiration trickled down my face and neck. The leaves of the corn plants hid the deep ditch in front of me and I fell into it, rolling heavily on my side and skinning my hands in the rough dirt. I lay there, breathing spasmodically.

Suddenly I felt a wrench of pain, as though giant hands were twisting my body, wringing it like a rag. My fingernails dug into the earth. For days I'd experienced little twinges and tightenings of my abdominal muscles, but never pain like this. Although I was carrying my first child, I'd attended other slave women in birth and I recognized the signs. My baby had chosen this time and place to enter the world.

The thought of giving birth alone frightened me; but at least, I thought, I would be away from Ixel's poisonous gaze and the leaves would shade me from the hot sun. I smoothed out the dirt with my hands, trying to make myself comfortable as I waited for the next pain to come.

If I had a son, I planned to ask Chilam to let me name him Tenepal after my own father. True, it was a strange name to the Mayan ear, but then I'd told him many times what a noble man my father had been. Chilam, if he cared for me, might choose to honor my wishes.

I leaned back against a mound of dirt and, needing something to take my mind off the pain, tried to bring into focus the features of the father I'd lost eleven years ago—the kind, homely face with its prominent hooked nose, the thinning gray hair, the stoop-shouldered body, the distinctive limp. I remembered walking hand in hand with him as a little girl through the marketplace of Oluta, my little chest puffing out with pride when people bowed low to him or saluted him by touching their fingers to the ground and then to their lips—

Another pain wrapped its cold fingers around me. My hands twisted the edge of my skirt, and I closed my eyes and clenched my teeth. It was good to be bringing this child into the world. My only regret was not being in Centla. As the pain subsided I could still hear the distant throbbing of drums and the blare of conch shells.

Had Quetzalcoatl returned? I wondered. You see, I still thought of the god by his Nahuatl name, although he was the same personage as the Mayan Kukulkan. It was my father who had first told me the legend of the white, bearded one who had promised to return to us in the year *ce acatl.* He'd been the most beloved of gods and the most widely accepted—Quetzalcoatl, Kukulkan, the Plumed Serpent, god of the east wind, of wisdom, knowledge and culture; he was the morning star, which died in the west and rose again at each dusk, symbolizing rebirth and resurrection.

But he was coming a year early! I counted carefully on my fingers. The Mayas used a system that was different from the Aztec sun calendar by which the people of Oluta had measured time. I counted the days, months and years by both systems. According to the Aztec dates, *ce acatl*—one-reed—

which occurred once during every fifty-two-year calendar cycle, would come next year.

Back in Oluta, the temple of Quetzalcoatl, a pyramid with a small *teocalli* at its summit, had occupied a secondary position to the newer and larger temple of the Aztec god, Huitzilopochtli, where daily sacrifices were offered to feed the sun on its journey across the sky. At the temple's foot, the market spread out into the square.

Waiting for the next pain, I moved my thoughts away from my body and tried to remember how the marketplace at Oluta had looked. To my childish eyes, it had been the most wonderful place on earth. My father had organized it after the manner of the huge market of Tlatelolco in the Aztec capital, which he'd visited for the coronation of the new emperor, Moctezuma II. But the thought of Moctezuma and of the market brought me no peace of mind. It was in the market of Oluta that my father had bought Itzcoatl to serve as my tutor and to keep an account of the tribute that was set aside for Moctezuma . . .

No, the slave market and Itzcoatl were such bitter memories that I could not let myself think of them while my child was being born. I opened my eyes and the vision dissolved into the blue, green and brown mosaic of sky, maize and earth around me.

The pains were coming harder than ever, shooting around my hips, creeping up my spine and down into my legs. I thrashed in a sea of helplessness now. Ixel or no Ixel, I was beginning to wish I'd made my way back to the house while I was still able to walk easily. With soundless lips I invoked the goddesses who were designated protectors of women in childbirth: the Mayan Ixbunic, the Aztec Temazcalteci, patroness of midwives, and Ayopechcatl, who had been worshipped as goddess of childbirth in Oluta. I remembered the chanting circle of women who used to gather around my mother, singing to beseech the little goddess's aid:

"Down there where Ayopechcatl lives, the jewel is born, a child has come into the world . . ." I whispered the familiar phrases through pain-locked teeth. "It is down there in her own place that the children are born . . ."

The maize stalks parted with a rustle and a small face peered between them. Was it Ayopechcatl herself coming to aid me?

"Malinalli! Thank the gods I've found you!" Tonaxel was out

of breath from running through the fields. "When you didn't come back—" She looked anxiously down at me and her delicate mouth formed a round little O. "The baby! It's coming now!" I nodded and her eyes widened with panic. "I've never helped with a baby before," she whispered.

"It's not hard." I tried to smile. "The baby comes by itself. Just do as I tell you when the time comes. Right now you can make a hollow in the earth and line it with clean leaves." I patted a spot on the ground next to me and Tonaxel began to dig frantically, like a little dog. "There's no need to hurry," I managed to say with a laugh. "There's plenty of time." In her fluttery presence I felt myself growing calm.

The tightening began again, welling up slowly from its center deep inside my body. I gripped Tonaxel's small, cold hand as the pain spread and hardened. By the time the contraction was finished, Tonaxel's eyes were wet with tears of sympathy.

"I'm hurting with you, Malinalli." She laughed shakily. "Don't you want me to run for the midwife?"

I shook my head emphatically. "No, don't leave me." Then, seeing the fear in her eyes, I added, "Don't worry, Tonaxel. Things are as they should be with me." I patted the little hand. "What's happening in Centla?"

"Chilam says that the women mustn't even see the strangers!" she exclaimed, a trifle petulantly. "We were shut up inside the houses. I had to sneak out to find you." We exchanged apprehensive glances. Unless the sight of the baby softened his heart, Chilam would be angry with us both.

"Did Chilam expect a battle?" I asked her.

"I don't think so. After what happened at Champoton, he's cautious. The plan is to wait and see if the strangers are friendly. Surely if they're gods— Malinalli, you're having another pain, aren't you?"

"Just keep talking to me," I whispered, pressing my back hard against the mound of dirt.

"Malinalli, I'd die if anything happened to you." Her fingers dug into the palm of my hand. "You're the only woman in Chilam's house who's been kind to me. Ixel hates me. I can see it in her eyes every time she looks at me." She gazed at me intently, the color deepening in her face. "Malinalli, when Chilam . . . when Chilam takes me, will you be jealous like Ixel is?"

"No, I won't be jealous, Tonaxel." I could say it honestly. I was Chilam's possession, to do with as he pleased. I respected him, yes, and I'd honor him by giving him a child, but as for any feelings that might give root to jealousy, I had none. I smiled reassuringly at her. "I'm happy that you've come to our house. It's like having a little sister."

"Did you ever have a real sister, Malinalli? I did."

"I didn't," I answered. "I was the only living child of my parents. But I had a friend who lived with us. She was almost like a sister. When I look at you, Tonaxel, I remember her."

"Tell me about her." Tonaxel leaned forward, eyes soft like a butterfly's in her tiny face.

So I told her about frail Miahuaxitl as I studied Tonaxel's face. Yes, something in the set of the eyes and the tilt of the cheekbones recalled memories of my friend. But Tonaxel's was the bright, darting liveliness of a hummingbird. Miahuaxitl had faded and drooped, I told her, like a blossom whose season has ended.

"She died, then?" Tonaxel asked.

"Yes," I said. "On the most terrible day of my life. Let's not talk about it now." The birth of a child was a happy event, not a time to dwell on painful memories. I crushed her hand in mine as new agony, stronger and more merciless than ever, surged downward through my body. "Soon!" I gasped.

Groaning with pain and effort, I crouched above the bed of leaves Tonaxel had prepared. I put all my strength into one final, excruciating push and felt my baby slide out into the world with a long, healthy wail.

"It's a little man! Oh, Malinalli!" Tonaxel leaned forward to study him in wonder where he lay blinking in his green cradle.

"Give him to me." I reached out eager hands.

Tonaxel carefully picked up the baby, still covered with the slime of birth, and placed him in my arms as I leaned back, exhausted, against a mound of dried cornstalks. I examined him minutely, counting his tiny, exquisite fingers and toes, looking into his eyes, ears and mouth, and stroking the thick mat of black hair. He was perfect. When the afterbirth came I took a strip of cloth torn from my *huipilli*, tied off the umbilical cord and, for want of a knife, severed it with my teeth. Then I moved him up to my breast and felt the little mouth groping for nourishment. As he nursed I looked at him, delighted. His nose, already large, was part Mayan and part Tenepal. The thin, blunt-ended fingers and the long, narrow chin were Chilam's, but the black eyes that gazed up at me were replicas of my own.

Tonaxel had taken off her own skirt and was ripping off a wide section of the clean inner part to wrap around the baby. "You can't stay here much longer, Malinalli. The sun's going down." She glanced anxiously at the sky, which was beginning to turn pink in the west.

She handed me the blue cloth and I put it across my lap and laid the baby on it. He was shivering, so I wrapped him quickly, tucking the ends around his tiny, kicking feet. I was anxious to get back to Centla. Even the birth of my son had failed to eclipse my excitement and fear over the arrival of the white gods, and I was hungry for news of them.

"Don't hurry so, Malinalli," Tonaxel said fretfully. "You'll hurt yourself. Here, give me the baby and I'll carry him for you. You're shaking." She took the baby in her arms, and I put my hand on her shoulder and followed her slowly between the rows of corn, back toward Centla.

As we entered the house, we heard Chilam's voice raised in annoyance.

"Look, Tabasco. These little green stones aren't jade. I can crush one into powder with this rock. See? They deceived us."

"So they aren't jade." Tabasco's high-pitched voice was calm. "Who knows? They may be something else just as good. Look how they catch the light."

The two chiefs were dining in the garden; Tabasco, fat and red-faced, was munching contentedly on beans and turtle eggs, but Chilam was eating only a little out of politeness. His lean body tensed as he squatted beside the mat. "I don't trust them," he said.

Tabasco shrugged his fleshy shoulders. "They seemed peaceful enough to me," he mumbled between bites. "Their interpreter said they were only looking for gold." He stopped chewing. "Are they gods, Chilam?"

"A god with his front teeth knocked out? I don't think so!" Chilam exclaimed. "But who can say? They don't look like my idea of gods, but then how are real gods supposed to look?"

Tabasco reached out for a slice of melon and bit into it, licking at the juice that trickled down his chin. "The toothless one who calls himself Grijalva," he struggled with the name, "invited us to board one of their boats tomorrow. I plan to do it. They're amazing things and I want to see their workings. What about you?"

Chilam frowned. "One of us should stay on shore in case

they're planning any surprises," he said. "Get rid of them, Tabasco. Tell them there's gold in Aztec country. Then let Moctezuma deal with them."

Although Tabasco's position as chief of the provincial capital gave him authority over his neighbor, Chilam was the older of the two and well known for his sagacity. Tabasco was wise enough to listen to his advice on most matters. "I'll do as you say," he answered with a note of reluctance in his voice. "If they're men, better to be done with them. If they're gods, nothing we say will make much difference."

A servant, a small, brown man named Potop, came out of the garden with an empty platter in his hands. I hissed at him from where we stood in the entryway. "Potop, were you at the river today?"

He nodded vigorously, grinning at the sight of the baby. "What a day! You should have been there." In a hushed voice he told us about the visit of the white gods. "And no matter what my lord Chilam thinks," he announced, "I, Potop, know gods when I see them. They were wonderful beings! Pale skin, hair like corn fibers. Some of them had eyes as blue as the sky. They wore metal clothing and carried grey metal knives as long as your leg!" His little eyes danced. "And you won't believe this, but they had a dog with them that was as big as a deer!"

The voices in the garden had fallen to a murmur. Potop leaned forward. "They had a Mayan interpreter who spoke their language, and Tabasco asked their leader if he was a god. The man laughed at the idea. He said they worshipped a god who couldn't be seen, that all other gods were false and wicked. I tell you, I could make no sense of—" He broke off, for Tabasco and Chilam had finished their meal. They rose to their feet, Tabasco patting his full stomach, and strolled back toward the kitchen. Potop hurried to the garden to clear away the dishes.

Chilam scowled when he saw us. "Where have you been? We needed you here this evening to serve the lord of Tabasco and neither of you could be found—" His face softened as he noticed the baby. "I see you've been occupied with other things!"

"You have a son, my lord." I put aside the folds of cloth to show him the baby. "Isn't he beautiful?"

"That he is," Tabasco murmured, and I, remembering what I knew of his habits, looked at him sharply and covered the baby again.

"Ixel, come and see!" Chilam called to his wife.

I cringed inwardly as Ixel came grumbling out of the kitchen, having been forced to prepare the meal in my absence. She would have nothing good to say. She looked from the baby to me, her narrow eyes brimming with hatred, saying nothing.

I turned to Chilam. "My lord," I said, "I'd like your permission to name him after my father, Tenepal."

"She can name him anything she likes," Ixel snapped. "His name's of no importance. In three days he'll be thrown into the sacred well as an offering to the rain god."

I clutched the baby, reeling with shock.

"What's all this, Ixel?" Chilam demanded. "I've no plan to sacrifice this child!"

She turned on him. "Have you already forgotten your promise?" She spat out her answer to Chilam's bewildered look. "Ten years ago! We were pleading with the gods to place a baby in my womb. You promised that if you were to take another woman your first child by her would be given in sacrifice so that the gods would be pleased and let me become pregnant."

"Ixel, this is foolishness!" Chilam shook her arm. "You're too old to have children now. Your fluids have dried up—you told me so yourself." His voice had begun to waver. A promise to the gods was not to be taken lightly.

"Take the baby, Ixel," I pleaded. "Raise him as your own son." I thrust my child at her but she made no move to take him. "Hold him in your arms," I begged. "If you're a woman, Ixel, you can't let this thing happen . . ." Tears were pouring out of my eyes and falling onto the baby's face.

Ixel pushed him away. "A vow to the gods is sacred," she said, her mouth a grim line. "To break it would bring disaster on our people. And you'd be responsible, my husband." She jabbed a finger into Chilam's chest. "Refuse to fulfill your vow and I'll take the matter up with the high priest!"

Chilam was weakening. "You're young, Malinalli," he said, looking at me with eyes full of despair. "We'll have other children. The gods will reward us—"

"No!" The words tore from my throat. "You'll have to kill me first! You can't have him!" Holding my son close, I pushed past Chilam and fled to my room. The baby had begun to cry and I lay down on the mat and put him to my breast, feeling the warm flow of life and love from my body to his.

"No one will take you," I whispered. "I won't let them. Tomorrow we'll run away." I kissed the top of his head. "Go to sleep, little rabbit, while I make our plans."

* * *

Chilam, accompanied by Tabasco and a retinue of slaves bearing gifts of food for the white gods, had departed for the river early the next morning. Ixel was busy at her loom in the garden. The other slaves paid little attention when I sauntered into the kitchen with a long cotton bag and began filling it with fruit, leftover maize cakes and dried fish. My only plan was to travel in the direction of the setting sun, back to my own people, back to Oluta. The journey would be long and dangerous, but I preferred death in the jungle to seeing my baby sacrificed.

I would have liked to say goodbye to Tonaxel but I realized that she'd be questioned when my absence was noticed. It would be safer for both of us if she knew nothing of my plans. Tonaxel had come to my room that morning with a steaming bowl of *atolli* for me, fussing over the baby and bursting into tears whenever our eyes met. It had been a relief when Ixel summoned her to go to the well for water.

Centla was quiet, for the market had been closed that day and nearly all the men had gone to the river. Only a few old men were about when I slipped out of the house with my baby on my back and a small bundle of provisions on my head. With the morning sun behind me, I followed a path that led through the maize fields and out into the forest. I moved unsteadily, still weak from the baby's birth, but the lure of escape and freedom urged me forward.

The trail disappeared in a maze of trees but I knew that I must keep walking. I intended to make my way through the forest for some distance, then cut north to the beach, emerging from the trees at a point beyond the area where the people of Centla came down to the sea. It would be easier walking along the shore than in the woods and I would be able to find shellfish and turtle eggs to eat along the way. My chances of getting lost would be considerably lessened, for I could keep the sea on my right hand. Later on, I could ask at each fishing village where to turn inland toward Oluta.

I trudged on, stopping to nurse the baby when he cried and to nibble on the provisions I had brought, torn between the desire to make the food last as long as possible and the knowledge that I had to eat in order to produce nourishment for my baby.

At last, toward evening, I heard the murmuring hiss of the sea ahead of me. Weary and aching, I stumbled out of the trees and onto the soft, warm sand. I was exhausted and the baby was hungry, so I sank down to rest and to feed him. As he nursed, I gazed out over the tranquil ocean and something on the distant horizon caught my eye. Far away, the strange, winged towers, four of them, were moving against the pink sky, carrying the white gods away from Tabasco. I watched them until they vanished into the thin line that divided sea from sky. Then my head dropped to my chest and I sank into oblivion with my baby beside me. . . .

The cry of a fishing bird awakened me. The morning sun was already hot on my cheek and I realized that I'd slept much longer than I'd intended. The baby's head was nestled in the hollow of my arm. Drowsily, I studied the delicate features, the long lashes, black as obsidian against flower-petal cheeks, the puckered, mauve lips. He stirred in his sleep and I brushed my cheek against his hair.

Suddenly I turned my head. Fingers of ice shot up my spine as I looked up into the sober face of Chilam. I clutched the baby with a start and he began to cry.

"Feed him," Chilam ordered. "Then we're going back to Centla."

I put the baby to my breast. My mouth was so dry that I couldn't speak.

"It wasn't hard to find you," Chilam answered my unasked question. "I knew you'd travel toward the setting sun because your people lie in that direction." He squatted down beside me and stroked the baby's hair with a fingertip. "I also knew that sooner or later you'd have to come out onto the beach, away from the snakes and wild animals."

I found my voice. "Let us go, Chilam. No one will have to know that you found me . . ."

Chilam looked down at the sand. "You've told me that you were the daughter of a chief, Malinalli," he said. "Surely he must have tried to make you understand the responsibility of a ruler toward his people."

I shuddered, remembering my father squatting on the floor of the sacrificial cage and refusing my childish efforts to set him free. Yes, he had tried to make me understand.

"Ixel was right," Chilam continued. "It's true that I made a promise. It was a fool's promise—I know that now—but I made it before witnesses. They'll remember."

"Tell them you found us dead in the jungle," I begged. "No one will know the difference. Let us go, Chilam!"

He shook his head sadly. "The gods will know, Malinalli. If I let you go they'll be angry. They'll bring down misfortune on Centla and it will be my fault. The responsibility is too great." He put his hands on my shoulders and now I saw the pain in his eyes. "Do you think this is easy for me?" he said brokenly. "Maybe you think I'm some kind of monster who enjoys sacrificing his own children. He's my son too, my firstborn child—and I'm not a young man. Every time I look at him I weep inside because of what I'm forced to do!" His golden eyes softened. "Malinalli, I have no choice. I must take the baby back to Centla. But I won't force you to return with me. You're free to go back to your people."

He let go of my shoulders and I fell back with a jerk. In the two years I'd been with Chilam I'd seen him display no emotion except anger, not even when he took me to the sleeping mat. Compassion was something for which he had no capacity, or so I'd thought. Yet he had just set me free. I only had to turn my back on him and on our son and walk away down the beach to a new life.

He looked down at his feet, avoiding my gaze. "I'll send a pair of armed guards to escort you back to your people if you like."

Strangely enough, the decision came to me easily. I'd lived for the day when I could return to Oluta, but I couldn't leave my son to die without me. However brief his time on earth, I wanted to be his mother until the last possible moment. And afterward, could I face my grief alone? Could I leave Chilam to face his?

I sat up. The baby had finished nursing and was blinking at us. I reached out and touched Chilam's cold hand. "I want you to know that someday I'll leave you," I said. "But not now, Chilam."

He let out his breath. "We'll walk back to Centla very slowly," he said as he helped me to my feet. "You're still weak. Do you want me to carry him?"

I hesitated. Every moment of my baby's life was precious now. "Yes, for a while," I said at last. "Carry your son." I handed the baby to him and we started walking back up the beach together. I concentrated on my own footsteps, trying to blot from my mind the vision of the high priest of Chac taking my child in his hands and flinging him out over the black water of the sacred well. It would be over quickly. Weighted down with gold ornaments, the baby would sink swiftly into the dark world of the rain god.

Chapter Five

Tabasco—1519

During the months that followed the death of my baby, I often thought about our light-skinned visitors. Indeed, I forced myself to think of them, trying to picture the details of their faces, clothing and weapons as Chilam had described them to me. My mind was groping for some preoccupation that would obliterate the grief that overwhelmed me with a pain more agonizing than any physical wound. My arms ached for my son. I couldn't wipe out the memory of tiny fingers clutching mine, petal-soft lips nuzzling my breast, serene black eyes gazing up at me trustingly as I handed him to Chilam to give to the high priest.

I found my thoughts returning to my own mother. Now, having loved a baby of my own, it was even harder to understand how my mother could give me life, raise me to young womanhood, and willingly sell me into slavery. I found little escape from my bitterness. Even sleep brought only nightmares in which my father, my mother, Itzcoatl and Chilam whirled through my tormented mind, appearing and disappearing like phantoms, as the owl-eyed priest flung baby after baby—all of them mine—to their watery deaths.

In spite of Chilam's attentiveness I hadn't become pregnant again. Chilam was disappointed, but concern for me was forced to the back of his mind after a time as new worries began to present themselves.

One evening Tabasco appeared at our house, accompanied by several servants and Nacontoc, the soft-eyed young boy who had been sold with me.

"Forgive me for intruding, Chilam," he apologized, "but I had to talk to you about something I heard in the market today. It may take some time to discuss, so I came prepared to spend the night." His reptilian eyes darted to the boy who stood near him fondling a long green feather.

"Our house is honored," said Chilam. "We were just about to dine. We'd be pleased to have you join us."

In fact the household had long since eaten, but Tonaxel and I were already hurrying to prepare another supper. Not to offer the chieftain a meal would have been an unspeakable breach of etiquette.

"Sit down," Chilam said. "We can talk while we wait for the women to serve us."

Tabasco lowered his thick body to the mat and scratched at the jade plug in his lip. "I met two soldiers from Champoton today," he said, and his expression was that of a man who had suffered great humiliation. The soldiers had made jokes with him about the return of the white men and had revealed that the Tabascans had become objects of ridicule in every village from the northern boundaries of Mayan territory to the island of Cozumel. "They've been laughing at us all this time!" Tabasco sputtered. "They're calling our warriors old women because we didn't fight the white men the way they did at Champoton." He gave a melancholy sigh. He was a proud man and his pride had taken a cruel flogging. "Were we wrong, Chilam?"

"You saw their weapons," Chilam said slowly. "It would have been foolhardy to fight them."

"Foolhardy even if they were men," Tabasco said, relieved that someone else felt he'd made the right decision. "If they'd been gods, it would have been even worse. I still think they might have been."

"Remember those missing teeth," Chilam cautioned.

"That makes no difference," Tabasco insisted, scooping up a paste of beans and chilis with his finger and sucking noisily. "If you go to the temple and break off the head of Kukulkan, does that make him any less a god? No, we were right, Chilam. Who knows what might have happened if we'd attacked them?" He paused to select a piece of turtle meat from the stew. "But, my friend, there's also the matter of pride. Everyone's laughing at us. They're saying that there are no men in Tabasco, only women, children and dogs. It's disgraceful. I can't stand their insults."

"Could you have found it easier to bear having your people die?" Chilam asked. "A wise decision isn't always a popular decision."

Tabasco sighed. "Perhaps. But that wise decision has made us all look like cowards in the eyes of our friends."

"No one who's been at my side in battle could accuse me of cowardice." Chilam fingered the jagged white scar that ran like a streak of lightning from his forehead to his chin. "I've won my victories not by being a brave fool who rushes in at every chance, but by weighing the odds and striking only when they were in my favor. I don't fight for glory and honor. I fight to win."

"Your reputation as a strategist is well deserved, Chilam." Tabasco wiped his greasy fingers on an embroidered napkin. "But this is different. Couldn't we at least have put on a show of strength—maybe shot a few arrows into their boats before we let them come ashore?"

"If we had, their weapons would have cut us all down," Chilam said. "What's the point in all this talk, Tabasco? The strangers have come and gone. It's too late to change the past."

"That's true," Tabasco admitted. "We may never see them again. But if they do come back, we've got to be ready for them. That's why I've come to you, Chilam. You're our finest military leader. I want you to take charge of fortifying our towns and training our warriors. Consider the advantages and disadvantages of our side and theirs, and prepare your strategy accordingly." Tabasco gazed at the moon, which had emerged out of the east just as the pale strangers had done. "If they come again we must stand against them for the sake of our honor."

"Honor's a poor reason to fight," Chilam said, "but you've handed me an interesting challenge and I accept it." He leaned forward, his eyes narrowed in thought. "Listen, Tabasco, their weapons look heavy to me. It must take a great effort to move the largest ones. If we gather on the shore in a mass, they only have to aim at us and kill us all. But if we can lure them into the swamps and fields where they'll have difficulty moving with their heavy weapons and armor . . ." Chilam picked up a piece of charcoal from the hearth and began to sketch his plans on the paving stones. I had been listening in fascination from the kitchen where Tonaxel and I were working. Now I turned reluctantly to making more maize cakes.

Tabasco's young companion wandered into the kitchen and stood watching us, twisting a piece of grass in his fingers. I smiled at him. I'd seen him from time to time in the marketplace of Tabasco and, because our misfortunes had been linked, there was a gentle sort of camaraderie between us.

"Is everything well with you, Nacontoc?" I asked, knowing full well that everything was not.

"Don't ask me that!" he exclaimed in a voice that had deepened noticeably since the day we'd been sold by the *pochteca*. "Look at me, Malinalli. I'm almost a man. I should be training to become a warrior, I should be watching the girls and looking forward to my marriage. That's what I should be doing!" He looked down at his own bejeweled hand with an expression of pure loathing. "Instead I'm nothing but a scented toy for that filthy old snake! He makes me wear flowers in my hair and paint my face yellow like a woman. I keep hoping he'll get tired of me, but he shows no signs of it." Nacontoc pulled the grass into several pieces and flung them onto the floor. "Malinalli, I'm not like Tabasco. I'm a man like other men! One day I'm either going to kill him or kill myself!"

"No!" Tonaxel cried, stepping around the cooking fire to Nacontoc's side. "Never speak of ending your life." She put her hand on his arm. "Can't you run away?"

Nacontoc gazed into the small, flowerlike face looking up at him. "Why, there are tears!" he exclaimed. Then he shook his glossy head. "No, I tried to run away once, not long ago. But I was caught and since then Tabasco's watched me like an owl. He says that if I go back to my village he'll burn every house in it. I keep hoping he'll lose interest as I become more of a man. If not, my only escape can be death—mine or his."

Chilam's voice interrupted from the garden: "The lord of Tabasco wants more *chocolatl*!"

"It's ready," Tonaxel called. She poured the bubbly whipped chocolate into a cup, stirred it a few more times with a wooden whisk, and hurried out of the kitchen.

Nacontoc's eyes followed her as she disappeared. "What a beautiful girl," he whispered. "Who is she, Malinalli?"

"Chilam bought her last spring," I told him.

"Is she—" the words came out painfully— "his concubine?"

"Not yet," I said. "But she will be as soon as she turns sixteen." I watched Nacontoc's face cloud with disappointment. "You see," I explained to him, "Chilam wants an heir. Ixel has always been barren. When she became too old to have children in any case, Chilam bought me." I squeezed the balls of *masa* dough between my fingers and patted them into flat circles for the *cumal* as we talked. "But Ixel has pressed the point that the child of a Nahua woman shouldn't govern a Mayan town. She's a forceful person. Chilam listens to her."

"I know. Potop told me what they did to your baby. I'm sorry, Malinalli."

I spread the flat cakes on the sizzling *cumal* and murmured something about the ways of fate and the gods. I could not even think about my baby without feeling pain. I continued, "Rather than argue with Ixel, Chilam went to the lord of Potanque and bought the daughter of one of his concubines. When Tonaxel gives him a son, the child will be pure Mayan and of noble descent on both sides. Ixel will have nothing to say."

"She's too lovely to be an old man's second concubine," Nacontoc said wistfully. "Forgive me, Malinalli, but life is so sad. Death is a welcome thing to a slave."

"Don't tell me you're talking about death again!" Tonaxel bustled back into the kitchen, fluttering from pot to pot like a bright little hummingbird. "What a morbid young man you are! Look around you! Walk out into the garden where the flowering vine has opened up its white blossoms. Listen to the crickets. They're singing with happiness just because they're alive! Ah! Here are the red chili peppers that the lord of Tabasco wanted, and they're still hot."

She scooped up a portion of the peppers from the cooking pot onto a plate and scurried out of the kitchen again. Nacontoc's adoring eyes followed her every movement.

Chilam and Tabasco continued their discussion until dawn.

March 1519

The months had passed quickly. Tonaxel, now approaching her sixteenth birthday, was looking ahead nervously to the consummation of her union with Chilam. I had made up my mind that on the day he took her as his concubine I would ask him to fulfill his promise to let me go back to Oluta. The timing of my plans had nothing to do with jealousy. I simply wanted to take my leave when the parting would be easiest.

Finding the time to tell Chilam about my decision was going to be the most difficult part. He was now fully occupied with the training of the area's young men for battle. There were more than forty villages and towns under the rule of Tabasco. Chilam visited each of them as frequently as possible to supervise the physical training of the warriors, the making of spears, shields, bows and arrows, and the construction of traps and fortifications around the towns. There was more at stake here than the wounded Tabascan pride. It was possible that if the strangers came again it would be not to trade but to conquer. Chilam was familiar with Moctezuma's practice of sending his *pochtecas* to assess the strength and wealth of new territory before launching his armies in conquest. It had occurred to him that the white men might use the same tactics.

"We'll let our land be our ally," I heard him say time and again. "The strangers are strong, but we will lure them into the swamps, into the forests and furrowed fields, so that we can fight them where their movements will be difficult."

On my treks to the seashore to gather shells and turtle eggs, I felt my eyes drawn irresistibly toward the horizon, where at any time the winged towers might appear again. I knew that by the reckoning of my own people the year *ce acatl*, in which Quetzalcoatl had promised to return, was now fully upon us. I thought of his coming with a mixture of dread and anticipation. Would it bring death and destruction or the power of a new life?

One day toward the end of the dry season, as I sat in the garden grinding maize to make *tamales* for a feast of supplication to the rain god, I heard the sound of running steps. A messenger, streaked with dust and sweat, burst through the garden entrance and collapsed in front of me.

"Get Chilam!" he gasped, his sides heaving. "The white gods—they've come back!"

There was no need to summon Chilam. He had heard and he was there at once, pulling the man to his knees as I brought him a calabash of water.

"Where are they?" Chilam demanded, shaking the runner by the shoulders. "Have they landed?"

"They're at Nonohualcos," the messenger panted. "When their interpreter asked us to bring food, we told them there was none, that they were to take their boats and leave or we'd cut them to pieces . . ." He paused to gulp the water I offered him. "They came ashore with their thundersticks. They chased us into our town . . . our fortifications were useless before them . . . we made our stand there, but when more of them appeared from another direction, we were lost. They've taken Nonohualcos." He began to sob. "Our warriors are all prisoners, dead, or hiding in the jungle!"

Chilam flung the messenger to the ground, where he sagged in a forlorn heap. "The fools!" Chilam raged, his eyes flashing amber. "They forgot everything I tried to teach them!" He began to bark orders to his assembled household. "Malinalli! Bring me my helmet and my padded coat. Ixel, my shield and my lance! Potop! Run to Tabasco. Tell him to ready his warriors but to do nothing until he sees me!"

Potop raced out of the house, only to return a moment later. "Tabasco's on his way here now," he reported. "I see him coming up the path with another man. A stranger."

The man who strode into the house beside the panting Tabasco was tall and thin. His face was plain to the point of ugliness, with protruding eyes, a long nose that drooped at the end, teeth like a rabbit's, and a receding chin. He was dressed only in the simplest loincloth. Chilam recognized him at once.

"You!" he exclaimed. "The interpreter!"

The man bowed. "I was captured by the Castilians two years ago, my lord. I've taken the first opportunity to escape." He spat on the floor. "They gave me the name of Melchor. They sprinkled water on my head, dressed me in their hot clothes, taught me their language and used me as a tongue to betray my own people! But I've run away from them, I've come to join you!"

Tonaxel and I listened, wide-eyed, from the kitchen.

"Tell us first of all," Tabasco commanded, "are your masters gods?"

"They are my masters no longer!" The man called Melchor spat again and rubbed the spittle into the floor with his bare heel. "Gods!" He coughed out the word. "I've seen them in their boats on the sea, when the motion of the waves made their faces turn yellow and their stomachs turn inside-out. I've seen them with boils and fevers. In the cities of the land they call Cuba, I've seen them drunk in the streets, and I've seen them with women. Gods?" He snorted. "I've even seen them die. They bleed and moan just as we do."

"So they're men!" Tabasco exclaimed, tugging nervously at the jade plug in his lip. "Then what do you advise us to do?"

"Fight them." Melchor spoke through clenched teeth. "Fight them to the last one of you. They'll stop at nothing to get what they want, and what they want is gold. It's like a sickness with them."

"But we have only a little gold here," Chilam protested.

"We said as much to the white men the first time they came."

"I know," Melchor said, licking his lips. "It was through my ears and tongue that your message came, remember? But it makes no difference to them. They'll ravage your land in search of gold, and in the process, they'll take away your women and your gods and soak the soil with the blood of your young men. You must stop them!"

"I've seen their weapons," Chilam said slowly. "Is it possible to defeat them?"

"They've been at sea for many days and they're tired. With their heavy weapons and armor they move slowly, especially over rough ground. Yes, you can defeat them, but only if you plan carefully."

Chilam agreed with him and now moved decisively, reaching for the rolls of bark paper on which he had sketched his maps and battle plans. "Look at this . . ." The three men bent over Chilam's sketches, muttering as they pointed out strengths and weaknesses of the plans. I brought another calabash of water for the runner, who was stretched out on the ground.

"How many of them are there?" Chilam asked. "How many boats?"

"Twelve boats, but four of them are too big for the river," Melchor replied. "The men, I think not over four hundred."

"Good," Tabasco exclaimed. "At least we'll outnumber them. Maybe we can . . ."

"You can!" Melchor insisted. "You must kill them all or lose your lives and freedom. I will lead you to—"

"You'll lead us nowhere," Chilam interrupted. "You've given us no proof that we can trust you. For all we know, your masters have sent you to spy on us or to lead us into a trap."

"Why, I give you my promise—"

"Promises have lost battles," Chilam retorted. "You'll be placed under guard here in my house. If we find that you've betrayed us, you'll pay with your life."

Melchor bowed his head in submission. "I understand your need for caution, my lord. I'll stay willingly. You'll find what I've told you to be true."

Tabasco thumped his fists together. "Ha! The man with the broken teeth won't find the same kind of welcome waiting for him as he did the last time!"

"Broken teeth?" Melchor raised his jutting eyebrows. "You're talking about Captain Grijalva. I wish it were he who'd come! Grijalva's an honorable man, but not too intelligent. He's predictable enough to be outwitted." He shook his head disdainfully. "No, the leader of these Castilians is no Grijalva. He's as cruel as a jaguar and as devious as a snake. His name is Hernán Cortés."

Chapter Six

March 1519

The black-hooded buzzards hopped about with hideous grace, defying those who had come to drag away the bodies. Spreading their broad wings and screeching hoarsely, they began their work, pecking hungrily at the eyes, tongues and open wounds of the dead and dying.

As I walked among the fallen victims of the battle, stepping over mangled limbs and shattered weapons, I saw no dead white men. What few there were had been long since carried from the field by their bearded comrades; but the blood of the warriors of Tabasco had flown like the waters of a river that day. Here and there I recognized a face I'd known, frozen in the terrible peace of death. The maize field where I'd given birth was now trampled flat and strewn with Mayan corpses.

The white men had chased a small party of warriors as far as the swamps and fields that separated Centla from the sea, and there Chilam's forces had been waiting for them. Tonaxel and I had climbed to the roof of the house to get a view of the distant fighting. I remember the first glint of metal through the trees as the first little band of the men Melchor had called Castilians emerged to confront the waving horde of Tabascans. The invaders were so few in number that even when their reinforcements arrived, victory for our forces looked easy. Even when the strangers unleashed their dreaded thunder-sticks, which flashed fire and roared with ear-shattering loudness, it seemed that sheer superiority of numbers would win out. Chilam had trained his men well and they fought bravely.

The turning point in the battle came when thirteen of the most frightening creatures I ever saw came pounding out of the trees toward the backs of our troops. To us, they looked as though they'd come straight out of hell—huge, snorting monsters of destruction with metal heads and men growing out of their backs. They trampled everything in their paths. Our poor warriors panicked at the sight of them. They fought on, but the outcome of the battle had been set from the moment those thirteen horsemen came crashing out of the swamp.

My ears still echoed with Melchor's screams. When defeat became inevitable, the priests came to the house and seized him by the arms and legs. They carried him, weeping and thrashing, to the top of the temple where they stretched him out on the sacrificial stone and ripped his heart from his body. Had he betrayed his own people or had he merely underestimated the strength of his former masters? No one could be certain now, but it no longer mattered. Melchor was dead and the Mayans were badly beaten.

What gaping wounds the white men's weapons left . . . I saw heads half blown away, arms and legs shattered and bodies torn open by the force of those metal balls. The back of my neck tingled as I picked up the end of a broken spear, heavy and oddly formed. I ran my hand along the shaft and felt the pointed metal tip with my fingers. The spear had been held in the hand of one of those fearsome white strangers. Sudden revulsion overcame my fascination, and I threw the spear to the ground again.

It was near the point where the battle had been thickest that I found what I was looking for. The white plumes of Chilam's helmet lay trampled in the dust and his body was sprawled nearby, his lifeless chest a mass of red. I picked up the helmet and flung it at an approaching buzzard, which flapped noisily away. I wondered if I should go get the helmet again—Ixel would like to have it, I knew. No, if Ixel wanted it, she could come and get it herself. Chilam's wife had been prostrate with grief when her husband had failed to return from the battle. She had sent me along with the other servants to look for him.

Bending closer, I gazed at the still face. The eyes were open, the mouth askew. His graying hair had been plastered to his forehead by the pressure of the heavy helmet. This was the man who had bought me for a piece of jade, the man who had fathered my child and stood at my side as that child, its tiny arms and legs flailing, disappeared beneath the black waters of the sacred pool. Looking at him for the last time, I felt curiously little—mostly a sense of finality, a realization that the life I had known had come to an end.

I straightened up and, looking about me, waved one arm above my head. A short distance away, Potop and another slave, carrying a litter between them, acknowledged my signal and trotted toward me, hopping over fallen weapons and corpses to bear the body of their master back to Centla.

Ixel had chosen to be buried with her husband. She was quickly strangled by one of the priests and then, with great haste, the two bodies were dressed in their finest robes. A piece of jade was placed in each of their mouths to represent their hearts. Then they were carried, along with some choice ornaments of gold, to the underground chamber Chilam had reserved for his burial. The priests and servants sealed the entrance and carefully camouflaged it with rocks and brush so that it would not be found and pillaged.

The rest of Chilam's possessions, including his slaves, were speedily rounded up by Tabasco, who ignored my protests that Chilam had freed me before his death. There had been no witnesses to my liberation, and I realized I could prove nothing.

"Please understand," Tabasco announced, "that I'm not taking the lord of Centla's property for myself. The Castilians have defeated us. It's only fitting that we deliver tribute to them."

Tonaxel shot me a terrified glance. We were huddled together in a room with eighteen other women. Most of them were slaves, but several wives of poor men, newly widowed by the battle, were included in their number. All, I noticed, were young and attractive. We trembled at Tabasco's words. One woman stood up and began to scream hysterically. A burly guard slapped her and she collapsed into a sobbing heap on the floor.

The worst fear of all, I believe, is the fear of things unknown, and it had taken possession of us all. The twenty of us were to be given to the white strangers. The thought of what they might do to us sent our imaginations into flights of horror. Remember, my daughter, we didn't even know what sort of beings they were. Many still believed them to be gods, and the traditional food of the gods was human flesh. That they might only want to possess us as men possess women was the least of our fears.

We were given new clothing and ordered to wash and arrange our hair. When this was done we were lined up behind forty slaves bearing gifts of food, cloth and jewelry, and were marched through the woods and down to the beach where the Castilians were camped, with their immense boats anchored offshore.

The first Castilian I saw at close range was a young sentry carrying a metal-tipped lance. His clothes and beard were caked with dust, and as he walked slowly back and forth outside the circle of cloth tents he scratched at a bloodstained bandage around his left thigh—a scruffy, pathetic god. Somehow the sight of him comforted me.

The sentry stiffened as we approached. He lifted a coiled metal tube to his lips and blew a blast of sound that made Tonaxel cower against me in fright. It was not so different from the noise made by a conch, I told myself, as, with the camp alerted, the sentry motioned Tabasco and the rest of us to follow him to its leaders.

Walking with downcast eyes, as was proper, I cast furtive glances about me to take in the world of bewildering sights, sounds and smells we encountered as we came within the circle of tents. The Castilians, in uncomfortable-looking clothing that fitted them tightly from neck to feet, were resting from the battle. I peered at them from under my lashes. White men. I'd expected dazzling whiteness, like clouds in a morning sky. Instead they were . . . faded. Like pieces of dyed cloth left out in the sun until the brightness of their colors had vanished. I saw pink skin, honey-colored skin, even skin with little brown splotches, but no skin that could be called white. Their eyes—all of them looking at us—were faded as well: brown as muddy water, blue like the sky, or green as *chalchihuitls*. But for all their strangeness, these visitors from another world looked reassuringly ungodlike to me.

They eyed us with interest as they stood around in small groups or sat on thick chunks of driftwood from the beach. One black-haired young man dressed all in brown, his beard carefully trimmed and combed, lounged alone against a tree. He was tall, so incredibly tall that I forgot my manners and stared right at him. He straightened to his full height. If I'd been standing next to him my head would barely have reached the bottom of his breastbone. From his lofty vantage point he stared back at me. Then his face lit up in a slow, lazy smile. One eye closed and opened with a mischievous wink.

Flustered and scared, I lowered my eyes. "Bernal! Bernal Diaz!" someone called. The tall man turned away in the direction of the voice. One day, after we'd become good friends, Bernal and I would look back on this first meeting and laugh.

Their camp was dotted with cooking fires, some of them tended by the men and others by women of two distinct types: brown-skinned, not unlike ourselves, and black as soot with short-clipped kinky black hair. They were dressed in long, full skirts and short blouses, mostly ragged and dirt-stained. I looked for white women but saw none. Closing my eyes, I breathed deeply, for my nose could often tell me as much about a place as could my eyes and my ears. I recognized easily the smell of roasting meat, but some of the spicy odors floating from the metal pots were new to me. The entire camp was permeated by the smells of sweat and smoke. Sick and wounded men lay on blankets on the ground, smelling of vomit and dried blood.

A sleek gray dog, as big as a puma, bounded toward us with ear-piercing barks. Never having seen a dog larger than cooking-pot size, we gaped at it with open mouths, drawing together fearfully. So awestruck were we that at first we didn't notice the stoop-shouldered man walking beside the dog. Nothing seemed remarkable about him until he drew closer; then I saw that he moved softly, lightly, like our own people. He was dressed in clothing that fit him as though it had been made for someone larger. And he was constantly pulling at it, looking at the plain brown sleeves as if they were made of gold. His skin was burned red by the sun, and the eyes that peered out from beneath his shaggy brows were pale blue. His graying head was newly and sloppily shorn.

He smoothed the bristling hair on the dog's neck and spoke to it softly. The animal stopped barking and obediently stretched out at his feet. "Don't be afraid of Esmeralda, my brothers. She's noisy but she's gentle." The sunburned Castilian in the badly fitting clothes had spoken to us in fluent Mayan. He made a low bow to the astonished Tabasco. "My lord," he declared in a formal voice, "I greet you on behalf of my captain, the most noble Hernán Cortés, whom you will meet presently. My name is Jeronimo de Aguilar, cast on your shores eight years ago when my ship sank in a storm and newly rescued by the grace of God and my countrymen."

"Tell your master we've brought an offering of peace." Tabasco returned the bow—though not too deeply, for this man was plainly an underling.

"He knows you've come and he's waiting," Aguilar said.

"This way, please." We continued through the camp. I kept glancing about us at the men—tall and short, fair and dark, shabby and well dressed—wondering which of them would turn out to be Hernán Cortés, whose presence already seemed to hang like smoke in the air about us.

"Malinalli!" I heard Tonaxel gasp. "There!" I followed her eyes to where a golden-haired man clad in scarlet stood conversing with two soldiers. He stood out like a jewel amid the grays, browns and dull greens that most of his comrades wore, and as he turned toward us his hair caught the sun's rays and seemed almost to blaze. He was not a big man, but there was an arrogant strength to the set of his shoulders, a brashness in the tilt of his splendid head with its handsome, hawklike features. He was clearly a leader, possibly Hernán Cortés himself, but for some reason I found myself hoping he was not. Instinct seemed to tell me even then that Pedro de Alvarado, for all his good looks and valor, had a dangerous streak of vanity and selfishness.

"He's beautiful!" Tonaxel whispered. "He must be . . ." Her voice trailed off as Aguilar passed by the man without giving him so much as a glance.

At last we came to the largest tent in the circle. In front of it was a massive wooden table strewn with papers and maps. The youth who was bending over to study them turned his head at the sound of our footsteps, revealing a thin face with long-lashed brown eyes, curly black hair that fell onto his forehead, a large, straight nose and a receding chin, partly hidden by a sparse beard. He was immaculately dressed in deep blue velvet, and the position of his body hid from sight the face of someone seated on the opposite side of the table.

"Noble lords of Tabasco," Aguilar intoned, "I have the honor to present to you our commander, Hernán Cortés."

For an unbelieving instant I thought he meant this slender boy whose shoulder blades jutted out like wings. Then I knew he did not, for the youth slowly straightened his body, stepping to one side to reveal the person who was sitting behind the table in a carved wooden chair.

The square-boned face was framed by wavy brown hair and a short beard. The eyes, round and deeply set, were intensely dark, sharp and probing as a ferret's, the shoulders broad and straight, the hands strong but finely molded. He was dressed in well-made clothing of soft gray that emphasized the pallor of his face. His only ornament was a little gold medallion on a thin chain around his neck. On the table lay his sword, and beside it was a delicate, silver cup with a stem like a flower's.

Was I looking into the eyes of Quetzalcoatl—the east wind, the morning star? Or was this merely Hernán Cortés, a man and a leader of men? Studying him, I suddenly realized that the answer didn't matter. Man or god, this vital, intense presence held my destiny in his hands, and even from that moment, I knew I would have no power to resist him.

Hernán Cortés rose to his feet. He was not tall. From my position behind the assembled chiefs and gift-bearers I had to stretch in order to see his face. After one of our priests had perfumed the air with his swinging censer of burning copal, Tabasco pressed his face to the ground and spoke in his most conciliatory tones.

"Great lord, we come before you in peace. We've brought you the choicest of all we have: gifts of gold, food fit for a god, the most beautiful girls in all the province of Tabasco. All we ask in return is your forgiveness!"

Aguilar interpreted his words for Hernán Cortés, who scowled. When he spoke, his deep, rich voice was stern. No interpreter was needed to convey our conqueror's displeasure. They had come in peace, he said through Aguilar, only to be met with arrows and spears. Why should they want to make peace with such untrustworthy souls?

"Great lord, we throw ourselves upon your mercy!" Tabasco implored, the color draining from his florid face.

"You're fortunate, lord of Tabasco," Aguilar translated for his commander, "in that you've been defeated in battle by one whose god compels him to look upon all men with the spirit of forgiveness." Tabasco heard these words and began to dry his tears. "But," Aguilar continued, "if you show yourselves to be treacherous again, I'll let loose my shooters of thunder against you. They are easily angered! Behold!"

Two soldiers touched a lighted straw to the base of a black metal tube that was as thick as a tree. With sickening suddenness a blast of smoke and flame shot from the weapon's mouth. The ground shook with ear-splitting thunder that echoed and reechoed against the hills. As I clapped my hands over my ears I was nearly knocked over by the retreating wave of Tabascans.

"Something else is angry too," Cortés announced after Aguilar had restored quiet. "It wants to speak with you." He nodded his head toward a grove of trees and a man came forward, leading one of the huge beasts that had turned the battle against us so quickly. Our jaws dropped as we stared at it.

The creature's head was not made of metal after all. There was no man growing out of its back, I realized, feeling a little stupid for having thought so. At close range it looked something like a deer, but no deer ever boasted such a massive body, such a powerful neck and legs. Its stonelike feet could have clubbed a man to death. As it came nearer it began to snort, tossing its head and rearing up on its hind legs. Even the husky fellow holding the lead rope was having difficulty controlling the animal. One of the soldiers who had fired the weapon ran forward, dodging the deadly feet, to help him. The monster plunged toward us, baring its ugly yellow teeth, its red-lined nostrils foaming. Forgetting dignity, forgetting ceremony, we panicked, trampling one another in our flight to escape this snorting, stamping terror.

Tonaxel and I were knocked to the ground by a portly priest. We lay where we fell, clutching each other for protection. Suddenly Tonaxel stiffened. "Malinalli, they're laughing at us! Look!" It was true. The assembled soldiers and officers, including the slim youth in blue and the towering Bernal Diaz who'd come to watch the action, were holding their sides, convulsed with laughter. Aguilar was biting his lip to maintain a semblance of seriousness while tears ran down his sunburned cheeks. Only Hernán Cortés remained impassive as he stood behind the table, his face a mask of severity.

Finally the horse was pulled away to a safe distance and Aguilar was able to restore order. He informed us for his master that the horse was angry with us and that Cortés would now go out and talk with it in an effort to convince the beast that we were peaceful.

Cortés strode out to where the two men held the animal's rope. Carefully sidestepping the horse's flailing feet, he stood at its side, stroking its neck and back, whispering softly to it. The horse stopped rearing, but continued to toss its head menacingly. The conversation finished, Cortés turned his back and walked away while the men led the reluctant beast back to its lair in the grove of trees.

Bernal Diaz was wiping his eyes. Aguilar was struggling openly to regain his composure, but Cortés's face did not even twitch. "The horse has told me," he announced gravely, "that it can't be pacified with mere words. To show it that your intentions are peaceful, the following conditions are to be met." The repentant Tabascans listened as Aguilar translated. First of all we were to return to our towns with our families as proof that we desired to live in peace. Second, we were to deliver up Melchor for his just punishment.

"We can't," Tabasco said in a quavering voice. "We've already burned his heart."

"Then justice has been done," Cortés declared, "but that brings me to the third condition. You must renounce your false gods and embrace the worship of Jesus Christ and his mother, the Blessed Virgin."

Renounce our gods! The chieftains looked at one another, stupefied. Even Moctezuma did not require conquered peoples to give up their gods. They were only asked to make room for the Aztec deities among their own. The priests' confused protests buzzed in the air.

Just as Cortés began to speak again, a gaunt man in a rough brown robe, his gray hair shaved at the crown, stepped out of the crowd and placed a hand on the commander's arm. He whispered a few words and Cortés nodded his assent.

"My brothers," Aguilar announced, "I give you our priest, Fray Bartolome de Olmedo."

The priest stood before us. His eyes were the color of the sky on a stormy day. He cleared his throat. "First of all, my beloved new friends," he said in a strange, mellow voice that carried a tone of authority in spite of its softness, "I want to make it clear to you that we force no man to accept our religion. True conversion comes only from the heart of the individual." Aguilar translated for him.

I had never had a high regard for priests of any religion. They were such mirthless creatures—pious, fanatical, often cruel—and this frail-looking Castilian in his ugly brown robe appeared no different from the rest. Yet there was something in his manner or his speech that struck a long-dormant note of response within me. What was it? I listened and suddenly I knew—it was his voice! Although I could understand none of the words, the priest's voice was so like the voice that had caressed, soothed, ordered, reprimanded and taught me through the days of my childhood. It was my father's voice speaking to me again in another tongue, and I listened with my heart.

"I know," the priest continued, "that it would be useless to ask you to give up anything unless we had something of greater value to offer in its place. Your gods demand the sacrifice of innocent blood. Our God asks only for the devotion of your spirits. Accept Him, my brothers, and I promise you happiness and peace beyond anything you've ever known in your lives."

While he was speaking, another priest, plump and red-cheeked, came forward carrying a cross and a doll-sized figure of a woman in a long, flowing dress with a child in her arms. It was then that I heard for the first time the story of the birth, death and Resurrection of Jesus. If anyone had told me then how many times in years to come I would find myself telling and retelling the same story to my people, I would never have believed it.

When the priest came to the Crucifixion and pointed out on the wooden cross where Jesus' hands and feet had been nailed, a gasp of horror rose from his listeners. Human sacrifice had its aspects of cruelty—no one could deny that—but at least having one's heart cut out was a quick way to die. The thought of those long hours of agony brought shivers of revulsion to even the stoutest Tabascan heart.

I found myself looking at the little statue of the mother with a strong sense of kinship. I, too, had given a son in sacrifice. The tiny, painted eyes that gazed back at me brimmed with sympathy and understanding.

But we all liked the part about the Resurrection; it was like a happy ending. Then Cortés came forward again and informed us that, although no man would be forced to accept the new religion, we must, as a condition of peace, clean and whitewash our temple and allow a cross to be erected in the place of the altar. Then he turned his attention to the women. "Lords of Tabasco," he said, placing his hands on his hips and looking critically at us where we stood in a line, "you do us great honor with this gift of your daughters." His eyes looked me up and down and I felt my cheeks growing warm. "However," he continued, "we can't accept any woman who worships heathen gods. All twenty of them must be baptized at once. Any woman who refuses will be sent back to her people."

Aguilar, after interpreting for his commander, now spoke for himself. "My sisters, if there are any of you who wish to show the willingness of your spirits by being the first to be baptized, will you please come forward?"

The women around me giggled nervously, glancing shyly at Aguilar and nudging one another. I stood aloof from them. Trembling, I stepped forward and looked into Aguilar's pale eyes.

"I'm ready," I said.

Aguilar smiled. He was a homely man with a broken nose and crooked teeth, but I felt even then that there was not a trace of unkindness in him. "What's your name, little sister?" he asked.

"Malinalli."

"Well, Malinalli, to signify the beginning of your new life, we're going to give you a new name."

I protested. My name was one of the precious few things that remained of what my father had given me. Aguilar whispered to the priest, who nodded. "Then we'll only change your name a little," he said. "Kneel, child."

I knelt obediently on the ground. Fray Olmedo was handed a basin of water from which he sprinkled a few drops on my bowed head. In the voice that brought memories flooding back to me each time I heard it, he chanted some strange words that Aguilar did not translate.

The ceremony was a short one. When the priest had stopped speaking, Aguilar reached for my hand and helped me to my feet. His eyes were moist. "Welcome, Marina," he said.

Looking back now, I can see the shallowness of that, my first acceptance of the Christian faith. A familiar voice, a story, a little painted statue—these simple things had prodded me along. And I won't rule out the possibility that my fascination with Hernán Cortés added to my eagerness. But in truth, my daughter, it was years before I became a true Christian, years of trial, sorrow and bewilderment before I even understood the meaning of the word.

Not long after you were born, María, I stood alone in the cavernous space of the new cathedral in the square. My life had come full circle, its pieces fitting together at last, like the links of a chain. I knelt down before the altar in that cool dimness and poured out my thanks to the Power that had guided my stumbling feet to their destiny. I felt a sense of completeness—almost. Yet one link in the chain of my life remained open. I had found myself thinking more and more of my childhood, of a wild, pagan promise that remained unfulfilled. I caught myself counting the years, wondering if I would live long enough to see the coming of the next *ce acatl.*

Then I looked up at the cross above the altar. It was not a little wooden one like the cross I first saw in Padre Olmedo's hand, but a grand one brought all the way from Spain, complete with a life-size painted carving of the crucified Christ. Admiring the workmanship, I studied the face, the dark beard against the ivory skin, the masterfully painted eyes that spoke of love and forgiveness even in the midst of suffering. The pain seemed very real to me at that moment, but I consoled myself with the knowledge that He had risen again, just as the star that falls in the evening rises again at dawn . . .

The huge church was quiet as a tomb except for the pounding of my own heart. I gazed up at the cross and a hoarse whisper worked its way up and out of my tight throat.

"Quetzalcoatl . . . ?"

The name echoed against the dark walls and the high, vaulted ceiling. Only silence answered. Silence and reason, telling me that I was wrong.

Yet, deep inside me, I had felt that last open link close to a perfect circle.

Chapter Seven

March 1519

The sea was in a playful mood, rocking the ships like toys as the wind that filled the huge, flapping sails propelled them through the waves. I had never ventured more than a few yards from shore in a canoe, so the sensation should have been exhilarating, but the memory of the night before had drained the brightness from the day for me. I stood by the rail of the ship, watching the white foam as it trailed past the bow. My lower lip jutted out petulantly.

"You didn't come to perform your devotions to Our Lady," scolded Aguilar, who'd moved over to stand next to me. "I waited for you. Did you forget?"

"No," I said in a flat voice. "I didn't forget. I remembered and decided not to go." I was disillusioned. Full of new faith, I had asked the little painted goddess for just one small favor and she'd ignored my prayers.

Aguilar had told us of the miracles that could be wrought by faith—how the blind had been made to see, the lame to walk. Compared to these near-impossibilities, I had asked for such an easy thing, but for all the good it had done me I might as well have been kneeling before one of the stone gods back in Centla. "If it's permitted for one to be angry with a goddess," I pouted, "then I am angry with your Lady."

Aguilar shook his head. "You child!" he exclaimed. "It's true that Our Lady can perform miracles, but she doesn't give us everything we ask for. If she did, there'd be no poor among us, no sick, no lonely ones. There'd be no need for us to work or perform our Christian duties to others." He ran a hand over his shorn head. "Think how life would be if we got everything we asked for."

I continued to stare out at the sea. His philosophizing wasn't making me feel any better.

Aguilar peered at me curiously. "Now what was it you asked for?" He scratched his ear. "Ah, yes, of course! I've got eyes and I've seen the way you look at our commander. You're out of sorts because he gave you to young Puertocarrero instead of keeping you for himself."

I felt my eyes smoldering as I looked at him. He'd guessed correctly. Against my prayers and wishes, Hernán Cortés had awarded me to the skinny youth in blue who'd stood beside his table.

"Come now," Aguilar coaxed. "Can't you see that for Cortés to take a woman before his men had them would have been a bad thing in their eyes? He did the only thing he could—he took none of you." He paused to watch a seagull drift past us and dive into the waves for a fish. "It wasn't that Cortés didn't like you—on the contrary! When he presented you to Puertocarrero he whispered to me, 'What a splendid creature. Mark my words, she'll make a man out of our young Alonzo!' "

Nobody, I reflected sullenly, could make much of a man out of Alonzo.

"You're not so poorly off," Aguilar said soothingly. "Alonzo Hernandez Puertocarrero's the son of one of the noblest families in Spain. Maybe that's why, when Cortés heard you were a princess in your own right, he decided that the two of you would be a fine match. Besides, anyone can see that the boy adores you. He'll never treat you badly."

Aguilar's words had failed to reach the depths of my disappointment. I watched the green water slide past the flanks of the ship and wished he would leave me alone. At least Tonaxel was happy. She'd been christened Antonia and given to her golden-haired god in scarlet, Pedro de Alvarado. The radiance of her face was almost blinding.

The dog, a greyhound bitch, sidled up to Aguilar and rubbed her muzzle against his hand. "Ah, Esmeralda," he crooned, rubbing her ears affectionately. "We understand each other, you and I, don't we? Just two rescued castaways, that's us."

"The dog too?" My curiosity was piqued. Aguilar had cast a different kind of bait to lure me out of my pouting this time, but I took it willingly. After all, I couldn't sulk all day.

"That's right." He squeezed the dog's muzzle with his hand. "Esmeralda went exploring on her own last summer when the Grijalva expedition stopped for water down the coast, and they had to sail off without her. Bernal Diaz was with them and he says he's positive she's the dog they lost. Cortés picked her up just a few days before they found me." Esmeralda turned over on her back and Aguilar squatted down on his haunches to scratch her belly with its two neat little rows of nipples. "You'd been pretty lonesome, hadn't you, old girl." He waited expectantly, and I knew he wanted to tell me about his own experiences.

"The story's a long one," he said when I'd asked him. "I'll tell you if you'll promise to stop blaming your troubles on Our Lady and come to mass tomorrow. Agreed?"

"Agreed." I leaned back against the rail. The breeze in my hair felt good. Esmeralda curled up in a ball at Aguilar's feet as he began.

"It was a storm that brought me to this place," he said. "The Caribbean's full of them, especially in late summer. I was with Captain Valdivia, sailing from Darien to Santiago de Cuba when our ship, a ship much like this one, was hit by one devil of a gale—but no! I'm convinced it was the hand of God himself stirring up those winds! In casting me on your shores and forcing me to learn your language, He made me His own instrument for the preaching of the true faith to the people of this land." Aguilar paused, breathing deeply to regain control of his emotions. He was totally sincere, I would come to find, in his belief that God had set his particular misfortunes upon him for some divine purpose.

I listened, absorbed, as he told me how the captain and most of the crew had been eaten by the natives who found them. Aguilar, being very thin, had been put in a cage to fatten. One night he and a sailor named Gonzalo Guerrero, who was strong enough to loosen the bars, were able to escape along with several others. They'd fled to Chetumal where they'd thrown themselves on the mercy of the old Mayan chief, Ahkin Xooc, who'd permitted them to live in his province, but only as slaves. Aguilar had been given to the old ruler's son, Taxmal, who succeeded to the chiefdom when he died.

I nodded excitedly, remembering that Chilam had mentioned Taxmal a number of times. "I wish I'd known about you," I said.

"Well, Chetumal is far from Tabasco." Aguilar continued his story with a melancholy expression in his eyes. After disease and exhaustion had taken their toll, the only Castilians who remained alive were himself and Gonzalo Guerrero. "Ay, it was strange, the two of us, so different from one another—he a man of the sea and of the world, and I who'd taken minor orders and hoped to join the Dominican brothers one day—and yet the strength to survive was present in us both.

"I'd taken vows of poverty, chastity and obedience, and I kept them all. Poverty and obedience were my natural lot—I had no choice in the matter. Now chastity—but that's another story. Not for your innocent ears, little sister."

I had to laugh at that. I'd been raped by Quauhtlatoa, spent two years as Chilam's concubine and borne his child and was now engaged in teaching a skinny lad how to behave with a woman. "Tell me," I teased. "If there's anything I don't already know, I'd best learn about it now."

"Oh, very well." He started off, his voice laden with misgivings. "My master and his comrades had noticed that I never so much as raised my eyes to look at a woman. Having learned their language by then, I explained my reasons. They should have understood—their own priests are celibate, as you well know—but for some reason my continence was a special source of amusement to them." Aguilar actually reddened under his sunburn. "Once, just to try me, my master sent me on a journey to bring back a special kind of fish. As my only companion, he sent along his own concubine, a most beautiful girl—and the mischievous devil had instructed her to make every effort to entice me.

"We had only one hammock between the two of us, and at night she'd string it between two trees, take all her clothes off and try to get me to lie down in it with her."

He'd been staring down at his feet as he spoke, but now he raised his head and looked me in the eye. "By all the saints, I swear that Our Lord himself, during his trials in the desert, was not besieged by a more persistent tempter. I cut stacks of wood for the fire. I recited the rosary. I sang all the songs that my mother'd taught me on her knee. Yes, I resisted that brown Jezebel. Then I flung myself down on the ground and slept like an infant, lulled to sleep by the songs of heaven." Proud of his resistance, he stood tall. "After that, my master trusted me totally. He placed me in a position of authority second only to his own. And so things remained until word reached me that my countrymen were waiting at Cozumel."

"What about your friend Guerrero?" I asked.

"He married a Mayan girl and became a chief in her tribe. After I'd been set free I went after him to bring him back here with me, but all he said was, 'Look at me, Brother Jeronimo!' He had jade plugs in his ears and lips; his face was tattooed. What would his own people have said when they saw him? I sat down and his wife brought me some fresh fruit and his little son and daughter climbed on my lap and began to play with my beard. Poor Gonzalo. 'They'd die in our world, my friend,' he said to me. 'And how could I go and leave them? Give me those green beads you brought for my ransom and I'll give them to my wife to wear around her neck.' So I gave him the beads and the other things I had and set out alone for Cozumel."

He leaned his chin on the rail, a faraway look in his washed-out eyes. One of the Tabascan girls strolled by on the arm of a tall, brown-haired officer. "If you're skeptical about miracles, Doña Marina, let me put your mind at rest," Aguilar said to me. "Going back for Gonzalo had taken me so long that by the time I got to Cozumel, Cortés had given up on me and left. You can imagine the desolation I felt. But then, not many leagues out, one of the ships, a perfectly sound one, began taking on water like a sponge. The leakage was so bad that the ship had to turn back to Cozumel for repairs, and by then I was waiting there for them." He turned his gaze from the sea and looked me squarely in the eyes. His voice dropped to a whisper. "Nothing less than a miracle, little sister, could have brought that ship back to find me!"

"God must have wanted you to be found," I agreed, duly awed by the story.

Aguilar chuckled. "By then I didn't look much more like a white man than poor Gonzalo did. When I saw the ship, I had an Indian paddle me out to it in his canoe. There I stood, with nothing but a dirty rag wrapped around my privates, sunburned as red as any heathen. All I had left of civilization was a battered Book of Hours that I carried in a net bag. They didn't even recognize me as one of them till I shouted out, 'Are you Christians?' " He lapsed into silence, a distant smile on his face at the memory of the reunion that had followed. I could have left him to rest then, but another question had surfaced in my brain and my curiosity was too urgent to deny it.

"There on the beach at Tabasco," I said, "when they brought the horse out to frighten us, I saw you laughing."

He came out of his reverie. "Oh yes. What a rotten trick for that fox Cortés to have played on you!"

"Now that I'm one of you," I demanded, "I think it's only fair that you tell me what was so funny." The revelation that it had been Cortés's doing only intensified my curiosity.

Aguilar puckered his brows and gave a thoughtful sigh. "Tell you?" He brightened suddenly. "No, come on, I'll *show* you."

I followed him down the slippery ladders and into the hold of the ship. It was frightening, like a descent into the belly of a creaking monster. Lanterns lit the way here and there, but shed only a dim, eerie glow. The hold smelled of seawater, rotting wood, stale fish, mold and the pungent odor of horses.

Rounding a corner, we came into an open area lined with wooden stalls. In each stall, huge and terrible, stood a horse. The beasts were surprisingly placid. Some were munching dried grass, chomping away with their big, yellow teeth. Others were snorting softly, stamping and shifting their weight with the motion of the ship.

"Come on." Aguilar took my hand and pulled me toward the horses. "Don't be afraid. They're as gentle as Esmeralda." He dragged me to a massive brown stallion, the very one that had thrown the Tabascans into such a panic. "Stroke his neck," Aguilar whispered to me. "He likes that. Don't be afraid. Who knows? One day you might sit on his back just like our captains do."

The horse's ears were pricked forward. The large eyes, glowing in the light of the lanterns, gazed softly at me. I reached out a trembling hand and ran it along the glossy neck, feeling the sleek coat and, under it, the rippling masses of muscle. The creature lowered its head and closed its eyes. Delighted, I moved my hand up to its forehead and then, timidly, down to the petal-smooth nose. Suddenly the horse snorted, blowing a cloud of moisture into the air and sending me lurching backward against Aguilar.

Someone laughed, a deep, hearty laugh, and a voice called out merrily to Aguilar. Startled, I looked quickly around. In a neighboring stall a man had risen to his feet.

He looked to be about thirty years old, not tall but well proportioned. His dark blond hair was streaked by the sun and his face and arms were tanned, contrasting darkly against his white blouse with its rolled-up sleeves. Even his deepset eyes spoke of a life in the open air, for they were creased at the corners as though he'd spent years squinting into the sunlight.

As he approached us, I saw that he'd been dressing the wounded leg of a black mare, for in one hand he held a wad of bloodstained cloth and in the other a cup of hot oil. I repressed a shudder, knowing that the oil was made from melted fat taken from the body of a dead Tabascan. He smiled at Aguilar, flashing white, even teeth, and said a few words to him.

Aguilar turned to me. "Juan Jaramillo wants me to say that he's sorry for having laughed at you, but your reaction to the stallion was so delightful that he couldn't help himself." He spoke a few sentences to the man. Although I couldn't understand him, I caught the mention of my own name and Alonzo's, and realized that Aguilar was telling him about me.

Juan Jaramillo acknowledged the introduction with an inclination of his head, glancing awkwardly down at the bandages and the cup of oil in his hands. The subtle glint of concern in his blue eyes told me that he'd remembered the source of the oil and its painful association with me, but when he spoke his manner was charming.

"He says," Aguilar translated, "that Alonzo Hernández Puertocarrero is the most fortunate man in all the Indies." I found my face warming, even though I knew the remark had been nothing more than one of the little gallantries these Castilians were so fond of. For some reason the amusement in those eyes aroused a streak of defiance in me. I stepped to the side of the stallion and began to stroke its neck once more, boldly caressing the hard, flat forehead and the velvety nose. When the animal shook its mane and snorted again, I steeled myself and remained unflinchingly where I was.

"So the creature's gentle," I said a bit haughtily. "You still haven't told me why you were laughing at us."

Aguilar turned to Jaramillo and translated my question. I fully expected the blond Castilian to laugh at me again, but this time he did not. "Doña Marina," he said simply, as Aguilar translated, "I hope you'll accept my apologies on behalf of my countrymen for a trick that was an affront to the dignity of your people." It was a surprising thing to say. I felt my defiance melting as he continued, "I wasn't there, mind you, for I had my duties here on the ship, but the men told me afterwards what had happened." He reached up to run his hand along the stallion's back. I noticed that a black sash was knotted around his upper arm. "You see, a female, a mare ripe for breeding, was hidden in the bushes behind you. Poor Arriero!" He patted the stallion's shiny rump. "He wasn't angry. He only wanted to get to his mate. Please forgive us, my lady." He regarded me expectantly as Aguilar translated for him, and I found myself wondering whether he was still laughing inwardly at me.

"I accept your apology on behalf of yourself," I said, "but

your commander can do his own apologizing." The glance that passed between the two men was enough to tell me I could expect no apology from Hernán Cortés. "Devious as a snake," the unlucky Melchor had described his former master. It was plain that the description was a true one; yet I was not repelled when I thought of him. If anything, I was all the more intrigued.

Aguilar had just opened his mouth to speak when he was interrupted by the sound of running feet and shouting on the deck overhead. I heard a cry of anguish in a familiar voice, followed by Cortés's bellowing for Aguilar. Forgetting Juan Jaramillo for the moment, I followed the bandy legs of the interpreter as he scrambled up the ladder, through the open hatch and into the sunlight.

There, with his arms pinioned by Bernal Diaz and Cortés's own blade at his throat, was Nacontoc.

The youth was barely recognizable. His face and body were streaked with sweat and dirt, and he'd hacked off his flowing hair at the shoulders. His face, contorted with terror, relaxed when he saw me.

"Malinalli!" he gasped. "The gods be thanked! Tell them I'm not their enemy!"

"They found him hiding in the food stores," Aguilar said.

"He's a good friend. Tell your commander to put away his sword," I said quickly.

At Aguilar's translation, Hernán Cortés's black brows rose, rippling his pale forehead. His reply was sharp, but he withdrew the point of his sword from the hollow of Nacontoc's throat and slid the weapon into its sheath.

Aguilar failed to conceal his smile. "My captain says that he's not accustomed to taking orders from a woman, but he asks you most humbly to enlighten him about the young man."

"He's a . . . slave of the lord of Tabasco." I decided not to embarrass the boy by revealing the nature of his function in Tabasco's household. "I've known him for years. He's been used most cruelly by his master. I don't blame him for running away and hiding on your ship." I glanced from Aguilar to the scowling face of Cortés. "Give him refuge," I said. "He'll be a grateful servant."

"Runaway slaves are nothing but trouble," Cortés snapped. "But if you two will be responsible for him, Aguilar and Doña . . . what's her name, Aguilar?"

"Marina, sir."

"Very well, Doña Marina. The lad's your responsibility. If he causes any problems I'll have you both flogged."

While Aguilar translated, Bernal released his iron grip on Nacontoc's arms and the young man pitched forward to fall at my feet, sobbing with relief.

"Come with me, little brother," coaxed Aguilar. "You can share my quarters and I'll teach you about Our Lord." He looked at Nacontoc and his homely features lit up. "I think I'll name you . . . yes, Esteban, after him who was the first to give his life for the holy faith." He took Nacontoc's hand and pulled him to his feet.

San Juan de Ulua—April 1519

Along the distant shore I could make out swarms of people who had come to see the spectacle of the tall ships as they rocked at anchor under a blazing sun. How long had it been since it was I who stood on the beach, gaping at the approaching vessels of Grijalva?

We'd been at anchor since dawn, deliberating the wisdom of attempting a landing, and Alonzo Hernández Puertocarrero was growing bored. Reaching out a thin arm, he pulled me closer to him. "Now let's hear it again," he commanded.

"This is a ship," I responded in halting Castilian. "That is the sky, that is the sea. You are Alonzo. I am Malina—no! Marina. Ma*rrr*ina." I liked the way the *r* sound, nonexistent in either Mayan or Nahuatl, tickled the tip of my tongue. I was grateful for Alonzo's interest in teaching me his language, even though I realized he did it not so much for my own benefit as for show. None of the nineteen other girls had learned any Castilian yet, except for their own names and the names of their respective masters. Alonzo was proud of my linguistic skill.

My mind, however, was not fully upon the language lesson. Two thoughts gnawed at my awareness. The first was the memory of the still-unchristened Nacontoc's face when I told him that Tonaxel, now Doña Antonia, was on another ship with her new master, the golden-haired Pedro de Alvarado. The boy had grown dejected, refusing to eat the strange food or to listen to Aguilar's earnest preaching.

"How can I accept a religion with so many puzzles?" he'd asked me. "Aguilar says that when the priest raises the little cake in the air it becomes the body of the god, Jesus, and the

Christians eat it. Yet I'm told they hate the eating of human flesh by our people."

"Is that so strange?" I reasoned. "According to the beliefs of our people, it's the gods who eat the flesh of men. Here, you see, the situation is just reversed, and it is men who eat the god's flesh." I hoped my explanation made more sense to him than it did to me. "Besides, the little cake tastes nothing like meat. The change takes place only in one's mind, I think."

Nacontoc had walked away and squatted in a corner with his head on his knees. I feared that when we landed once more and he saw Tonaxel, so happy with her dashing captain, his attitude would only grow worse.

The other thought that plagued me on that hot afternoon was the memory of the dream I'd had the night before—a dream that had transported me back to Oluta. Unnoticed, I'd walked the familiar streets and roamed the marketplace I had so loved. I was exquisitely happy. Then I began to look at the people around me—my people. They were ragged and ill; their eyes were hollow eyes of death, and they began to stare at me and point at me with fleshless fingers. I tried to run, but my legs had turned to water and would not carry me. With my people swarming over me, I began to crawl along the ground toward the base of the pyramid of Huitzilopochtli. I looked up toward the *teocalli* and saw my father standing on the topmost step. The stones of the pyramid were as hot as flames, searing my hands and knees as I inched my way upward. When I reached the *teocalli* at last, my father was gone. Looking down, I saw my people gathered at the bottom of the long flight of steps, crying and reaching up toward me with their bony hands. As I turned away from them, I found that I was able to stand on my feet at last. Fearfully, I entered the *teocalli*. There, coiled on the altar, were two great, hissing serpents: one of them slender, its tongue darting in and out; the other hideously fat, its indolent eyes half closed. I cried out and the two serpents turned their faces toward me. One was Itzcoatl and the other was Cimatl, my mother. They reared back their heads and struck at me, and I stumbled backwards out of the *teocalli* to pitch down the endless steps, screaming . . .

Alonzo had awakened me and for the rest of the night I'd lain close to him, my eyes wide open, grateful this one time for the comfort of his frail arms.

The dream troubled me. I'd have taken it to a soothsayer

for an explanation, but here there was no one who could help me. Aguilar put little store in dreams and had dismissed my tale with a shrug of his shoulders. "It was only the devil trying to pull you back into idolatry," he'd said. "Don't dwell on it, little sister."

A squawking pelican bent its wings and dipped into a wave. Alonzo's beautiful eyes caressed me from head to feet, lingering in those places of which he was fondest. Suddenly he took hold of my arm. "Come, Marina," he whispered, pulling me away from the rail.

I resisted. The thought of the stuffy cabin, filled with flies, the rumpled bed and Alonzo's hot, sticky body and groping hands, was unbearable.

"Marina, come!" he ordered churlishly, dragging me behind him down the steps and through the door of his tiny, windowless quarters. Many pairs of knowing eyes had watched our disappearance and I was scarlet with humiliation. I was Alonzo's property to do with as he wished, but I moaned inwardly at his lack of discretion. The indignity was too much for the daughter of a *tlatoani*. This time I would not submit. Maybe my refusal would teach this Castilian puppy a badly needed lesson.

He shoved me onto the bed and began to unbutton his blue velvet doublet. I sprang to my feet again. "No!" I exclaimed. Alonzo's face reflected surprise, but he only laughed and tossed me back onto the bed. "No," I repeated, struggling to my feet again. Instead of being discouraged, Alonzo seemed delighted at the challenge. Half undressed, he hurled himself against me, his force sending us both tumbling among the tousled bedclothes. Gritting my teeth, I pushed him firmly away from me.

Overhead on the deck something was happening. I heard the thud of running feet and the murmur of excited voices.

"Aguilar!" Cortés was roaring. There was a thump, like the bow of a canoe touching the hull of the ship. Someone was coming aboard. I thrashed to free myself from Alonzo's embrace.

All sound from above died away except for one voice, the voice of a stranger. "I am Teuhtile, *tlatoani* of this land, and I have brought with me the personal representatives of the *uei tlatoani*, Moctezuma. We wish to speak with your leader." No one answered. Teuhtile repeated the statement again. The only response was a confused babble of voices. Where was Aguilar?

Then I heard him. "We give you greetings," he was saying loudly in Mayan. There was a note of desperation in his voice. "Can't any of you understand me?"

With a surge of strength I shoved Alonzo away from me. The realization had hit me like a bolt of lightning: the stranger was speaking in Nahuatl, not Mayan. We had entered the domain of the Aztecs. Aguilar spoke only Castilian and Mayan, whereas I— By the four hundred rabbits, could it be that I, Marina, was the only person on the ship who understood Nahuatl? Leaping from the bed, I bolted through the door and raced up the steps and onto the deck, smoothing my disheveled hair and tucking the end of my skirt under my sash.

The strangers were Aztecs. My first glimpse of them confirmed it. They were dressed in cloaks of jaguar skin and crowned by the plumes of their offices. Their proud faces were grim with consternation.

I slipped through the closely packed throng to Aguilar's side and nudged him to get his attention.

"Brother Jeronimo," I hissed, "I understand them."

He glowed with relief. "Come!" he exclaimed, taking my hand and leading me to where Cortés stood. He exchanged a few rapid words with his commander, who suddenly fixed those dark, penetrating eyes on me as though he were seeing me for the first time. His gaze warmed me to the soles of my feet. Smiling, he spoke to me.

I looked expectantly at Aguilar. "My captain wishes to ask you," he translated, "if you are an angel sent to him from heaven?"

As I took my place, trembling, between Aguilar and Hernán Cortés, my eyes caught a glimpse of a disheveled figure slouched against a mast. It was Alonzo Hernández Puertocarrero, his face drawn into a sullen expression.

Chapter Eight

San Juan de Ulua—May 1519

I slipped into the river, shivering as the cool water rippled over my naked body. How good it felt! With powerful kicks I moved out into the middle of the pool at the foot of the small waterfall and dived at its deepest point, my hair streaming out behind me, the water blurring my eyes until I broke into the sunlight again. The girl christened Isabel was washing her master's clothes on a nearby rock, scrubbing and pounding with the aid of the fruit of the *copalxocotl*, which the Castilians—or Spaniards, as they were also called—had named "the soap tree."

"And tell us about your master, Malina," she grinned impishly, her Mayan tongue still unable to master the elusive *r* sound.

"Yes, tell us about your skinny Alonzo with his beautiful eyes," echoed another, Juanita, who was washing her hair at the pool's edge, "We've been comparing to see which of us is the luckiest. Tell us, does he give you presents? Is he good at pleasing a woman?"

I splashed water on her and submerged. Although I enjoyed these times when the other women and I were allowed to go to the river and bathe, I didn't want to talk about Alonzo. The poor fellow had been racked by dysentery since the landing and had hung about the camp, growing thinner and more miserable each day. Juan Jaramillo, who ministered to men as well as to horses, had given him a purge that had helped for a day or two, but now Alonzo was worse than ever, and peevish because I was neglecting him.

He had no reason to be so resentful, I brooded. Was it my fault that my new duties as interpreter for Hernán Cortés occupied so much of my time? Was it my fault, I asked myself, that I felt little more than a gentle sort of motherliness for Alonzo? That I was truly alive only when standing at the side of the pale, dark-eyed commander, molding his words from Aguilar's Mayan into Nahuatl?

As much as I liked Aguilar, his slow tongue was an encumbrance at times, and I was attacking my study of Spanish with zeal in the hope of eventually being able to translate directly. At the same time, Cortés had ordered me to instruct Aguilar in Nahuatl, for, life and fate being so precarious, he knew the folly of total dependence upon any one individual.

When I surfaced again, the women were admiring a necklace of blue beads that Pedro de Alvarado had given his Antonia.

"Ah, but you're the luckiest of all, little one," Isabel gushed. "Your master is not only handsome, but he's generous. Does he please you?"

Antonia only blushed. Love had ripened her prettiness to dazzling beauty. The unhappy Nacontoc had not dared approach her, but followed her about the camp from a distance, sick with longing.

Seeing her swollen breasts, faintly laced by blue veins, I realized that my friend was pregnant. I swam, then waded over to where she stood waist-deep in water and touched her hand. "We never have time to talk anymore, Tonaxel," I said softly, using the old name. "Are you happy?"

"Beyond anything I ever imagined," she answered dreamily. "Oh, my life isn't always perfect. Yesterday, when he discovered that I'd let the blade of his sword get rusty, Pedro was so angry that he slapped me." A shadow of pain crossed her pretty face at the memory. "But we made love afterwards and everything was all right. Malinalli, when I think of how it might have been with Chilam . . ."

"We all think of how it might have been," Isabel interrupted with a laugh. "As for me, I prefer my Castilian master to my Tabascan one, even if Cristobal is so hairy that it's like climbing into bed with an animal." Isabel had been given to Cristobal de Olid, a boar of a man with a split lip and a bellow for a voice.

"It's not the hair that bothers me," said Juanita. "But I wish they'd bathe more often. Ugh! I think they must wear the same clothing till it rots on their bodies."

"You're a quiet one today, Malina," observed another girl, Leonor. "Maybe you're thinking of our handsome commander instead of your Alonzo. I'm surprised that he hasn't taken you for himself."

"He'd never do that," I said. "He loves Alonzo like a son." I told them what Alonzo had told me, through Aguilar—that back in Cuba, Hernán Cortés had sold the gold buttons off his cloak to buy him a good horse.

"And now poor Alonzo's too sick to ride," Isabel chimed in. "Gonzalo de Sandoval's been exercising his horse for him. Now there's a man for you! He rides as if he'd been born on a horse!"

"And his legs look as though they'd done their growing around a horse's middle," Antonia said with a giggle. "But I like him. He's a good friend of Pedro's. What a pity he has no woman."

"Neither does the tall one called Bernal Diaz," added Juanita, "nor Cristobal Corral—" she struggled with the *r's*— "the strong one who carries the banner, nor that good-looking Juan Jaramillo—I've caught him watching you, Malina. What a shame there are only twenty of us . . ." She twisted the water out of her black hair and began to comb it with her fingers. "When do you think Hernán Cortés will take a woman?"

"I don't know," I answered, feeling a strange little stab in the pit of my stomach. "Aguilar says he has a wife in Cuba, and a daughter by a slave woman." Aguilar had probably made a point of telling me that to discourage my feelings toward his commander.

"Ha!" Isabel hooted. "I've heard about his wife. According to what Aguilar told *me*, the men say she's got a tongue like the bite of a gila monster. They say she forced him to marry her and he hates her for it."

Now this was something Aguilar hadn't told me. I turned this new tidbit of information over in my mind. Cortés wasn't the only man with a wife back in Cuba. Marriage hadn't prevented some of the officers from taking Tabascan girls, and I guessed that when the time came it wouldn't stop Cortés either. Aguilar, when I'd asked him, had explained our status to me. My friends and I were *barraganas*—more than mistresses but less than legal wives. "The *barraganía's* a useful institution," he'd declared. "Let's say that it protects the sanctity of marriage but at the same time makes allowances for the . . . natural weaknesses of men. There's no dishonor in it, little sister, and it prevents a good deal of sin." He'd looked at me sharply. "Of course I, being a servant of God, have no need of such things." I nodded my understanding. It seemed simple enough. We were concubines, as most of us had been before we'd left Tabasco.

Concubines, priests who have no women, a god who gave himself in sacrifice and asks men to eat his flesh . . . The more I learned of the white men's ways the more amazed I was, not because of their differences from our own ways, but because of their similarities to them.

"Doña Marina! Doña Marina!" The piping voice came from behind a discreet clump of bushes. It was twelve-year-old Orteguilla—"little Ortega"—the youngest of the pages who waited upon the Spanish officers. The youngster had an astounding gift for mimicry and had already picked up enough Mayan from the women to carry on a simple conversation. He was also learning Nahuatl from me, and a quick bond of affection had grown between the two of us.

"Doña Marina, Señor Cortés needs you back at camp."

"I hear you," I called back, "and I'm coming." I stepped up onto the mossy bank, wound my skirt around my dripping body, gave my hair a quick twist to wring out the water, and slipped on my sandals and my *huipilli*. The boy was waiting beside the trail.

"Is anything wrong?" I asked him.

"Five men!" he answered, bouncing with excitement. "Strangers, not Aztecs! Bernal Diaz brought them in. They have blue stones here—" he pointed to his lower lip. "Hurry!"

I trotted along behind him, praying that the newcomers were friendly. We needed allies now more than ever, for the followers of the local *tlatoani* had become sullen toward us. Their daily offerings of turkey and venison, fruit and the flat maize cakes that the Spaniards had dubbed *tortillas*, so abundant at first, had dwindled and disappeared, leaving us helpless and hungry. The salt pork and cassava bread brought on the ships from Cuba had become too rotten to eat.

The growing hostility of the natives had put the Spaniards on edge. Hernán Cortés had ordered that the guard around the camp be doubled. The men slept fully dressed, their weapons by their sides.

Moctezuma's ambassadors had vanished as well, into the misty highlands that rose to the west, leaving behind them gifts of indescribable beauty and value. Among other things, they'd presented Cortés with the headdress of Quetzalcoatl, which was made of jaguar skin with a long cape of leather feathers trailing behind it, and the spectacularly plumed helmet of Tezcatlipoca. Aguilar had reacted with horror, refusing to translate my suggestion that Cortés need only don these sacred vestments and proclaim himself a god, and all Mexico would be at his feet. "God forbid, little sister, that my captain would ever perform such an act of blasphemy!" he'd gasped.

But even I had cringed when they'd presented a slave dressed as a nobleman, whom they'd brought along to offer the white gods in the event that they were eaters of human flesh. The slave was sent back to his masters, with total disregard for the fact that acceptance of him would have strengthened Cortés's god-status considerably.

The Aztecs had sniffed about our camp like curious hounds. They'd even brought along an artist who sketched our men and horses on sheets of *amatl* paper. They all became excited when one of them noticed a rusty helmet that belonged to a poor soldier. The helmet, they'd declared, was a duplicate of one worn by their god, Huitzilopochtli. They wanted to borrow it to show to their *uei tlatoani*. Cortés feigned reluctance. Finally, after some thought, he had given them the helmet, asking just as an afterthought if it could not be returned filled with gold.

The messengers had departed and returned again, the *tlamemes* bent low with their burden of gifts: two great circle calendars, one of gold representing the sun, and one of silver like the moon; load after load of embroidered cloth-and-featherwork capes that made me gasp at their beauty. There were chains of gold, jewel-encrusted necklaces, earrings and lip plugs. The rusty helmet was there, filled to the brim with grains of unworked gold. Hernán Cortés had received these offerings with no more outward elation than he would have shown if the Aztecs had brought him a few baskets of corn, but I felt the tide of excitement surging among the men as they gaped at this display of splendor. I knew that this same raging current leaped in the soul of our commander, held in check only by his iron will.

With the gifts came Moctezuma's greetings and his expressed desire for friendship with the white strangers. With the gifts came also the warning that we were not, under any circumstances, to try to visit him in Tenochtitlan. I smiled at the thought of their words. Would one offer a jaguar a bite of venison and then admonish the beast not to kill any deer?

I tried to imagine Moctezuma, squatting on his heels in his palace at Tenochtitlan, surrounded by priests and sorcerers, his eyes bulging with fear as he listened to the reports and looked at the drawings his scouts had made. He would remember the omens, the disasters that had taken place in recent years: the drowning of eight hundred warriors in a river; the storm that had set the waters of the lake surrounding his capital to churning like the sea; the fire from the sky that had burned the twin temples atop the great pyramid. I knew of these events because my father had told me. I knew as well of the mystical bird a fisherman had caught and brought before his emperor. On the bird's head was a smoky black mirror, and when Moctezuma had looked into it he'd beheld the destruction of his people.

What thoughts must have been passing through the *uei tlatoani's* mind with the coming of these white, bearded strangers in the year *ce acatl*? Certainly he would be torn between fear for the safety of his kingdom and the realization that these strangers, if they were gods, should be welcomed and worshipped. Why else would he vacillate between adoration and hostility as he seemed to be doing now?

I walked swiftly, letting the sun dry my hair. The nightmares that had plagued me so had ceased, for I had felt destiny reaching down to take me by the hand. Through Hernán Cortés and his small army I would be a tool to help liberate my people from Aztec oppression. The seeds of hatred for Moctezuma and all that he stood for had been planted in my heart by my father, and they were alive and growing. We're coming, Moctezuma, I thought, to shake you loose from your death-grip on my people! Wait for us and tremble!

"Hurry, Doña Marina," Orteguilla urged.

The five newcomers were standing in a little cluster. Bernal Diaz glowered down at them from his great height, but it was obvious that they had come of their own will and had no intention of escaping. All of them were short and plump, with shiny paunches protruding above their loincloths. Gold rings set with blue stones hung from their ears, noses and fleshy lower lips. Hernán Cortés waited, glancing impatiently down the trail toward us as we hurried up to him. Pedro de Alvarado and the barrel-chested young Gonzalo de Sandoval hovered nearby, talking in low tones.

Aguilar looked flustered. "I can't understand them, little sister. They're not speaking Mayan, and it doesn't sound like Nahuatl either."

He was right. To my dismay, the strangers greeted me in a language I'd never heard before. My only chance lay in the hope that, since they came from territory ruled by the Aztecs, some of them might speak Nahuatl as a second language. When I asked, two of the men stepped forward, and our communication problem vanished. The shortest one, who had a mole on his fat cheek, acted as spokesman.

They were Totonacs, he said, from the province of Cempoalla which lay three days' march away. Their *tlatoani*, the illustrious Chicomacatl, had heard of our coming and sent them to welcome us, but they had not dared to approach our camp while Moctezuma's men were there. They'd been watching us from the forest for days, waiting to be certain there was no danger.

I translated for Aguilar, who fashioned my words into Spanish. Standing next to Cortés, I felt his breathing quicken. Some spark was beginning to ignite in his mind. "Ask them, Marina," he commanded, "whether they are enemies of Moctezuma."

I had understood, and passed the question deftly on to the Totonacs. The man with the mole looked pained. "We have the misfortune of being his vassals," he said heavily. "And Moctezuma keeps our people in a state of misery. His *calpixque* drain us of our food and goods, his soldiers carry off our young men to be sacrificed, and they rape our wives and daughters before our eyes . . ." The Totonac's fingers whitened against his staff. His voice choked with emotion. "Great lord, our *tlatoani* begs you to come with us to Cempoalla where he will welcome you as a brother. Use your powers to rid us of these Aztec bloodsuckers!"

Cortés listened quietly to the translation, but a vein in his forehead was twitching, a sign of agitation that I had come to recognize. "Marina, can we trust these fellows not to lure us off into the jungle and kill us?" he asked me through Aguilar.

"I don't doubt their story," I answered. "The same words could have been spoken by my own father."

His face relaxed as it always did once he'd come to a decision. "Tell them to inform their *cacique* that we'll accept his invitation," he said. Then he turned and strode toward the camp. The air rang with commands, jarring the lethargic company into a frenzy of activity.

"Olid, ready the troops to march at dawn. We'll take four hundred men overland, along with the horses and two of the lighter cannon. Alvarado, you'll take the ships, along with their crews and the heavy gear, and sail them on up north to Quiahuitzlan, where Montejo found that harbor. Wait for me there. Maybe you'll find a good site for our city. Sandoval, go find Escalante and Avila, and Velásquez de Léon. Tell them to see me at once. Marina, is your Alonzo well enough to ride? If not, he'll have to go on the ship with Alva—*Santiago!* Not that gun, the smaller one! Have the rest of them hoisted onto the ships. You don't know *what*? Dolt! Well, go find Jaramillo—he can rig anything. Curse it, man, watch that cannon!"

I congratulated myself on having understood most of what he'd said.

After more than twenty days of languishing on the hot sands of San Juan de Ulua, where thirty-five men had died of wounds and disease, Hernán Cortés was back in action and it was glorious. After twenty days of flies, mosquitoes, sickness, boredom and quarreling, the men were happy to be on the move, and as they marched along behind our Totonac guides, young Cristobal Corral, who carried Cortés's black, red and gold banner on its heavy staff as lightly as if it had been a flower, broke into a rousing hymn that was quickly picked up by those who followed him.

In spite of his illness, Alonzo had chosen to travel by land. I suspected it was because he didn't want to let me out of his sight. He alternately walked and rode his trim bay mare—either way being too uncomfortable to endure for long. Gonzalo de Sandoval rode beside him on Motilla, the splendid copper-colored stallion that had been assigned to him because of his superb horsemanship. Aguilar and I walked between the mounted Cortés and the two Totonacs, our tongues ready if needed.

The sun blazed white-hot in the cloudless sky as our guides led us into the cool green maze of the forest where the fragrance of damp moss and hanging blossoms tantalized our nostrils; where butterflies drifted through the air like winged flowers, and flame-hued birds scolded at us from branches and thickets. Orteguilla could not contain his delight and he ran easily twice the distance of the morning's march, chasing bugs and lizards or scrambling after flowers, which he brought to me in grubby hands.

Now and again the forest opened to reveal neat little *milpas* where cornstalks grew in carefully tended rows. Beside them were clusters of thatched huts—always deserted, for their occupants fled at our approach.

Hernán Cortés sat astride Arriero, the big chestnut stallion that had frightened the Tabascans. He'd bought the horse from Ortiz the musician after his own mount had sickened and died at San Juan de Ulua. I glanced up at him from time to time, thinking what a splendid pair they made, the man and the horse, both of them bursting with strength and vitality. His stirrup brushed my arm and I shot my eyes upward to find him smiling down at me. Hot-faced, I lowered my eyes and felt myself quivering. Aguilar was looking at me quizzically. Had he noticed anything?

"Brother Jeronimo," I said, trying to appear calm, "I'm beginning to catch a few words of Spanish now. Did I hear our commander say he was going to build a city?"

"You did indeed. Villa Rica de Vera Cruz—" He savored each word. "The Rich Town of the True Cross. He's already drawn up plans for the place and chosen the officials. Your Alonzo's to be one of the *alcaldes*. Now all we have to do is find a likely spot and sink our spades." He trotted along in silence, with the stealthy gait of one who has lived long in the forests. "Ay! What a commotion this talk of a town's caused among the men. But it's been a victory for Cortés—a victory as hard-won as any fought on the battlefield."

I'd sensed something during those long weeks on the beach, seeing the conflict in men's eyes and feeling the tension among them. I'd supposed it was just restlessness, but when Alonzo had been summoned to Cortés's tent in the night I'd realized it was something more. I asked Aguilar for an explanation.

"I'll try," he said, and he told me how the expedition had been sent from Cuba by the governor, a man named Velásquez. "A fat, pompous turkey, if I'm to believe the way some talk about him. He's a kinsman of our captain, too, since their wives are sisters. But the only blood between those two is bad." After appointing Cortés as leader of the venture, Velásquez had become suspicious of him and changed his mind. "And this was after our poor captain had sold everything but his soul for ships and supplies, after he'd signed up his own crews and was ready to cast off."

I could guess what Cortés had done. He'd take his ships and sailed away, leaving the governor ranting on the shore. "I have the feeling he didn't leave all his problems in Cuba," I said.

"Wisely put, little sister! Many of the men who came with him are still loyal to Velásquez." He glanced back over his shoulder and lowered his voice to a whisper. "Velásquez de León, Morla the scout, Ordaz the stutterer, Escudero, even one of the priests, Padre Juan Diaz—"

"The fat one?"

"That's the one. They're all the governor's men. So was

Montejo until our captain persuaded him to change his stripe. Cortés is a hard man to resist." He cocked an eyebrow at me, trying to discern whether I'd caught his double meaning. "He'll win them all over in time. Never fear."

"And what about the city?" I asked, wanting him to go on.

"Ah, yes, I'm coming to that. Velásquez gave no authority for a settlement. He only sent the expedition to look for treasure and scoot on back to Cuba. That's what the governor's men want to do. They're afraid for their skins. They miss their *ranchitos* and their women. But why should Cortés want to go back to Cuba? Velásquez would clap him in irons for so long that he'd never see daylight again. Beides, he smells big game in Tenochtitlan. He wants to build a good base here on the coast and then move in all the way to the throne of Moctezuma himself."

I felt my spine tingle at his words. "The governor's men must have howled when Cortés suggested building a city," I speculated.

"Cortés *suggested*?" Aguilar chuckled. "You've underestimated our dear captain. He's as cunning as a spider. No, he told his men that they were all going back to Cuba and *they* suggested it, as he knew full well they would. And the more he protested, the more they insisted, thanks to a few well-placed men like your Alonzo and Pedro de Alvarado."

It annoyed me slightly that he always referred to *my* Alonzo, but I didn't say so. Instead I wondered aloud what would happen if the governor sent more ships under his own orders.

"That's just what Cortés fears," Aguilar said. "His only hope is to petition for direct authority from the king of Spain. It's only then that he'll be safe from Velásquez. But to reach the king, to win his blessing and return with the signed charter . . . by the saints, I've known men who've waited months even for an audience. It could take forever."

Later that day we crossed a river, stopping to hack down trees for building rafts or climbing into the shaky dugout canoes that had been left on the bank. The current was wild, and as brown as *chocolatl* with silt washed down by spring rains. Men strained at their stout poles to keep the rafts from washing downstream as their human cargoes clung to the lashed logs with all their might.

Orteguilla, never quiet, tried to shift his position on the raft, lost his balance and tumbled into the swirling water. His cry for help ended in a gurgle as the waves washed over his head. I leaped into the river where he had disappeared, seeing in my mind the image of another much smaller child, weighted down with chains of gold, sinking into a pool as black and still as obsidian.

With muddy water filling my eyes I groped for him. My hand clutched at his shirt, but he was thrashing so wildly that he tore it loose from me. Now I had him again, this time by the arm, and I held tight. My toes touched the slippery rocks on the bottom. It was not so deep after all, but I had to get the boy's head above the water at once and he was struggling hysterically, his panic giving him unbelievable strength. The powerful current pulled me off-balance, dragging us both farther and farther away from the raft. My feet were slipping on moss and I felt the river tugging him from my arms. A wave washed over my head, filling my nose and mouth with the choking brown water. The boy was being torn from my grasp . . .

Suddenly arms of iron closed around us, raising us both out of the water. As I gulped the precious air, I heard Orteguilla coughing.

"Now pull!" It was Hernán Cortés himself barking the order. His arms were around me, as strong as I had known they would be. He had a line lashed to his waist and the men on the bank were pulling us, hand over hand, toward shore. My strength spent, I relaxed against him, feeling the rise and fall of that broad chest, the wet beard against my cheek.

Alonzo, who had swum his horse across the river, was waiting on the grassy bank with hands outstretched to take me when Cortés let me go. Guzman, Cortés's steward, held out a blanket for his master, his young face pale with concern. Orteguilla was spitting water and limp with fright, but was otherwise none the worse for the dunking. Cortés took the proffered blanket and wrapped the boy in it.

"There, you little monkey," he chided good-naturedly. "You'd best be more careful. I almost lost two valuable tongues in that river. Puertocarerro! Get a cloak for Doña Marina. Can't you see how she's trembling?"

The well-groomed fields and orchards could only mean that we were nearing Cempoalla at last. What a beautiful place, I thought, my eyes passing over a garden where humming-birds, the jewels of the air, hovered above yellow blossoms. I drank in the beauty of the countryside, which was crowned by a soaring white mountain, trying to forget my weary feet and the night we'd spent in a deserted town where the steps of the temples were slippery with fresh blood and flies swarmed on the severed limbs and heads of recent sacrificial victims. "Abomination!" Cortés had thundered and, tired as we were, none of us had slept that night except the exhausted Orteguilla.

I had even more forgetting to do. Try as I might, I couldn't blot out the memory of those moments I'd spent in the river with the arms of Hernán Cortés around me, his face against my hair and his heart beating in my ears.

"You mustn't think about it!" I told myself angrily. Cortés had given me to Alonzo with his own hand. He was interested in me only because I could translate. Before he knew that I spoke Nahuatl, I'd been nothing more to him than another of the soldiers' women. Yes, I belonged to Alonzo, to gentle Alonzo who had spoken so wistfully to Aguilar and me of the bare hills of Spain, who only last night in his sleep had cried out the name of his mother.

Now, as I looked out over the countryside surrounding Cempoalla, I suddenly spied Cortés's scouts riding hard across the fields toward our caravan.

"We've seen the town and, *Santa Maria*, the houses have walls of silver!" Dirt exploded under the hooves of the horses as the two scouts wheeled their mounts alongside Cortés's stallion. Walls of silver! The words swept back through the ranks like fire through dry grass.

"Walls of silver?" Aguilar repeated the words to me and we burst out laughing. Not even the palaces of Moctezuma had walls of silver—I knew because my father had told me—but when the sun shone on newly washed lime, it could sparkle like silver. "You'll see for yourselves," Aguilar told the men with a wink.

Even though it proved not to have walls of silver, the city of Cempoalla was a paradise. Its flower-smothered houses gleamed with fresh lime; its streets were immaculate; verdant gardens were everywhere, and well-fed citizens thronged the streets arrayed in their colorful best. In no time we were awash in a veritable sea of fruits and flowers pressed upon us by our eager hosts. Pineapples, berries, fragrant *anones* and juicy *zapotes* were given to every man. Incense filled the air with its cedary, smoky smell. Cortés was bedecked with garlands of flowers.

The *tlatoani* was nowhere to be seen. "My lord begs your forgiveness," one of the Totonac nobles who had met us on the road with bouquets of roses had explained to us. "He would have come out to greet you but he's too fat to walk this far." The excuse had amused some of the men, but no one could fault Chicomacatl as a host. He had insisted on waiting until we'd eaten and rested from our strenuous march before receiving us in his royal chamber.

I slipped a scarlet *huipilli* embroidered with feathers, one of Chicomacatl's gifts, over my head and braided my newly washed hair with red blossoms for our audience with the ruler whose subjects had greeted us with such warmth. Then, beside Cortés and Aguilar, I walked along a path of flower petals. Pausing at the foot of the low palace steps, we looked up to see Chicomacatl emerging through the door to greet us.

A ripple of laughter swept down the ranks, but one angry glance from Hernán Cortés was enough to quiet it. The noble Chicomacatl was the fattest man we'd ever seen. His body, wrapped in a mantle the color of the sky, was immense, and great curtains of flesh that trembled whenever he moved drooped from his upper arms and chin. His eyes were almost hidden in the folds of his fat face, but when I gazed into them I sensed intelligence and kindness looking back at me. A golden helmet festooned with yellow plumes was on his head, and in his bearing there was true majesty, He bowed before Cortés, as low as his physique would permit, but the first words he spoke were to me.

"Your name, child." His voice, speaking fluent Nahuatl, was powerful, deep and clear.

"Marina, noble one." I touched the ground and put my fingers to my lips in the traditional greeting. "It's my honor to present to you my master, Hernán Cortés."

At that moment Cortés stepped forward and flung his arms around Chicomacatl's ample shoulders in an enthusiastic embrace. My jaw dropped in horror. To touch a *tlatoani* in such a manner was unthinkable! I groaned inwardly, telling myself I should have anticipated this. The Spaniards were always slapping one another on the back, greeting each other with *abrazos* and handclasps. They were a nation of "touchers," whereas my own people touched one another only when necessary, and to lay hands on a person of high rank was to court death. A guard reached for his *maquahuitl.*

It was Chicomacatl's own remarkable dignity that saved the situation. With no loss of composure he returned the embrace as heartily as it was given.

"Malintzin," he addressed me, adding the suffix to my

name as a sign of honor, "please tell your commander to bring his men into the palace where we can talk and have some refreshment."

Mats had been spread out on the polished stone floor and two *icpalli*, little chairs that had backs but no legs, were set out for the leaders. There, through the ears and tongues of Aguilar and myself, the messages flowed back and forth. Cortés spoke of the all-powerful King Carlos V in Spain whose vassals we were, and of Jesus whom we worshipped. There were admonitions against idolatry and human sacrifice—something of which we'd seen evidence even in this paradise.

Chicomacatl listened politely, nodding his assent. Then it was his turn to speak, and from his gold-studded lips poured a torrent of bitterness against the depradations of the Aztec overlords. His eyes filled with tears as he repeated the all-too-familiar tale of excessive tribute taxes, of sons and daughters carried off to sacrifice or slavery.

Chicomacatl leaned forward, his voice quivering with emotion. "Our province alone can promise you fifty thousand warriors, and there are other tribes, as oppressed as we are, whose fighting men will flock to your banner if you will only agree to help us."

I translated for Aguilar, who repeated the words for Cortés. There it was, the vein throbbing in his forehead as he savored the possibilities that were opening like blossoms before him. I could almost read his thoughts. Moctezuma was not absolute lord of this land after all. He had enemies, many of them, who might be persuaded to unite under the black and red banner. Then, when it was over, when Moctezuma had been vanquished, who would be the ruler of this lush land where gold and silver seemed to flow as abundantly as water?

Day stretched into evening. Chicomacatl had invited the entire company to a banquet where his servants heaped gifts of finely made robes upon his new allies and stuffed them with exotic delicacies. When he discovered that the men liked *octli*, or *pulque*, the white liquor that came from the distilled pulp of the maguey plant, he dispensed it freely; and I, reared in a society where intoxication was forbidden except to the very old, was discomfited when some of the men drank too much. Cortés only sipped at the stuff. Never, in all the years I was to know him, did I see him drunk.

Surveying his guests with an expression of satisfaction, Chicomacatl clapped his hands once more. Eight young women minced out from behind an embroidered curtain and stood before Cortés with their heads bowed. An expectant hush fell over the men, for the girls were obviously gifts, just as my friends and I had been. That they were beauties by Totonac standards was evident in Chicomacatl's proud smile. All of them were well rounded—some more than others—with hair so tightly pulled back from their faces that it made their narrow eyes slant. Some of our men wrinkled their noses; others shrugged. After all, they were women at least. The eighth girl, however, was quite lovely. She was more slender than her companions and dressed all in white; her hair was elaborately coiled atop her elegant little head and garnished with a single white blossom. Her only piece of jewelry was a wide collar of hammered gold. Her skin glowed like the surface of a shell. Seeing her, I felt a twinge of envy. Perhaps the time had come for Cortés to select a woman of his own, and who could resist such prettiness?

"Malintzin." Chicomacatl had turned to me. "Tell your master that these girls, all of them maidens of noble families, are for his captains. It's our wish that they have many fine sons and daughters to enrich our tribe."

Cortés offered his thanks to the lord of the Totonacs, and then, with the usual explanations, the girls were baptized by Padre Olmedo and given Christian names.

The first girl was awarded to Montejo, the second and third to Juan Velásquez de León and Diego de Ordaz, adherents of the governor whose favor Cortés wished to gain. The rest went to those captains who had distinguished themselves in battle or shown exceptional loyalty to their chief. At last, one maiden stood alone: the beauty in white. The men held their breaths. Bernal Diaz, hopelessly outranked, had hovered nearby throughout the proceedings, appraising each girl with a bold eye.

"Poor Bernal," Aguilar whispered in my ear. "Such an appreciation of fine horses and fine women and neither the money nor the position to enjoy either."

"But he's one of the bravest," I whispered back. "Maybe Cortés will—" I didn't finish the sentence, but for Bernal's sake and for my own, I wished fervently . . .

"And this lovely lady, Doña Francisca, I give to my loyal friend, Alonzo Hernández Puertocarrero," Cortés announced with a flourish of his velvet cap.

Stunned silence hung in the air for a moment, followed by

a low, angry buzzing. With so many womanless men, why give two women—the best-looking ones to boot—to Puertocarrero?

I stood numb with surprise and bewilderment while a blushing Alonzo stumbled to his feet and came forward to claim his unexpected prize. Alonzo's eyes met mine for an instant, puzzled, embarrassed, and then he had to look away. He took the girl by the hand and led her to a seat beside him. My frozen thoughts warmed to life again. I inspected my own feelings carefully, but I saw no jealousy. My attachment to Alonzo was hardly strong enough for that. There was only . . . relief. Yes, and an unanswered question so awesome that I was afraid to face it squarely. Surely Cortés didn't intend to let Alonzo have two women at the same time. Why, then, had he given the girl to Alonzo except to offer him a replacement for me? Could it be that . . . ? I dared not even put my hope into words.

But Chicomacatl had not finished with his gift-giving. "Malintzin, tell your chief that I've saved the best present of all for him." He paused, beaming, while Aguilar and I translated. "It's my desire to unite your blood with my own," he said to Cortés, "for then we would truly be brothers. Unfortunately, I have no marriageable daughters to offer you. Instead I give you my niece, the daughter of my own sister." He turned to me. "Tell your master to treat her lovingly, Malintzin, for she's the jewel of my life."

Eyes fixed on the floor, I translated, trying not to hear the words or to feel their impact. I willed myself to look at the quivering curtain as it parted to reveal a bejeweled figure in yellow.

No one could doubt that this girl was the niece of Chicomacatl, for the family resemblance was strong. She was well on her way to becoming as fat as her illustrious uncle. The two of them stood side by side. Identical gold rings drooped from identical lumpy noses. The two pairs of eyes that looked so brightly out at the world from between folds of fat were the same. The girl glanced at Cortés and smiled shyly. Her arm, laden with bracelets of gold, shook as she extended it to her new master.

Cortés took her hand with an air of solemnity. "I'm overwhelmed by the generosity of the lord of Cempoalla," he declared reverently. One of the common soldiers, a drunken seaman named Trujillo, had the effrontery to let out a loud guffaw. Cortés's glare cut him down like a sword. "This young lady is a princess and will be treated as such by every one of you," he said slowly. There was no more laughter. The girl stood nervously, twisting the hem of her *huipilli* and nodding uncomprehendingly while I explained the basic principles of Christianity to her, and then Padre Olmedo stepped forward to administer the baptism, a basin of holy water in his hand.

"And the young lady's name?" The priest looked expectantly at Cortés.

"What? Her name, you say?"

"Yes, my captain. Would you like to choose a name for the princess?"

"Oh, of course. Catalina. Doña Catalina." There was an odd note to his voice.

Bernal Diaz was standing just behind Aguilar and me, close enough for us to hear him mutter, "*Santa Maria*! What a rascal!"

We both turned to look at him, puzzled.

"Catalina," Bernal whispered, shaking his head. "He's named the poor girl after his wretched wife back in Cuba."

"Please try to understand, Marina *mía*." We were standing in the palace garden. Alonzo, his face obscure in the darkness, had cupped his hand under my chin. "I'm only doing it out of duty," he pleaded. "I didn't ask Cortés to give her to me. When we leave this place, Doña Francisca will stay here with her family and things will be the same between you and me, I promise."

I looked back at him, only partly understanding his speech, but guessing the meaning of the words. I was glad the night hid the expression of wry amusement in my eyes. Poor Alonzo . . .

"I understand," I whispered in the best Spanish I could manage. "Now go. Go to her and don't worry about me." I shoved him gently away from me and he was gone, his heels clattering on the paving stones.

The moon had drifted into a space among the clouds, illuminating the tinkling fountains and the huge white lilies that only opened their faces at night. Chicomacatl's garden was lush with ferns and creeping vines, and fireflies flitted in and out among the foliage like little winged stars.

It wasn't so bad to be alone sometimes, I reflected. I only wished my mind would forget that Hernán Cortés was somewhere in the palace with his plump little Catalina, no doubt making the best of the situation. Oh, I was a fool to think of him, I berated myself.

Something moved in the shadows. "I've been looking for you, Marina," said the voice of Hernán Cortés.

Startled, I turned to face him. He was wearing an open-collared blouse the color of the lilies, of a soft, thin material that rippled like water when he moved. I hated him.

"Do you need me to translate for you?" I asked in a dull voice.

"Good Lord, no!" He laughed roughly, then took a deep breath, filling his powerful chest. "I only wanted to tell you . . ." He stopped, fumbling for the few words that he knew I would understand. "I only wanted . . ." He stopped again, frustrated.

"Oh, the devil with it!" he exploded, and suddenly his arms were pulling me hard against him. His mouth thrust against mine with a force that drained away my strength and made the stars spin. I could only cling to him, feeling the impact of that long, brutal kiss as I had never felt anything in my life. Abruptly, he drew away from me and stood holding me at arm's length. His eyes were melancholy in the moonlight. He shook his head.

"I can't stay," he said. "Forgive me, Marina." Then, like Alonzo, he was gone, his footsteps echoing in the darkness. My legs would not hold me. I sank down on a stone bench, trembling, feeling suddenly like a stranger to myself and everything I had ever known up until this night. My very soul belonged to this man, to this fiery blend of iron and quicksilver. Yet I think I knew even then that he would never permit me or any other woman, to possess him fully.

I put my hand to my head. The red flowers in my hair had wilted.

Chapter Nine

Quiahuitzlan—May 1519

The fortress-town of Quiahuitzlan was set on a high, rocky promontory overlooking the harbor where the eleven ships waited to meet Cortés's land expedition. Its streets were white with the rubble of the centuries' accumulation of broken shells that crunched under the feet that walked over them. The lime had flaked from the low mud buildings, showing the brown earth underneath in spots where the sea-wind struck. Gulls and terns wheeled in the sky and flocked above rubbish heaps that were rich with the smell of fish.

I sat on the edge of a well, removing a pebble that had lodged in my sandal during the long climb and raised a painful blister on my foot. The place had been deserted when we arrived, except for a few priests, chanting and waving censers of copal incense in an effort to cast a protective spell over their little town; but our Cempoallan escorts had been quick to convince the population to return to their homes and welcome their new allies.

Alonzo had stayed in Cempoalla, suffering from a severe recurrence of his illness, brought on perhaps by the previous day's feasting. His lovely Francisca was nursing him.

Hernán Cortés, occupied once more with his duties as commander, had avoided my eyes. Well, what else did you expect? I chided myself angrily. I remembered the sight of fat little Catalina standing forlornly on the porch of the palace as the army marched away in the dawn, her adoring eyes following her new master until he disappeared from her sight. At the same time, I remembered his strong arms crushing me close, his rough beard against my face. Now that moment seemed as remote as the birth of Quetzalcoatl. I shook my head to clear my mind.

"Doña Marina, come look over the wall!" Orteguilla was so convulsed with laughter that he could hardly talk. Still holding my sandal, I limped to the edge of the fortification and peered over it and back down the hill in the direction from which we had come that morning. There, struggling up the rocky slope, groaning with effort, were eight bearers, staggering under a litter on which Chicomacatl sat, as dignified as a mountain and almost as big. He was grunting encouragement to his bearers, reaching over to flick them with a little feather fly-whisk. A train of puffing nobles followed him. As they came closer, I saw that the *tlatoani*'s face was furrowed with anxiety.

A runner whom he'd sent ahead of him reached the gates first and, recognizing me, raced to my side. "The *calpixque* are in Cempoalla," he panted. "Five of them! They came for the tribute and arrived just after you left. When they found out we'd welcomed you . . . Ay! May the gods help us!"

Chicomacatl now stood before Cortés in the bare room that had been given us for our headquarters. An aide stood on either side of the chief to support him. "Malintzin, your lord must help us. The *calpixque* are furious. They'll demand retribution!" His massive body trembled with fear. "They always do. You can't imagine . . ." A slave wiped his sweating forehead. "If the tribute is short, they demand ten sacrifices. If they don't like the food we serve them, one sacrifice or even two. They have the power to take whatever they want from us."

As I translated for Aguilar, a second runner flung himself through the door of the room. He fell on his face before Chicomacatl, pouring out a torrent of words in the Totonac language. The *tlatoani's* face turned pale.

"The *calpixque* are here in Quiahuitzlan. They followed me all the way from Cempoalla! Now you'll see . . ."

Looking through a window, we could see the five tax-gatherers in the square outside. Like all princes of Tenochtitlan, they were draped in embroidered robes, with jewels dangling from their necks and ears. Their hair was swept upward and tied at the crowns of their heads. Each carried a carved stick with a hook on the end, the badge of his office, in one hand and a bouquet of roses in the other. They walked with the flowers held near their noses to protect their senses against the salt-fish stink of Quiahuitzlan. Behind them marched a long retinue of attendants, wafting incense and waving heron-plume fans. The town chiefs were already bowing low before the five Aztecs. Chicomacatl, ashen with dread and leaning heavily on the arms of his aides, waddled outside to join them.

"What kind of allies are these?" Cortés growled, raising his eyebrows as the whole procession swept grandly past the building where we were quartered and into the tribute-house where hastily gathered refreshments were awaiting them.

Chicomacatl was back again a short time later, more shaken than ever. "Now what are we going to do? The *calpixques* want twenty young men and women brought to them for sacrifice. And that's not all! They're going to take all your men as slaves and when you've gotten their women pregnant, they'll put you on the altar." He wiped his eyes with the back of his hand. "It's all my fault, dear friend. In wanting to make you welcome, I've put your people and mine in danger."

Cortés appraised him calmly. "Chicomacatl," he said, "you've got to make a decision. If you want to join us, just tell me so and do what I ask of you. But if you haven't the courage to keep your promise of friendship, I'll take my men and march away. The Aztecs can do what they want with you." His dark eyes seemed to peer into the very heart of the poor, fat chief. "Well, which is it to be?"

Cortés waited calmly as Aguilar and I translated for the lord of the Totonacs. I watched him amazed, for though our lives might depend on Chicomacatl's answer, he was relaxed, rocking back on his heels as though he knew that whatever the outcome, it would be in his favor.

Chicomacatl drew in his breath and let it out again slowly, his shoulders sagging with the strain he was under. "Malintzin, tell your commander that I'm his man. He has only to command me and I'll do as he asks."

"Very well, then." It was the answer Cortés had expected. "The first thing you must do is order your soldiers to arrest the tax collectors."

"Arrest them! By all the gods, Moctezuma will annihilate us!"

"Noble one," I interrupted, "you've placed yourself in my master's hands. Trust him."

Chicomacatl set his jaw. "I've given my word to obey, Malintzin. Summon my warriors."

It was not long before five astounded Aztec princes found themselves taken prisoner, with leather collars around their necks and their hands and feet tied to wooden poles. Their attendants were herded into a compound and placed under guard.

Scarcely able to believe what they'd done, the Totonacs crowded into the square to gape at the spectacle of Moctezuma's own representatives trussed up like common slaves. It had been so easy. The *calpixque* had been so unprepared for such an act that by the time they'd gathered their wits about them, the deed had been accomplished. Cortés stalked out into the marketplace where the prisoners were tied, looking them up and down, a scowl on his face. The crowd pressed closer, murmuring louder. A shout rose from the edge of the square, and the throng took up the cry, surging toward the Aztec princes.

"What are they saying?" I whispered to Chicomacatl, who stood between me and Cortés.

"Sacrifice!" exclaimed the chief. "And why not? Our gods will be pleased with such choice offerings. Besides, the dogs mustn't live to return to Moctezuma with tales of what we did to them."

But sacrifice was not part of Cortés's plan. He frowned when Aguilar relayed my message to his ears. "You've placed yourselves under my command," he rumbled, "and I tell you now that the sacrifice of these prisoners is not to my purpose. They're mine and I order that they be imprisoned in my own quarters."

The command was translated from Cortés's Spanish to Aguilar's Mayan, then into Nahuatl by me and into Totonac by Chicomacatl. The prisoners were made to hobble into the building set aside for us and were shut into one of the small rooms. Slowly the murmuring crowd dispersed, cheated of the ultimate thrill of seeing their enemies die on the altar, but elated nonetheless over the events of the day.

I stirred in my sleep. The crowded room was black in the night. There was no sound except the far-off howl of a dog and the clink of the sentries' armor as they patrolled the street outside. Someone was shaking my shoulder. I opened my eyes to see Jeronimo de Aguilar crouching over me with a candle.

"Come on," he whispered. "Cortés needs us."

I got up and followed him, stepping over slumbering bodies until we reached the little room where the five Aztecs had been tied. There Cortés waited, pacing restlessly.

The five captives stood disheveled and forlorn in the dim light. Their jeweled necklaces and earrings had been plucked from them in the first moments of their arrest, and their hair hung down around their faces in scraggly little tendrils. Their wrists and ankles were rubbed raw where the leather thongs had chafed them.

Cortés motioned us nearer. For a fleeting moment his eyes met mine over the flame of the candle he held; in them I read tenderness and a plea for understanding. "Wait," his look seemed to say. "Be patient until the right time comes for us."

Then Cortés rolled his face toward the ceiling, and with an expression of total innocence he began: "I want you to ask these poor men why they've been treated so disgracefully by the Totonacs. Tell them I know nothing of the reason for their imprisonment, but it grieves me most painfully to see them so mistreated, for they're the representatives of Moctezuma, to whom I've pledged my friendship."

I'd marched beside this man for days, and I'd thought I was beginning to know him. Now I realized that I knew him no more than one who, seeing the jungle from a distance, knows its paths and trails. My face expressionless, I translated Aguilar's words for the five *calpixque*.

"We don't know what made the Totonac filth arrest us, noble lord," one of the captives whined. "But if you've pledged your friendship to Moctezuma, then prove yourself by letting us go."

"I can't release you all," Cortés hedged. "The Totonacs will suspect trickery if they find all five of you gone." He looked the Aztecs up and down coolly. "I'll let two of you go. As for the three of you who stay here, I'll defend your lives with my own." He drew a dagger from its leather sheath at his hip. The blade flashed, reflecting the candle flame. "There. Now tell your Moctezuma that I, Hernán Cortés, cut your bonds with my own hand to set you free."

The two tax-gatherers, haughty princes of Anahuac, fell on their faces before their liberator and kissed the floor. Taking the hand of each, Cortés raised them to their feet again. "Go now, my friends," he whispered, "before the Totonacs hear us. Remember that you carry word of my friendship to your emperor."

With a quick gesture of farewell, the two Aztecs slipped from the room. The remaining three, still bound, looked at one another muttering.

"They're afraid," I explained. "They're saying that the Totonacs will sacrifice them in the morning."

"Tell them not to worry," Cortés said. "Tomorrow I'll have them transferred to one of my ships. Later on, when it's dark, they'll be taken ashore where they can escape." He smiled. The dancing candle flame made eerie shadows on his face.

Villa Rica de Vera Cruz—July 1519

The Rich Town of the True Cross had sprouted like a cluster of mushrooms out of the narrow plain that lay beweeen Quiahuitzlan and the harbor. Hernán Cortés himself had carried the first baskets full of earth to be kneaded into adobe by the Cempoallan laborers; he had lifted the first stones and been the first to strike his pick into the earth at the site of the new church where the little yellow-haired goddess was now properly housed.

Officers, foot soldiers and sailors brought ashore from the ships had followed their commander's example that no man among them should fancy himself too noble or too important to work with his hands until the town was completed. Now the *alcaldia*, or town hall, stood across the square from the church. Here was a granary, there an arsenal, a stable, a store, a slaughterhouse, and quarters for the men. A pillory had been erected in the square for the punishment of minor wrongdoers. The whole town was surrounded by a stout wall with stations for men and cannons.

Stripped to the waist, his tanned, muscular torso and his blond hair gleaming in the early-morning sun, Juan Jaramillo was occupied with erecting one of the walls of the town jail. Carefully, he lifted each heavy adobe into place, stopping now and again to test the structure for perfect straightness with a small lead weight tied to a string.

I basked on a pile of stones nearby, enjoying the sunshine and the presence of this quiet man whose hands and mind never seemed to be idle. I had been with the Spaniards for four of their thirty-day months now and my mastery of their language, while far from complete, had progressed to the point where I conversed easily with the men. From the jumble of bearded faces, scores of individuals had emerged for me. Among my favorites were the lanky, blunt-spoken Bernal Diaz, who had given me a mischievous wink when I first came to the Spaniards' camp, the expert horseman Gonzalo de Sandoval, just twenty-one and already one of the most respected men in the company, and Cristobal de Guzman, Cortés's fair-haired steward who was so shy that he blushed if I so much as smiled at him. I cared less for Tonaxel's handsome Captain Pedro de Alvarado who had been named Tonatuih—"the sun"—by the Aztecs, but I made an effort to like him for my friend's sake.

The men in the ranks ran the gamut from nobleman to knave. Orteguilla had been instructing me very seriously in the matter of discerning one from another. A man who was well born, educated, and mannerly was distinguished as an *hidalgo*. It was a status that could be acquired only by the proper birth and upbringing. Wealth made no difference. Alonzo Hernández Puertocarrero, so poor that Cortés had bought a horse for him, was an *hidalgo*. The foppishly dressed Fernando Salcedo, who had sailed into port with his own ship, was not. "It means 'son of something,' " Bernal Diaz, a non-*hidalgo*, had explained to me. "Spain's boiling over with them—second sons of second sons whose noble ancestors left them nothing but blue blood, pride, and a disinclination to work for a living. Conquest is the only worthy career that's open to them."

So Orteguilla and I had made a game of picking out the *hidalgos* in our company. Cortés, of course, was an *hidalgo*; so were Alvarado, Velásquez de León, Escalante, Montejo and several of the other captains. Olid and Sandoval were not. I was learning.

"What about Juan Jaramillo?" I had asked Orteguilla one day. The boy had looked at me incredulously.

"Certainly!" he'd answered with a ring of indignation in his voice. "Can't you tell?"

I could not. Jaramillo puzzled me. He was not one of the officers. Yet when any sort of trouble arose, from a lame horse to a fever to a tangled rigging or a malfunctioning firearm, he was usually the first to be summoned. The men had a saying: "For death, you call a priest; for a real emergency, you call Jaramillo!" He did everything well. I'd seen him on horseback and he rode almost as expertly as Sandoval, but he seemed most at home on the deck of a ship. He was modest, soft-spoken; yet I'd watched him deliver a withering reproof to one of the grooms who'd mishandled a horse.

"They always give you the worst jobs to do, Juan Jaramillo," I said now, tilting my head so that the sun glinted on my hair. "Tending sick men and sick horses, unloading the cannon, building this ugly jail . . ."

"Ugly!" He laughed without turning his eyes from his work. He was always friendly to me; indeed, he seemed happy to have me with him. Yet there was a wall of reserve around him that I'd never been able to crack, and at times I felt he was almost wary with me. "So you think my jail is ugly, do you? Should I be insulted? The whole town's ugly, isn't it, Doña Marina?"

"It's just—" I groped for words— "it's just that everything's so plain. It's so different from the cities I know."

"Do you want us to build pyramids and palaces like the ones in Cempoalla? This is a Spanish town. We build what we know with what we have, and what we have is mud and more mud." The sardonic undertone that I detected so often in his speech vanished for a moment when he said, "Now if you could only see Seville . . . Toledo . . . Granada . . . Ay! You'd love the Alhambra, the Moorish palace in Granada. The stonework looks like lace. When the Christians took it away from him in 1492, the Moorish king wept like a baby." He hefted another adobe into place and paused to study the alignment. "This isn't Spain, Doña Marina. It's just a grubby little outpost in the New World, and for now this ugly jail will have to do. I count it a blessing to be able to work on it."

"You like to keep busy, don't you?" I asked, hoping he'd reveal a little of himself to me. I felt an inexplicable need to know this man.

"I have to," he said. "I have my own definition of hell. It's a place where the poor damned souls have nothing to do but sit and think and remember."

I shivered. Aguilar had told me about the blazing inferno where unworthy beings would spend their eternities. Jaramillo's hell was no better. I glanced at the black arm sash, tossed on the grass beside his white linen shirt, and began to understand a little.

"Black is the color of sadness among your people, isn't it?" I said.

"I wear it for my wife," he said quickly. "She died a year ago in Cuba." He picked up the plumb line and dangled it along the edge of the wall.

"Do you ever talk about her?" I had time for a story. The Aztecs had gone; Cortés, Alonzo and the other officers were readying the treasure for shipment back to their king in Spain. No one needed me.

"Sometimes. It's a form of penance, maybe."

"Penance? But why?"

He turned toward me then, fixing me with his blue eyes. "Because, in a way, you could say I killed her."

He'd wanted to shock me. I was determined not to let him. "You couldn't mean that the way it sounds," I said.

"Almost." He bent to his work again. "I suppose I owe you an explanation after an opening like that."

"You don't owe me anything," I said. "But won't you tell me as a friend?"

He glanced up at me quickly and I saw that those blue eyes could warm. I settled back against the stones, contented. "My parents died when I was fourteen," he began, working as he talked. "So I was raised by my mother's uncle—a saint of a man. His wife had died giving birth to a daughter, and that little girl was all he had. My good uncle! He wanted to give me the best possible education, so at fifteen I was sent to the university in Salamanca for two years." He glanced at me over his shoulder to make sure I'd understood, for my mastery of Spanish still had some gaps. I nodded my understanding and he went on.

"Well, I enjoyed learning and I wanted to please my uncle, so I concentrated hard on my studies, at least at first." He paused to nudge another adobe into place. "You can't imagine how it was in those days. Cristobal Colón had sailed west and discovered the new Indies, Vasco da Gama had gone around Africa, ship after ship was coming back to Spain still smelling of the places they'd been! To stay in a dusty room with only books for company . . . God forgive me, but it was impossible. I said goodbye to my uncle and signed aboard a merchantman out of Sanlucar."

He worked in silence for a few moments, hands and eyes carefully aligning the sun-baked bricks. "India, Africa, the lands of Muhammad, England, the north—a hundred ports, each with its own sights, sounds and smells, its wines, its women. After ten years at sea I knew them all. It was only then that I finally came home to visit my uncle.

"I found him in frail health and his little daughter grown up. She was beautiful, just sixteen years old, modest, shy, pure as a white violet. I wasn't fit to touch her, and when I asked my uncle for her hand he very rightly said no. I should have gone back to my ship and sailed away for another ten years, but I was a stubborn fool. I stayed and courted her behind my poor uncle's back." He glanced up at me with an expression of bitterness. "Oh, it was easy. She was so innocent and I knew all sorts of ways to please a woman. One night when her father was asleep, I took his precious Teresita and ran away with her. We boarded a ship bound for Cuba, where I'd heard there was land for any man willing to work it. The captain married us."

He put down his tools and sat on the ground, facing me. "*Madre de Diós,* what I put that girl through! We were so poor—the sheep and pigs on her father's estate lived better than we did. She worked at my side like a common field hand. Every ship that left Cuba carried a letter from Teresa to her father, but he answered none of them. A few months after our arrival we got word that he'd died. My little wife never recovered from the blow. She'd always been frail, and Cuba, with its hot, wet air, its insects, its diseases, was the worst place I could have brought her. A few days after we got the news about her father, she was dead too."

He cleared his throat, rose to his feet and turned to the wall again. "So in his great ledger, God can credit the deaths of two good people to the account of Juan Jaramillo, the fool!"

"A fool," I snapped, suddenly exasperated with him, "is anyone who has the arrogance to blame himself for the workings of fate!"

He raised an eyebrow. The barrier had fallen firmly into place again. "Part of your native philosophy, Doña Marina?"

I glared at him. He acknowledged my irritation with a little nod and returned to his work while I sat there fuming, yet wanting desperately to close the gap that had opened between us. A hummingbird, no longer than my little finger, paused in its darting flight to hover an arm's length from Juan's ear, inspecting him curiously. On tiny wings that were no more than blurs, it hung in the air, glowing like a piece of living jade.

"Don't move!" I whispered. "You'll frighten him!" We sat like statues for those few precious seconds until the exquisite little creature, with a final chirp, took its leave and soared out of sight. I followed with my eyes. "Little warrior," I breathed.

Juan Jaramillo gave me a quizzical look. I *had* him. "When a young man dies in battle," I explained, "his spirit goes to live with the sun for four years. Then he returns to earth once more as a hummingbird. That's why we must always treat them with respect."

A smile tugged at the corners of his mouth. "I know what the priest would say to that. But it's a charming idea. I like it."

"Tell me how you became a physician," I said.

"I didn't," he answered. "Oh, I can dress wounds, mix a few purges, apply leeches—much as I hate the things—but I'm no physician. You might call it the workings of fate again." Unexpectedly, he grinned at me. "It was on a voyage around Africa. The ship's doctor—heaven knows what training he'd had but he was better than nothing—took a fever and died. Those of us who could read and write drew lots to see who'd replace him. You might say I won." He shrugged his suntanned shoulders. "At least the old man had kept notes, stacks of them. I spent the next few days poring over them to learn what I could. It was lucky I did because less than a week after that there was an accident on the ship and I had to cut a man's leg off."

I put a shaking hand to my cheek. "Did he live?"

"Yes, thanks to God."

"Thanks to you," I said. "You accept blame, so you have to accept credit as well, Juan Jaramillo."

He only smiled, shook his head slightly and turned his attention back to the plumb line. I sat on the pile of stones in silence for a time, watching the deft, sure movements of his hand as he worked and trying to picture the fragile girl he'd loved. I had never seen a Spanish woman, but I envisioned her fair-haired and sweetly melancholy of face, like the little statue of the Virgin that stood in the new church. "Pure as a white violet," Juan had said. I contemplated my sturdy brown fingers and sighed. My own purity had vanished long ago beside a forest stream that was too wide to leap.

Raising my eyes, I saw Orteguilla running across the grass to summon me.

"I've been remiss!" Hernán Cortés thundered, slamming his fist onto the table, making the silver goblet dance. "Why did we come to this land, eh, Padre? To bring the True Faith to these poor heathens. And God forgive me, I've been neglectful. But no more. It's time we erected the cross in Cempoalla." Cortés was a man of great calmness in most things, but when he spoke of religion his eyes took on a fanatical gleam. At such times he almost frightened me.

Padre Olmedo nodded, his gaunt face retaining its expression of quiet thoughtfulness as he replied to Cortés's outburst. "We've treated them like brothers. Maybe this time we can do it by gentleness, by persuasion. That's how Our Lord would have done it."

"Of course." Cortés spread his hands palms up. "You know how I've always condemned the use of force in these matters. Conversion comes only from the heart."

"But for the love of all saints, haven't you seen what they're doing?" put in the baby-faced Padre Juan Diaz, his pink cheeks quivering. "A fortnight ago I visited their market. A man in a booth was selling human legs cut into sections! Every day, under our very noses, they sacrifice four or five poor souls to their filthy gods!"

Padre Olmedo shook his head sadly. "And yet they're such children. Whatever you do, my son, do it kindly."

Cortés's mind was already racing ahead. "I'll need you, Marina, and Aguilar. And both of you, Padres." He turned to the swarthy Captain Olid. "Assemble two hundred men. We'll march to Cempoalla within the hour. God and Saint Peter be with us!"

"Destroy our gods?" Chicomacatl stood on the steps of the temple, supported by his aides, eyes twitching incredulously in his fat face. "But why, my brother? How have we offended you? I thought we were friends. Why, not even Moctezuma would force us to give up our religion!"

The Cempoallans, mute with horror, crowded the square before their temple, overflowing onto the steps of the palace and into the side streets. Silent, powerless, their stone gods gazed down upon them from the top of the pyramid.

"You don't understand," Cortés went on insistently, as Aguilar and I waited to translate for him. "I'm not forcing you to give up your gods. I only came to tell you that we can't live in the midst of idolatry and human sacrifice. You have a choice. If you choose your gods over your friendship with us, we'll be forced to go away and leave you." He swept his eyes over the grotesque forms that towered above us. "Do you think these lumps of stone will protect you from Moctezuma when we're gone?"

I saw Chicomacatl's massive body sag under the weight of the invisible burden. It was no secret to him, I knew, that Cortés had released the two Aztec princes and that their return to Tenochtitlan had averted a full-scale attack against Spaniards and Totonacs alike. His spies could not have missed the fact that a royal delegation from the emperor had visited our settlement the month before and that Cortés had produced the three remaining captive *calpixques*, safe and well, as proof of his goodwill. Poor Chicomacatl! He knew he was being used but he was trapped. The departure of the Spaniards would leave his people open to retaliation from Moctezuma, and this he dreaded above all else.

He sighed mightily, the breath rushing from his body like a melancholy wind. "Very well," he whispered hoarsely. "Work your will. Demolish our gods—our lives! But you must do it yourself, you and your men. Don't expect my people to help you."

A groan went up from the Cempoallans as the soldiers, shouting with triumph, tossed a rope around the neck of the tallest stone god and began to pull, bracing themselves along the steps of the temple. Chanting, they heaved against the lines. The sound of crumbling rock was heard as the idol began to sway. The Cempoallans wailed and pounded their own heads with their fists.

Suddenly an arrow whined through the air and glanced off the altarstone. The Totonac priests, like a flock of black vultures, were swarming across the square to the foot of the temple, armed with bows, clubs and slings. Their long hair and robes were caked with human blood, their faces twisted with hate. It was not for them to stand by while upstarts defiled their gods. Closer they came, hurling rocks and arrows and shrieking at the people to join them. Now the Cempoallans began to follow priests' lead, surging toward the steps, their voices raised in angry taunts.

Cortés moved swiftly. In an instant he was behind Chicomacatl, one hand pinioning the chieftain's arm behind his back, the other pressing a dagger against his neck.

"One more step and he dies! Tell them, Marina!"

I called out his message above the din, knowing that few of them would understand me. But words were hardly necessary. Seeing their leader in danger, the Cempoallans hesitated at the foot of the steps, shaking their weapons at us.

"Tell him to order them back," Cortés growled. "Tell him that if even one of us is harmed, our cannons will level his city!"

As I spoke to Chicomacatl, my heart went out to him. His little eyes bulged with indignation. Tears were trickling down his face. I knew that he would gladly have given his own life to preserve his gods, but he would not endanger the lives of his people. Weakly, he called out orders to them in their own language and they began to shuffle back into the square, leaving a wide area vacant at the foot of the steps.

"Continue!" Cortés barked, his blade still at Chicomacatl's

throat. Quickly, his men seized the ropes again. The idol swayed, toppled and came rolling and bouncing down the steps, breaking into several pieces on the way. One after the other, the remaining stone gods followed until the lower steps of the temple were heaped with rubble. At last it was done.

"This den of filth is to be scrubbed and whitewashed," Cortés ordered. "Then it's to be decorated with flowers so that it might be fit to house the cross." Smiling with satisfaction, he looked out over the silent throng. "But first, our priest, Padre Olmedo, will preach to you heathens the loving gospel of Our Lord!"

Villa Rica de Vera Cruz—late July 1519

Seabirds screeched and wheeled above the harbor where the fittest of the ships floated at anchor, rigged for departure. Safe in its hold lay the glittering cache of Aztec treasure, an offering designed to win the favor of Carlos V in Spain. Although the king was traditionally entitled to his "royal fifth" of the booty from conquered lands, Cortés had persuaded his men to send Carlos nearly all of Moctezuma's gift, each man giving up his own share, so imperative was it that the king give his official blessing to our venture and protect Cortés from retribution at the hands of Cuba's Governor Velásquez.

Cortés had chosen two of his most trusted aides to accompany the treasure and carry his plea to the king. The first was the eloquent Francisco de Montejo, who had switched his loyalty from Velásquez to Cortés, and the second, I had learned only a few days earlier, was to be Alonzo Hernández Puertocarrero.

"It's because I have relatives at court, Marina *mía*," Alonzo had explained proudly. "The Duke of Aguilar is my father's cousin, and that's important. The king won't grant an audience to just anyone, you know. Some folk, especially commoners, have to wait months just to speak with him." He paused to brush a speck of lint from his blue velvet tunic. How thin and pale he was. I knew that Hernán Cortés had more than one reason for sending Alonzo back to Spain. He feared that his young captain would die if he remained much longer in this land.

There was another reason as well, I admitted to myself. Not that Cortés had spoken to me about it—it would have been wrong to do so while I belonged to Alonzo—but I knew from the warm gaze of his eyes when they met mine and the pressure of his hand when he touched me that when Alonzo was gone I would be his woman. Catalina, in spite of her robust appearance, was too delicate to stand the rigors of life in the new settlement and had already gone back to her family in Cempoalla.

Now, in the chill of early morning, Cortés, Alonzo and I stood on the newly built jetty, waiting for the return of the little boat that had already conveyed Montejo to the ship and would presently carry Alonzo. In addition to the treasure, the ship would carry letters, specimens of birds, small animals and plants, samples of Aztec picture writing, four captives rescued from the sacrificial cages of Cempoalla, fifteen sailors to man the ship, and the pilots, Alaminos and Bautista.

"Bautista will be missed—he's a good man. As for Alaminos," Cortés snorted, "I'll be glad to be rid of the haughty bastard! Just because he sailed with Cristobal Colón, he thinks he's too good for the likes of Hernán Cortés! I'll show His Majesty more gold than the Admiral of the Ocean Sea ever dreamed of!"

"More of everything!" Alonzo's eyes were moist.

"Now, mind you, you're to head straight for Spain." Cortés wagged a finger under Alonzo's nose. "Some of the crew might want to see their families—Montejo might even want to check on that plantation of his that he's always talking about. But you all have your orders! I can't tell you what the consequences would be if Velásquez got wind of our plan."

"Trust me, sir." Alonzo looked at me and suddenly drew in his breath as though he'd been wounded. "I'll worry about Marina," he said to Cortés. "She'll have no one to protect her and some of the men are . . . well, rough, if you will, and crude. It would put my mind to rest if you'd see that she goes to a good man." He lowered his lashes and the color crept into his pale cheeks. "If you were to take her yourself, that would make me happy."

Hernán Cortés swallowed hard. "You're a good lad," he whispered fiercely. "Don't worry. I'll take good care of her for you. Now, here's Sanchez with the boat. You'd best be on your way."

Alonzo took my hand and squeezed it painfully. I looked into his peaked face. No, I hadn't loved him. In my mind I'd ridiculed his weaknesses, his inexperience, and now I was sorry. In spite of all the things that had made him unattractive to me, he was a good man.

"Goodbye, Alonzo."

"Goodbye, Marina. I'll never forget you." He released my hand and stepped quickly down into the waiting boat. "I won't let you down, sir."

"A fine lad," Cortés murmured, and I saw that his cheeks were wet. "Curse it, I just have to say it to someone! Marina, what I'm about to tell you is for your ears alone. Understand?"

I nodded.

"This is probably no surprise to you," he began, "but the days of my young manhood in Spain were . . . most adventurous. I'd had my first woman before I got my first whisker, and by the time I was fifteen, tall for my age, mind you, and husky, I was climbing in and out of bedroom windows like a tomcat." He slipped his arm around my waist, a simple gesture of possession. "Ah, but I was nearly killed once! Some roof tiles came loose and fell to the ground, taking me with them. The lady's husband heard the commotion, and came rushing out in his nightshirt. Before I could get to my feet he had his blade at my throat. It was the old mother-in-law who saved me. I can hear her now. 'No, Rodrigo! Spare him! Can't you see he's only a boy?' " He mimicked the old woman's voice, laughing. "That was one house I never returned to!"

The sun was coming up out of the sea, washing the tips of the waves with gold. Cortés half-closed his eyes and rocked backward on his heels, tasting the memory. "I remember in particular a fair in Medellín, where I was born and raised . . . people laughing, dancing, drinking wine . . . it was easy for one to get carried away with the merriment. There was a beautiful lady there in a white mantilla. She'd lost her duenna in the crowd and I was too willing to assist her. I couldn't believe my luck! I knew her, but I'd never had the courage to speak to her. She was married, you see, to an old *hidalgo* who kept her sequestered away like a nun. I'd seen him earlier, drunk as a winemaker's goat, so I had little to fear." He let out his breath in a long happy sigh. "That was one of the sweetest afternoons of my life! But I left Medellín shortly after that. I never saw the lady again . . ."

He was silent, but I knew better than to interrupt his thoughts. I studied his face, the unruly brows, the small, sensuous mouth, and waited for him to speak again.

"Many, many years later, I met Alonzo in Cuba. When he told me he was from Medellín I became interested in him, and when he told me the names of his parents . . . well, naturally I couldn't resist asking the date of his birth. You can guess the rest, can't you? Of course, I can never be sure, for the lady did have a husband, old as he was. And certainly I would never even suggest it to Alonzo, or to anyone else except you."

He gazed out across the harbor where the ship, its unfurled sails reflecting the pink light of dawn, was already disappearing into the mist.

"Aye, he's a fine lad," he whispered. "A fine lad indeed."

Chapter Ten

Villa Rica de Vera Cruz—August 1519

"Cortés! . . . Cortés!"

The words came probing into my dreams, causing me to stir between the linen sheets. I shifted my position, feeling the reassuring, naked warmth of Hernán's body beside me, hearing the sound of his breathing.

"Cortés!"

He was awake instantly, feet thrashing to the floor, hand on the hilt of the sword he kept by his pillow.

"No! No, my general," gasped the voice in the darkness. "Don't be alarmed! It's I, Coria!"

I wrapped myself in a blanket and lit a candle from the firepot. The flickering light revealed a crouching figure huddled fearfully in the doorway. It was Bernardino de Coria, a scurrying mouse of a man of whom I knew little except that he was one of the supporters of the Cuban governor. His little dark eyes darted from Hernán to the open doorway and back again.

"What is it, Coria? Speak." Sitting on the edge of the bed, Hernán leaned forward impatiently.

"They're taking one of the ships . . ."

"They're *what*? Blow out that candle, Marina! Who's taking one of the ships?"

"Padre Juan Diaz, Escudero, Cermeño, Gonzalo de Umbria, others . . ." He was almost strangling with fear. "The ship's already rigged and provisioned for a trip back to Cuba. They plan to tell Velásquez about your treasure ship, in hopes that a fast vessel from Cuba might still be able to capture it."

"Traitors!" Hernán rumbled. "How did you learn about this?"

I could almost feel Coria's cold terror through the darkness. "Forgive me, my general," he whined. "I was to go with them

. . ." He paused, then stumbled on, relieved that Hernán hadn't struck him dead on the spot. "They're leaving within the hour. There's just time for you to trap them. I can't stay, or they'll miss me and get suspicious. I told them I was going back to look for this—" He held out his palm; a tiny gold trinket glittered in the moonlight.

"Go back to them." Hernán was slipping on his clothes. "Say nothing. When they go to board the ship I'll be there."

Coria nodded mutely and crept away to join his cohorts.

"Get into bed, Marina," Hernán ordered me. "No one's to know I'm not here with you."

I climbed obediently under the covers again. "Take care," I whispered.

"Don't worry. If it's a trap, I'll have plenty of good men along to get me out of it." He shoved his feet into his shoes. "I'd have expected something like this of Escudero, and probably Cermeño. But Juan Diaz? *Madre de Diós!* How am I going to punish a priest?"

The traitors stood before the company, bare heads bowed in the cold morning light.

"Happy is the man who can't write, if it saves him from such business as this!" Hernán exclaimed, putting his quill back into the inkwell. He had just signed the death warrants for Cermeño and Escudero, who had been sentenced to hang. Umbria was to have both feet cut off and the others were to be flogged.

Padre Juan Diaz stood apart from the rest, all expression erased from his cherubic face. It was he who'd been the real instigator of the plot, but, protected by his priestly cloth, he'd escaped punishment. Bernardino de Coria had conveniently disappeared at the moment of the others' apprehension.

"Carry out the sentence at once!" Cortés snapped to Juan de Escalante, who had been designated as the new *alcalde* now that Alonzo had left. "I'm going to Cempoalla to join Alvarado. Send two hundred men on foot to follow after me." He looked at me sharply. "Marina, you're to go with them and meet me there." Without another word he flung himself into the saddle of his waiting horse and galloped furiously away, as if to flee from the screams of Umbria, whose feet were even now being laid on the wooden chopping block. Nearby, a white-faced Juan Jaramillo was already heating two spear tips in a forger's fire to cauterize the bleeding stumps.

* * *

Like a man possessed, Hernán Cortés paced up and down the polished floor of Chicomacatl's palace. Alvarado, Sandoval, Ávila, Olid and I watched him apprehensively, each of us knowing better than to speak.

"If the rebellion had been confined to the few men we caught and punished, I could have dealt with it easily," he muttered. "But others, so many others, knew about the plot and approved—men I've trusted, men I need!" His expressive hands punctuated his every word. "We're so few, four hundred against hundreds of thousands. Any disunity and we'll be wiped off the face of this land."

He continued to pace silently, furiously, like a jaguar in a cage. He stopped abruptly, wheeled about and gazed at us, dark eyes glowing in his impassive face. I knew that look. The disjointed problems and ideas whirling about in that complex mind had suddenly fallen into place. He had found his plan.

"The ships," he said calmly. "How could anyone hope to make it back to Cuba in those worm-eaten hulls? Every last one of them would sink as soon as it hit the open sea."

"Even Salcedo's ship? But he just got here!" Cristobal de Olid blinked stupidly.

Alvarado, who had grasped his commander's train of thought at once, glared at his less astute comrade. "My good Cristobal, didn't you see the way Salcedo's ship was listing when he sailed into the harbor? Taking on water like a sponge, the men said. They were lucky to have made it to port without foundering."

"We have to protect the lives of the men." Young Sandoval spoke with a slight lisp, eyes bright with agitation above his curly, nut-brown beard. "It would be suicide to venture out in one of those rotten ships!"

"Besides," Cortés added, elation creeping into his features, "there are so many items from the ships that could be put to better use in Villa Rica—cabinets, beams, windows . . ."

Pedro de Alvarado's green eyes took on a look of amused speculation. "My general," he said very slowly, "wouldn't it be a wise move to inspect the ships for seaworthiness and scuttle those that prove unfit?"

All eyes were on Cortés. With a wild look in his eye and a faint smile on his lips, he nodded once, twice, three times.

"You're all mad!" exclaimed Alonzo de Ávila in his high-pitched voice. "But whatever you do, count me as your man!"

"Good!" Cortés answered. "In that case, Ávila, you ride back to Villa Rica at once. Instruct Escalante to order an immediate inspection of the ships by men we can trust to see things our way. Make sure he understands what's to be done. We can count on him."

Standing with one hand on the hilt of his sword, Cortés looked beyond the faces of his captains, beyond the doorway to where the unclouded sky met the horizon. "For years to come—for generations," he whispered, "when they talk of Caesar's crossing the Rubicon they'll speak as well of the day Hernán Cortés destroyed his ships." He turned, breaking the spell. "Remind me to tell you about Caesar someday, Marina *mía*."

We lingered in Cempoalla for several days, discussing with Chicomacatl the impending march inland toward Moctezuma's capital. "Go to Tlaxcala," the fat chief had admonished us. The Tlaxcalans, he went on to explain, were a warlike people, so fierce that Moctezuma had never conquered them. His territory surrounded their nation, cutting off all trade with the outside. They had no cotton, no salt. Moctezuma made war on them just often enough to capture men to feed to his hungry gods. "They hate him," Chicomacatl insisted. "Win their friendship and you'll have a powerful ally—something you're going to need, I assure you. Your army and mine together are not enough to beat the Aztecs."

It occurred to me that he might not be telling the truth, but I dismissed the thought. The poor man had no reason to see us defeated now that he had broken with Moctezuma. In spite of all we'd done to him, he had no choice except to give us the best advice he had to offer.

Laden with information and crude maps, we returned to Villa Rica to find all the ships except Salcedo's drying on the beaches, their masts tilting crazily, sails and rigging already removed and stored. Governor Velásquez's men were in a fury, for enough evidence had been discovered to convince them that the dilapidation of the ships had been helped along with the liberal use of a brace and auger.

"For shame!" Leaping onto a stack of barrels, Hernán confronted the angry mob. He railed away at them for at least half an hour, his deft tongue lashing his men, stabbing, cajoling, caressing, playing upon their emotions as a master musician plays upon his instrument. He extolled the untapped glories of the new land, the rewards waiting for any man who stayed to fight at his side. For those faithless cowards who wanted to leave, he offered to provision the remaining ship, Salcedo's, which was actually in fine condition, at his own expense. As he concluded, the air reverberated with cheers. "So!" he exclaimed, "wouldn't it be well to destroy the remaining vessel and make a safe, clean thing of it? I see that there are no cowards here!"

The men roared their approval and Hernán, riding the tide of their enthusiasm, did not waste a moment.

"With your permission, Señor Salcedo? You'll be well compensated, of course."

"All that I have is at your disposal," Salcedo answered, twirling his mustache jauntily around one finger.

"Very well, then we're all agreed." Cortés waved an arm toward the harbor and by prearranged signal the sails were instantly unfurled and a fresh breeze began to blow the stately ship toward the beach.

I felt a catch in my throat. It was like watching the death dance of a goddess. Sails and pennons fluttered gracefully. The elegant bow rose and fell over the crests of the waves. It was hard to believe that the vessel was only a lifeless thing of wood, rope and canvas. How could anyone, thrilling at the sight of those billowing sails and that dark hull cutting so trimly through the water, deny that a ship had a life of its own? The breeze picked up and the ship hastened toward us. Then, suddenly, with an agonizing scrape of wood against sand and a final, heartbreaking death-lurch, the deed was done. The last thread linking the stout *conquistadores* to Cuba and safety had been severed. A few of the men furtively brushed tears from their cheeks.

"Dismantle her!" Cortés barked. "Escalante, you'll head the garrison here at Villa Rica. The rest of us will march for Tlaxcala."

Climbing from the muggy coastal plain to the lush slopes of Mexico's vast central plateau, we followed the land, marveling at the bewitching changes; the fruit trees, the flowering vines, the pine trees with their long silky needles that grew more abundant as the altitude increased. Finches and long-tailed anis with their heavy bills twitted us from the branches.

Most of the time I walked, but once in a while, when Hernán wanted me near him, he would reach down and swing me up behind him onto the horse. If the truth be told, I only tolerated being on horseback. Arriero swayed, snorted and smelled of musk. Gripping his flanks with my knees made me so stiff I could barely hobble along. But being close to

Hernán, pointing out new birds, animals and plants to him and listening to his gruff whisper amply compensated for my discomfort.

At night the small canvas tent would be pitched and the bashful Guzman would serve our supper and shuffle away, eyes on his feet, leaving us alone. I can't deny that I looked forward to these times. After having experienced Quauhtlatoa's brutality, Chilam's indifference and Alonzo's ineptness, I found myself possessed at last by a man to whom lovemaking was sport and art. I was totally his. That he was never totally mine didn't matter. Hernán was my sun, and I was content to bask in his radiance.

Sometimes during the long days of marching I'd drop back in the company to visit with Aguilar and the sullen Nacontoc who carried his provisions. To Aguilar's consternation, the youth still refused to be baptized. I suspected that his stubbornness was, for the most part, a manifestation of his discontent. He had run away from Tabasco for two reasons: to escape his odious role as his master's concubine and to be with Tonaxel. He had succeeded in his first aim, but in his second he'd fallen woefully short of his mark.

Tonaxel had come along on the march, her tears winning out over Alvarado's protests that she was in no condition to make the journey. Under her *huipilli*, her body had begun to bulge with the growing baby. Despite her weariness at the end of each long day's walking, her pretty little face with its flattened Mayan forehead glowed with the joy of being near her Pedro. Nacontoc's eyes, full of naked longing, followed her whenever she came within his sight. Yet, seeing her happiness, he never approached her.

"I know I should forget her," he confided to me one day. "She's happy with her golden god—she cares nothing for me and she never will. But what can I do? Since that first moment I saw her in Chilam's house I've thought of no one else. Every time I see her now I just lose myself all over again. You see, Malinalli, I know what a fool I am!"

He paused to adjust the leather head strap from which the burden on his back was suspended. Aguilar's possessions were few and so the load was not heavy. He sighed. "Every day I see the walls of my cage getting smaller," he said. "It wasn't so bad at first, but I don't have your gift for languages, Malinalli. I count on my fingers the number of people I can even talk to. You fit in so well, but to me, everything is still strange. I can't make myself accept the white men's ways, their manners, their religion. I've run away from one misery to another."

"Accept Christ," Aguilar put in. "Then you'll be happy. That's what I keep telling you, my stiff-necked young Esteban." Aguilar insisted on calling Nacontoc by the Christian name he'd chosen for him, despite Nacontoc's refusal to give up his "heathen" ways.

"I know you keep telling me," Nacontoc responded crossly. "That's all you *ever* tell me."

Aguilar and I exchanged unhappy glances and walked on in silence.

Our company included a number of black slaves from Cuba, two hundred *tlamemes* from Cempoalla, and a fair-sized army of Cempoalla's Totonac warriors, among whom were forty ranking chiefs. Although the chiefs had joined the march willingly, their true function, however well disguised by Cortés's flattery, was to serve as hostages against the possibility of the Cempoallans attacking the scanty garrison at Villa Rica. Most venerated among them was the graying, battle-scarred Teuch. He must have been ugly even in his youth—even before time and warfare had ravaged his face into a mass of lines and furrows. Now he was as tough as an old cedar and he overflowed with blunt wisdom.

The occasional towns through which we passed had been friendly, for the Aztecs had ordered that we be welcomed and provided for. But without exception, the townspeople had advised us against going to Tlaxcala. "They're barbarians!" one village chieftan had exclaimed upon learning our plans. "They'll have your head on a skewer before you can even tell them who you are. Go south by way of Cholula instead. The Cholulans are the most cultured people in the empire. They'll give you a fine welcome."

"Maybe I should have listened to him," Hernán muttered through chattering teeth. "The road to the south couldn't possibly be as bad as this." He clutched his cloak more tightly around him and leaned against Arriero's neck for warmth. We were toiling up the steep slope toward a mountain pass, so high that even the pines found it inhospitable and so cold that the water turned to ice in the calabashes. The climbers gasped for breath and clutched their throbbing sides in the thin air. Several Cuban slaves had died the night before.

"What do you think?" I asked old Teuch, who was striding along beside us, suffering little in his warm armor of quilted cotton. "Should we have gone the other way?"

"I've made this journey more times than I can count, Malintzin," the old man answered. "The worst of it's nearly over. The pass is in sight above us now. After that we'll have to march three or four days in the cold, but the walking will be easy because there will be no more mountains." He looked at me thoughtfully from under his grizzled eyebrows. I was bundled up in Hernán's extra wool cloak, with cotton rags wrapped around my feet, and was trying hard, out of pride, to control my own shivering. "You know, Malintzin, when your master's people came to Cempoalla I looked at them and thought, 'They must be gods! Men don't look like that!' I know better now. I've seen them sicken, suffer, die. Why, if they were gods, they'd fly over the tops of these mountains and strike at Moctezuma with bolts of lightning!" He glanced up at the shivering Hernán. "A god takes no chances. He can do whatever he wishes. True bravery belongs only to mortal men, and for this I respect your master and his followers."

I translated this for Hernán, who beamed with pleasure. "Ask him what we can expect from the Tlaxcalans, Marina," he said.

"First I'll tell you about the Cholulans," Teuch insisted, his breath making little puffs of white as he spoke, "so your master will be content that we're not going their way." And he told us about opulent Cholula, the Aztec empire's religious center with a temple for every day of the year, including the largest pyramid in all Mexico, which was dedicated to Quetzalcoatl. The paving stones of every street were stained red from countless sacrifices. "It's true the Cholulans are cultured," Teuch admitted. "They dress in fine cloaks embroidered with gold and silver and they walk with their heads and hands like so—" Thrusting his nose into the air, he minced along, hands dangling at the ends of his raised wrists in mock grace. I laughed. Hernán did not. "They sing and dance and write poetry. They're also as slimy as worms and as treacherous as quicksand, and they're so loyal to Moctezuma that if he told them to cut off their testicles and burn them on the altar of Huitzilopochtli, they'd do it to the last man!"

Teuch spat on the ground to show his contempt. "Now, the Tlaxcalans are as different from the Cholulans as the top of a mountain is from a swamp. I know them, because I served as ambassador to Tlaxcala for years. Still, I fear them. They're a harsh people, full of anger. They take such pride in being free that they acknowledge no king, not even among themselves.

Instead, they're ruled by a council of four chiefs."

I translated Teuch's words. "Ask him if they're wealthy," Hernán demanded eagerly. "And what about their military strength?"

"If your commander's looking for gold, he won't find it in Tlaxcala," Teuch answered, a note of disgust in his voice. "Moctezuma cuts them off from outside trade, so all they have is what they raise out of their own soil. It's too cold to grow cotton there, so they weave cloth out of maguey fibers. They gave me one of their cloaks once, but it was so scratchy that I only wore it to please them." He smiled at the memory.

"As for their military strength, every male who can walk can fight like a cornered ocelot. Listen to me, Malintzin. If your chief can win their friendship, they'll die for him. They're insanely loyal. If not, he might as well count himself dead right now."

Tlaxcala—September 1519

The bodies of more than a score of Cuban slaves slept behind us, buried in the cold, alkaline wasteland we'd crossed days earlier. Now we marched across the dry, sweeping plains of the Anahuac plateau, moving ever nearer to the boundaries of Tlaxcala. We had sent four Cempoallan chiefs ahead of us as ambassadors, each wearing the traditional cloth tied slantwise around the body and knotted twice in back, and carrying a dart and buckler in one hand, the traditional badges of office that would be recognized and guarantee them safe conduct throughout Mexico.

"This country looks like Spain." Bernal Diaz had moved up alongside me, his eyes sweeping from horizon to horizon as he spoke.

"No wonder you left," I teased. "I don't like it. It's dry and it's cold."

"So's Spain. When I look at these plains, I can almost imagine . . ." His eyes clouded wistfully. "But then we go through one of their towns and I remember where I am. *Diós*, did you see the collection of bones in that place we went through yesterday? There must have been a hundred thousand skulls on those racks."

I nodded, remembering. "I'm glad the padre talked Hernán out of trying to leave a cross there," I said. "Who knows what they'd be doing with it now?"

"Who knows what the Tabascans and Cempoallans are doing with *their* crosses?" Bernal snorted in disgust. "I won't be fooled into thinking that a few sweet words from a priest are going to change things overnight. The last time I was in Cempoalla I saw blood on one of the altars."

"I saw it too." I bit my lip. I'd said nothing until now because I didn't want to risk another confrontation like the one that had taken place when we pulled down their gods.

"Well, maybe their children will be Christians, or maybe their grandchildren, but I'm not looking to—"

He broke off. The six-man scouting party headed by Hernán himself reappeared over the ridge ahead, and they galloped down on us, raising clouds of dust as they pulled their horses to a stop.

"A wall!" Hernán exclaimed. "By my conscience, what a wall! High as a young tree, thick as four men laid head to foot. And it runs all the way across the valley."

Teuch wagged his head knowingly. He needed no translation, for there was only one thing on the path ahead that could cause so much excitement. An apprehensive smile played about the twisted old lips. He grunted a single word: "Tlaxcala."

The wall was enormous, like something built by giants playing with stones and mud. Hernán Cortés led his small force, each man's heart in his throat, through the semicircular laps of the gate. The rolling hill country of Tlaxcala spread out before us like a vast yellow-gray carpet. Not a living thing was in sight.

The dead quiet was more frightening than the howls of a thousand warriors. "I don't like this," Cortés muttered. "No sign of the ambassadors we sent, no one to welcome us. I smell trouble." Choosing ten horsemen to go with him, he spurred his mount and galloped out ahead of the main force, disappearing quickly over a rise.

The long moments dragged by as the rest of us continued to march forward. I found myself clenching and unclenching my hands as I walked. My palms were damp with perspiration.

Suddenly the stillness was shattered by the rumble of hoofbeats as Lares exploded over the horizon.

"*Madre mía!*" he gasped, pulling his horse up alongside Sandoval's. "Four, five thousand of them! Hurry!"

Sandoval's bellowed orders echoed and reechoed down the ranks. The column of soldiers instantly separated itself from the women and baggage and sped forward, cannon and arquebuses ready. The accompanying body of Totonacs moved with them. Ordering the women and the *tlamemes* to stay where they were, I took Aguilar, the two priests, and Teuch, who was too old to fight, and we ran off to a high ridge from which we'd be able to see the battle.

We shaded our eyes with our hands. The enemy swept forward in a single wave toward the little force of mounted Spaniards. The wild drumbeats and war cries sent chills up the back of my neck. Their obsidian spear tips glistened in the sun. Teuch studied them, eyes narrowing into two creases in his weathered face. "Otomi," he grunted. "The Tlaxcalans have set their dogs on us."

"They're not Tlaxcalans?" I crouched down beside him.

"The Tlaxcalan banner—a white heron on a red field—it's nowhere in sight. But they're here in spirit, all right. The Otomi are their vassals. They wouldn't attack us without orders." He ran forward a few steps for a better view. "Look! Your infantry's joined the horsemen! I've been wanting to see how your Castilians fight. Pray to your god, Malintzin."

I grasped the little cross on its silver chain that Alonzo had given me and prayed silently. Below, on the plain, I could hear the first shouts of battle as the opposing forces collided.

"Lure them into the swamps, into the furrowed fields . . . where their movements will be difficult . . ." Chilam's words came back to me now, spoken so long ago in that other world I had known. How right he had been. The Spaniards had won even in the treacherous fields of Tabasco, but here, on the open plain where cannon could maneuver, where infantry and cavalry could charge freely, they were in their own element—back in Spain almost, as Bernal would say. Here, they were the equal of any fighting force on earth.

I watched, my breath coming in gasps, as Hernán led his horsemen again and again into the waving body of Otomi warriors, our riders cutting them down like so many stalks of maize. The hills echoed with the roar of cannonfire; and with each volley the Otomi fell back, only to surge forward again. I was scarecely aware of the thin silver chain biting into the flesh of my neck as I twisted the cross anxiously in my hands.

"I think . . . yes! They're falling back!" Aguilar breathed. "We've won!"

"Not yet," Teuch muttered. "Not if I know the Tlaxcalans."

Miraculously, we emerged from the battle with no loss of life, but there were many wounds to tend. At Juan Jaramillo's suggestion, I pressed the more capable women into service, translating as he instructed them in tending the wounds with melted fat and wrapping them with strips of clean cloth. After watching the long battle, powerless to do anything, I was relieved to be active again, and Juan's occasional smile and quiet, sure manner as we worked together were a calming influence.

After the Otomi retreat, a delegation from Tlaxcala had visited the camp. They were tall and spare in their rough robes, with a visible toughness born of their rigorous existence. They'd brought with them two of the four Cempoallan ambassadors, whom they returned unharmed. The Otomi attack had been a mistake, they insisted, and they were sorry. If we wanted to proceed ahead, we could do so freely.

"I don't trust them," Teuch growled when they'd gone. "They were too pleasant."

We marched on, coming at dusk to a deserted Otomi town whose temple reeked with the odor of slaughter. The townspeople had carried away every last grain of food. Only a few small dogs remained to yap at the intruders. They were unlucky dogs, for they were soon roasting on spits over our fires. The hungry Spaniards ate them without a complaint.

Hernán had been ill with dysentery for the past several days, and now, after the incredible strain of the day's battle and the misery of sitting astride a galloping horse, he collapsed on his cot.

"Another day of this and life won't be worth living," he groaned. "Tell Jaramillo to mix up a purge of chamomile for me, Marina."

"You know what this will do to you, don't you?" Juan addressed his patient as he crushed the herbs and mixed them with boiling water. "This purge won't take effect until tomorrow. When it does, everything inside you will try to come out at the same time. Afterward, you'll be too weak to walk. You'll be useless for at least half the day."

"Damned well worth it if it cures me!" Hernán raised himself on one elbow and eyed the greenish liquid. "Besides, there shouldn't be any trouble tomorrow. They said we could go ahead."

"Teuch doesn't trust them," I warned.

"Well, by my conscience, I hope he's wrong," he sputtered, quaffing the bitter stuff with a grimace. "They fight like tigers, don't they, Jaramillo? Once or twice out there I thought they had us. Two horses gone! Curse them, I could more easily afford to lose ten men!" He shivered and spat into the dirt. "One horse got its head hacked off by those beastly obsidian-edged clubs. What're they called, Marina?"

"*Maquahuitls,*" I said, wiping out the cup Juan had used to mix the purge.

"I gave orders to bury the horses. If the Indians get hold of the bodies and find out they're only flesh and blood, that will take some of their fear away. We can't afford to let that happen." He stretched his aching limbs. "Strange. Those devils could have killed me ten times over out there, but they wouldn't even strike at me. Not even to save themselves. They just kept trying to pull me off the horse."

I kicked myself for not having thought to tell him. Among the Aztecs, and undoubtedly among these people as well, the main objective in any battle was to take prisoners for sacrifice. The more captives a warrior could take, the greater his honor, prestige and rank. Killing a man counted for nothing. "They wanted you alive," I said. "What a sacrifice you'd have made, Hernán!"

"Then I've got their bloody customs to thank for my life!" He lay back, his head on the pillow. "A civilized man would have run me through on the spot. Well, I'll consider it all a lesson and use it." He closed his eyes and fell into an exhausted sleep. Juan Jaramillo slipped quietly out of the tent, leaving me alone with him.

Marching cautiously along in the gray dawn of the next morning, we came to a body of a thousand Otomi warriors waiting for us at the top of the next hill.

"Pray they're friendly this time," Hernán muttered, still unaffected by the purge. In the presence of pompous little Godoy, the king's notary, who duly recorded and legalized any official action, he sent three of our Otomi captives back to their comrades with a proposal of friendship. With nerves as taut as bowstrings, we waited for an answer. It came in the form of a shower of stones and arrows.

Cortés sprang into Arriero's saddle. "Santiago and at them!" His battle cry rang out over the plains as his men rushed at the enemy.

The first shock of the attack seemed to jar the Otomi backward. They fought with less bravery than had those of the previous day, retreating slowly, step by step, their faces still toward their adversaries, who followed them zealously.

Again, Aguilar, Teuch and I had left the baggage carriers and climbed a ridge. Running along its top, we could keep pace with the battle at a safe distance. We groaned at what we saw. The Otomi had led their pursuers up onto a rocky crest where horse and cannon began to falter on the rough ground. A much larger force suddenly came swarming up from the other side.

We were near enough so that I could hear Hernán's voice. "Forward! Keep to the banner! Hold it high, my good Corral!" Hacking their way to the top of the hill, the Spaniards suddenly stopped. We raced along our ridge, trying to see what lay ahead.

"Blessed Mother!" I heard Aguilar gasp. There, waiting in the next valley, was a veritable sea of warriors. They covered the valley from one side to the other, a forest of a hundred thousand spears. At the sight of our little army coming over the top of the hill, they began to shriek and shake their weapons, the great brown mass pulsating in the sun. I gave a little cry as I saw their banner, an angry white heron on a red field, a symbol of the republic of Tlaxcala.

A tall figure in a red-plumed helmet strode before the huge body of warriors, one arm upraised, waiting to give the attack signal. Teuch cursed. "It's young Xicotencatl! I know him—he's never been beaten. We're dead men, Malintzin!"

"No!" I protested, my new faith suddenly welling up inside me. "Their general's never fought against our God. He'll protect us, won't he, Brother Jeronimo?"

"His will be done," murmured the trembling Aguilar, eyes half closed in silent prayer.

The battle raged through the day. Our forces had fought their way back to smooth ground, staying close together, a solid wedge in the midst of the Tlaxcalan swarm. They managed to hold their own, striking whenever possible at the chiefs, who were easily distinguished by their headdresses, and taking good advantage of the Tlaxcalan practice of carrying the dead and wounded from the field as they fell. Again and again, the cavalry plowed into the midst of the foe, leaving a path open to the infantry, who followed close on their heels. The Tlaxcalans were able to surround one of the horses, a fine mare, and pulling the rider from the saddle, they stabbed the animal to death with spears and *maquahuitls*. The rider was rescued by the infantry, but the horse was dragged triumphantly from the battlefield as a trophy, for all to see that it was a mere animal with no more mystical powers than those possessed by a dog or a deer.

But such small victories were few for the Tlaxcalans. Toward the end of the afternoon, their forces scattered and many of their chiefs killed, they retreated like a great brown wave washing back to the sea.

The slaves, carriers and women had made a rude camp by the time the soldiers returned, infantrymen dragging their exhausted limbs, horses wet with foam and blood. Wonder and elation were written across weary faces. There'd been just fifteen Spaniards wounded, and only one of them was in grave condition. Cempoallan losses were heavier, owing to their greater numbers, their unprotected bodies and the fact that they were less prized as live trophies.

Hernán came clattering into camp on Arriero, his face glowing. "We've won the day!" he exclaimed. "But they'll be back. There's no time to be lost. We've got to make more spears, more straw matting. The guns have to be cleaned, the powder measured." He stirred uneasily in the saddle. "And there's no food. Ávila, organize a foraging expedition at—at—" He doubled over and slid from his horse, racked with pain and nausea, as the purge finally took its effect.

The next morning, a renewed Cortés led raids on six villages, returning in triumph with food and four hundred captives, who were placated with beads and dispatched to Xicotencatl with another offer of peace.

After what seemed a long time, two Tlaxcalan messengers came trotting back over the hills. Both of them were young. They strutted defiantly into the camp, heads high, eyes scornful; but I noticed how their staves shook in their hands.

One of them spoke. "Xicotencatl the Younger sends word that we will celebrate peace in Tlaxcala tomorrow." He paused for dramatic effect, giving me a chance to translate. Hearing the words, the men's faces relaxed into smiles. They were on the verge of cheering when the messenger raised his hand for silence. "We'll celebrate our peace by burning your hearts on our altars and simmering your flesh over our cooking fires—with chili peppers to give you better flavor!" He swaggered back and forth, licking his lips in mock pleasure. A wave of shock went through the listeners as I translated, trying to keep my own voice from shaking. "Use this night to say goodbye to your friends," the gloating young messenger added. "Sleep with your women, those of you who have them, for the last time."

Hernán stood beside me. I could almost feel the tension vibrating in his body, but when he spoke his voice was calm, almost pleasant. "Tell your *cacique* that we and our God will be waiting for him." He bowed politely.

The last two of the four Cempoallan ambassadors had escaped and come back to us that night, weeping tears of indignation. The Tlaxcalans had violated the protection of their insignias and had them bound and imprisoned. But they brought us some encouragement. Only two of the four ruling chiefs were in favor of fighting us. The others, Maxixcatzin, the noblest of men according to Teuch, and blind, aging Xicotencatl the Elder, father of our enemy general, wanted to declare peace and welcome us as allies. They'd argued for days. The Otomi attack had been a compromise measure, designed to feel us out without direct Tlaxcalan involvement.

The campfires flickered late into the night, illuminating long lines of men waiting before the two makeshift confessionals—little more than blankets thrown over tree limbs—where Padre Olmedo and Padre Diaz helped each soul make its peace before the coming battle. The waiting was tedious, for these bold voyagers carried some heavy sins on their shoulders. After the cleansing of the spirit, each man returned to the sharpening of his sword, the padding of his armor, the cleaning of the cannons.

"You've not gone to confession, Marina *mía*?" We were seated on a log in the open doorway of the tent, huddling close to the small fire for warmth. Under my *huipilli* Hernan's calloused hand caressed the curve of my back. I closed my eyes to isolate the sensation.

"I haven't gone," I admitted. "It's as if I want to say to God, 'I'm not expecting to see You tomorrow!' "

"You blasphemous little witch!" He pinched my shoulder blade till I winced. His touch and voice were playful. He leaned over and tickled my ear with his beard. "I didn't go to confession either," he confided, "and for the same reason. Call it an act of faith. Besides, I confessed last Sunday and since then I've been too busy, too tired and too ill to sin."

"Oho! Brother Jeronimo says you can sin even in your thoughts."

"I haven't even had time for a sinful thought!"

A chilly breeze struck us. I moved closer, leaning my head against his bulging shoulder. I wondered idly if the Tlaxcalans in the other camp were confessing to Tlazoteotl, the Eater of Sins. The Christians had no monopoly on confession. Nahua people had been unburdening themselves to that fierce goddess for centuries. But where the Christian God listened and forgave time after time, the less patient Tlazoteotl allowed each man just one absolution. For that reason, when a man laid his sins before her, it was usually in the belief that he was going to die soon.

I shifted my weight on the log, suddenly uncomfortable. This talk of sin had reminded me of something that was troubling my conscience.

"Hernán?"

"What is it, my little savage?"

"Padre Diaz told me that I was living in sin."

"What?" He stiffened.

"I and the other women, too. Because we're not married to our men. He says we're sinning."

"Why that pious little—" He halted until he'd regained his composure. "Does that bother you, Marina?"

"No . . . well, yes, a little. We're all decent women, Hernán. We're trying our best to be good Christians. It's not our fault that our people gave us to you and your men. Most of us would like to be married if we could be, and now your priest says we're sinning." I was overwrought now, I knew.

Hernán patted my shoulder. "You know why I can't make you my wife, don't you, Marina?"

"Yes," I said. "You're already married. That's nothing new to me. I was a married man's concubine in Centla. No one accused me of sinning then."

"Well, we're all sinners in the sight of God." He put his arm around my shoulder and pulled me closer to him. "Don't worry about it, Marina *mía*."

"But what about Pedro de Alvarado?" I persisted. "He doesn't have a wife. Why doesn't he marry my poor little friend? And what about some of the others?"

"The questions that come from that pretty mouth!" His hand had returned to my back and the caresses were stronger now, more demanding. "I can't answer for my men. I only know that in times like these, when home's far away and danger's near, a man needs the warmth of a woman. God, in his wisdom, must know this and look down on us with understanding."

"Hernán. . . . ?

"No. No more questions." His mouth covered mine, warm, moist, compelling. One hand tugged at my sash. "Lower the tent flap, Marina," he whispered.

* * *

The white heron of Tlaxcala spread its angry wings on the banner that rose above the undulating sheet of warriors. They were fresh troops, half again as many as we'd faced two days before. The sound of their drums made the very hills vibrate.

"Well, I've pissed and made the sign of the cross," said Bernal Diaz. "Let the devils come! I'm ready!"

Arriero danced nervously, Cortés pulling back hard on the reins as he addressed his little army.

"There's no hope for us unless we can outwit them," he said. "They don't seem to have much of a battle plan, and that's to our advantage. We'll make them chase us, tire them out. Then and only then will we take the offensive." He patted Arriero's neck. The horse, covered with steel and bullhide, looked more like a machine than an animal. "Now, stay close to the banner! Hold it high, Corral. If you falter—"

"I won't falter, sir," said the husky Corral, his plump, boyish face pale. The drums had stopped and the silence was more terrible than any sound could be.

"Here they come! Follow me! Follow the cross!" Hernán spurred Arriero to a canter, weaving back and forth at the head of the ranks as they moved cautiously toward the screaming wave of Tlaxcalans that spilled over the hills and flowed with frightening speed into the valleys.

Even the sun climbed high to watch as the two armies clashed again and again, the huge Tlaxcalan force pushing our little band farther and farther back up the hill toward the camp.

Surely we'd turn on them soon! I could already distinguish the colors of the war paint on Tlaxcalan faces and hear the *thunk* of lances against plaited-reed shields as the forefront of the battle crept nearer. The camp was in a state of panic. A woman shrieked as an arrow struck the earth near her running feet. Two *tlamemes* fought over a discarded shield. "Help me, Teuch!" I shouted. "They'll be on us soon!"

The old chief had assessed the situation. "Pile the baggage over there!" he roared. "Get the women and the wounded behind it! You, *tlamemes*! You may not be warriors but you're men! Collect the extra weapons! Hurry!" After a lifetime of commanding, Teuch knew how to make himself obeyed. Within moments his orders had been carried out and the baggage had been arranged to form a low fortification between the camp and the approaching fray. The *tlamemes* brandished staves and broken spears.

A stone glanced off my shoulders as I grabbed Orteguilla and darted for cover behind a pile of empty pots. I wondered if it wouldn't have been wiser to abandon the camp and flee back into the hills, but there were wounded men who could not be carried and valuable supplies that we couldn't afford to lose. Better to stay and fight. The battlefront was coming up the slope now, and I could see the backs of our troops intermingled with the brown skin of the Cempoallans and the quilted, brine-soaked armor of their chiefs as they retreated, battling all the way. There was Corral with the banner, blood streaming from his arm as he staggered back. A wounded Bernal Diaz, whose towering form made him an easy target, defended Corral with sweeping blows of his sword, assisted by the smaller, more agile Juan Jaramillo. The mass of lean Tlaxcalan faces, smeared with red, white and ochre, each in the design of its own fighting unit, pressed ever nearer. A Tlaxcalan in a plumed helmet swung his *maquahuitl* and severed the arm of a Cempoallan, whose blood spurted over them both as he fell. Here and there a horseman bobbed above the melee. Pedro de Alvarado had lost his helmet. His golden hair, blazing in the sun, made him the most desired trophy on the battlefield. His mare reared and plunged, hooves clubbing the band of Tlaxcalans who were trying to drag him to the ground.

Gonzalo de Sandoval charged his splendid Motilla again and again into the thickest part of the fray, moving to aid the wounded Ávila, then to rescue Lares who'd been pulled from his horse, chopping a circle of safety around the animal till its rider could remount.

Clutching Orteguilla to me and choking on my own heart, I saw Hernán struggling up the hill on Arriero, Tlaxcalan warriors swarming over him like ants, grasping at his arms and legs, flailing away at the stallion's armored flanks. Sandoval plowed his way to his commander's side. Gripping Motilla with his legs, Sandoval used both hands to cut through the mass of brown bodies that surrounded Hernán. The air was fetid with the odors of blood, dust, horse sweat and gunpowder. My ears echoed with the roar of cannon and arquebus, the shouts of men, the screams of horses, all blending into one great blur of noise that bore down on me and shook me to the core. In a moment the battle would be upon the camp. Crouching next to Orteguilla and clutching a little dagger, the only weapon I'd been able to keep for myself, I waited for the enemy. There was no use in running. If we lost, there'd be no place to run. Knowing what they'd do to him, I couldn't let the boy be taken alive. I gripped the little dagger tightly and prayed for the strength to use it if I had to. The heap of pottery, our fortress, grew lower and lower under the barrage of arrows and stones until we lay flat against the earth.

"Santiago! Santiago and at them!" The battle cry of Hernán Cortés rang out above the din. There he was, beside Corral and the banner now, rearing his horse high in the air. "At them!" He lowered his lance and galloped forward. The men rallied behind him.

They surged forward once more. The startled Tlaxcalans, caught off-guard, were driven swiftly back down into the valley. Fresh reinforcements were waiting for them and they rallied in turn, but the retreat had given the Spaniards precious seconds to reload the arquebuses and rewind the crossbows. The next charge of Tlaxcalans was met by a deadly hail of arrows, propelled with such force that they pierced the quilted armor. A befeathered chieftain, swinging his *maquahuitl*, charged an arquebusier and had his head blown off in an explosion of bitter yellow smoke.

At last it was the weary sun that chose to end the battle. As it dropped behind the hills, the Tlaxcalans, who didn't fight at night, melted away into the growing darkness, leaving our men to drag their aching bodies back to camp.

"What's this?" chuckled a tired Hernán, seeing my little knife. "Were you going to kill a chicken for our supper, Marina?"

Teuch had sent his most intrepid spies on a mission to the enemy camp, their identities disguised in the battle gear seized from dead Tlaxcalans during the fight. The three of us, Hernán, Teuch and I, waited far into the night for their return, huddled around a campfire in the chilly darkness. It wasn't until the first gray streak of dawn appeared in the black sky that the two men returned.

The news they brought was not unexpected. The Tlaxcalans planned to finish us off that coming morning with even greater numbers, freshly arrived from the capital. Xicotencatl the Younger was determined not to let us hold him off again.

Still, there was a thread of hope. The Tlaxcalan general was losing favor because he'd failed twice against us. Opposing forces in the capital and in the camp were growing in strength and vehemence. Maxixcatzin and old Xicotencatl were drawing converts from among the elders to their side, and among the

Tlaxcalan troops there was talk that Cortés was a god and that his men were invincible.

We could only pray for a miracle—Hernán and I to Our Lord, and Teuch to the old gods of his ancestors. Our forces were weak, wounded, exhausted. Without divine help we could never hope to hold our own against the multitude of fresh Tlaxcalan troops that waited out on the plain for morning and for us.

The sun rose again, blinking through the clouds over the eerie stillness that ruled where there had been chaos the night before. In battle formation, weapons ready, our battered forces waited for the expected attack; but not one Tlaxcalan appeared over the hills. Not one drumbeat disturbed the air.

"Sandoval." Cortés spoke softly, hardly daring to break the silence. "Ride up to a good vantage point. Try to get a look at their camp."

Motilla's hoofbeats rang out startlingly as he bore his master away. All eyes were on Sandoval as his horse climbed to the top of a high ridge. Every ear was strained to hear the first shout of warning.

Sandoval waited on top of the ridge, shading his eyes with his gloves. He leaned forward and shook his head in utter disbelief. Then, at last, he wheeled his horse and came galloping back down toward us as recklessly as the slope would permit, shouting at the top of his lungs. "By the saints, they're leaving! They're marching off in all directions! There's no banner left down there except Xicotencatl's!"

As two antagonistic dogs gradually arrive at understanding after growling, bristling, sniffing one another, then jumping back to snap and snarl, so did Cortés and Tlaxcala move cautiously toward peace.

Hernán began the day by raiding ten more Tlaxcalan villages, burning the huts and capturing their occupants. Xicotencatl retaliated with a night attack, something almost unheard of in the annals of Nahua warfare.

Later we learned that sorcerers had told the Tlaxcalan general that we drew our power from the sun and were thus vulnerable in darkness, but Xicotecatl's troops were easily beaten off, thanks to our sentries.

Xicotencatl's next move was to send fifty "ambassadors" to our camp with gifts of food and five old slave women. "They're spies," Teuch whispered to me. Watching them as they questioned the Cempoallans and fingered the weapons, I had to agree with him. We alerted Hernán.

"This will be the last time that dog sends anyone to spy on me," he thundered, and he ordered the hands of the leaders and the thumbs of the rest chopped off. Amid their screams and the pungent odor of seared flesh, he ordered them sent back to their general. "Mild punishment," he replied to my shocked face. "If I'd killed them all no one would have thought the worse of me for it."

The Aztecs had not forgotten us. As soon as word reached them that we'd survived our encounter with the Tlaxcalans, they sent an embassy, laden with gifts and entreaties to beg us to leave these treacherous plains and go to Cholula with them. I could understand their concern. An alliance between Cortés and Tlaxcala could portend disaster for Moctezuma. We accepted their gifts and remained where we were. Another delegation of Aztecs was more surprising. Younger and more plainly dressed than the other groups, they came not from Moctezuma but from Ixtlilxochitl, a prince of the city-state of Texcoco.

"An upstart!" Teuch warned me. "This young Ixtlilxochitl rebelled when his older brother, Cacama, was put on the throme of Texcoco by Moctezuma. He wants Texcoco for himself and he'll side with anybody who'll help him get it."

So the days dripped past—literally, for the rainy season had now arrived. We camped in the cold, wet mud on the plain while Hernán played balancing games with the three opposing native powers—the Tlaxcalans and the two Aztec factions. The Tlaxcalans sent visitors to us daily, begging us to come into their city and insisting that Xicotencatl the Younger had acted against the orders of the council.

"Can we trust them?" Hernán would have me ask Teuch after every visit.

"I put my trust in one man," said the old chief. "Maxixcatzin. I've known him since we were young warriors. When he comes in person with his promise that you'll be welcome in the capital, that's when I'll feel safe."

So we waited, shivering, as Hernán sent back one embassy after another. At last, one morning in the midst of breakfast, we looked up to see a long procession bearing three litters coming over the next hill. I gripped Teuch's arm. "The *tlatoani*!"

"Yes, Malintzin . . ." He was grinning broadly, showing several missing teeth, as his eyes took in the dignified figure seated in the first litter. "There's my friend, Maxixcatzin."

Chapter Eleven

Tlaxcala—September 1519

While the Tlaxcalan welcome was less lavish than the one in Cempoalla had been—for fruit and flowers were scarce in this harsh land—it was no less sincere. The Spaniards, in full battle regalia, marched up the principal street as the populace cheered themselves hoarse and jostled one another to gawk at these pale-skinned god-strangers and their steeds. Walking beside Arriero, I gazed about with interest at the people and their buildings. The most noticeable characteristic of both was their lack of ornamentation. Any addition beyond the functional, either in construction or in costume, was an excess the hard-pressed Tlaxcalans could not afford. Their gods had been stingy with them.

The four *tlatoani* waited for us on the steps of old Xicotencatl's palace. Although three of them had come out to our camp the day before, they were meeting us officially for the first time. Teohuayacatzin and Tlehuexolotl, both middle-aged, returned Hernán's handclasp somewhat coolly, but the older Maxixcatzin embraced his new ally enthusiastically. He was a remarkably handsome old man, graceful and vigorous as a youth. "I knew that if my friend Teuch was with you, you couldn't mean us any harm," he exclaimed happily. "It's pained my heart to know that our warriors were fighting you."

Xicotencatl the Elder had been too feeble to make the trip to our camp. Shriveled and blind with age, he was led forward to touch Hernán's face with his bony fingers. "You don't feel like a god," he said in a voice that was surprisingly clear and steady, revealing the strength he'd once had. "What are you, my friend?"

"A man and your brother!"

"As for you, child," he addressed me, "I've no need to touch you. Your voice tells me you're young and pretty. But

I've heard so much about those big animals you've brought with you, I'd like to inspect one."

A docile mare was led forward, the high-strung Arriero having been judged too great a risk to the old chief's safety. Sensitive hands explored the contours of the mare's face, the eyes, the petal-like softness of the nose, the arch of the glossy neck, and measured the length and breadth of the animal's body, stroking the rounded belly and feeling the strength of the sinewy legs.

"It's like a deer, isn't it?" The old man laughed with delight. "How unafraid it is!"

Xicotencatl the Younger stood in his customary place behind the four chiefs, watching his father's antics with disgust. He was older than his name had led me to believe, about forty perhaps, a lean man with a sober, jutting-jawed face and coarse-textured skin. His hair was cut squarely at the shoulders and he carried his red-plumed helmet under his arm.

Hernán, who bore no grudges, took a step toward him. "At last we meet as friends," he exclaimed, extending his hand.

Xicotencatl ignored the outstretched hand and turned eyes full of hatred on Hernán. "We've opened our gates to an army of monsters," he snarled. "I tried to warn my father and the others but they wouldn't listen. They're fools. You'll destroy us one day. But the council has ruled that you be accepted as allies, and as a son and subject of Tlaxcala, it's my duty to abide by their decision. You may expect no further trouble from me." He turned and stalked away.

The exchange of gifts took place the following day, after a night of feasting in the palace. After Padre Juan Diaz had said mass, standing in for the ailing Padre Olmedo, Hernán presented his new allies with beads, trinkets and a few of the much-prized cotton robes given us by the most recent Aztec delegation.

Xicotencatl the Elder apologized for the meagerness of his gifts: seven little fish made of gold, some rough robes and several stones that were said to have magical powers. "We're a poor people, Malintzin," he said, using my name to address Hernán. "But please accept these unworthy trinkets with our love." Hernán assured him that the gifts meant more to him than would the gift of a roomful of gold from Moctezuma.

Xicotencatl continued, smiling, "But for these next presents, I need make no apologies. The sun does not shine on any lovelier women than our daughters."

All heads snapped at once to the back of the room, where five young women had entered, escorted by their slaves.

"I hear you, my flowers," called the old chief. "Come forward."

I watched apprehensively as the five women glided toward us in their simple robes, wondering if one of them would turn out to be another Catalina. It would be painful if it proved to be so. At least I'd felt sorry for the fat little Totonac princess, but there was no need to pity any of these girls. They were beautiful, taller and more slender than the Totonac women and without the prominent noses and flattened foreheads of the Mayans—a feature which, Bernal Diaz had confided to me, the Spaniards found unattractive. These women were Nahuas, physically and linguistically of the same stock as myself.

Old Xicotencatl beckoned the girls close to him, reaching out to take the arm of the nearest one. "You are . . . of course, Zicuetzin. Malintzin, this maiden is Maxixcatzin's niece. She's for one of your brave captains."

Hernán accepted the girl and awarded her to Juan Velásquez de León. Three more princesses, all daughters or nieces of the four chieftains, were given to Cristobal de Olid, Jorge de Alvarado (Pedro's brother) and a deserving Gonzalo de Sandoval. Just one girl, the prettiest one, remained. I braced myself for what I knew must surely be coming.

"To you, Malintzin, I give my own daughter, Tecuilhuatzin." I translated, my heart thumping convulsively. "I hope you'll fill this palace with grandchildren for me." Xicotencatl thrust the girl gently toward Hernán.

He was silent for a moment. Get it over with, I thought furiously.

Hernán glanced at me. "I'm honored," he murmured. "But I can't rightfully take the girl for myself. You see, I already have a wife."

My heart soared. He wasn't going to take her! When I translated, trying to hide my own elation, the old chief's face fell. Hernán, I knew, would have to find a way to please him.

He looked quickly around at his captains. Pedro de Alvarado, in his scarlet tunic, amply justified the name he'd been given by the Tlaxcalans: Tonatuih, the sun. Hernán put an arm around his shoulder. "My friend and brother," he declared. "Some say he's even braver and better-looking than I am. Will you do me the honor or accepting him in my place?"

"I'll accept any man of your choosing," Xicotencatl answered graciously. "Tell him to come closer, so my fingers can see his face."

As Pedro de Alvarado stepped forward, a little cry was heard from the back of the hall. There, standing with the women in our party, was Tonaxel, her body swollen with Alvarado's child and her little flat-browed face ashen. She turned with a sob, tore herself loose from the women who tried to stop her, and ran out of the building. There was a shout. "She's fallen down the steps!"

Hernán seized my arm to keep me from running after her. "Let me go to her," I begged.

"No, Marina," he insisted. "I need you here for the baptisms."

"How could you have done it?" I stormed. "You could have chosen anyone but him!"

His fingers tightened painfully on my arm. "Don't make a scene," he said under his breath. "Would you rather I'd taken the girl for myself?"

Several of the women had hurried outside after Tonaxel. I heard no screams, so I could only hope she was all right. "They'll take care of her. Forget about it," Hernán said.

Dawn was bleak and chilly in Tlaxcala. The first beams of gray light awakened the turkeys and dogs in their pens and the little black and brown birds that chirped in the trees. The rough-handed women of Tlaxcala arose and breathed the embers of the cooking fires into flames. The white-robed priests in the temples blew their conches and pierced their ears with thorns to welcome the sun before taking the captives from their cages and cutting out their hearts to feed and sustain him in his journey across the sky.

Lying awake beside the sleeping Hernán and listening to the sounds of the morning, I distinguished the light footsteps of Orteguilla as he hurried over the stone floor toward our room.

"Doña Marina," he whispered outside the curtain that covered the door. "Juan Jaramillo says he needs you. Hurry!"

I slipped on my clothing and sandals and smoothed my hair. "What is it?" I asked, pushing aside the curtain and stepping softly through the doorway.

"I don't know." He was still rubbing his own eyes. "I think someone's sick. Señor Jaramillo didn't want to wake you himself." We tiptoed through the cool hallways of Xicotencatl's palace, where sleepy Spanish sentries waited for the end of their watch, and went down to the rooms that had been set aside for the quartering of the troops.

Juan was waiting anxiously for us outside one of the tiny storage rooms. "It's Doña Antonia," he said. "I'm afraid she's going to lose her baby." He caught my questioning look. "Alvarado brought her here in the night—wanted me to take her in repayment of a few pesos I'd lent him to pay a gambling debt in Villa Rica." He ran his fingers through his tawny hair. "I told him to forget the money, I didn't want the poor girl. He just walked away. I tried to get her to go back and stay with the other women but she wouldn't go—just sat in the corner rocking back and forth. Finally I realized she was in pain . . ."

He drew aside the curtain. Tonaxel lay on a mat against the adobe wall of the little room. Her face was almost gray and huge beads of perspiration stood out on her forehead.

"Malinalli . . ." She was so weak she could barely raise her hand to greet me. Her pretty little mouth tightened as she glanced down sadly at the mound her body made under the rough blanket. "It's too soon, isn't it?" she whispered.

"Yes." There was no reason to lie to her. "Hold my hand, Tonaxel. You'll have others."

"Not Pedro's," she breathed. "He's given me away . . ."

"Don't try to talk," I said, my eyes stinging with tears. "Save your strength."

I sent Orteguilla away with instructions to tell Hernán where I was when he awakened. Then I sat beside Tonaxel, gripping her hands as she moaned and writhed, remembering a sun-splotched maize field in Tabasco where, little more than a year ago, Tonaxel had held my own hand as I gave birth to Chilam's baby. From time to time I wiped the pale face with a damp cloth. Juan crouched morosely beside me, straightening the blanket, wringing out fresh clothes. He was practically useless and he knew it. Yet he stayed.

"Damn!" he said. "I've never felt so helpless. Alvarado ought to be hanged!"

The sun was climbing high in the sky now. Outside, feet hurried back and forth as soldiers and servants went about their business. Tonaxel grew weaker. "Malinalli," she whispered, "I'm not big enough to have this baby. I'm going to die too."

"No!" I choked, looking down at her narrow hips and realizing she was probably right. "The baby isn't that big yet, Tonaxel."

Juan couldn't have understood what we said, but he'd watched a woman die before. I looked at the black sash against his white sleeve and remembered. "Do you want me to find the padre?" he asked softly. I reached over and touched the back of his hand.

"Not yet. That would frighten her."

Tonaxel moaned, twisted on her mat and suddenly began to hemorrhage, soaking her skirt and the woven matting with blood. The curtain at the door rustled. It was Nacontoc, breathless from running. "They said she was here," he panted. "They said he'd given her away! Malinalli, I've told Brother Jeronimo I'd be baptized if I could have her—"

I'd gone to the doorway to talk to him. I put my hand on his arm.

"My poor Nacontoc. She's dying."

A sound like the cry of a wounded animal tore from his throat as he flung himself through the curtain and onto his knees beside Tonaxel, calling her name, pressing her cold hands against his face. She was lying in a pool of blood now. Her eyelids fluttered once and froze as her tense body suddenly went limp in Nacontoc's arms. She was dead. He cradled her for a moment, staring at the still face in disbelief. Then, slowly, he lowered her back to the mat, his face contorted with an emotion too awful to bear.

"I curse the Castilians!" he whispered hoarsely. "I curse their god! I curse Tonatuih—he killed her!" He rose to his feet and stumbled out of the room.

Juan and I looked at Tonaxel's body in silence, both of us too drained to cry. He leaned forward to cover her face with the blanket, but I stopped him with my hand on his arm. "I'll wash her," I said. "You can get the padre and tell Alva—"

"My sword!" he exclaimed. "It's gone!" The empty scabbard leaned against the wall next to the door. Only one person could have taken it. We looked at each other in instant comprehension. "Come on!" He grabbed my hand. "We've got to find Alvarado!"

Through the dim corridors we ran, searching, asking. "Pedro de Alvarado? I saw him out in the square," answered a soldier with a bandaged head. We rushed out into the glaring sunlight.

A crowd was already gathering at the far side of the square, men running from all directions to swarm around something we could not yet see. I followed the path Juan's body made as he shouldered his way through the mass of onlookers.

Pedro de Alvarado was wiping the blood from his sword

with a linen handkerchief. He looked nonchalantly at the circle of shocked faces around him.

"What else could I do?" he said with a shrug. "The idiot tried to kill me. You saw it."

Nacontoc sprawled on the paving stones, blood pouring from a deep wound in his chest. Juan's sword, still clean, lay an arm's length away where he had dropped it.

Juan knelt beside him, inspecting the wound. He ripped off his shirt and thrust it against the fountain of red, but the shirt was quickly saturated. He shook his head sadly. "We're too late, Doña Marina."

Jeronimo de Aguilar thrust his way through the crowd with the priest, Juan Diaz, in tow behind him.

"Here he is, Padre. Quick, there's no time to lose. He's dying."

Pushing Juan Jaramillo aside, the round-cheeked padre knelt over Nacontoc's body, a basin of holy water in one hand. With the other hand he sprinkled a little water over the unconscious boy's head and repeated the one Latin phrase I had come to recognize:

"In the name of the Father, the Son and the Holy Ghost, I baptize thee, Esteban."

Someone held a feather against Nacontoc's nostrils. It fluttered once and then all movement ceased. Aguilar clutched his rosary and gave a long sigh of relief that Nacontoc's short and unhappy life had at least come to an end with the hope of salvation.

October, 1519

"Why do they call me Malinche?" Hernán asked me.

"They call you by my name because I speak for you," I answered. "But it's not Malinche, it's Malintzin. Malina because they can't say the *r*, and the 'tzin' to honor me." I shifted my weight on Arriero's rump. "To honor both of us."

"Malin-tz . . . tz—I can't even say it properly. You'll have to be content with Malinche from me."

I was seated behind him, riding at the head of a long column of marchers that now included five thousand Tlaxcalans. We'd already passed over the southern border of Tlaxcala and now we were making our way through a countryside of pastel greens where well-tended fields were separated by rows of spiny maguey plants. The snow-capped summits of the conical Popocatepetl and the graceful Ixtaccihuatl seemed to float above the landscape, their bases a hazy blue in the distance.

"You're still angry with me, aren't you?" he said. "You haven't smiled at me since we buried your two friends."

"It wasn't your fault," I said tonelessly. I didn't want to revive the quarrel I'd had with him that morning three weeks ago, when I'd come in from the square with Tonaxel's blood still on my fingers. He'd been taken aback when I'd lashed out at him with a fury I didn't know I possessed.

"She'd have died anyway, you little fool," he'd growled at me.

"At least she'd have died happy," I'd flared back. "Four hundred men and you had to give the girl to Alvarado!"

"The old chief wouldn't have settled for just anyone. I had to choose somebody who'd impress him."

"Impress him! The old man's blind, Hernán!"

"That's enough," he'd snapped at me. "I make my decisions for the good of the company, not to spare the feelings of some pregnant little Indian slut. If you don't like it, that's your privilege."

We'd slept apart for the next few nights—but who was I to resist the persuasions of the man who'd talked his company into demolishing their own ships? There was a hypnotic quality about Hernán, a dark intensity in all his actions and beliefs that elicited a fascination and loyalty among his soldiers. Even had I not been his concubine and thus bound to serve him, I knew that Hernán, whom so many saw as a leader—even as a god—was a man who needed me. And so I'd relented.

"I'm not angry," I said now. "Only sorry."

"Well, by now you've seen me at my worst, Marina." He reached back and patted my knee. "Do you think I'm a cruel man?"

"Cruel? No," I said. "Stubborn? Wilful? Contrary? Absolutely. Why else would you be going to Cholula against the advice of our friends?"

I felt his body shake with laughter. "You know me, don't you, you little witch! You knew I'd have to see the place for myself."

"I still wish you'd go back to Tlaxcala," I said. I was worried. Moctezuma's repeated, honeyed invitations to visit Cholula held the promise of treachery, I was sure. Yet Hernán paid no attention when I tried to warn him.

"Another week in Tlaxcala would've killed us all," he said.

"Adversity's meat and drink to these good comrades. Too much kindness and they get as soft as overripe pumpkins." He glanced affectionately back at the long line of marchers that stretched out behind us. With the exception of Xicotencatl the Younger, the Tlaxcalans were so passionate in their friendship that when Hernán had insisted on marching on, they'd offered him the service of every soldier in the republic. He'd declined all except these five thousand seasoned troops. By his own choice, Xicotencatl was not among them—which was as we preferred it to be.

"Marina, what about that young prince who sent his ambassadors to us? Can we count on him?"

"Ixtlilxochitl?" I shook my head. I'd questioned everyone from Moctezuma's envoys to Maxixcatzin about the young rebel who'd offered us his friendship. No one had had anything good to say about him. When he was twelve, he'd led a gang of young toughs who roamed the city of Texcoco, making mischief and terrorizing the citizens. Only his princely rank had saved him from execution. He was power-mad, I'd been told, and he'd join with anyone who might help him wrest control of Texcoco from his older brother, Cacama. It was whispered that his ambition extended beyond Texcoco to the very throne of Moctezuma.

Hernán listened as I told him all I knew. "I'll reserve judgment till I've met him," was all he said, lapsing into thoughtful silence, but I saw the old twitching of the vein in his forehead.

I bounced along behind him, my hands wet where they gripped the cool metal cuirass. I wished he'd turn back. I wished he had at least taken more warriors with him.

He stiffened in the saddle. Still distant, Cholula lay before us, its three hundred sixty temples glistening white in the morning sunlight. One enormous pyramid towered above the rest, and from the *teocalli* at its top a black plume of smoke rose against the crystal sky. I could hear the faint blare of the conches and the pulsing of the big temple drums; I could even smell—or was it only my imagination?—the blended odor of copal incense and roasting flesh.

Pale, fragrant smoke, billowing out of censers that swung from priestly hands, enveloped us as we marched down wide streets lined with chattering, bustling men and women in fine robes.

I'd dismounted for the entry into the city. Now I walked at

Hernán's stirrup, taking in the sights with wide eyes. The priests were almost as numerous as the townspeople. I'd never seen so many white robes. The Cholutec lords who'd come out to meet us escorted us past the base of the great pyramid of Quetzalcoatl, where they paused to surround Hernán with clouds of incense. The priests waited as if they were expecting him to mount the steps of that huge structure and claim the *teocalli* as his own. I wondered what our welcome would have been like if he'd openly claimed to be Quetzalcoatl, as so many people believed him to be.

The temple itself fascinated me. It was so old, according to Teuch, that no one even knew what people had begun it. Every fifty-two years, at the close of each calendar cycle, a new facing had been built over the old one until the pyramid had grown to mountainous size. The Cholutecs boasted that a powerful torrent of water lay hidden in its heart, ready to gush forth and engulf any invaders who threatened the city.

Pedro de Alvarado and Gonzalo de Sandoval rode behind us. "Look at all the gold!" Alvarado marveled. "That man's necklace alone must be worth a fortune."

"You can look at the gold all you like," Sandoval answered curtly. "As for me, I'm keeping one hand on my sword."

The woman was plump and middle-aged; her features bore evidence that she'd never been a beauty. She was dressed in an orange *huipilli* edged with varicolored feathers, and her neck was circled with a gold chain. As I stood on the porch of the palace where we'd been quartered, she caught my eye from the square below. Now she beckoned furtively, looking about her to see if anyone was watching. A boy of about fourteen stood beside her, his arms laden with bundles from the market. She beckoned again, hastily, nodding her head to emphasize that she wanted me to come to her.

Warily, I slipped down the steps and into the crowded square. For the past two days since we'd entered the city, I'd been trying to quell a growing panic inside myself. The very air seemed thick with apprehension. Food, scanty even in the beginning, had not been offered to us at all that day. A new Aztec delegation had informed us that the road to Tenochtitlan was impassable and we could not leave the city. Worse yet, Teuch's Cempoallan spies, who circulated freely, had brought back reports that pits and barricades were being constructed in the streets. The Tlaxcalans, who'd been made to camp outside on the plain, had sent a rumor in to warn us that they'd seen women and children leaving the city, their arms loaded with provisions.

As my feet touched the bottom step, I glanced back up at the elevated porch. Bernal Diaz stood in the shadow of a pillar, chatting with Juan Jaramillo. Both of them had seen me go. I felt safer.

The woman grinned, revealing a missing front tooth, as she took my arm and led me around a corner of the palace. The boy followed us. "I thought I'd never get a chance to talk to you alone, Malintzin," she whispered. She took my hand, an intimate gesture for a stranger. "I've been watching you. You're pretty, intelligent, clearly well born. I've been thinking what a fine wife you'd make for my son!"

I glanced at the young boy, amused.

"Oh, not that son!" The woman laughed nervously. "I have an older one, handsome as a god. You'll like him." She tugged at my sleeve. "Why should you wait, Malintzin? Come with me now."

I drew back. "Little mother, I don't know your son. I need time to think about it."

She grabbed my sleeve again, impatient. "There is no time! Can't you see I'm trying to save your life? Stay in that palace one more day and you'll die with your masters!" She knew this from her husband, who was an important city official, and she told me that her warrior son had sworn to kill Hernán with his own hand.

It was as I'd thought. Steeling myself to be calm, I took her arm. "The gods must have sent you!" I said. "But how can I go to your son empty-handed when my masters have given me so much gold and so many fine robes?" I watched the woman's little eyes gleam hungrily. "Let me go back and get what I can," I whispered. "I have one *huipilli* trimmed with feathers and jade beads that would be lovely on you. Wait here. I won't be long." I squeezed her hand and hurried away, dizzy with fear.

The woman was waiting when I returned with a heavy bundle on my head. "Did you get everything?" she asked, clutching me.

"I couldn't carry it all," I said. "There's so much."

"No matter. My husband says he'll get a share of your master's goods when they're dead. Moctezuma will reward him—" She caught her breath in horror as Bernal and Juan stepped around the corner. She looked helplessly at the two men. When the boy tried to run, Bernal seized him by the arm. "I'm a stupid old woman," she muttered. "I should have known your heart belonged to your master."

I patted her shoulder. "I'm still your friend," I said. "Come inside. Tell us what you know and you won't be hurt."

Hernán was waiting for us, growling with impatience. While I'd been involved with the woman, two Cholulan priests had come into the palace. They were huddled together in Hernán's room. Aguilar, whose Nahuatl was passable at best, welcomed me with relief. I left the woman with Juan and Bernal for the moment and lent my attention to the matter at hand.

"They won't tell us what they want," said Orteguilla. "The only thing I can understand of what they say is 'Quetzalcoatl.' "

"See?" Hernán said. "I let you out of my sight for a few minutes and next thing you know I'm lost. Find out what they want, Marina."

The timid faces of the two priests contrasted oddly with their bloodstained white robes and long, matted hair. The older of the two spoke, almost apologetically: "Forgive us for troubling your master, Malintzin, but there's something we have to know." He looked down at his scarred hands. Every day of his adult life he'd shed a drop of blood for the god he served. "Malintzin, is your master Quetzalcoatl, as so many claim him to be?"

I weighed the question before I translated for Hernán.

"Tell them I'm a man as they are," he said, as I knew he would. "But I serve a god who's greater than a thousand Quetzalcoatls."

I turned to the priests. "He says that he is Quetzalcoatl," I lied, "and because you've recognized him, you should be rewarded." I took two *chalchihuitls* from one of the little cotton bags I'd carried out to the woman and pressed them into their hands. "And now you must tell me what your people plan to do to us."

The priests looked at each other, imagining, no doubt, that we had some unearthly power that told us what people were thinking. Their story came pouring out, along with the woman's. Between the two stories we pieced together the facts. Moctezuma had indeed lured us to Cholula to trap and kill us. He had wanted to garrison his own troops in the city but most of the Cholutec leaders, fearful of occupation by such a large force, had expressed their willingness to carry out the plan themselves. The attack was to take place the next morning. The ropes and stakes for binding us had already been prepared.

Ten children had been sacrificed to Huitzilopochtli to gain his favor.

"We hope we've done the right thing . . ." The younger priest looked at me worriedly. "To have our people rise up against a god . . ."

"Quetzalcoatl is grateful," I assured them. "And now we must ask you to stay with us until tomorrow, for your own protection."

The priests nodded happily, raising the flies that had settled on their blood-matted hair. Hernán strode out of the room to summon his captains.

Aguilar wagged a finger at me, his homely face taking on a look of mock severity. "Shame on you, little sister. I heard that monstrous lie. You'll have to do penance for that!"

"Brother Jeronimo," I sighed, "when we're out of this cursed city I'll gladly do penance twenty times over."

Having decided on a course of chastisement for the Cholulan treachery, Hernán had me summon the rulers of the city. He was disgruntled with the shabbiness of the city's hospitality, they were told, and he and his men wished to depart the following morning. They would require the accompaniment of two thousand Cholutec warriors and the appropriate number of *tlamemes* to carry their goods. The Cholutec captains, with sly glances at one another, accepted the request almost too eagerly.

After they'd gone, our men worked stealthily throughout the night, readying and positioning the cannon at strategic points around the square, which was surrounded by buildings on all four sides. No attempt was made to conceal the cannon, for the Cholutecs, never having seen them fired, would not realize their function until it was too late.

One by one, the moments of darkness crawled by. No man slept. Swords and pikes were sharpened, guns cleaned and loaded, crossbows wound and in readiness. The Tlaxcalan forces that were camped outside the city had been alerted.

Dawn came at last, and with the first blare of the morning conches a huge body of Cholutec warriors and carriers, even more than we'd requested, filed into the square, led by forty of the town's high officials and priests. The Aztec envoys who had accompanied the Castilians from Tlaxcala were summoned to witness what was about to take place and report it to Moctezuma.

As soon as the Cholutec officials stood before him in his chambers, Hernán confronted them with their treachery.

"You invited us to your city and we came in good faith!" he thundered. "Now I see that from the beginning you intended to kill us all. I dare you to deny it."

The chiefs and priests huddled together, buzzing frantically among themselves. "It was not our doing, Great One," one of them said in a quavering voice. "Moctezuma ordered it!"

"Yes, it was Moctezuma," murmured the rest. "He forced us."

"You're even worse than I had thought," Hernán exclaimed with a purposeful glance at the Aztec envoys. "How dare you blame your treachery on my noble friend, Moctezuma? He'd never stoop to such trickery! I'll punish you not only for your attempt to deceive me, but for the betrayal of your own emperor!"

The woman who'd befriended me had given me the names of those chiefs, including her husband, who had been opposed to the plot, and these were quietly separated from the others and herded into another room.

"Go! Back to your men in the square!" Hernán ordered those who remained. "Wait for me there while I decide what sort of fate is cruel enough for you."

Eyes downcast, the Cholutec leaders walked down the steps. The instant their feet touched the stones of the square, Hernán dropped his raised hand and deadly volleys from arquebuses and cannon flew into the body of warriors. Arrrows whined down upon them like hail, felling them where they stood. The square was filled with churning panic as warriors and priests stampeded toward the narrow exits. Finding them blocked, many tried to scramble up the sides of the temples and other buildings lining the square, but the sides were slippery and they fell back into the bloody pit below. The street nearest the *tlamemes* had been left open long enough to allow most of the innocent carriers to flee, but those warriors who tried to follow them were cut down by the crossbowmen. The paving stones were slimy with blood. Screaming men fell over the twisted bodies of their fallen comrades as the awful missiles ripped into them.

Sick with horror, I crouched at the top of the steps behind the remains of a shattered idol and tried to focus my eyes on Hernán as he drove Arriero again and again into the densely packed square, his sword cutting a swath of destruction. In the distance I heard the screams of battle at the point where the Tlaxcalans had entered the city and were now quenching their long thirst for revenge against their old enemies.

The crowd had broken out of the square and the fighting now spread to the streets. The fleeing Cholutecs fell into the trenches they'd dug to trap the Spaniards. Their bodies filled the holes to the top as their panic-stricken comrades trampled over them in their flight.

The pyramid-temples were natural places of refuge and the Cholutecs clung to their sides like monkeys. Our men drove them down with a rain of balls and arrows, setting fire to the temples at the tops until the city blazed with a hundred torches.

I had seen death and violent battle, but never had I witnessed slaughter like this. Leaning against the base of an idol for support, I stared at the carnage around me in disbelief, my legs too weak to hold me. In the distance I could see the immense pyramid of Quetzalcoatl. A score of priests had fought their way up its sides and were laboring to remove the stones that were said to hold back the flood of water. The stones were large and heavy, but fear gave the priests strength as they lifted them aside, one by one. Finally the last stone was removed and they stepped back, waiting.

Nothing happened. The dry empty hole mocked their faith and their efforts. Now the Spaniards, led by Hernán himself, were swarming up the steps of the pyramid toward them. Cursing, the priests scrambled upward toward the *teocalli*.

"Surrender at once!" Even at that distance I recognized Teuch's bellowing voice. "Surrender and we will spare your lives!"

For answer, one of the priests paused to pick up a loose stone from the temple's steps and hurled it at the attackers. It skittered down the sides of the pyramid, striking no one.

Someone tossed a firebrand onto the thatched roof of the *teocalli* and the dry palm leaves erupted into flames. White-robed priests burst out through the entrance, scattering like a flock of herons. Many of them flung themselves from the topmost steps of the pyramid to shatter their bodies on the broad slopes or to be impaled on the waiting pikes.

Suddenly the sticklike form of the high priest of Quetzalcoatl appeared atop the blazing roof. The shouting and struggling ceased for a moment and all eyes were drawn upward to him as he stood amid the flames, magnificent in a headdress of gold and flowing quetzal plumes. His voice screamed defiance again and again as, shaking his fist at the sky, he became a livng torch. A dark column of smoke rose into the air as his body blackened and crumpled before thousands of horrified eyes.

I drew in my breath. The smoke stung my throat and penetrated every pore of my skin. My legs would not hold me. The bloody world of smoke and pain and screaming men began to whirl crazily. I closed my eyes, and blessed oblivion came crashing down upon my senses.

"She's all right, sir. She's opening her eyes."

Guzman's serious young face seemed to float above me, the setting sun making a halo of his fine hair. Juan Jaramillo appeared as if from nowhere and placed a cool, damp cloth against my aching forehead.

"You gave us quite a scare," he said softly. A red cut ran from his temple, across his cheek and disappeared in his short blond beard. He's going to have a scar just like Chilam's, I thought drowsily. And his eyes are the color of the sea on a sunny day . . .

Suddenly I sat bolt-upright. "Where's Hernán?" I said. "Is he . . ." Dizziness hit me like a double-up fist and I fell back.

"He's fine," Juan said. "He's out in the square, I think. Guzman, go tell him that Doña Marina's awakened." He replaced the cold cloth that had fallen to the mat when I sat up. "Lie still now. You've got a bruise on your forehead as big as a turkey egg. We found you on the steps. You've been unconscious all afternoon. I—we've been worried." There were shadows under his eyes. "You must have fainted or been hit by a stone during the . . . battle." He choked on the last word.

I remembered the pyramid, the old priest. "What's happened?" I asked.

"Good Lord! We butchered them, thousands of them. We chased them through the streets and slaughtered them like cattle! With us on one side and the Tlaxcalans on the other, the poor bastards didn't have a chance." His voice shook. "I look at these hands of mine and when I think what they did out there today—"

"You always blame yourself," I said. "They were going to kill us, Juan."

"I envy you." He leaned forward, his chin on his hands. "I envy anyone who can accept life and death as they come. Bernal says I take things too seriously."

I reached up and touched his face where the fine cut stood out, red against his tanned skin. I smiled. "You have a trophy now. Something you can show your grandchildren. You were lucky. A *maquahuitl* doesn't usually make such a nice clean cut. It just takes half your face off!"

He winced at my touch and my words. "*Maquahuitl!* I wish that's what it had been—that would even things a little." He touched the red line gingerly with his fingertip. "It was Olid, damn him, waving his sword around like a windmill. He caught me with the point of his blade."

Under different circumstances I'd have laughed. I didn't laugh now. "What did you do then?"

"What could I do? I insulted his ancestors and went on killing." He glanced back over his shoulder. "Ah, here's Cortés." He moved away from me almost reflexively, and his eyes took on a guarded look.

Hernán had come into the room, still striding energetically. He was untouched by the battle. "See to my horse, Jaramillo," he barked. "He has a wound on his shoulder—not serious, but I don't want it to fester."

"Right away." There was a tinge of irony in Juan's voice. His footsteps echoed away down the hall.

"So! We have another casualty, do we?" Hernán chuckled tenderly, bending over to lift me in his arms. I clung to him, the one solid object in a room that was spinning. "You little idiot, why didn't you have sense enough to find some shelter? I couldn't worry about you out there."

"I wanted to see. Hernán, it was terrible . . ."

"It could have been worse. I gave orders to spare the women and children and the wards whose leaders hadn't plotted against us. Those orders were obeyed, for the most part. The worst of it was holding back the Tlaxcalans. By my conscience, they'd have carried off every man, woman and child in Cholula if I'd let them. They're still out there, looting the town. Food, weapons, cotton cloth—funny, but the greatest prize of all is salt. Salt! I saw one man drop a load of feathered robes and jewelry to pick up a bag of the stuff."

I nestled my throbbing head against the cool metal cuirass that covered his chest. "You'd better put me down," I said. "I think I'm going to be ill."

He kissed the ugly bruise on my hairline before he laid me down on the mat. His lips were dry. A messenger hurried into the room and whispered something to him that I couldn't hear. His face was incredulous at first, then he broke into roaring laughter.

"Can you believe this, Marina? It's Xicotencatl the Younger! He's come with twenty thousand additional Tlaycalan troops to help us fight the Cholutecs. That haughty devil's just in time to help carry the goods back to Tlaxcala and he won't even have to strike a blow. I suppose I should go and meet him. Can you come with me, Marina?" He shook his head impatiently when he saw that I was lolling helplessly on the mat, shaking with nausea. "Oh, all right. I'll try and make do with Aguilar. Better yet, I'll find Orteguilla. He's supposed to be with the women, but who knows where the little monkey's gone since the battle . . . " He drifted out of the room, talking half to the messenger and half to himself while I sank slowly into pain-racked sleep.

It was dark by the time he returned to me, his face downcast. "They brought some news from Villa Rica," he said dully, sinking down beside me on the mat. "The Aztecs attacked Cempoalla and the garrison at Villa Rica. Our men drove the dogs off, saints be thanked. But Escalante, my good noble friend, is dead—" He buried his face against my shoulder and his body shook with silent grief.

Chapter Twelve

November 1519

The long column of men and horses snaked its way along the base of the towering cone of Popocatepetl, the fire-belching old god whose snow-crowned head rose into the clouds high above. In the blue distance, the sinuous curves of his goddess-wife, Ixtaccihuatl, the White Woman, seemed to float above the valley as she reclined in eternal slumber, her snowy robes spread around her.

During the three weeks we had spent at Cholula, Diego de Ordaz, whose stammering tongue belied his intrepid nature, had formed an expedition of nine men. To the horror and amazement of Cholutecs and Tlaxcalans alike, he'd climbed the summit and gazed into the very mouth of fiery Popocatepetl. The adventure had nearly cost him his life, but he'd returned a hero, his feat strengthening the god-status which Hernán Cortés and his men now enjoyed among the Aztecs and their allies.

Those three weeks of rest had brought about not only my own recovery but a surface healing, at least, of ravaged Cholula. Three thousand corpses had been burned or buried in the days following the massacre. Now the streets of the city were clean once more, businesses and markets functioning as usual. Although Padre Olmedo had persuaded Hernán that the Cholutecs were not yet ready for full-scale conversion to Christianity, a simple stone cross now stood atop the huge pyramid of Quetzalcoatl, guarding the spot until the day when a church would be erected there.

". . . And the strangest thing to come out of it all," Hernán remarked, "is that Tlaxcala and Cholula have exchanged ambassadors and begun to trade."

"It's been mostly our doing," I said. I was seated close behind him astride Arriero's back, my arms laced around his body. He'd been tender with me these past three weeks, and I'd responded in kind. I held onto him tightly. At the same time I swung my eyes from the green valley below us to the summit far above, my senses drinking in the beauty of our surroundings and the warm, musky scent of Hernán's hair and the sound of his voice, trying desperately to drown the memory of blood, smoke and screams that still echoed in my head, and my lingering sadness over the senseless deaths of Tonaxel and Nacontoc.

A pass lay far ahead of us, between the old god-mountain and his wife. Our guides had told me that when we reached it we'd be able to see the valley of Mexico, with Tenochtitlan at its center.

"And what's waiting for us there?" Hernán patted my hand. "Look into the future and tell me, Marina *mía*."

I had no gifts of prophecy. I could only piece together the bits of information I'd gleaned from my father, from my Aztec-sponsored education back in Oluta, and from talking with those who'd been to Tenochtitlan. The Aztec capital, with its companion city of Tlatelolco, set on an island in the middle of a shallow lake, connected to the mainland by several causeways. The island was interlaced with canals, where the people went about their business in canoes. My father had told me that it was possible to paddle a canoe into the very palace of Moctezuma.

I told Hernán about the structure of the Aztec government, so tedious when I'd memorized it in school. The power rested on an alliance among the three major city-states: Tenochtitlan in the middle of the lake; Tlacopan on the western shore; and dispute-ridden Texcoco on the east. He who ruled Tenochtitlan—Moctezuman, in this case—was *uei tlatoani*, the supreme "speaker."

"But is Moctezuma absolute ruler? Doesn't he share his power?" Hernán's thoughts pursued mine, darting, probing. By now I knew him well enough to anticipate his way of thinking: find a little crack and drive a wedge into it; look for jealousies, petty rivalries, traces of frustrated ambition, and use them.

I'd spent an afternoon with Maxixcatzin discussing the Aztec political structure and the individuals who comprised it, and I told Hernán everything I'd learned. Moctezuma's second-in-command was known as the *ciuacoatl*—the woman-serpent—although he was neither serpent nor woman. While the *uei tlatoani* enjoyed luxury, adulation and absolute authority, it was the *ciuacoatl*, as supreme judge and administrator, who supervised the intricacies of running the Aztec empire. "But I see no possibilities with him, Hernán," I said. "His authority comes from the emperor. No *ciucoatl* has ever succeeded to the throne."

"Then who would succeed Moctezuma?"

"A council, headed by the *ciuacoatl*, would decide. Most likely Moctezuma's brother, Cuitlahuac." I analyzed the past pattern of succession to the Aztec throne. Moctezuma's father, Axayacatl, had been succeeded first by his own brother, Tizoc, then by another brother, Ahuitzotl, and only then by Moctezuma himself. Cuitlahuac ruled Itzapalapan, a powerful city at the south end of the lake. The king of Tlacopan was of less importance and had given up his place in the trio of principal rulers to Cuitlahuac.

"Texcoco . . . ?" Hernán's thoughts kept pace with mine.

I told him all I knew. The royal line of Texcoco preceded that of Tenochtitlan by many generations. In my childhood I'd learned poetry composed by the Texcocan king, Nezualcoyotl, grandfather of the present ruler, Cacama, who was also the son of Moctezuma's sister.

I knew what Hernán was thinking then. If there was a chink in the Aztec armor it would be Texcoco. The kingdom had been torn in two by the dispute between Cacama and his younger brother, Ixtlilxochitl. Cacama was young, vulnerable perhaps. Cuitlahuac was neither.

We climbed as we talked. It was growing cold and windy. Hernán had Guzman bring me a cloak from the baggage. Tomorrow, our guides had told us, we would reach the pass.

"By my grandmother's bones!" exclaimed a panting Bernal Diaz, gaping at the vast plain that spread out below us. "I'd never have believed this!"

From the time we'd first heard the name of Tenochtitlan, each of us had carried in his mind his own vision of the valley of Mexico. No amount of dreaming could have prepared us for the sight that awaited us when we reached the crest of the mountain pass.

The valley was richly green, dotted with pines, cypress and clumps of *tenocha*, or prickly pear, from which the Aztecs had chosen the name of their capital. The landscape was punctuated by little towns that became progressively larger in size near the lake, which was surrounded by cities. Even at this distance we could make out the three causeways that ran from the mainland to the island in the lake's center, where the fabulous Tenochtitlan and its twin-city of Tlatelolco glittered whitely in the sun.

Eagerly, fearfully, we descended into the valley. I felt as if I were walking into a cage. Teuch and our Cempoallan allies had returned to Villa Rica to defend it from the Aztecs, and our army of four hundred Spaniards and six thousand Tlaxcalans seemed pitifully small. I realized, as we all did, that if we were to survive and conquer here, it would be by luck and cunning, not by force.

The descent down the steep slopes was laborious. Soon it was evident that the lake, which had seemed so near when viewed through the crystalline air atop the pass, lay at least two or three days' march from where we were. The journey was pleasant, however, for the people of the outlying towns and cities welcomed us warmly, pressing gifts of food, gold and slaves upon us. Although they publicly declared their allegiance to Moctezuma, many of them came to us in secret to complain about the burdensome taxes, the sons and daughters carried off to slavery or death. Hernán was elated. Even here, in the heart of his empire, the Aztec ruler had his enemies.

At last we came to the southeastern tip of the lake, where the towns of Chalco and Ayotzinco stood, half on land and half on pilings over the green-brown water. There was more traffic in the canals than in the streets. Long dugout canoes floated along the waterways, loaded down with flowers, vegetables, goods for trade in the market, and brightly dressed citizens who gawked at us as we passed.

We spent the night in Ayotzinco and it was there, next morning, that a plumed messenger arrived to announce the coming of Cacama, the lord of Texcoco. I hurried to change the simple *huipilli* and skirt I'd worn on the trail, and put on a beautiful robe of red and blue feathers, which Moctezuma's emissaries had given me. There was no time to braid my hair, so I quickly thrust a red blossom behind one ear.

"No one's going to look at Cacama!" Bernal Diaz said with a grin as I bustled past him on my way to join Hernán. We strained our eyes toward the glittering procession that was approaching us on the road from the north. First came a train of priests and nobles, clad in jaguar pelts and feathered cloaks. The plume fans they carried waved like petals under a ruffling breeze. There were warriors, the most distinguished of whom were wearing the costumes of the two elite military orders:

the "eagle knights," dressed from head to toe in feathers, with beak-shaped helmets; and the "jaguar knights," wearing spotted jaguar skins with the heads covering their own and the sharp teeth protruding down over their foreheads.

Next in the procession came eight burly nobles, identically dressed, bearing on their shoulders a gold-covered litter on which, dazzling, arrogant and beautiful as a young god, sat Cacama. When he dismounted and walked slowly toward us, priests perfumed the air around him with incense. Two pretty slave girls with reed brooms cleared every wisp of straw and every pebble from the path of his royal feet. A canopy made of green feathers and studded with gems was supported over his head by his attendants, who moved forward with him as he proceeded toward our party.

Although he was no taller than Hernán when the two stood face to face, Cacama's heavy-lidded gaze and the proud tilt of his head made him appear to be looking down at all of us. His movements were calm and unhurried as he bent to touch the earth with his palm and raise his hand to his lips in the traditional Aztec salute. When he spoke his voice had a peculiar singsong quality, as though he were reading symbols from a scroll.

There was nothing new in his message. Moctezuma sent his greetings but still forbade us to enter his capital. However, Hernán was undaunted. We had come this far, he explained, and nothing would stop us.

"I see you're not to be dissuaded," Cacama said gloomily. "In that case, my instructions are to inform you that Moctezuma will welcome you as a brother in his palace. Proceed ahead with your guides and have no fear." He turned abruptly, was assisted onto his litter, and departed with his golden parade in the direction from which he'd come.

He took with him Hernán's present of three clear stones called Margaritas, shabby gifts compared to the wealth of gold and featherwork that the Aztecs had heaped upon us. But then, Hernán had left Cuba prepared to trade with primitive savages. How could he have known the manner of men he was to find?

Wary, distrustful, we continued on our way, marching along the shore of the lake and then taking a short, narrow causeway to a charming little island city where we were welcomed. Here, for the first time, we saw flowers and vegetables growing on floating mats of woven reeds and earth called *chinampas*. The people of the lake, where land was precious, had created their own floating gardens, which they tended in canoes. Some of the *chinampas* were large enough to support families in thatched huts.

We passed by causeway onto land again, a long, narrow peninsula that divided the southern portion of the lake from its central part. Houses and people were everywhere now. Farmers in white loincloths tended patches of maize, maguey, squash and beans, and straightened in amazement as we passed by. Flowering trees and vines spilled over the edges of hidden courtyards. Children ran screaming out of our path. The crowds became larger and more curious now, but they kept a healthy distance between themselves and the horses. They pointed and jabbered at us. "Look upon my son!" cried a woman, holding her squirming baby above her head. "Bless him with good fortune!"

We had just sighted the towers of Iztapalapan, the city that was ruled by Moctezuma's brother, Cuitlahuac, and that marked the beginning of the main causeway to the island, when a shout came up from behind that a large party was approaching our rear. Sandoval twisted in the saddle and peered back over his shoulder. "*Maldito!* They're armed!"

Alarm swept through the ranks. They'd cornered us with the lake on two sides and Itzapalapan on the other. With Hernán roaring commands we formed for battle, swinging the cannons around toward the rear.

The strange army came closer, still making no move to attack. We relaxed a little, for we could see that despite the long spears they carried, their faces were unpainted. Above the muffled sound of their footsteps I could hear the cadence of the *teponatzli*, but the drum's rhythm was gentle, marking the metered tread of the warriors. They carried a litter on which sat—no, reclined indolently, like a snake in the sun—the slender form of a man.

"Moctezuma?" Hernán's whispered question hung in the air.

"It couldn't be," I said. "Look how plainly they're dressed."

As the litter drew nearer we saw that its passenger was young, no more than twenty. Thin green plumes drifted from a gold helmet to frame a narrow, foxlike face. As the litter was placed on the ground, he uncoiled his graceful body and sprang to his feet with a burst of energy, striding toward us with his eyes upon me.

"Malintzin!" he exclaimed, touching the ground lightly and kissing his palm. "Kindly tell your master that Ixtlilxochitl, rightful ruler of Texcoco and his only true friend in this land, has come to welcome him to the valley of Mexico."

Mats were quickly spread on the ground, and a canopy was erected to shade the two leaders as they talked. Our Aztec guides, who were Moctezuma's men, hovered nearby, anxious to catch any word that would pass between the two. A servant handed out cups of *chocolatl*.

Ixtlilxochitl squatted on the mat, a position comfortable and socially acceptable to Aztecs of all classes. I did the same. Hernan sat crosslegged, awkward in his armor and tight clothing, resolving that he would order chairs the next time he talked with a native ruler.

The young prince leaned toward us. His eyes were narrow and so closely set that the tips of his brows met above his high nose. "Malintzin," he whispered, speaking this time to Hernán, "we can't talk openly. Too many big ears." He flicked his amber eyes toward our Aztec guides. "I've only come here to see you for myself and to tell you that you can depend on my help when you need it. Until you do, our friendship can best be served at a distance."

He looked about him and raised his voice so that he could be heard clearly. "So! I travel this far to invite you to come to my city and you refuse! I'm disappointed in you, Malintzin. You may regret your decision."

"Tell the prince I'm sorry, Marina," Hernán rejoined, playing Ixtlilxochitl's game skillfully, "but my heart is so eager to clasp the hand of my brother, Moctezuma, that I can't think of delaying our meetings any longer. At some later time perhaps . . ."

"At a later time you might not be invited," Ixtlilxochitl snapped. "You've made your choice, Malintzin. I've nothing more to say to you." With a single, liquid movement, he rose to his feet and turned and motioned to his bearers. As they hoisted his litter onto their shoulders he pointed an indignant finger toward us. "One day," he hissed, "you may wish you'd not treated my offer of friendship so lightly."

As the rebel prince was born away into the distance, Hernán couldn't hold back a chuckle. "Forgive me, Marina *mía*. I know you warned me about that fellow, but so help me, I like him."

"Naturally," I muttered under my breath in Nahuatl. "He thinks the way you do."

* * *

We spent the night in Iztapalapan, a city of breathtaking beauty whose sparkling white palaces and lavish gardens were said to be superior even to those of Tenochtitlan. Moctezuma's brother, Cuitlahuac, stern and cold, had formally welcomed us to his city. After a long evening of feasting and gift exchanges, Hernán checked to see that the guards were posted and then he and I retired to our room. He lowered the curtain that covered the entrance, blew out the candle I carried and, laughing, seized me in his arms. "*Ay de mi!* What a long day it's been," he murmured, "and the best part's yet to come!"

It was then that a shadowy figure stepped out from behind an embroidered hanging.

In a flash, Hernán's sword was out of its scabbard. "Who are you?" he whispered hoarsely. "What do you want?"

"Ah, you react quickly, Malintzin!" The voice, speaking in Nahuatl, was as smooth as flowing honey. "Don't trouble yourself with wondering how I got in here. Ixtlilxochitl goes wherever he pleases." He chuckled. "No, don't make a light. I'm alone." In the moonlight that filtered through the tiny window I could make out his sharp features. He was smiling, showing small, uneven teeth. "I want to compliment you on your performance this afternoon. It was almost as good as my own, and I'm an old master."

Hernán found his voice and I translated for him. "You come here at great risk, my friend."

"Life gets dull without risks, does it not?" Ixtlilxochitl lowered his body to the mat. "I see that Cuitlahuac was here to welcome you, that old owl! Believe me, if he'd had his way your heads would be on Moctezuma's skull rack by now. Don't believe anything he tells you." He tilted his head. The moonlight made the whites of his eyes flash as we crouched down beside him. "You should have seen the council chamber, with Moctezuma moaning about prophecies and fate, Cuitlahuac screaming for your blood, and my poor brother, Cacama, vacillating from one to the other. Cacama . . ." He said the name slowly, flicking each bitter syllable off the back of his tongue and out between his lips, tasting his own rancor. "I have a hundred brothers. Why did Moctezuma have to put that witless turkey on the throne of Texcoco?"

"Ask him about Moctezuma," Hernan urged me.

"My poor uncle!" Ixtlilxochitl ran a hand over his square-clipped hair, caressing his topknot, the badge of the experienced warrior. "You realize he's terrified, don't you? The omens, the prophecies of doom in the stars . . . He believes he's powerless against you."

I studied him, this strange young man who seemed to have no loyalties except to himself. "And what do you believe?" I asked him.

He replied without hesitation. "I believe in Ixtlilxochitl," he said. "Gods are for fools. We guide our own destinies. Moctezuma could kill you all if he tried, but he won't try because he's afraid." He rose to his feet. "I have to go. A sister of mine, Mazatl, is one of Moctezuma's concubines. If you need to get word to me, go to her. She can be trusted and she'll know where to find me." He paused at the curtain. "Don't worry about my safety. There's a secret way past your sentries. They won't see me." He slid through the doorway and was gone, with no sound of footsteps.

As our feet marched at last over the beaten earth of the causeway that led from Iztapalapan to Tenochtitlan, a sense of helplessness teased at our tight nerves. Knowing that once we were on the causeway we'd be vulnerable to capture or slaughter, we'd commended ourselves to God that morning. Padre Olmedo, his eyes weary from the night of confession-hearing, had given us his blessing, his voice rich with the tones that so reminded me of my father. Then, with our courage somewhat fortified, we'd turned our steps toward the city that beckoned so terrifyingly from the middle of the lake.

Hernán led the procession, his armor polished so brightly that I could see my face in it. Tiny bells had been tied to Arriero's bridle and the stallion pranced along as if aware of the sensation his appearance would create. Aguilar and I walked on either side of him, flanked by the Aztec guides who had accompanied us all the way from Cholula.

"If your people attack us, you'll be the first ones to die," I'd warned them that morning, but they'd reassured me over and over that Moctezuma's intentions were nothing but friendly.

Behind us rode Cristobal Corral, carrying our banner. Although the strapping youth generally walked, Lares had graciously offered his horse so that the flag might be better displayed. Alvarado and Sandoval rode on either side of him, along with the other captains on horseback. The infantry stretched out behind them, followed by the Cholutec bearers and the warriors from Tlaxcala.

The causeway had been cleared of all traffic, but flower-bedecked canoes by the hundreds, filled with gaping citizens of every rank, flocked around us in the water, providing a show of their own. Here was a fat *pochteca* whose boat rode so low in the water that it looked as if it were going to sink. There was a fancily carved canoe filled with *auianime*, the women who served as companions to the unmarried warriors. Their faces were smeared yellow with *axin* and heavily rouged on the cheeks; their perfumed hair hung loose down their backs. They were exquisitely dressed, and with their teeth—stained red from cochineal dye—they chewed little balls of *tzictli*, making a soft clicking noise that accompanied the rhythmic movement of their jaws. Next to them a small canoe carried a peasant family whose small children clung to their parents in fright. A ragged old woman with one blind eye and a crippled leg paddled her tiny boat from one canoe to the other, begging for food. A large boatload of black-robed priests disdainfully looked the other way when the beggar woman came near them. The vendors of *tamales* and *tlaxcalli* were doing a brisk business, receiving handfuls of *chocolatl* nibs in exchange for their wares.

Arriero was sweating heavily, as though the tension in those around him had transferred itself to his massive body. Walking beside him, I inhaled his pungent odor. The familiar scent was somehow reassuring. I reached out and patted the stallion's glossy neck. How could I ever have been so afraid of this gentle beast? I wondered, remembering the day Juan Jaramillo had apologized for the trick that had been played on me and the slave women of Centla.

The causeway was not made entirely of earth. Here and there it was broken by spans of water over which sturdy wooden bridges had been built. This, as one of the guides explained, was to allow for the fluctuations of the lake, which became turbulent in the rainy season and would flood the causeways if it could not pass through them. Although no one mentioned it, I realized that removal of the bridges could make Tenochtitlan a true island, preventing either invasion or escape by land. I shivered as the hollow sound of our footsteps echoed over the planks of the first bridge.

I looked up and saw Hernán smiling down at me. Whatever this day was to bring, we would meet it together. The tiny fortress-island of Acachinanco loomed ahead of us on the causeway, its high gates hiding the road ahead from view, so that when we'd passed through we were startled to see the grand procession coming toward us. The dignitaries of the city, more than a thousand of them, dressed in an array of jewels and gold so dazzling as to make the eyes drunk, had come out to meet us. Hernán was obliged to stop while each man filed past to give him the traditional salute.

"Where's Moctezuma?" he growled nervously in my ear.

"You're to wait for him at the next bridge," said one of our guides.

After the nobles had passed, we advanced to the bridge, dismounted and waited. The strain of anticipation was almost unbearable. Horses stamped and fidgeted. Sandoval cursed under his breath. Esmeralda, the greyhound, sniffed along the water's edge, growling at the canoes. We peered down the causeway until our eyes ached. At last we saw the royal procession emerging from the city and making their way toward us.

I don't know what I had expected. Wealth, certainly, and it was there in abundance. After the opulence of Cacama's train, it was no surprise to see that Moctezuma's entourage surpassed it in splendor. But here was more than mere show; here was reverence. The nobles who preceded the emperor's litter walked with bare feet and bowed heads. When the *uei tlatoani* passed, the people in the canoes bent low. Not one eye was raised to look upon the royal face. It was so quiet that I could hear the shuffling feet of the litter-bearers as they came toward us.

I strained to see Moctezuma's features through the haze of incense that floated before him. In my mind he'd always been a monster, more of a thing than a person. Now he was moving closer with every step, the being I'd hated since the days of my childhood. Moctezuma Coyoacan was stepping from his litter and walking slowly toward us, with Cuitlahuac and Cacama supporting him on either side.

The three rulers were dressed in identical sky-blue *tilmatli* cloaks, edged with gold and knotted at the shoulder. They wore helmets of gold to which green plumes were fastened, but while Cacama's and Cuitlahuac's plumes hung down their backs in long cascades, those on Moctezuma's helmet stood out from around his face like the rays of the sun. I'd made up my mind not to bow to him. Instead I looked squarely into his face with defiant eyes, studying him openly as he came closer, trying to strip away the kingly raiment and see him as the man he was.

His face was pleasant enough. The forehead was high, the nose straight and narrow. The jaw was finely chiseled, almost feminine, but well formed and fringed by a sparse, black beard. The mouth was unremarkable, but the eyes were large, soft and liquid like a deer's. Frightened eyes.

He was of average stature, with the well-developed muscles and catlike walk of the trained warrior. As his golden sandals stepped across the carpets that were laid on the ground before him, I saw that his legs were lacerated like a priest's.

In a gesture that was almost childlike, he extended a bouquet of roses to Hernán. "Welcome to Tenochtitlan, Malintzin," he said in a musical, singsong voice. "Everything we have is yours."

Hernán responded appropriately. Then he took from his own neck a showy necklace made of glass. "It looks funny on you," I'd commented earlier that morning, watching him take the necklace from its musk-scented box and fasten it behind his head. I knew it wasn't valuable, but it was the best thing we had and it would have to do as a gift for the emperor.

Cuitlahuac and Cacama stirred uneasily as Hernán leaned forward to fasten the clasp around the royal neck.

Then he opened his arms. "My brother!" he exclaimed, reaching out to clasp Moctezuma's shoulders in a warm *abrazo*. Cacama stepped between them and put out a restraining hand that pushed Hernán backward a couple of steps. "One does not touch the *uei tlatoani* in such a manner!" he said in a shocked voice.

Hernán looked at me with a little shrug. "Apologize for me, Marina," he said. I glowered at him. He knew better! He'd deliberately tested the lengths of familiarity to which he'd be allowed to go. I apologized for his supposed ignorance of royal customs, feeling strangely like a parent whose child has shamed him in public.

Chapter Thirteen

Tenochtitlan—November 1519

The central square of Tenochtitlan was dominated by a huge pyramid that formed a base for the dual shrines of Huitzilopochtli and the rain god, Tlaloc. The three-tiered temple faced west and and a double flight of one hundred fourteen steps (Bernal Diaz had been the first to count them) rose from base to summit, where the two *teocalli*, built with high, sloping roofs, rose side by side. Although they were identically constructed, the two shrines were decorated differently. Tlaloc's temple was trimmed in blue and crowned with a motif of shells, while that of Huitzilopochtli was red, with butterflies carved on its roof to represent fire and sun. The ever-present convex altar stone, stained deep red with dried blood, sat in front of the two temples.

On ground level, directly in front of the pyramid, rested the cylindrical stone of Tizoc, almost as high as a man and twice as thick as it was tall. It was here that the most valiant of the warriors delivered for sacrifice were tied by one ankle, supplied with wooden weapons, and given the chance to fight for their lives against two Aztecs armed with *maquahuitls*. The outcome of these battles was never in doubt. The mortally wounded captive would be cut loose and carried to the top of the pyramid, where the priests were waiting to rip his heart from his body.

There were other temples in the square, including a building dedicated to Quetzalcoatl. Its entrance was carved to resemble the gaping mouth of a serpent. "Like the jaws of hell," Bernal had muttered the first time he saw it.

The most gripping sight of all was the *tzompantli*, the enormous rack on which the sacrificed skulls were displayed. It was as high as a two-story building. From its many slats, row upon row, thousands upon thousands of gleaming white skulls looked out onto the square with their hollow eyes and bare, grinning mouths. Those which were newly attached still had flesh on them, but eventually all were picked clean by birds and insects.

To the south of the pyramid stretched Moctezuma's palace, an expanisve maze of rooms, hallways and courtyards. Correspondingly, on the north sat the similar but older palace of Axayacatl, which had been vacated for our use.

Standing alone on the palace steps, I ached with a weariness that had crept into every bone and muscle. It was not so much a physical tiredness, for my body had been toughened by weeks on the trail. It was more a state of mental and spiritual exhaustion. For an entire week I'd done nothing but transfer platitudes from Hernán to Moctezuma and back again. Hernán was no nearer to the culmination of his conquest than when he'd entered the city. The two leaders spent their time reassuring each other of their friendship and good intentions, while both of them bristled inwardly with distrust.

Even with the delights of the palace and the gifts of gold, robes and slaves that Moctezuma lavished on our warriors, they were getting restless. Hernán maintained battlefield discipline. Here, in the midst of hospitality, the soldiers slept with their swords beside them and posted sentries at all hours.

Dark clouds rolled across the sky, a prelude to one of the swift evening storms that lashed the valley during the rainy months. In the growing twilight the square was filled with people going about their business. Some of the torches had already been lit, and were blazing in brackets along the palace walls. Their flames cast an eerie glow, throwing the temples and the skull rack into startling patterns of light and shadow. On an impulse I slipped down the steps and into the square. Hernán had forbidden his men to leave the palace, but this wouldn't be the first time I'd bent his rules to suit my own inclinations. He was in conference with his captains and wouldn't miss me for these few moments.

With my Spanish companions, I was an object of curiosity and instant recognition. Alone, dressed in a simple white *huipilli*, I blended into the crowd. Anyone who looked at me would see no more than a tall girl in white with her hair hanging down her back in a single braid. I breathed deeply, filling my lungs with the chilly night air, savoring the biting scent of pine and copal smoke and the mossy, musty odor of the lake. A curious bliss crept over me as the people bustled past. Bare arms brushed against mine. I felt the warmth of flesh, of skin that was brown like my own. All around me were proud, high-nosed faces, dark eyes and straight hair, as black and shiny as obsidian. My own kind. They were beautiful—more beautiful, I realized, than the Spaniards with their pale skins that burned where the sun touched them, their washed-out eyes and hairy bodies. Not even the handsome Pedro de Alvarado could compare with these people, I thought bitterly, remembering how callously he had treated Tonaxel and Nacontoc. Only Juan Jaramillo had been moved by the incident and had understood its effect on me. The others, even Hernán, had seen it as of no account, for it had not happened to one of their own.

I could run away, I thought recklessly. I could hide among my dark brothers and sisters and never be found. My own kind—like Itzcoatl and my mother, Cimatl? My own kind had sold me, passed me from one master to another like a bag of *chocolatl* beans. The white men treated me with respect and kindness. I was bound to them by gratitude, by friendship, by the common bond of Christainity, and most of all by my devotion to Hernán. No, I didn't belong out here in the square. Not anymore. I found myself wishing I'd known Aguilar's friend, Gonzalo Guerrero. He too had forsaken his beginnings and lived between two worlds.

Hernán would be needing me soon. When he did, I would be there. I turned my steps back toward the palace of Axayacatl and suddenly found my way blocked by a bulky figure in a feathered cloak.

He was tall, so tall that my gaze collided not with his face but with the ornate pendant that was suspended from his neck by a gold chain. Surrounded by a filigree of gold and pearls, it was a large *chalchihuitl* of near-perfect quality. I had seen only one other stone as fine, the one Chilam had used to buy me from—

It was the same *chalchihuitl*! The design and color were unique! Trembling, I forced myself to look up into the mocking eyes of Quauhtlatoa.

He laughed. "What tricks the gods play, Malinalli! I thought I'd never see you again, and here you've come to me. What do you have to say to an old friend?" He took hold of my shoulder.

"You never could keep your hands off me," I sputtered, twisting away from him.

"Ha!" He grinned. "You're still as feisty as an ocelot and just as beautiful. Relax. I'm not going to ravish you here in the middle of the square, much as I'd like to. I've been watching you for days, just hoping to get a chance to talk to you." His voice softened. "At least stay and walk with me for a little while. What harm could that do?"

I relented. What could happen to me here, right in front of the palace with people all around us? Besides, he wouldn't dare harm the concubine of Hernán Cortés. "Is your father well?" I asked, for although I had no affection for the *pochteca*, I remembered that he had dealt fairly with me.

"As well as could be expected under the circumstances," Quauhtlatoa said. "Last year he took an Otomi arrow through the heart and died. One of the things he left me was this *chalchihuitl*. Do you like it?" He smiled innocently, then laughed at my consternation. "Yes, I know where it came from. That's why it's my favorite piece. I can't look at it without thinking about you." He reached for my waist to pull me close to him, but I moved quickly away.

"Your father sent you home to be married," I said, "but I see you haven't changed your ways."

"What can I say?" He shrugged. "I told you about her once and she's no different. At least I don't have to trade for a living like my father did. I don't have to do anything." He kicked at a loose paving stone with his toe. "As for children—my wife's barren. She won't let my buy a concubine, and I can't go against her wishes because everything we have comes from her father."

He was quiet for a few steps. Then he looked over at me and his mouth stretched into a grin. He still had the same arrogant, self-satisfied bearing, but he'd put on weight since I last saw him and he had the beginnings of a double chin. "Malinalli!" he exclaimed. "I always imagined you raising a flock of little Tabascans somewhere. How do you think I felt when you walked into the square with your white gods and I realized that you were the famous Malintzin? I wanted to climb to the top of the temple and shout to the whole city that I'd been the first man to love you. I wanted everybody to know that before you belonged to them you'd belonged to me."

"I never belonged to you!"

"You offered me yourself and Oluta once, remember?" He was guiding me away from the palace, toward the skull rack.

"If I'd accepted, I'd be a happier man than I am now—unless, of course, you were planning to have me killed as soon as I'd gotten you back to your people. Were you, Malinalli?"

"Yes," I answered, not knowing whether it was true or not.

"Well, all that's in the past." He shrugged again. "Tell me about your white gods. Are they really gods?"

It occurred to me then that he might have been sent to get information from me. "You've seen them," I hedged. "Judge for yourself."

"I already have. They look like gods. They do things that I never thought mortal men could do . . ." His sandals made scuffing noises on the stones as we walked across the grisly shadow of the skull rack and paused. "Then I see the way you look at the one called Cortés. I know you, Malinalli. You're a woman of flesh and blood, warm, alive . . . You'd never be happy as the consort of a god." His hand stole up my arm to my shoulder. "Your Cortés is no more of a god than I am, and the thought of what he has makes me sick with envy."

I shook my shoulder loose from his grip. Suddenly he spun me around, pinioning me with both hands against a corner-post of the skull rack.

"You always thought you were too good for me," he snarled. "Well, listen to me, little princess. The time will come when you'll scream for your white gods and they won't hear you. You'll *beg* me to be your friend then! You'll kiss my feet!"

I stared at him, remembering Cholula and the woman who'd warned me.

"See," he said with a smile. "Your eyes are pleading with me already. What will you give me to tell you what I know?" He pulled me hard against him, his hands kneading my flesh, forcefully molding my body to his. "You'd give anything to find out, wouldn't you? And then you'd go running to tell your white master." He pressed more tightly against me. The empty eyes of a hundred thousand skulls laughed down at us.

"I'm not that stupid," he said. "There's only one way I'll tell you. Come with me! Now! I have a house in Pochtan that belonged to my father. My wife's family doesn't even know about it. You'll be safe there."

I struggled in his arms. "Let me go!" I raged. "Cortés will kill you! Don't be a fool!"

"You're the fool. I'm trying to save you. Do I have to beg you to come?" Furiously, I stamped on his feet with my sandals. He only laughed. "Come on, Malinalli. I can't believe you hate me that much for what I did to you. Women like it, I'm told. You want me now! Deny it!"

I relaxed against him just long enough for him to drop his guard. Then, with every bit of my strength, I brought my knee up between his legs. He staggered back, cursing. By the time he lunged for me again I was gone, my feet flying over the stones of the square. Dodging clusters of people, I finally reached the broad steps of the palace.

Behind me the storm broke in sudden fury. Lightning snapped in the sky. The booming laughter of Tlaloc, the rain god, echoed across the valley as the torrent fell, churning up the placid water of the canals, sending men, women and children scurrying for cover and driving the birds and ants from their grim work at the skull rack. The rain poured in rivers from the edge of the palace roof. I hardly dared look back the way I'd come. Water was everywhere. I couldn't see Quauhtlatoa, but the thought that he might be following me, just as he had so long ago, threw me into a panic. I ran blindly into the palace and through the maze of corridors, fear gobbling up my reason.

I told Hernán about Quauhtlatoa that same night. I suppose I'd expected him to be jealous, protective, but his reaction hurt me. He was only interested in the fact that I'd gotten wind of a plot.

"It's too bad you botched it," he said. "The only thing you can do now is go back out there and try to learn more."

"Tonight?" I sat there blinking like an idiot, my hair still damp from the rain, thinking that this had to be some wild dream.

"Oh, the devil with it! It's too late and it's raining," he snapped. "And tomorrow's no good either. We're having dinner with Moctezuma. Let's hope it can wait till the next night, and that you haven't scared him off. I'll double the guard."

I was still dazed. "Just what do you expect me to do?" I asked.

"Anything you have to, Marina *mía*. Whatever's left of your virtue can't be more important than four hundred lives."

He didn't touch me for the rest of the night. I lay on the mat beside him, staring into the darkness until morning.

The greatest privilege Moctezuma could bestow upon a visitor was that of watching the emperor dine. He never invited anyone to sit down and eat with him—that would have been an unthinkable familiarity—but when he was finished he sometimes honored an important guest by allowing him to select untouched tidbits from the royal plates.

In honor of the occasion Hernán had brought along not only me, but Aguilar and Orteguilla as well. For show and for protection, Alvarado and Sandoval were there, as well as Bernal Diaz, whose height always made an impression.

Moctezuma's attendants seated us on *icpalli*, the Aztec version of chairs, which had seats and backs but no legs. We watched in respectful silence as the monarch entered and took his seat. An embroidered screen was removed from in front of us, revealing an incredible array of delicacies on black and red plates from Cholula. The dishes—Bernal, who had a penchant for counting, whispered that there were more than three hundred—were spread out in a wide circle on the floor, with pathways arranged among them so that the four pretty serving girls who waited on the emperor could quickly reach any item he asked for.

The variety of foods defied the imagination. There were dishes of turkey and dog, simmered in different types of sauce. There were six different kinds of *tamales*, seven kinds of maize cakes; roast venison, wild pig, rabbit and iguana, snails and agave worms in hot pepper sauce; ducks, pheasant and partridges, doves, roast fish, oysters, crabs, and turtle meat from the coast; frogs, newts, tadpoles and fresh-water shrimp from the lake, and clusters of water-fly eggs called *ahuauhtli*. There were ants and grasshoppers, smothered in tomato sauce or roasted to crispness, yams, peppers, beans, and an assortment of soups, sauces and fruits.

Moctezuma dipped his hands into two calabashes of water held by one of the serving girls, and the other two girls dried his hands on a white napkin. Seated on an *icpalli* before a low table covered with a white cloth, he began his meal as the humblest peasants in all Mexico did—with fresh *tlaxcalli*, flat maize cakes still warm from the *cumal*.

In spite of the abundance of food, Moctezuma ate sparingly and with great delicacy, wiping his fingers on a clean napkin whenever they became soiled. He spoke to no one except for an occasional word to the serving girls. At last he finished the meal with a cup of sweetened, whipped *chocolatl*, and then, with a gesture and a slight smile, he indicated that the dishes were to be passed to his guests. Hernán and the others selected turkey and venison. Orteguilla couldn't restrain a grimace when, tired of such tame fare, I chose tamales stuffed with snails and agave worms.

"Sometimes I almost forget where you came from," Hernán muttered, eyeing my plate, "but every now and then you do something to remind me."

The dishes that remained were carried away by servants to feed other visitors in the palace, as well as the priests and the palace staff. Moctezuma's table was also removed and he leaned back against the *icpalli* to watch us. As we sipped our *chocolatl*, our ears caught the light patter of sandaled feet on the polished stone floor of the corridor leading from the women's quarters.

Suddenly a little girl of about eleven burst into the hall. She giggled and skipped her way across the room, a butterfly in human form, wearing a bright yellow *huipilli* and blossoms in her hair. Laughing, she danced over to where the emperor sat, gave a little spring, and landed in his lap.

Moctezuma smiled apologetically. "My daughter, Tecuichpo," he said. "She's bright, her teachers say, and learns everything well except good manners. I have other children—older, more accomplished and—" he gave one of her braids a little tug—"better behaved. Look at her, then, and tell me why she's the one who rules the heart of the *uei tlatoani*."

We studied the little girl as she sat on her father's knees, smiling shyly at us. She was small for her age, and from the crown of her head to the soles of her little gold sandals she was exquisite. Beauty we had seen in abundance, but here, in the features of this little princess, was perfection. She must have been spoiled. Who could deny anything to such a little jewel?

"I see that you enjoy children too," said Moctezuma, looking at Orteguilla with interest. "Is the boy your son, Malintzin?" He'd addressed the question to Hernán, but it was I who answered him.

"The boy's an orphan. He serves us as a messenger, but with his quick tongue, he's becoming a good interpreter too."

"Boy . . ." Moctezuma fixed his soft eyes on Orteguilla. "If you can understand me, come over here and sit down."

Orteguilla, showing no fear, stood up, trotted over to the platform where Moctezuma sat, and seated himself on its edge. The emperor smiled down at him. "I need a small person like you to instruct me in the ways of your people. Would you like to stay here in the palace with me—with your master's permission?"

The boy nodded. His pink cheeks and sun-streaked hair contrasted starkly with the golden darkness of the monarch and his daughter. I translated the question for Hernán.

"But of course," Hernán said quickly. "As a bond of friendship between us!" I knew that he was thinking what a valuable little spy he'd have.

Moctezuma beamed his satisfaction. "My son—if I may call you that—maybe you'll teach my daughter a few words of your language. She has a quick tongue, too. I, unfortunately, do not." He picked the little girl up by the waist and stood her on the floor. "Show your new friend the palace, Tecuichpo. The talk here will only bore you." He gave her a gentle shove in Orteguilla's direction. She took his hand shyly and tugged at it. Then, in sudden understanding, the two laughed at each other and ran off together down the hallway.

It was only after they'd gone that I noticed the presence of a slight, gray-haired man who had come into the room unannounced and seated himself not far from the emperor. He was dressed in a plain, rough *tilmatli*, as all subjects wore when they came into Moctezuma's presence, but this man was distinguished not only by his proud bearing, but by the fact that he wore shoes. Except for the rulers, Cuitlahuac and Cacama, only one man in the kingdom was not required to bare his feet before his emperor, and that man, I knew, was the *ciuacoatl*.

I'd seen him before, but only from a distance and only when his long black and white robe and elaborate headdress all but masked his features. Although my mind had long since reduced Moctezuma to flesh and blood, I could not yet quell a sense of awe in the *ciuacoatl's* presence. While the *uei tlatoani* wielded supreme power and received the adulation of his subjects, it was his second-in-command who was actually responsible for the intricacies of running the nation. It was the *ciuacoatl* who acted as supreme judge, who decided which warriors would be rewarded and promoted, who organized the armies and appointed their commanders, and who, at the death of a *uei tlatoani*, presided in his place until a permanent successor could be chosen by a council that he also organized and commanded.

He was a plain man, some years older than his chief. His penetrating black eyes and high forehead, crowned by thin, silver-streaked hair combed straight back instead of being cut in a fringe above his brows, gave him an air of wisdom. He was unusually thin and not tall . . . I suddenly realized that I'd been staring at him.

"Many years ago," Moctezuma said, "when my grandfather, Moctezuma I, was *uei tlatoani*, he named his brother Tlacaeletzin as the first *ciuacoatl*. He served so ably that from that time to this, Tlacaeletzin's descendants have performed their duties at the side of their emperors. As they served, so Tlacotzin now serves me."

Tlacotzin rose from his place, touched the floor and raised his palm to his lips. "I've been most anxious to meet you." He spoke rapidly, in a low, well-modulated voice that lacked the singsong quality of his emperor's. "I may try your patience. You'll find me a most inquisitive man!"

The *cuiacoatl* then proceeded to prove that he'd described himself well. Far into the evening he bombarded Hernán with questions about everything he'd seen and heard about him. ". . . How many vassals does your king have, Malintzin, and what sort of tribute do they pay? . . . Is it an alliance he wants, or have you come here to subjugate us? . . . How much tribute would he want? . . ." Even the evasive Hernán was no match for his astuteness. When an answer did not satisfy him he would rephrase his question. ". . . Your thundersticks interest me, Malintzin. What makes them work? . . . Magic? Oh, come, I know every trick of magic that our people can do. Each has its secret. What's yours? . . . Well, then, if you took one apart, what would you see? . . ."

Moctezuma said little but listened intently as the *ciuacoatl* pried and probed, asking how steel was made, whether it was possible to breed and raise horses, what the the extent of the Spanish empire and the size of the sea the Spaniards had crossed. He was especially fascinated by the idea of sails, and declared that he wanted to experiment with a sail on one of the royal canoes.

"You see, Malintzin," he explained, "ours isn't an old civilization. Two hundred years ago we were nothing but vagabonds, living in the reeds, eating frogs and lizards. But we learned from the other tribes that were here in this valley. We copied everything they had. Now they're gone and we're still here." He clasped his expressive, spider-thin hands around his knees. "If we're to survive as a great people, we have to keep on learning. There are those—" he glanced at Moctezuma—"who don't agree with me, but the law that governs my own life is this: One grows or one dies. And now—" he paused—

"I would like for you to tell us about your god."

The relief on Hernán's face shone through clouds of frustration. He'd been striving to reveal as little information as possible under the *ciuacoatl's* barrage of technical queries, but religion was another matter and he spoke volubly. The *ciuacoatl* interrupted him with frequent questions.

"You say, Malintzin, that it's wrong to worship more than one god. Yet you pray to a Father, a Son, a Holy Spirit and a little statue of a woman. That makes four gods."

"The Father, the Son and the Holy Ghost are one spirit," Hernán explained carefully as the *cuiacoatl* raised a skeptical eyebrow. "As for the Virgin, we don't really worship her. She's our intermediary with God. But we consider her sacred because, Tlacotzin, without having known a man she became the earthly mother of God. Do you find that hard to believe?"

The *ciuacoatl* leaned forward, eyes sparkling with interest. "Not at all!" he exclaimed. "I find that fascinating. Our own Huitzilopochtli was born of a virgin too. His mother, Coatlique, was sweeping the path in her garden one day when a ball of feathers fell out of the sky. Just to get it out of the way, she tucked it into the neck of her *huipilli*. Later, when she looked for the ball of feathers to throw it out, it was nowhere to be found—but she was pregnant. Who knows, perhaps your god and mine are brothers of sorts."

Hernán reddened as I translated. The vein in his forehead began to throb. "Blasphemy!" he whispered hoarsely. "How can you say that? You worship gods of death, stone idols. We've brought you the God of Life. Why won't you accept him?"

"But Malintzin," Moctezuma interrupted, "I've never said that we wouldn't accept your god. We welcome new gods. We disagree, you and I, only when you so stubbornly insist that we give up the gods we already have. *That* we could never do."

"Put yourselves in our place, Malintzin," the *ciuacoatl* said soothingly. "Our gods have been kind to us—even you can see that. How can we leave them for an unknown god who's never done anything for us?" He gestured in the direction of the square. "When you go outside tonight, look around you. You'll see the temples of Huitzilopochtli and Tlaloc standing side by side. You'll see Quetzalcoatl's temple to the east and Tezcatlipoca's to the south, and the *coacalco* that houses the gods from our other cities and provinces. Our gods live together in peace. If your god is so jealous that he can't tolerate having other gods beside him, then keep him for yourselves. We'll never try to take him away from you." The *ciuacoatl* spoke pleasantly, for years of service as a judge, diplomat and administrator had disciplined his voice and manner. His calmness only intensified Hernán's exasperation.

"Your gods drink human blood! Human sacrifice is an abomination! We want to free you from it."

"My dear Malintzin." The *cuiacoatl* spoke as though he were quieting an angry child. "Didn't you tell me how your Jesus offered himself as a human sacrifice for the good of all people? You'd never call his sacrifice an abomination. It was an act of supreme unselfishness. Can't you see that our religion gives many people the privilege of doing what He did?"

Hernán clearly needed my help, so I spoke, this time for myself. "My father, Tenepal, *tlatoani* of Oluta, was so privileged. His death was a waste of a great man's abilities."

"Tenepal . . ." the *ciuacoatl* mused. "I remember hearing about him. It was some years ago, wasn't it? A brave man, as I recall, but lacking in prudence." He shifted his weight, suddenly uncomfortable. "So you're his daughter! The gods have been mischievous."

"I understand that the present *tlatoani* is most loyal to us," said Moctezuma. "It's getting late, Malintzin. One of my reasons for asking you here this evening was to invite you to visit the market at Tlatelolco with me tomorrow. You've confined yourself too much to the palace. Perhaps if you see more of the way our people live, you'll gain a better appreciation of our ways."

"We'd be honored," Hernán said with a slight nod of his head.

Aguilar, Alvarado and Sandoval had listened to the long conversation with interest, but Bernal Diaz was openly bored. He'd spent the time gazing around the hall, his lanky body stirring restlessly. Finally his eye had alighted on one of the pretty serving girls who had returned to the room to bring the emperor a clay pipe filled with a strong-smelling herb called *tabac*.

As her royal master puffed away at the pipe, the girl remained, straightening the mats, gathering up the last of the dishes. She kept her eyes modestly lowered, even though she couldn't help but be aware of Bernal's warm gaze, which followed her wherever she went.

Moctezuma smiled, amused. "Malintzin, this tall companion of yours—is he a brave warrior?"

"Brave as a lion," Hernán said, beaming and once more in possession of his good nature.

"Brave as a . . . jaguar," I translated, unsure of what a lion was.

"And is he noble in character as well?" The emperor's eyes twinkled.

"A prince." I gave my own answer.

Moctezuma motioned the girl to his side. "I've seen how this tall Castilian admires you, little Xochitl. Would you like to be given to him?"

The girl looked at the floor, color flooding her pretty face.

"Malintzin, tell your warrior the girl is his if he wants her."

I translated, trying not to laugh at Bernal's ill-concealed delight.

"Tell the emperor that Bernal Diaz del Castillo is his friend for life," he said with a low bow.

Having bade goodnight to Moctezuma and the *ciuacoatl*, we walked back across the square by torchlight. Xochitl was with us, stepping along silently beside her new master, mouth tight, eyes glowing. I hoped Padre Olmedo would not grumble at being awakened in the middle of the night to perform a baptism.

Remembering my childhood fascination with the market at Oluta, I smiled to myself as I surveyed the huge marketplace of Tlatelolco from atop its pyramid, which was even bigger than the one in the sister city of Tenochtitlan. Grand as my native market had once seemed to me, it could have been lost in a small corner of this vast square where shoppers and traders moved about like thousands of varicolored ants below us. The market was neatly laid out in sections, with one area reserved for the sellers of vegetables, another for dealers in animal pelts, another for feather workers, another for live birds, dogs, reptiles and so forth. The variety of goods and services for sale dazzled us. There were shops where one could sit down and buy a meal of *tlaxcalli, tamales* and beans, places where hair was cut and arranged, booths where sandals and robes were repaired. A buyer could choose from fine cloth, gold, pearls, jade, shells, sandals, little household gods for every purpose, herbs, charms, quails for sacrifice, slaves and every imaginable variety of food. Indeed, there was nothing available throughout the kingdom that was not sold here at Tlatelolco. At one side of the market there were even barges filled with human excrement that could be bought for fertilizer and for tanning hides.

"You see, Marina," Hernán broke into my thoughts, "young Orteguilla's already proving his worth. I wanted Moctezuma's permission to climb to the top of this *cu* and he got if for us. The emperor's so taken with him he can't deny him anything."

"Moctezuma thinks you want to see his gods," I said. "If he knew the real reason you wanted to come up here he'd have refused even Orteguilla. How does it look to you, Hernán?"

He surveyed the city and the lake, spread out below us. "It's an invader's nightmare." he muttered unhappily. "Look at the causeways. All they'd need to do is take out the bridges and they'd have the world's biggest moat. They could keep almost any enemy out."

"Or in," I reminded him.

"And the canals! The place has more waterways than streets. To move cannon and cavalry in a mess like this . . ." His heavy brows curled in thought as he looked out across the island metropolis to the shallow, brownish-green waters of the lake. "There's got to be a way . . ."

We stood there outside the *teocalli*, each of us lost in his own thoughts—Hernán in his plans for conquest and I in the fearful mission I was to perform that night. I'd prayed for strength. I'd almost prayed that I wouldn't find Quauhtlatoa when the time came.

The others who had come—Alvarado, Sandoval, Olid, Bernal, Juan Jaramillo and several more—joined us now, just as Moctezuma came out of the *teocalli* where he'd gone in ahead of us. Ostensibly we'd come to see the temple of Huitzilopochtli. I steeled myself for the ordeal, but at least I knew what to expect. The others were less fortunate. We followed the emperor through the thick stone doorway into the gloomy interior of the *teocalli*. A flame burned in a large brazier filled with copal, sending our shadows dancing crazily on the walls and ceiling. We stopped in front of a high, tasseled curtain.

Moctezuma turned and glanced at us warily. "Malintzin, I'm still not sure I should have let you come," he said. "What you're about to see is sacred to us. Will you promise me, at least, your respect?"

Hernán nodded, impatient to be done with the experience.

A young priest drew the curtain aside. I heard Sandoval catch his breath at the sight of the apparition looming above us. The god was a twisted mass of human and animal forms, blending into a single grotesque entity. The jewels that covered it only intensified its hideousness. In a brazier before the idol there were three fresh hearts sizzling in the flames. The walls of the temple were coated with blood. Bernal Diaz pulled a handkerchief out of his pocket and held it against his nose.

And old priest tended the burning hearts. He kept his back turned, as if to convey to us that anything less than his god was not worthy of his attention. As he poked at the coals of the fire with a short, engraved stick, I noticed the embroidery on the edges of his bloodstained robe—a sign of high priestly rank. His bony old hands were scarred from bloodletting, as were the spindly legs that showed below his robe. Long gray hair, caked and matted with blood, hung below his waist.

I stole a quick look at Hernán. The dancing vein just above his left temple told me that he was raging inside. ". . . Ghastly," he murmured. "Moctezuma, you're an intelligent man! How can you bow down to an abominable hunk of stone like this?" I put a hand on his arm, trying to caution him, but he wouldn't be still. "Just let me put the cross and Our Lady's image in these temples. Then you'll see these idols shake and topple of their own accord!"

Something in Moctezuma's expression told me that it would do no good to lie about what Hernán had said. "Malintzin," he breathed. "If I'd known you were going to insult our gods I'd never have let you come. Our gods are good. They give us health, sustenance, victory, whatever we need. You're not to say another word against them!"

The old priest had overheard his emperor. He turned to face us. His eyes flashed hatred, but he directed his venom not at Hernán but at me. "You wicked woman," he snarled. "I can understand your master's ignorance—but you! These are your own gods you're using your tongue to blaspheme! Traitor!"

My throat tightened as I recognized him.

I'd been a child at our last meeting, so he would not have remembered me. But as for him, the years had only increased the gauntness of his frame, the prominence of his hooked nose and the hollowness of his sunken eyes. Cozcaquauhtli had merely aged into an exaggeration of himself.

I spoke slowly, hurling each word at him and enjoying its impact. "Cozcaquauhtli, I turned my face away from your gods years ago in Oluta, when you raised your knife to kill my father."

I'd caught him off-guard, but only for an instant. "Ah, yes," he hissed, "little Malinalli. My leg still carries the marks of your teeth. I should have killed you too. Who knows what it would have spared us!"

"Our God would have found other ways," I retorted.

Moctezuma stepped between us. "We've offended the gods enough," he said. "Must you fight in their presence? Malintzin, I insist that you leave this place at once. Visit the market. Go back to the palace. I'm staying here to punish myself for having let you come!"

Hernán retreated, murmuring apologies, but the *uei tlatoani* had turned his back on us. The old priest handed him a long thorn to use in drawing blood from his legs.

We walked out into the sunlight.

Chapter Fourteen

Tenochtitlan—November 1519

After the way I'd treated Quauhtlatoa, he might not even come to the square again, I told myself as I strolled cautiously past the steps of the pyramid and turned toward the *tzompantli*, where the naked skulls gleamed in the torchlight. I wondered what Hernán would have done if I'd refused to go tonight. Not that it mattered. I couldn't refuse him anything. Besides, he was right. My own feelings, when measured alongside the lives of four hundred men, shrank to their proper significance.

Still, Quauhtlatoa had precipitated the most humiliating experience of my life. My skin crawled with distaste at the thought of being touched by him again. I willed myself to concentrate on the old priest, forcing my heart to pump its hatred into every vein . . .

"It's a good thing for you, Malinalli, that I'm such a persistent man." His voice came from behind me and I whipped around to face him. "I knew you'd be back," he said laughingly. "But I should have realized that it would be on your own terms. Still very much the *tlatoani's* daughter, aren't you?" He looped a possessive arm around my waist and I forced myself not to pull away. "Didn't you bring anything with you?"

"I couldn't," I said. "They watch me like a prisoner. If I'd done anything to make them suspect I was running away—" I looked up at him and forced a smile. "But it doesn't really matter, does it? We'll be able to go back and take what we want after they're dead."

Quauhtlatoa did not take the bait. "It's not important. As long as I keep my wife happy I'll have enough *quachtli* to buy you a new robe for every day of the year. The house is small, but it's pleasant. I'll see that you're not bored." He chuckled and squeezed my arm. "Malinalli—you, here with me! I can't believe I'm not dreaming!"

We walked along the bank of a small canal, past an occasional torch-lit canoe, then turned into a maze of streets and alleyways that marked the beginning of Pochtan, the traders' quarter.

I said little, for my mind was busy trying to memorize the winding route our steps had taken. It was possible that I might have to return along the way we'd come.

"These streets will be our friends," he said. "If your old masters come after you, they'll never find you here. And that's not the only advantage. I can approach the house from any one of several directions. No one will see me coming and going regularly, and so no one will carry any tales to my wife and father-in-law."

"I'm afraid . . ." I clung to his arm. "You don't know Hernán Cortés. If he finds me, he'll kill us both. How long will we have to hide from him?"

He ignored my question. "Oh, you'll be safe enough. No stranger could come near the house without causing a stir. And there's a secret room under the floor. My father built it for his treasures. It's dangerous for a *pochteca* to show off his wealth, you know. He's liable to lose it."

Was he as innocent as he sounded? Or was he merely playing a game, knowing full well what I wanted him to tell me? My spirits sank as I walked beside him, listening to his cheerful conversation. He knew. He had to know. Quauhtlatoa wasn't stupid. He'd bring me along, secretly laughing as he tested the lengths to which I was willing to go to get information from him, information he might not even possess. After all, he was neither warrior nor statesman. Why should he be privileged with secrets. Yet his father-in-law was an important man, and perhaps Quauhtlatoa had overheard something.

"Here it is." We'd entered a tiny alleyway and now we passed through a narrow opening into a courtyard, untended and overgrown with vines, but wildly beautiful in the moonlight.

Turning me toward him, he ceremoniously lifted the chain of the *chalchihuitl* from around his neck and slipped it over my head. The heavy green stone rose and fell with my breasts. Its weight seemed to press me into the ground.

"Every time I've looked at this *chalchihuitl* I've envied the man who used it to buy you," he breathed. "But now I'll never envy any man again." He crushed me in his arms, his hands searching my body. "Malinalli," he panted, "I can't wait any longer. Come inside."

I stifled a scream as he dragged me into the house and flung me down on a mat. He paused to yank off his *tilmatli*, his loincloth and the long obsidian dagger that was tied to his waist by a thin cord. The dagger clattered as it hit the floor. He moved toward me, crouching.

Suddenly something snapped inside me. The house was gone and I was in the jungle again, parrots and monkeys screeching above my head, wet moss against my back. Once more I fought him with all my strength, kicking, scratching, tasting blood where I bit his shoulder.

He slapped my face hard. "Not again, Malinalli!" he muttered. "You're not going to fight me this time!" The blow stunned me but I kept on struggling against the aggressive weight of his body, against the hands that were tearing away my *huipilli*. The dagger was there, beside the mat where he'd dropped it. Stretching agonizingly, I grasped its carved handle. Then, in a frenzy of rage and panic, I drove the blade straight down into his back.

He tensed, bellowing with pain and surprise, and slowly his face twisted into a grotesquely grinning mask. His fingers locked around my throat. Tighter and tigher he squeezed, choking off my breath. I felt the tissues yielding to his strong thumbs. My body screamed for air. As the darkness closed in on my senses, I heard a shout and glimpsed the flash of moonlight on a steel blade. Suddenly, Quauhtlatoa's body went limp and he fell on top of me. Blood trickled down his shoulder and onto my hair. With the last of my strength I shoved him to one side and rolled clear of his weight.

Juan Jaramillo stood over me, the sword in his hand still dripping blood. "Marina!" His voice shook. "*Diós mío*, if he's harmed you . . ."

Dizzy and light-headed, I rose to my knees. My *huipilli* hung from my shoulders in shreds. "I'm not . . . harmed, Juan," I whispered, surprised that I still had a voice. "And if I were, what could you do to him? He's dead." A shaky laugh caught in my throat. I began to tremble uncontrollably.

"Good Lord, how could Cortés have let you do this?" Juan knelt swiftly beside me, unfastened his cloak and wrapped it around my bare shoulders. I tried to speak, but now the only sounds that came from my lips were painful little gasps. Suddenly I was in his arms, sobbing.

He held my tenderly, as one holds a child, accepting my

nearness without question. The tears poured from my eyes, soaking the front of his shirt, as I sobbed out my humiliation at the hands of Quauhtlatoa, my fear, my weariness. I cried for all the times I'd been afraid to cry, for the horrors of Cholula, for Tonaxel, for Nacontoc, for my son, even for my father. At last the tempest inside me was spent. I rested my head on Juan's chest, and listened to the drumming of his heart against my ear.

"Juan," I said, suddenly wondering, "how did you get here?"

"Cortés had me follow you." I felt his muscles harden under my fingers. "He didn't even tell me why. 'Keep a discreet distance,' he told me, 'and don't interfere except to save her life.' Why, that—" His words trailed off helplessly. "Damn it, if I'd known what you were going to do—! First I lost you in this confounded tangle of streets. I couldn't tell where you'd gone until I heard that brute cry out. If I'd gotten here half a minute later he'd have killed you!" His arms tightened around me.

"I've failed," I said dejectedly. "Why didn't I just go through with it, Juan? I'm not the trembling virgin defending her honor anymore."

"Stop it," he said. "You're not that kind of woman."

"Oh, but I am," I said ruthlessly. "It wouldn't even have been the first time with—"

"Stop it!" Something in the gruffness of his voice made me draw back and look up at him. "Stop it, Marina," he murmured, and then he was kissing me, with a gentle hunger that sent tremors of sweetness all the way down to my toes. I felt my arm slipping up and around his neck.

He kissed me again, in a mounting crescendo of fierceness that left us both gasping. "Marina," he whispered against my hair, "God help me, but I've loved you from the first moment I saw you! Don't you know that?"

Wonderingly, I pressed close to him, quivering with new emotion as his warm lips moved over my face to my throat, my ears, my tear-swollen eyes. How I wanted to block out the awful storm of reality that swirled around us both, to isolate this moment in space and time from the world that awaited us outside these walls.

With a sigh of reluctance he stepped back, holding me at arm's length. His eyes were blue wells of sadness. He glanced down at Quauhtlatoa's corpse and nudged it with the toe of his boot. "We've got to get rid of him," he said. "Someone could have seen one of us come in. There could be trouble if the body's found." Only then did it occur to me that he'd taken a great risk in following me here alone.

"There's supposed to be a secret room under the floor," I said.

The house was small, and a brief search revealed a trapdoor hidden under a mat. Juan lifted it, exposing a stairway leading down into a black, cobweb-shrouded hole. Juan walked back to Quauhtlatoa's body and picked up the sandaled feet. I moved forward to help him. He shook his head. "No, don't touch him again, *querida*." He backed toward the stairway, Quauhtlatoa's lifeless face bumping along the stone floor after him. I found a strip of my torn *huipilli* and began to sponge the blood out of my hair.

A series of dull thuds told me that Juan had shoved Quauhtlatoa's body into the hole. The trapdoor grated back into place and Juan came back, looking a little pale. "I've got to get you back to the palace," he said. I nodded. We both knew that our time together was over.

Silently, we made our way out of the house and into the maze of streets. Juan had a sailor's sense of direction and he guided us back toward the square without missing a turn. We said little, for there was little to say. He was taking me back to the palace and Hernán. There was nothing either of us could do about it.

We reached the edge of the central plaza. Torches gleamed from the porches of the palace of Axayacatl. Juan beckoned me into a shadow. "Marina—" He took my hand and pressed the tips of my fingers to his lips. "Listen to me, *querida*," he said. "I'd rather die than hurt you. What happened back there was . . . a dream. It has to be. Do you understand?"

I shook my head. "What happened, happened, Juan. We can't change the truth."

"The truth is there." He looked across the square at the palace. "You can't betray him and I won't betray him. It was my fault. Forgive me, Marina." He let go of my hand. "Don't make this any harder than it is. Put on a nice face and run, like a good girl, back to the palace. I'll watch till you're safely inside. Then I'll come in another way."

As I trudged away from him I battled the urge to run back to his arms one last time. I struggled feebly against it and lost. Turning, I took a step back toward him.

"Juan—"

He stood his ground. "Marina." His voice was edged with

pain. The black sash stood out sharply against the white of his sleeve. "If you want to destroy us both, just take one more step."

He was right. Almost hating him for his strength, I turned and ran across the square and up the steps of the palace.

The halls were deserted, which was puzzling. Worriedly, I slipped inside the room I shared with Hernán. It was empty, but everything was in order. I realized then that I was still wearing Juan's cloak over my torn *huipilli*. Folding it tenderly, I placed it on top of a chest before getting out a change of clothing.

As I was winding a long sash around my waist, Hernán hurried into the room, his face flushed with excitement. "I saw Jaramillo," he said. "He told me he'd brought you back."

"Did he tell you I'd failed?"

"He told me that by the time he caught up with you, you'd nearly killed the *cabrón*, and that he had to finish him to save you." He put his arms around me and pulled me close. "My poor Marina, I've been in torment from the moment I let you go, wondering if I'd done the right thing."

"I didn't learn a thing from him, Hernán," I said. "Maybe there was nothing to learn."

"No matter, then. Don't think about it. Just remember that as long as I live I'll never forget what you were willing to do for me tonight." He kissed me lightly on the lips. His eyes were glittering. "Come with me now. I've a sight to show you that would make anyone forget his troubles!"

He took my hand and led me down the hallway to the large chamber we'd chosen for our chapel. There was now a gaping hole in one of the inside walls, as high and as wide as a man's body. Several of Hernán's men moved away from the hole as we entered the chamber.

"Yañez, the carpenter, was looking for a spot to place the cross," Hernán explained, "and he noticed that one section of the wall had been plastered over recently. I ordered the spot dug away and . . . look for yourself, Marina." He pushed me through the jagged opening.

"Hernán!" The torchlight revealed a room heaped with glittering treasure. Chests of polished wood overflowed with chains of gold and piles of pearls and precious stones. Little gold statues and trinkets of the most exquisite workmanship were everywhere. Folded robes were stacked to the ceiling. There was more wealth here than one man could count in a week, more than the imagination of even the greediest could grasp.

"Look well, all of you," Hernán announced to the men who thronged around the entrance. "But don't take anything. Not yet. We'll have Yañez close the wall again." He nodded toward the stocky carpenter who stood nearby. "But look at this, and remember what lies in store for the faithful followers of Hernán Cortés!"

Later, I lay beside him in the darkness, too exhausted to sleep. I listened to his deep, regular breathing and was grateful that he hadn't tried to make love to me. Wide-eyed, I stared into the blackness above my head, trying to comprehend all that had happened to me tonight.

I hardly thought of Quauhtlatoa, for his brutal attack had somehow broght about a miracle. Juan loved me. I trembled with the total unexpected joy of it. Juan. I closed my eyes and concentrated, trying to bring back the warm strength of his arms around me, the rough tenderness of his lips on mine, I turned his words over and over in my mind until they developed their own rhythm, their own music.

A mosquito whined above me, closer and closer until it landed on my forehead. I brushed it away, my sudden movement causing Hernán to stir next to me. What I felt for Hernán was devotion, respect, even awe. But love? I wasn't sure. As I looked back over the time I'd spent with the Spaniards, I realized that it had always been Juan I went to when I needed the warmth of understanding. And somehow he had appeared at my side in my darkest moments, when I most needed a comforting presence.

What was I thinking? I was feeding a monster that could destroy us all! Juan was right: one weak link in the chain of loyalty that bound us both to Hernán, one small breach in the ranks of our little army, could make the difference between victory and defeat. I could not let my own feelings provide that one vulnerable spot. My encounter with Juan tonight had been a dream, just as he'd said. We could never let ourselves dream again . . .

The moon emerged from the clouds long enough to point a finger of light through the tiny window of the room. Something gleamed on the floor, next to the heap of clothes I'd discarded when I undressed. Sliding carefully off the mat, I reached out with my hand and touched the cold chain of the *chalchihuitl* that Quauhtlatoa had given me. Holding it, I shivered. It had bought me once, and tonight it had nearly bought me again. I studied it by moonlight. Its workmanship was beautiful, but the sight of it brought back memories of slavery and death. Hernán might want to have it, though. He liked jewelry and it was a heavy enough piece to look good on a man. I rummaged about for the chest in which he kept his most valuable treasures, opened it, and placed the *chalchihuitl* carefully beside the pink shell necklace with the golden shrimp that Moctezuma had given him on our arrival in the city. Reverently, I closed the lid of the chest and slid it out of sight. Now the *chalchihuitl* belonged to Hernán, and so did I. All was as it should be. One day I would tell him where it had come from.

I crept back under the blanket, expecting a mental peace that didn't come. Rising up on one elbow, I looked at Hernán slumbering beside me. He read men the way I could read a tribute scroll. He could easily have known what Juan felt for me when he had sent him to protect me on my dangerous errand.

I traced each line of his face with my eyes. Had he been moved by concern, sending the man to guard me who could best be trusted with my life? Or had it been a perverse desire to punish Juan by forcing him to watch me with Quauhtlatoa? "Interfere only to save her life . . ." Those had been his instructions. A convulsive shudder seized me as I looked at him and realized that neither motive was beyond him.

Then he moved in his sleep, moaning softly. His eyelids fluttered open. "Marina," he whispered.

"I'm here, Hernán."

"Marina, as God as my witness, I'll never send you away like that again. When I think of what might have happened to you . . . Forgive me, *preciosa*. I must have taken leave of my senses to let you go."

I cradled his head between my breasts, unable to speak.

"Listen, Marina." He was fully awake now. "I see only one course of action open to us. We've got to act quickly. I'll need your help."

"What is it, Hernán?"

"We'll have to take Moctezuma as a hostage. There's no other way if we want to leave Tenochtitlan alive, much less conquer it."

My heart was pounding. "When?"

"As soon as I can make plans with my men. Tomorrow, if we can be ready. Or the day after. Are you with me, Marina?"

"After all this time, you have to ask?" I whispered.

He pulled me to him, running his hand along the curve of my hip. "Marina," he murmured huskily, "before I take you, you've got to make me a promise."

"Yes . . . to whatever it is you want."

"Promise me that you'll never leave me. Never."

"Never . . ." I was grateful that the darkness hid my tears.

Chapter Fifteen

Tenochtitlan—January 1520

The jaguar paced back and forth in its bamboo cage, growling deep in its throat. Under the gleaming mottled coat, the muscles rippled with each padding step. I felt a stab of pity for this monarch of the forest who would never know his kingdom again.

I gazed at the caged animal and thought once more of the captive emperor who now held court in the palace of Axayacatl, surrounded by his Spanish guards. The royal apartment was a far cry from a bamboo cage, it was true. Moctezuma had even been allowed the company of his favorite wives and concubines, and no physical comfort was lacking. He received ambassadors and ordered his subjects about as always but the bars, invisible through they were, were present nonetheless. The *uei tlatoani's* power was now in the hands of Hernán Cortés, who ruled his every movement.

The deed had been accomplished easily. The first step had been to find an excuse for our action, and the Aztec attack on Villa Rica under the leadership of a chief named Quauhpopoca had provided it, for the chief would not have acted except on Moctezuma's orders. With sentries planted at strategic posts outside the palace and in Moctezuma's audience chamber, Hernán had taken Alvarado, Sandoval, Francisco de Lugo, Alonzo de Ávila and Velásquez de León, heavily armed, to confront the emperor.

Moctezuma had been at his most gracious that morning. He announced that he's chosen the choicest jewels from among his nieces and his own harem to give as companions to his Castilian brothers. The captains had waited, champing at the bit like nervous stallions, while the women were distributed. Then, with a flourish, the emperor had produced one of his own daughters for Hernán, a girl whose face maintained a vapid expression like a rabbit's, although she was otherwise quite pretty. To my relief, Hernán had protested that he already had a wife.

Moctezuma had laughed at that. "Look at me, Malintzin!" He spread his hands to encompass his whole palace. "I'm surrounded by women and I keep all of them happy. You're my equal in so many things—surely you could do as well. Why not sow your seed in many hills, just as I do?" He thrust the girl toward Hernán. "Take her. Give me some fine grandchildren."

I translated expressionlessly.

"Oh, very well." Hernán cocked his eye at the girl. "I'll take her. Why not? Tell the emperor he's made his point, Marina."

I thanked Moctezuma, rather coldly, wondering how Hernán would dispose of her—and never doubting that he would.

With these niceties finished, we'd gotten to the business at hand. Hernán had produced a letter from Villa Rica in which Moctezuma was accused of instigating the attack in which several of Hernán's men had perished, including Escalante.

Moctezuma had denied all knowledge of the attack. It had all been the doing of Quauhpopoca, the local chief, he insisted.

"I'm accountable to my king for the lives of those men," Hernán said. "If you say you're not guilty, my noble friend, I believe you. But wouldn't it be wiser if you come with us to our quarters and stayed till we can get Quauhpopoca here to prove your innocence?" He smiled confidently at the emperor. "It would be for your own protection, of course. My men are upset about their lost comrades. I can't guarantee your safety here."

At first Moctezuma had reacted with outraged dignity. His royal person could not be treated in such a manner. He simply could not go with us. Then, seeing the determination in Hernán's eyes, he'd begun to plead, offering to send his wives and children—even Tecuichpo and her brother Asupacaci, the royal heir—as hostages in his place. The tears ran down his cheeks. "Malintzin, I beg you on my knees not to let this disgrace fall upon me!" He was so pathetic that I could hardly bear to look at him.

"Why should it be a disgrace?" Hernán answered him. "The palace of Axayacatl is yours. Just tell your people you've gone for a visit."

But Moctezuma had continued his pleas, offering us anything in his possesssion if we'd allow him to remain in his palace. The men grew uneasy. I heard Velásquez de León behind me, breathing rapidly and shuffling his feet, until he could stand it no longer.

"The wretch is going to talk all day!" he exploded. "Let's either take him or run him through and be done with it."

The emperor couldn't understand the words, but there was no mistaking their tone. His soft deer's eyes wide with fear, he'd turned to me to ask the meaning of what he'd just heard.

I had hated him all my life, yet when I spoke to him now, pity gave root to gentleness. "You mustn't delay, my lord," I said. "They're getting impatient. If you don't do as they ask, they'll kill you."

Defeated, he had sent for his litter.

The jaguar coughed again, a gutteral, breathy sound that sent a herd of deer racing around their pen at the other end of the large compound, crashing wildly into the sides of the fence. Moctezuma's menagerie, located at the rear of the palace, contained every imaginable kind of beast—pumas, ocelots, wild pigs, monkeys, snakes—languishing in bamboo cages or in deep pits, all under one vast roof.

"I'll never understand why you like to come to this hellhole," muttered Bernal Diaz. "I'd rather escort you through a band of howling human savages any day than brave the kind of nightmares this place gives me."

"It passes the time." I smiled up at him. "And look, some of them are beautiful." I paused before the cage of a sleeping ocelot that was curled up into an exquisitely mottled ball, and watched the subtle changes of light and shadow on its body as it breathed. "It's sad that they're not free, yes, but you never get to see them like this in the forest."

Bernal followed me around a walled pit where several boa constrictors coiled and slithered. "Ugh!" he grunted. "The only person I know who likes this place as much as you do is Juan Jaramillo. He says it's interesting! You should have asked him to come with you and spared me the experience." He was watching my face as he spoke, and his sharp eyes caught the subtle rise of color in my cheeks. "Ha! Just as I thought." He grinned. "You two are hiding something, aren't you?"

"What has he told you?" I looked up at him in alarm.

"Nothing—on my word of honor. Don't look so startled. He doesn't need to tell me. I've got eyes, and I know him. We've been like brothers since we signed on this rooster-chase back in Cuba. The man's miserable."

I leaned over a low fence to scratch the back of a snuffling tapir.

"Let's go outside," Bernal said gruffly. "I can't hear myself think in this bedlam, and the smell's turning my stomach." He took my arm and guided me through the maze of pens, through the gateway of the compound and out into the small garden that divided the beast-house from the royal aviary.

"Now listen to Bernal," he said. "I'm not one to meddle, but I've got to say this. I think Cortés has treated you abominably, putting on that pious long face of his and moving in with Moctezuma's daughter as if it were some noble sacrifice. Setting you aside like a piece of baggage until the time comes when he needs you again." He sat down on a low wall, his knees jutting upward in their long brown hose. "Oh, the men talk, all right. Most of them feel the same as I do . . ."

"What are you trying to tell me, Bernal?"

He cleared his throat. "That no one would blame you," he said slowly, "if you paid Cortés back in his own coin."

"With Juan?" My face and voice were composed; my heart was not.

"Naturally! Oh hell!" He pummeled the side of his leg with his fist. "What right have I to talk to you like this? It's just that I'm so happy with my Francisca, but Juan, the poor devil . . ."

I put my hand on his arm. "You're a good friend, Bernal," I said. "You mean well, but listen to me. If I were to do as you suggest, I'd only be using Juan to . . . to repay Hernán in his own coin, as you say. I couldn't do that, especially when I'd always have to go back to Hernán." My reply had come easily. I'd crossed that same bitter bridge in my mind the first night Hernán had left our room to go to Moctezuma's daughter, Doña Ana. Alone on my mat, I'd fought temptation and won, using the same arugment against myself. I picked a pink blossom from a flowering vine and shredded it in my fingers. "I'd only hurt Juan," I said softly. "And I care about him too much to do that."

Bernal patted my hand. "Then you're a rare wench," he said. "I don't know whether to feel sorry for Juan or envy him."

Tenochtitlan—February 1520

Tecuichpo, lovely in a pale blue *huipilli* edged with green feathers, sat crosslegged at her father's feet. From under her long, thick lashes she watched the flight of the little golden *totoloque* balls. She, along with her mother—Moctezuma's legal wife—and some of her father's favorite concubines, had been moved to the palace of Axayacatl, which was now the emperor's prison. Her half-sister, Doña Ana, lounged on a mat nearby, her nose twitching in its rabbitlike way as she munched tidbits from a bowl of fruit. Her languorous eyes brightened with interest only when Hernán Cortés took his turn at the game of throwing the small balls at the metal targets set up on the floor some distance away.

From out of the corner of my eye, I studied her and wondered idly whether she pleased Hernán. Ana was not as pretty as some of the girls Moctezuma had given the Spanish officers, but still she was a far cry from dumpy little Catalina back in Cempoalla. Hernán had shown no inclination to leave her and return to my bed. He'd offered little explanation, although I saw him constantly during the day in my capacity as interpreter. "Look upon it as duty, Marina *mía*," was all he'd said. "It's not for long. You know that my heart always remains with you."

For the first time in months I'd remembered Ixel, my Tabascan mistress. Now I understood her better, for I was walking in her shoes. I struggled through one difficult day at a time, trying to keep my thoughts away from Ana and away from Juan.

Now that his position in the Aztec capital was temporarily secure, Hernán had become curious about the resources of the rest of Moctezuma's kingdom. He'd sent out small expeditions of Spaniards and Aztec guides to explore and report back to him; one group went sourthwestward to Tochtepec, and another, headed by the footless pilot, Gonzalo de Umbria, traveled southwest to Zacatula. There was also a need for a better harbor than the one at Villa Rica, and Diego de Ordaz, who had braved the heights of Popocatepetl, had offered to lead a party to the coast to search for one. Hernán had authorized him to select ten men whose knowledge of ships and sailing would enable them to recognize a good harbor if they found it. Among the ten chosen was Juan Jaramillo.

Juan's farewell had been public and brief, for I'd been standing beside Hernán when the little party had marched off into the dawn. For a dizzying instant he'd clasped my hand as his eyes devoured me. Then, with my whispered "*Vaya con Diós*," he'd marched away with Ordaz and the others. My eyes had followed them down the causeway until they disappeared into the mist.

"I win!" Hernán crowed as one of the balls clinked against its target. "That makes five points for me."

"Five points!" Moctezuma rolled his eyes in mock dismay. "Surely not, Malintzin. By my own count you only have four points. The game isn't over yet."

"No, five points! Five!" protested Alvarado, who was keeping score. Laughing, he held up five fingers.

The emperor feigned displeasure. "A less trusting man than I would suspect your friend of adding to your score, Malintzin," he said. "Very well, I'll pay our wager." He clapped his hands and a servant carried in a chest filled with little rings of gold. Counting out twenty of them, he presented them to Hernán who, smiling benevolently, tossed them one at a time to Moctezuma's servants.

Such was the practice in these long days of the *uei tlatoani's* imprisonment. When Moctezuma won at games, he distributed the winnings among his Spanish guards. Sometimes Pedro de Alvarado played and when he won, as he usually did, he would keep his winnings for himself. When he lost, he made a great show of paying his Aztec opponent in *chalchihuitls*, which were of no value to him.

While a servant passed around cups of fragrant *chocolatl*, two elderly musicians entered the chamber, one with a clay flute and the other with a prettily carved *teponatzli*. They squatted like two old shorebirds. The first musical tap on the drum sent Tecuichpo flying to her feet with the lightness of a butterfly. She was a gifted performer, and she knew it. Laughing, she danced in a growing circle, moving with a delicate skill that was spiced with her own natural exuberance and love of rhythm. The iridescent green feathers on her costume gleamed until she seemed less a little girl than a tiny hummingbird flitting over the surface of the polished stone floor. Soon this giggling, dancing child would be a woman. What a prize she'd be, I reflected. A consort for an emperor, a gift for some lucky conquistador—what would be her fate? What would be the state of her world by the time she reached marriageable age? I looked at Moctezuma and glanced rapidly away, pretending not to notice the tears in his eyes.

"They're going to try and get him free again, Doña Marina. A tunnel this time, into the garden." Orteguilla had sidled up to me and, with his eyes on Tecuichpo, had whispered the message. He'd remained in Moctezuma's quarters since the emperor's arrest, with instructions to keep his eyes and ears open.

"What, again?" I sighed. All the other escape attempts had failed, but Moctezuma's henchmen never gave up, even though the emperor himself had slipped into an ill-concealed state of hopelessness. His last flicker of resistance had died the day Quauhpopoca, who had led the attack that killed Escalante, was tried by Hernán and burned alive in the square, along with his son and fifteen of his staff, on fires made of weapons and shields looted from the city's arsenals. As punishment for his own involvement, Moctezuma had been forced to watch the immolation with iron shackles on his wrists and ankles, an unspeakable humiliation for someone regarded as a near-god. Afterwards, the shackles had been removed, with many tears and protestations of love from Hernán, who had even embraced the royal personage. But the spirit of the proud monarch had been crushed once and for all. Now he fawned on his captors like a beaten dog.

The public executions had had a shattering effect, even on a populace so accustomed to death. At last, even the most naive of Moctezuma's subjects realized that the *uei tlatoani* had not gone to the palace of Axayacatl on a friendly visit. Though the affairs of the kingdom still functioned smoothly under the capable administration of the *ciuacoatl*, the very air tingled with unrest. Hernán kept his royal captive out of sight as much as possible, and on the rare occasions when Moctezuma did leave the palace, he did so under heavy guard. The tedious days were passed in games, contests of skill between Spaniards and Aztec warriors, and infrequent hunting forays to the forested hill area of Chapultepec, which lay on the western shore of the lake. Even these trips were used to advantage by Hernán, who carefully noted the construction of the acqueduct that carried water from the streams of Chapultepec to the fountains and cisterns of Tenochtitlan.

"The tunnel's almost finished," Orteguilla whispered. "I heard the *ciuacoatl* telling Moctezuma this morning. I pretended not to understand."

"I'll tell Velásquez de León. He'll know how to put a stop to it. Thank you, little brother. I know this isn't easy for you." I frowned thoughtfully. Perhaps seizing the *ciuacoatl* would put an end to the escape plot, but without Tlacotzin to manage the complex machinations of the kingdom, the delicate balance between control and chaos would be upset drastically, turning the situation to our disadvantage. He was of more use to us at liberty.

"Doña Marina . . ."

"Don't worrry, *hermanito.* Moctezuma won't be harmed."

"Doña Marina, he's been so kind to me . . . I only remember how my own father used to beat me. The emperor treats me like a son. He loves me. Please don't let him be hurt!"

I put an arm around his thin shoulders and squeezed him affectionately, marveling that this orphan cub could view Moctezuma in a light so different from the one in which I had seen him at the same age.

Tecuichpo's dance had reached its climax. With the final trill of the flute she sprang high into the air and landed, kitten-like, in a graceful pose. Cheeks flushed and eyes sparkling, she looked about the hall for approval and suddenly spotted the slender youth who had just entered.

"Asupacaci!" Decorum forgotten, she hurled herself toward him, leaping up to fling her arms around him neck. "Asupacaci, I never get to see you anymore."

Moctezuma's legitimate son and heir strove to maintain some dignity as he disentangled his sister's arms from around his neck. I'd seen him only a few times before, for he lived not at the palace but at the *calmecac*, the priestly school for young Aztec nobles, which his father had attended before him. Asupacaci, whose long hair indicated that he was untried in battle, had inherited his father's fine features, along with a robustness that seemed to have skipped Moctezuma's generation. His handsome young face was frozen into a scowl. What he thought of us was clear.

Moctezuma hurried forward to greet him, and as the two embraced, Asupacaci whispered a message in his father's ear. I was unable to hear it, but no one could have missed the wave of shocked amazement that rippled over the emperor's features. Drawing himself up to his full height, Moctezuma turned to face us.

"Malintzin," he announced, "as a friend and brother I want to warn you that your life is in danger. Take your horses, your thundersticks your Tlaxcalans, even the treasure—yes, I know you've found it—and flee Tenochtitlan before it's too late!"

Hearing my translation from his seat beside Doña Ana, Hernán paled slightly.

"If you don't leave," Moctezuma continued, "the time may come when I can't be responsible for your safety." His voice faltered. "My son has just told me that my nephew Cacama, lord of Texcoco, had begun a revolt—against you and—" He choked, then went on, ". . . against me!"

* * *

As the weeks passed, it became apparent that Cacama's rebellion was not being supported as wholeheartedly as the haughty young ruler might have expected.

True, Cuitlahuac had pledged himself to the cause, but suspecting that Cacama had designs on Moctezuma's throne, he had furnished fighting troops only in token quantities. Likewise, Cacama's own brothers, including Ixtlilxochitl, gave him little more than lip service. The cities at the far northern end of the lake were aligned behind Cacama, but the chiefs at the lake's populous southern end, most of whom had already secretly tendered their allegiance to Hernán, refused to join in the revolt.

Cacama's activities had little direct physical effect on life inside the palace of Axayacatl, except to increase the high pitch of tension that already existed. Doña Ana had announced her pregnancy, and I functioned at Hernán's side with all the animation of an earthenware doll. Now that he had accomplished his duty by the emperor's daughter, I half expected that he would return to me. I reacted with both resentment and relief when he did not.

There was time for introspection in these long days, and I realized that the strongest factor in my present attitude toward Hernán was my own wounded pride. For these past months, I'd been "the commander's woman"—honored, envied and, I'd thought, even loved. Now I realized that Hernán did not love any woman. He was a man who took whatever was at hand and used it as he had used me—and as he was now using Ana. Women were little more than tools to him, and the final awareness of this truth stung like salt in an open cut.

I'd been stunned by his abrupt acceptance of Ana on the heels of his tenderness the night I'd come back from Quauhtlatoa, the night he'd made me promise never to leave him. I'd wanted him to forsake her and return to me on his knees, begging forgiveness. Now, knowing Hernán as I did, I realized that this would never happen. When he tired of Ana, or when her usefulness to him was ended, he would be back. And I, fool that I was, would be waiting. He needed me, and I was caught up and bound by the power of that need. I had promised never to leave him. Whatever happened, I would keep that promise.

And Juan? I longed for him as a caged bird longs for the sky. I ached for the sweetness of those brief moments I'd spent in his arms. Yet even as I cursed the wisdom that kept us apart, I recognized the rightness of it. Our feelings for one another, if allowed to run unbridled, could only destroy us. Hernán and Juan. I cared for them both, but there was no reason to compare the two of them, to weigh, judge or make a choice. Life and fate had long since made that choice for me.

I had gone to sleep early, tired from the strain of the day and wondering why Doña Ana had suddenly begun to look at me with eyes full of poison. She had no reason to, I reflected, for Hernán's behavior hadn't visibly changed toward either of us. Perhaps it was her pregnancy. Some women, I knew, were more prone to jealousy at such times. Actually, it was I who had more reason to be jealous. If only God had favored me with Hernán's child, at least I could have glared back at Ana on an equal basis.

I slept fitfully, dreaming once more of gold-bound babies sinking into black pools, of hollow-eyed priests with blood dripping from their stone knives, of my own hand driving the dagger into Quauhtlatoa's naked flesh . . .

"Malintzin! Wake up!" It was a woman's voice, buzzing softly in my ear. I opened my eyes. One glance at the figure crouching beside my mat in the moonlight told me that I had never seen the woman before, but something about the sharp, narrow features, the slanting eyes and graceful, animal-like posture stirred my memory.

"I'm Mazatl, Malintzin. I have to speak to your master."

Mazatl? I groped in the fog of my sleepy mind and suddenly remembered.

"Ixtlilxochitl's sister?"

"Yes," she answered a little impatiently. "I have a message from my brother. Can you help me?"

"Hernán isn't here. He's . . ." Embarrassed, I let my voice trail off.

"Oh, you don't have to tell me. I listen to palace gossip. I know where he is." She reached out and patted my arm with a cool hand. "Don't be ashamed, Malintzin. We know how men are. Look at me. I'm Moctezuma's concubine, but I've only shared his mat twice in the past year. Come on!" She tugged at my coverlet.

Rumpled and barefoot, I followed the shadowy form through the palace. "Mazatl," I whispered. "Doña Ana's room's in another wing, not this one."

The slanting fox-like eyes flashed in the darkness. "Doña Ana's room?" She laughed softly. "Oh, Malintzin!"

I blinked at her, sleepy and uncomprehending. Then the absurdity of the situation suddenly dawned on me. So this was the reason behind Ana's venomous glances. She thought Hernán had gone back to me. Instead, the wretch had fooled us both! I forced a nervous chuckle.

Mazatl stopped before a heavily curtained doorway. Uneasily, I turned to her. "I can't go in there and wake him," I protested.

"Shhh! By the four hundred rabbits, you won't have to." She gave me a disgusted look. Then she drew out a handful of pebbles from a drawstring bag around her neck. Moving a little distance down the hall, with me beside her, she flung one of the stones at the curtain. It struck the cloth with a soft thud and skittered onto the stone floor. The sound of stirring was heard from inside the room. "He sleeps lightly, Malintzin," Mazatl murmured, flinging a second pebble. Abruptly, the curtain was thrust aside and a tousled Hernán, a blanket twisted around his waist, lunged out into the hallway. The long blade of his sword gleamed in the darkness.

I tried to lessen his chagrin and mine by getting at once to the business at hand. "There's word from Ixtlilxochitl," I whispered.

"All right. Come down here away from this doorway." He avoided my eyes.

Mazatl delivered her message as I translated. "My brother is ready to deliver Cacama to you tomorrow night if you wish."

Hernán caught his breath as she continued.

"He's persuaded Cacama to come to Tepetzinco for a conference to make final plans for the attack on Tenochtitlan. Tepetzinco is right on the lake. Soemone could seize Cacama and bring him here by canoe. It could be done very quietly . . ."

"Then do it," Hernán declared. "Even Moctezuma'd go along with us. He's as worried about Cacama as we are. Do you think he should be told?"

"He has to be told," Mazatl answered. "How would it look if Cacama's own brother were to bring him to you?" She glanced down the hall, the faint light silhouetting her sharp profile. "No, it has to be Moctezuma's men who take him. He can arrange things, and he will."

"Then let's go and wake him." Hernán turned and took two eager strides down the hallway.

"No—" Mazatl stopped him wth her hand on his arm. "Tomorrow's soon enough. There'll be time for him to get his agents to Tepetzinco before nightfall."

"And in return," Hernán guessed, "I'll wager your brother wants the throne of Texcoco."

Mazatl smiled. "Oh yes, except that it's not in your power to give it to him. Cacama's successor will be appointed by the council. Moctezuma still has some influence—he'd never let Ixtlilxochitl be chosen. But we have a younger brother, a boy still, who's here in Tenochtitlan now. He's too young to have many enemies, so the council would probably accept him."

"Then what can I do?" Hernán asked.

"Anything you can to influence Moctezuma in favor of the boy. He's on our side." Mazatl smoothed her hair back at the temples. Her eyes darted like a ferret's from Hernán to me. "I know what you're thinking," she said. "Cacama's my brother, too. You're wondering how I can betray him like this." She wet her lips with a pointed tongue. "Our father, Nezhaupilli, died without naming an heir. When Moctezuma used his power to make Cacama ruler, our family was cut in two. It became necessary to choose one side or the other, and I chose to follow Ixtlilxochitl. When I did, Cacama ceased to be my brother." She stepped back from us, her eyes gleaming like black gems. "I have to take your message back across the lake," she whispered. "If you ever need me, look for me in the women's quarters . . ."

Her voice faded away as she disappeared like some creature of the night. Hernán and I stood in silence until we heard the faint, distant splash of a canoe paddle.

I drew in my breath. He tensed, expecting an attack that did not come.

"Marina *mía*, would it do any good to explain?"

"Why should you?" I said, my mouth set. "I don't own you, Hernán. "I don't even want to know who she is."

"But you'll wonder, won't you?" He looked at his bare feet. "She belongs to one of the men who went with Umbria. When he returns she'll go back to him."

"You didn't have to tell me that," I said. "I'm going to my room and forget where I found you."

"My beautiful Marina!" He pulled me close and I stood stiff and unresponding in the circle of his arms. "Forgive me! I'm a man of flesh and the flesh is weak, but my heart always returns to you. You know that, don't you?"

I drew myself up, locking my gaze with his. "Hernán, when

your body decides to follow your heart, I'll be waiting. You made me promise not to leave you, remember?" Laughing, he lowered his head to kiss me. "No!" I snapped, so fiercely that he straightened again. "I want you to do a foolish woman one favor."

"Name it." He grinned confidently.

"Leave me this one little shred of dignity, Hernán. Don't humiliate me by hopping into my bed on your way to someone else's. When you come back to me, come to stay. Until you're ready to do that, leave me alone."

His arms released me. "*Ay de mí*, but you drive a hard bargain, Marina! You'd ask a bee to gather all his honey from one flower. But very well. I suppose I owe you that much." His brows furrowed in an expression of pain and he shook his head sadly. "If only you knew how much it hurts me to have to talk to you like this."

"You think it only hurts you?" I answered. "*Hasta mañana*, Hernán. We can't afford to be enemies, you and I. Now go back to her." I turned to walk away.

"Marina!" He caught my hand, pulling me back toward him and crushed me against his chest. His lips consumed me, draining away my resistance, shattering the barrier's between us. I felt myself responding as intensely as ever. My pride was crumbling. No! I would not yield to him! By a supreme act of will I tore myself away from him, shoving him backward with both hands. He looked at me, stunned.

"Hernán, what I said . . . I meant every word of it."

He nodded ruefully. "Yes, I believe you did. *Hasta mañana*, Marina *mía*." Whistling softly, he turned and walked back toward the curtained room.

Chapter Sixteen

Tenochtitlan—March 1520

Several royal captives now languished within the lime-washed stone walls of the palace of Axayacatl. Moctezuma continued to occupy his spacious suite, surrounded by servants, wives and concubines, while in another part of the palace the arrogant Cacama raged against his iron shackles and Cuitlahuac paced the confines of his cell like a panther. With Ixtlilxochitl's unobtrusive help, Hernán had managed to round up most of the leaders of the revolt, which, afterward, had died out quickly. The young Cuicuetzcatl, to almost everyone's satisfaction, now ruled Texcoco in Cacama's place.

After a five-week absence, Umbria's party had come back with grains of gold panned from the rivers. A certain mysterious lady had presumably been returned to her master, but Hernán remained at large. I studied the dark-eyed beauty who'd been given to Ordaz and tried not to wonder if she was Hernán's new mistress. The return of the Ordaz expedition to the coast was overdue. There'd been no word from them since that misty morning of their departure, when Juan had gripped my hand so tightly in his. Worry had begun to gnaw at the men's tough crusts with its relentless teeth. A special mass had been said the previous Sunday. I went about with a knot of fear in my throat, not even daring to put my anxiety into words.

Just after prayers on a morning when sunshine poured over the city like liquid gold, a tired messenger came jogging over the causeway with a letter from Ordaz. The company crowded around Hernán, anxious to hear the news. He read silently at first, frowning, making me want to scream with impatience. Finally, he cleared his throat and began to read aloud.

The little party had spent several weeks scouring the coastline, the letter reported, but had yet to find a promising harbor. They had mapped the area, however, and established some trade with the natives. ". . . I regret, *señor*, that we have no more encouraging news than this," Ordaz concluded, "but at least, thanks to God, the Indians are friendly and all of us are safe and well."

I turned away to hide the tears of relief in my eyes.

Later, after the morning's audience with Moctezuma was over, I found myself alone. Hernán was briefing his captains on the day's orders and, for these few moments, did not need me. The solitude was welcome. Happy for the first time in weeks, I wandered out into a small porch overlooking a garden and sat down on one of the steps. The sun soaked into my skin, warming me to the bone as I drank in the honey-smell of pink and white blossoms. Lazily, I watched two vultures soaring above the lake. Strange, how gastly they were on the ground, yet how elegant in flight. "All of us are safe and well," the Ordaz letter had said. Safe and well. *Salvo y sano* . . . it was like a song.

"So here you are! I've been looking all over the palace for you." Bernal Diaz's voice startled me. "Ay, but it's the kind of day that makes a body want to sit in the sun and dream, isn't it?" He sat down beside me, his brown eyes glinting with merriment. "You're just glowing," he said. "I've never seen you look so happy. I can't imagine why."

I looked down and wiggled my toes, saying nothing, but thinking how glad I was that he knew about Juan and me. It would have been difficult indeed without someone with whom I could share my secret. "You said you'd been looking for me," I ventured. "You must have had a reason."

"I can't keep anything from you, can I?" He chuckled. "The messenger who carried Ordaz's letter brought something else—something for me!" He drew a yellowed paper from the folds of his doublet and crackled it enticingly under my nose.

"Bernal!" I snatched at the paper but he lifted it out of my reach, laughing and shaking his head, his black hair shining in the sun's glare.

"What will you give me if I read it to you?"

I glowered at him. "What will I give you if you don't!"

"You've made your point and I yield, my lady." He grinned as he unfolded the letter and began to read:

19 February 1520

My good friend, Bernal,

Ordaz has granted me the kindness of allowing this letter to be sent to you along with his report to Cortés, and for that I thank him. I hope you won't find it too hard to read. My penmanship was the despair of my teachers at Salamanca, and it's not improved by this rough rock that serves as my writing desk.

We have a comfortable camp. As I look about me, I see Ordaz putting the finishing touches on a map with his quill, and García Holgún mending his shoe. Martín López is counting our remaining trade supplies and the others are busy tending a haunch of venison that's roasting over the fire. Our guides kill birds and monkeys with blowguns and their accuracy is amazing, but I shot the deer myself with our one crossbow.

The Indians are friendly, probably because we have Moctezuma's men with us. Two days ago we passed through a large, fine town. The guides told me it was named Oluta, or something similar. I became interested at once, for we've all heard how Doña Marina was sold into slavery by her own mother, and as I remember she gave Oluta as the name of her native place. We met the present *cacique*, a proud, handsome fellow, but most unpleasant with us, and also his wife and young son. The wife, to whom I paid particular attention, was middle-aged, but something in her big black eyes and the set of her chin spoke to me so strongly of Marina that I was stunned. Since we communicate with the Indians only by sign language, I was unable to question her, but I went away convinced that I'd seen the wretched woman who'd sold her daughter to the slavers.

Bernal paused in his reading and met my eyes. "What do you think?" he asked me. "Could he have really found your mother?"

My jaw tightened so hard that the muscles ached. "Juan may have found the woman who gave me birth," I said, "but I have no mother. Read the rest, Bernal."

Bernal nodded and continued:

My friend, I ask you as a special favor to look after Doña Marina, as I would want to do if I were there. Cortés has treated her badly in view of all she's done for him. I fear for her in the light of what might lie ahead, and I worry that Cortés, with so many matters at hand, might fail to protect her if danger comes.

"See?" Bernal grinned triumphantly. "I knew he cared for you, the poor devil! . . . Oh, *Santa Maria*, you're not going to cry, are you?"

I bit my lip and shook my head determinedly. Bernal went on with his reading:

> God willing, we should be back in Tenochtitlan within a few weeks, and then I'll be able to keep you awake all night telling you about our adventures—but what am I saying? How could any wild story of mine ever compete with Francisca for your nights?
>
> Take care, Bernal, my friend. We're safer here in the jungle than you are in your palace. I worry about you and our comrades more than I can say. The page is nearly full, so I'll make an end of this. Give my warmest greetings to all.
>
> Juan Jaramillo

Bernal and I sat in the sun. I watched the two vultures and he watched me. "I thought you might like to have the letter," he said at last, handing me the paper. I took it and smiled my thanks. "It's a pity you can't read," he said.

I studied the lines of bold, sprawling script that contained Juan's thoughts. "I'll learn," I exclaimed. "Why not? A year ago I'd never heard a word of your language and now I speak it as if I'd spoken it from birth. I'd ask you to teach me, Bernal, but you save most of your spare time for your Francisca, don't you?"

He smiled at my reasoning. "You're right," he said. "But what about Aguilar? He's less than a soldier, less than a priest, and I've yet to see him lower his eyes below the level of a woman's neck. Surely he'd be willing . . . Oho! Your eyes are dancing the *zarabande*! If Juan could see you now, he'd be lost!"

I walked at Hernán's shoulder, dressed in a long *huipilli* covered with red, yellow and orange feathers. "You look like a flame," he whispered to me as the procession was forming outside Moctezuma's audience chamber. I forced a smile.

Only yesterday he'd openly taken another of Moctezuma's daughters, a pretty girl christened Doña Inés.

"This place is a rabbit warren," Aguilar had grumbled when I'd come to him for my reading lesson the previous evening. "It wouldn't surprise me if Our Lord were to rain fire down on the lot of us. I've never seen so many women in a camp of good soldiers."

"At least Hernán's made an effort to keep order." I defended him just as I'd resolved to do. "He's had the number of slaves restricted to one for each man."

"Well and good," snorted Aguilar, whose only female companion was the greyhound Esmeralda. "Now if only Cortés would follow his own orders . . . Ay! I can see that I've offended you, little sister. A thousand pardons, but your loyalty to the man astounds me."

"Here, look at my letters," I'd said not wishing to pursue the subject. "I've been practicing them every morning before prayers. Aren't they getting better?"

My mind snapped back to the present as I heard the gruff tones of Valásquez de León behind me, blended with Ávila's near-falsetto.

"Do you think Moctezuma will give us any trouble?"

"That beaten whelp? You're joking. But I'm more worried about some of his *caciques*. What will those proud devils do when he surrenders his authority to Cortés and the king?"

"What can they do? If they try anything we'll butcher the lot of them. Cortés should have done this a month ago."

"By the saints, what an occasion! Pity Sandoval's not here to see it!"

I too missed the earnest young Sandoval, who'd been sent back to command Villa Rica after one Alonzo Grado, who'd succeeded Escalante as *alcalde*, had turned out to be a strutting incompetent. Sandoval's simple forthrightness had always provided a welcome contrast to the swaggering of the other captains.

Hernán glanced back at the line behind us. "Olid! Alvarado! Is everyone here? Ready, Tapia? Let's get on with it."

Two stout slaves held aside the embroidered curtain as we entered the large room, which was filled with chiefs from all the major towns and provinces in the valley. They stood proudly, their feet bare and their rich clothing covered by rough cloaks, as was proper in the presence of their *uei tlatoani*.

With my eyes darting about under lowered lashes, I picked out a number of leaders whom I recognized. Young Cuicuetzcatl was there, representing Texcoco. The falcon-faced Cuitlahuac, still a prisoner, stood beside his brother Moctezuma. Next to him I saw a handsome youth whom I guessed to be his nephew, Cuauhtemoc, son of the lord of Tlatelolco. Cacama was conspicuous by his absence, but several of the chiefs who'd been arrested along with him had sworn allegiance to our side and been released. Ixtlilxochitl stood at the back of the room, his sharp countenance a carefully arranged mask of impassivity. Many of the faces were unfamiliar—proud young faces, faces creased with age, faces with high foreheads and haughty noses, faces adorned with gold earrings and with jade lip and ear plugs.

Moctezuma stood on a raised platform, wearing the same sumptuous green-plumed headpiece he'd worn on the day the white gods first marched over the causeway. Orteguilla, his young face showing strain, sat at the emperor's feet.

We filed into our places. At Hernán's ear, I whispered the meaning of Moctezuma's words as he addressed his assembled vassals.

First of all, the *uei tlatoani* spoke of his intense love for all the peoples of his empire, a traditional love that the Aztec rulers had always held for their subjects. "To serve my people and my gods," he declared, "this has always been my duty and my joy. Now I find that it is the will of the gods that I make a great personal sacrifice."

He went on to relate the legend of Quetzalcoatl, the god of the morning star, and his promise to return one day, with others of his race, to claim this land as his kingdom. Here the eyes of a number of the chiefs shifted cautiously to Hernán and his captains, whom some of them were seeing for the first time. They were not unprepared for their lord's announcement. He'd informed them of the problems at hand in a private gathering held the previous day and witnessed only by Orteguilla, but the most stout-hearted of them could not help but be moved by the *uei tlatoani's* plight.

"Hence I pray," Moctezuma concluded, his singsong voice now a hoarse monotone, "that as you have hitherto held and obeyed me as your lord, so you will henceforth hold and obey the great King Carlos for he is your legitimate ruler, and in his place accept this captain of his. All the tribute and service you have given to me, you must now give to him, for I also have to contribute and serve with all that he may require. In doing this you will fulfill not only your duty, but give me great pleasure."

The last words were almost lost in the sobs that his humiliated soul could no longer stifle, and for long moments these sobs, blended with those of the young Orteguilla were the only sounds in the great hall.

The forge of Lares, the smith, glowed in the darkness of the little courtyard as the hissing bellows fanned the flames to red-hot intensity. Nearby lay a waist-high mound of golden trinkets, waiting to be melted down into gold bars bearing the royal seal of Spain. I picked up the figure of a hummingbird whose wings scarcely spanned my palm. Its jewel eyes had been pried out, but it was still beautiful. Every tiny gold feather had been etched in exquisite detail by some patient craftsman. Before the night was over, the delicate form would be blended with a hundred others into a massive golden lump.

"In my wildest dreams I couldn't have imagined the amount of gold that's passed through these hands in the past week," the smith exclaimed. "Faith, I've lost count!"

"Well, I'll wager Cortés hasn't," grunted Trujillo, a coarse, common seaman who squatted beside the fire, picking his teeth with his fingernail.

"The *huevos* of that bastard—taking his fifth of the treasure off the top of the heap just like the king himself. Cortés's own royal fifth! And the *hijo de puta*'s living like a sultan—the pick of the women, the pick of the gold!"

"Quite, you fool," the smith hissed, having noticed me standing nearby. "You're the one with the nerve. Since that incident of your peeing against Moctezuma's wall while you were on guard duty, I'm almost ashamed to be seen with you."

"Well," Trujillo said, chuckling, "his highness gave me a fine piece of gold when he sent young Orteguilla to ask me to desist."

"And so you did it again. *Por Diós!*" the smith groaned. "He didn't give you another gold piece, did he?"

"No, but I don't have to guard the dog anymore, and that's almost as good!" Trujillo roared with laughter rocking on his heels.

"You're an idiot," exclaimed Fernando Estrada, a well-dressed young man who was warming his hands beside the fire. "Don't you know that Pedro López was flogged for speaking no worse of the emperor than you just did?" He paused to brush a fleck of soot from his sleeve. "Besides, I hear that Cortés is going to relinquish his fifth of the booty and take only his share as *capitán-general.*"

"Fat difference it makes." Trujillo spat into the fire. "By the time the gold's parceled out to pay the expenses of this cursed venture, along with extra shares for the horsemen, arquebusiers and crossbowmen, there'll be nothing left for us poor *chinches* at the bottom of the ladder."

"I suppose you're right," Estrada said with a sigh. "I should have stayed in Havana with my wife and lived like a gentleman."

"You have a wife?" The smith was surprised.

"Oh, indeed I do. María's her name and a fine, strapping woman she is. She's a few years older than I am, but what does it matter? She's got plenty of money."

"Aha!" Trujillo exclaimed. "A widow lady, I'll wager."

"That's right. Married to a rich old grandee who wasn't even man enough to give her children. When he died she chose me to fill the empty space in her bed. It hasn't been a bad life. My body's kept her happy and her money's kept me happy. A fair exchange, is it not?"

"I have only one question," Trujillo growled. "What in hell's name are you doing here?"

Estrada scratched at his thatch of straw-colored hair with a slender finger. "Well, it's not easy to explain, but after a time any man who's a man gets tired of living like a leech. Besides, I could see that María's inheritance wasn't going to last forever, the way we were spending it, and she's a real lady. She deserves to live well, bless her. Anyway, I heard of this expedition and persuaded her to let me go and become a rich man in my own right. She bade me farewell with many tears and kisses, and here I am. *Ay de mí*, what I wouldn't give to be in her big, soft, white bed this minute!"

I wandered back to the glittering heap of gold, and fingered the little figure of a butterfly. The filigreed wings were as thin as paper.

"You look troubled, my daughter." Padre Olmedo, out for an evening stroll had come into the courtyard to stand beside me. I welcomed him with a smile.

"Every time I hear your voice I think of my own father," I

said to him. "But I've told you that before, haven't I, Padre?"

"More than once. What are you thinking, standing here scowling at all this gold?"

"Only how lovely these things are. It seems such a shame to destroy them." I stroked the wings of the little butterfly.

"You're right, but you mustn't think of it that way," the priest said. "Who knows how many idols we're melting out of existence? It's been a long time since I've seen you at confession, *hija mía*,"

I looked at my hands. How could I find words to tell this man, God's personal representative, of the turmoil in my soul?

"Come and walk with me," he said. So I walked with the thin priest, matching my steps to his, through the long palace corridors and out into another garden, where at last I found my voice.

"You'll be angry if I tell you what's troubling me, Padre."

"Nonsense. It's a priest's duty to understand."

"I groped for a way to begin. "Since I was the first to accept the faith, doesn't it stand to reason that I should be one of the strongest?" I whispered.

"And aren't you, child?"

I shook my head miserably. "Sometimes I think Nacontoc was right in refusing to be baptized until he understood your teachings."

Padre Olmedo's brow wrinkled with concern. "Is it that you don't believe?"

"I believe with all my heart," I said quickly.

"Then—?" He waited expectantly, fingering his brass crucifix.

"How can I say it? You tell me about the wonderful things that Jesus taught us—love, unselfishness, purity . . ." I clenched my hands together into a tight ball. "Then I look around me. Not only at others, but at myself! I'm not a true Christian, Padre. I see so few real Christians here. Oh, you, of course, and Aguilar perhaps, but as for the rest of us . . ." I turned toward him. "Sometimes I think it's easier to feed hearts to Huitzilopochtli than it is to be a good Christian."

"Oh, you're right." The priest rubbed the top of his shorn head. "If I told you that I knew the answers to all of life's mysteries, I'd be either a liar or a fool. But I'll try and explain a few things to you. Look, do you see the mountain?" He stretched his arm and I followed his pointing finger with my eyes to the silvery summit of Popocatepetl, floating like a cloud in the distance. "Imagine if you can, Doña Marina, that the top of that mountain represents the ideal of love and purity of which Christ spoke. Tell me now, is it easy for anyone to climb to the peak?"

"Certainly not. Ordaz was almost killed."

Padre Olmedo gave an impatient little chuckle. "You needn't be so literal, child. We're not really talking about the peak you can see with your eyes."

"Of course not. Forgive me, Padre." I felt a little foolish. "Is it possible for anyone to climb your peak?"

"Only one man sits at its pinnacle," he answered, "and that's Our Lord Himself. As for the rest of us, we're only climbers. Some are high on the mountain, even to the point of touching the white snow, but most of us are still struggling up the lower slopes, falling back, finding our way again. The thing that matters is that all the climbers on the mountain, all those who look toward the peak and strive to reach it, are followers of Christ."

"That was beautifully said, Padre," I murmured affectionately. "But I must be climbing up a rockslide. I try to be a good Christian, but so many things interfere."

"What sort of things, *hija*?"

"Things that I know are sins. You know that I've killed a man—at least I began the killing."

"I know. You did it in your own defense. No one would call that a sin."

"There's more." I twisted my hands. "I hear you speak time after time of forgiveness. Padre, there are . . . people I can never forgive. My mother, my stepfather, the old priest who sacrificed my father—he's here in Tenochtitlan. I've seen him and I won't be satisfied till he's dead. So how can I call myself a Christian?" I exclaimed angrily.

"Patience, daughter." Padre Olmedo shook his head sadly. "Keep climbing the mountain and one day you'll find that the chains of bitterness have fallen from your soul. When that day comes, then you'll know the meaning of true joy."

"I wish it were as simple as you make it sound."

"Now . . ." He cocked his head like a wise old wolf and looked at me with eyes that seemed to peer into the roots of my conscience. "Isn't there anything else troubling you?"

With a sigh, I divested myself of the last of my burdens. "I try to be faithful to Hernán, as I would be if I were his proper wife," I whispered. "It isn't easy when he shames me with other women, but maybe I deserve it. I'm not blameless myself."

Padre Olmedo gazed at me questioningly, as if he were afraid that a word from him might frighten me into silence.

"I love another man," I said brokenly, and as soon as the words had spilled out I knew they were true. "It began even before Hernán took Doña Ana." My heart began to pound. "Padre, must I tell you who he is? Please don't ask me to!"

"You don't need to tell me," he said gently. "The morning the Ordaz party left for the coast I was there to bless them, remember? It would have taken a blind man to miss the look in your eyes when I touched his forehead with holy water. I've guessed correctly, haven't I?"

I clasped my hands together and said nothing. My face felt hot.

"A good man, Jaramillo," the padre said musingly. "A decent man. Incapable of dishonor, if I know him as well as I think I do." He gazed quietly at the top of a flowering tree. "It's no sin to be tempted, daughter. Our Lord himself suffered forty days of temptation in the wilderness of Judea, but he resisted and triumphed. So must you." He raised his eyebrows. "By my faith, you haven't—?"

"No, I swear it, Padre. We've done nothing!"

"God willing, Jaramillo and his comrades will be returning soon. Then you'll have to take care not to open the door to temptation. You mustn't allow yourself, or him, to be placed within reach of the Evil One. Do you understand?"

"Yes, Padre."

"And don't judge Hernán Cortés too harshly." Padre Olmedo had begun to walk once more. "His is the responsibility for delivering an entire nation into the hands of Our Lord. You know as well as I do the weight of the burden he carries."

"That's what I keep trying to remember," I said.

"I spoke with him just this morning. He's decided that the time has come to strike a blow against idolatry. He plans to have the images taken out of the temple in the square. Pray for him, *hija*. He's going to need it."

The steps of the towering pyramid were stained with blood. I shivered with apprehension as my thin sandals brushed them. Our party consisted of twelve men—thirteen souls, counting myself. Was it faith or idiocy that drove Hernán toward the twin temples above us?

"What if the priests scream for help?" I whispered to him.

"Ávila has his orders," Hernán said, jerking his head in the direction of the palace where his captain waited just inside the walls with reinforcements. "But I want to surprise the bloody devils. Marching up these steps with an army would only draw a crowd."

"I'll be glad when this business is over," Andrés de Tapia muttered, panting with the effort of pulling his stocky frame up the steep, narrow steps. "But it's high time we brought those cursed idols down."

You can tell your grandchildren about it some day!" Bernal Diaz flashed a reckless grin as the painted roofs of the temples of Huitzilopochtli and Tlaloc loomed into sight above us. Acting on my advice, Hernán had chosen midafternoon for his assault on the pyramid, when the high-ranking priests would most likely be absent.

Only a handful of startled novices met us at the summit. The drawing of a few swords was enough to frighten them into horrified silence as Hernán, leaving two sentinels outside, strode boldly into the *teocalli* where the statue of Huitzilopochtli was housed. The idol itself was hidden from sight by a heavy curtain fringed with pellets of gold.

"Pull it aside."

Bernal and Olid tugged at the curtain but it resisted their efforts.

"The devil with it! Cut the cursed thing open!" Hernán roared. Swords flashed and the curtain was ripped asunder. Hernán Cortés, white with indignation, stood face to face with Huitzilopochtli. The idol was spattered with fresh blood, a clear violation of Padre Olmedo's edict against human sacrifice.

"One more step and you die!" croaked an ominous voice. There at the foot of the idol, the front of his robe soaked with red blood, old Cozcaquauhtli crouched like a cornered owl, spitting his defiance at us.

"Get out of the way, old man," Olid snapped, giving the priest a whack with the flat of his sword that sent him sprawling. He struggled back onto his spindly legs again, but rough hands dragged him into a corner and held him there as he shrieked in helpless rage.

I had never seen Hernán so pale. The vein in his forehead was purple and throbbing violently as he cried out in a strange, hoarse voice, "Oh God! Why dost thou permit the devil to be thus honored in this land?" He whirled around to face the old priest. "This den of filth is to be cleaned, these foul images thrown out! Before this day ends, the cross will stand on this spot!" He jabbed his arm toward the altar. Cozcaquauhtli yowled his fury at my translation.

Huitzilopochtli, a grotesque lump of twisted forms with a face like a bear's, looked down impassively on the scene below. The god stood as tall as the ceiling of the *teocalli* and was made of a cement that had been mixed, supposedly for strength, with the blood of sacrificed children.

"Touch our god and you'll pay with your soul!" the old priest screamed.

"His words only goaded Hernán to new heights of anger. Seizing a heavy metal rod used for tending the fires, he sprang with almost superhuman strength and, with a mighty swing of the rod, knocked the golden mask from the face of Huitzilopochtli. It fell to the floor with a hollow clatter. The old priest began to wail hysterically.

One of the sentinels hurried in from outside. "Half the town's down there in the square!" he reported breathlessly. "They've gotten wind of something."

"We're trapped up here like cats in a tree," Olid said with a curse.

I put my hand on Hernán's arm. "Send for Moctezuma," I urged him.

He swept his arm in the direction of the faceless god. "Tear it down," he croaked. "Break it to pieces and the other one as well!"

"Don't be a fool!" Olid exploded. "We'll have the whole city on our necks!"

"Hernán, for the love of God," I pleaded. "Get Moctezuma up here or we'll never leave this place alive."

He gave me a sidelong glance with eyes that were slightly glazed. "So even you oppose me, Marina *mía*," he said sadly. "All right. Send a runner for Moctezuma." Then he turned back to the battered idol and the vigor returned to his voice and stance. "But I'm not leaving till this filthy thing's broken into a thousand pieces."

We waited, nerves stretched to excruciating tautness as the emperor, under heavy guard, made his way across the crowded square and up the steps. I watched him as he entered the *teocalli* and stood gaping in mute anguish at what he saw.

"Tell him, Marina," Hernán snapped, "that we're going to tear this demon apart with our own hands."

"Malintzin!" Moctezuma's spectral whisper floated out of the depths of his dismay. "Wait. Let me talk to the priests.

Surely we can . . . make some arrangement that will please you."

Hernán, to my relief, nodded. For a few moments the emperor exchanged frantic whispers with his priests in a corner of the *teocalli*. When Moctezuma came forward again, his face was etched with grief.

"We'll give you the temple, Malintzin," he said. "But only if you'll let us take down the gods with our own hands and agree never to touch them again."

I felt the tension ease out of Hernán as I translated. "Agreed," he said cautiously. "But it's got to begin at once—and no tricks. Get on with it."

"This is a sacred process, Malintzin." Moctezuma's soft brown eyes were wet. "I beg you, let us do it . . . lovingly. Take your men and leave." He cringed at the gathering storm in Hernán's scowl. "My word as a man and an emperor, Malintzin. The gods will be moved by the time the sun goes to sleep."

We posted guards at the bottom of the pyramid and marched back across the square in triumph, only to stop and stare at the scruffy figure waiting for us on the front steps.

"*Hola!* It's Ordaz! He's back!"

"Well, praise the saints! Ordaz, you dirty dog!"

Ordaz's beard was unkempt, his armor rusty, but he was grinning jubilantly. Hernán ran forward to embrace him. My own heart had begun to pound wildly with the joy of their sudden return. "What about your men?" Hernán asked eagerly.

"Fine, all except Jaramillo," Ordaz answered. I caught my breath in alarm as Ordaz went on, his explanation slowed by his stammer. "Snakebite. Right after I wrote to you. He almost died. That's what took us so long. The fool kept begging us to leave him, but we brought him back. He's going to be all right, thanks to God."

I felt suddenly weightless. "Bernal, isn't it . . . ?" I turned toward the spot where the tall soldier had been standing behind me, but he'd already dashed into the palace.

I saw Bernal in the hallway a few minutes later. He was beaming.

"You've seen him?" I whispered anxiously. "How is he?"

"Skinny," he said, eyes twinkling. "Pity you're so determined not to get involved with him. Otherwise I'd tell you where he is."

"Bernal," I muttered.

"Oh no you don't! If you think Bernal Diaz del Castillo is going to have any part of setting your feet on the road to sin—"

"Damn it, Bernal," I exploded. "I only want to see him."

"Ay! Curses from such a lady! What you need is some prayerful contemplation, some time to meditate on the merits of gentler language. I know just the place for you." He winked solemnly. "The garden behind the aviary—it's always quiet this time of day."

His rollicking laughter followed me down the hallway.

"Walk," I commanded my feet, but they wouldn't listen. They flew, carrying me pell-mell through the long corridors toward the rear of the palace. I passed a dark figure in a doorway: Padre Olmedo. I paid no heed. Even the promise I'd made him could not slow my flight.

Juan was standing in the garden, sunburned, tousle-haired and terribly thin, wearing a mud-stained vest of the quilted cotton the Aztecs used for armor. One leg was bandaged. Without a word, I ran into his arms.

He smelled wonderfully of sweat and salt water and he held me tightly against his chest, whispering my name over and over.

"Marina, *querida mía*, you shouldn't have come. I shouldn't have wanted you to—"

"Hush. Nothing could have kept me away." I buried my face in the deep opening of his shirt, tasting his salty skin with the tip of my tongue. "Ordaz told us about the snake. Juan, I'd have died if you hadn't come back . . ." I ran my hand up his arm and noticed then that the black sash was missing.

"It's gone," he said. "I was out of my head for a week, they told me, and while I was lying there I fancied that my Teresita, my poor little wife, came to me. She leaned down and kissed me and then she untied the sash and took it away. When I came to my senses it was *really* gone." He kissed the spot where my hairline came to a peak in the center of my forehead and I wondered how I could be so base as to be jealous of a dead woman. Juan gave a little laugh. "I was pretty shaken by the whole thing until I found out that one of our Indians had taken the sash. He thought it was magic. I had an extra one in my gear, so I took it out and gave that one to him as well." He raised my chin with one hand. "It was time, *querida*."

With a little moan of joy I opened my lips to meet his. He crushed me close. He was mine and I, for as long as life would allow, was totally his. I pressed the length of my body against him, almost choking with happiness as he kissed me—kissed me until his chest heaved with emotion, until the deepest parts of me throbbed with longing.

"Juan, yes . . ." I whispered wildly.

There was a spot in a corner of the garden where willows hung so low over the grass that they formed a little cavern. Weak as he must have been, Juan lifted me in his arms and strode toward it. I clung to him dreamily. He would take me here in the soft, cool shade of Moctezuma's garden, his love wiping out the memory of every other man who'd ever touched me.

Suddenly he stopped in mid-stride, cursed under his breath and gently lowered my feet to the grass again. "Oh, Marina, love, we can't do this," he murmured in an anguished voice.

As he held me, softly now, the world faded back to its real colors. I remembered Hernán and my promise to Padre Olmedo. "Why does it have to be this way?" I said bitterly.

"We can't answer that." He pressed his cheek against my hair. "But I won't hurt you. I won't toss you into the hell of pain and guilt that's waiting for us if we weaken. I want you, Marina—so much I can hardly stand it—but it's got to be the right way."

I reached up and traced the fine scar that ran down his temple toward his shaggy blond beard—the scar that Olid had given him the same day that I'd awakened from the nightmare of slaughter in Cholula to find Juan at my side. Juan would always blame the death of his wife on his own impetuosity, and now he'd steeled himself against another mistake. If I pushed him into making love to me, and if the consequences proved to be tragic, he'd be devastated by guilt. The padre was right. If I loved Juan, I'd spare him that torment.

He mistook my silence for dissent. "What if I got you with child, *querida*?" he said. "What then?"

Blessed Lady, I'd be the happiest woman alive! I thought. But I didn't say it; it would only have made things worse. "What can we do, Juan?"

"I could ask Cortés for you. I'm not afraid."

"It wouldn't do any good. He wouldn't let me go and he'd resent you for asking. Maybe someday, but not now."

He sighed miserably. "Then all this is leading to just one answer, Marina."

"I know," I said slowly. "The same as before. Nothing." I stepped back a little. How it hurt to say it! "Juan, the palace is full of beautiful girls. Take one of them and forget me."

"Damn it, it's not that simple, Marina. Not for me, at least." He pulled me gently back toward him. "I'm a weak man, *querida*—not strong enough to put you out of my mind and not strong enough to tell the whole world to go to hell and take you here and now. What can I do?" He looked at me hopelessly. "Things were easier before you knew."

"Before I knew, I was only half alive!" My arms slipped around him again. He was so thin that I could have counted his ribs. "I wouldn't go back. Not for anything. I love you, Juan."

He held me fiercely, whispering curses at the fate that made all this so painful.

"I can't live without seeing you," I said. "Can't we . . . talk sometimes at least—like we always have? Like friends? It's better than nothing."

"It won't be easy." He lifted my hand and pressed the palm to his lips. "I'll try, if that's what you want." He forced a little grin. "But knowing the way I feel when I'm with you, we'd better find ourselves a good duenna."

"Who?" The idea made me smile.

"Oh . . ." His arms released me. "How about Bernal?"

"Bernal!" I sputtered in mock indignation. "A fine duenna he'd be! Do you know what he—?"

"I know. Why do you think I thought of him?" Juan's eyes failed to join in his laughter. "Come on, my friend." He took my hand and led me toward the palace. "Let's go find him before my resolve gives out."

Still holding hands, we walked back through the garden, Juan pacing determinedly and I nearly trotting to keep up with him. We were doing well until we reached the palace entrance, where paused for a moment and our eyes met.

"Oh, hell," he muttered, catching me in his arms again and holding me tightly. I felt the tears squeezing out from between my eyelashes as I listened to his heartbeat and wished fervently that we could stop the movement of time.

"You've got to go back inside," he whispered. "Leave me here, *querida*." He let me go and stepped back. "Please, love."

I didn't have the strength to restrain myself to a walk. I ran.

* * *

Tenochtitlan—April 1520

The dry season had lingered, staying on fearfully late. All around the lake, the hills gleamed like brittle gold under a sky of blazing turquoise. The brown dust of the *milpas* covered the withering corn like a powdery blanket. In the city there were growing whispers of famine.

By now the cross and the Virgin had been established atop the pyramid where Tlaloc and Huitzilopochtli had held their grim court, and the shrine had been washed clean and guarded against mischief. Surely, the people murmured, this drought was Tlaloc's own revenge. In his new temple, the god stubbornly ignored their tears and prayers, their secret sacrifices. Even so, it came as a surprise when a delegation of nobles and priests came to us with a challenge to ask our God for rain.

I perched on the edge of the big, map-strewn table after they'd gone, contemplating Hernán as he leaned back in his chair and twirled the stem of his silver goblet in one hand. His eyes were far away but the vein at his temple was twitching subtly. Padre Olmedo shuffled the maps and toyed with his crucifix. It was a little like waiting for a volcano to erupt.

"Elijah!" The eruption came in the form of a breathy whisper. "Remember?" Hernán whirled in his chair. "Elijah and the priests of Baal! By my conscience! Tell Marina about it, Padre."

So the priest related the story of the fiery prophet, the drought and the challenge: how the two altars were prepared with sacrificed animals and how the wicked priests of Baal spent the entire day crying to their idol. "They even cut their arms and legs to let their blood flow onto the sacrifice. Doesn't that sound familiar, child? They tore their robes and yanked out their hair—all for nothing." The good padre paused for effect, his plain face shining. "Then Elijah, that man of faith, had his own sacrifice soaked with water. He cried to the Lord and, lo, the altar was covered with sacred flames . . ."

"And the rain?" I was awed.

"It came that very evening. In torrents."

Hernán's eyes gleamed. "Why not here!" he exclaimed. "Why shouldn't God send us another miracle?"

"You'd be so bold as to try God?" Padre Olmedo's face wore a look of stunned skepticism.

"Not *try* him, only *ask* him. Think of it—a special mass atop the pyramid, where the whole city can see it." He thumped the table for emphasis. "It's got to rain sooner or later. Maybe our timing's inspired."

The priest sighed. "My son, I'm no Elijah. I'm only poor Bartolome de Olmedo and every week I have to do penance for my worldly thoughts. Don't expect fire from heaven for my prayers." He shrugged. "But a special mass? Yes, that's quite within the range of my humble abilities."

So here we were, trooping back down the steps of the pyramid after an especially showy mass attended by most of the little company of Spaniards, dressed in our best and carrying flowers to heap upon the small altar. Padre Olmedo had been in exceptionally fine voice. As the padre chanted the words of the mass, I'd glanced at Hernán kneeling beside me, elegant in the same simple doublet of gray wool he'd been wearing the first time I saw him. Although most of his captains were weighted down with gold, his only ornament was a medallion of the Virgin that hung from a slender chain around his neck. His beautifully chiseled hands had clutched it fervently during the prayers. Raising cautious eyes to his face, I'd been stunned by the intensity of his expression. To me this particular mass was little more than a show, a display staged to impress the townspeople, but I could see that to Hernán it was much more. His eyes were closed so tightly that they creased at the corners. His lips moved slightly as he followed the padre's words, and tiny beads of sweat stood out on his pale forehead. I could almost feel the tension in his body beside me. My heart flooded with wonder and a strange tenderness for this man, this demonic saint, this angelic sinner, who had made me his tool and possession.

As we came out of the dimly lit temple into the glaring sunlight I walked beside him. Doña Ana and Doña Inés had remained in the palace with their father. Juan, still weak from his ordeal, was absent as well. Later, when Hernán could spare me, I would go to him and we would talk, sitting carefully apart, avoiding any intimacy of word or touch, yet savoring the sweetness of the pain that shot through our souls each time our eyes met.

"Marina!" I caught Hernán's hoarse whisper beside me. "Look, there above the mountains. It's . . . a cloud!"

"It . . ." I shaded my eyes with my hand. "It is—but it's so small!"

"Small, and, *Madre de Diós*, the shape of a man's hand!"

"Look! It's growing!"

"I can't believe it! Feel the wind!"

By the time the company had reached the bottom of the steep stone steps, the sky was boiling with black clouds. Lightning and thunder split the heavens and echoed from horizon to horizon as, like a celestial bucket of water overturned upon the earth, the rain came down in sheets, washing away the dust, flowing from the rooftops in torrents, drenching the multitudes who filled the square. They pressed backward to make a path for us as we made our way back to the palace in the downpour.

"See," I heard an Aztec near me exclaim, "Tlaloc never fails us!"

"Glory to God!" boomed a Spanish voice somewhere behind me.

"Praise to Tlaloc!" echoed the murmuring crowd. Now I knew why Elijah had asked for flames on his sacrifice.

I looked up at Hernán through a curtain of water. The rain was running in rivulets down his hair and beard and dripping off his heavy brows as he stared at the sky. Suddenly he looked down at me as if I'd touched him. I jerked my gaze away, but too late. He had caught the intensity of my expression.

"By my conscience, but it's a hard bargain you've driven with me, you wench. Even hard for you sometimes, I'll wager." Then he threw back his head and laughed, laughed at the rain, at the gods and at me.

Chapter Seventeen

Tenochtitlan—April 1520

"What could the royal wretch want at this hour?" Hernán grumbled as he hurried toward Moctezuma's chamber, flanked by Olid and myself. "Faith, I hope it's worth interrupting dinner."

I looked at him, concerned. Ordinarily, Hernán would have flogged any of his men for speaking so disparagingly of the emperor, but the strain of the past weeks was beginning to tell on his nerves and everyone else's. The city seethed with the hostility of citizens who'd seen their ruler captured and humiliated, their gods desecrated and deposed. Unrest was growing with each day. How long had it been—two weeks, perhaps—since Moctezuma had summoned us to announce in his most imperious manner that his subjects were massing to attack and kill the hated Castilians to the last man?

"But I love you, Malintzin." The *uei tlatoani's* voice had mellowed.

"I've given you my daughters and you've honored me by filling their bellies with children. That makes you my son." He cast a melancholy look at Doña Ana and Doña Inés, who lounged at one end of the hall. By now both of them were pregnant. "My poor little flowers . . . Do you think I'd wish your death on them, Malintzin?" He'd turned back toward us, once more the haughty ruler. "Take your men, take your Tlaxcalans—we've grown sick of feeding them. Take your horses, your weapons, all the treasure you can carry. I can promise you safe conduct back to the sea if you'll give me your word to leave this land."

"Without ships?" Hernán was confident that the emperor was bluffing. "You expect us to swim away like fish, or fly through the air like birds?"

"I'll help you build some." Moctezuma's eyes pleaded with us. He'd have given anything to restore things to what they'd been before the white men came. "I'll give you the timber, the workmen, protection for your builders. But you'll have to hurry. I can't hold my people off forever. Not with the way young Cuauhtemoc's been stirring them up."

So Hernán had summoned his chief carpenter and shipbuilder, the stout Martín López, and sent him, along with an Aztec guard, back to Villa Rica with instructions to delay the completion of the ships as long as possible.

Now, once more, we'd received an urgent summons from the emperor. Nerves stretched to the snapping point, we tramped down the hall to the royal chamber. Ávila, Lugo and Bernal Diaz fell into step behind us as we entered.

Moctezuma's face wore a rare smile. In his hand he held a roll of *amatl* paper. His slender fingers plucked uneasily at one corner of it. "I have good news for you, Malintzin. It seems you won't have to finish your ships after all. You can leave at once."

We stared at him, alarmed, as he unrolled the paper. "A runner from the coast just brought this to me. Look! Your friends have come in their ships, just in time to take you away with them."

We crowded around the paper for a look. Yes, there on the paper was a drawing of a ship with eleven little circles beside it. Eleven ships. We studied the complicated drawing, counting figures of men, horses. "They're from Spain, I'll wager," Ávila said, grinning broadly. "I knew Montejo and Puertocarrero wouldn't fail us!"

"Praise the saints, they'll double our force. Triple it, maybe," Olid exclaimed. His ugly face, with its heavy, scarred features and split lip, was flushed with excitement.

Hernán, however, stood like an island of gloom in the midst of the jubilation. I touched his arm. "What is it?"

He gave an impatient huff. "If the ships are from His Majesty, all well and good," he said. "But what if they're from Cuba? That fat old dog, Velásquez, might have sniffed out our plans. What if he's sent an army to take it all away from us, eh, lads?"

Their faces sagged. Olid muttered an obscenity. "We'd better find out fast!"

Hernán shrugged. "We'll know soon enough. We're sure to get word from Sandoval. If we don't hear within a few days, I'll send someone to find out."

"What should I tell Moctezuma?" I asked him.

"The truth. We can't make a move till we're sure the men

on those ships are our friends. By the time we know for sure, we'll have found some other excuse to stay, never fear."

"Curse it all, I should have known." Hernán thumped a heavy fist against the tabletop. "How could I even have dared hope they wouldn't be from Cuba?"

Messages had come, not one but two: one from Sandoval in Villa Rica, and another from Velásquez de León, who'd been gathering tribute with a small force in a nearby province. The news was all bad. The ship carrying Alonzo and Montejo back to Spain had stopped in Cuba, against all orders. The expedition that had landed near Villa Rica was indeed sent by Governor Velásquez. Its leader was one Panfilo de Narvaez.

"Narvaez—that strutting donkey! Wouldn't you know!" Hernán shook his head with a bitter chuckle. "He's an old acquaintance, Marina *mía*."

"And I'm guessing he's not a friend," I added.

Narvaez's first official act upon setting foot in Mexico had been to send his two notaries to Villa Rica to demand the surrender of the garrison. In reply, Sandoval had had the two notaries trussed up in net hammocks and carried between *tlamemes* back to Hernán in Tenochtitlan. Hernán had welcomed them, restored their ruffled dignity, and was even now wooing them with gold and promises. However, when Narvaez had moved on Villa Rica with his full army, the prudent Sandoval had taken his meager troops and fled to the hills.

From Velásquez de León had come word that Narvaez had taken over Cempoalla as well, intimidating the confused Chicomacatl into supplying him with food and treasure. Narvaez's captains had even taken the brides our captains had been given.

"I wonder which one of them got little Catalina!" Bernal Diaz said with a wink. "By my faith, I hope it was old Panfilo himself." He was careful to make this remark out of Hernán's hearing, but I gave him a warning glance to quiet him as I turned back to Hernán.

Hernán was most deeply wounded by the disobedience of his order not to stop in Cuba. "The fools!" he ranted. "Can't I trust anybody? Alonzo, of all people! And Montejo! Look at the trouble they've caused. Worse, what if Velásquez gets word back to Spain ahead of our ship? He's got an ally there—Bishop Fonseca, who's in charge of His Majesty's affairs in the whole damned West Indies. If Fonseca gets wind of all this before we can get to the king . . ." He put his fist to his forehead.

"Alonzo wouldn't betray you on purpose." I tried to soothe him. Only I knew the depth of his disappointment. "Montejo—he had land in Cuba and was Velásquez's man to begin with. And the crew could have wanted to see their families. How could Alonzo have stopped them alone?"

"It doesn't make much difference now, Marina," he said glumly. "The damage is done. Guilty or not, you know what Alonzo is to me. I'll never feel anything toward him but love. But, curse it all, why couldn't they have obeyed one simple order?" He sat with his head in his hands, brooding. I straightened the maps on the table and fussed with the hangings on the walls.

"Oh, what the devil." He raised his head and suddenly grinned at me. "We can still save it, can't we, girl? Just wait! Poor old Velásquez might be surprised to find he's dropped another army right in my lap."

May 1520

Moctezuma had been puzzled at first by Hernán's hesitancy to join his comrades on the coast, until I explained to him that the newcomers were brigands, no better than outlaws: ". . . As inferior to my master and his men as the Otomi are to the Aztecs," I'd added with a touch of honey in my voice, and he'd understood at once.

Hoping to win by entreaty before resorting to force, Hernán had sent the most persuasive and inoffensive member of our company, Padre Olmedo, as an envoy to Narvaez and his troops. The priest's departure left an unexpected void in my own existence.

The two notaries, now converted for the most part to our side, were sent back to Narvaez with gifts and conciliatory letters. Reports flowed in from Sandoval's mountain stronghold. Most of the men in the Narvaez company, Sandoval's spies had learned, were loath to fight against their own countrymen. It was only Narvaez himself who was determined to bring his rival to defeat and disgrace at any cost. Padre Olmedo's mission had been successful inasmuch as he'd secretly won over a large number of the soldiers and officers, but he'd narrowly escaped arrest at the hands of Narvaez. He was now in the mountains with Sandoval.

"Look at this letter." Hernán laid the creased paper on the table and smoothed it with his fist. "It looks like our friend Panfilo's his own worst enemy—they're flocking from his camp to Sandoval's! Not that I'm surprised. He's got the disposition of an old bull alligator."

"And I hear that when it comes to money his fists are as tight as two clams," Alvarado exclaimed, arranging the three rings on his left hand so that the stones all pointed upward.

"Well, then, maybe if we wait long enough our problem will take care of itself." Olid rubbed his thick black beard with a hairy hand.

"Now that, my good Cristobal, would be asking too much of providence," Hernán said. "We can't wait for the dog to gather his strength and march on us here. The time's got to come when we confront him face to face, and it's got to come soon. He unrolled a crude map on the table and weighted the corners down with an inkwell and an earthen platter. "Sandoval's here, not far from Villa Rica. Velásquez de León's down here," he said, pointing with a blunt-ended finger to an area near the coast. "With enough warning he could be at this point to meet us and march with us on Villa Rica. *Compañeros*, it seems to me that Narvaez is about ready for a comeuppance."

"Ha! I can already feel my good Toledo steel between the scoundrel's ribs!" Alvarado made a few imaginary thrusts with his arm. "Let's march! Tomorrow's none too soon for me."

"But, Pedro, my eager warrior, this march isn't for you." At Alvarado's open disappointment, Hernán continued, "Who else could I trust to keep matters under control here while I'm gone? I can't be in two places at the same time. Moctezuma's even more vital to our mission than Narvaez is. I'll take Aguilar and leave Marina and Orteguilla here to help you, along with . . . what do you think? Would a third of the army be enough?"

"More than enough," Alvarado said, flattered at being entrusted with so great a responsibility. "Take all the men you need. "As long as we've got Moctezuma we'll be safe from the jackals outside."

Hernán nodded approvingly. "I'll leave you the men who still might have thoughts of going over to Narvaez. It won't make your job any easier, but I can't risk taking them back to the coast with me. As for the rest of you—" gravity weighed upon his face and voice—"I'll have no talk of killing. We're marching against our own countrymen—men who, once they've been won to our cause, will swell the ranks of our own army. Every one of their lives is precious to me. We're to win our victory with as little bloodshed as possible. Do you understand?" He paused, sweeping his eyes around the circle of bearded faces. "Good! Then we'll march as soon as we're ready."

Juan Jaramillo orgainzed his gear with a seaman's concern for weight and space. I watched dejectedly as he spread clothing, utensils and weapons out on the floor, assembling them into compact bundles according to size and need. He hummed little snatches of sea songs as he worked with a grim animation that dismayed me.

"I think you *want* to go," I said, pouting.

"I do, in a way." He wiped the rust from a short-bladed knife. "But it's not that I won't miss you, Marina."

"How can you go? You're not even well yet." I sounded as desolate as I felt.

"*Querida*, I'm *too* well." He picked up his boots to inspect them for holes.

"I don't believe it," I argued. "You're still so thin."

He put his boots down on the floor with a thud, turned around and fixed me with a look that was as near to a glare as anything I'd ever seen on his face. "Marina," he said in an exasperated tone, "I'm fine. I'm so damned healthy that I can't even look at you without wanting to drag you under the nearest bush. *That's* why I can't stay. Now please stop looking at me like that and hand me that little bag of chamomile."

I didn't move. With a mutter of hopelessness, he got up and walked over to put his hands on my shoulders. "Can't you see that this isn't working, love?" he said in a gentler voice. "I want you. I'm sick of pretending to be some kind of saint when I'm not."

I parted my lips to speak, but he pressed a finger against them. "No, don't say anything. Just listen to me," he said. "Have you looked around this place, Marina? Have you counted the women? Have you heard them talk, Bernal and the others? The whole palace of Axayacatl is just one big breeding shed, and here I sit with you, day after day, not even trusting myself to hold your hand."

He dropped his hands from my shoulders, turned and paced the length of the room. "Oh, there are plenty of other women. It's not that I haven't had opportunities." He shook his head at the involuntary narrowing of my eyes. "But how could I face you the next day? How could I look into those big black eyes, knowing how hurt you'd be if you found out? No, better to vent my lust in the heat of battle, as they say, than lose my mind in this perfumed prison."

The words stung my pride and I turned on him. "You think you're so good!" I spat out. "You're so proud of your honor! A curse on your honor! All it does is make us both miserable—"

"Don't, Marina." I could sense the pain in his voice, but he didn't try to touch me. "Don't make things any harder than they already are. I can't stay." He crouched down and began to arrange his things on the floor again. "If you're wondering why," he said, "It's because I love you. Now maybe you'd better go before we ruin everything that's good between us."

I glowered at him, too angry to feel anything but the hurt.

"Marina!" he exploded. "What have you learned from seeing the way these *cabrones* treat their women? Do you think I want you passed to me like a platter of meat at a banquet? Listen to me!" His eyes caught mine and held them. "If you come to me, it's got to be for good—not to go back to Cortés or to be handed on to someone else. Until I can have you on that basis, it's best that we stay apart. That's why I have to leave."

He was right. He was always maddeningly, infuriatingly right. But he'd wounded me. I felt resentment bubbling up inside me like hot lava. "So!" I hissed. "You've got to have it all your own way. If you don't get what you want, you just up and leave and whatever stays behind can go to the devil. Well, go then. Just don't expect to find me waiting when you come back!"

I'd drawn blood. I could tell by the look in his eyes. Not wanting to give him a chance to reply, I whirled and stalked out of the room. I didn't even look back to see if he was watching me go.

"If you come to me, it's got to be for good," Juan had told me. I strode angrily down the hall, his words ringing in my ears with haunting familiarity. Then, with a jolt, I remembered the night when, proud, defiant and trying to hide my own shame, I'd said the same thing to Hernán.

I had never liked Pedro de Alvarado. I'd felt ill at ease in his company from our first meeting and, though neither of us spoke of it, I'd never forgiven him for abandoning Tonaxel and he knew it.

I functioned mechanically at his side, quietly carrying out his gruff commands, saying little except what was required of me. Hernán had always asked my advice on matters concerning Moctezuma and his subjects; Alvarado asked for none. I found myself wishing that Hernán had sent Alvarado to govern Villa Rica and left the genial, competent Sandoval to manage affairs in Tenochtitlan.

I wrapped myself in a cocoon of loneliness, for those to whom I'd grown closest in the past year—Hernán, Padre Olmedo, Aguilar, Bernal and Juan—had all marched off to Villa Rica. I thought often of their early dawn departure, the feathery mist floating above the lake, the jingling, snorting horses who seemed glad to be in service again after long, lazy months, the gleam of the sun's first rays on polished lance-tips, helmets and cuirasses, the roughness of Hernán's beard against my cheek as he leaned down from Arriero's back to kiss me goodbye.

I'd avoided Juan's eyes, making a show of looking away when he passed me, stubbornly denying myself even as much as a glance before he and the rest of the company disappeared over the causeway into the mist.

"You're a fool," I'd berated myself when it was too late. "When Juan comes back you're going to beg his forgiveness on your knees. When he comes back . . . Blessed Lady, *if* he comes back." And I'd sunk into a depression of spirit that drained the color from the world around me.

Ironically, the only remaining person with whom I felt comfortable was the unhappy emperor himself. I found myself lingering in his chamber after Alvarado had gone, and seeking him out when trivial problems arose. There were even times when I nearly forgot how much I'd always hated him.

"Where's Tecuichpo?" I asked him one day, realizing that I hadn't seen her for more than a week. "This hall suffers for want of her beauty."

Moctezuma beckoned me to come close, away from the hearing of his guards and courtiers. "Tecuichpo's become a woman," he whispered, eyes gleaming with fatherly pride. "I can't let her come here anymore, Malintzin. All these men . . . do you understand?" He sighed. "I've given freely of my daughters, my slaves, even my own concubines, but Tecuichpo—she's the child of my heart, a consort for an emperor. If one of your soldiers were to ask me for her, or worse yet, take her without asking, it would kill me. She's so young."

"Orteguilla must miss her," I said, my eyes traveling to the far end of the hall, where the young page was chatting in fluent Nahuatl with a group of amazed and amused visitors.

"Yes," he said, "They were good friends. But it's for the best, I think. Oh, if your own master were to ask for her, perhaps . . ." He stopped speaking, for he'd caught the shadow that had passed across my face. "Ah, it's true then. You weren't pleased when I gave him my daughters."

My embarrassed silence answered him.

"For shame, Malintzin." He laughed. "Jealousy's such a useless emotion. You should be honored to belong to a man who has the strength to take on more than one woman. Look at me. I have more than a hundred sixty concubines. They don't seem jealous or unhappy, do they?"

"How can they," I asked, "when each of them sees so little of you?" On an impulse, I decided to tell him. "I might even have been one of them," I said. "The *pochteca* who bought me planned to sell me to you."

Moctezuma raised an eyebrow. "And why didn't he? No doubt, I'd have made him a rich man."

"The gods willed it otherwise," I answered evasively, remembering, with a shudder, the corpse lying at the bottom of a dark stairway in the trader's quarter.

"Well, I'd call it a pity," Moctezuma said. "You'd have brought me more pleasure on the mat than you do as the tool of my jailers." Cocking his head, he looked down at me with his velvety eyes. "Don't you ever have regrets?" he asked me. "Don't you ever feel guilty for the way you've turned against your own people?"

"My own people," I said slowly, "let my father be sacrificed by your priest. My own people sold me into slavery."

"And the Castilians treat you like the princess you are—that's not hard to understand. But does even that justify what you've done?"

"What I've done!" I flared indignantly. "I've only made it possible for you and Cortés to talk to each other. Don't you think that without me he'd have found some other way? Why blame it all on me?" Uneasily, I smoothed the fringe of blue feathers that edged my *huipilli*. "Besides," I said, "my being here is partly your own doing. It was your decree that killed my father."

"Mine?" His eyes widened. "Ah, now I remember. That day at Tlatelolco, the old priest. But I didn't even know your father, Malintzin. Cozcaquauhtli's a good subject, loyal, pious, most zealous in the service of his god. When he sent word to me that there were stirrings of rebellion in Oluta, I authorized him to arrest the upstarts and deal with them as he saw fit. If that makes me responsible for your father's death, then yes, I'm guilty—and you're exacting your revenge on me twenty times over." He sat quietly for a time, leaning his head on one arm as he studied me. "Malinalli." He pronounced my name slowly, syllable by syllable, in his singsong voice. "Wasn't that what the old priest called you? I have some knowledge of names and fortunes, my child. That's a dreadful name, an evil name!"

"I know it is," I said, remembering the story of how my father, in his dogged love of truth and simplicity, had named me for the date of my birth, *ce malinalli*, the first day of the grass. The town soothsayer had come to the house, unrolled his book of days and signs, and begun to wail and shriek as if someone had died. "A wicked sign!" he'd howled. "She'll be feared like a wild beast!" For a fee of four turkeys the old man had offered to change my birthdate in his book, to deceive the gods into thinking that I'd been born under a more favorable sign, but my father would have none of it. He would not begin his daughter's life with a lie, he'd declared. Looking back, I recalled that he was also most careful with his wealth, including turkeys, so Malinalli I remained. "You should have known my father," I told the emperor. "If you had, you'd never have let him be sacrificed."

"If he'd shown a little more loyalty, he might still be alive."

I leaned toward Moctezuma, determined to make him see himself as so many wretched others saw him. "If he was less than loyal to you, it was your own doing, don't you see?" I insisted. "The way you treat your provinces breeds disloyalty. You bleed them dry with your demands for tribute. You carry off their children, their wives . . . Do you think Cempoalla and Tlaxcala would have gone to Cortés if you'd treated them with kindness? Why, they'd have driven him back to the sea and perhaps you'd have ruled this land to the end of your days."

The *uei tlatoani* drew in his breath sharply. "It's too late to change anything now, isn't it, Malinalli?" He lowered his handsome head, trembling with the effort of overcoming the welling tears. At last he conquered his emotions. "There's another matter I need to discuss with you and Tonatuih, if you'd be kind enough to mention it to him," he said with forced brightness. The name "the sun" had clung to the golden-haired Alvarado since the days of Tlaxcala.

"The Feast of Tezcatlipoca?" I guessed. Orteguilla had mentioned that the emperor had some misgivings about the coming festival.

Moctezuma nodded. "You know it's the most important celebration of the year," he said. "Feelings are bound to run high."

"But you've got Hernán's permission to hold it. He gave it before he left, on condition that there be no sacrifices."

"That's true, Malintzin, and we plan to do as he wishes. But there are other problems. The symbols of your god stand atop the temple where our own gods once stood. Your god might be offended at the sight of our worship going on all about him. Wouldn't it be better to take down the cross and the little goddess until after our festival's finished?"

"I'll ask Tonatuih for you, but I expect he'll refuse."

"The Feast of Tezcatlipoca is a time of strong emotion. My people are bitter. There might be trouble." His voice wavered. "I feel their anger pressing in on me like some dark, heavy thing. I can't control them anymore." His head sagged with the weight of his beautiful golden headdress.

"It's out of the question," Pedro de Alvarado snapped, flicking his leather gauntlets against the side of the table. "Cortés wouldn't let the cross and the Virgin be taken down and neither will I. I'd slaughter the bloody lot of them before I'd see that happen, and you can tell Moctezuma I said so. That puffed-up bastard, if he thinks he can dictate to me—"

"He wasn't trying to dictate," I protested. "He's worried. I think he's honestly afraid something's going to happen out there."

We were alone in Alvarado's suite, except for the servants and Alvarado's woman, the Tlaxcalan princess, Doña Luisa, daughter of Xicotencatl the Elder and sister to the fiery Tlaxcalan general. She was young, pretty, and as devoted to her dazzling master as even Tonaxel had been. Now she hovered near us, visibly agitated. "Malintzin," she said, tugging at my arm. "I've wanted to warn Pedro but he doesn't understand, and I can't speak his language well enough to tell him yet. I've heard things . . ."

"What things?"

"Rumors. Gossip. People whispering. The travelers coming into the city for the festival are bringing arms with them. There's talk that they plan to attack the palace."

Quickly, I translated for Alvarado.

"*Diós!* I knew something was afoot," he excalimed. "Find out everything she knows. Ay, it's a good thing I've treated that wench right."

"Does Moctezuma know about this?" I asked Luisa.

"I don't think so." Nervously, she twined one braid around her fingers. "You've separated him from his people for so long that he's no longer part of what they do."

"And the *ciuacoatl*?"

"I don't know. I've already told you everything I've heard. It's just palace gossip, things the servants talk about."

"We've got to know more," Alvarado growled. "Round up the servants. We'll get the story out of them any way we have to."

The air swam with copal incense. Thousands of feet shuffled through the streets and courtyards of Tenochtitlan, compelled to rhythm by the throb of *teponatzli* and the shrill cry of flutes. Colors ran wild: tall headdresses of red and blue plumes that bobbed among the crowd; faces painted black and red; sumptuously embroidered robes of every hue; the black and white striped flags carried by the dancers; the flowers twined in the hair of those too poor to have any other adornment; and the wreaths of toasted maize crowning the heads of the young priests and priestesses—all blended into a whirling vision of light and sound. Here and there, garishly painted trains of priests wound their way through the jostling crowds, bearing glittering idols on their shoulders. The largest procession was led by two flawless young men dressed as the gods Huitzilopochtli and Tezcatlipoca. These two envied youths, who had lived in luxury for the past year, would normally expect to die on the altars at the climax of the celebration. Watching them, I wondered whether this year would be different. I'd heard whispers that Hernán's prohibition against sacrifice was not to be heeded.

One courtyard had been set aside for the nobles of the city, and here they performed their own dance before a huge representation of Huitzilopochtli, molded of *tzoalli* dough and interlaced with human bones. The dancers, about six hundred of them, moved in a circle, a gigantic human whirlpool with the old men at the center and the younger lords and princes surrounding them on the outside. They were so heavily adorned with gold and jewels that the circle glittered like an enormous sun. Chain after golden chain hung from aristocratic necks; wrists and arms gleamed with rows of jeweled bracelets; long plumes waved like grass from hundreds of gilded headdresses.

"I didn't realize we'd left them so much gold," Pedro de Alvarado muttered from his vantage point on the steps of a temple. He looked like a god himself, with his golden beard jutting out below his handsome face and his helmet and cuirass gleaming in the sun like mirrors. The sleeves of his doublet were deep scarlet, and the fingers of the powerful, hairy hands that held his lance were adorned with showy rings. "The servants told us that the attack's to come when they carry that idol of bread into their temple," he said under his breath. "If it's true, we shouldn't have long to wait."

"The servants would have told you anything after what you did to them," I whispered, my voice cold with disgust. "It sickens me that I was forced to be part of it." My stomach tightened into a knot as I remembered heated irons applied to the bottoms of bare feet. I could no longer even pretend to have any respect for Alvarado, and I wished fervently that Hernán could be here.

Alvarado glanced back over his shoulder at the clusters of armed Spaniards and Tlaxcalan warriors who had ostensibly come to the square to see the dancing, but who had been warned to be ready for a fight. "I suppose you'd rather they killed us all," he snarled. "Sometimes I wonder whose side you're on. You've been damned friendly with Moctezuma lately."

"Hernán would never have let it come to this," I hissed back at him. "He'd have done what I advised you to do—found the leaders and arrested them, taken hostages, paid bribes, whatever he had to do to put down the unrest without an open confrontation. Now all we can do is stand here and try to be ready in case they attack us."

"Cortés is in Villa Rica and I'm here," he answered haughtily. "And what makes you think I'm stupid enough to wait for them to fall on us? Hernán Cortés had his greatest victory at Cholula. I'll have my own victory here."

Victory! As the meaning of his words penetrated, I remembered the square at Cholula, the screams, the blood . . .

"No! Alvarado, for the love of God—" I grabbed his shoulder but he shook me loose, shoving me off-balance. Slowly, in exquisite, dreamlike silence, I saw him raise his arm to give the signal.

The wedge of soldiers, their drawn blades glistening, surged into the mass of unarmed nobles. For an unearthly instant they appeared to be part of the dance. Then the sound of human screams rose above the shrilling of flutes. The Tlaxcalans waded in with their *maquahuitls* and panic surged through the sea of dancers and the hundreds who had gathered to watch. The openings on the courtyard had been sealed off to prevent both escape and outside aid. Those who plunged toward these exits found their flight blocked. Shrieking, they stampeded in one direction, then another, trampling those who fell under their heedless feet, slipping on the blood that already flowed in rivers over the paving stones, stumbling onto the cruel points of the pikemen who guarded the sides of the death trap.

Alone on the steps now, I clung to a pillar of the temple for support. I realized now why Alvarado had brought no firearms to the square, something I'd questioned earlier. The thunder of cannon and arquebus would attract fighters from other parts of the city. Blades of Toledo steel, *maquahuitls* edged with obsidian, clubs, pikes, lances—these were silent and effective. There was no sound except for the screaming of the doomed and the clash of metal against metal as the carnage mounted. The pavement became a red, writhing mass of blood and bodies, dismembered limbs, heads and entrails, where the warriors of Castile and Tlaxcala waded up to their knees in gore, slashing at everything that moved.

My stomach was churning; my ears roared with screams and I felt, without really hearing, my own hysterical shrieks tearing loose from my throat. I could do nothing. I begged for the blessing of unconsciousness that had come to me at Cholula, but it was not be granted. I watched as men I'd known for a year left the Tlaxcalans to finish the slaughter and flitted among the dead like vultures, gathering up necklaces, bracelets and helmets from mutilated corpses, until they staggered under the weight of bloodstained gold.

The sound of approaching clamor was almost welcome. "They're coming!" someone shouted, "Half the city, and they're armed!" Pedro de Alvarado, his beard stained red and his arms filled with booty, straightened over the body of a dead prince from which he'd just removed a neckpiece of hammered gold. "Retreat!" he bellowed. "Back to the palace!"

I was swept along in the press of hot, blood-soaked bodies as they rushed back toward the palace of Axayacatl, staggering under their prized burdens. They'd lingered over the treasures too long. A mob of warriors came howling into the square, pelting us with stones and arrows. Packed tightly together for protection, we raced toward the palace, which, although it lay just across the square, seemed almost out of reach. The soldiers raised their bucklers to ward off the missiles as the screaming band bore down on us, but they could not fully protect themselves. I saw man after man lurch back as the deadly rain struck. My own arm was bleeding where a dart had grazed it. Pedro de Alvarado, hacking his way through the suffocating crowd, was hit by an arrow that lodged deeply in his neck, the shaft protruding above the top of his cuirass. He reeled and collapsed into the arms of his aides, who dragged him up the steps of the palace. Here the cannons were waiting. The moment our troops were safely out of the square the guns spat roaring death into the mob, driving them to retreat.

Safe at last, we looked back from the portals of the palace at the way we'd come. The square was littered with corpses, most of them Aztec, although I recognized a number of Tlaxcalan crests among the fallen. Although most of us were wounded, I noticed no one missing until I heard a groan of dismay from a bloodied soldier who stood next to me.

"Look! *Por Diós*, it's Estrada!"

There in the square, beyond the reach of even the bravest, lay the trampled body of Fernando Estrada, the young man who'd spoken so wistfully of his rich wife back in Cuba. His head, severed by a *maquahuitl*, lay an arm's length away from his bloody torso.

Chapter Eighteen

Tenochtitlan—June 1520

For many days Pedro de Alvarado had drifted along the river of death, struggling against the current that threatened to carry him away. I had removed the arrow and dressed the wound in his neck myself, using rendered fat as I'd seen Juan do, but my trembling hands had been unsure. Deep inside, I think I wanted him to die. His Luisa and Padre Diaz had nursed him faithfully, the woman weeping, the priest clicking the beads of his rosary. It was a deep wound. Blood had oozed out day after day without stopping, but he had the strength of a stallion. Slowly, unbelievably, he had rallied until now he was sitting up in bed, as surly and impatient as ever.

The palace was under seige. Only the presence of cannon at each portal discouraged Moctezuma's subjects from rushing in and overcoming us. Supplies of food had stopped, and what little remained in the palace was strictly rationed. The scarcity of water had forced us to dig a well in one of the courtyards, but the water that oozed up through the ground was brackish like the lake, almost undrinkable.

Upon hearing the news of the massacre in the temple courtyard, Moctezuma had gone into seclusion, refusing to see anyone except his own servants and the *ciuacoatl*, Tlacotzin, who hurried in and out of the palace without interference. Although he had as much reason to be bitter about the slaughter as did his emperor, the pragmatic Tlacotzin continued to function as intermediary between the *uei tlatoani*, the Spaniards, and the people of Tenochtitlan, all of whom recognized his indispensability.

I saw him now, striding up the steps in his long black and white cloak, a scroll of *amatl* paper tucked under one arm. "Malintzin," he hailed me soberly. "How's Tonatuih feeling today?"

"He's ranting to get out of bed," I said, "but the Padre's convinced him that he should rest a little longer, I think."

"That's good." His voice was expressionless. "Maybe he'll stay in bed long enough to keep anything else from happening before your master returns."

My eyes darted over Tlacotzin's impassive face. The *ciuacoatl* had lost a son in Alvarado's orgy of killing, but his manner toward me remained as deferential as ever. "You've had news!" I exclaimed.

"Yes, Malintzin. I just received this by runner." He took the scroll out from under his arm. "I don't see any reason why I shouldn't show it to you."

I studied the drawings on the scroll, groping for the correct interpretation. Since the Aztecs had no language of written letters as the Spanish did, it was sometimes difficult to convey exact meanings on paper.

"See, Malintzin, there's your master on his horse." Tlacotzin pointed to the central figure in the drawing, a bearded man on horseback with his lance piercing the eye of a man who'd fallen to the ground. "He has his victory. It was an easy fight, the runner told me. Your master's enemy lost an eye and now he's a prisoner." He pointed to the sketch of a figure in chains.

I whispered my thanks to the heavenly powers.

"Look," Tlacotzin continued. "Here's the *tlatoani* of Cempoalla paying his homage." The drawing of Chicomacatl was amusing. I recognized Catalina standing between Hernán and her uncle with a big smile on her plump face. Well, that doesn't surprise me, I told myself.

"Do you know how soon he'll be here?" I asked anxiously.

"He's on the road. He may even have come as far as Tlaxcala today. The runner says he's bringing back more men and horses." The *ciuacoatl's* eyes twitched, the only indication he gave of the dismay the news must have brought him. "But look at this, Malintzin. Could they be bringing one of their women back with them?" He pointed to a beardless person on horseback, her hair pulled into a knot on the back of the head. "I've been curious about Spanish women," he said musingly. "Do you suppose they look like the little goddess they keep in their temple?"

"I don't know," I said. "But they'll be here in a few days, thank God."

Tlacotzin shook his head sadly. "You may thank your god, Malintzin. As for me, I fear that our own gods have turned their backs on us. I won't be sorry to greet your master again. Anyone's preferable to Tonatuih. But what does it matter? I see nothing ahead for our people except tragedy."

"Isn't there any hope for peace?" I asked, realizing at once that it was a fool's question.

"Malintzin," he answered gravely, "there's not a leading family in Tenochtitlan that isn't in mourning for a son, a father, a brother. How can you dare hope they might forget what's been done? Myself, I am wrung dry of tears. I've seen more sadness than my heart can bear, and still I have to go on living. Maybe those who died so quickly under Tonatuih's long knives were the fortunate ones." The *ciuacoatl* rolled up the long piece of *amatl* paper and put it under his arm once more. His eyes were dull. "And now, Malintzin, permit me to leave you. I must take this message to my emperor."

With the news that Hernán was on his way and would be arriving within a few days, life in the palace and in the city slipped into an uneasy limbo. Pedro de Alvarado waited, steeling himself for the fury that was bound to strike when his commander learned of the massacre. The soldiers waited eagerly, looking forward to the arrival of supplies and ammunition, the strengthening of their numbers and the welcome faces of old comrades. The *uei tlatoani* and the *ciuacoatl* waited helplessly, realizing that the fate of their kingdom was now out of their hands and that, for the present at least, they were at the mercy of a bearded, dark-eyed demon who knew no fear.

I also waited, my mind in turmoil. For more than a year I'd stayed at Hernán's side, living his life, carrying out his every wish, accepting banquets or crumbs as my due from the table of his affections. So deeply had I immersed myself in his identity that the two of us were called by the same name. Now, separated from him these past weeks, I'd been forced to stand alone, to see myself once more as an individual, and what I saw puzzled and disturbed me.

When I looked into the little glass mirror Hernán had given me, I saw black eyes, a straight nose, a firm chin, high cheekbones, skin of a deep honey brown: the face of a Nahua woman. I walked with the gruff, bearded Spanish soldiers, shared their simple meals and their bawdy jokes, and they were my brothers. I spoke with the troubled Tlacotzin and his sorrows were my own.

When I drew from among my treasures the letter Juan had

written to Bernal, and traced the letters of each word with a fingertip, lingering in places where he'd written my name, I belonged completely to Juan and I ached to have him beside me. I only hoped that he had forgotten my angry farewell, that he had forgiven me. Yet I knew that the moment would come when Hernán Cortés would come galloping over the causeway, swing himself out of Arriero's saddle, and sweep me away in the force of his presence.

I was Marina and Malintzin, everything and nothing. I was Malinalli, the grass, which bent with every wind, the plaything of fortune. When I looked at myself, I did not like what I saw.

Then there was the matter of the Spanish woman, depicted in the drawing as riding beside Hernán. Who else could it be but his wife, Catalina? What other woman would be willing to risk the dangers of a wild land? Who else would be permitted to make such a journey? And yet, if the woman was Hernán's wife, would she have permitted his reunion with her namesake, the plump little Cempoallan princess? In any case, I was burning with curiosity about her. Would she be pale and dainty, like the little statue of the Virgin? Would she be jealous of me? Would I be jealous of her? I wondered and waited.

I was in my room, taking a few moments to practice my letters with a strip of *amatl* paper and a stick of charcoal from the firepot, when I heard the trumpets heralding Hernán's arrival.

"They're coming, Malintzin, from the north causeway!" It was Bernal's Francisca, flying past my doorway. I paused to check my appearance in the little hand mirror, tucking a stray wisp of hair into my braid before hurrying after her. I heard the salutes of cannon and arquebus and shouts of welcome as, a few minutes later, Hernán clattered into the square with Sandoval at his side and Olid, Ávila and Velásquez de León riding behind him. They were followed by more men on horseback, many of them strangers. Among them, on a gray mare, sat a woman in a long dress, her face veiled against the sun.

The palace's defenders were laughing with relief. "Sandoval! What a sight! Did you miss us?"

"Look there—Tapia's lost weight, he's marched it off!" They waved and called out as the captains rode into the square.

"Say, López! Your woman wasn't lonely while you were gone!"

"Sánchez! *Hombre!* I thought you'd never leave Cuba. What're you doing here?"

I waited on the palace steps, wondering whether Hernán expected me to run and meet him. I could tell by the thunderclouds in his eyes that he already knew what had happened here.

The foot soldiers, nearly double the number who'd marched away, were filing into the square. Francisca gave a squeal of delight as she spotted Bernal among them. My own eyes darted down the ranks once, then again, searching for one face among hundreds. After the infantry had trooped into the main courtyard of the palace I saw Juan at last, talking with Martín López, the burly shipbuilder. His back was turned to me, and a new helmet, which had kept me from recognizing him earlier, now swung by its leather strap from one hand. I stood staring at the back of his head and cursing the circumstances that kept me from rushing headlong down the steps and flinging myself into his arms, just as Francisca had done with Bernal. If only he'd turn and look at me, at least, before I had to join Hernán; Blessed Lady, if only he'd smile . . .

Martín López had turned away, and now Juan was sweeping his eyes around the courtyard, looking for someone. I stood breathlessly quiet, praying he wouldn't still be angry with me over my outburst before his departure.

His eyes met mine. Blue is the coldest of colors, and I fully deserved to be frozen by his gaze. Yet I was warmed, melted. He was smiling the tenderest of smiles. I was forgiven. Bliss overcoming discretion, I took a step toward him.

"Marina? Blast it, there you are!" It was Hernán, just dismounting at the far end of the courtyard. "Why are you hiding over there? Come here!"

With a stricken look at Juan, I turned and ran in the direction of Hernán's voice.

"Name of heaven! How could you have let it happen? Wasn't there some other way you could have handled it?" Hernán was white with rage. Pedro de Alvarado, to his credit, did not cringe before the fury of his commander. He'd gotten out of bed and dressed in his finest to meet the onslaught, and now the two faced each other across the long table in the council room.

"I felt it was justified," he said coldly. "There was a plot to murder us all, but I managed to strike before they did. Would you rather have come back to find us all dead?"

Hernán paced back and forth, whipping at his leg with his gloves. "The city was like a graveyard when we came through the streets. We expected them to come howling out of the alleys at us any second. How are we ever going to repair the damage you've done to our position here?" He paused to glance at me where I stood quietly against the wall, and then turned on Alvarado with fresh anger. "And to take Marina out there with you! Don't you realize what we'd have lost if she'd been killed?"

"I wanted her where I could keep an eye on her," Alvarado said. "Who knows, she could have run to Moctezuma with stories of what I was planning."

Hernán was livid. "Good Lord, man, you'd suspect her of treachery?"

"Look at her," Alvarado growled. "Her skin's as brown as theirs. If it came to it, she'd choose the lives of her own people over ours. Why, she even tried to stop me."

"I could kill you for that—" Hernán took a step toward him, and the situation would have come to blows if the Spanish woman had not hurried into the room at that moment, wringing her hands. "I can't find him!" she cried. "Fernando's not here and nobody will tell me what's happened to him. Please, señor, I know something's wrong."

Hernán inclined his head in a little bow. "Captain Alvarado, Doña Marina, I wish to present to you a noble lady, Doña María de Estrada."

I felt my taut nerves slacken. So the woman wasn't Catalina after all.

Alvarado made a low bow over her hand and pressed it to his lips. "Fernando? Fernando Estrada, you say? Ah, my poor lady! Alas, your husband gave his life most bravely in defense of his comrades. How sorry I am to have to tell you." Hernán glared at him, knowing it was Alvarado's brashness that had cost Estrada his life.

Estrada . . . I remembered the fair-haired young man who'd longed to return to his María in Cuba. I remembered his headless body lying in the square, the body no one had dared retrieve for a Christian burial before the Aztecs dragged it away. The woman stood there in stunned silence. Beyond her given name, she bore no resemblance to the little image in the chapel. María de Estrada was forty perhaps, black-haired, swarthy and as plump-breasted as a quail. Her eyes, large and lustrous, were her best feature. Below them, her face was dominated by a broad, flat nose and an oddly delicate mouth crowned by a downy fringe of black above the upper lip. The mud-spattered brown traveling dress she wore was simple but finely made, like Hernán's own doublets.

A new widow of my own race would have burst into the wailing death chant. Instead, María de Estrada crossed herself, pulled a lace kerchief from her bosom and dabbed at her eyes.

"I knew it," she said with a sigh. "From the moment he walked up the gangplank of that ship, I knew I'd never see my Fernando again." She sniffed deeply. "*Señor*, with your indulgence, I'd at least like to visit his grave. Would you please have one of your men show me where he's buried?"

If a shadow passed across Alvarado's face, it was too brief to be noticed. "We buried him in one of the inner courtyards, my lady," he purred. "I'll summon Trujillo to escort you to his grave. It's a lovely spot. I'm confident you'll approve of it."

I threw him a horrified glance. A fortnight ago one of the mares had delivered a stillborn foal. Alavardo had ordered the animal buried in the courtyard. "I've instructed Yañez to make a fine cross to mark the grave," Alvarado added hastily. "When he's finished it, you may have the honor of placing it there."

"Thank you," María de Estrada said quietly. "You're so kind."

Hernán would forgive Pedro de Alvarado. The impetuous captain was, after all, only guilty of emulating his general's performance at Cholula. Besides, under present conditions Alvarado was too valuable a man to alienate for long. Instead, Hernán vented his contempt on the miserable Moctezuma. On the first day of the return, when Moctezuma had come out of his suite to welcome him, Hernán had swept imperiously past the poor emperor without a glance in his direction. To add to the *uei tlatoani's* pain, Hernán had received his ambassadors with insults and had even called him a dog in their presence.

"I'll build a golden statue of Malintzin on his horse and cover it with jewels if he'll only be kind to me," the pathetic monarch had begged.

Hernán, in brusque reply, had ordered Moctezuma to reopen the markets so that food could be procured, but the emperor's command no longer carried any weight with his subjects. In desperation, Hernán had released Cuitlahuac with orders to see to the market's opening, but Moctezuma's brother had done nothing and had never returned to the palace. Our men were finally forced to forage for supplies in dawn raids on the city. Those who returned reported barricades in the streets, bridges removed from the canals in strategic spots, and caches of weapons hidden in buildings.

The palace of Axayacatl was now a fortress, besieged day after day by painted attackers who yowled their hatred as they bombarded the former gods with stones, arrows and firebrands, setting the palace's thatch roof ablaze and filling the rooms with smoke. Water was so scarce that we extinguished the fires by throwing dirt on them.

Hernán tried time after time to drive the Aztecs back from the palace, charging out of the gates with guns and horses, but his men were always trapped by the barricades and the open canals that lay where there had once been bridges. They were pelted with a hellish rain of missiles from the rooftops and beaten back into our fortress once more, dragging their dead and wounded.

Moctezuma was now *uei tlatoani* in name only. Outside, a new figure reigned in the streets, a new name flowed from the lips of the people. Cuitlahuac, lord of Iztapalapan and brother of Moctezuma, stern Cuitlahuac who had hated the white strangers from the moment their feet touched Mexican soil, now ruled in the city. His streaming emerald plumes rode the crest of every attack on the palace his own father had built. Second to him in command was the fiery Cuauhtemoc, whose courage and youthful beauty inspired near-worship among his followers.

Inside the palace, Juan and I saw little of each other, for the days of leisure and longing were past. I spent much of my time tending the wounded men, but María de Estrada, who ministered with the skill of a physician and the tenderness of a mother, had relieved Juan of his duties in this capacity, freeing him for more dangerous assignments.

Despite María de Estrada's lack of beauty it was clear that the men adored her. All bickering and cursing ceased when she passed among them. The wounded suppressed their moans and smiled at her through clenched teeth, the dying gripped her hands. I too, as I hovered near her, translating her orders for the Tlaxcalan nurses, was warmed by her presence and we soon became friends.

However strong the friendship, I always made excuses when

María de Estrada asked me to accompany me on her daily pilgrimage to what she still believed was her husband's grave. The spot where the dead foal had been buried was covered with fresh flowers and watered by a widow's tears. No one, not even I, could bear to tell her the truth. But after a time, somehow it didn't seem to matter. Eventually, in everyone's mind, the mound of earth in the courtyard became the grave of Fernando Estrada, and when Yañez, the carpenter, finished the prettily carved little cross, no one murmured of sacrilege when María planted it there. Day after day, other fallen comrades took their places beside it until the grave was only one of many.

"Ay!" María de Estrada fussed for the hundredth time as she brushed the dust from her brown skirt. "To think I didn't even bring along a black dress and veil for *luto*. What would my friends in Cuba think if they saw me mourning my Fernando in grays and browns?"

"Is the color that important?" I asked her. "No one questions what you feel inside."

"Those Cuban ladies would. Even my friend, Doña Catalina Juárez de Cortés, would click her tongue and say, 'María, how could you forget such a thing?' I still want to laugh when I remember how you thought I might be Catalina when I came here."

"But what else was I to think? Would Hernán let just any woman come to a place like this?"

"Look, Hernán Cortés would let the devil himself ride with him if he brought along enough gold and his own horse. But Catalina? *Madre mía*, you couldn't *drag* her to a place like this!"

"What's she like?" I'd been wanting to ask María about Catalina from the moment I found out she knew her. "Is she beautiful?"

We were walking down a long corridor toward the makeshift infirmary. We made a strange pair, I in my fringed *huipilli* and deerskin sandals, my black braids twined atop my head, and the stout Spanish woman, dressed too warmly for the day, gliding along as though she had wheels under her long dress instead of feet. Shafts of light flickered down on us where the roof had burned through.

"Yes." María tilted her head, a delicate, birdlike gesture. "Oh, not in the same way you are, of course. You're like some lovely little forest creature, all life and movement and mystery. I can see why Hernán Cortés couldn't resist you—not that he's the least bit resistant to any woman. But yes, Catalina's beautiful. She's tall, much taller than I am, with reddish brown curls, green eyes and white, white skin. She never lets the sun's rays touch her. And when she was younger she had the smallest waist in all Cuba." María patted my arm. "Don't look so envious. She's almost as old as Hernán himself, and they haven't been happy together for years."

"Is it true that he was forced to marry her?"

"Almost. The rascal'd promised to marry her, but then after he'd gotten what he wanted, he tried to wriggle out of it. Governor Velásquez, who'd married her sister, made things hot for him until he kept his promise. Oh my, he even put him in jail." María de Estrada pulled a black lace fan from her sleeve and fluttered it near her sweating bosom. "A fortuneteller once told Catalina she'd marry a great man and for many years she put on such airs that most of us thought the prophecy'd gone to her head. But now, who knows? That gypsy may have been right."

"But—" my lips formed the words slowly—"does she still love Hernán? Does she know about me and the . . . others?"

"The other women? Come, child, I'm not deaf. I've heard the men talk. I know what Cortés is and nothing he does surprises me. I'd not put it past him to have a harem as big as Moctezuma's." She registered her disapproval with a deep sniff. "Catalina knows about you, at least. The ship that stopped in Cuba carried many tales and that was one of them. It's nothing new to her. He had a daughter by a slave woman in Cuba, you know—a lovely young thing and there are no secrets about who her father is. But as for love . . ." María tapped the edge of the fan against her palm. "Well, Catalina surely loved him once, but when he refused to marry her it broke her heart and turned her whole system to gall. They've been getting revenge on each other ever since."

"How sad for them both." I could think of nothing else to say.

"Now, you mustn't be hard on poor Catalina." María wagged a plump finger under my nose. "She's not a bad person, but a man's cruelty can do awful things to a woman's nature. Hernán Cortés hasn't done well by her. And don't you get your hopes up either. No matter how many women that he-goat takes on, he still has only one legal wife and she won't let him go as long as there's breath in her body. She'll hang onto him for her honor, for her religion, for the promise of being a great lady, and for pure spite. You can depend on it!"

"I never thought it would be otherwise," I said quietly. A wife had power and security. We *barraganas* had to be content with whatever our men gave us. "Some of the girls are hoping their masters will take them to the padre one day," I said. "Not I. I know that's not possible."

"Those poor fools . . ." María clicked her tongue. Tell me, have any of them done it, or even one?"

"No."

"I thought not," María said tartly. "Do you know what the dream of every man here is? Every mother's son of them down to the grubbiest foot soldier? It's to win a fortune in gold, go back to Spain or at least to Cuba, and marry into Spanish nobility. Even Bernal Diaz with his sweet little Francisca, and Alvarado, Sandoval and Velásquez de León with their Tlaxcalan beauties. They'll *never* marry them." María's silver earrings danced as she shook her head vigorously. "They're all saving themselves for the daughter of some Spanish duke. I know it's not a kind thing to say, but I feel it's my duty. These men are all alike!"

"I understand," I whispered, and my thoughts rose above the palace walls and flew to the streets outside where four *mantas*, hollow wooden towers on wheels, were now rumbling over the stones. They'd been built to combat the enemies who gathered on the rooftops. Inside one of them, Fighting for his life, would be a man who'd told me that I came to him he'd want me to stay forever. Did that mean that Juan was different from the others, or was María de Estrada right? I closed my eyes for an instnat and felt the heart-twisting pain that came with her words. Then I followed her on down the corridor and into the infirmary, where the wounded were waiting.

"A curse on those *mantas*," muttered Juan, who sat on a low stool while I dabbed at a cut on his forehead. The wound was not serious enough to warrant so much attention, but it provided me an excuse to be with him. He winced at the touch of the rough cloth. "They bogged down at the first canal! It the infantry hadn't held them off while we retreated, the devils would have fired the *mantas* and roasted us inside. What a waste—"

"Hold still," I said, steadying his chin with one hand and savoring the first physical contact we'd had since his departure for Villa Rica. The infirmary was a beehive of activity. Bandaged men and Tlaxcalan women, weary from nursing, bustled about us. Gonzalo de Sandoval, limping from a leg wound, nodded as he passed.

"It was hell out there today, eh, Jaramillo?" he lisped. "We're lucky to be alive."

"I'm counting each day as a gift," Juan said. His eyes were red from smoke and fatigue and his face was smeared with soot. "How much longer can we hold out?"

Sandoval frowned above his thick beard. "How long can we live without food? We'd leave if we could secure the route to one of the causeways."

"We've been trying to do that all week," Juan said. "It's like carving a tunnel through Hades!"

"What about Moctezuma?" I asked. "Can't we use him to bargain?"

"Cortés is thinking about that." Sandoval paused as he wiped the soot from his cheek. "Hasn't he talked to you about it?"

"I've hardly seen him. He's busy with the fighting and I spend most of my time here in the infirmary." I brushed back a stray lock of hair.

"Well, get ready for something," Sandoval grunted. "We can't hole up in this place forever and it's beginning to look like we can't fight our way out either." With a shrug he limped off in the direction of Hernan's quarters, just as María de Estrada hurried up to us, twisting her hands.

"*Señor* Jaramillo, thank heaven I've found you! It's young Sanchez. He's going to die if that arm of his doesn't come off. I can handle almost anything else, but, Blessed Mother, not that! Can you help me?"

Nodding, Juan rose wearily to his feet. "Fill the lad up with *pulque*. Then get someone heavy to hold him. Corral'd be good; he's done it before." He rubbed his eyes with the back of his hand. "And get Lares to heat some irons . . ."

"I'll help too, if you need me." My voice and hands were shaking.

He leaned so close to me that his short, singed beard brushed my ear. "No, this isn't for you, *querida*," he whispered. "We'll need a couple of strong men just to hold him. The *señora* and I can do the rest." He took my hand and held it tightly for an instant. Then his eyes darted about the room. "There he is. Corral, we can use you!" And he hurried off after the husky banner-carrier, leaving me alone. I began folding the unused bandages.

"Doña Marina!" Orteguilla, breathless from running, burst into the room. "Cortés needs you."

I followed him. The page had grown as pale and thin as the wisps of fog that drifted over the lake. "He wants you to talk to Moctezuma," he said.

The emperor reclined listlessly on a low platform. His apartment had been sealed off from the commotion that engulfed the rest of the palace, and was tomblike in its quietness. The footsteps of Olid, Padre Olmedo and myself echoed eerily through the empty audience chamber.

"So you've come to me at last." Moctezuma's voice was dull and weary. "I'd have thought Malintzin would at least have presented himself in person to apologize for the way he's treated me."

"He couldn't come," I said, marveling that this man's foremost concern was with his own treatment. "He's busy defending this palace against your subjects."

"Ah, well. I see he's sent two whom I love best in his place." His eyes, in his unmoving face, flicked from Padre Olmedo to Olid, who had taken one of the emperor's daughters, in addition to Doña Isabela, the talkative young woman Hernán had awarded him in Centla. "What does he want? Why can't he just leave me to die in peace?"

The tenuous thread of my patience broke. "Peace!" I snapped. "Whose peace? Don't you know what's happening outside?"

Moctezuma lowered his eyes. Padre Olmedo, who'd caught the anger in my tone, laid a restraining hand on my arm. "Let me try, child," he whispered. "Ask him whether he'd rather die with his people fighting ours or live on as a great peacemaker."

In response to the question, Moctezuma only sighed dejectedly.

"We only want you to talk to your people," Olid pressed. "Tell them that if they'll put their weapons away and go home we'll release you and leave the city peacefully. You have Cortés's promise on that."

"Malintzin's promise . . ." A bitter smile played about the royal lips. "A bit of scum on the lake has more value. Kill me and be done with it."

"You're still *uei tlatoani*," I urged. "Think of how many lives you'll be able to save if you intercede for us."

"If you refuse we might not be able to stop our men from

taking reprisals." Olid rubbed his chin and looked sideways at the emperor. "We have several of your children, you know, including your son. Some of our men are . . . emotional. One Aztec's the same as another to them. We can't be responsible."

"You have Asupacaci?" Moctezuma straightened, charged with anxiety. "You're lying! I had him kept away from the palace for his own safety!"

"We caught him yesterday, in the street." Olid spoke slowly, letting each word strike with its own impact. "Trying to prove himself as a warrior, I suppose. He's a feisty young cub."

"But we don't want to use him to threaten you," Padre Olmedo said soothingly. "Just do as we ask and we'll release him to you. You can have him here in your quarters for as long as you like."

The emperor sighed, stretched his limbs and stood up. His eyes had the glazed look of a dying animal's. "Very well. Malintzin always gets his way with me in the end, doesn't he? But do you really believe I can accomplish anything? My people listen to Cuitlahuac now, not to me.

"So!" Moctezuma snapped at a servant, beckoning him from his station. "If I'm going to speak to the people as their emperor, I want to look the part. Bring me the royal headdress and the blue *tilmatli* edged with gold, my golden sandals . . ." The servants scurried to do his bidding.

The painted warriors filled the square, shrieking their hatred as they pelted the palace of Axayacatl with stones, arrows and firebrands. They surged like a dark wave amid the timbers of the skull rack. They covered the rooftops and the steps of the temples like swarms of insects, screaming, cursing the white men, waiting for the moment when the palace defenses would crumble and they would rush in for the kill.

A ripple of surprised silence passed over the throng as the heavy wooden gates we'd built to seal off the palace entrance creaked open and Moctezuma was prodded through them and out onto the elevated porch. He was surrounded by his guards, who protected the royal body with a barrier of shields. Cacama, Asupacaci, and several other captive chiefs stood behind him, also under heavy guard.

I took my place at Hernán's shoulder as Moctezuma raised his arm for attention. When the crowd had quieted, the guards lowered their shields, exposing him to full view of his subjects.

"My children!" The monarch's voice was strangely high. Standing there in his turquoise cloak, quetzal plumes radiating from his head, he made a figure of touching magnificence. Restless, mistrustful, the crowd stirred.

"You're in arms, my children," he said, his voice quavering, "in hot battle. Why? You'll only be killed, and this land will echo with the cries of widows and orphans. You want to set me free, and for that I thank you. You don't turn away from me in anger, and I thank you for that as well. You haven't chosen another *tlatoani* in my place, and for that too I thank you. Such an act would displease the gods and bring destruction upon all of us!" Moctezuma spread his arms, turning slightly from side to side to show that he was not chained or held. "See!" he exclaimed. "I'm no prisoner. I'm free. By divine command I must remain the guest of our friends just a little longer. You mustn't attack them, for soon they'll be leaving us to go back to the land from whence they came." His voice caught. "Alas, my people, my country, my crown—" With these last words he broke into sobs. His body contracted with shame so that he seemed to shrivel before the eyes of his people.

Among the captive chiefs standing behind him was Itzquauhtzin, ruler of Tlatelolco and father of the young Cuauhtemoc who stood below in the throng, red plumes bristling like flames from his helmet. I saw the eyes of father and son meet across the distance and lock in understanding as Cuauhtemoc threw back his head and shrieked, "Moctezuma is a coward! A woman to the Castilians! We spit on him!"

"Rabbit!" "She-turkey!" "Murderer of your own nobles!" The cries were taken up on all sides until the multitude was roaring its contempt for the ruler they'd once worshipped. A rock ricocheted off the edge of the top step.

"Raise your shields!" Hernán croaked. "Get him inside!" But the soldiers who leaped to obey him could not move faster than the fist-sized stone that came whistling through the air to crunch home between Moctezuma's eyes. The emperor blinked incredulously. Then his head sagged forward, his knees buckled and he collapsed into the arms of Cristobal de Olid, who dragged him inside amid a torrent of stones and arrows.

"Damn, we've lost this one!" Hernán cursed. "Is he alive?"

Olid bent an ear to Moctezuma's chest and nodded. "But that was quite a blow. Who knows what it's done to his head!"

"Well, get him to his room—fetch Jaramillo. And close

those doors!" A stone struck him on the ankle. "Curse it! Close those doors!" he bellowed.

Moctezuma thrashed in his twilight sleep, moaning softly as his fingers tore at the dressing Juan had applied to his head. His son, Asupacaci, squatted beside the mat, silent, sullen, his eyes as hard as granite.

"The fool!" Juan's voice rasped with exhaustion. "Marina, can't you make him understand that he'll die if he doesn't let us take care of him?"

"I've tried, but that's exactly what he wants. He welcomes death."

"In that case, I wish he'd die and get it over with! I should be out there on the pyramid with the others, not sitting here watching some idiot who won't even let me touch him." Juan rubbed his face with his palms. "Ay, forgive me, Padre, Marina. It's just that, like everyone else, I haven't slept for days."

I sat on the floor and watched him, thinking that I'd give anything to pillow that tired head in my arms and stroke the sun-streaked hair with my fingers.

Moctezuma whimpered and clawed at the dressing on his head again. He got it loose and flung it feebly onto the floor, exposing an ugly blue-red wound that oozed blood and pus. Juan got up from his chair and moved toward him with a handful of clean bandages.

"No, stay back. Let me die . . ." the emperor moaned.

"Not while I'm here," Juan muttered. "Help me hold him, Padre."

Asupacaci, eyes glittering with helpless hate, watched silently as the two white men held his father down and replaced the bandage on his head.

"That wound's an ugly one," said Padre Olmedo, "but it doesn't look bad enough to kill him."

"It isn't," Juan agreed, "but he's killing himself. The fool hasn't eaten in the three days since we dragged him in here, and every time he rips the dressing off his head he opens up the wound again. If he wants to die, then I fear he's going to have his way."

Two flies settled on the edge of the dressing. Moctezuma did not even try to brush them away. Orteguilla crept into the room without a sound and knelt beside the emperor. His pink-cheeked face was now white and pinched, streaked with tears from his reddened eyes.

Moctezuma managed a wan smile. "Don't cry, little friend. This life no longer holds anything for me. But I want to speak to Malintzin one last time. Would you get him for me?"

"He's not in the palace," the page whispered. "He's out in the square with his men, trying to drive your warriors off the big pyramid."

Moctezuma's sigh was almost a whine. "See what a failure I am? I couldn't stop the fighting. Bring Malintzin to me as soon as he's back in the palace. There's so little time left . . ."

"Sh! I hear something!" Juan exclaimed softly. We listened. Shouts were coming from the square.

"Well, run and see what it is," said the padre, nodding at both of us. "The boy and I can watch Moctezuma."

I raced beside Juan, through the long palace corridors to the front entrance that opened onto the square. There, coming toward us, we saw the little Spanish troop, shouting and waving their bloodied swords and lances in triumph. Behind them, the temples of Tlaloc and Huitzilopochtli sent twin pillars of smoke and flame billowing toward heaven. "Hernán was holding his left hand carefully in his right. His leather glove was soaked with blood.

Seeing us, Bernal Diaz broke ranks and came leaping up the steps. "*Santa María*, what a fight you missed, Jaramillo! The saints were out there with us. Talk about miracles!"

"Bernal's not exaggerating." Hernán had come up beside us. "God was on our side today. They rolled logs as big around as horses down at us, and the damned things went shooting through us lengthwise!"

"You'd better let me see that hand," Juan said.

"Yes . . . in a moment." Hernán turned to me. "We only took two prisoners, but you might be interested in seeing them, Marina." He jerked his head toward the cluster of men who'd come into the palace and they moved aside, revealing the two captives who stood in their midst. I gasped.

The *ciuacoatl* stood before me, dignified even in captivity, his black and white cloak torn and stained with blood. Beside him, eyes smoldering with hatred, spitting and snarling like a bobcat, crouched the old priest, Cozcaquauhtli.

Chapter Nineteen

Tenochtitlan—Late June 1520

Moctezuma's eyes had sunk into blue hollows above his cheekbones. The skin that stretched over his frame was waxen yellow, his breathing barely perceptible. No one, not the assembled chiefs who stood beside his mat, not the Spanish captains in their polished armor, not Padre Olmedo, who stood by with a basin of holy water in hopes of a deathbed conversion, not even the little page who wept helplessly in one corner, could deny that the *uei tlatoani* was dying.

"Malintzin . . ." he whispered hoarsely, beckoning to Hernán with a flutter of his fingers. With me at his elbow, Hernán bent low over the platform where the emperor lay. Hernán's left hand was bandaged. He'd lost two fingers in the assault on the pyramid.

"Malintzin, my son . . ." Moctezuma spoke with great effort. "I ask two things of you—protect my children, that is the first. Cherish my daughters. Tell their babies about their grandfather . . ." He paused to recover his breath. The wound on his head was a ghastly mass of purple. "My grandchildren . . ." he whispered. "Tell them the good things, not the bad . . ."

As I translated for Hernán, I glanced up at Doña Ana and Doña Inés, who stood nearby wiping their eyes. Both were pregnant, Doña Ana enormously so. I looked quickly away.

Painfully, Moctezuma cleared his throat. His breath already smelled of death. "The second thing I ask . . ." His voice was scarcely audible. "Avenge my death. Punish those who . . . turned against me. My people."

"As you wish," Hernán murmured, motioning to Padre Olmedo, who came forward with the basin. "My brother," he urged, "it's not too late to accept Christ and find a place in His heaven."

"Heaven . . ." The emperor smiled faintly. "Are there Castilians there?"

"Most assuredly," said Hernán. "Heaven's only for Christians."

"Then," Moctezuma gasped, "I want no part of it. Leave me with my own gods." And he shut his eyes and closed out the world.

In the early evening, several minor nobles and priests had been released to carry Moctezuma's body back to his people. The Aztecs had greeted the little procession with hoots and insults, driving it through the streets until at last the corpse fell into sympathetic hands and was properly cremated.

"His death was a mercy," sighed Hernán, leaning against a pillar of one of the inner courtyards for a moment of rest. "But what are we going to do without him, eh, Marina?"

I sat on the steps near his feet, limp with weariness, watching the fireflies blink in and out among the white blossoms. During the past few months I'd avoided being alone with him, even though I'd been beside him almost constantly in the company of others. Now the magnitude of danger and despair had reduced the differences between us to trivialities.

"He wasn't of much use in the end," I said. "We still have the others—Cacama, Cuauhtemoc's father, the *ciuacoatl* . . ."

Hernán shook his head. "Cuitlahuac wouldn't bargain for Moctezuma and he won't bargain for the rest of them either." He leaned over and rested his uninjured right hand on my shoulder. His strong fingers massaged the tight, aching muscles in my neck. It had been a long time since I'd let him touch me.

"Tomorrow," he said, "I'm going to try to take the Tlacopan causeway. It's the shortest one, and if we have that we'll at least have a lifeline out of here. Then the hostages might be of some help in getting us off this accursed island." He wound one of my braids around his finger. "What about the old priest, Marina? Say the word and we'll slice off his ugly head for you."

"That can wait," I said. "As one of the ranking priests of the city, he might be of some use to us. Why waste him?" In truth, my mind had been in a quandary from the moment of Cozcaquauhtli's capture. Ever since my father's death, I'd dreamed of revenge. Hernán had made it clear that the old man was mine, to deal with as I pleased. Why, then, had I hesitated so long in giving the fatal order? I thought of the priest as he huddled in his cell, peering owlishly from under his thatch of blood-clotted hair, spitting defiance at all who approached him. He expected death, I was sure. Yet I found myself wondering whether my hunger for vengeance was more nourishing than its fulfillment would be.

A caged jaguar in the animal compound gave vent to its frustration with a coughing explosion of sound. A puma answered with a melancholy screech. I felt Hernán's hand tremble against my neck. "I've been told they're fed human flesh," he whispered.

"Bernal hates them," I said. "He says he's going to kill them all someday."

"By my conscience, he'll have his chance!"

"Malintzin's taken the causeway!" The young Tlaxcalan who'd slipped into the gate of the palace was jubilant. "They've even got men on the mainland."

It was splendid news. The palace's defenders cheered and clapped one another on the shoulders. Now our retreat would be secure. That morning's portion of the seige had been fought bitterly, with the enemy hurling themselves again and again against the battered walls. The little force Hernán had left behind had been hard-pressed, but then the Aztecs too had been divided between the square and the Tlacopan causeway.

On the heels of the good tidings came a plumed Aztec messenger with an offer to discuss terms of peace. A runner was sent with a written message to Hernán, who came galloping back with half his troops, the remainder having been left to hold the causeway under Velásquez de León.

"Marina," he greeted me inside the gate, swinging down off the panting Arriero, the midday sun gleaming on his helmet. "Tell me I'm not dreaming. How could our luck have changed so much?" He squinted at me in the sunlight. "You're frowning. What is it?"

"They're making it too easy," I said. "Be careful, Hernán."

"I'm always careful." He dismissed my worries with a shrug of his shoulders. "Did they tell you their terms?"

I nodded. "If we promise to make no reprisals, they'll promise to restore the causeways and let us leave peacefully."

"Fair enough. Is that all?"

"No. The whole agreement rests on one demand. They want the *ciuacoatl* and the old priest back at once. I don't like it, Hernán."

"I see." He smoothed his beard with a gloved hand. "Marina, surely you'd forgive me if I let the old priest go in order to save our lives."

"You think that's what's bothering me? What do you think I am?" Hernán smiled at my indignation.

"Well, what is it then, my little spitfire?"

His flippancy in the face of my concern infuriated me, but I gulped down my anger and tried to answer him calmly. "Moctezuma's dead. The Aztecs are without a *uei tlatoani.*"

"So? What about Cuitlahuac?"

"He's the natural successor, but he's uncrowned, don't you see? Ceremony means everything to these people. Cuitlahuac can't assume full power without a coronation, and for that they need the old priest and the *ciuacoatl.* As long as we've got them, Cuitlahuac's hands are tied."

"I still don't see what difference it makes," Hernán answered subbornly. "Marina, I've already made up my mind to let them go. It's a small price to pay for our lives. You've done your duty and now let's hear no more of it. I'm sending an order for their immediate release." He pulled off his gloves and unfastened his helmet. "As for me, I haven't had a decent meal or a good night's rest in two weeks. Order the cooks to serve me the best meal they can concoct out of whatever we have left. I'm going to enjoy every bite!"

The priest and the *ciuacoatl* had walked out into the square amid cheers from both sides of the palace walls. Hernán had removed his armor, washed his face and hands, and was just sitting down to eat when a bloodied Tlaxcalan runner stumbled through the gates and collapsed at my feet.

"They're attacking the causeway again," he gasped. "We . . . we're too few to hold them back."

The palace burst into a pandemonium of shouting voices and running feet. Hernán cursed as Guzman buckled him back into his cuirass. In a flash, the horsemen, with Hernán in the lead, were thundering through the gates in the direction of the causeway, with the infantry following at a run.

Standing in their dust, I clutched the tiny silver crucifix around my neck and whispered a prayer. Juan was among those who'd stayed to guard the causeway.

Those of us who remained in the palace waited into evening with no word of the battle except for the taunts of the Aztecs in the square. "Make peace with your god!" they howled. "We've taken your soldiers and tomorrow we come in after you!" "We'll feed your flesh to our children!" "You'll smell your friends' hearts burning on our altars!"

I translated reluctantly for the men. "Don't believe them," I admonished. "They only want to scare us." But inside myself I was sick with fear. I knew that on the narrow causeway where horse and cannon had no room to maneuver, the Aztecs, with their canoes and vast numbers, would have the advantage.

A new ripple of excitement surged through the crowd outside the walls. "Malintzin is dead!" shrieked a painted warrior. "Malintzin is dead . . . dead . . . dead . . . !" the mob chanted flinging themselves with new fury against the gates.

"What are they saying?" Lares the smith demanded.

"Only more of the same," I whispered, grasping the little silver cross so tightly that the edges bit into my fingers.

I waited in dread, willing myself not to believe the chants of the Aztec mobs. At last we heard the sound of trumpets above the din in the square, and the retreating Spanish forces appeared, dragging their exhuasted bodies before the pursuing Aztecs. Fear loosened its stranglehold on my throat as I saw Hernán bringing up the rear. They fought their way across the square and through the gates, which ground shut behind them. By torchlight, my searching eyes found Juan at last. His clothes were drenched with lake water. An ugly red stain had spread across one shoulder and his eyes burned like two miniature hells in his haggard face. I clutched at a pillar to keep from running to him.

"Not one word of reproach from you, Marina?" Hernán, blood flowing from a gash at the knee, was being eased off his horse with the help of Gonzalo de Sandoval. "You were right," he said, grimacing with pain. "I should have listened to you. As soon as they had what they wanted, they hit us again."

"You should have seen him out there, Doña Marina." Sandoval's eyes were as adoring as a puppy's. "He was the last one off the causeway. The brown devils were swarming all over him. Ay! Just when we thought we'd lost him, he tore loose and leaped this huge gap with his horse . . ."

"Any credit for saving my life goes to Arriero." Hernán patted the stallion's neck. "If he survives long enough, I'm going to build him his own palace. But, curse it, we lost twenty good men out there, and now we're trapped again." He struck the pommel of the saddle with his fist.

"Señor Cortés, you shouldn't be standing on that leg,"

María de Estrada fussed. "To the infirmary with you! Someone help him!"

Hernán's captains surrounded him as María bandaged his knee. His face matched the gravity of theirs. We were nearly out of food and were hoarding our ammunition like gold. Once we lost the use of our cannons, nothing could stop the Aztecs from storming the palace. "The longer we wait the weaker we become," he said. "We can get out of here at once or we can stay and die."

"Botello's consulted the stars." Alvarado indicated a lean, swarthy soldier who hovered nearby. Botello was looked upon with awe by his comrades because he spoke Latin and professed a knowledge of astrology. "He says the signs are favorable for our leaving tonight."

"You know I don't hold with such things." Hernán winced as María cleaned his wounded knee. "But in this case, I agree for reasons of my own. The Aztecs are celebrating today's victory. They're less likely to be on guard and they won't expect any sudden moves from us after the licking we took today." María de Estrada finished the bandage with a tidy little knot. Sandoval handed Hernán a staff and he rose painfully to his feet. "Marina, turn one of the prisoners loose with a message for them. Offer them all the treasure we have if they'll let us leave in eight days. That'll lull them a bit more. After that, inform the Tlaxcalans that we're going tonight."

I hurried off toward the section of the palace where the prisoners were kept. Juan passed me in the hallway. Someone had bandaged his shoulder.

"We're leaving tonight, did you hear?" I whispered.

"I heard, love. That sort of news spreads fast."

"Botello says the stars are favorable. Can he really read the sky, Juan?"

"I wish I knew," he said quietly. "I just talked to Bernal. He says he heard that Botello saw something else in the stars as well, something he was afraid to tell Cortés."

"What was it?" I could hear my heart.

"His own death."

By the light of a single small candle, I rummaged through the chests in my room. I threw aside the elegant feathered *huipillis* and embroidered skirts I loved to wear. They would have to remain behind, for I could not travel with a heavy burden. Groping amid stiff cotton and feathers, my fingers touched something soft. I pulled out the dark brown cloak that Juan had wrapped around me the night of Quauhtlatoa's death. I would wear it. It was warm and its dark color would make me less conspicuous in the night. I put it on and, quickly fastening the clasp at my throat, hurried to the chapel where Hernán had opened the treasure room.

The two pitch-pine torches that had been stuck into brackets on the walls of the vault cast a rippling glow about the heaps of gold and jewels, which reflected each dancing flame a thousand times over. By the time I arrived, Hernán had set aside the royal fifth for the king and a generous portion for himself and his captains. Since no more carriers could be spared, he'd invited the men to help themselves to what was left. It was a bizarre sight that met my eyes as I peered through the hole that had been broken out of the chapel wall. Scores of men were wading through the treasure, snatching up choice pieces and stuffing them into bags or into their clothing, draping chain after chain around their necks and jamming jeweled rings onto their fingers. I noticed that, without exception, those most heavily loaded with treasure had come with the Narvaez expedition. The veteran conquistadors were satisfied with a few easy-to-carry pieces.

"Look at the idiots," snorted Bernal Diaz, who stood nearby with a trembling Francisca clinging to his arm. "They're loading themselves down like burros. Their riches are going to drag them to the bottom of the lake."

"Didn't you take anything for yourself?" I asked him. "I don't see a trace of gold on you."

"Look . . ." Bernal produced a kerchief in which he had wrapped four perfect *chalchihuitls*. "Where we're going, these will be worth more than gold. I've enough here to purchase a few meals, shelter for a night, and maybe my own life if necessary. What more do I need?"

Plans for the evacuation had been made earlier. Fifty men, under an officer named Margarino, were to carry a portable wooden bridge that had been assembled hastily out of lumber from the *mantas*. Pledged to stay at their posts until the last man had crossed, they would remove the bridge from each gap in the causeway and carry it to the next until all three stretches of open shallow water had been crossed. Sandoval, with a force of two hundred infantry and twenty horsemen, would lead the stealthy procession. After him would come the most cumbersome part of the train, consisting of the baggage, the sick and wounded, the hostages, the women and the treasure. They would be guarded by a large force under

Hernán himself, as well as most of the six thousand Tlaxcalans. Alvarado and Velásquez de León would bring up the rear with thirty horsemen, a hundred experienced soldiers and most of the men from the Narvaez expedition.

After Padre Olmedo's short mass, I caught Juan's eye across the crowded chapel. He broke off from a conversation with Ordaz and Corral to make his way to my side.

"Have they told you where you'll be marching?" I asked him.

"I'd expected to go with Sandoval," he said, "but Cortés just put me in charge of a hundred men assigned to guard the treasure. I suppose I should be flattered by such trust." There was a sardonic glint in his eyes.

"At least I'll know where you are," I said.

"Listen, Marina." He leaned toward me. "If they catch us on that causeway, there'll be hell to pay. Stay close to Alvarado's woman, if you can. Her brothers will protect her with their lives. Promise me you'll do it."

"I promise." I looked up into eyes that were bloodshot with weariness. My mind caressed each feature of his battle-scarred face. With the crowd milling around us, we dared not even touch fingertips.

"God go with you, *querida*," he whispered huskily.

"God go with us both." I watched him as he turned away and was lost in the crowd as it surged toward the courtyard to assemble for the exodus.

Thank God for the rain, I thought, for the cold, drizzly mist enveloped us like a cloak as we crept through the streets toward the causeway. It was after midnight, a time when darkness and the miserable weather would keep the city's inhabitants shut up in their houses, but the marchers in the ghostly procession scarcely dared breathe for fear of waking even one sleeping Aztec who could arouse the entire city with his cries. I glanced back at the line of prisoners. Cacama, Moctezuma's son Asupacaci, Cuauhtemoc's father and the other chiefs were tied together in single file, with Tlaxcalans marching on either side of them. They'd been tightly gagged to prevent them from crying out a warning to their people. Against my advice, Hernán had allowed Doña Ana and Doña Inés to go unbound and unmuffled. They were loyal to him, he'd insisted, and in any case, how could it be possible for a woman to betray the father of her own child? When I'd tried to press my argument further, he'd accused me of jealousy and so, seeing that he could not be moved, I'd given up. The two women walked just in front of me, Doña Ana moving awkwardly with the bulk of her unborn baby. Looking ahead into the mist, I could just make out the cowl of Padre Olmedo, the stoop-shouldered frame of Aguilar, and Orteguilla's tawny head bobbing between the two. Somewhere behind me was the treasure, with Juan and his men guarding it. Hernán himself rode silently back and forth alongside the ranks, making certain that all was moving as it should. He passed us now on Arriero, pausing for a concerned glance at the toiling Doña Ana. I avoided his eyes and quickened my step to keep up with Alvarado's Luisa, who was walking next to her warrior brothers. The two young men, friendlier than their older brother Xicotencatl, were well known for their fierceness in battle.

I counted the canal bridges as we passed over them. Echoing under my feet now was the fifth one. The sixth and last would take us onto the causeway. By now, Sandoval's company and the men with the portable bridge would be on the narrow roadway that led across the lake, approaching the first open gap where the bridge would be placed. Here, near the causeway entrance, the houses were vacant, for the inhabitants had fled the fighting that had taken place there earlier. All was quiet. The evacuation of the city was going incredibly well.

We passed over the sixth bridge, through streets as still as death. As my feet touched the earth of the causeway, Doña Inés spun around, threw back her head and screamed, a shattering warning that echoed through the empty streets. She screamed again. I lunged for her, but I was not as fast as the Tlaxcalan who split the head of Moctezuma's daughter into two pieces with one blow of his *maquahuitl.* As her body rolled down the bank, the tones of the big snakeskin war drum atop the temple of Tlatelolco shook the air, startling the city into wakefulness and sending our band of refugees tumbling frantically onto the causeway. We crushed and pushed one another, shoving some down the slippery banks and into the lake. Remembering my promise, I clawed my way through the packed bodies to Luisa's side. As I fought for balance I heard the splashing to a thousand canoe paddles and saw black forms moving swiftly toward us over the surface of the lake. From the shouts of battle up ahead, I guessed that Sandoval was already being attacked, but the train continued to move forward; that could mean that Margarino's men had been able to place the bridge across the first gap. The canoes crunched against the bank and the painted warriors sprang out of them to fall upon the Tlaxcalan guard. Shrieks split the air as spears and *maquahuitls* found their targets.

I saw Hernán on his horse, flying back to where the treasure was being carried. "Jaramillo!" he roared above the din. "Get them moving! Follow me! We're taking the treasure ahead, all the way to the other side! *Diós mío*, don't look at me like that! Make a wedge!"

"Move back—get them out of the way!" I recognized Juan's shout as, moments later, Arriero came plunging down the center of the causeway, crowding both attackers and attacked toward the edges. The lightly packed wedge of infantry and treasure-bearing *tlamemes*, leading and pushing a mare loaded with the royal fifth of the treasure, came charging through in his wake. I glimpsed Juan's face beneath his helmet. He was cursing as he flashed past without seeing me. The outward surge of the crowd pushed me onto the slope. I dug my fingers into the mud to keep from sliding into the lake. Someone stepped on my hands and I screamed as I felt something clutch my leg, dragging me down. I heard the swish of a *maquahuitl* and a wail of agony as one of Luisa's brothers chopped into the arm that had seized me. Grasping Luisa's outstretched hands, I pulled myself back to level ground.

The mass of struggling bodies narrowed and I felt wood under my feet. We were on the bridge, packed so tightly together that I had to fight for breath. Canoes swarmed around both sides of the bridge, where the enemy was harvesting victims for later sacrifice, jerking them off the sagging platform and into the waiting canoes. A woman fell into the lake, screaming. Moments later we poured off the bridge and onto the second section of the causeway. Shoved from behind, I fell flat over the wet, lifeless mass of a dead horse. My hand pushed against a face that was almost buried in the mud. I sprang back, horror giving me strength. The face was Cacama's.

Two Aztecs had spotted Asupacaci, Moctezuma's son, and were trying to rescue him. They chopped their way through the crowd but they were too late. The prince's head went flying through the air to land in the lake with a splash and his body crumpled into the mud. I could not even see who had killed him.

All forward movement had stopped. The fleeing mob jammed tighter and tighter against the end of the causeway's second section as a cry went up from the rear. "The bridge—they can't move the bridge! It's wedged in!" Groans of dismay filled the darkness.

Hernán appeared out of the black mist, his horse and clothes dripping with water. "Go to the right!" he shouted. "There's a ford there. Don't be afraid, it isn't deep."

Even in the midst of the panic, I remembered my duties. I called out his instructions in Nahuatl, praying to be heard above the clamor. People began to spill off the end of the causeway into the lake, where the Aztecs were waiting to drag them into canoes or club away at their heads until they sank. Salcedo, the dandy who had joined us so long ago in Villa Rica with his own ship, lunged out of the water at one of the canoes, overturning it with his weight. As one of the canoe's occupants attacked him, Salcedo pulled out his dagger and the two grappled together in the water until they disappeared beneath the surface. A cloud of red spread over them and diffused in the murky water.

Clutching Luisa's hand, I stepped off the end of the causeway and into the lake. The waves lapped at my legs. It was suprisingly shallow. I moved forward, suddenly sickeningly aware of what was under my feet. The softy, lumpy mass just under the surface was not the lake's bottom. I was walking on a thick carpet of debris and corpses that was filling up the gap in the causeway. No bridge would be necessary here.

Luisa screamed as an Aztec canoe bore down on us. Two warriors were in it, *maquahuitls* raised to strike. I jerked Luisa under the water with me. The terrified girl thrashed wildly, but I held her down, pressing both our bodies against the piled-up dead and praying that I wasn't drowning her. The canoe passed over us. As we surfaced, gasping, we saw that Luisa's brothers had upset the canoe and were clubbing the two Aztecs to death in the water.

We dragged ourselves onto the bank on the other side, Luisa still coughing and spitting. As soon as her brothers had joined us, we struggled on along the causeway. The crowd was thinner now and movement was easier, but we were more exposed to danger than ever.

Stragglers were beginning to catch up from the rear. "They're all dead back there," I heard someone say. A wounded Velásquez de León staggered past us. He'd lost his horse. I saw his Tlaxcalan princess, Doña Elvira, just ahead. A burly Aztec was dragging her toward his canoe. Velásquez de León plunged toward them. He was almost too weak to raise his sword, but his weight knocked the warrior off-balance. He gathered Elvira in his arms as six or seven Aztecs clambered over them like ants, hacking them both to pieces with their *maquahuitls.* I heard myself screaming uncontrollably. I stumbled backward over something bulky, my hands groping for balance. The thing behind me had a strangely swollen feeling to it. I turned around. The head had been crushed beyond recognition, but I recognized the royal robes and pregnant body of Doña Ana. My stomach began to churn. I fought for self-control.

Crowds were jamming against the end of the second portion of the causeway, providing easy prey for the Aztecs who howled against their flanks, striking freely. Word had come back that the crossing ahead was deeper and wider than the others, but someone had found a single long, narrow beam on the mainland, and those who were afraid to swim were teetering across the chasm on it, one at a time. Many of the swimmers, exhausted, wounded or weighted down with treasure, were disappearing beneath the black water.

One of Luisa's brothers glanced around desperately. "Come," he hissed, tugging his sister and me toward the side of the causeway. An overturned canoe was floating there. Quickly we righted it, and the two brothers helped us climb inside. "Lie down," one of them commanded. "We'll stay against the sides and push."

The young Tlaxcalans were strong swimmers and they had the floating canoe to sustain them. With excruciating caution, they slipped among the other canoes and out into the open lake, making a wide circle around the fighting. Luisa and I clung together in the canoe's bottom. The battle sounds grew fainter. The motion of the swimmers changed just enough for me to realize that they'd touched bottom and were walking rapidly toward the shore of Tlacopan.

The canoe scraped against the sand and I leaped out and helped pull it ashore. All was dark and quiet where we'd landed, but in the distance to the south we could hear the fray and see the occasional flare of a torch. Luisa and her brothers collapsed on the beach, but I could not rest. Thanking my friends, I began to run along the shore in the direction of the causeway.

I strained my eyes to make out details, but I could see only that the fighting seemed confined to the causeway itself. The Aztecs were not pursuing the survivors onto the mainland. Suddenly I collided with a lean figure whose rough robe blended with the darkness. I nearly cried with relief when I looked up into the pale face of Padre Olmedo.

"Doña Marina! By all the saints, I feared we'd lost you too."

"Aguilar? Orteguilla?" My chest contracted with dread.

"Alive. God's arm was around us."

"And Hernán?"

"He's indestructible. He must have ridden down that causeway at least three or four times to help the others get to the mainland. The last time I saw him he'd gone back to look for Velásquez de León."

"He won't find him," I said dully. "What about the others?" I hardly dared ask who we'd lost.

"Lares the good horseman, Salcedo, Salazar, to name a few . . ." The priest sighed. "Many, many of the soldiers who came with Narvaez, all the hostages, and most of the women are lost—and no one's seen Pedro de Alvarado."

The news was even worse than I'd expected. "What about María de Estrada?"

"Ay! What a woman! You should have seen her, Doña Marina, standing over her dead horse with a sword and buckler she'd picked up, shouting, 'Take that, you devils! Take that for my Fernando!' She must have wounded four or five of them by the time Pero Farfán got to her. He almost had to drag her off the causeway."

Padro Olmedo regarded me with one eyebrow cocked and and shook his head. "Go ahead and ask me, child. The question's written all over your face. Jaramillo's alive—took an arrow in the thigh, but it wasn't enough to put him out of action."

I lowered my eyes, my relief momentarily dulling the horrors of the nightmarish escape.

"I must say he's busy," the padre added. "Cortés put him in charge of the defenses at this end of the causeway, including everyone and everything that makes it to shore alive. Most of the survivors have been gathered in the square at Tlacopan. I'll take you there, but first I want to go back to the causeway and let Cortés know you're all right. He's been beside himself."

"Does he know about . . . the others?"

"Doña Inés and Doña Ana? Yes, he knows. He grieves for them, of course, but it's you he's really frantic about. He asks everyone who comes across if they've seen you. Come, child."

The black sky was washing out to gray in the east and the fog was lifting. It was now possible to see a little distance down the causeway, but Hernán was not in sight. A battered Gonzalo de Sandoval hailed us. His splendid Motilla was caked with dirt, foam and blood.

"Padre! And Doña Marina! *Gracias a Diós!* We all thought you were dead." The brown eyes that peered out from under his helmet were rimmed with red. He wiped beads of mist from his beard with the back of his hand. "Things are coming to an end here. The poor devils who haven't made it across by now must be either captured or killed. Cortés heard shouts out there and went to see if he could help out the stragglers. Damn! Why does he take such chances when we need him so much?"

"Any word of Alvarado?" asked the priest.

"None. We've given up hope. Most of the men in his section were lost. Ay, did you hear about the fools who hadn't made it onto the causeway before the fighting started? They turned around and ran back to the palace—a hundred, maybe a hundred fifty of them. They're trapped like stinking rats back there. The Aztecs will starve them out if nothing else."

I shuddered. "How many do you think have come across?"

Sandoval shrugged. "Who knows. Half the company perhaps." His voice broke, despite his efforts to control it. "We've sent most of them to the square to form up under Jaramillo. Maybe someone there will dare to count them."

Bernal Diaz had come up beside us, leaning on a broken lance for support. His face was the color of ashes. "Look at the sky," he said hoarsely. "If we're not out of here by daylight we'll have the whole country on our heads."

"It's a wonder they've not chased us past this point," the padre said.

"They lose their advantage once we're off the causeway," said Sandoval. "Then there's the gold we were carrying. They're probably too busy looting the bodies to follow us."

"Well, whatever the reason, we should use it to get out of here before it's too late," Bernal growled.

I moved to his side and quietly took his hand. His huge fingers gripped mine like talons. "Bernal," I whispered, "where's your Francisca?"

Bernal didn't answer. His empty, burning eyes told me all I needed to know.

By now we could see as far as the nearest and last gap in the causeway. Hernán's mounted form emerged out of the dark mist. He was herding a small cluster of wounded men before him, protecting their rear as they dragged themselves along. The beam was still in place across the gap, but it was slimy with mud. The men had to inch their way across it, some of them crawling on their bellies like worms. Among them I recognized Botello, the self-professed astrologer. He'd misread the stars both in terms of the propitiousness of our escape and the prediction of his own death. Hernán eased Arriero into the water and began to swim him across the chasm. Botello was the last one to cross on the beam. He teetered precariously, waving his skinny arms for balance. Suddenly a javelin came whizzing out of the mist, striking him in the back and piercing his body through. He walked on with an unearthly stagger, the point protruding from his chest, then toppled onto the bank just as the others rushed to him. He was gurgling blood and babbling out something that sounded like "The stars!" when he died.

Arriero heaved himself out of the water with a splash, and trotted wearily down the last finger of the causeway to the mainland. It was only then that Hernán saw me. "Marina!" He vaulted out of the saddle and at the end of two long strides his arms were around me, crushing me against the cold wetness of his armor. He was unsteady on his feet and shivering as he whispered my name through chattering teeth.

"Marina . . . Marina *mía*, thank God you're alive. From the beginning I told them to watch for you . . . I watched for you myself when I could. No one saw you come off the causeway, and so I thought . . . we all thought . . ." He held me painfully tight. "Marina, we've lost so many. Lares the horseman, Salcedo, Velásquez de León, Alvarado . . . What will we do without them?"

"You've found Alvarado's body?" Sandoval asked.

"We found no trace of him, but the rear end of the column was massacred. Hardly anyone got through. Alvarado'd have made a great prize for some glory-seeking young buck. By my faith, I hope they didn't take him alive . . ." I held him as well as he could be held in the heavy cuirass and tried feebly to comfort him.

All at once a crescendo of war cries echoed down the causeway. Pedro de Alvarado burst out of the fog with a band of twenty Aztecs in screaming pursuit. He'd lost his horse, his sword and his helmet. He had nothing but a lance, which was almost no defense at all against so many. "Alvarado! Come on!" Hernán roared, springing into the saddle to gallop back toward the opening.

Alvarado was covered with wounds. Every step must have

been agony, and yet he was running full-tilt toward the last gap in the causeway. The Aztecs were closing in. A few more paces and they'd have him. Hernán and the others rushed helplessly toward the other side of the crossing. The beam could be traversed, but only slowly. Alvarado was going to be captured before our eyes.

He sprinted the last distance to the gap, still holding his lance. Then, in an astounding climax of effort, he thrust the tip of the lance into the watery opening, where it struck the debris-piled bottom and propelled him through the air like a catapult. Miraculously, he landed safely at the edge of the water on the other side. Murmurs of "Tonatuih!" arose from his stunned pursuers.

Hernán himself reached down to help him up the steep bank. Alvarado clambered up into the saddle behind Morla and they took advantage of their enemies' shock to move quickly out of range, but not before the gallant Morla stiffened in his saddle and fell dead with an arrow through his chest. There was no time to weep for him.

"Is anyone left alive out there?" Hernán demanded.

"No, I swear it! They're all dead. No fool could pass over that causeway and live except me." Alvarado was coughing for breath.

"Then I suppose we've done all we can. Pray for their souls, Padre." Hernán said quietly. "We may as well go back to the square. If Jaramillo has everyone ready to march we can be in the hills before sunup. No, put the wounded men on Arriero, my good Sandoval. I'll walk with Marina." He laid his arm heavily across my shoulders and pulled me close to his side. Weak with exhaustion, defeat and despair, he leaned on me, drawing my strength as we walked back toward Tlacopan. I knew that the moment he stepped into the square, Hernán Cortés would blaze to life again, decisive, energetic, in total command of himself and his men; but for this short time he needed me and I bowed under the burden of that need.

The previous day's fighting had driven the inhabitants of Tlacopan from their city. Yet, chilly as the night was, our battered forces had lit no fires in the square. Even the flicker of a candle might be seen by the enemy. The survivors had been organized into squads, a reflection of Juan's natural sense of order. Only the wounded were allowed to rest. Those who were fittest patrolled the streets. Others assisted the bedraggled María de Estrada in tending the wounded, or inventoried our pathetic store of supplies and weapons. The degree of inprovisation was amazing. Cloaks and shirts had been torn into strips for use as bandages, or lashed between spears for stretchers to carry the wounded. The houses around the square had been ransacked to the last kernel of maize. But no amount of activity could lighten the sense of shock and sorrow that rode so heavily on each man's shoulders, or mask the hopelessness in eyes that had seen enough horror in one night to last a hundred lifetimes.

Juan cantered his borrowed horse across the square toward us. Relief flooded his tired face when he saw me. His lips formed my name.

"I knew I could count on you to have things well in hand here, Jaramillo." Hernán had released me from his arm. The vigor had returned to his voice. "How many are we?"

"About five hundred Spaniards and no more than two thousand Tlaxcalans. A few stragglers are still coming in." Juan spoke mechanically, making, I realized, a great effort to control his emotions. "We've lost more than half of our men, and two out of three Tlaxcalans."

"And the treasure?" Hernán leaned forward confidentially.

"The mare with the royal fifth made it across. Most of the rest went to the bottom of the lake with the *tlamemes* who carried it."

Hernán's features sagged perceptibly. "Horses? Weapons?"

Juan closed his eyes briefly, as if trying to force his fatigued mind to concentrate. "Twenty-four horses, counting your own, most of them wounded. The carriers dropped all the artillery and ammunition into the water." He fought to keep the despair out of his voice. "We've come up with only a dozen crossbows and six or seven arquebuses with no powder. We've only our swords and pikes left. I'd expected you'd want to make a run for the hills, so I've told the men to be ready to march at your order."

"If there's no one behind us, there's no use in waiting," Hernán rumbled. "Unless we get out of here we'll have all Tlacopan to fight. Let's move. Look at the sky—we'll be racing the sun to the hills!"

Chapter Twenty

Otumba—July 1520

Following the advice of a Tlaxcalan chief, we'd taken a course north from Tlacopan on a line parallel with the lake shore. Hungry, exhausted, and with the Aztecs snapping at our flanks, we'd struggled sixteen leagues from Toltepec to Teuculhuacan to Citlaltepec, and had finally turned our course eastward in the direction of Tlaxcala. It was the seventh day of July and the seventh day of our flight from Tenochtitlan, and now we threw the last of our strength into a desperate thrust to reach Tlaxcala and—we hoped—safety before the day's end.

With so many wounded, our progress was slow. Food and rest we'd snatched wherever we could find it, and there'd been precious little of either. Hunger gnawed at our innards, draining away strength of body and spirit. The previous day, we'd eaten a horse that had died of its wounds after a skirmish with the enemy. In that same skirmish, Hernán had been badly wounded in the head and the left arm.

It was the head wound that worried me. A sharp rock, fired by a sling from below and at close range, had hit him in the forehead, leaving a bloody depression in his skull. I had swallowed a gasp of horror as Juan washed away the blood and we realized that the wound had penetrated the outer covering of the brain. Incredibly, he was still able to ride. His bandaged head bobbed like a banner at the front of the column and he frequently galloped back to the rear to prod and encourage the stragglers. I dared not take my eyes off him, for there were times when he would put his hand to his face and sway dangerously in the saddle, clutching at Arriero's neck for support. Still, he refused to be carried on a litter. "Most of the wounded are worse off than I am," he'd say through clenched teeth. "So who am I to expect to be coddled?"

The adoring Sandoval clung to his commander's side like a burr, his bushy eyebrows meshed with concern, ever alert for ways in which he could share and ease the burden of command. I appreciated his attentiveness, and told him so as I walked beside him in the chill of early morning.

"Some are loyal to Hernán out of concern of their own safety," I said softly, "others because they admire him or because they share his ambition. But as for you, Gonzalo de Sandoval, I think you follow him out of love."

Sandoval flushed and looked down at his feet. At twenty-two, he was by far the youngest of Hernán's captains, and the esteem shown him by the rest of the company seemed to embarrass him at times. "I've never met anyone like him," he murmured. "Who else could have brought us this far? And he's not beaten, Doña Marina. He'll return to Tenochtitlan one day and I, God willing, will be at his side." As his foot struck a prickly pear, Sandoval cursed and bent over to pull the spines out of his boot.

I smiled at his irritation. "You must miss your Motilla."

"Ay, but God outdid himself when he made that beast . . ." Motilla, I knew, was back in the train with three wounded men on his back. Sandoval hitched up his boot and caught up with me. "But while I still have two good legs to carry me, I'd best use them," he said.

"Those bandy legs look out of place on the ground, my Sandoval." Hernán's voice boomed down from above our heads. He was trying to smile but his pain-ravaged face looked like a grinning death's head. The bandage that bound his wound was crusted with dried blood.

Sandoval forced a laugh. "If my bandy legs carry me for this one more day, they'll have served me well enough. I understand we've only got to cross the next valley and we'll be close enough to spit across the border into Tlaxcala."

"True," said Hernan. "But our troubles may not be over even then. How will they welcome us in Tlaxcala? Look how many of their sons and brothers we've lost. We may have to fight our way back to Villa Rica."

"That's a joke," Sandoval grunted. "Look at us. We couldn't fight our way out of a flower bed." He exaggerated but little. Our army was so weak from wounds and hunger that we could barely trudge along from one day to the next. We had no cannons, no guns and no ammunition. I wondered when the Aztecs would decide to move in and finish us.

The top of the ridge was in sight, the unrisen sun turning

the sky pearly above it. From its crest, our allies had told us, we would be able to look out over the valley of Otumba and see the peaks of Tlaxcala in the distance. In spite of our weariness, we strove eagerly toward the rocky summit. The ground itself—dry, rocky, bristling with its own spiny cactus claws—seemed hostile to my blistered feet. The friendly mountains would be a welcome sight.

Hernán was first to gain the ridge. Sandoval and I struggled up behind him, followed by others. We looked out across the mist-shrouded valley and suppressed the urge to shout for joy at the sight of the goal—Tlaxcala!

A limping Bernal had moved up beside me, a smile on his face as he gazed toward the rising sun, shading his eyes with his hand. Then he looked down into the valley and the hand dropped like a stone. "*Diós mió*—"

The mist had begun to dissolve in the morning light, lingering only in the cool hollows of the land. The sun's first rays glinted upon a distant forest of spear tips! Padre Diaz crossed himself. Hernán leaned forward in the saddle. Others clambered up besides us to watch, transfixed, as the warming air cleared to reveal hosts of warriors spread out over the plain like grass.

"How many, do you think?" Hernán whispered hoarsely.

Sandoval squinted into the sun. "Who knows? A hundred fifty thousand at least."

"Closer to two hundred fifty thousand's my guess," Bernal muttered.

"Maybe more. *Diablos!* What difference does it make? Do you think they've seen us?"

"Probably." Hernán ran one finger under the edge of the bandage on his head. "They know we're coming or they wouldn't be here." He turned in the saddle and looked back at his pathetic army. "Sandoval, assemble the men around me," he said quietly.

I stood beside him, ready to translate his words for the Tlaxcalans. My eyes passed over the ragged little group, lingering on Aguilar, who had an oversized sword strapped to his waist, his hand gripping the leash of the dancing Esmeralda; Padre Olmedo with his arm around young Orteguilla; Olid on horseback, dirty bandages covering an ugly leg wound. I saw Alvarado leaning on his Luisa; the coarse Trujillo with one useless arm; proud Ávila in a hammock strung between two Tlaxcalan carriers; Ordaz with wrappings covering his head and one eye. Most of us are already half dead, I thought. Bernal Diaz, towering a full head above the others, leaned heavily on his lance to ease the weight on his wounded foot. Juan stood beside him, quilted armor stained red where his shoulder wound had reopened. My eyes stung as they met his. We'd hardly spoken since *la noche triste*—"the sad night," as the retreat on the causeway had come to be called—for Hernán had kept me with him constantly.

"*Compadres* . . ." The strength in Hernán's voice belied his condition. "You've seen what's waiting for us down in that valley. After all we've been through, how many of you are ready to die?"

The men looked at one another. There were some nervous stirrings but no one spoke or made a sign. "Good," Hernán declared. "If we march on down there with our hearts resigned to death, there's not one of us who'll come out alive." He paused to let the force of his words penetrate. His eyes swept the sky. "Brothers," he said in a hushed voice, "we have Christ and all his angels on our side! As long as we conduct ourselves like soldiers of the cross, we can win against any odds!"

What blind, mad faith, I thought, what insane courage. Yet, we had no alternative except to fight. Escape was impossible, surrender fraught with unspeakable consequences. I saw María de Estrada standing beside Pero Farfán, a genteel, graying soldier who'd distinguished himself by being the first to lay hands on Narvaez. Doña Maria's torn, soiled gown hung loosely on a frame that hardship had reduced to bones and sinew. She wore a sleeveless vest of quilted cotton, the native armor, and a rusty helmet sat lopsidedly on her head. When her eyes met Farfán's, her homely face softened into near-beauty. I prayed silently that both of them would live through the day.

"Now, listen and listen well," Hernán continued. "There's not one of you here who hasn't seen a man die. Think then of a man, a mighty, boastful man, who can take an arrow in his hands and snap it like a twig. Yet, that same arrow, when shot from a crossbow, can be driven through his heart to kill him where he stands. Which is the stronger then, the man or the arrow?" He paused, fever-bright eyes boring into each man's soul. "I tell you, the arrow in itself is nothing. But given the bow . . . given the archer . . .

"My comrades, our little army must be that arrow. A deadly missile shot with the swiftness of courage from the very crossbow of God, straight through the heart of that mighty host. Our cavalry's to be the barb, thrusting with lances at the faces of the enemy, driving them back and opening up a path for the infantry, the shaft of the arrow, who'll strike at their bodies with swords and pikes. We'll stay together, all of us, in one solid mass with the wounded and the women in the middle and the strong on the edges. Keep the column narrow—no more than four lance-lengths wide. That way a good part of their spears, arrows and stones will pass over us and fall on their own troops on the other side. Press always to the east. That snow-capped peak to the south—keep it on your right. Let no one think of death. Think only of God, who has delivered us this far and won't forsake us now!" He surveyed the crowd, satisfied that his words had had their desired impact.

The ranking Tlaxcalan chief, the tough, scar-faced Calmecahua, stepped forward. "We'll protect your rear," he offered, "and we can put two of our warriors at the side of each of your men."

"Done," said Hernán. "By my faith, I've never seen such allies!"

Calmecahua scowled as I translated. He and his men had even more at stake in this battle than did the Spanish. Defeat would lead to harsh reprisals against their homeland; Cuitlahuac would show their loved ones no mercy. He spat in the dust. "In our land," he said disdainfully, "when a man takes his woman to the mat he tells her, 'Give me sons to kill the Aztecs!' "

Hernán's eyes embraced the forlorn ranks. He motioned to Padre Olmedo, who led us in prayer, invoking the aid of the Virgin and our special patron, Santiago. Then, hastily, we formed for battle as Hernán directed: horsemen in front, grouped in fives, with infantry forming a compact shaft behind them. Someone handed me a sword. It was long and heavy, awkward in my hand. I passed it on and accepted a *maquahuitl* from one of the Tlaxcalans. The short wooden club, edged with razor-sharp chunks of obsidian, felt more natural to me. I prayed for the strength to use it.

On the way to his place in the line, Juan brushed past me. "No heroics from you, Marina," he said. "Stay in the middle where you'll be protected. Promise me." I nodded. "God keep you, *querida*," he whispered. I answered him with my eyes. Then I moved into place beside María de Estrada, who raised her eyebrows and shook her head. The sharp-eyed lady had missed nothing, but I didn't care. If I died within the next hour, I'd die happier with the whole world knowing that Juan loved me.

We marched down the other side of the ridge and out onto the plain of Otumba, our little army consisting of less than five hundred Spaniards—most of them wounded—twenty-three horses and about two thousand Tlaxcalans. Waiting for us was a host outnumbering us nearly a hundred to one, a vast force of Aztec warriors, superbly trained and equipped, well fed, rested, and sensing the final kill. They spread out across the plain like a human sea, the choicest troops of all the kingdom, the flower of Aztec military society. There were fresh units from the lakeside cities of Iztapalapan and Tlacopan, from Tlatelolco, from Tenochtitlan itself, and from the hills and plains. Their insignias waved above their heads. There were princes and generals, their elaborate headdresses weaving like blossoms among the warriors. The sun glittered on helmets of gold, on freshly painted faces and dancing spear tips chiseled from obsidian. Black-robed priests moved among the ranks, blessing the coming battle with their swinging copal censers.

As we moved closer, the din of the drums and conches rose to a deafening shrill, but the advance of the massive army was slow, cautious, as if they were still uncertain as to whether the white gods had been stripped of their powers. Hernán waited till the glistening tide had nearly engulfed us. I could see the painted designs on their faces, the intensity of their expressions.

"Santiago! Santiago and at them!" Hernán bellowed, and the calvary spurred their horses to a gallop, charging in spearheads of five into the mass of the enemy, striking first in one direction, then another, their lances sending a shock wave through the Aztecs. The enemy fell back, jammed solidly together, many unable to move as the infantry waded in with pikes and slashing swords. Following Hernán's instructions, we strove to keep the column moving forward en masse. Our troops made no attempt to engage in individual hand-to-hand combat. Rather, we hacked from the sides of the shaft, wedging our way through the wall of warriors, striving to push them back.

Our forces had thrust deep into the body of the enemy, but the struggle for life had only begun. The entire column was surrounded now, and we battled for every step forward. With the small size of our tightly packed unit, only limited numbers of the enemy had contact with us at any given time, but the Aztecs were able to pour layer after layer of fresh warriors against us. The Tlaxcalans, fighting one on either side of each Spaniard, took the force of the impact, giving the Spanish blades and lances time and room to strike.

María de Estrada fought with the fury of a jungle cat, using both hands to strengthen the blows of the heavy sword, pausing to shout encouragement to those around her. She had moved to the outside of the column alongside the men, exposing her scantily protected body to the fighting. Hoping to reach her before she was killed, I struggled through the column, dodging upraised swords and clubs. I stretched out my hand and caught hold of her dress. "Don't be a fool, María!" I shouted, but it was impossible for my voice to be heard above the clamor of battle. María's body suddenly went limp. A rock had thumped against her helmet, leaving a dent. An Aztec warrior seized her by the arm to drag her away. Lunging forward, I swung my *maquahuitl* and felt a wild, sickening exhilaration when it crunched into muscle and bone. The howling Aztec fell backward. Crouching down, I wrapped my arms around the body of my friend. But even as thin as she had become, her large frame was heavy and it took all my strength, lifting, pushing and pulling, to get her back to the middle of the column. Orteguilla saw us and made his way forward to help. We were able to support the semiconscious María on either side with our shoulders and keep moving slowly ahead with the rest.

Sandoval, once more astride his Motilla, seemed to be everywhere at once, spearheading the thrust with blows from lance and hooves, moving alongside the column in the thick of the fighting, roaring encouragement to his comrades, and always keeping one anxious eye on his commander. Hernán led charge after charge. He battled mightily and his voice rang out as strongly as ever. Only a handful of us—Sandoval, Juan, myself and a few others—knew how deeply he drew from his last reserves of strength.

Suddenly I saw Arriero stagger with pain. The horse's muzzle frothed with blood and he lurched and bucked uncontrollably, nearly throwing Hernán from the saddle. The pressure of the bit was unbearable in the stallion's wounded mouth. Several men formed a protective circle and others held him long enough for Hernán to dismount. No sooner had his master's feet touched the ground than Arriero broke loose and bolted straight ahead into the thick of the enemy, tearing an open swath through the startled Aztecs. "After him!" Hernán bawled. "Forward!" Sandoval paused long enough for Hernán to climb up behind him. The half-charge, half-chase was successful. They recovered Arriero had forged a deeper path into the midst of the enemy, but Hernán was still without a horse. Declining Sandoval's offer of Motilla, he sent an urgent message back to the rear where one available mount remained. The soldiers shook their heads as *El Pícaro*—"the rascal"—was led up the center of the ranks to the head of the column, but they moved aside to clear a respectful path. The horse was as vicious as he was ugly, a yellow brute whose penchant for kicking and biting had always consigned him to the baggage train.

El Pícaro stood still while Hernán mounted, but his little eyes glittered with malevolence. The instant his rider's weight settled in the saddle, the horse exploded into a tornado of hooves and snapping yellow-green teeth. Tugging mightily at the reins, Hernán aimed the animal where his bad temper could accomplish most, and charged.

The sun climbed high in the hot blue sky, blazing down on the combatants and evaporating their strength, but the battle raged on. It was plain to see what the outcome would be. Although our soldiers and allies fought like furies, we were exhausted. With their vast reserves, the Aztecs would be able to send wave after wave of troops against us. It was little more than a question of time before heat and weariness would hand the victory to the brown-skinned multitude.

The Tlaxcalans, with their unprotected bodies and vulnerable position at the rear, had taken the brunt of losses. They'd fought like demons, dropping one by one until the original two thousand had dwindled to a few hundred. We who survived owed them our lives.

María de Estrada was conscious, but dizzy from the blow on her head. She still could not walk without support. Rivulets of perspiration trickled down under my *huipilli* as Orteguilla and I labored along under her weight. Warm, stinking flesh pressed against us from all sides. The air reeked with odors of blood, sweat and incense, and rang with the clatter of weapons and screams of pain and fury that dulled the ears and hammered the brain. We moved along at a caterpillar's pace in the blistering heat.

I felt a soft touch on my shoulder, a touch apart from the shoving of fevered bodies. Even without turning my head I knew Juan was beside me. I looked up at him. There was a red gash across his cheek. He looked unspeakably tired. Tears burned my eyes as I read the despair in his face and realized why he'd moved in to be near me. The end was coming. Our forces were so spent that the next wave of fresh Aztec troops would likely overwhelm us. Juan would die protecting me.

I had no idea how far our little army had traveled across the plain—half a league at the most, surely no more—our progress was so slow. As I raised my head for a gulp of air I saw him over the forest of waving arms—the commander of the Aztec army. He rode on a litter above the fray, surrounded by his chiefs. His feathers were unfamiliar, but from the banner of gold net and the insignia hanging from a tall staff attached to his back I guessed him to be the lord of nearby Teotihuacan. A splendid figure in gold-studded armor and multicolored plumes, his curiosity had drawn him close enough to see the death blow that was about to be dealt to his enemies. Too close. Hernán spotted him.

I heard his bellow over the melee. "After him! In the name of God and Saint Peter, follow me!" Hernán plunged his ugly horse through the enemy ranks with such vigor and suddenness that they were caught off-guard and fell back. The cavalry thrust in after him, pushing their advantage, and the entire column, renewed by the prospect of victory or at least of revenge, poured into the breach they left in their wake. The fury of our charge swept Juan away from me once more.

The *tlatoani* saw us coming. Rising on his litter, he leaned forward to lash at the shoulders of the bearers with his little staff, but they were scarcely able to move in the pressing crowd. Before they'd taken twenty steps the horsemen were on them. As the defenseless bearers crumpled or fled, the litter began to pitch. The *tlatoani* clawed at its edges, scrambling for balance like a cat on a slippery roof, as his chiefs died around him. It was a mercy when one of our soldiers charged in and caught the royal chest with his lance tip, lifting the *tlatoani* off his feet with the impact of the thrust. Then the weight of his body pulled the lance downward until, lifeless now, he slid off the bloodied end and collapsed on the trampled grass. With the skill of an acrobat, the soldier swooped low in his saddle and snatched up the golden banner, giving a whoop of triumph as he thrust it into Hernán's waiting hand. Someone cut off the head of the fallen chief and raised it on a pike.

Hernán flung back his white-swathed head and the cry that rose from his throat sent chills up my back. His voice rang with exultation and blood lust. Our whole company took up the shout and, forgetting wounds, pain and danger, surged like madmen into the enemy. The Aztecs reeled backward in a body, twitching with shock like the newly decapitated corpse of their leader. Then panic shot through their ranks and they began to scatter in wild disorder, dropping weapons in their haste and leaving wounded comrades behind them. Our forces bore down on them like a band of avenging devils in a whirlwind of slashing blades, pounding hooves and stabbing lances. Those Aztecs who chose to stay and fight were cut down by the score, and even those who ran, if they did not run fast enough, were overtaken on horseback and pounded into the dust.

I dragged María and Orteguilla over to the fallen litter and we crouched behind it for protection. I had seen three thousand die at Cholula, I'd seen Alvarado butcher six hundred at Tenochtitlan—and I'd been sick with horror both times. Now, with the slaughter multiplied at least fivefold, I found that I had lost all sense of remorse. Along with the rest of the company I had gone a little mad. I watched in jubilation as every man who could walk, even the wounded, even the priests, even my gentle Juan, who'd been so repulsed by his own part in the Cholulan massacre, waded into the slaughter with compulsive vengeance. The killing went on and on until every Aztec who'd not been able to flee into the surrounding hills, some twenty thousand of them, lay dead on the plain.

The moon had risen, covering the bleak hills with silver. We were camped in the deserted town of Temalacayocan, where we'd marched after holding religious services and gorging ourselves on enemy provisions left behind at Otumba. Hernán, his blood still racing with the day's frenzied excitement, had been unable to sleep, so he had offered to stand watch over his exhausted men. He walked with the lightness of a cat, moving shadowlike past the glowing embers of campfires, stalking the camp's outer fringes, ears alert for the slightest indication of trouble.

I walked beside him, trembling with exhaustion. He had wanted me near him. Juan was stretched out on the ground with the others in the deathlike slumber of one whose strength was long spent. Fate was strange, I thought. Except for an occurrence that could only have been the result of heavenly intervention, Juan and I would have died together. Now here we were alive and apart.

Coyotes yipped from the direction of the battlefield. I wondered whether the beasts were scampering among the dead, poking their sharp noses into the open wounds, or if the Aztecs had returned to carry away the bodies of their comrades.

Hernán filled his lungs with the cool, smoke-tinged air. "I almost hated to see this day end, Marina. Men will talk about this battle for centuries to come."

"And they'll talk about you. I've heard what your troops are saying. They give credit first to God, then to Cortés."

He laughed modestly, but I knew he liked praise. "Oh, everyone's to be credited—the cavalry, the infantry—they fought like lions."

"And the Tlaxcalans," I added quickly. We owed them an overwhelming debt. Their two thousand warriors had dwindled to a mere handful, a few hundred at most, including their intrepid general, Calmecahua. The Spanish troops had escaped with incredibly few seriously wounded men.

"And tomorrow, God willing, we cross into Tlaxcala." Hernán shook his head despairingly. "How are they going to welcome us, Marina? We left their capital nine months ago with six thousand of their sons, fathers and brothers. Now I could put all the survivors into a few good-sized tents. They'll curse the day they opened their gates to us."

"You can trust men like Maxixcatzin and old Xicotencatl," I said, trying to buoy his spirits. "They'll give us shelter or at least safe passage."

"I lean on your faith, Marina *mía*." He pulled me close with one bandaged arm and bent down to kiss my forehead. "Remember your little ultimatum? I think you've won. I'm all yours again."

I found myself suddenly discomfited by his announcement. "You can't have been thinking about that all week," I said lightly, groping for some distraction. "If I know you, Hernán, you've got our next move all planned out. What's it to be?"

His body shook with silent laughter. "You're right, you little witch. You *do* know me. My mind's been busy nearly every step of the way." He released me and began to talk, his eyes bright with enthusiasm. "Listen. Tenochtitlan's an island, even with its causeways. And there's only one way to conquer an island. Now let's see how bright you are. What am I thinking?"

"Canoes?" I guessed.

"Canoes!" He snorted. "You're thinking like an Indian. Use your imagination." He chuckled at my silence. "Ships, Marina."

"Ships . . ." I was dumbfounded. "But how would you—?"

"How would I get them to the lake? Think, Marina. There's plenty of timber between Tlaxcala and the coast. The rigging, the sails, the tackle, screws, bolts—all the things we'd have trouble making ourselves, we already have, salvaged from our old ships at Villa Rica. We'll build the ships at Tlaxcala, in sections that can be carried to the lake and assembled. They couldn't be big ships, of course. Brigantines should be small enough to transport, yet big enough for cannons. We'll need a cannon for each ship, that'll limit the number of vessels . . ."

"Look at us, Hernán." I tried to tug him back toward reality. "We're half dead and you're talking about ships."

"Oh, there'll be time, Marina," He said. "We'll mend our wounds, build up our strength. We won't strike till we're ready. Think of it! Hannibal crossed the Alps with an army of elephants. Years from now, centuries from now, they'll talk about the way Hernán Cortés crossed Mexico with his own armada—"

Suddenly his fingers dug into my shoulder and he doubled over, one hand clutching his head. His face, in the firelight, was contorted with awful pain.

"Hernán!" I whispered, suddenly frightened. "Is it your head?" He nodded, teeth clenched, eyes squeezed shut in agony.

I pulled at his arm. "You've got to lie down."

"No," he muttered. "They mustn't see, they mustn't know. Just hold me, Marina—" He burrowed his face between my breasts, quivering with pain as I wrapped my arms around him. "Hold me," he moaned. "Don't let anyone see . . ."

He was in the saddle again the next day, sitting masterfully astride the unruly Pícaro as we entered the Tlaxcalan town of Hueyotlipan. First to come swarming into the streets were the women, for a fair portion of the Tlaxcalan force had come from this place. As word of the tragic losses spread, the houses were filled with the wails and shrieks of mourning families.

We clustered together, weapons ready, fearful of the dark flashes of resentment in the eyes that peered out at us from windows and alleys. Finally, however, I was able to negotiate with the town chiefs for provisions in exchange for gifts of booty taken from the vanquished at Otumba. Cautiously we sat down in the square to eat.

"If we get this kind of reception here, what will things be like in the capital?" Bernal Diaz grunted between bites of tortilla.

"I don't think we'll have to wait long to find out." Olid was staring over his shoulder. "I'd say the capital's come to us."

We sprang to our feet as the conches blared to announce the arrival of the delegation of chiefs from Tlaxcala, now coming down the narrow street toward us. A regal figure on a litter headed the procession. "Maxixcatzin . . ." I breathed a little prayer of thanks.

"But look behind him—it's young Xicotencatl and he looks like a thundercloud," Hernán hissed in my ear. "Be ready for anything."

The litter was lowered to the ground. Maxixcatzin, with his marvelous youthful grace, stepped off and hastened toward us, his arms outstretched. No one could misread the compassion on his weathered face as he hurried forward to enfold Hernán in a warm embrace. The clouds of apprehension lifted. We were among friends at last. The troops cheered.

"We got here too late," said Maxixcatzin sadly. "Just outside this town, there are thirty thousand warriors I'd gathered to help you when we heard about your plight. Except for some unfortunate delays—" he glanced angrily at Xicotencatl—"we'd have been there to fight by your side at Otumba."

"Our God and your brave sons gave us the victory," said Hernán. "But with your thirty thousand we could have wiped out the whole army. One Tlaxcalan's worth at least ten Aztecs. In all the world I've seen none to equal your warriors in bravery, old friend. I only weep that we've returned with so few."

"I weep too." Maxixcatzin rested a hand on Hernán's arm. "But we're a nation of warriors, Malintzin. Death walks with us. It sleeps on our mats and eats at our firesides like an old friend. Our sons and brothers gave their lives worthily in the destruction of the Aztecs. We have many more pledged to give their lives for you if you need them. Come now and see the presents we've brought for you and your men."

I translated, moved to tears by his words. This man sits high on Padre Olmedo's mountain, I thought, even though he doesn't recognize the One who stands at its peak.

* * *

Despite the mourning for the lost warriors, the reception in the capital of Tlaxcala was tumultuous. Tlaxcalan citizens filled the streets and clustered on rooftops to cheer the small band who'd brought such disgrace to their enemies. Our welcome was marred only by the sullen face of Xicotencatl the Younger, who sulked at the fringe of the crowd, saying nothing.

Mounted on his horse, Hernán received their adulation with waves and nods. I walked as near to him as El Pícaro's nipping teeth would let me, glancing up at him frequently, sick with worry. He'd passed a fitful night, unable to sleep because of the pain in his head. He was upset as well by news of Aztec reprisals throughout the country, and he fretted for the safety of the little garrison at Villa Rica and for our allies at Cempoalla. I'd held him in my arms as he writhed on his mat, moaning and whispering incoherently until I feared for his mind. And yet, the next morning he was on his feet, determined to ride smiling and erect into Tlaxcala.

Maxixcatzin walked beside me as a gesture of homage. We were marching in the direction of his own palace, where'd he'd invited us to stay.

"Don't worry, child." He'd noticed my concern. "We've just a little way to go now. I've sent word ahead to ready a bed for your master. He's worse off than he'd have us believe, isn't he?"

"Much worse. He may die if we don't get him out of this hot sun." I reached over and clasped the strong old hand in gratitude.

Finally we rounded the last corner and fanned out into Maxixcatzin's courtyard, where we were sheltered from the adoration of the crowd. Servants bustled out to show us to our quarters.

Still mounted, Hernán clawed at the chin strap on his helmet with his bandaged hand. "Someone get this steel oven off my head," he groaned. I reached up to help him. His face, usually so pale, was crimson, his skin as dry as parchment. He leaned toward me, swayed in the saddle and slowly slid off, unconscious, into my arms.

Tlaxcala—July 1520

We've done all we can, Marina," Juan folded the bloody discarded bandages and handed them to a waiting servant.

"His life's out of our hands," he said softly. He had just opened Hernán's wound and removed broken slivers of bone to release the pressure of the fluid on his brain.

Hernán lay between us on a raised platform, as quiet as death. His face was flushed with fever. The clean dressing on his head was already beginning to darken with the fluids oozing from his wound. I had lost count of the number of days and nights I'd kept watch at his bedside while Juan and María de Estrada alternated in tending the festering hole in his skull. An anguished Maxixcatzin had hovered as near as he dared, afraid of being in the way.

Sometimes Juan would sit down and share my vigil for a few hours, but being together in such a way was torture for us both. The body of the man to whom we both owed life and allegiance always lay between us. We said little, for pleasantries seemed out of place and to talk of reality was too painful. Instead we would sit quietly, avoiding each other's eyes, both of us guiltily trying to forget that Hernán's death would leave us free to be together.

"You've got to get some rest. I don't need two patients." Juan's voice reflected his concern. "How long has it been since you've slept?"

"I doze for a few minutes at a time. It's enough." I looked down at my clenched hands to avoid meeting his eyes. "I can't bring myself to leave him until he's . . . out of danger." I consciously opened my fists and smoothed my skirt over my knees. "You've seen Alvarado, haven't you? How is he, Juan?"

Splendid. The brute's as tough as a Spanish bull. Did you know his Luisa was pregnant?"

"No." With a little pang I remembered Tonaxel. "I'm happy for her," I said. After all, there was no reason for me to hold Luisa's happiness against her.

Hernán stirred, whimpering in his delirium. Maxixcatzin entered quietly and stood looking on him with a stricken expression. "No changes, I see."

"None. But the fact that he's lived this long's a good sign." I tried to cheer him. "I fear less for his life every day."

Maxixcatzin shook his head. "A nephew of mine had such a wound. He lived, it's true, but now his mother and sisters have to feed and dress him like an infant. Better if he'd died . . ." He clapped a hand over his own mouth. "Forgive a foolish old man, Malintzin. I've only made you feel worse. Isn't there anything I can do?"

"Nothing, my friend." I patted his hand and tried to smile.

Maxixcatzin had brought some news. His spies had returned from Tenochtitlan with word that Cuitlahuac's coronation had taken place as expected with the appropriate number of sacrifices. The old chief's eyes met mine in grim understanding as he told me this, for we both knew that the prisoners taken on the causeway would be foremost among the victims. The first act of the new *uei tlatoani* had been to initiate a purge of all those who'd been friendly toward us. Even the *cuiacoatl* had been in danger, but at the last moment Cuitlahuac had spared his life and restored him to his position.

I translated for Juan. "Cuitlahuac's no fool," he commented. "Without the *cuiacoatl* the whole kingdom would bog down."

"And Tlacotzin could talk his way out of anything," I added, remembering the chief judge with an unexpected surge of fondness.

There was more news. Young Cuauhtemoc, Moctezuma's nephew, had been named high priest of Huitzilopochtli, a position that would give him more power than ever and place him next in succession to the throne.

"What about the coast?" I asked him. "What have you heard about Villa Rica?"

"From what I've been told, your little colony's safe for the present, Malintzin," he said, a vague uneasiness creeping into his voice, "but the reports from Cempoalla distress me most deeply. There's talk of some strange curse there."

"What sort of curse?"

"A curse on men's bodies. Boils on the skin that burn like fire. Fever and death. Not many have escaped it. My old friend, Teuch—" Maxixcatzin broke off, his voice unsteady. "He was one of the first to die from it."

"Marina, what is it?" Juan had read the alarm in my eyes.

I told him. The color flowed from his face. "Good Lord!" he burst out. "It's the *viruelas*—the pox! A slave who came with Narvaez had it at Villa Rica. Damn it, I told them to put him back on his ship and leave him there—it must have been too late even then!" I stared at him, not really comprehending. "Marina, have you ever heard of anything like this in your country before?"

I shook my head. I had never seen Juan so upset.

"Every Indian in Mexico could get it." He ran an agitated hand through his hair. "Marina, tell Maxixcatzin to close his frontiers between here and the coast. He mustn't let anyone through who's been near Cempoalla or Villa Rica in the past two weeks."

Maxixcatzin was as perplexed as I was. "It may be too late already," he said. "A caravan of traders came up from the coast just yesterday. That's how I heard about the curse."

"Were any of them sick?" Juan asked him. Maxixcatzin shook his head. "You've got to isolate them," said Juan. "Put them in some house—better yet, make them camp outside the city. Will you let me go and look at them? I've seen enough of the curse, as you call it, to recognize the early signs."

"I'll take you to them," said the old chief. "I spoke to them just this morning. If they've already passed the curse to me, there's nothing I can do."

I caught Juan's arm as he turned to leave. "No," I whispered. "Stay away from them, Juan. I'm afraid for you."

The blue eyes mellowed. "There's no danger for me, *querida*," he said, squeezing my hand. "Anyone who gets the *viruelas* and recovers is protected for life, and I had it as a boy in Spain." His face clouded at the memory. "My mother, my father and I came down with it. Both my parents died . . . You're not to leave this room till I return, Marina."

As his footsteps echoed down the hall, I dropped my head and buried my face against the rough blanket that covered Hernán's leg. I was tired. My eyes smarted and every muscle and bone in my body ached. Hernán whimpered again and I felt his limbs tense as if straining against invisible chains. I sat up and straightened the blanket where it had slipped down off his bare shoulders. His skin was hot to the touch. Fever had consumed his flesh until he looked like the emaciated Christ on the little crucifix that Padre Olmedo wore.

I remembered his strength, his audacity, his ferocity at Cholula, his courage at Otumba. I would gladly have given my life now to save him. Being a Christian is difficult at times like this, I thought. Were it not for my baptism I could sacrifice ten turkeys or even a slave to appease the god of death. I sighed. This new God of mine demanded sacrifices of a different sort. What was it the padre had said? A contrite spirit and a broken heart—that's what pleased Him most.

I knew what I had to be contrite about. I knew it every time I looked at Juan Jaramillo and felt my whole being swell with longing. True, I'd not been given to Hernán as a proper wife, but I had gone to him with the understanding that I would be faithful. I had betrayed him, not with my body but with my mind and heart. I had sinned, and now could it be that God demanded my repentance in exchange for Hernán's life?

I straightened my spine and gulped down the lump that was forming in my throat, and resolved that if God wished for a broken heart I would give him one. Clenching my fist around the tiny silver crucifix I prayed aloud:

"*Santa María, Madre de Diós*, give me strength. Cleanse me of my sin as I cast away my desire . . ." Tears pressed their way out from under my closed eyelids. "I promise to renounce my feelings for . . . for any man except Hernán Cortés. I promise to vanquish from my heart the memory of my unfaithfulness . . ." Thoughts of Juan inundated my mind—his blue eyes creasing at the corners when he smiled, the gentleness and skill in his suntanned hands, the feel of his hard body against mine, his lips, his voice . . . No more! I would shove such memories into the dark pit of unconsciousness and seal them over forever. "Forgive me, Blessed Lady," I prayed. "Forgive me and grant me the gift of Hernán's life . . ."

My head fell to rest against the surface of the blanket once more. I lay there for a time, breathing deeply, striving to empty my mind of all unworthy thoughts.

"Marina—"

The hoarse whisper was louder than a thunderclap in the little room. I sat bolt-upright. Hernán's eyes were focusing with clarity on my face. His hand crept feebly across the blanket to rest on mine, the palm damp with perspiration. I touched his forehead. He was sweating profusely, the best of signs.

I buried my face against his chest and wept.

Chapter Twenty-One

Villa Rica de Vera Cruz—October 1520

"Come walk along the quay with me, Marina. The sea air will do you some good." Hernán tugged at my hand to keep me abreast of his long strides.

I doubted his words. The smell of refuse and rotting fish along the dock would only aggravate my nauseated stomach, I was sure, but I went along. I wanted to please Hernán and to view the newly arrived ships he'd lured to join him.

With the terrible head wound now only a fresh, pink scar against his hair, Hernán was once again riding the crest. The disaffection among the men, especially those of the Narvaez party, upon learning of his plans for reconquest, had been quelled with his silver-edged tongue. So effectively had he cajoled those soldiers who'd had enough of horror and bloodshed and wanted to go back to Cuba, that any word against him was now looked upon as cowardice. To the few who could not be convinced to stay, he'd given permission to leave, so that the remainder would be solidly loyal. The ranks were swelling week by week with arrivals of new vessels, men and horses. While Hernán was still recovering in Tlaxcala, a Captain Barba, who'd been sent to arrest him in a small ship with thirteen men and two horses, was deceived into coming ashore and won over to the cause. A band of refugees from an ill-fated expedition to the north, sent by Governor Garay of Jamaica, had also arrived at Villa Rica, half by land and half by sea. Those who'd come by land were so ill and bloated that they were dubbed "the green stomachs." Still another little ship with eight men, one mare, and a large supply of provisions and material for making crossbows, had sailed into the harbor only the day before.

The army had not been idle during this time. As soon as he was well enough to ride, Hernán had launched a campaign of subjugation against those surrounding provinces that were allied with the Aztecs. It had been a relatively easy task, for allies were plentiful now and most of the fighting had taken place in the open plains country where horses and cannon could be used to their best advantage. Not only that, but the miraculous victory at Otumba had so enhanced the reputation of the Spaniards that the mere sight of them was enough to send shivers of panic through any native army. The provinces had fallen one by one until the mass of territory between Tlaxcala and Villa Rica had been wrested from Aztec control.

It was no wonder, then, that Hernán walked with a spring to his step. His fortunes were crowned by the discovery that I was pregnant, and he was tender, solicitous, delighted.

I appreciated his consideration, for the pregnancy showed signs of being a difficult one. I was racked by constant nausea, as I had never been with my first baby. Still, I counted my condition a gift from the Virgin, a clear sign that I'd obeyed divine will in returning to Hernán with undivided devotion.

Juan had received the news of my promise gallantly, as I had expected he would. "I've always known you'd go back to him," he told me. "I haven't lost you. You were never mine to lose. Be happy, *querida*." He'd opened my hand and kissed the palm, the pressure of his lips sending tremors of anguish through my whole body. "I hope your decision brings peace to us both, Marina," he'd said, and I'd turned and walked away from him so that he wouldn't see my tears.

I'd seen almost nothing of him since. He'd taken Aguilar as an aide and interpreter and gone to Cempoalla in hopes of helping prevent the spread of the *viruelas*. He might just as well have tried to stop the flow of a river with his bare hands. By now the pox had spread throughout the countryside, its deadliness intensified by the native practice of bathing in cold streams to ease the burning. In Cempoalla, death had claimed not only our good friend Teuch, but poor little Catalina and thousands upon thousands of others. Fat Chicomacatl had survived the disease but was left hideously scarred.

Terrified people fled from one town to the next, carrying the pox with them. Bodies were left to rot where they fell, for no one dared come close enough to dispose of them. The flapping black vultures, unaffected by the disease, grew fat; the flies flourished. Juan had returned to Villa Rica in despair and disgust, burned his clothes, and set out for Tlaxcala with the shipbuilder, Martín López, to scout for timber to build the brigantines.

I prayed that the curse could be kept out of Tlaxcala. We

owed this as a debt of gratitude to the Tlaxcalan people in general and to Maxixcatzin in particular. During the early period of Hernán's recovery in Tlaxcala, a delegation of six Aztec lords had come in secret to present an offer of peace and alliance to the Tlaxcalan council for the purpose of driving the white men from their land. The Aztecs had acquired a ready advocate in the person of Xicotencatl the Younger, whose resentment toward Hernán still smoldered. The Tlaxcalan general had presented a strong case for alliance. The men of the lake and those of Tlaxcala were of the same blood, he'd arrgued, while the Spaniards were foreigners, far removed from them in customs and appearance. Which, then, would be the more natural course of alliance? Besides, the stony-faced general had insisted, it was easy to see that the strangers could not be trusted. Their awesome powers could so easily be turned without warning against their friends. Now, while they were weak, was the time to strike them.

The council had been swayed. They were discussing in earnest the possibility of an Aztec alliance when Maxixcatzin stepped forward. With all the eloquence at his command, he lashed them with reminders of their old enmity toward the Aztecs, of past outrages against Tlaxcala, of the years of cruelty, privation and murder they'd suffered from Aztec hands. He'd stirred their anger skillfully, whipping away at their pride and patriotism. With help from their Spanish friends they would have power in their hands to destroy the long-hated Aztec empire. When young Xicotencatl protested, Maxixcatzin struck him across the face and the council cheered. In the end, the Aztec envoys beat an ignominious retreat and Xicotencatl was severely censured by the members of the council, including his own father.

Now, as I walked beside Hernán on the quay, my thoughts were interrupted by a sudden wave of nausea brought on by the smell of rotting fish and seaweed. Laughing at my discomfort, Hernán tightened his arm around my shoulders. "So you've had enough sea air, have you, little girl? Very well, it's back home with you then."

We walked back along the muddy street and through the square. The Rich Town of the True Cross had grown during its first year of life. There was now an inn, with its adjoining *cantina* where the fiery native *pulque* was served in earthenware mugs and a fading beauty named Isabel Rodriquez danced on a tabletop in a red dress. There were other Spanish women too, most of whom had arrived with Narvaez, a few wives and sweethearts of the men and several others who painted their faces and worked in the *cantina*.

With the influx of new arrivals, housing was in short supply. Ramshackle shelters clustered against the backs of the town's original buildings, lean-tos of old planks and native thatch where men sweltered in the heat and shivered in the rain.

The veterans of the conquest had pitched in and built a neat little house of adobe for the newly married María de Estrada and Pero Farfán, a house that soon became the social center for the town's elite. María bubbled with happiness, her tongue and hands never quiet. "I was married the first time to an old man for money," she told me, "the second time to a young man for—well, never mind. Now at last I have a man of my own age and it's bliss! For the first time in my life I feel loved for what I am, not for my youth or my money . . . Tch!" Her head bobbed like a chickadee's. "My friends in Cuba would be shocked. To be proper, I should have had at least a year's mourning for Fernando, but they'd never understand how short life can be in this new world. One must fill every moment with pleasure, for that moment might be one's last, *verdad?*"

As Hernán and I passed the *cantina*, Olid hailed us noisily, a mug of *pulque* in his hairy fist. "Aguilar's looking for you," he rumbled. "He asked me to tell you he'd be waiting at your house. I don't know what he wanted. The old *cucaracha* seemed out of sorts when I asked him."

Hernán's own dwelling was a spacious, two-story affair with strands of ivy already curling around the gates and doorways. Aguilar was waiting in the muddy street, his homely face tense with the importance of his message but his pale blue eyes looking thoughtful.

"Bad news, brother?" Hernán asked, trying to read his expression.

"The worst news and the best news—I don't know where to begin." Aguilar shuffled his feet and the mud oozed up over the toe of one shoe. "There's a runner from Tlaxcala waiting outside the gates. When I heard what he had to say I thought it best not to let him come into town . . ."

"The *viruelas*?" I felt myself turning pale. "It's spread to Tlaxcala?"

Aguilar nodded grimly. "Maxixcatzin has the pox. The runner says he's dying."

"*Diós mío!*" Hernan choked. "What in the name of heaven could be good news after that?"

"Maxixcatzin wants Padre Olmedo to come to Tlaxcala at once, to . . ." Aguilar drew a long breath to calm his emotions ". . . to give him the rites of baptism. He wants to become a Christian!"

November 1520

The word of Maxixcatzin's death sent the entire community of Villa Rica into mourning, with Hernán donning black and declaring that he'd lost a father. Padre Olmedo and Aguilar returned from Tlaxcala within a fortnight, bursting with news.

"The pox is everywhere." Padre Olmedo shook his head. "The streets and houses are full of corpses. There are more recoveries among those who've followed our instructions and stayed out of the streams, but we can do so little . . ."

"Alvarado's woman has it," Aguilar put in. "She's not so badly off as some, but she'll be scarred if she lives."

Poor Luisa! That night on the causeway had formed a strong bond between the Tlaxcalan princess and myself. "What about her baby?" I asked worriedly.

"I've seen healthy infants born to women who'd had the pox, so there's hope for the child if the mother doesn't die," the padre answered. "Alvarado hasn't left her side. I never realized he was so fond of her."

"Any news from the Aztecs?" Hernán asked.

"I was coming to that," said the priest. "The *viruelas* has traveled all the way to the palace. Cuitlahuac's dead."

There was a moment of dazed silence.

"Well, at least *that's* a piece of good news." It was Ávila's highpitched voice among the murmur of the crowd that had gathered around us in the square.

"Good news!" Aguilar scoffed. "Can't you guess who's taken his place?"

The men looked at each other, their foreheads wrinkled. There was only one possible answer: Cuauhtemoc.

"That young devil hates us even more than Cuitlahuac did," Sandoval muttered.

Orteguilla had squirmed his way through the forest of legs and trunks. His voice piped up timidly, "Padre, did you hear anything about Tecuichpo? Do you know if she's all right?"

The priest placed a hand on the boy's shoulder. "The little princess is in the best of health from what I've heard my son.

But it seems that to strengthen his claim on the throne, Cuauhtemoc has made her his wife."

Again there was a startled hush. Lovely, laughing little Tecuichpo and the fierce Cuauhtemoc—a wedding of flower and flame. I couldn't help wondering about the nature of the marriage. Moctezuma had told me several months before that the little princess had achieved her womanhood, but Tecuichpo was only twelve, still a child in so many ways. The young emperor was twice her age and surely the union had no motive other than the political one.

Orteguilla turned and walked away slowly, his shoulders drooping, one foot kicking a stone ahead of him.

December 1520

"Not so tight, María—you'll hurt the baby. This is crazy!"

"Nonsense." María de Estrada de Farfán knotted the laces of the corset with practiced fingers. "This isn't tight, Marina. Why, when I lace for a *fiesta*, my face turns purple. Besides, you're only four months along—hardly showing a thing, and what little sticks out's below the waist, not up here where I'm lacing you."

"I can't move. I should never have let you talk me into this."

"Well, you're not backing out now, *chiquita*. Not after all the hours I spent taking in my blue dress to fit you. Blue was never my color, but on you, with that skin, it will look divine. What luck I left that trunk of clothes here in Villa Rica!" María stepped back to admire the effects of the lacing, cocking her head critically. "That will do. Now for the dress. Sancha! *Caspa de San Pedro*, where is that girl?"

Twelve-year-old Sancha, with a face that was all huge, melancholy eyes, peeked timidly around the edge of the doorway. She would have been a pretty child except for the big letter *G*—for *guerra*, war—still raw and unhealed, which had been burned into her forehead.

The branding of captives was a sore point between Hernán and me. "It's horrible," I'd gasped after seeing the first results on a group of prisoners from the Tepeyacac campaign. "Even the Aztecs don't do this. And on the face, Hernán!"

"It's customary, Marina," he's retorted coldly. "These people are renegades, cannibals. They deserve even worse than this. We took them fairly in open warfare and they're our property."

"Then why don't you brand me too?" I snapped at him.

We'd slept without touching that night. Once Hernán made up his mind to do something, no one could change it. More captives were branded the next week, and still more the next. Then they were distributed as slaves among the Spaniards and their allies. The young girl who'd been renamed Sancha had been given to María and Pero Farfán.

"There she is," María sputtered, catching sight of Sancha in the doorway. She'll be worthless until she learns to understand what I tell her. Marina, what's the Indian word for 'dress'?"

I shrugged. "There's no such word. We don't have dresses."

"Of course, how stupid of me!" Maria fluttered her hands.

In the end, feeling oddly light-headed in the tightly laced corset, I went and got the dress myself. "*Vestido,*" I said slowly, looking at Sancha and indicating the dress. "*Ves-ti-do.*"

"*Ves-ti-do,*" Sancha repeated painstakingly.

I smiled my approval. "María, Hernán's offered me a little girl from Cuba—a black. She's bright and willing. Why don't we make a trade? I'll give her to you and take Sancha in her place."

"Consider it done." María sighed. "I've been at my wits' end with that little urchin. Now for the dress . . ." She held up the pale blue cloud of material. "I can't wait to see how you look in it. Hold out your arms . . ."

The dress floated into place. I held my breath as my friend did up the long row of buttons that held the back together.

"But you're beautiful!" María exclaimed.

I looked down at the new form my body had assumed, feeling like a newly emerged butterfly. The dress, charming in its plainness, clung to my upper toso, defining a tiny waist and high, swelling breasts. The bodice was cut generously low, to reveal tawny shoulders and just a hint of softly curving bosom. The full skirt stood out like the petals of an upside-down flower.

"Now sit down and let me do your hair," María ordered. She lifted the black cascade of my hair and twisted it experimentally. "Something high, I think, to show off that long neck, but not too elaborate. And it needs a necklace. I have a simple strand of opals and pearls that will be perfect.

Tch! I can't wait to see the look on Hernán Cortés's face when you walk into the room."

"María, I'm scared. What if he doesn't like it?"

"Doesn't like it? Impossible! No man could resist you in that dress. Now hold still or I'll pinch you."

The fiesta was a dual occasion. We were celebrating the departure of one of the vessels for Spain with letters and gifts for His Majesty, along with two other ships bound for Cuba, bearing the dissident soldiers and letters requesting settlers, livestock and arms. It was also to provide a festive send-off for Hernán and the bulk of the army, who would soon be returning to Tlaxcala to renew the war of conquest against the Aztecs. The spacious hall in the *alcaldia* had been decorated with cotton streamers, garlands of flowers and lanterns from the ships. Their lights flickered out into the square, and the twang of guitar and mandolin mingled with the murmur of voices punctuated by laughter as María and I made our way through the darkness.

"Does your husband know what we've been doing?" I asked her. I was short of breath from the tightness of the lacing.

"Oh yes. Nothing escapes Pero. I told him to go ahead without us, but he won't tell. It will be a surprise." María lifted her skirt of elegant plum-colored velvet to keep it from dragging in the mud. I copied her. We mounted the steps and I paused at the door, held my breath and closed my eyes for a moment. I felt as if I were about to plunge naked into an ice-cold spring.

The long room, so stark in itself, glowed with color. The lanterns cast flickering shadows on the whitewashed walls. The hues of the streamers were echoed in the robes of the native belles who had come on the arms of their masters. Here and there a billowing Spanish skirt flared amid the crowd. The men, far outnumbering the women, stood in clusters, elegant in muted grays and browns. Subdued laughter floated in the air, blending with the notes of the mandolins.

Bernal Diaz, lounging near the doorway, was the first to see me. His eyebrows shot up and the next moment he was bending over my hand. He was pale and thin from a long bout with fever but his eyes twinkled as he spoke.

"I can't believe my eyes! You're a real *señorita!* I've always thought you were beautiful, but tonight you're a vision. It's a good thing Jaramillo's in Tlaxcala."

I frowned at him.

"Oh, all right," he said, chuckling. "I won't tease you anymore. Juan told me it was all over between you two. But the sight of you in that dress would light a fire in any man."

I fluttered my white lace fan the way María had taught me. "Be honest with me Bernal. Do I really look all right, or should I run home and throw on a *huipilli* before Hernán sees me?"

"My girl, you look ravishing. Everyone who sees you will be enchanted, even Cortés—although I must say he was in a black mood when I last saw him. He'd overheard some of the men complaining that he'd taken all the choicest slaves for himself and his officers."

I sighed. That sort of thing always made Hernán angry. "Just when he thought he'd quieted all the grumblers," I said. "Were you one of them, Bernal?"

"Not this time," he replied, taking a sip of *pulque*, "but not because I wasn't unhappy about it too. I was so far down the line that when my turn came to pick a slave there were none left in the compound but a few old women. I'm now the proud owner of a fifty-year-old corn grinder. At least she can cook and wash, but she's not very decorative."

Pero Farfán came over to claim his wife. "*Qué bella!*" he exclaimed, twirling his gray mustache. "María, your handiwork's superb."

"See, I told you," María said proudly. Then she swept away on her husband's arm, leaving me to face the admirers who crowded around me.

"By my faith!" Sandoval raised my fingers to his lips. "You look like a different woman, but I like it."

"You'd better not dress like that for the march to Tlaxcala," teased Ávila. "If you do, the men won't be able to stay in line."

A hush fell over the crowd as Hernán entered the hall from the other end. They fell back, leaving an open path between us. He had seen me, but no flicker of pleasure lighted his eyes as he strode the length of the hall and stopped before me.

Now he smiled, but his mouth looked as though it had been pasted on a scowling face. He greeted me with a slight inclined of his head. The coolness in his eyes made my skin shrink. He strolled about the hall with his arm linked in mine, pausing to greet friends among the merrymakers, making a great show of joviality without saying a word to me. Finally, after two or three turns about the room, he led me out onto the patio and spun around to face me. "Marina, I want to make a bargain with you," he said. "If you promise to go home at once and take off that ridiculous dress, I will promise not to reprimand María for her part in this little farce."

I glared at him. "The others like it!"

"The others have no reason to be embarrassed. I do. Marina, anyone who pretends to be someone he is not makes a mistake. You've made such a mistake in dressing as something you are not and never will be. By now you should know your place. Stay in it and be content."

Never in my worst moments had I imagined that Hernán could speak to me with such contempt in his voice. "Whatever you say, I will do," I spat out. "Forgive me for the times I fail to remember that I'm your slave and your property. I'll go home. I'll take off this beautiful dress that my friend worked so hard on and I'll never wear it again. But don't ask me to come back here tonight. That's something I *won't* do."

"As you wish, Marina," he answered calmly. "Don't wait for me at home. I may be spending the night elsewhere."

He always had to have the last word. Well, let him, I thought furiously, as I turned away from him and stalked back into the hall, composing my features quickly as I passed through the doorway. Bernal, one eye cocked, had seen me come in. I nodded silent thanks as he offered me his arm. Fluttering my fan, I smiled gaily up at him.

"So it was that bad, was it?" he said. "Well, Cortés can be a real jackass when he wants to be. You caught him at a bad time."

"No, I'm the jackass, Bernal," I whispered, flashing my smile at everyone we passed. "Would you walk me to the door?"

"I'll walk you all the way home if you like, my sweet lady."

Quickly, I shook my head. "We'd be the talk of Villa Rica."

"Say, that might be fun," he said with a wink. But he released my arm when we reached the front steps and I whispered a speedy good night to him.

The challenge of negotiating the muddy ruts and puddles in the dark occupied my mind until I reached the house. With trembling hands I managed to undo enough of the buttons to allow the dress to slip over my head. The relief from the tight laces was bliss. In a long, loose robe I curled up on the bed to lick my wounds.

I'd learned something tonight. In spite of the friendliness, the pretty speeches, the lovemaking, there was a barrier between Hernán's race and my own. I'd taken a step through that barrier and suffered the consequences. My loyalty to Hernán was the same loyalty he inspired in his men, but Hernán was the conqueror, and I, as much as the Aztecs I'd fought, was among the conquered. No matter how useful I might be to the white men, no matter how much I pretended to be one of them, I was *not* one of them and would never be. I remembered María's observation that even the meanest foot soldier dreamed of marrying into the Spanish nobility. Hernán and his men had been given the daughters of kings, beautiful young women who were unfit for marriage to their Spanish conquerors because their skins were brown. And I, Marina, was one of them, a Nahua woman, an Indian, as they called my people. I was what I was and I would not be ashamed of it. Hernán had been cruel tonight. He had also been right.

I lay back and felt the child fluttering deep in my body like a tiny fish. Poor little one, I thought. At least I know what I am. What will you be?

The hours passed and Hernán did not return. I remembered one of the prisoners from Itzocan, a girl so lovely that Hernán had made a single exception and allowed the *G* to be burned onto her shoulder instead of her face. I did not sleep. As the blackness of the sky was beginning to fade in the east, Hernán came into the room. He removed his clothes, crept into bed and gathered me close to him. His body smelled strangely of sweat and flowers.

"Forgive me, *preciosa*," he murmured into my shoulder. "How could I have been so cruel and thoughtless? It must have been the wine. Wear the dress. Do whatever you like. If I ever hurt you like that again, I'll cut out my tongue. Promise you'll forget every word I said . . ." His voice trailed off. He was fast asleep.

January 1521

In a fur-lined cloak and hood I nestled between Hernán's arms and tried to be comfortable as El Pícaro jogged over the rough trail. Sitting sideways across Hernán's knees was not particularly comfortable, for I had to twist my body forward to equalize my weight, but he would no longer let me sit astride behind him. "I once overheard my mother scolding a pregnant cousin about that," he'd said, patting the bulge that was beginning to creep up past my waist. "She said it was one of the worse things a woman in such a condition could do, so no more of that for you, my sweet."

It had begun at last! Behind us lay the muggy coast and the pox-ravaged plains of Tlaxcala. We were going back to the lake, back to victory or death. The long train of fighting men glittered behind us—five hundred fifty infantry divided into nine companies, and forty cavalry in four squads, with nine small artillery pieces, eighty crossbows and arquebuses. Cuirasses and helmets gleamed in the morning sun, casting beams of twinkling light against the dark pines. Tiny bells jingled on the edges of the bullhide body protectors the horses wore, and on their bridles. The icy air was invigorating. Little puffs of vapor issued from the red-lined nostrils of the horses. Snow sparkled down from the pine branches as the men and their mounts brushed past them. The men were in high spirits. Glancing back at them from time to time, I saw smiles, heard joking remarks and raucous laughter. It was almost possible to forget that this festive procession was in reality an instrument of terrible destruction going forth with one purpose and design: to kill.

Surpassing even the Spaniards in magnificence were the hundred thousand Tlaxcalans in their armor of quilted maguey cloth, whose ranks stretched farther than my eyes could see. The multitude looked like a gigantic, undulating plumed serpent that bristled with long spears and pikes. Its scales were shields of plaited reeds, adorned with feathers of every hue. Plumes rose from its back, shooting up above the bejeweled helmets of the chiefs and warriors. For all its splendor, this serpent was armed with fangs of death.

I remembered Tlaxcala with a little sigh. Despite the warmth with which the people had received us, I'd been unhappy for the fortnight we'd spent there. The smallpox epidemic had subsided, but its depredations were everywhere. The back streets were still littered with rotting corpses to be swept into piles and burned in stinking fires by those who had survived the disease. The land of the white heron had become the land of the vulture. The flapping, screeching black horrors filled the skies and clustered on the rooftops, plastering the thatch and walls with their droppings.

Because the danger from the pox had not entirely passed, Hernán had not allowed me to leave Maxixcatzin's palace. I'd roamed the halls restlessly as he drilled the troops outside in the square. My only visitor had been Alvarado's Luisa, whose once-pretty face was now a mass of pock-marks. She was a welcome visitor, her nature as sunny as her brother Xicotencatl's was austere. Luisa had brought her baby son, a striking child with his mother's black eyes and hair almost as fair as his father's. "People pity me because of the way I look," said Luisa, "but I lived when so many died. I have a beautiful, healthy son, and Pedro is still good to me." She giggled. "He says that the way I look in the dark hasn't changed and he wants to give me ten sons as fine as this one." Looking at the happiness on Luisa's ravaged features, I felt my thoughts revolve in a puzzling circle. That the rough, violent Alvarado I knew could bring such radiance to anyone's face amazed me.

Deny it though I might, I'd looked forward to seeing Juan again. I'd tortured my emotions to the point where even the pain of his eyes seeing my body growing big with Hernán's child would have been more welcome than this awful void I'd lived with for months. I'd searched for his face everywhere I was permitted to go until Bernal had mentioned one day that Juan was at Atempan, where the parts for the ships were being built, and that he had no plans to come into the capital.

He's staying away on purpose, I'd told myself angrily, even though I realized he was probably doing the right thing. I hated him. I loved him. Life without him was less than life. I sighed again. Juan was still at Atempan and would not be joining us until the ships were transported to the lake for assembly.

My days at Tlaxcala had not been completely idle. There was the matter of settling a dispute over the succession to Maxixcatzin's chiefdom between followers of his only legitimate son, a twelve-year-old boy who bore his father's name, and his older, more experienced brother-in-law. At my suggestion, Hernán had solved the problem by naming the boy as chief but appointing his uncle as regent until the lad grew to manhood, which pleased both sides. The young Maxixcatzin had been baptized by Padre Juan Diaz. Xicotencatl the Elder had become a Christian as well, much to the undisguised contempt of his son.

Looking back around Hernán's mail-covered shoulder, I could see Xicotencatl's scarlet crest bobbing at the head of the long Tlaxcalan column. I recalled the first time I'd seen him, when I'd realized that his designation as "the younger" was misleading, for he was in his forties and there was nothing of youth in his stern bearing. Further acquaintance had not softened that impression. Even I, who did not frighten easily, was a little awed by his fierceness. I shivered in my fur wrappings, remembering the encounter I'd had with him just a few days earlier in the palace. I'd passed him alone in the hallway with a glance and an uneasy nod, for I never knew what to say to him. Hurrying silently on my way, I'd been startled to hear him speak my name.

"Malintzin, wait!"

I'd turned, thrusting my chin up at him. He was tall for his race, and broad-shouldered. "I've wondered since the first time I saw you," he said, "How a woman of your intelligence could be so deceived by white men's lies."

"What do you want from me?" I had demanded, not wanting the conversation to go on.

"Nothing. Only to tell you you're a fool. There was a time when I'd hoped you could be convinced that you were wrong, but I see now what binds you to the man called Cortés. You're carrying his child." His upper lip had curled with contempt. "You're just like my sister. Look at her—her face ruined by the curse that followed the white men's coming, and a child in her arms that belongs to no nation."

"Luisa's happy," I'd argued.

"She's an idiot and so are you. Women are like dogs. They'll follow any scum who'll give them a pat on the rump."

By then I was seething. "May I remind you," I said hotly, "that neither of us had any choice? We were handed over to the Spaniards like sacks of corn—by men like you! But there are *none* of us who'd go back. They treat us better than our own people ever did."

"Spoken like the traitor you are," he said coldly.

"Traitor! Traitor against whom? The Spaniards are allies of your people, not enemies, Xicotencatl. As for the Aztecs, I grew up hating them as much as you did. If Maxixcatzin were still alive he'd be quick to point out which of us is the traitor."

His jaw had tightened angrily. "I chose the lesser of two evils, Malintzin. Maxixcatzin and my father were proud old men. They let their hatreds blind them to a danger greater than anything we've ever faced at the hands of the Aztecs. Do you see the slaves taken in battle, the ones with the marks burned onto their faces?" He'd leaned close to me, his hard brown eyes boring into mine. "Remember my words, Malintzin—if these white men are not stopped, we who follow them will live to see the same marks on the heads of our own children."

With a swirl of his long red *tilmatli*, he'd left me standing speechless in the corridor. But for all his words, he was here now, marching resignedly at the head of his army. I was afraid to let him out of my sight. My warnings to Hernán had been lightly dismissed. "Xicotencatl's still smarting from the thrashing we gave him last year. He'll come around like the rest of them." Hernán has laughed. He was laughing now, as El Pícaro twisted his neck around in an effort to nip my foot.

"So many fine horses to choose from and you have to ride this beast," I mumbled.

"Please, *vida mía*, you'll hurt his feelings and make his disposition even worse. Pícaro's earned the right to lead our little army. I'd rather ride him into battle than the most splendid steed in the company." His beard tickled my cheek. He was in high spirits.

"I miss Arriero," I said. "Bernal told me that he may never be fit for riding again, with that tender mouth."

"True. Now he's only good for one thing. Every mare in Villa Rica that comes into season will carry his seed in her belly." He chuckled and slid one hand across my growing bulge. "Marina, my little witch, pray that when war's made an old man of me, there'll still be enough left to put out to stud, just like Arriero." The baby gave a vigorous thump against his palm. "Ay! The little rascal kicks like a mule. Only a manchild could pack a clout like that."

"You're sure?" I was amused.

"Well, almost. If wishing could make things happen, then you could wager I'd be sure. I've never knowingly fathered a son, you know. At least not one I've been able to claim. I like children, Marina. Someday I plan to surround myself with a whole brood of them." He pulled me so tightly against him that I could feel the texture of his mail through my cloak. "Do you have any idea how happy you've made me, Marina *mía*?"

I felt suddenly uncomfortable with his elation. "The guides say we'll be in sight of Texcoco by this time tomorrow," I said.

"By my conscience, I hope so. This mountain road's taken so many turns, it's gotten so I hardly know the back end of my horse from the front."

"That shouldn't be so hard," I said tartly. "It's the front end that bites."

"And it's so damned cold. Sometimes I wish we'd gone by way of Cholula again.

"It's best this way," I said, shaking my head. "We're less likely to be attacked." I leaned back against him and wondered about Texcoco. It was essential that we take the lakeside city first, for it would be the best base of operations for the assault on the other cities along the shore and on the island capital itself. Remembering the attacks that Cuauhtemoc, the new *uei tlatoani*, had led against us before the *noche triste* in Tenochtitlan, I knew he would be as fearsome and devious an enemy as Cuitlahuac had been before the *viruelas* had claimed him.

"If only there'd been a way to get word to Ixtlilxochitl," Hernán mused, echoing my thoughts. "Then I'd feel more confident about gaining Texcoco."

"Forget him," I scoffed. "Where was Ixtlilxochitl during the seige? Where was he on the causeway and at Otumba? He only used you to get rid of Cacama for him." I caught my breath as a small party moved into sight over the ridge above us and began to descend.

"What a comfort to know you can be wrong, Marina," Hernán exclaimed. "You've misjudged our foxy friend. Unless I've forgotten the sight of his banner, that's Ixtlilxochitl himself."

The prince was on foot, striding toward us with remarkable vigor. He was swathed from head to toe in jaguar skins. "Malintzin!" he hailed Hernán gleefully as the latter dismounted to embrace him. I slid carefully from the saddle. Ixtlilxochitl was smiling, showing small, pointed teeth in his vulpine face. "So you're marching on Texcoco!"

I frowned. The guileful wretch had spies everywhere.

"I don't know how you found out," Hernán answered my translation, "but it's true. Can I count on your help?"

Ixtlilxochitl threw back his head and yipped with laughter. "But you won't need my help, Malintzin. Not much, at least. The city's yours for the taking." He shook his head in mock sorrow. "You know what my family's like by now. You put my younger brother on the throne of Texcoco before you left. Now my eldest brother, Cohuanacoch, has killed him and rules in his place."

"I don't see how that can help us," Hernán said.

"Oh, but you will. Cohuanacoch is his own worst enemy. He's piled heavy taxes on the people and he licks Cuauhtemoc's hand! The people of Texcoco hate him, my friend. Go on into Texcoco and chase him out. The dog hasn't enough followers left to put up a good fight against you."

As I translated, I glanced at the little group that had come with Ixtlilxochitl. His sister, Mazatl, was the only woman among them. She was cloaked in golden puma furs. Her slanting eyes flickered when she looked at Hernán.

Texcoco—February 1521

Ixtlilxochitl had spoken the truth. The wariness with which we'd approached Texcoco had been unnecessary. We'd met with only token resistance. The lakeside city was now ours and Ixtlilxochitl had used his persuasion to soothe the city's frightened populace into returning to their homes and resuming their normal lives. Cohuanacoch had slipped through Hernán's fingers and fled to join Cuauhtemoc, taking his family and followers with him. In his stead Hernán appointed yet another brother, a young boy this time, who'd been baptized a Christian.

If Ixtlilxochitl was displeased over not having been selected himself, he gave no indication of it. "The throne of Texcoco's a slippery place. I'm in no hurry to climb onto it," was all he said. He must have realized that no non-Spaniard would be allowed any real power in Texcoco. In truth, the new ruler was little better than a prisoner. A tutor and a staff of palace guards were appointed from among the Spanish army, and María and Pero Farfán took residence in the palace as his guardians.

Exhausted by my pregnancy and the strenuous march over the mountains, I was installed in the suite next to María's, where she and Sancha could look after me. Hernán would have little time to see to my comfort. With Texcoco assured, he was already looking toward Iztapalapan, the city controlling the entrance to the south causeway.

Iztapalapan, once ruled by Cuitlahuac, would not be as easily taken as Texcoco had been. I knew this and I watched apprehensively from the porch of the palace as Hernán rode off to the south at the head of the army.

"Come inside," María fussed. "It's going to be a long day for you, *niña*, and it's not good for you to be on your feet so much. You worry me. Expectant mothers are supposed to blossom, to fill out all over. Your arms are as thin as broomsticks, and you should see those dark patches under your eyes! Now that I've got you under my finger you're going to get some rest and some decent food."

"You worry too much, María," I said, looking anxiously toward the south end of the lake and wishing I could see the temples and towers of Iztapalapan. "Pray for an easy victory today . . ."

That day and the next had dragged into darkness before Hernán returned with a small portion of the army. Tossing sleeplessly on my mat, I heard his arrival and ran out into the courtyard. His clothes were damp and he was shivering when he took me in his arms. "We almost had them," he said. "Then they broke one of the dikes and flooded the whole damned city. We nearly drowned! It must have taken us three hours to fight our way out of the water." He glanced around as a pair of *tlamemes* trotted into the courtyard with a stretcher between them. "Get María de Estrada," he said. "Tell her she's got a life to save if she can."

The bloody, sodden mass on the stretcher scarcely looked human. Long legs dangled so far off the stretcher's end that they almost dragged on the ground. I stifled a little scream as I recognized Bernal Diaz. Spinning around, I raced to the Farfáns' quarters to awaken María.

Bernal was covered with blood. A spear had been thrust into his neck, miraculously missing the jugular vein by a hair's breadth but tearing into the windpipe and surrounding tissues, doing double damage when his adversary jerked it out again. "All we can do is try and stop him from bleeding to death," María muttered as she sweated over the white face. "Only God himself can put together what's been ripped apart in there. *Madre mía*, I don't know how he lived long enough for them to carry him all the way from Iztapalapan!" She took a clean cotton pad from my hands and pressed it against the ragged wound. "Sit down, Marina, and get some rest. Someone else can help me."

"Don't ask me to go," I begged. "It's true that I'm tired, and if it were anyone else . . . but Bernal's like a brother. I can't leave him."

"Oh, very well." Her busy fingers shifted the dressing to a dry spot. "And I suppose Juan Jaramillo's like a brother as well?"

My eyes shot open with surprise.

María continued to soak up Bernal's blood. "I have eyes," she said, "and ears too. I wasn't far from you at Otumba." She pressed a fresh pad against Bernal's neck. "Ay, but what am I saying? Forgive a meddlesome, old woman. You've got troubles enough without me making things worse by prying. Don't answer me when I ask such questions!" She shook her head sadly. "I just wish we had Señor Jaramillo with us right now."

The hours of the night crept on into a pink dawn. Young Sancha scurried back and forth like a mouse, carrying bandages and hot water while the two of us labored over Bernal's still form. At last, when the sun was high in the sky, he slept, breathing deeply. The bleeding stopped and the color returned slowly to his cheeks. We leaned against the walls, limp with exhaustion and relief.

"Go to bed, Marina. You can send Sancha for someone to watch him. God willing, I think he's going to live."

"Thank you, dear friend. I'll do that." My legs and body ached with every move. "And you too. Your husband will be wanting his breakfast."

"Marina . . ." Her dark eyes regarded me sharply. "I know I said I wouldn't pry, but it would set my mind at rest if you'd answer one question." She paused, then continued hurriedly, "You know that what you answer will never leave this room . . ."

There was no need for her to say more. I'd read the question in her face before she asked it. "The baby is Hernán's," I said wearily. "It couldn't be anyone else's."

Chapter Twenty-Two

Texcoco—March 1521

"They're coming, Malintzin," Sancha cried out. "The men with the ships! Hear the lookouts!"

I roused myself from my nap in the hammock and laughed at the little girl's excitement. This was not the same shy, fearful Sancha who'd come to me from the Farfán household. At that time, moved by the child's wistfulness, I'd offered to return her to her people. "My whole family's dead of the curse, Malintzin," she'd replied. "Let me stay with you."

"The ships, Malintzin! Hurry! Everyone's running to see them and we'll be left!"

"Well, I'll have to puff along as best I can," I said, standing up carefully and taking a moment to smooth out my braids. Under my *huipilli* my body bulged out awkwardly. The baby kicked, protesting the sudden change of position. "Forgive me, little cub," I whispered, patting the roundness.

Hernán strode into the patio, all smiles. "Come on, my fat *calabaza*. This'll be the grandest parade you've ever seen and I want you by my side. Your litter's already waiting."

The huge train would be too cumbersome to pass through the narrow streets of Texcoco, so the grand review would have to take place on the outskirts of the city, where a shipyard with a large pond had been built.

By now my advanced pregnancy would not even permit me to climb onto a horse, and Hernán had forbidden me to tire myself by walking long distances. He rode beside my litter as the bearers trotted along through the flowing crowd of festively dressed Tlaxcalans and Texcocans, his men forming a double line behind him.

The procession was already in sight, a spectacular parade that stretched back beyond the horizon. Warriors and gear-laden carriers marched to the music of flute, conch and drum.

Plumes and banners dangled limply in the heat. Sandoval, who'd come up from Villa Rica with fifteen horsemen and two hundred foot soldiers to provide an escort, waved joyously from his horse. Martín López, the shipbuilder, rode beside him, beaming with accomplishment. The air rang with *vivas* and shouts of "*Castilla y Tlaxcala.*"

The pounding of my own heart in my ears drowned out the sound of the drums as I searched each face that passed. Juan disliked pomp, I knew. It would be like him to melt into the ranks of the soldiers for the triumphal entry, but I hadn't seen him. I looked down at my protruding waist and realized that he might not even know I was pregnant. What would he think when he saw me? What would I say to him? Suddenly I wanted to crawl under the litter and hide.

The long timbers for the keels of the ships were now passing, borne on strong, brown shoulders. Down the line I could see spars, masts, bundled sails and great coils of rope for rigging moving toward us. The line seemed interminable. We'd been watching all morning. I still hadn't seen Juan and I was beginning to worry. Maybe he was in the rear—but then the rear was nowhere in sight. It was hot. My feet and hands felt puffy. A little stream of sweat trickled its way down the side of my neck. Faces were beginning to swim before my eyes.

Hernán leaned toward me. "What a shame Bernal Diaz wasn't well enough to come."

"María almost had to tie him to his bed to keep him from coming," I said, smiling at the scene Bernal had created. "Hernán, the sun's getting hot and there's still so much to see. Would you forgive me if I took the litter back to the palace to wait for you? I could check on Bernal."

He patted my shoulder solicitously. "By all means. I don't want you becoming ill, my sweet."

Hernán had been excessively concerned about my health lately, I reflected as the bearers trotted back through the empty streets with my litter on their shoulders. He seemed to want to isolate me, to cushion me against the strain of his own busy world. We'd occupied separate apartments since our arrival at Texcoco, for, as he said, he didn't want to disturb my rest or do anything that might harm the baby. I'd felt overprotected, useless. Time had crept by slowly, leaving me restless.

I'd go see Bernal, I thought as the litter was lowered to the porch. He would be chafing for news of the ships' arrival, and perhaps a visit with him would lift my spirits.

The coolness of the palace was welcome after the hot sun. As I pattered toward Bernal's room I could hear his voice echoing down the hallway. "Name of heaven, don't make me laugh like that! It hurts!" Wondering who had stayed with him, I hurried into his room and stopped short as a lean, muscular figure in a leather jerkin turned and rose to meet me. It was too late to run or to hide my swollen body. Juan's warm eyes gazed down at me. At least there was no surprise, no revulsion in them. I flushed and tried to look at my feet. I couldn't even see them.

Bernal came to my rescue. "See, Jaramillo, didn't I tell you what a pretty little mother she'd become?"

"You did," Juan said, "and for once you didn't exaggerate. But as for you, old friend, you're as skinny as a starving mule. What are you feeding him, Marina?"

"Whatever he can swallow," I said, "and that isn't much."

Bernal pulled a face. "Corn gruel, mare's milk, mashed-up squash—ugh! I could barely choke down garbage like that even before that brown devil tried to put my head on a spit. I'd sell my soul for a good chunk of beef."

"I heard a rumor that the last ship to reach Villa Rica had a cow on board," Juan said. "But it would cost you more than your soul if you tried to get a slice off it."

"It might be worth it." Bernal's shoulders shook until the tears came to his eyes. "See what you're doing to me? Marina's going to bar you from my room till my wretched neck heals and I can laugh without crying." Bernal looked at me, then at Juan, and an awkward silence filled the little room. He cleared his throat. "You'll forgive me," he rasped, "if I have the sudden urge to take a walk. There are things a man of dignity must do by himself." He got out of bed, wobbling a little, and shuffled barefoot into the hallway, the tails of Pero Farfán's borrowed nightshirt flapping above his knees.

Juan shook his head. "What a sight! I don't think I could have stood it if that spear had killed him, Marina." He studied me, one eyebrow raised slightly. "You don't look well, *querida*."

The old endearment plucked at my emotions, making me tremble. "I feel better than I look," I said. A tear formed in the corner of my eye and spilled over to run down the side of ny nose. "I thought you'd hate me when you saw me," I whispered.

All at once he was standing very close to me. He raised my chin with his fingers and brushed a chaste kiss onto my forehead. I was painfully aware of the bulk of Hernán's child between us.

"Hate you?" he murmured. "Don't you know me better than that, Marina?" He released my chin and stepped back a little. "Nothing's changed. Heaven knows I've tried, but I still can't close my eyes without seeing your face."

My heart was racing. "There's no way we can be together, Juan. Not—" I glanced down at my body—"not anymore. I promised the Virgin Mother."

"I know that. And I wouldn't let you break such a promise. Why do you think I've stayed away so long?" He looked down at his hands and pressed the tips of his fingers together. "It hasn't been easy, but it's better for both of us. I'm resigned to more of the same."

"You're right," I said softly. "I don't think I have the strength to be with you and still keep my promise."

He made a slight movement toward me, then checked himself. "I won't be far away, Marina," he said. "If you need me—for anything—I'll be nearby."

I wanted to throw myself into his arms, to beg him not to leave me. Instead I bit my lip and nodded. We heard Bernal's footsteps shuffling down the hall toward us. The Blessed Virgin must have sent him back in my moment of weakness, I told myself.

May 1521

The sound of hoofbeats clattering into the courtyard woke me in the night. I heard the muffled tread of many footsteps and the babble of voices in the street. God willing, Hernán and his men had returned from Chalco. I rose quickly, dressed and hastened outside as fast as the heaviness of my body would let me.

The city of Chalco, which lay on the southern extension of the lake, had been a problem since March, when its rulers had willingly tendered allegiance to the Spaniards. The area was an important source of food and other supplies for Tenochtitlan. Its defection had so aroused the wrath of Cuauhtemoc that he'd rained destruction down upon it. Sandoval had already led two expeditions to relieve the

Chalcans. When these had failed to establish safety for them, Hernán himself had marched south, accompanied by a large force under Ixtlilxochitl, to teach the Aztec emperor a lesson.

The stone floor was cold under my feet as I hurried out into the night air. In the torchlight I saw Guzman helping Hernán down from his horse. There was a blood-soaked bandage on—oh, Blessed Lady, no!—his head! I ran to his side. He laughed at my frightened face. "Calm yourself, Marina. It's only a little cut. You know how head wounds bleed." His arm was bandaged too. I looked at the circle of bearded faces around us and saw deep lines of fatigue on them all.

"He can smile about it now," said Alvarado, "but we almost lost him out there. His horse fell with him. The Aztec devils were about to drag him off when one of Tlaxcalans came to his rescue."

"See that the man's rewarded," Hernán broke in. "We've plenty to give him." Peering into the surrounding darkness, I realized that the army was laden with booty. Many of the men wore gold chains about their necks and carried jewelry, plumed headdresses and feathered robes. A large cluster of prisoners, some of them female and pretty, stood roped together at one side.

Hernán patted his horse's muzzle. "Poor old Pícaro needs a rest. I've almost ridden him to death. Ay! That march around the lake with our powder gone and those dark demons knowing it—! But we whipped them at Chalco, Marina, and then we sacked Xochimilco and burned it for good measure."

With Guzman's help, a disheveled María managed to hustle Hernán inside and into a chair, where she removed the dirty dressing from his head. "No, the wound is not so serious," she agreed. "You were lucky, Señor Cortés. But *caramba*, hold still and stop talking or I'll wrap this bandage around your mouth!"

Hernán ignored her. "Bring me the map, Marina," he commanded. I obeyed, unrolling the crude map on the table in front of him and holding it flat with my hands. It showed the lake with its surrounding cities—Texcoco on the eastern shore, Tlacopan on the west. Iztapalapan, Chalco, Xochimilco and other cities at the southern end and the twin cities of Tenochtitlan and Tlatelolco on the island in the center. He placed a finger on Texcoco and moved it north in a sweeping line around the lake.

"All this is secure now, Marina," he said, "all the way down here to Tlacopan. We occupied Tlacopan for six days last month—proof enough, I think, that we can take it for good when we have to. Chalco is on our side, Xochimilco's destroyed, Iztapalapan is weakened. Most of the others have already joined us. I think it's safe to say we can have Cuauhtemoc surrounded within the next few weeks. Maybe then he'll listen to reason and surrender without a fight."

"From what he's shown us, there's not much hope of that," I said, remembering tales of the blind loyalty of the *uei tlatoani's* warriors. "He wouldn't even talk with you at Tlacopan. Remember what happened to those two runners you sent back with peace proposals during Passion Week . . ."

"I'd like to forget," Hernán grunted. Cuauhtemoc had sent us back their hands. Hernán rolled up the map, patted the end with his hand, to even it, and tied it up with a strip of leather. He yawned, and slumped into his chair. "By my conscience, I'd like to sleep for a week, but the rest of tonight will have to do. Don't worry about my head, sweet, it'll be healed in a few days. No, you needn't help me, my dear Guzman. I'm quite capable of walking to my own quarters." He made his way out of the room, mumbling instructions to his young chamberlain.

I walked out into the darkness. The sky was just beginning to pale in the east. A body of Texcocan troops had gathered in the courtyard to divide their spoils before returning to their homes. My eyes caught the slender grace of one figure cloaked in white. Puzzled, I studied the oddly familiar movements. All at once the lithe form turned and in the dawn's light I glimpsed the slanting fox eyes of Ixtlilxochitl's sister, Mazatl.

"You're so surprised, Malintzin?" The mocking voice at my shoulder made me jump. "Of course my sister came along with us," chuckled Ixtlilxochitl. "On dark, dangerous nights like these, a man needs a woman by his side. At her own suggestion, I offered Mazatl to your master and he took her. Come, now, don't look so shocked. In your condition, what could you offer him?"

Still gaunt from his recent brush with death, Bernal lounged in the sun, and I, so clumsy in my last days, nearly tripped over his long legs.

"Careful!" He laughed, steadying my hand. "The last thing you need is to fall down on top of a bony old warhorse like me. You look so tired. Sit down. It's been two days since we got back from Xochimilco and I've hardly seen you."

"You're looking much better. Being back in action agrees with you." I lowered myself carefully to the top step.

"I think you're right, but no one will ever compliment me on my beautiful neck again. I'm growing my beard a little longer to cover the scar. See?" He cocked his chin for my admiration. "I took a good long walk this morning, all the way out to the shipyard. Someone out there asked about you." Eyes twinkling, he watched for my reaction. I gave him none.

"How are the brigantines coming?" I asked evasively.

"Fine. Practically finished. They're quite a sight, all thirteen of them sitting there in the pond like a gaggle of fat geese. Juan took some time to show me around, which I appreciated since he's busier than a bat in a mosquito swarm." Bernal scratched the scar on his neck. "He's picked up quite a bit of your lingo. Orders those Indian workers around like he's done it all his life. You know he still loves you, don't you?"

"Bernal . . . please!"

"All right—I deserve to be hanged. Here's another piece of news, though. Cortés has named the commanders for the brigantines, and Juan's to be one of them." He stretched lazily. "Oh, Juan tried to make a small thing of it when he told me. You know how he is. But I could tell he was excited. I happen to know he's wanted a command ever since the idea of the ships came up."

"Then I'm happy for him," I said, wishing I could talk about Juan without hurting. "Tell me, Bernal, were you able to get a younger slave this time?"

"Ha! This time I didn't even try. The pretty ones were whisked away so fast by the officers that I hardly got a look at them. Some of the officers even hid their prisoners and claimed they'd escaped so they wouldn't get skimmed off the top. The same with the gold. If Cortés doesn't do something about the situation, he's going to have a rebellion on his hands." Bernal leaned toward me confidentially. "The men have been grumbling for weeks, but this Xochimilco affair's brought things to a head. There's even talk of trying to replace him as *capitan-general.*"

"And are you one of the grumblers, Bernal?"

"I? Heaven forbid! Oh, I see the unfairness of it and I complain. After all the officers wouldn't even be alive if it weren't for lowly soldiers like me. But I'm no fool. No one but Cortés could have brought us this far with our skins in one piece, and I'll back him to my last breath. But there are others—Narvaez's men, mostly—and they're influencing the new arrivals. They're saying Cortés is a mad fool and that we'll all wind up on Cuauhtemoc's altars. Their leader's a dog named Villafañe. Cortés should have him watched." He shot me an alarmed look. "*Madre mía*, but you look strange. Are you all right?"

"I . . . I don't know. A pain . . ." My face relaxed as the spasm passed. "If you'll excuse me, Bernal, someone had best go find María de Estrada."

His eyes were wide as he helped me stand. "We'd better get you to bed."

"No," I protested. "It was just a little twitch, Bernal. It might not even be the real thing. I think María's out in the square. Go and find her for me and I'll go to my room. Don't look so worried, Bernal. It was nothing."

I had lied to him. The pain had ripped and twisted its way through my body like a dull knife. I'd wanted to scream with the agony of it. I watched Bernal until he disappeared in the direction of the square. Then I turned and made my way unsteadily inside the palace and down the corridor. I walked as fast as I could, praying that I'd reach my room before the next pain seized me. But I'd waited too long. Again I felt the tightening that heralded another contraction, this one even worse than the first. I sank to my knees next to a doorway, hands twisting my skirt, biting my lip to keep from shrieking. As the pain subsided I heard the whispers of two voices just inside the doorway.

". . . So it's got to be tonight, then. *Caramba!* This scares the hell out of me! We'll be dead men if we fail!"

"And rich men if we succeed. Think of the juicy reward Villafañe's promised us when they're dead. And it won't be so hard. When Cortés and the others sit down to dinner, López hands him the letter, saying it's from his father. He won't live to find out that it isn't."

"But, good God! Sandoval! Alvarado! Olid and the rest! I'd rather fight a pack of wolves with my bare hands!"

"So we won't use our bare hands! As soon as Cortés opens the letter we'll just slip out of the curtains behind them and stab them in the backs. *Vaya*, José, if you're not man enough to do it, there are others who will."

I shrank back against the wall. I would have to get to Hernán to warn him, but the men would see me if I tried to steal past the open doorway. I'd have to go back the way I'd come and take a roundabout way to Hernán's suite. Praying that I would find him while I was still able to walk, I backed down the hallway. If seen, I wanted to appear to be coming from the opposite direction.

The two men had stepped to the door. One of them looked down the hall and saw me, ostensibly walking toward them, trying to look as if nothing was wrong.

"Ay! Doña Marina, of all people," Muttered the man called José. "That's a bad sign. You don't suppose she heard anything, do you?"

"You're like an old woman today!" growled the other, "Stop fussing, José. She's too far away."

I passed them and turned the corner to double up with pain again. When the agony had passed I raced as fast as I dared to Hernán's quarters. He was there, thank heaven. From outside his room I could hear his voice raised in anger, along with another voice, crying, pleading. Just as I was about to burst through the doorway I caught myself. I'd recognized the second voice. It was José, the man I'd just heard plotting to kill Hernán.

I peeked through the doorway. José was sprawled on the floor facedown at Hernán's feet. "Mercy, my general," he was wailing. "I was fool enough to be taken in by Villafañe, but I've known all along that I couldn't go through with it. Spare me and I'll help you catch the others—by my mother's grave!"

Hernán jerked the man to his feet, clutching the front of his shirt in his powerful fist. "The others," he snarled. "Their names, dog, and I'll save you from the noose."

"I only know a few," quavered José. "Villafañe has a list in his breast pocket . . . a list, *señor*, of every man involved in this devilish plot. Spare me! Don't punish me with the others—"

"Stop caterwauling. Of course I'm going to spare you. But there's no time to lose. We've got to find Sandoval and the others. Come on, I'm not letting you out of my sight."

Hernán exploded through the doorway, dragging the whimpering José behind him. He glanced at me where I stood against the wall. "Whatever it is, Marina, it will have to wait," he muttered as he clattered off down the hall.

I leaned back, limp with relief. It was all right. He knew. Perhaps the sight of me in the corridor had been enough to frighten the already uneasy José into going to Hernán with his story. The shadow of pain passed over me again and I sank to the floor, writhing.

A frantic María de Estrada found me there a short time later.

* * *

I struggled against the pain, thrashing with each new wave that swept over me and threatened to drag me down. I remembered squatting in a cornfield to give birth to Chilam's baby. It had been so easy then, nothing like this time. Every instinct told me that something was terribly wrong, that this baby of Hernán's was having great difficulty in making its way into the world.

I supposed that it was night, for a torch had been lit in its bracket on the wall, but the measure of time had eluded me. I could not tell how long I'd tossed and strained on my bed. I was barely aware of the pale, haggard face of María de Estrada bending over me to smooth back my hair and wipe my sweating forehead, and the enormous black eyes of Sancha, who fluttered helplessly about the bed like a forlorn little insect.

I heard a rush of footsteps in the hallway outside and moments later, through a cloud of pain, I sensed a pair of sea-blue eyes looking worriedly down at me. Was I dreaming or had Juan come into the room?

"How . . . did you know? How did you get here?" I spoke with effort. My own voice sounded far away to me.

"Bernal. He brought me a horse. Hush, Marina, save your strength." He looked around at María. "Where's Cortés? Why isn't he with her at a time like this?" he demanded.

"I've sent Sancha to look for him twice. She can't seem to find him and I don't dare leave myself." The woman twisted her hands. "It's been so long, Señor Jaramillo, and she's getting so weak . . ."

"Someone has to find him. I'll go myself." He stepped toward the door, turning for one more look at me.

"Juan," I whispered, reaching out my arms toward him, "Don't leave me!"

He hesitated for an instant, glancing uneasily at María. Then he moved quickly back and knelt by my side.

I managed a feeble smile. "It's all right, Juan. She knows. Just hold my hands—quickly!" Massive talons of pain gripped my senses once more, almost tearing me apart with their intensity. I concentrated on the cool hands grasping my hot ones while my body contracted into a knot of agony. The contraction receded and I felt something wet oozing between my legs. María, at the foot of the bed, raised the sheet and motioned Sancha to come close with a candle.

"I feel something," she grunted as she probed my body, "but it isn't the head. *Madre mía,* this is worse than I thought

. . ." She took a deep breath. "Get her to relax if she can, Señor Jaramillo. I've got to try and turn the baby somehow—if the pain doesn't kill her . . ."

I bit my lip until the blood flowed as María, panting with the effort, twisted at the unyielding lump inside me. Juan stroked my hands. "Don't be so brave, love. Scream if you want to, if it helps . . ." His cheeks were wet.

I screamed—from the deepest wells of pent-up agony, from the depths of my tortured body. ". . . That's right, love, go ahead . . ." Juan was whispering as I screamed again and again, and felt something shift in the center of the pain.

María leaned over me. "It's better, I think. Now, when the next pain comes, Marina, push. Push for your life!"

The tightening was already beginning. At the height of the contration I pushed, my nails digging into Juan's flesh, every muscle in my body straining to its upmost. Nothing moved. I rolled my head back and forth in frustration. "I can't!" I sobbed. "I can't do it!" Another pain followed in the wake of the last one. I took it limply, without fighting. María shook her head.

"Sancha! Run, girl, and don't come back without the padre."

The padre . . . They thought I was going to die. The strange thing was that I was too tired to care. Juan was cursing under his breath. He took hold of my shoulders almost angrily. "Damn it, Marina, we're not going to lose you! Now, when the time comes, push! Hold my hands and push, *querida* . . ."

The pain mounted to an awesome crescendo. It tore at my body, it wrenched and twisted and stabbed. With my last strength I pushed hard. Something was moving, withdrawing from me. I closed my eyes, utterly spent, and waited for the cry of new life. It did not come. I heard the sound of María slapping something, but Juan was holding my head tight against his shoulder so that I couldn't see.

"Something's wrong," I gasped. "There's no cry! There's no cry! Juan, let me go! I want to see my baby—"

I felt the shaking of his head as he held me, trembling. "No, Marina, lie still. The baby was born dead, *querida*." There were tears in his voice. "Lie still, *mi amorcita,* my little love . . . if you move you'll make the bleeding worse." He held me while I sobbed quietly.

"I hear someone coming," María whispered. "It's Cortés! Señor Jaramillo, perhaps—" she looked imploringly at Juan.

"I'm not leaving," he said. "Not yet."

Hernán came striding into the room with Sancha and Padre

Olmedo on his heels. His face paled as he saw María wrapping something in white cloth. "The child?" he whispered hoarsely.

María shook her head. "Dead, *señor*."

"A son?"

"A daughter, *señor*. A little girl."

Hernán's shoulders sagged as the breath hissed out of his lungs like air from a bellows. He turned toward the bed. "Ah, it's you, Jaramillo. It was good of you to come. How's Marina?"

"Alive, but little beyond that." Juan had risen to his feet. "She'll need a good deal of rest and care if she's to get well."

"Then she shall have it." Hernán knelt down next to the bed and took my hands in his. Juan moved aside for him. "Marina *mía*," he whispered. "Ay, I'll never forgive myself for not having been with you, my poor little girl."

I remembered the plot. "Villafañe . . ." I murmured. "He was going to have you killed."

"It's all right. We caught him. He's dangling from the second floor of his house with a rope around his neck."

"The list . . ."

"I have it. He tore it up but I pieced it back together." He put his hand to his face. "The names . . . men I'd have trusted with my life, Marina. I still can't believe it! If I punish them all we'll be left immeasurably weaker. I've got to win them back somehow—but I'm tiring you. Jaramillo says you have to rest. Don't be sad, my sweet, we'll have more children. I promise you." He lifted my hands and kissed them. Out of the corner of my eye, I saw Juan slip quietly out of the room.

Late May 1520

The launching of the brigantines was an even bigger event than their arrival, in pieces, had been some three months earlier. A huge multitude had assembled on the shore of the lake: the men, women and children of Texcoco, the new allies from the lakeside cities and the vast Tlaxcalan force numbering into the hundreds of thousands, gloriously plumed and painted. Not to be outdone, the Spanish army gleamed with the polish of steel and brass. Hernán, in velvet-covered mail, pranced his jingling horse back and forth in front of the troops. Padre Olmedo stood ready to bless the ships, flanked by Padre Diaz and a newcomer, Fray Megalrejo, who'd come on the last ship from Cuba, bearing a generous supply of papal indulgences to sell. "He's come to the right place," Bernal had commented cynically upon Megalrejo's arrival. "This little company of sinners is going to make him a rich man."

There was even a choir, which Padre Olmedo had been rehearsing for weeks to give forth with a rousing *Te Deum* at the moment the dam on the pond was smashed, launching the brigantines down a narrow canal and into the lake.

I had made a remarkable recovery. Now, only two weeks after the loss of the baby, I was able to travel out to the shipyard on a litter to watch Hernán commission the captains of the thirteen brigantines and to see the vessels launched upon the lake. I'd mourned deeply for the child I had carried and lost. I'd sat for days beside the tiny mound of fresh earth in the courtyard, watering it with my tears, until I realized that I was crying not for the baby, who was now at peace, but for myself. After that my mind had begun to heal along with the rest of me. Today I felt more alive than I'd felt since the beginning of my pregnancy. The rains had come, washing out the dust-laden air and brushing the plains and hillsides with fresh emerald. A lively breeze raised scores of banners on their staves and mastheads and whipped my hair into tendrils around my face. It molded my red *huipilli* against the curves of my figure and fluttered the garland of scarlet and purple feathers that Sancha had woven into my hair that morning. For the first time in months I felt pretty.

I had no chance to speak to Juan, but our eyes met often during the ceremony. He was openly delighted to see that I was well enough to have come, and I was proud of his new commission. A reckless abandon, brought on perhaps by the spring wind, possessed my spirit. Whenever I felt his eyes on me, I returned his gaze with my boldest, most radiant smile.

My eyes wandered to Xicotencatl, possibly the only person in the whole assemblage who did not look pleasant. He sat under a canopy of plumes, stiff-backed and scowling, beside the co-commander of the Tlaxcalan army, the brave Chichimecatl. From time to time Xicotencatl cast poisonous glances at his companion. I knew there was bad blood between the two. Xicotencatl openly resented having to share his command with another. He grumbled whenever Chichimecatl was given an assignment of greater authority than his own. I had even heard rumors that the two generals were in love with the same woman. Their conflict could lead to nothing but trouble for Hernán.

I said as much to Hernán that same night after vespers, as we walked alone in one of the gardens. He had stayed doggedly at my side all evening. When I'd turned away to retire to my room he'd taken my arm instead and led me out into the flower-sweetened night. I walked beside him, talking nervously, enormously aware of his closeness, of his proprietary hand on my waist.

". . . I'd advise you to separate those two, Hernán, before they kill each other. Leave Xicotencatl here where you can watch him and send Chichimecatl to Chalco or Tlacopan. If you don't keep them apart they'll be too busy fighting each other to fight the Aztecs."

Hernán smiled. "Spoken like my wise little counselor. I'll do as you suggest, but it can wait till morning. You looked especially fetching out at the lake today, Marina. Made me realize that I've been neglecting you."

I looked down at my hands, wondering what was coming next.

"But there was something different about you today, Marina *mía*. A mystery, a sort of wildness, you might say. It was most intriguing. I sensed somehow that you were not thinking of me. You were casting your smiles elsewhere, my dear."

My heart sank. So that was it—I'd behaved idiotically.

"I won't embarrass you by naming names, *niña*, but I want you to understand something." His hand traveled up my spine to rest on my shoulder. "There's no room in my life for jealousy, Marina—no time, no energy to spare in chasing off rivals for what's mine. You belong to me and I expect you to remember that and conduct yourself accordingly. There'll be no more shaming me before my men by flirting like a tavern strumpet. Do you understand?"

I nodded, my face flaming with humiliation.

"Tomorrow we begin the assault on Tenochtitlan itself. There'll be no time for petty emotions then, but as for tonight, Marina, I think it's time you returned to my bed."

I gave an involuntary gasp. "Hernán, it's so soon . . ."

"By heaven, don't you think I know that? What kind of an animal do you think I am? I'll try and keep enough control over my baser instincts to leave you alone till you're ready, but I want you beside me nonetheless! And one thing more—there'll be no more leaving you behind in Texcoco when I march away. You're coming with me. Have Sancha pack your things in the morning."

I found myself wanting to hurt him. "You don't trust me here alone, is that it?"

"You little fool! I *need* you."

"What about Mazatl?"

"Oho! So you know about her? A mere diversion. I've long since tired of that skinny vixen."

"And suppose I refuse to come with you?" I pushed him, amazed by my own daring.

The short fuse of Hernán's patience sputtered and burned down to powder. He spun me around and jerked me brutally against him, his iron embrace crushing the breath out of me, his lips bruising mine and traveling downward, devouring my neck, my shoulders, draining away my spirit.

"You won't refuse, Marina," he murmured in my ear.

We were awakened early the next morning by a timid knock on the door. I stretched my aching body. Ugh! He hadn't even been gentle. It was my own fault for trying to argue with him.

At Hernán's rumbled "*pase,*" Guzman thrust his blond head through the doorway. "I'm sorry to bother you, *señor*, but there's a man outside who says that Xicotencatl's gone."

"Gone!" Hernán cursed, swung his legs over the edge of the bed and slipped into the brown velvet robe that the young man held out for him. "Show him in."

I recognized Captain Ojeda, a polished young fellow whose rapid mastery of Nahuatl had elevated him to the position of inspecting officer of the native forces. His face wore a look of perplexity.

"Xicotencatl's gone, you say?" Hernán growled. "What got into the son of a dog?"

Ojeda shrugged and shook his neatly trimmed head. "I'm not sure. There was an incident last night . . . one of our men struck a cousin of his. If I hadn't been there, there'd have been a real fight. The cousin was in such a rage, I thought it best that he leave, sir, so I ordered him back to Tlaxcala. I just found out that Xicotencatl and his personal retinue went back with him. They could be a quarter of the way home by now."

Hernán paced the floor. From the bed, with the covers drawn up to my chin, I could see the old pulsing of the vein in his forehead. "You realize, Ojeda, that we can't just let him walk off and leave us like this. Why, if he gets away with it, half the Tlaxcalan army could follow him."

"I know, sir. I was about to ask your permission to go after him."

"Of course!" Hernán snapped. "Take three or four swift horsemen. Don't try to force him, not yet at least. Appeal to his honor. In the meantime I'll order Chichimecatl and the bulk of the Tlaxcalan force to march south with Alvarado today. It's just as well they don't know what's happening."

That evening Ojeda returned without Xicotencatl. "He won't come," the young captain reported. "He says that if his people had listened to him they wouldn't be the tools and slaves of foreigners. He was most insolent, sir."

Hernán's face darkened. "By my conscience, I've had enough of that bastard. He's guilty of flagrant desertion and there's only one punishment for that—death."

The ominous word sent a chill into the room. I looked from Ojeda's grim visage to Hernán's. "He's an important man," I said. "Kill him and you risk alienating the whole Tlaxcalan nation!"

"You're right, Marina." Hernán's chest rose and fell with impatience. "But we've got to get rid of that troublemaker. We've got to make an example of him or we'll have our allies running home whenever the fancy strikes them." He brooded for a moment, his broad back toward us. "Ojeda!" He wheeled around again. "Take along a letter to the four chieftains. Go to them first and explain that in our army the penalty for desertion is death. Ask their permission to bring Xicotencatl back here to Texcoco and punish him justly. If they don't grant it—then we'll have to think of some other way."

Ojeda departed promptly, this time with an *alguacil* to make the official arrest and a number of loyal Tlaxcalan nobles to strengthen Hernán's position. In his absence, Hernán was confident enough of the outcome to erect a towering gallows in the square. "I want this to be seen," he muttered as his eyes traveled the height of the long beams.

Ojeda was back in a few days, with the glowering Xicotencatl, bound and gagged, in tow behind one of the horses. "It was almost unbelievable, sir," he reported. "Even his father condemned him. They told me that the penalty for desertion in Tlaxcala is death, too, and we were to take him and punish him as we saw fit."

Hernán did not even bother to remove the gag from Xicotencatl's mouth. "Why should we listen to any more of his venom?" he said coldly, and motioned the guards toward the gallows.

I turned my head away, but Hernán watched as the defiant figure was prodded up the high steps and the hangman tightened the noose around his neck. I heard the thud of the trapdoor and the twang of the rope as it took his weight. When I finally found the courage to look, the still-twitching body was being hoisted to the top of the gallows for all to see, the head tilted to the right of the heavy knot, the hands still clenched, the limp feet revolving in a graceful little arc.

Chapter Twenty-Three

Xolox—July 1521

The fortress of Xoloc stood at the intersection of the Coyoacan and Iztapalapan causeways, controlling the southern access to Tenochtitlan. That fierce little clump of rock, crowned by stout walls, battlements and turrets, had been captured by Olid early in the campaign. Hernán, seeing its strategic advantages, had been quick to make it his new headquarters. It was here also that I was housed. From the fortress towers I had watched the daily progress of the assault on the heart of the Aztec empire. Things were moving well for us. Only the island capital itself remained outside our grasp. Hernán now ruled the lake and the circumference of its shore. He owed the greatest part of his success to the brigantines.

I had stood beside Hernán on the deck of Captain Villafuerte's flagship, the *San Pedro*, on the day the fleet's guns had aided Sandoval and forty thousand allies in the taking of Iztapalapan. That same day Hernán had gone ashore with a hundred and fifty men and, under cover of the cannon, overthrown a fortress on a rocky promontory afterward known as El Peñol del Marquez, putting all but women and children to the sword. Immediately afterward, a flotilla of five hundred Aztec canoes had poured out of the island's canals and begun moving toward us, painted prows reflecting in the glassy surface of the lake. When Hernán and his band of marauders had regained the brigantines, he'd ordered them rowed into a line.

The ships, each with a crew of twenty-four, were clumsy hulks compared to the trim Aztec war canoes. They bobbed upon the placid water like fat ducks, sails hanging limp in the windless air as the painted fleet glided toward us.

Hernán was cursing. When rowed, the brigantines were unwieldy lumps of wood. It would take wind in the sails to bring them to life. As the canoes closed in, the brigantines stayed in tight formation. From the *San Pedro* I could see Juan on the deck of his own ship, the *Santiago*. I could even hear his terse commands as he pressed his rowers and readied the guns and crossbows. But where was the wind? Where was that capricious element that would fill the sails and send the ships winging down on their foes like angry eagles? By now I could make out the painted designs on the canoes. I could recognize individual features, details of shields and helmets.

Suddenly a fresh breeze struck my face. A great shout went up from the crews of the ships as the sails began to billow. The brigantines took wing and swooped toward the canoes. The two lines met. Cannon and arquebus roared. I smelled powder and heard human screams and the crunch of wood on wood. Then we were past the canoes, looking back on a vast, floating field of wreckage. Those native vessels that had not been destroyed were speeding back toward their island stronghold. The decks of the brigantines rang with cheers.

With that one brief encounter the Aztecs had surrendered their domination of the lake. Now, from a parapet of the Xoloc fortress, I watched day after day as the brigantines, each escorting a flock of allied canoes, prowled the waters. I'd learned to distinguish one from another, for each had its own colors and slight peculiarities of construction. The *San Pedro* carried Hernán's own black and red banner. Juan's flag, like his eyes, was blue. Captain Holgún's *San Mateo* flew a yellow flag; Captain Briones's *Santo Tomas* a green and gold one; and so on with the rest of the little fleet.

After that first dramatic victory on the lake, I had entertained hopes that the men on the brigantines would enjoy relative safety throughout the rest of the campaign. Alas, it was not to be. The Aztecs were quick to discover that the vessels, when immobilized, were vulnerable to attack. They would plant tough, pointed stakes on the shallow bottom, just below the surface of the water, and rush out to swarm over any brigantine that was unlucky enough to blunder onto them. Nights were especially dangerous, for it was then that the lake came alive with foraging parties from Tenochtitlan attempting to run the Spanish blockade and bring back supplies from the mainland. Some of these groups acted as decoys to lure the brigantines into tight channels or onto the stakes where their comrades were waiting in ambush. Captain Barba had already lost his life in such a trap. I began each day with a climb to the parapet and an anxious scanning of the lake for the sight of the *Santiago* with its blue banner.

Today I rested my chin on my hands and gazed wistfully at the tiny speck of blue as it disappeared in the direcion of the late-afternoon sun. The fleet had been broken up, with vessels going to assist the troops at strategic points around the lake. The *Santiago* and two other ships were headed for Sandoval's camp on the north causeway, carrying Juan out of my sight once more. Perhaps it was for the best, I told myself. If only I could keep from thinking about him so much . . .

"Marina, come down here!" Hernán's voice rumbled up from the courtyard below. "Must you sit up there all day like a cat in a tree, especially when I need you?" Conscience-stricken, I flew down the narrow stairway to his side. "That's better," he grunted, encircling my waist with his arm. "Come look at the map with me. I need the advice of my trusted little counselor."

The map was already laid out on the table of the council room. Small moveable figures of wood indicated the position of the army divisions and the brigantines.

"Have our spies reported back, Marina?"

"They have. Tenochtitlan's on the verge of famine." I forced my mind away from the vision of women and children starving in the streets. The population had been weakened by the *viruelas* before we came, and now, with food supplies from the mainland cut off and the acqueduct from Chapultepec broken, the food-and-water situation was growing desperate.

"That's what I expected." Hernán nodded his satisfaction. "I knew what I was doing when I sent Olid to cut through that acqueduct." He studied the map, scowling. "What about Cuauhtemoc? Hasn't the plight of his people moved that stony heart in the least?"

"They say he's determined to die rather than surrender, Hernán."

Leaning on the table with his fists, Hernán sighed heavily. "Twice already I've entered his accursed city by the south causeway and penetrated all the way to the plaza. The second time I burned the palace of Axayacatl and that infernal house of beasts and birds—*Santa María!* You should have heard the howls coming from that place. I've slaughtered their warriors like a wolf in a herd of sheep, and still that arrogant son of a devil won't even talk to me."

I put my hand on his arm and felt the tautness of each muscle fiber. "Could it be that he still hopes he might win? After all, he drove you out both times."

"The darkness drove me out," Hernán snapped. "Those

cursed canals—our horses and cannon can't pass over them, so we have to fill in each one as we cross. By the next day those dogs have opened them up again and made new traps. I want to put an end to it, Marina. I want to go out and finish this hellish business now!"

"You said you needed my advice." I waited quietly.

He gazed through me, his mind focusing on some distant point. He looked tired, I thought. The hollows around his intense black eyes were deeper, the faint, white streaks at his hairline more pronounced. "My captains think I'm being too cautious," he said at last. "They're pressing me for an all-out assault to take the city. If we could gain the market at Tlatelolco and establish a base there, they say, the capture of Tenochtitlan itself would be an easy step."

I realized he was hesitating, weighing the odds, fearful of losing such a gamble. "You're in command, Hernán," I said, "not your captains."

"I knew you'd say that, Marina *mía*," he said wearily, patting my hip. "Your heart's always with mine. But isn't it possible that we could both be wrong this time? By my conscience, I wish I knew."

"Alvarado's already tried to take Tlatelolco from the Tlacopan causeway," I reminded him. "The Aztecs undermined one of the bridges and collapsed it under most of the company." I'd talked to Bernal afterward and he'd told me how they'd fallen in and how he was almost captured. "It was a disaster, Hernán," I said.

He sank into a round-backed chair, shaking his head. "Disaster or not, Alvarado's being touted as a hero for daring to try it—but he had only his own division, Marina. Suppose we hit Tlatelolco with the whole army, from all sides at once?"

It was clear to me then. He was afraid of losing face. "You'd be risking everything," I cautioned.

"Yes, but if we won, Marina, we'd advance their surrender by weeks, even months! And the men are so impatient—"

I stepped behind him and began to massage the tightness out of his shoulders with my fingers Hernán had made his decision without me. There was nothing more to be said.

The plan was to enter the city from the Tlacopan causeway and assault Tlatelolco from four principal streets. Jorge de Alvarado and Juan de Alderete, newly arrived as the king's treasurer, would lead one party, Andrés de Tapia another;

Sandoval and Pedro de Alvarado would join to head a third, and Hernán himself would lead on the most difficult approach.

On the morning of the attack I was up on the parapet at the first light of dawn to watch as the brigantines, with their accompanying flotillas of allied canoes, cleared the nearby causeways of all traffic. The *Santiago* had returned and I was so intent on the maneuvers of the blue flag that I did not realize Padre Olmedo had climbed up beside me until he spoke.

"Are you wishing for wings, *hija*?"

"Wings?" I smiled at the priest and made room for him along the wall.

"Wings to fly out over the lake like an angel and view the coming battle from a better vantage point."

I decided to ignore the implication of his words. "Padre, I'd be content with a pair of magic eyes that would let me see all the way to Tlatelolco."

"Are you worried?" He looked down at my white-knuckled hands where they clutched the parapet wall.

"Yes."

The padre leaned on his elbows beside me. "I don't blame you. Cortés really didn't want to do this thing, did he?"

"He's not a reckless man by nature," I said.

"Still," Mused the priest, "I've heard talk that he's only dragging his heels to protect himself in case of failure."

"Failure! Don't speak of it, Padre!" I leaned forward, peering into the dawn mist. "They should be moving along the causeway into the city by now. If it weren't for this accursed mist we might be able to see them . . ." I cupped a hand to my ear to catch a faint tremor of sound. "Listen . . . shouts. Do you hear them?"

"I don't hear anything. You have ears like a deer. No, wait—cannon fire. It's beginning." He patted my arm. "Have faith, child. Remember Otumba."

The words were of little comfort. At Otumba we'd had the firm plain beneath our feet and nothing above us but God's own sky. Today Hernán and his men were marching into a hell of canals, ditches, undermined streets, and death on every rooftop. "Padre, I'm afraid," I whispered.

By the time the sun had cleared away the mist, the distant Tlacopan causeway was empty, a pale thread against the blue horizon. The brigantines hovered around the edges of the island city of Tlatelolco, taking care to avoid the treacherous stakes along the shore and at the canal entrances. Except for the faraway echo of gunfire and battle shouts, the vista from the fortress of Xoloc would have been pleasant, even peaceful. As it was, the suspense was sheer torture. The priest and I strained our eyes and ears for any telltale sight or sound that might indicate the tide of the battle. There were other watchers on the parapet now—the wounded, the women, the servants. All waited in silence, some twisting strings of rosary beads in anguished hands, some moving their lips to pray or to curse.

"Listen!" someone exclaimed. We leaned forward to catch the new sound: the sonorous throb of the great snakeskin drum atop the central pyramid at Tlatelolco. Its cadence sent chills over the flesh of those who had heard it once before on the *noche triste*. Was it an alarm, an attack signal? The battle sounds rose to a new pitch. I gripped Padre Olmedo's arm so hard that he winced.

Suddenly a dark line began to spill out onto the Tlacopan causeway, flowing along the narrow roadway like blood. "They're retreating," croaked a wounded young soldier next to me, a boy of no more than seventeen. "They're running . . ."

Even at such a distance it was evident that the retreat had lost every trace of order. The dark mass surged out onto the causeway, spilling over the edges and into the water. Aztec canoes clustered around the fleeing forces, dragging away captive after captive. More Aztec canoes came pouring out of the canals. Quickly the brigantines moved in to cover the retreat, some of them sweeping dangerously near the shore.

"The stakes," I gasped. "They're getting too close!"

One ship, bearing a green and gold flag—that would be the *Santo Tomas* under Briones—was already in trouble. It had crunched into a row of stakes near one of the canal entrances and was firmly wedged. Canoes came swarming out from the canal to drive off the allied canoes and surround the ship. Brown-skinned warriors clambered swiftly aboard, overwhelming the twenty-four-man crew. I saw the body of a Spaniard drop over the side and land in the water with a splash. Two Aztecs were hauling another man into a canoe. The man was screaming.

The causeway was packed with the fleeing horde now. Many were swimming in the shallow water, easy prey for the waiting canoes. The fugitives were beginning to trickle out onto the south causeway as well, moving toward us at Xoloc.

As we looked on in helpless dismay, the battle continued to rage aboard the besieged *Santo Tomas*. Now another brigantine was speeding to assist the trapped vessel. I gasped when I saw that the second ship carried a blue flag.

The Aztecs were too near the *Santo Tomas* to be driven off by cannon fire. Juan's first pass was breathtaking—so close that the bow of the *Santiago* swamped several canoes. His crossbowmen and arquebusiers were able to fire off some accurate shots before the ship's momentum took them out of range. The *Santiago* wheeled and swept down upon the enemy again. This time several of her crewmen were able to leap to the deck of the *Santo Tomas* to aid their comrades. the Aztecs began to desert the ship for their canoes, where the *Santiago's* guns drove them into a wide circle around the two brigantines. I clawed at the stone under my hands. The stakes were all along the shore. If Juan's ship ran up against them, both vessels would be lost.

The crew of the *Santo Tomas* jumped overboard with axes to chop away at the stakes as Juan swung his ship back and forth in an arc to make a protective shield for the stricken brigantine. After an achingly long time the *Santo Tomas* was free. The two vessels came plowing through the circle of canoes and returned to guarding the causeway. The watchers on the parapet cheered. Padre Olmedo nudged my shoulder. "Your friend's a good sailor," he whispered. I flushed with pride. If only . . .

I looked out toward Tlacopan at the routed troops jamming the causeway and toward the north at the forlorn stragglers making their way toward Xoloc. Beside me, the young soldier with the wounded leg was sobbing, his face buried in his hands.

The first group to reach Xoloc in a body was Andrés de Tapia's company. I ran down to meet Tapia as he slid exhausted off his bleeding horse. "I still don't know what happened," he gasped. "Things were going just as they should have—then suddenly they hit us from everywhere. Name of heaven, don't you have any news of Cortés?" There was something beyond fear in his round eyes.

"Nothing," I said, my throat tight. "What is it?"

Tapia's voice broke. "They threw heads at us—white men's heads! And they shouted 'Tonatuih! Sandoval! Malinche!' . . ."

I clutched his arm. He was shaking. "They were other men's heads—but some of us knew them. And we've had no word from Cortés. No word." The brave captain fought to keep back the tears.

"Come inside and rest." I spoke calmly, trying to hide my

fears from the distraught man. "There's sure to be news soon."

Tapia shook his head. "Not till I've found Cortés. I'll take three horsemen and ride to his camp at once. When I find him I'll send word back to you."

"God go with you then, Captain." Uninjured horses were recruited and Tapia, with three aides, galloped off toward the mainland. With a silent prayer I watched him go. It was beginning to get dark and the victory drums were pounding away in Tenochtitlan. The city was so near that we could see the torches and make out figures atop the great pyramid. Flames were dancing before the *teocalli*. A procession of priests in full regalia was winding its way toward the summit. I joined the other watchers on the parapet, even though I knew with a sickening certainty what we were about to see.

A line of prisoners, appeared, led by priests and prodded on their way by Aztec warriors with spears, winding their way up the side of the pyramid. Their faces were smeared with paint. Plumes were tied to their heads.

A Spanish woman standing beside me began to scream. "They're white! Mother of God, they're white! They're ours!"

The first group of prisoners was prodded into a circle. The priests made them dance by jabbing at their legs with firebrands. "Who is it? Can you recognize them?" someone asked.

"Impossible. With all that paint . . ." The answering voice deepened into a moan as the first prisoner was forced onto his back over the convex altar stone. The priest—I gave a little cry as I recognized his wild gray hair—took the obsidian knife and raised it above his head with both hands. As he plunged the dagger straight down into the chest of his victim and scooped out the still-beating heart with his bare hands, the Spanish woman standing beside me screamed again and again.

Someone carried her below. I stayed with the others, close to Padre Olmedo where I could hear the comforting murmur of his voice as he whispered a prayer for each Christian who died on the altar. Some met death meekly, with the lethargy of hopelessness. Others had to be carried, kicking and thrashing, to the bloodsoaked stone. Awaiting his turn to die next was a youth, slender and very white. As he turned his head, I caught a glimpse of pale golden hair. I bit my lip to keep from crying out. Only one man in the entire company was so fair: Cristobal de Guzman, Hernán's own chamberlain. As Cozcaquauhtli stretched him out on the altar I buried my face in the folds of the padre's robe, remembering young Guzman's gentleness, his shy sweetness in my presence. I tasted tears. Then a new horror clutched at me. They had Guzman. They could easily have Hernán as well. He could be there, watching his men die, awaiting his own ghastly end. I watched in terror. They would save him for last, for the climax of the ceremony. The hearts of the men would be burned on the altars. The bodies, I knew, would be flayed about the heads and torsos and the skin used to dress the priests during special ceremonies. The flesh would be eaten by the victors and their families.

I was startled by the sound of hoofbeats from below. In the torchlight I recognized one of the men who'd gone with Tapia. Seeing me, he called out, "Cortés is safe! So are Sandoval and Alvarado!" I sagged against Padre Olmedo in relief.

The Aztecs killed sixty Spaniards that night. The rest of the sacrifices were brown-skinned—Tlaxcalans, Texcocans, Chalcans and other allies. It was dawn before the killing stopped.

It was midmorning when Hernán trotted his mount wearily into the enclosure of the fortress. Hurrying out of the infirmary, I took two running steps toward him and stopped short. His eyes stared at me, through me and past me, like two burned-out black coals in cavernous sockets. His cheeks were hollow like an old man's, and his clothes and beard were caked with dust. He looked like a body that had just emerged from the pit of hell, leaving mind and soul behind.

I recovered from my shock and ran to his side. He would need me more than ever now. While a soldier held the horse, I helped him dismount, remembering how Guzman had always been there to attend him. He leaned upon me, his heavy armor creaking as I helped him to his room, where I removed his helmet and helped him out of his cuirass. He collapsed onto the edge of the bed, sitting with his head in his hands while I poured him a cup of wine.

At last, with the red liquid warming his throat, he spoke. "I begged them to leave me, Marina *mía*," he whispered hoarsely. "I pleaded with them to let me stay and die with my men . . ."

"No!" I sat at his feet and pressed my face against his knee. "We'd all be lost without you, Hernán."

"The devils had me once. They were carrying me away in their arms and I wanted it, Marina. I *wanted* it. Then young Olea flung himself at them and they let me go. It cost him his life. And Guzman . . . I'd lost my horse, poor old Pícaro, and he was bringing me another when they took him. Either of those fine young men was worth ten of me."

I looked into his ravaged face with my eyes full of tears. "How did it happen?" I asked him in a whisper.

He shook his rumpled head. "I don't understand it all myself. I'd sent a good part of the men in ahead while I stayed to see to the rear. They had strict orders to fill in every canal they crossed. Ay, they were so eager and impetuous that they didn't have time for such dreary tasks. When the Aztecs hit them from inside the city and drove them back, those empty canals were waiting like traps, covered with little more than sticks. It was living hell, Marina, with the front guard stampeding back against the rear and those screaming devils raining death on us from every rooftop. And afterward . . . those priests!" His hands shook so violently that I had to take the half-empty cup from him.

"We saw them too," I said quietly. "Lie down and rest, Hernán. It wasn't your fault."

"In the name of heaven, what does it matter whose fault it was now?" He buried his face in his hands once more, refusing to be comforted. I sat silently by his feet, watching the convulsive rise and fall of his shoulders.

After a time he was still, and after a very long time he spoke again. "Marina," he said in a hollow voice, "I swear by all that's holy, I'll never again send my men into that death-trap of streets and canals!"

I waited, not daring to question him. Could he, after all this time and effort, be giving up the conquest?

"There's only one way to take a hellish maze like Tenochtitlan." The vein in his forehead was twitching. "I'll go in with an army of laborers and level every house and building from one end of the island to the other. As we go, we'll use the rubble to fill in those accursed canals for good." His voice quickened. "I'll not leave one stone upon another, Marina. I'll create my own battlefield of open ground, and on open ground no one can beat me! Bring me the map, *vida mía*."

August 1521

"Smoke! Smoke from Tlatelolco!"

I heard the cry of the lookout and ran up onto the parapet.

A slender black column rose into the blue distance, growing rapidly heavier until it thickened into a billowing cloud. The *teocalli* atop the great pyramid was aflame, proclaiming to all the valley of Anahuac that the forces of Hernán Cortés from the south and Pedro de Alvarado from the north had met in the marketplace at last. Except for the formalities of surrender, the siege of Tenochtitlan was over.

I was ready and waiting when an escort of Tlaxcalan warriors and carriers arrived a short time later to convey my litter to Tlatelolco. As they trotted over the causeway to what remained of the island city, I surveyed the destruction on all sides. I'd watched the demolition of Tenochtitlan at a distance from my parapet at Xoloc, house by house, street by street, but at close range the destruction was worse than I'd ever imagined. We marched across a wide field of rubble. Buildings, streets and canals had vanished as if a mighty hand had swept them all into dust. The light, porous *tezontli* stone from which most of the city had been built had been broken and crushed by Hernán's force of a hundred thousand native laborers who'd performed the destruction while the Spanish troops kept the Aztecs at bay. Fragments of homes, businesses and temples crunched under the sandals of my litter-bearers.

The sickly sweet stench of death rose everywhere. Arms, legs and heads protruded from the rubble, alll picked clean by the black vultures that wheeled about the sky and screeched as they flapped around each new find. I filled my eyes, ears and nostrils with the signs of death. To turn away and deny its reality was impossible. I remembered the first time I had passed over the same road amid the splendor of Moctezuma's welcome. This time Hernán would be waiting for me in ravaged Tlatelolco.

Within the more recently conqured parts of the city, the human suffering was worse and much more evident. Bodies lay thick in the streets, their flesh melted away by starvation. The hollow-eyed living crawled about and gnawed on the limbs of the dead. The monster of hunger had stolen their minds. I saw that there were no children left alive, and no old ones. Flies swarmed blackly on the rotting corpses, which companies of native laborers were already shoveling into piles to be burned.

The pyramid of Tlatelolco, its temple in smoking ruins, loomed above us as Hernán strode out from a nearby palace to meet me. His face was grim, but I recognized the spring of victory in his step.

"What about Cuauhtemoc?" I asked anxiously as he helped me from the litter.

Hernán gave a snort of disgust. "One small part of the city still belongs to the Aztecs and he's holed up there like a rat, the bastard. Why doesn't he surrender and end this misery? You see what's happened to his people? That's *his* doing, not mine. He was the one who chose to let them starve." He led me up the palace steps. Soldiers stood about in groups, resting from the battle and comparing their exploits. Bernal Diaz, who'd been with Alvarado, greeted me with a wave of his hand.

"I've been expecting Cuauhtemoc to flee by way of the lake," Hernán continued. "The brigantines are out there waiting for him if he does. Ay, these devils who don't have the sense to give up . . ."

"He's a proud man and a brave one, Hernán," I said, making no effort to hide my grudging admiration for this fiery young ruler to whom freedom was more important than life.

"Hmph!" Hernán grunted. "Oh . . . Ojeda tells me they have your old priest."

"Cozcaquauhtli?" I caught my breath. "Who has him?"

"The Tlaxcalans. I don't know what they've done with him, but Ojeda said that some of them claimed to have recognized him atop the pyramid on that awful night when they put so many of our men and theirs on the altar. I told him that if that was true, they had my permission to do anything they damn well pleased with him. I trust you'd approve, my sweet."

"Yes . . ." I'd been right, then; it was Cozcaquauhtli I'd seen from Xoloc. "But I want to find out what's happened to him, Hernán."

"Go, then. I've a conference with my captains and they're waiting for me. The band that took the old man is camped over in the northeast corner of the square. Hear the drums? They've some sort of celebration going on. Should I get someone to go with you?"

I shook my head. "I always feel safe with the Tlaxcalans. When I've finished, I'll have someone show me to your quarters."

"Do that, Marina *mía*. I've been too long without you."

I walked toward the wild throbbing of the *teponatzli* that came from the center of the Tlaxcalan camp. The sound made the hair on the back of my neck stand up like a cat's. I nodded greetings to arrogant warriors who stood beside fires where human arms and legs were roasting, and to bedraggled slave women who sweated over their *metatls*, grinding corn and chiles. The crowd of warriors, hideously painted, grew thick as I neared the central point of the revelry, but they moved aside respectfully and let me pass, opening up a path to the very heart of their celebration. The pounding of the drums filled my ears, my head.

Someone with his back to me was dancing. I recognized my old enemy, his long, gray, blood-matted hair swishing and swinging with each wild leap of the dance. Such agility for an old man . . . Suddenly, with a mighty lurch of my stomach, I realized what I was seeing. The dancer whirled in my direction and I saw his face-within-a-face. A nimble young Tlaxcalan was dancing in Cozcaquauhtli's flayed skin!

So this, at last, was the consummation of my vengeance. Rooted to the spot, I watched the dance, expecting a feeling of jubilation that did not come. Instead, my knees began to liquify and I felt my stomach begin to churn with nausea. I made my flight with as much dignity as possible, nodding at everyone I passed, until I found refuge at last behind a tall heap of rubble. There I allowed myself to be totally, unbecomingly sick.

Afterwards I sat down on a loose building stone and held my head in my hands to keep it from spinning. How strange it was, the way life revolved in circles. The flayed skin was all that remained of a bitter, lifelong enemy, the man who had killed my father with his own hand. Yet, had it not been for Cozcaquauhtli's treachery I would still be no more than the daughter of the *tlatoani* of Oluta, living out my life as I had once planned. It was the old priest's actions that had set my feet upon the path over which I had returned to destroy him and his world. And Quauhtlatoa, whose body was now no more than bones buried under the ruins of the traders' quarters? His first act against me had freed me from a future as Moctezuma's concubine and sent me to Tabasco and my destiny. His second had thrust me into Juan's arms, where I had found my only moments of real love and happiness. And the others . . . Itzcoatl . . . my mother . . .

I shivered suddenly feeling that all my steps had been—somehow guided. Something too large for me to grasp and understand was hanging above the realm of my thoughts, something frightening and wonderful that had no name.

When Hernán had summoned me to Tlatelolco, I'd assumed that the fighting was over. I'd been wrong. Like maddened, cornered beasts, the Aztecs continued to battle for every street, every house. Delegation after delegation of captured nobles sent to Cuauhtemoc's little quarter with offerings of peace returned with haughty assurances that the *uei tlatoani* preferred death to life under the rule of the white man.

Starvation and pestilence crawled through the streets. The people had eaten frogs, worms, insects, the scum from the lake, until even these were no more. At the very last, their minds gone, they'd begun to prey upon one another.

I stood beside Hernán and Alvarado on the palace steps, choking on air that was putrid with smoke and death. A group of five nobles, the last to be sent to Cuauhtemoc, had promised us that the emperor would come to the square the following morning.

"You know that son of a female dog won't come," Alvarado snapped. "Why not go in there, kill the bastards and be done with it?"

"You think I wouldn't like to have it over with, my good Pedro?" Hernán wiped his sweating face with his sleeve. "But I need Cuauhtemoc. Look at these loyal sons of Spain who've fought so bravely at my side—do you think they've done it out of love for me? Ha! I've dangled the promise of riches before their noses all the way from Cuba. They'll be content with nothing less than the feel of gold between their fingers, and if I disappoint them I'll have *another* war on my hands. You've seen the wealth of Anahuac, you know how much gold we left on that bloody causeway . . ."

"And Cuauhtemoc knows where it is?"

"If I didn't think so, I'd crush him like a fly."

The next day we waited in vain for Cuauhtemoc and the five nobles to appear. At last, toward afternoon, in a fury of exasperation, Hernán unleashed the full force of his own army and the two hundred thousand allies upon the pitiful remnant of the Aztec nation. In the incredible butchery that followed, more than forty thousand sick, starving Aztecs died.

Despising my own cowardice, I fled from their screams to Hernán's quarters in the heart of the palace, but there was no escape. The shrieks, the wails, the horrible, choking black smell of burning bodies followed me. I ran wildly down the empty halls, not knowing or caring where I was going, until my way opened up into a small inner garden of the palace. The garden was bare, the fountain in its center long dry. The flowers, the leaves on the trees and vines, even the grass had been ripped away by the hands of the starving. I flung myself onto the ground, tasting dirt and remembering how the hunger-maddened Aztecs had filled their bellies with the earth itself.

Suddenly I became aware of the ludicrousness of my situation. People were dying like locusts in the streets outside, and here was poor little Marina, tearing about like a crazed rabbit because she couldn't endure it! Well, I lashed out at myself, what *was* the proper behavior for someone witnessing the death throes of a nation? Should I stand at Hernán's side and smile? Should I take a sword and join in the carnage? Should I fall on my face and beg to die with my own people . . . ?

"I've been looking for you, child." Padre Olmedo had come quietly into the garden and bent down to touch my shoulder.

"Why?" My voice was dejected, almost hostile.

"In the hope that, in this dark hour, you and I might be of some comfort to each other."

"You need comforting, Padre?" The idea struck me oddly, coming from one who was himself such a comforter.

The priest sat down on the ground beside me, crossing his legs before he spoke. "Picture if you will, *hija*, a great field of ripe wheat—no, corn, so you'll understand. Picture the harvester, wading in with eager hands, rejoicing at the richness of the crop. See him as he goes from plant to plant and finds, to his dismay, that the ears are diseased, rotten, eaten away by worms. No more than a few kernels are saved. The rest of the field must be cut down and burned, and the harvester watches the flames and weeps." Padre Olmedo fingered his brass crucifix. "I entered this venture with such hopes of bringing a nation of souls to the foot of the cross . . . not by force, but by kindness, by good example. I wanted to show them that the way of Our Lord was the way of peace and love. What a dreamer I was! What a fool!" He bowed his shorn head and stared down morosely at his sandals.

I put my hand on the roughness of his sleeve. "At least you came with a noble purpose, Padre," I murmured. "I came looking for vengeance. And I've found it—a hundred thousand times over! Oh, Blessed Lady . . ." Bitter sobs forced their way up out of my throat.

"Calm yourself, daughter. You're trembling. This isn't your doing. You couldn't have prevented it."

"But . . . how can I make you see it? That's my own blood flowing in the streets out there. Whatever I say, whatever they've done to me, they're *my* people. Xicotencatl called me a traitor and I denied it, but he was right. I used to think I hated them, Padre, but now part of me's dying with them." I felt myself shaking uncontrollably. "How could I have known it would come to this? What have I done?" I buried my face in my hands, choking with sobs.

The priest placed his hand on my head, the loving hand of a father. "Listen to me, child." There was a strange quality, a glow in his voice. "You were the first in this land to accept Our Savior, and I've taken great pride in you. I've tried my best to teach you his ways, praying that you would understand, hoping that you would not only come to know his words, but to feel the power of his love." He paused and I realized that he was weeping. "My daughter, my heart has never been filled with more pride than at this moment, for I know his love has touched you—the same love that moved Our Lord, in his agony upon the cross, to look down upon his crucifiers and pray 'Father, forgive them . . ."

"But I'm the one who needs forgiveness."

"But only from yourself. This day will end, child. The black vultures of death will fly away. Then your people will need you more than ever, and you'll find your forgiveness . . . Yes, go ahead and cry, my little one. Shed your sweet tears for all of us."

August 13, 1521

Even the previous day's slaughter had failed to flush Cuauhtemoc. Now Hernán brought forward his three heaviest cannon, resolved to blast the stubborn monarch from his hiding place. One last delegation of captured nobles was sent to plead for his surrender while Hernán, the army and the cannon waited.

At last the nobles appeared again, emerging from the smoking maze of streets like gaunt spectres. A commanding figure stood in their midst.

"Cuauhtemoc!" exclaimed Captain Alderete, who had not been to Tenochtitlan with the original party.

"No . . ." I caught my breath as I recognized the tattered black and white cloak of the *ciuacoatl*. I checked the impulse to run forward and embrace him like a long-lost uncle.

Tlacotzin's flesh was stretched over his bones like the skin of a drumhead. He moved slowly, as though using his last strength for each step, but his eyes still flashed like a hawk's in the sun and his voice still rang with authority as he commanded his aides to present Hernán with a fine gold chain.

"Malintzin." He bowed his head gravely. "To me has been entrusted the duty of surrendering our city into your hands. The victory is yours." The honey-smooth flow of his voice was unbroken. I marveled at his self-control. When I translated his words, the troops cheered wildly.

"Tell him I want Cuauhtemoc," Hernán growled.

"All in good time, Malintzin." The *ciuacoatl* dismissed the demand with a wave of his skeletal hand. "Surrender is a most complicated business and we've much to discuss. The first thing you'll want to do is establish the amount of tribute you expect to be paid as a token of your victory. Then there's the matter of safe conduct for our women and children . . ."

Even Hernán was no match for the *ciuacoatl's* silver tongue. Tlacotzin held sway most of the morning, expounding each tiny detail of the surrender, repeating himself so cleverly that the sun was at its zenith before it occurred to anyone that he was merely stalling for time. I grew hoarse from translating. Hernán's repeated insistence that Cuahtemoc appear was deftly turned aside until his short-fused Spanish patience snapped.

"Marina," he exploded, "tell this evasive devil that unless Cuauhtemoc is standing here before me within the hour, these cannon will blast him, his emperor and what remains of his city into dust!"

A flicker of a smile played about the corners of Tlacotzin's thin lips. "Malintzin, he will not come," he said in his quiet, cultivated voice. "My lord Cuahtemoc has surrendered all to you save his freedom, and that he will not give up. And now, if you'll give me leave, I wish to return and die with my *tlatoani*."

"Seize him," Hernán commanded. "If we lose the eagle, at least we'll have this oily-tongued hawk in our cage."

Two burly guards moved in to take the *ciuacoatl* prisoner. "That won't be necessary, Malintzin." He raised a frail hand and the dignity of the gesture was enough to hold his captors at bay for a moment. "So little remains of my life that it matters not to me where I end it."

So we left him alone and allowed him to stand impassively beside us as the cannonballs roared into the last fragile bones of the city, smashing the houses into powder. Most of the dwellings appeared to be empty. The *ciuacoatl's* long discourse had purchased enough time for the inhabitants to vacate the doomed quarter and flee onto the causeways—time spent in vain, for the Tlaxcalans and their allies were waiting there to perform the final slaughter.

Suddenly the booming of cannon in the city was answered by a salvo from the lake. The signal! The long-awaited signal that Cuauhtemoc had at last attempted his escape and had fallen into the net of waiting brigantines. The order to cease firing echoed down the ranks amid cheers.

Sandoval, now in command of the fleet, had orders to bring the royal prisoner to Hernán immediately, In anticipation of this, an area in the square was speedily cleared, swept and decorated with banners. The captive's progress from the shore of the lake, through the streets and into the square was easy to follow, for Cuauhtemoc's enemies went wild with glee at the sight of him walking in the midst of his captors. Crowds flocked into the square, eager to see the death-blow dealt to the Aztec empire.

They entered the plaza amid cheers. Cuauhtemoc, bareheaded and clad in nothing more than a tattered loincloth, walked erect between Sandoval and Captain García Holgún of the *San Mateo*. Sandoval and Holgún were glaring at each other and I guessed—correctly, as I later learned—that they'd quarreled over who was to take credit for the emperor's capture; Sandoval as commander or Holgún as the one who'd made the actual apprehension.

A long file of captured Aztec nobles and their families stretched out behind them. Surrounded by guards was the tiny form of Tecuichpo, daughter of Moctezuma, wife of Cuauhtemoc, and last empress of the Aztecs. Hunger had sharpened the exquisite little features, but her beauty had not fled. Her enormous eyes stared straight ahead at her husband's back as he came face to face with Hernán and stopped. The *ciuacoatl* fell to his knees before him in a last gesture of homage.

The young emporor was as emaciated, ragged and dirty as his subjects but he stood with dignity before his conqueror and his voice was dispassionate when he spoke. "Malintzin, I have done everything I could possibly do in the defense of my city and my people. There is nothing, save my life, that I have not lost, and now I wish to lose that as well. Take that knife out of your belt and kill me with your own hand." As I translated, he reached forward and touched the hilt of the poniard that hung at Hernán's hip.

Hernán recoiled in mock horror. "Take the life of such a

noble adversary! I wouldn't think of it! This country's going to need men of valor and integrity like yourself, Cuauhtemoc. Join with me. We'll restore this devastated land together and you can lead your people to new greatness." He beamed with magnanimity.

"My people are dead," Cuauhtemoc said bitterly, "and since you refuse to grant my wish to join them, I must die the slow way, day by day. I ask only that you give shelter to my empress. Knowing that she's safe will give me peace." He glanced back at Tecuichpo and I caught the fleeting tenderness in the look he gave her. Tecuichpo gazed at him, her thirteen-year-old eyes brimming with secret emotions, the nature of which we who watched could only guess.

Then the two of them were led away separately.

The victory was celebrated that night with music, laughter and freeflowing *pulque*. There would be time for religious services in the morning. The main hall of the palace at Tlatelolco blazed with torches. Those who could not fit inside staged their own festivities in the hallways and patios, drinking, roaring with merriment, and watching the native women dance. Hernán joined in the revelry with his officers, but I, still repulsed by drunknness, felt ill at ease in their company. Stifling, I sought the night's coolness and wandered aimlessly through the palace, lost in thought.

I found myself at last on a high balcony that faced west toward the lake. Leaning my chin on my hands. I watched the turbulent black clouds froth across the face of the moon like sea foam. The air smelled of coming rain. From my vantage point I could see all the way to the lake, where the brigantines were moored. Lanterns hanging from their masts cast rippling beams of light onto the surface of the water. I wondered which of them was the *Santiago*, for I could not tell in the darkness. I had not seen Juan at the celebration below, so it was likely he'd stayed aboard his ship. Was he alone? I wondered. Was he thinking about me? I imagined myself leaving the palace, making my way through the ruined city to the shore of the lake to find him waiting. I closed my eyes, wanting to bring him near, to feel warm and safe in his arms again. With a melancholy shake of my head I opened my eyes again and stared into the darkness. What a fool I was . . .

The wind eased into a great, breathy sigh that rose to a moan, then to a shriek, like the lament of some anguished monster in the sky. It lifted the dust of the crushed city into a choking cloud that drove me back against the wall in search of shelter. It rose to a howling crescendo, and then, with a heaven-splitting burst of thunder, the rain began falling in solid sheets, whipping against the collapsed buildings, pelting the bodies of the slain, freshening the ghastly perfume of death. Lightning yellowed the sky, illuminating the desolation below. I stood with my face turned up to the rain, letting the stinging droplets wash death's fingerprints from my skin.

Someone was beside me. I gave a little scream then felt foolish as I recognized the *ciuacoatl.* "I thought they'd locked you up," I said.

"What for?" He shrugged. "Where could I go?" A flash of lightning outlined the sharp contours of his skull-thin face. He leaned out over the edge of the balcony. "Listen, Malintzin . . ." he whispered. "Listen!"

At first I heard only the wind. Then the sound was more than wind. It was the wail of voices in a hundred different keys, a death-chant as immense as the sky itself, a howling lament that filled the very universe. I was trembling. "What is it?" I whispered, hoarse with awe.

Tlacotzin's eyes were fixed on the sky. His voice seemed to come from somewhere outside his body. "Huitzilopochtli," he murmured. "Tlaloc, Tezcatlipoca . . . Xipe Totec, the Lord of the Flayed . . . Tlazoteotl, the Eater of Sins . . . the four hundred rabbits . . . even Quetzalcoatl . . ." He blinked away the raindrops. "The gods are leaving us, Malintzin. All of them. Forever."

Chapter Twenty-Four

Tlatelolco—June 1522

"You can still smell it after every rain." Don Juan Velásquez inhaled deeply of the cool, evening air. His aristocratic nostrils quivered. "Death, Malintzin," he answered my quizzical look. "Even a sprinkling brings it out of the earth again. Smell it. It's sweet, like incense. Not at all what you'd expect from the dust of men's bodies."

"I'd always thought it was only the flowers," I said slowly, leaning against the edge of the parapet and remembering how the two of us had stood in the same spot less than a year before to watch the storm's fury sweep over the death-ravaged capital.

Tenochtitlan had changed, emerging from its baptism of fire and rain with a new name, *La Cuidad de México*. Gone were the canals, the temples, the garish *tzompantli* with its hundred thousand grinning skulls. Gone was Moctezuma's palace and the palace of Axayacatl, where the captive monarch had languished and died. Gone were the drums, conches, flutes, feathers and blood. In their place an air of bustling serenity reigned as crews of Indian laborers. working under their Spanish *jefes*, reorganized the loose blocks of *tezontli* stone into the elements of a Spanish city. A commodious municipal palace was planned for one side of the central square. The walls of a huge church were already rising upon the spot where the pyramid had stood, with its twin temples of Tlaloc and Huitzilopochtli.

Don Juan Velásquez was himself a symbol of his kingdom's transformation. I studied him with affection. The high, bulging forehead, the silvered hair, the stark nobility of features had changed little, and he retained the simple dress of his people. The only outward change was manifested in a golden object that dangled from a chain around his neck: a finely worked crucifix, a gift from Hernán to Don Juan on the day of his christening. Like the crucifix, the name was new. Yet, although his plumed helmet and black and white cloak of office had vanished with the past, the eloquence and authority of the *ciuacoatl* remained, and it was still Tlacotzin who gazed out through Don Juan's eyes.

He'd been indispensable in the days following the conquest, although he'd declared that it was his people, not Cortés, whom he served. Under his leadership, the remnant of his tribe had been gathered and reestablished in Tlatelolco, which Hernán had reserved for his Aztec vassals. Homes had been rebuilt, gardens planted, markets reopened. Hundreds of Indians had followed him in baptism even though, as I well understood, his conversion was born less of faith than of resignation. The pragmatic Tlacotzin had served his old gods while they lived for him, but finding them no more, he had turned as a matter of course to the new god who now ruled Mexico.

"And how fares my emperor?" His voice was so devoid of expression that he might have been asking about the weather. How well he hid his anguish over the treatment Cuauhtemoc had suffered.

"Well, when I saw him last . . ." I lied, wanting to spare him.

"The truth, Malintzin. I prefer bad news to falsehoods."

I looked down at my hands. "The burns on his feet are so severe that he may never walk again without pain. The lord of Tlacopan is no better." Cuauhtemoc's torture had been the talk of Mexico. I had witnessed it out of necessity, and I was still haunted by the pungent odor of oil burning on flesh, by the moans of the lord of Tlacopan and the hatred in the eyes of the young emperor as the two men had borne the agony of their blazing feet. Hernán had gripped my hand so hard that I could hear my bones crunching. The sweat had run down his face as he suffered torments of his own. "Enough! For God's sake, you'll kill them!" he'd cried out at last, and the "questioning" had stopped.

"You know it wasn't Hernán's wish that the thing be done," I said to Don Juan.

"He could have refused to allow it."

I defended Hernán stubbornly. "It was Alderete, the king's treasurer, and the pack of dogs who follow him. They wanted more gold for the king and for themselves, and they forced him to do it. Alderete has friends at court in Spain who could influence the king at a time when so much depends on his favor . . ."

"But what did they gain? A few gold pieces hidden in a garden? My emperor speaks the truth, Malintzin. Moctezuma's gold lies buried in the ooze at the bottom of the lake, where your master's own men dropped it that night on the causeway."

"Hernán cares little for gold except in terms of what it will buy." I plucked a white flower from a vine that had wrapped its tendrils over the edge of the parapet. "Gold? All he talks about now is the land. Seeds, tools, settlers, animals from Cuba—and such animals, Don Juan! Tame pigs as plump as this—" I made a fat circle with my arms. "Horned beasts as big as horses that give their masters milk and the best kind of meat. Short-legged deer with coats like cotton that can be cut off and spun into cloth. My ears can hardly believe everything he tells me, the dreams he has for this country!"

A rare smile played about the corners of Don Juan's mouth. "He's like the man who comes to ravish a woman and stays to marry her," he said. "He's not conquered Mexico. Mexico has conquered him. But it's all too easy to dream, Malintzin." Don Juan leaned on the stone railing and drew a fingertip along a beaded line of raindrops that flowed together at his touch. His expression grew pensive and I knew he was thinking of the abuses and injustices that, in spite of Hernán's good intentions, had been heaped upon his people. The defiant Xicotencatl had not been far wrong in his bitter predictions.

Don Juan, still silent, looked down at the street below where my litter-bearers lounged, awaiting their mistress's pleasure to return to Coyoacan and Hernán. "The jaguar is lord of the forest," he said deliberately. "Yet when he makes a kill by virtue of his strength and cunning, the vultures, coyotes and foxes come slinking in to claim whatever they can seize—not because they've earned the right to it, but because that's nature's way. Sometimes these scavengers can become so ferocious and so many in numbers that they drive even the king of beasts from his own prey. Has man come so far from the jungle, Malintzin?" He lapsed into quiet once more, leaving me to ponder his words as he gazed out over the distant lake.

After a long time he spoke again. "Does Cuauhtemoc still refuse to see me?"

The truth was cruel, I knew, but there was no way to evade it. "The last time I spoke to him about it he refused to listen. He called you a traitor."

Only a sigh betrayed Don Juan's pain. "To die for the sake of one's pride is a luxury only the noblest can afford," he murmured. "If my emperor sees it as treachery that I have chosen to live and serve our people, then so be it. What he calls me is what I am. By all that's holy, wouldn't I have shared his imprisonment, even his torture, if it could have accomplished one iota of good? It's a curse to have been born a practical man, Malintzin . . ."

"A curse to whom? Where would your people be without you, Don Juan?"

He shrugged off my praise. "Have you seen the little empress?"

"Tecuichpo—Doña Isabel—" I corrected myself, for Moctezuma's daughter had recently been baptized—"grows lovelier each day. But they keep her in such seculsion that she's not even heard about the burning of her husband's feet. I was ordered to ask her about the treasure, but she knows nothing, I'm sure of it."

"Surely they wouldn't—"

"Oh, no! Never! Hernán would rather die than let them harm her!"

As it was beginning to grow dark, I took my leave of him. The six carriers trotted along the avenues toward the causeway leading to Coyoacan, where Hernán and I had taken residence in a native palace. I leaned back in the litter and closed my eyes, aware of a new tiredness that had seeped into my bones of late—new, but by no means strange. I had not yet told even Hernán about the precious burden I carried within my body. He'd know soon enough, I reflected, if this pregnancy proved to be as difficult as the last one. I wondered if he would even take the time to be happy amid his preoccupation with the struggle for mastery of the land he'd conquered. The human counterparts of Don Juan's vultures, coyotes and foxes were moving in hungrily, and nothing less than the royal hand of King Carlos V would be strong enough to hold them off. I visualized Fray Megalrejo, who'd come selling indulgences during the conquest, a vulture incarnate in his black robes; Alderete, the treasurer, as cunning and avaricious as any fox; and the forgiven Narvaez, who slunk about the fringes of Hernán's circle, spreading his own gall. There was Cristobal de Tapia, overseer of His Majesty's gold foundries, who'd arrived with authority to take over the government of New Spain, a weak man whom Hernán had bought off with gold. There was Governor Garay of Jamaica, whose ambitions toward the northern coast of Mexico had prompted Hernán to extend his conquest to the province of Pánuco which lay in that direction. Each new vessel to sail into the harbor at Villa Rica carried a cargo of potential usurpers.

The long-awaited letter from Alonzo in Spain had plunged Hernán into despair. Alonzo Hernández Puertocarrero—had it been three years or three hundred since I'd stood on the quay with Hernán and watched his ship vanish over the eastern horizon? The ship had indeed touched Cuba before proceeding to Spain. Governor Velásquez had sent his swiftest vessel in pursuit of the fugitives and the treasure. Alaminos, the pilot, who'd first sailed those waters as a cabin boy on the ship of the great Cristobal Colón, had escaped with ease, but could do nothing to prevent the governor's ship from reaching Spain ahead of them. Velásquez's captain had alerted his old ally, Bishop Fonseca, who'd seized the treasure and the two young envoys the moment they stepped ashore.

Finally, free but penniless, Alonzo and Montejo had rejoined Alaminos and journeyed to Medellín where they'd enlisted Hernán's own father, Don Martín Cortés de Monroy. From there they'd followed the king's itinerant court to Barcelona, to La Coruña, and at last to Torsedillas, where Alonzo's powerful relative, the Duke of Bejar, was able to get them an audience.

The young Carlos, however, distracted by problems closer to home and heart, had listened to the stories of the conquest with no more than half an ear. Even the sight of Moctezuma's treasure, which arrived at court some months later, failed to move him to the point of naming Hernán as his legal representative. With other matters on his mind, the king had left Spain in May of 1520 for the more cheerful capitals of his empire.

Hernán had read and reread Alonzo's letter, shaking his head in disbelief. "By my conscience, it would have been such a small thing for His Majesty. A word, the signing of his name on a piece of paper . . ." He'd sat at the table for a long time with his face in his hands.

"At least my father's well," he'd said at last. "And there's still hope when the king returns to Spain, if only I can outlast those jackals who're tearing at my flanks. And Alaminos! Remember when I called him an arrogant bastard, Marina? What a true friend he's been!" In characteristic fashion, Hernán had plunged into readying a new embassy, headed by Diego de Ordaz, the intrepid young warrior who'd scaled Popocatepetl, to plead his cause with the king.

The evening air was chilly. I drew my cloak tighter around my shoulders and let the gentle motion of the litter, the rhythmic shuffle of the carriers' sandals and the lapping of waves against the sides of the causeway lull me into reverie. It was, for me, a dangerous state of mind. At such times my imagination was prone to wander onto forbidden paths and stumble into dreams where the stars in the darkening sky became Juan Jaramillo's eyes, and the caressing wind his touch upon my hair. Juan had accompanied Hernán as a captain in the Pánuco campaign, and for his services had been awarded an *encomienda*, a grant of land and Indians at Xilotepec in the Otomi country some ten leagues to the north. It had been months since I'd set eyes on him, for the demands of his land kept him away from the capital. Our meetings on those rare occasions when fate brought us together had been constrained and bittersweet, always overshadowed by Hernán's presence. Bernal Diaz, however, brought me reports of him on his frequent visits to Coyoacan.

The abundance of land compensated somewhat for the scarcity of gold as a reward for faithful soldiers, and Bernal had been given an estate in Coatzalcoalcos, not many leagues from Oluta. Had Francisca survived the *noche triste*, he might have been content to live with her on his estate, but his natural gregariousness and love of excitement made it difficult for the tall cavalier to keep his hands in the soil. He found endless excuses to journey to the capital, always by way of Xilotepec.

"Juan's peppering me with questions about you before I even climb down from the saddle," he'd teased me. "And you're almost as bad. *Válgame Díos* I wish the two of you would either get together or forget each other. I'm weary of playing *medianero*."

Forget! Blessed Lady, how we'd tried . . .

The lights of Coyoacan twinkled from the end of the causeway. I could see the second story of the palace, aglow with moving torches. I strained forward to make out what was going on. Such frenetic activity in the palace at this normally tranquil hour could only mean that something was amiss. With a whispered command, I hurried my carriers to a run.

Even from the street outside, I could hear the sounds of scurrying feet and Hernán's irritated bellow. "No, you idiot, the bed goes in the other room with the wardrobe that matches! That big mirror too! And find a better carpet . . . ."

I could hear the scraping and bumping of furniture being moved overhead into the patio. A servant bustled past, carrying a wicker chest on his head that I recognized as one of my own.

"I stopped the man by seizing his arm. "What's happening?"

"By the four hundred rabbits, I don't know, Malintzin," the servant answered in Nahuatl. The whites of his eyes showed all the way around the pupils. "Our master got a message by runner just as the sun was going down, and he's been yelling and cursing like a madman ever since. He's ordered your things taken out of his room and put in the south wing of the palace. You'd best talk to him yourself . . ." He scuttled away, the chest teetering on his head.

Perplexed, I walked slowly across the patio toward the stairway leading to the palace's second floor. In my preoccupation, I barely saw the gray stallion tethered in the shadows of the garden. Ordinarily the sight of the horse would have stopped me in my tracks like a bullet. Juan had bought the animal in Villa Rica this past spring and had made one of his rare trips to Coyoacan just to show it to me. "He's a barb," Juan had explained, "from Africa. Runs like a deer. I've wanted a horse like this since I was a lad. See that white spot behind his left rear hoof—the Moors call that the mark of swiftness." I'd never seen Juan so delighted with anything. He'd pulled me up behind him for an easy canter around the square and his closeness had been pure, exquisite torment.

"Marina!"

The husky whisper stunned me.

"Marina, over here, *querida*!" I turned, afraid to believe my ears. I took an incredulous step toward him where he stood in the shadow of a vine, and in the next instant Juan's arms were holding me. I closed my eyes and melted into his warmth, too happy for the moment to question his lack of restraint or his reason for coming.

"Listen, my sweet," he murmured against my hair. "Hasn't anyone told you what the commotion's about?"

I shook my head, rubbing my nose against his shirt.

"Cortés's wife. Doña Catalina. She landed at Ayagualulco a week ago and Sandoval's escorting her over the mountains. They could be here any day."

I stiffened against him. "Ay, Hernán didn't know!"

"Judging from the racket up there, I'd say he just found

out." We heard a heavy thump from above, followed by a muffled curse.

"Then it wasn't you who told him?"

"I just got here, *querida*, and I wanted to see you first.

"Then how did you—? Of course!" The answer had dawned on me by the time I'd finished the question. "Bernal."

"They spent a night at his place. He burned up the road to get word to me."

"And you?" I glanced at his horse. "Why did you come, Juan?"

"Because I know Catalina. She'll scratch your eyes out if she finds you here, love." His arms tightened fiercely around me. "But there's no need for her to find you at all. By the time Catalina arrives in Coyoacan, we can be married and on our way to Xilotepec." He lifted my chin with his fingers and bent down to meet my lips with his, searching for an answer in my response. For a moment I let myself pretend that it could be so. I burst into flame under those urgent, seeking lips. I wanted to sing, "María, you were wrong . . . wrong . . .!"

"You'll come with me, won't you *querida*?" he whispered. "How could Cortés refuse to let you go at a time like this?"

"You've spoken to him?" I was trembling. It was beyond all hope. The secret that was growing inside my body would shackle me to Hernán like a chain of iron.

"I wouldn't speak to him without knowing what you wanted," Juan said. "The decision should be yours, not his." He drew back a little and looked expectantly into my face. He was so open, so vulnerable. I thought of the fire licking Cuauhtemoc's feet.

"Leave me, Juan," I said bitterly. "Go back to Xilotepec. Look for some nice girl to marry and forget me! I can't go with you!"

I could read the sting of my words in his face, but he didn't let me go. "Look at me, Marina," he said. "Look straight into my eyes and tell me you don't love me. Then I'll believe you and I'll do as you ask." His eyes, blue even in the darkness probed into mine like gentle fires. His hands gripped my shoulders with all the intensity of his emotion. "Tell me you don't love me, Marina," he whispered. "Say it and I'll go."

The false words struggled and died in my throat. I lowered my eyes and the tautness of his grip softened.

"Juan. I'm with child," I said.

Did a shadow cross his face, or was it only a cloud passing

over the moon? "Name of heaven, is that all?" he said. "I'd take you with ten children, Marina, and I'd give you ten more!"

"Would you?" I shook my head. "Would you watch my body growing bigger day by day and not resent me because the child wasn't yours? Could you love Hernán's baby as your own?"

"Give me a chance," he said. "Children aren't hard to love. No, you've got to do better than that, Marina." Juan released me with a sigh. "It's Cortés, isn't it? Does he know about the baby?"

"Not yet. But we couldn't keep it from him, Juan. He can count. And even if I could deceive him, I wouldn't, and neither would you. He wants a son, an heir, to carry on his name. He's told me he'll never get one with Catalina."

Juan muttered something under his breath. "Hernán Cortés has bastards strung from one end of Mexico to the other, and that's no secret to anyone," he snapped. "Why, even in Pánuco . . . all he'd have to do is pick out the most promising, declare him legitimate, and he'd have his—" Juan paused in mid-sentence. "Forgive me, Marina. I've been rattling on like a self-centered idiot. You're thinking of the child, aren't you, of the doors that would be open to him as the son of Hernán Cortés." He turned, took two long paces, and pivoted back around to face me again. "And here I am, asking you to give that up for him. My poor Marina."

"It's not just the child," I insisted. "It's you and me. Hernán's not the only one who can count. Our names would be on the tip of every wagging, vicious tongue in Mexico."

I saw his face in the moonlight, his expression a blend of disappointment, pity and tenderness. "Marina . . ." He held out his arms. "Do you love me?"

One step was enough to bridge the gap between us. "Yes!" I whispered savagely, as my arms locked around him. "Yes, by all the saints, I love you! With every breath of my life I love you, Juan!" Whatever else I denied him, I could not deny him that.

He stroked my hair. "You've defeated me, *querida*. I can't force you to change your mind, but I'll wait. It won't be easy for you with Catalina here, especially when she finds out about the baby. She's a jealous woman. The day may come when you'll wish you were safe in Xilotepec. If it does, send word to me. I'll be here as fast as I can ride the distance."

"Don't wait for me," I said. It would be kinder to end it

now. I loved him too much to fill him with false hope. "I have an affliction, one that goes along with being a *tlatoani's* daughter. From the earliest days of my childhood, all I wanted was Oluta. My father's kingdom. For me it was the whole world. When my stepfather took it way from me I got drunk on my own vindictiveness. Then Hernán came along and suddenly Oluta wasn't enough. It was all Mexico I wanted. Now, what I once wanted for myself, I want for my son! Call it wicked, Juan. Call it vain. But that's the way I am."

I reached up and traced the thin white scar he'd worn since Cholula, running a caressing fingertip from his temple to his beard. "Loving you was never a part of my plan," I whispered. "It was an unexpected gift God chose to give me. A jewel to wear in my heart. Now we must leave it at that, my dearest. You must go away and find someone who has no ambition beyond making you happy."

He held me quietly. I closed my eyes and tried to drown myself in the warmth of his body, the strength of his arms, memorizing the sound, smell and texture of him, so that when he was gone I'd be able to remember . . .

The rumble of moving furniture above us had stopped, and the sound of footsteps on the stairs drew us apart instantly.

"Jaramillo!" The geniality in Hernán's voice contrasted with what we'd heard a few moments before. "What a surprise, *hombre*. I was beginning to think you'd sprouted roots in Xilotepec. What brings you to Coyoacan?"

"I was just passing by," Juan said, a little awkwardly, "and I thought it would be pleasant to see you—and Doña Marina—long enough to pay my respects."

"But you'll stay the night, won't you? *Cómo no*! We can relive the whole Pánuco campaign over a bottle of good Málaga! I'll have Manuel ready a room for you." He swept his eyes upward toward the ceiling. "You'll have to forgive the uproar. I just got word that my wife's on her way up from the coast. It was unexpected, to say the least. Nothing's ready for her, and Catalina's accustomed to the best. Marina, would you find Manuel and tell him—"

"No, please," Juan protested. "I'd like to stay but I have pressing business at home and I'm anxious to get back. I'd planned to spend the night on the road."

"Oh, very well. A man knows his own mind. But I've been wanting to talk to you anyway, Jaramillo." Hernán leaned comfortably against a tree. "You see, I've secured permission from the Cuban authorities to purchase some cattle and pigs to bring over. That fat oaf Velásquez still thinks Mexico's part of Cuba, and just to keep us licking his boots, he's allowed us to take only male animals. Wants to keep us dependent, you see. But it's better than nothing. Who knows?" He smiled at Juan. "Maybe the inspectors can be pursuaded to let a few females slip past their eyes. Gold can do some amazing things. That's where you come in, Jaramillo. I know I can count on you to pick quality stock for the fairest possible price and to load them for safe transport back to New Spain. I'll have a ship readied by the end of the month. You're to be on it."

Hernán had begun to pace excitedly. "I don't have to tell you what these animals mean to me. New Spain's my country now, and I'll not have a nation of freebooters who'll do nothing more than strip away her wealth and run! No! There are to be farms, towns, cities—Spanish cities peopled with respectable citizens. That's why I've given *encomiendas* only to men who want to make their homes here. That's why I've insisted that they pledge to stay on their land for at least eight years and to marry and start families within a year and a half. Now that's another thing, Jaramillo." He stopped abruptly in front of Juan and touched an admonishing finger to Juan's chest. "Xilotepec's a lonesome place, and from what I've seen of those Otomi women, I'd just as soon bed a wildcat. I want you to take all the time you need in Cuba. Pick yourself a likely wench, do a little courting, and come back to New Spain with a bride. That, *señor*—" he winked—"is an order!"

"Now that I can't promise." Juan's attempt at lightness was not lost on me. "I've been away from civilized ways so long that I fear I've become something of a bumpkin, and I don't know what sort of wench would have me. But I'll see what I can do." He glanced quickly at me. I knew what he was thinking. If he did not ask for me now, the chance would be gone. I gave a barely perceptible shake of my head, almost flinching with the pain that tore at my heart.

"By the end of the month, you say?" With an easy motion, Juan bent down and untied the reins of his horse from the loop of a gnarled vine. "Then I'll put things in order at Xilotepec and wait for your word to proceed to Villa Rica. I've a good overseer who should be able to handle things while I'm away."

"Oh?" Hernán raised an eyebrow. "Spanish?"

"Otomi," said Juan. "Heathen as old Baal himself, but I swear he could grow corn on bare rock."

"Then you'll have no fear of tarrying in Cuba as long as

necessary to complete my orders," Hernán said with a sly undertone. "If you can make it to Villa Rica early to help ready the ship, I'd appreciate it. I'll send you a letter giving you the details on the animals when I've worked them out myself."

Juan put his toe in the stirrup and swung into the saddle. "I'll do what I can to hurry things. Now, if that's all, with your permission I'll be taking my leave." He raised his gauntlet in a fleeting salute. "*Hasta la vista*—" he inclined his head—"Doña Marina." His expression betrayed nothing.

My eyes drank him in desperately.

"Godspeed, Jaramillo!" Hernán returned the salute as the gray stallion wheeled and galloped out of the coutyard and through the gate.

"Why the sad face, Marina *mía*?" Hernán slipped an arm around my shoulders and led me toward the stairway. "Is it Catalina, eh? Is it the thought of losing your place as the lady of this house?" He leaned down and pecked my cheek. "Never fear, my sweet. I may have to move you out of my bedroom, but I've not moved you out of my heart. Your quarters in the south wing will be as fine as my own, and I'll be seeing as much of you as I please, Catalina or no Catalina. Ay, I don't suppose I've done too well by the old girl. The least I can do is give her a chance at playing the conqueror's wife. She always did want to be a great lady, and when I was no more than the *alcalde* of a grubby little Cuban town, she never let me forget it!"

He leaned on me a little as he guided me up the stairs. "So come along, Marina. My big bed's empty and I want to enjoy what may well be the last contented night I spend in it."

Trying not to hear the distant ring of hoofbeats, I matched my steps to his. Tonight I would tell him about the child.

Catalina Juárez de Cortés arrived in a downpour that flooded out the welcome her husband had planned to stage for her. She swept into the entryway with Sandoval's cloak over her head and stood there dripping and wheezing while Hernán bowed gallantly and kissed her hand.

"Now, cursed if I'll have you slinking around hiding from her, Marina," he'd declared just prior to Catalina's arrival. "Go and make yourself pretty and be prepared to present yourself along with the rest of the household. She knows about you, to be sure, so there's no need to be secretive."

Thus I was there along with the retinue of stewards, butlers, maids and secretaries, all craning their necks for a glimpse of their new mistress. In a last-minute attack of cowardice I'd melted into their ranks, hoping Hernán would not be so bold as to single me out.

Alas, I'd hoped in vain. After a rather stiff embrace, a perfunctory kiss and a polite inquiry as to his lady's health, Hernán found me with his eyes and sternly beckoned me forward.

"Catalina, my love," he said, clearing his throat, "it gives me the greatest pleasure to present my friend and comrade, Doña Marina, who has, perhaps, done more than any one individual to help me lay this land at your feet."

Friend and comrade! *Caspa de San Pedro*, what next? I curtsied as I'd seen Spanish ladies do, and took Catalina's proffered hand. It was cold. My eyes crept upward to the woman's face. Yes, it was true that Catalina was beautiful. The rain had curled her auburn hair into ringlets around her plump face, setting off the fashionable pallor of her skin. But the handsome green eyes were set in puffy shadows above a high, thin nose, and the childish lips were frozen into a pout. Glancing at her figure, grown only a trifle stout with maturity, I realized with a start that the russet traveling dress was threadbare in spots. She wore no jewels. It was obvious that Catalina was not a wealthy woman. Hernán had exhausted his Cuban fortune, I knew, to outfit the original expedition and since that time had sent his wife little or nothing to live on. She'd probably had to raise the money for passage to Mexico herself! I felt an unexpected twinge of pity.

"Ah, yes." Catalina coughed imperiously. "The men speak most highly of you, child." Abruptly, she withdrew her hand and tossed the cloak back to a waterlogged Sandoval. "Can't the rest of the staff wait until tomorrow, Hernán, my dear? I'm exhausted. This air!"

She leaned on his arm as they skirted the edge of the inner patio, where the rain drizzled in torrents off the edge of the roof. The rest of us followed. Suddenly, in the midst of mumbling something about the weather, Catalina's frame stiffened. Her breath sucked sharply in and she began to gasp—powerful, wheezing gasps that sent jerking spasms through her body. Hernán, supporting her with one arm, glanced about frantically.

"Here!" A sullen-faced man, who resembled Catalina so closely that I guessed him to be her brother, rummaged through a satchel and pulled out a tiny glass vial. Twisting out the cork stopper, he waved it under Catalina's nose. She inhaled spasmodically, her nose twitching as her body relaxed and her breathing returned slowly to normal.

"You gave me a fright, my dear." Hernán kissed her cheek solicitously. "I confess I'd quite forgotten about your illness."

"It's this accursed thin air," Catalina muttered.

"Thin air? Nonsense. You've laced yourself too tightly, that's all."

"No." She shook her head emphatically. "It's the air. I tell you, I feel as though I'm going to die in this place."

"You're overtired, love. Let's get you upstairs and out of those wet clothes." He led—or rather, dragged—her toward the stairs. "Someone bring her chest. You—" he motioned to one of the maids—"come along and help undress her." Slowly, they mounted the stairs and disappeared. I heard a door open and close behind them. The welcoming party began to disband.

All at once, from the bedroom, an enraged shriek split the air. "How dare you?" Catalina's voice floated plainly through the open window. "How dare you have her here waiting when I arrive! The dark-skinned trull! You only did it to torment me, Hernán Cortés! But I'm mistress of this house now, and I tell you, I'll not have her—"

Gonzalo de Sandoval, his hair and clothes steaming wet and one bushy eyebrow cocked with disdain, offered me his arm and led me gallantly out of earshot.

Chapter Twenty-Five

Coyoacan—September 1522

As there was a shortage of Spanish-speaking maids, Hernán had persuaded me to give over the now-fluent Sancha to Catalina's service. In doing so, I unwittingly acquired an avid little spy who flitted from Catalina's suite to my own, wide-eyed with tales of her new mistress's ways.

"She drinks, Malintzin. Not wine. Something brown, like amber, and afterwards she falls into bed like this . . ." Sancha pantomimed melodramatically. "Usually she goes right to sleep, but sometimes, after I've been sent out, I can hear her through the door, begging our master to come to bed with her."

"Sancha, please," I said in a huff, "I don't want to hear this."

"She cries like an animal, Malintzin. But he won't come. He sleeps in the next room and hasn't spent one night with her. He only says 'Go to sleep, Catalina.' Then she curses him—and you too, Malintzin. Last night she called you a—"

"That will do, Sancha!" I ushered the little girl out of the room with a spank. "This tale-bearing of yours does no one any good," I said sternly.

It was evident, however, that Catalina wielded some power over her husband, for despite Hernán's declaration that he'd visit me as often as he pleased, I'd seen almost nothing of him in the weeks since Catalina's arrival. I passed the loneliest time of my life in the isolated south wing of the palace with only my maids, the birds and a greyhound puppy for company. It was by choice that I withdrew, for I wanted no confrontation with Catalina that might lead to the banishment of myself and Hernán's unborn child. I would do everything in my power to see that my son—and some instinct told me it was a male I carried—was born under Hernán's roof and properly acknowledged as his. For my baby I would endure

Catalina, loneliness, humiliation and even—the thought continued to torment me—life without Juan. I had thought for a time that perhaps after the baby was born, with no dispute as to his parentage, then I could set myself free to go where my heart beckoned. But now my calculations told me that Juan would long since have landed in Cuba. If he'd obeyed Hernán's instructions, he might already be sailing hime with his new wife. Why shouldn't he, I asked myself repeatedly, when I'd begged him to forget me?

I was shaken from my limbo one afternoon when Hernán strode into the garden, where I was sitting with one end of my loom tied to a tree and the other end strapped behind my back, and trying to remember the things old Atototl had taught me about weaving.

"There you are, little mother." He bent down and swept me playfully up in his arms.

"Be careful, Hernán! You're tangling the threads—"

"The threads be damned." He brushed my face with his beard. "Get yourself out of this witch's trap and give me a proper kiss."

I complied, gingerly extricating us both from the snarled loom. He ran his hands vigorously down the length of my body. "By my conscience, you're growing. I can feel it. Does he kick yet?" Hernán's children were always "he" until proven otherwise.

"Not yet. It's too soon. I've missed you, Hernán."

"*Ay de mí!*" He sank down on a stone bench and pulled me to his side. "She shrieks if I step out of her sight. 'Which one are you going to see this time, my husband?' " He imitated Catalina's high-pitched whine. "And she has me watched by her maids—I'm *sure* of it. Marina, I've wanted to slip off and see you, heaven knows . . ."

"Slip off? Why? You're master in this house, not Catalina." I said, pouting. After all, Hernán had never made much effort to conceal his visits to his other mistresses from me.

"Appearances, my girl! New Spain's becoming civilized!" He slipped one arm around my shoulder. "A thousand eyes are watching to see that my conduct toward my beloved wife is beyond reproach, and Catalina knows it. She's not above using a little bribery to keep me in line. The tale back in Cuba is that I'm living like a sultan with a whole harem of Indian beauties. If I want public support, I've got to prove otherwise. By many people's standards, even one Indian beauty is too many." He nibbled at my ear.

I frowned. The battle for my baby's recognition was taking shape already. "That didn't stop you from coming here today," I said.

"Ha! I've created a diversion. I suggested to Catalina that we give a gala reception in the old throne room. A ball would have been nicer, but there's such a shortage of women who know how to dance . . . Anyway, she's so busy with plans for the Coyoacan social season that it gave me a minute to get away." Hernán gazed down absently at his hands. They were soft and white, so free now of the callouses of reins, sword and buckler that one would think the two missing fingers of his left hand had been nipped off by a surgeon's knife, not by a *maquahuitl* on the slopes of a heathen pyramid.

"Marina," he said, "I want you to be at the reception."

I jumped back, pulling away from him a little. "What for? Your wife goes rabid at the sight of me."

"Appearances, Marina," he repeated with a sigh. "This time even Catalina's in agreement. You've become something of a legend, you know, and our guests will be wanting to meet you. If you're not there, there'll be talk." He shook his head to emphasize that talk was just what he wanted to avoid. "Now, if you put in an appearance, it will show everyone that there are no bad feelings between Catalina and you—that there's nothing in my relationship with you that would arouse her ill will. After all—" his expression was as guileless as a child's— "you know as well as I do that since her arrival, my behavior's been absolutely proper."

"Proper!" I felt like slapping him. "I'm going to have your child, Hernán!"

He looked at me blandly. "So you are, love, but there's no need for concern yet. You won't be big enough to show for another couple of months. We can wait till then to worry about where to hide you. Just wear something loose and flowing—I always liked you in red, you know—and who's to suspect?"

By a supreme act of will I suppressed the urge to fly at him like a hawk with bared talons. "Until now," I said quietly, measuring each word, "I'd thought you were pleased about the baby."

"Pleased is hardly the word. I'm delighted, Marina," He took both my hands in his. His eyes were full of pleading. "But you've got to understand my position. If I'm to keep control of this land I need the support of the Spanish population. Oh, to be sure, my old comrades would do no more than wink, but the new settlers, especially those who've brought their wives—and I don't need to tell you how a disapproving wife can sour her husband—they're a bunch of snot-faced prigs. And the Church! I've got to dance to its tune, Marina *mía*, for its power's growing. A word in the wrong place, a rumor, a whisper in His Majesty's ear . . ." He shook his head. "Once I get the king's letter confirming my powers as governor, I can tell them all to go to hell. Until then, I'm riding the back of a greased pig."

I listened thoughtfully, indecision gnawing away at my resolve. If Hernán was right about the need for public support and its dependence on his personal conduct, then the problem of securing recognition for our child was a sticky one indeed. What Hernán lost for himself would be lost for his son as well. Still, having been reared in a world where a ruler's popularity was enhanced by a multiplicity of concubines and offspring, and having observed firsthand that many of the bold *conqusitadores* were inclined in a similar direction, I found it hard to believe that these new arrivals could be so restricted in their views. I suspected that Hernán was exaggerating. Could it be that he still hoped for a legitimate heir from Catalina? I remembered Sancha's whispered reports and wondered whether they were accurate. After all, Catalina was still an attractive woman and not too old to bear children.

"Does Catalina know about the baby?" I asked him.

Hernán blanched. "No! And she's not to be told, at least not yet. She's been in such a state since her arrival here! Keeps insisting that I didn't really want her to come. Normally she'd probably accept it—I've a lovely daughter in Cuba, you know, by an Indian slave woman—but of late I can't seem to guess *what* Catalina's going to do next." He leaned toward me and lowered his voice to a conspiratorial whisper. "We haven't shared a bed in years, by her own choice, and it's just as well. I've no taste for her, and if she were able to have children she'd have conceived long ago, so what's the use?" He reached down and squeezed my knee. "But let's not dwell on it now, Marina *mía*. You'll be happy to know that I've invited María and Pero Farfán to come over from Texcoco for the party, and I've ordered the servants to ready the rooms next to yours for their stay. Does that please you?"

Did it please me! María after all these lonely weeks! Putting my annoyance aside, I hugged him enthusiastically.

* * *

María had never been known for her reticence. "You're an idiot, Marina," she sputtered when we were finally alone after the initial flurry of greetings and respects to Hernán and Catalina. "I've known men to do foolish things out of pride, but women generally have more sense. You astound me." She'd grown as plump as a contented hen. Her black eyes danced and her white lace fan fluttered almost as fast as her tongue.

"Now don't give me those innocent eyes!" She waggled a perfumed finger under my perplexed nose. "You know what I'm talking about." The white lace fan closed with a snap, accompanied by an impatient little sigh from its owner who, despite her frown, had obviously been looking forward to deliverings this lecture. "Juan spent a night with us on his way home from here, and by the saints, I've never seen a man look so unhappy. Oh, he tried not to show it. Made jokes with Pero over supper and talked about his *encomienda,* but he didn't fool me for a minute."

I listened silently, my emotions in a turmoil as my friend opened up the fan and commenced to flutter it again.

"Afterwards, I cornered him alone and insisted that he tell me what was wrong. I knew he'd just come from seeing you. Well, Juan's not an easy one to open up, but you know me. If they'd just turned *me* loose on poor Cauahtemoc, there'd have been no need to burn his feet. Finally Juan told me you'd decided to stay in this spider's nest rather than go with him. *Niña!* Knowing how you feel about him, I could hardly believe it . . ."

"Didn't Juan tell you why I wouldn't go?" Even speaking his name was painful.

"Of course he did, but I still think you're a fool. You've chosen to let your baby be born in a house with a woman who'll hate him, when you could have given him a chance to grow up on a fine ranch with a mother and father who care for one another."

The blade had been twisted so sharply that I cried out. "Stop it, María! You don't understand. The baby's Hernán's. As long as I stay with him, there'll be no doubts and no arguments when and if Hernán decides to legitimatize him. If I went with Juan, he'd be no one's child, don't you see? Juan would know who his father was, and I'd know—but as for anyone else, there'd be a thousand wagging tongues to suggest that Juan and I might have . . . So help me, María, sometimes

I wish we had!" My voice shook. "But I won't have my son—Hernán's son—grow up under such a shadow."

"*Basura!* Rubbish! What does it matter? Why, in this wide-open country, any boy with a strong arm and a good head can make his own way. And who says it's to be a son? If it's a girl, then it won't make a turkey feather's worth of difference. And what if . . ." María de Estrada hesitated, not wanting to be unkind. "What if you lose this one too? Then you'll have thrown Juan away for nothing."

I shook my head stubbornly. "It's going to be a son and he's going to live. If I'm wrong . . ." My shoulders rose and fell. "I'd thought once I could go to Juan on my knees and beg him to take me, but now it's too late. Do you think he's married yet, María?"

"Who knows? I don't think so, *niña*. Not if he loves you as much as I think he does. But he's got to marry eventually or lose his *encomienda*. He can't wait forever, and after all, you did send him away."

She rose to her feet, folded her fan once more and smoothed her skirt. "And now I'll be off to visit Catalina before she gets piqued and wonders where I am. She's my friend too, you know, and I'm expecting to hear a long tirade against you. I'll be sympathetic. You're not to blame for her troubles, I know, but Hernán's not been much of a husband to the poor woman. I can't condemn her for being the way she is." She bent down and gave me a motherly squeeze about the shoulders. "If I were you, and Juan came back without a wife, I'd be in Xilotepec before you could wink! *Hasta la noche*, Marina."

With a rustle of petticoats, María swept out of the room. I sat looking after her, my mind in turmoil. Curse it, why was I so easily swayed? Until now, I'd been so certain I'd made the right decision. Now here I was, full of doubts again, my heart crying out more pitifully than ever for Juan. María was right in a way. It would have been best for me, best for Juan and best for Catalina if I'd left—and even Hernán would have survived. But my son—that was another matter. I wanted it known without doubt from whose seed he'd sprung. If Hernán would only acknowledge the child before reliable witnesses, nothing more would be necessary. I'd be free to go to Juan, if he'd still have me. But could Hernán be persuaded? He seemed so reluctant, it wasn't likely. Could he be bribed? Tricked?

I paced the room with growing anxiety, my thoughts shooting off into erratic, tortuous trails that circled and wound their way time after time back to the same point. To Juan. Always to Juan. I remembered a small incident that had happened a few months ago, before Catalina's arrival. I'd been putting Hernán's array of jewelry in order, sorting the various pieces according to color and style, untangling the twisted chains, when I noticed that one necklace was missing: the large *chalchihuitl* Chilam had used to buy me, and that Quauhtlatoa had given me the night Juan had killed him. I'd placed it among Hernán's things myself that same night in a gesture that, to me, had symbolized my painful recognition that I belonged to Hernán just as surely as if he had bought me. It had been one of the few articles to survive the flight from Tenochtitlan, for I'd seen it several times since; but Hernán had never worn it and I'd never found the right time to tell him where it had come from. Puzzled, I'd asked him about it.

"Oh, that," he'd answered offhandedly. "If I'd known you fancied it, I'd have given it to you. It was a costly piece, no doubt, but I never cared for it. It was so heavy and had such a . . . well, such an Indian look about it. Dashed if I can even remember who gave it to me." He scratched his head in thought. "But I know what happened to it. I gave it to Jaramillo. It was right after Pánuco. You know how valuable he was to me then. Well, one day I was thinking I'd like to reward him, so on impulse I pulled out a chest and offered him a choice of anything in it.

"At first he declined. Seemed a trifle embarrassed by the fuss I was making over him. He's a modest sort of fellow and I rather admire him for it. But suddenly his eyes fell on that necklace. He picked it up, looked at it for a long time with the oddest expression on his face, and then he said he'd like to have it. I gave it to him gladly. As I said, I never cared for the thing. I thought he was going to wear it, but instead he coiled up the chain and put it in the pocket of his shirt. And that's the last I saw of it. Are you satisfied, Marina *mía*?"

I'd tucked the incident into my memory where it had remained half-buried until now, when it suddenly sprouted and burst into flower. Restlessly, I pulled the wicker chests that held my wardrobe out into the middle of the floor. I'd occupy my mind with choosing a costume for the reception. Something loose, Hernán suggested. Something loose, indeed! All *huipillis* fit like tents. I thought of padding my still-slender figure with a cushion to advertise my pregnancy to one and all, then laughed at the idea.

I had no shortage of beautiful robes from which to choose.

They'd flowed in as tribute and gifts from the *tlatoanis* of a hundred towns, some of them exquisitely simple, their beauty contained in the skill of their weaving; others studded with pearls and tiny beads of turquoise, or alive with the flashing hues of bird plumage. Hernán had suggested red, but this blue one, edged with feathers in a deeper shade, was lovely; and the yellow one, plain except for a fringe of jade beads at the hem . . . I tossed one after another aside with a carelessness that was foreign to my usual attitude toward clothes. What difference did it make? I'd close my eyes and choose one and be done with it. Then I'd call my maids to fold the rest up and put them away.

Impatiently, I opened up another chest and dumped the contents and into a heap. These would do as well as anything. I closed my eyes, stirred up the pile of robes, reached into their midst, seized one resolutely and pulled. But what was this? It was not the crispness of new cotton but the soft, rough warmth of wool that my fingers touched. I opened my eyes to find my hand gripping the dark brown cloak, Juan's cloak, which he'd wrapped around me the night he'd rescued me from Quauhtlatoa; it had covered me that black misty night on the Tlacopan causeway. I drew it toward me. Despite careful washing, it still smelled faintly of lake water and blood. I smoothed it tenderly. Then, suddenly with a little gasp and a convulsive jerk, I clutched the cloak tight against me and buried my face in its folds.

In the end, to indulge Hernán, I'd decided to wear red. I'd selected a scarlet *huipilli* interwoven with threads of gold and trimmed with iridescent amber-red plumes. The maids had coiled and braided my hair, skillfully entwining it around, below and over the small matching headdress until it formed a graceful crown of its own. A wide collar made of hundreds of tiny interlocked pieces of gold framed my neck, making it look even longer and more slender than it was. I surveyed my appearance in the big mirror of polished obsidian that had once hung in Moctezuma's harem, and pronounced myself satisified. Hernán would be pleased. Catalina would not.

The music, unlike anything I'd ever heard before, caught my ears as I walked along the portico toward the reception hall, María and Pero Farfán on either side of me. I was grateful they'd waited for me, for I quaked at the thought of entering Catalina's domain alone, and Hernán had neglected to send anyone to escort me.

"What's that?" Pero Farfán raised his eyebrows and flicked the corner of his trim gray mustache. "Bless me, but the Spanish court's come to Coyoacan. I haven't heard music like that since I left Madrid. It looks as though Catalina's made an effort to import some culture to this wild land."

"Now don't make fun of her, Pero," his wife cautioned him. "Let poor Catalina have her night. Heaven knows, she's had little enough happiness in her life."

"You're right, *querida*," Farfán murmured. "Why begrudge the poor soul if she wants to play at being the great lady, especially when we'll be drinking her wine. Ah, there's Sandoval! He looks as uncomfortable as a monkey in a velvet suit."

We paused on the threshold of the hall to take in the scene before us. Only one who was acquainted with both the New World and the Old could fully appreciate the dazzling array of incongruities. Candles gleamed in crude chandeliers made of native clay. Guests sipped *pulque* and minute quantities of rare Spanish wine from someone's priceless collection of dainty crystal goblets. A *tlatoani* in a feathered robe strolled past the quintet of musicians, casting a wary eye at their strange instruments. Those Spanish ladies who, like María, had brought their finery with them to New Spain stood out like jewels in their silks, laces and velvets. Others, less fortunate, had improvised gowns out of colorful native cottons.

I saw the *ciuacoatl*, standing alone in a corner and viewing the spectacle with an air of amused disdain. Ixtlilxochitl, now the undisputed ruler of Texcoco, strolled past with his beautiful Papantzin, who had once been married to Cuitlahuac. Across the room his sister, Mazatl, striking in a full-skirted gown of yellow lace, walked arm in arm with her fat Spanish husband. Other local chieftains, less at ease in such a setting, clustered at one end of the hall, goggling at the unfamiliar sights.

Many officers and soldiers of the conquest were there with their Indian wives and *barraganas*, who gazed enviously at the dresses of the Spanish belles. Alvarado stood beside another captain, sipping *pulque*. His Luisa was back in Tlaxcala, expecting their second child.

Sandoval, whose Tlaxcalan princess had died of the *viruelas*, was alone. Seeing me hesitating in the doorway, he came forward with a courtly bow.

"Doña Marina," he lisped, "if you'll do a poor soldier the honor . . ." As he looked up at me his eyes twinkled impishly under the unruly brows. He was, I realized, just a little bit drunk, but I was grateful for his company. Smiling, I took his proffered arm.

"Ah," he chuckled. "A few drops of good red wine to warm my insides, and the company of the most beautiful lady in Mexico. Sandoval, my good fellow, what more could you ask of life, eh?" He scowled briefly at the crowd that flowed and bobbed around us in a river of color. "Not much like the old days, is it? Look at them, all those nice soft bellies and bottoms. We knock down the hive and get stung, and they come crawling in to lap up the honey!" He paused to greet the foppishly dressed Alonzo Grado, the man he'd once replaced as commandant at Villa Rica. Grado had edged his way back into Hernán's favor since then, and was rumored to be first in line for the hand of Tecuichpo, should her marriage to Cuauhtemoc be declared invalid.

"*Caramba!*" Sandoval plucked a minature goblet of wine from the hand of a passing servant and emptied it in one gulp. "If some of these lace-trimmed *asnos* could have seen how it was—sleeping in the muck with our swords in our hands, seeing the heads of good old comrades stuck up on poles in the square! It was hell, but damned if there wasn't a sort of honesty about things then. Life was hard, but you knew who your friends were. Now you turn your back and some *maldito* will stick a knife in it."

"Why don't we sit down?" I suggested. "I think you've had too much to drink, my friend."

He ignored me. "Look at Cortés over there, all washed and perfumed, with Catalina's leash around his neck. Does he look happy? I've seen more sincere smiles on skull racks. Don't you think he'd welcome the feel of a lance in his hand once more? Why, even Motilla's getting too fat."

Poor Sandoval! I resolved that the next time I had a chance to speak to Hernán, I'd recommend some action for the restless young captain.

"Ay! Forgive me, Doña Marina." Sandoval clapped a hand to his perspiring forehead. "Ordinarily I'm not a man of many words, but a little *pulque* can do funny things to of a fellow's tongue." He glanced around the hall. "Where's *El Galán*?"

"Bernal?" I smiled at his use of the nickname that the men had pinned on their lanky friend because of his newfound love for flashy clothes: *El Galán*, "the dandy."

"I really thought he'd be here," I said. "He hates to miss any party."

"And what's a party without him? Ah, well, all the more for the rest of us." Sandoval downed another goblet of wine. Despite his joviality there was a bitter set to his jaw, a sardonic tilt to his heavy brows. I realized he was slowly steering me toward the spot where Hernán and Catalina were standing to greet their guests. I tugged at his arm and shook my head, a slight but adamant motion.

"But we ought to pay our respects to her majesty, oughtn't we, Doña Marina?" Sandoval argued, pushing me relentlessly toward his goal. "You're not afraid of her, are you? *Diós*, you've been ten times what she ever was to him. It's you who should be standing there at his side, not Catalina. Come on." His lisp was more pronounced than ever. "We'll spit in her face, you and I."

Catalina was exquisitely dressed in a billowing satin gown that matched the emeralds at her white throat. Her middle was laced to excruciating tightness. The soft paleness of her bosom bulged out above it, nearly spilling over the generously cut bodice. Catalina, someone had said, was especially admired for her pretty, plump shoulders and arms, and the dress was designed to show them off to their best advantage.

I had to admit she was a splendid sight. "Her majesty," Sandoval had scoffed. But at this moment she was as near as any woman to being the queen of New Spain. Was it more than a coincidence that the emerald tiara nestled among her auburn curls bore a presumptuous resemblance to a crown?

Catalina was glowing. She'd obviously been living in anticipation of this night. Hernán, in russet velvet, stood beside her, his face a mask. Was he happy? Proud? Bored? Embarrassed? Even I, who knew him so well, could not read his expression.

Sandoval was nudging me closer. "Smile," he hissed in my ear. "I had to endure the bitch all the way up from the coast."

He was using me, I realized, but it was too late to remonstrate with him or to turn and melt into the gay crowd. Catalina had swung around toward us with a smile that quickly faded. Her eyes, as green as Alvarado's and almost as green as her dress, narrowed defensively.

"Señor Sandoval. Doña Marina." She inclined her head only slightly. She was nearly as tall as Hernán himself. "You're enjoying yourselves, I trust?"

"My lady's hospitality is most gracious." I murmured the phrase I'd heard others use and made an awkward little bow.

Sandoval, eyes overflowing with mockery, bent in an exaggerated bow and raised Catalina's hand to his lips.

"The sweetness of your wine is exceeded only by the sweetness of your company, my lady." The last syllable was punctuated by a slight hiccup. He turned toward Hernán and suddenly his eyes misted. Whatever little sarcasm he'd been about to utter died in his throat in the presence of this man whom he'd worshipped for years.

"Gonzalito!" Hernán stepped forward and clasped both his hands warmly. For a moment the two stood transfigured in a bond as strong as the love between a man and a woman. I stole a glance at Catalina, expecting to see anger on her face. The woman suddenly looked my way and her eyes met mine for the first time. In them I read more pain than jealousy, more fear than anger; the quick stab of pity that had struck me upon first noticing Catalina's threadbare traveling gown thrust into me again, so sharply that I had to lower my gaze.

Surely it would be over soon. Sandoval would take his leave of Hernán and escort me to the obscure safety of the other end of the hall. But now they were chatting animatedly, each happy to be in the presence of the other. I looked past them and out the open doorway that led to the garden and from there to the street beyond. A tall, mud-spattered scarecrow figure had just stepped through the entrance. Bernal!

He'd failed to measure up to his nickname tonight, for he looked as though he'd just dismounted after the long, rough trip from the coast. His clothes were stained with the mud of the road. His face wore a haggard look I'd not seen on him since that black night on the causeway when he'd lost his Francisca. He was looking around the hall, searching frantically for someone, perhaps for me. At last I caught his eye. He beckoned furtively.

I took a quick step toward him, but by then Hernán had seen him too and sensed, as I did, that something was wrong. The two of us reached Bernal's side at the same time, with Sandoval at our heels. As agonizingly as he would pull a dagger out of his own flesh, Bernal drew an unsealed letter from his jerkin. Although he spoke to Hernán, his bloodshot eyes remained fixed on me.

He handed Hernán the letter. "This arrived in Villa Rica on the last ship from Cuba. It's from the *alcalde* at Trinidad. I offered to carry it to you myself."

Hernán unfolded the letter and cleared his throat with a

slight cough. ". . . Greetings . . . sends his regrets . . ." he mumbled maddening as he read. ". . . that your ship which left this port on the nineteenth of August under Captain Jaramillo with a cargo of . . . God in heaven! Sunk in a hurricane with all hands!"

My skin turned cold. I looked at Bernal and his eyes confirmed what I'd just heard.

Hernán, wiping tears away with one hand, finished the letter. A passing ship, it said, had found enough wreckage and dead animals to establish the lost vessel's identity, but had picked up no survivors. "Even in peacetime I send men to their deaths," he muttered, crumpling the letter viciously. "The servants will see to your needs, Bernal Diaz." He turned on his heel and started back toward Catalina.

Bernal, his eye brimming, leaned down to comfort me. "By the Blessed Virgin, if only I could have told you myself, in private . . . What can I say? I loved the man too."

I scarcely heard him. My thoughts were turned inward upon myself, and in my stricken imagination another storm raged with waves like mountains and wind like the breath of some wrathful god. I saw the ship tossed about like a plaything, heard human screams and the death cries of animals as they crushed one another in the rolling hold. I saw the vessel split open like a milkweed pod, spilling its contents indiscriminately into the boiling sea—cattle, pigs, barrels, boxes, good men, sinners and Juan Jaramillo.

The vision blurred and I tried to focus my eyes on my surroundings once more, but the candles and bright gowns spun and whirled into twisting rainbows. Faces became yawning caverns into which I felt myself falling . . .

I realized afterwards that I'd fainted. It must have been Bernal or Sandoval who caught me, but when I opened my eyes Hernán was holding me in his arms.

"You're not well, Marina," he whispered. "I'm taking you to your room." He lifted me with ease in his strong arms. The crowd was silent. Every eye was turned on him as he carried me across the floor.

"Come back here, Hernán Cortés," Catalina hissed as we passed her. "Let the servants take her. How can you disgrace me like this in front of our guests?"

Still holding me, he turned toward her. "Be still, Catalina," he said in a hushed voice that was nonetheless audible to those around him. "Doña Marina is carrying my child."

* * *

Coyoacan—October 1522

The nightmares began after that, so inevitable and so terrifying that I dreaded sleep. The old gods of my childhood came back to haunt me. I would find myself wandering through the watery realm of Tlaloc, where the spirits of those who died in his element were taken. My feet would stumble over sleeping skeletons that would suddenly take flight like schools of fish, shrieking mournfully as they floated upward and away from me. One of them, a tiny one, its bones interlaced with chains of gold, would wrap its bony arms around my neck in a stranglehold and whisper, "Stay . . . stay . . ." Terrified, I would wrench myself free and run, slowed in my motion by the water, crying out for Juan until the liquid world trembled with the vibrations of my voice. I would search for him endlessly among the drowned, running, calling, never finding him. At last I would awaken, exhausted and tearful.

Sometimes I dreamed of Chilam's wife Ixel, who would laugh wildly as she hurled naked infants into deep black pools. Sometimes Catalina's face would appear on Ixel's body and the baby falling to its death would not be the child of my past but the child of my future, which I now carried within me. As I screamed, Hernán would stand by as impassively as Chilam had once stood beside me on the brink of the sacred well.

I grew pale and wan, moving listlessly through each day, taking nourishment only for the sake of the baby. Hernán expressed his concern for me on his infrequent visits to my suite, but his mind was heavy with his own problems. While he waited helplessly for word from Spain, his enemies grew bolder, opposing his policies openly and disobeying his edicts. Catalina too had become unmanageable since the night of the reception. Her vitriolic tongue hounded him without mercy. It was whispered by Sancha that she was drinking more than ever.

I cursed my own self-pity. Juan was beyond pain. The crueler fate, along with the burden of acceptance and recovery, was my own. That some unknown young bride might have died with him no longer mattered. At least if it were so, I told myself time after time, his last days had been happy.

I was stirred from my shadowy world one morning by the sound of timid footsteps in the hallway outside my room. Alone and unannounced, Catalina stood in the doorway.

Hernán's wife looked ill. Her eyes were puffy, her skin drab, and she seemed to have difficulty breathing. She was wearing a purple gown that made her face look yellowish by contrast. Around her neck she wore a string of gold beads that she twisted with agitated fingers. "I had to talk with you," she said. "Heaven knows it isn't easy."

"Come in," I said. "You know I've never borne you any ill will, Doña Catalina."

The "Doña" seemed to please her. She sank onto the proffered wooden chair with a little sniff. For a few moments she sat looking at her own clenched hands. "You probably think I'm some kind of wtich," she said at last. "I came to tell you that I'm not. I'm only a woman who loves her husband." Her plump chin trembled. He'd broken her heart from the beginning, she sighed, when, after taking from her a woman's most precious gift, he'd refused to marry her. An outraged Governor Velásquez had thrown him in jail. The forced wedding that followed had been the governor's idea, not Catalina's. "He was married to my sister, you see, and he couldn't stand the idea of a scandal. I'd never have forced Hernán myself. I wanted him to love me!"

I listened in silence as Catalina, her voice on the brink of a sob, told how a bitter Hernán had exacted full revenge for his entrapment. While his bride languished alone in their bed, he'd spent his nights in the brothels of Santiago or in the slave huts of his plantation. Frome one of these unions had come a half-Indian daughter who was also named Catalina—not after his wife, but in honor of another Catalina, his mother.

"They all think I'm barren!" she cried. "But Hernán could get me with child if he wanted to. Instead he's punished me all these years for something that wasn't my fault." Oh, he'd made a public show of treating her well. When he was an *alcalde*, he'd lavished money on her for gowns, and they'd had the finest carriage in the Indies. In the company of others, his manner toward her was always courtly, but their private life together had been an empty hell. Still, as a beaten dog loves its master, she'd continued to love him.

"You think—everyone thinks—that I only came to New Spain to be a great lady. It isn't true," she whispered, dabbing at her eyes. "I came hoping that the years had changed him, that he'd forgiven me. I was fool enough to think we might find another beginning to this new land. Instead I found you."

"What do you want from me, Doña Catalina?" I asked softly.

"Let me have another chance with him," she said. "I'll give you everything I own if you'll promise to go away. You and your child will never want for anything."

I looked past the woman to the sunlit garden, where two hummingbirds flitted among the blossoms of a trumpet vine. I shook my head. "I can't help you," I said.

"You can't!" Catalina snapped. "You mean you *won't*."

"I can't," I said. "If what you've told me is true, do you think my going would make any difference? He'd only find someone else, and that wouldn't be hard. Surely you don't think he's been true to me all this time."

Catalina gazed at me in mute, sullen acknowledgement.

"I only want peace," I said. "I'd willingly do as you ask except for one thing." Catalina's eyes followed mine down to the swelling bulge that rose beneath my *huipilli*. "I will stay, Doña Catalina. Not for myself, but for my child."

"Then you won't even consider—"

I shook my head.

Catalina rose stiffly. "Then I've nothing more to say to you except that you may come to regret your decision." She started toward the door, swaying a little. I realized then how much she'd been drinking.

"I'll call Sancha to help you," I offered.

The woman turned on me. All the hidden venom surged up into her eyes. "I'll ask no help from you, you dark-skinned sorceress! You daughter of the devil!" she spat. Then she lurched out the door and disappeared.

It was that evening after vespers that Sancha hurried in, all out of breath. "You should have been at dinner tonight, Malintzin. The whole palace is talking about it!" She hopped on one foot with excitement.

"Now, Sancha . . ." I assumed my most disapproving frown. "Remember what I told you."

Sancha, as usual, ignored me. "There were guests all around the table, Malintzin, and all of them heard it. The *señora* was complaining to Señor Solis, the overseer, about her Indians. She said they hadn't been working on the jobs she'd given them"—Sancha broke off when she saw the plate of fruit at my side. "I'm still hungry. May I have that slice of melon?"

"If it will stop that mischievous tongue." But I was at Sancha's mercy by now and she knew it. Between bites of melon she continued her story.

"Señor Solis told her that it was Don Hernán who put the Indians to doing other work. Then she got angry, Malintzin, and she puffed up like this!" Sancha demonstrated by drawing up her shoulders and bugging her eyes. "And she said in a very loud voice, 'I'll soon see that no one meddles in what belongs to me!' "

Sancha paused to take a few nibbles of melon, spitting out the seeds into the garden. When she'd established a sufficient degree of dramatic suspense, she went on. "Well, Don Hernán just looked at her with his eyes half closed, like this—" again there was a demonstration— "and then he said—"Sancha took a deep gulp of air—" 'Madam, I want no part of anything that belongs to you.' "

I let my breath out in a little whistle. Whatever else he'd done to her, I'd never known Hernán to insult his wife in public. Sancha grinned at the astonishment her story had produced.

"Is that all?" I demanded, shamelessly intrigued.

"Yes, that's all, except that the *señora* got up and left the table. Don Hernán stayed until the guests had finished eating, and then he followed her to her room." She swallowed the last of the melon. "I have to go back now. It's my turn to sleep outside her door tonight. Thank you for the melon. I wish I could be back with you again, Malintzin."

That night I slept fitfully, alternating between wakefulness and horrible dreams filled with ghostly, screaming faces. I was running through a dismal hell, looking for Juan, searching, calling, never finding him.

I awoke, drenched with sweat, to find Sancha shaking my arm. The little maid's ebullient manner had vanished. She was trembling, eyes huge and staring in the darkness.

"Malintzin, wake up! It's the *señora*—she's dead!"

Hysterically, Sancha sobbed out the story. She and another Indian maid had gone to sleep on their mats outside the big double doors of Catalina's bedroom. In the night they'd been awakened by the sounds of a noisy quarrel from inside. Suddenly, Catalina's voice had gone silent and they'd heard Hernán shouting for someone to open the door. Knowing it was locked, they'd gone for Violante Rodríguez, Catalina's personal maid, who had a key. When the door had swung open, the candlelight revealed Hernán holding his wife's dead body in his arms. "She looked . . . just awful, Malintzin. Her face was all twisted. Her necklace had broken and spilled gold beas all over the floor. And her neck! There were red marks on it—"

I clutched at my own throat. Blessed Mother, it couldn't

have been the way it sounded! I was still dreaming. Yes, that was it . . .

But Sancha sobbed on. While they were busy examining Catalina, Hernán had disappeared. His pages and grooms had found him in his dressing room, screaming and pounding his head against the wall. They'd sent for Padre Olmedo.

"Sancha, be still. I hear something!" I strained my ears and caught the soft brush of footsteps coming across the garden. "Who's there " I called softly. There was no answer and the sound had ceased. "Leave me alone, Sancha. Go back and help the others," I commanded. The girl ran off at my bidding. No sooner was she gone than a wild-eyed Hernán stepped into my room.

"Marina!" In an instant he was kneeling at my side and I was cradling his battered head against my breasts. "Marina, my love, my refuge, my sanity! They'll all think I killed her," he moaned.

"But you *didn't,*" I whispered fiercely, wanting desperately to believe my own words. "You couldn't. Not you. What really happened, Hernán?"

"I don't know. God help me, but I don't remember! We were arguing one minute and the next thing I remember I was holding her and she was dead—" He pressed tightly against me, shaking like a newborn fawn. "She wasn't well, you know, and she drank herself senseless. It could have been anything. God, it could have been me! I just don't remember!" he sobbed, clutching at me frantically.

"Hush," I soothed him. "The Padre will be here soon. He'll believe you. He knows you, Hernán. Now rest. Stay with me."

Chapter Twenty-Six

Coyoacan—October 1524

I sat at my loom in the garden and watched Martín toddle from flower to flower on his sturdy little legs, like a plump earthbound bumblebee. He squatted down to investigate a pebble, picked it up with his pudgy hand and gravely put it into his mouth. Finding it not to his liking he spat it out and flung it onto the path once more, muttering to himself in his own mysterious language.

Had a year and a half really gone by since I'd stood beside Hernán while Padre Olmedo held our newborn son over the font and christened him with the name of Hernán's own father? Babyhood was so fleeting. Already, Martín seemed anxious to escape from my arms and get on with the business of becoming a man.

The past two years, I reflected, had ranked among the more tranquil times of my life, but they had not been free from trouble. Catalina had been buried and properly mourned, her death attributed to a form of plague in which red spots did indeed appear on the neck. Only her dour-faced brother had dared suggest that it might have been otherwise, but few listened to him, especially since, within days of Catalina's passing, the long-awaited letter from Carlos V had arrived, confirming Hernán as governor-general of New Spain. The appointment was less than the viceroyalty he'd hoped for, but at least his position was now secure. The following Christmas, however, when Hernán's old rival, Governor Garay of Jamaica, suddenly took ill and died during a visit to Coyoacan, the anti-Cortés faction became loud in their cries of "Murder!" It had done little good to point out that not only had Garay's illness been diagnosed plainly as pneumonia, with symptoms no poison could produce, but his visit with Hernán had been congenial to the point of arranging a marriage between Garay's son and Hernán's Cuban daughter. His enemies heard only what they wanted to hear.

As Martín plodded past me, I snatched him up in my arms and covered his face with a flurry of little kisses. He gazed at me with his big, sober eyes, neither responding nor resisting. He was such a solemn little fellow, this young Martín Cortés. Juan would have loved him, I thought, with a fresh surge of the sorrow that welled from its own hidden spring within me and never seemed to run dry. Juan's death was something I had never been able to accept fully. I had even hired a young man to manage his *encomienda* at Xilotepec and care for his prized horse to keep the animal and the land from passing to other hands.

The love that was not lost in grief I lavished on Martín, who accepted it with stoicism. Now I tickled him playfully under his chin, an indignity he endured unsmilingly. He had his father's paleness and his intense, dark eyes, but the wide mouth, high cheekbones and thick mat of black hair were a clear legacy from me. I blew on his hair. "My little owl, my fat little frog," I murmured in Nahuatl.

"Marina." I did not have to turn around and look at Hernán to know that he was frowning. "How many times must I tell you, I want you to use only Spanish with the boy? Sometimes I think you disobey me deliberately."

I put Martín down and he resumed his investigation of the garden. He was wearing an embroidered cotton smock that hung to his chubby knees. I would have preferred to let him run naked and free as Indian children, did, but Hernán had insisted that, as a young Spanish gentleman, he be properly clothed.

"Forgive me, Hernán." I smiled as engagingly as I could. "He's so precious that I forget myself. Tell me the little love-words that Spanish mothers say to their children and I will use them."

He ignored my request. Perhaps it embarrassed him, I thought. Once he would have laughed at me, or at least smiled. Now, in the time since Catalina's death, there'd been a noticeable cooling of his affections toward me. I suspected the reason why. Wasn't it a logical assumption that, with his wife gone, he might be expected to marry his closest companion, the mother of his son? At first I had almost expected it myself. But then, knowing his ambition and remembering

María's words, I realized that the possibility was far from his mind.

"Every one of them hopes to marry into the Spanish nobility one day," María had told me long ago. How right she'd been. In the past months, Hernán had maintained a close, rather furtive correspondence with his father in Spain. I suspected that the elder Cortés was helping his son arrange an advantageous marriage with some wealthy young Spanish *doña*.

Hernán had told me nothing, yet I was aware that I was being edged slowly out of his life. I'd not shared his bed since before Martín's birth. My delicate condition, my need for rest—he'd always had his excuses. It was just as well, since I'd had no spirit for it and he'd been busy elsewhere. A Spanish tavern maid in the capital was reportedly with child by him, and I'd heard rumors that his restless eye had fallen on Tecuichpo, now a breathtaking sixteen. My pride urged me to pack my possessions and leave. I was wealthy enough in my own right to live without his support. As for the pain of it, Juan's loss had left me so benumbed that I sometimes wondered if I would ever feel anything again. I stayed, yet for Martín's sake and out of a stubborn loyalty that refused to let me go.

"Martín looks tired. Have you forgotten his nap again, Marina?" Hernán's tone was reproachful. "If you'd just allow Violante to put him on a proper schedule—"

I scowled. The idea of Hernán assigning Martín's care to the prim, middle-aged Violante Rodriguez, who'd been Catalina's maid, when I, his own mother, was here, rankled on me even after all this time. "He's not sleepy," I said. "Look at him."

"He's going to whine all through dinner. You're spoiling him, Marina. A young boy needs discipline. Now, Violante—"

"She's not his mother, I am."

"Well, if you had a mother's concern, you'd want him brought up like a gentleman, not like some little savage."

The argument ended as many of its predecessors had, with Hernán stalking out of the garden and Violante sweeping in like an old hen with ruffled feathers to bear her howling charge off to his nap.

I was left alone in the garden to reflect on Hernán's temper, which was growing shorter by the day. His anger, I knew, wasn't really directed at me. It was only one expression of the frustration that filled his life. The man whose wits and daring had conqured an empire was being picked slowly to pieces by an army of petty officials, rivals and discontented friends. The man who had brought wealth and glory to his king was forced to live under the scrutiny of that same king's hired busybodies, who took delight in reporting anything that might discredit him.

And now a blow had come from another front, an insult almost too grievous to bear. Some months earlier, two large expeditions, illustriously led, had been sent to explore the territory south of the Aztec domain. Pedro de Alvarado had marched into Guatemala on the west, and Cristobal de Olid had taken his force to Las Hilbueras on the eastern coast. Now word had come back that Olid, one of the heroes of the conquest and a trusted friend, had declared his independence from his general. It was an act painfully reminiscent of Hernán's own rebellion against Governor Velásquez, and Hernán was outraged. He had quickly dispatched a kinsman of his, Francisco de Las Casas, to deal with the rebel. Even so, from the day of Las Casas's departure, it was plain that Hernán was having second thoughts about not having gone in person.

"You ought to forget about it. You've enough to do right here," I told him that evening after supper, as I sat in a high-backed chair of woven rushes, enjoying the song of crickets in the garden. The turbulence caused by the clash over Martín had dissipated, at least for the present. I snuggled into my red woolen shawl, for the night air in the high valley of Mexico was chilly.

Hernán would not sit. He strolled along the garden's edge at a leisurely pace, only the twitching of the vein in his forehead betraying the struggle that was being waged inside him. I contemplated the powerful figure, my mind asking the same questions he probably asked himself when he stood before his mirror each morning. Had he grown a trifle stout about the middle? Were the gray hairs creeping into his dark head with increasing profusion? He was nearly forty, no longer young, yet with the possibility of half his life stretching ahead of him. "By my consience," I could almost hear him saying to himself, "is it all to be downhill from here?" I read his thoughts and I agonized with him.

"Do you ever think of how it was, Marina?" He ran his hands along the back of my chair. "Lying back under the stars with the campfires blazing and Ortiz playing his lute? Sleeping on the earth with you on one side of me and my good sword on the other? Singing as we marched along in the sunshine?" He was clad from head to toe in black, still mourning the wife he'd neglected while she lived.

"I remember," I said, and as I spoke I also remembered blood, fever, insects, cold, exhaustion and Juan Jaramillo. What glorious hell it had been!

"It's all gone sour now," he sputtered. "In those days we ate dog meat and wild berries, and it tasted like manna from heaven. Our bellies were growling with good, honest hunger, and we enjoyed every bite because we never knew whether it would be our last. Tonight I had a meal fit for an emperor. All it gave me was an upset stomach."

"I know what you're thinking," I told him. "It won't be the same, Hernán. You've changed. We all have. Las Casas can handle Olid. Leave him to it."

"Olid!" he snarled. "That's where it rubs me. After I've handed him the world, he thinks he can cut loose from me and make his own empire. What I wouldn't give to face the dog myself! He'd howl for mercy then!"

I'd known all along that he would go. Preparations began at once. The next day he was sending off runners with letters to his old comrades. Sandoval declared that he could be ready in the time it took to buckle on his sword. Bernal Diaz sent word that he would join the march when the company passed through Coatzalcoalcos. There were a few others, ill at ease with the soft complexities of colonial life, who responded eagerly to their general's call. But I had been right. It would not be the same. Many well-remembered faces would be missing. Olid, of course, was now the enemy. Alvarado was in Guatemala, Ordaz in Spain. Death had taken Escalante, Velásquez de León, Lares, Morla, Salcedo, Guzman and a host of others. Andrés de Tapia, Alonzo de Ávila and Jorge Alvarado were busy with their *encomiendas*. Padre Olmedo was burdened with religious and administrative duties. Aguilar had recently died in a monastery, his dream of becoming a dominican brother fulfilled. Pero Farfán was in poor health.

It came as no surprise when Hernán anounced that I was to go with him. Although my presence as an interpreter was no longer essential—by now there was an adequate supply of both Nahuatl-speaking Spaniards and Spanish-speaking Indians—I'd been a vital part of Hernán's conquest and he could not recapture its spirit without me.

The thought of leaving Martín behind was infinitely painful, but Hernán would not think of exposing his son to the dangers and rigors of such a journey. When the moment of departure came, Violante Rodriguez smirked triumphantly. Fighting tears, I pulled myself loose from embracing him and deposited the sniffling child in her arms. "Now he'll be properly cared for," her prim gaze seemed to say.

The procession was already beginning to move. I hurried to my litter, looking back to wave at my unsmiling little son as the bearers hoisted the poles to their shoulders. Violante Rodriguez took hold of his hand and waved it for him until the litter rounded a bend in the street and we were lost from each other's sight: I wiped my eyes. Violante was a good woman, devastatingly capable. She would give Martín everything he needed except love.

I looked ahead and behind, shaking my head in amazement. Hernán had spoken wistfully of sleeping under the stars and feasting on dog meat and wild berries. What a joke! The long train of mules and *tlamemes* stretching out to the rear carried, among other things, his disassembled bed and mattress, his personal tent, a tent for myself and my maids, and tents for his captains. There were scores of chest loaded with suits of clothing, jewelry and dishes. In Hernán's suite there were a steward, a chamberlain, a butler, two toastmasters, a pastry cook, a larder-master, a man in charge of gold and silver services, a doctor, a surgeon, eight grooms, two falconers, five musicians, two jugglers, three muleteers and at least a dozen pages, including Orteguilla, now a slender youth of sixteen. Bringing up the rear was a huge herd of pigs, a sort of marching larder. With the servants and equipment brought along by his captains as well, the company's progress resembled the mass migration of some opulent city. All this to punish one rebellious captain.

Out spiritual welfare was to be under the care of two Flemish priests from the court of Carlos V—stubby, rosy-cheeked little men whose Spanish was nearly unintelligible. I would miss the earthy wisdom of Padre Olmedo, but I admonished myself to be fair. The two priests could not help it if their speech and mannerisms were so strange to me. They too were men of God, I told myself.

Hernán had not overlooked the possibility of an Indian uprising in his absence. As hostages he had brought along Cuauhtemoc, Ixtlilxochitl's brother Cohuanococh, who was the deposed ruler of Texcoco, the lord of Tlacopan, and even the *ciuacoatl,* as well as other prominent chiefs.

As we waited for the servants to prepare the midday meal, the *ciuacoatl* came and sat down beside me. "Has Malintzin lost his mind?" he said, glancing about to see if anyone was listening. "Doesn't he realize that the vipers he left behind in the city are more dangerous to him than twenty Captain Olids?"

"I tried to tell him the same thing," Don Juan, I murmured. "He doesn't listen to me anymore."

"He only listens to his enemies, and if those two snakes who ride on either side of him mean him well, my eyesight is failing."

I followed Don Juan's gaze to where Hernán stood chatting with Salazar and Chiriño, the king's two principal agents in New Spain. Salazar was a handsome man, strikingly so, even though his complexion was almost too fair, his lips too red and too delicately shaped. He was taller than Hernán by half a head and he dressed immaculately, though a bit foppishly for my taste. Chiriño was shrunken by comparison, nothing but sinew and raw, darting nerves. It was whispered that he suffered from a disease that consumed his flesh and left him with that eerie twitching about his eyes and hands, but I doubted it, for I had once seen him beat a disobedient Indian servant almost to death with those hands alone. If one were to judge by appearances, Chiriño seemed to ooze villainy from every pore of his body. Yet from what I knew of him, the charming Salazar was the more dangerous of the two. Hernán seemed blind to everything about him except that very charm.

I shivered. "I don't understand him anymore," I said to Don Juan. "He suspects friends who've been loyal for years and embraces those who'd sell his life for a peso. I told him he was wrong in bringing you with us, but he paid no attention to me."

"I've never called him a friend." The *ciuacoatl* twirled his gold crucifix between his thumb and forefinger. "But I'm not such a fool that I don't realize what would happen in this land if he were removed. He's the only man strong enough to keep the vultures from tearing the country apart and flying away with the pieces."

"I'll return your compliment for him, Don Juan. He considers you one of the few men capable of leading a revolt against him. That's why you're here."

"He's wrong, you know. I couldn't and I wouldn't. The white men are here to stay—a fact that only a dreamer would deny—and in its present circumstances, Mexico needs Hernán Cortés." He glanced sideways at Salazar, who'd placed a lace-edged arm around Hernán's shoulders. "Mexico needs him and he's deserting her . . ."

Our cumbersome army moved over the land at a slug's pace. We seemed to spend more time making and breaking camp than we did marching, and so it was that nearly two weeks had gone by before we reached the town of Orizaba, nestled among the skirts of a towering white peak. There we stopped to rest and it was there, two days after our arrival, that I saw Salazar and Chiriño organizing their gear for departure.

At last, I said to myself, Hernán's come to his senses and sent them packing! I found myself wanting to talk with him. That was something I'd avoided during most of the trip, keeping to the company of my maids and bearers while he rode ahead with his captains and the two royal agents. Perhaps sensing my disapproval, he'd sent for me only when necessary.

I hurried anxiously toward his tent. Sandoval was coming from the opposite direction, so preoccupied that he nearly walked into me. He looked as if a thunderstorm were taking place behind his eyes and I asked him what was wrong. "Salazar and Chiriño," he muttered.

"They're leaving," I said. "I just saw their servants packing. Things are bound to improve once they're gone."

Sandoval stared at me. "Good Lord, you haven't heard?"

I listened to him with growing disbelief and alarm as the story came out. Letters had arrived at the camp informing Hernán a of a violent quarrel between Estrada and Alborñoz, the two deputies who'd been left in charge of the government in his absence. "Our friends Salazar and Chiriño," Sandoval concluded, his lisp more pronounced with his anger, "are returning to the capital with authority from Cortés to take over the government of New Spain."

"He's mad!" The words sprang to my lips without thought.

"I pray you're wrong," said Sandoval. "But to save me, I can't think of any other explanation."

Hernán was still seated at a leisurely breakfast when I burst into his tent. "I see someone's told you the news," he said with studied pleasantness. "Sit down, Marina *mía*. Have some chocolate."

I remained standing. "It would have helped if you'd told me yourself!"

"You'd only have argued with me. That's all you've done lately. You've become quite the little bitch, my girl."

I'd intended to approach him rationally, to appeal to whatever common sense remained in his head in hopes of persuading him to recall Salazar and Chiriño. Now as I faced his nonchalance, all my self-possession was consumed in a flash of hot anger.

"You must be insane!" I exploded. "They'll ruin you and all you've done!"

"You're overwrought, Marina." He took a sip of melon juice from a silver goblet. "You're talking to his excellency, the Governor of New Spain, remember? I do as I please and I don't need you to give me orders. It so happens I wasn't looking forward to having those two meddlers hanging on my sleeves for the rest of the trip." A page brought him a linen napkin and he dabbed at his mouth. "They didn't want me to go in the first place, you know. But I can't just command the king's own lapdogs to take their tails and go. No, I had to wait for some good excuse to get rid of them. The trouble back in the capital gave it to me."

"But those two! They'd cut you to pieces to feed their own ambition. Now you've given them the power to do just that."

"Oh, calm your feathers. They'll do nothing. My friends wouldn't let them if they tried. You're being silly." He pulled back his chair and rose to his feet, the usual signal—even for me, of late—that the interview was over.

Indignation choked my voice to a whisper. "I've nothing to lose by being silly! But you have everything to lose! This whole expedition's a fool's errand!"

"If that's what you think," he said coldly, "then why don't you go back to the capital with them?"

Somehow I made it back out into the sunshine, where I stood blinking with helpless rage. I'll go see the *ciuacoatl,* I told myself. Maybe some of Don Juan's imperturbability would rub off on me.

The hostage chiefs were confined to one central area of the camp under heavy guard. Their living conditions were comfortable, but very restricted, for Hernán was fearful of any contact between them and the Indians of the neighboring towns.

The sentries, most of them young men enjoying their first taste of adventure, recognized me and let me pass without challenge. The Indian tents were simple affairs consisting of lengths of cotton hung on wooden frames, in contrast with the big Moorish tents used by Hernán and his captains. They were arranged in a tight circle around a well-swept open area where morning campfires smoldered and servants bustled here and there bearing baskets of food on their heads, or round clay pots filled with water for their masters' baths. I could not see the *ciuacoatl*. He was probably bathing, I reminded myself. I'd come at an awkward time. The only chief in sight was Cuauhtemoc himself, sitting crosslegged on a mat in front of his tent. The position was considered undignified for a man, but I knew that because of the damage to his feet he could not assume the customary squat without pain.

He was staring sullenly at the ground, probably a common pastime for the vanquished emperor. Bitterness and cruel treatment had aged his handsome features far beyond his twenty-eight years. He was as gaunt as a starving wolf, hollow-eyed and snarling. I wanted to avoid him.

"Malintzin!" His voice was a half-whsiper, half-growl. He'd seen me and would not let me pass without flinging a few taunting barbs in my direction. I braced myself for the venom that was sure to come next.

"Malintzin . . ." He was dressed in an unadorned white *tilmatli* and as he paused he licked his lips, savoring the hatred that was all he had left to him. "Do you know that among our people, when we want to call a man traitor we call him by your name?" He regarded me coolly, calculating the impact of his thrust. "Who are you, Malintzin? You're not one of us. Do you think you're one of the white gods?"

I said nothing. I'd long since learned that to answer him was pointless.

"If you think you're one of them, you're a fool," Cuauhtemoc continued in a low tone. "They think brown skin is dirty. They'll flatter and pet you as long as you're useful to them. Then when they don't need you anymore they'll spit on you!" He looked at me with eyes like dead coals. "You don't look happy, Malintzin. Have they begun to spit on you already?"

It was uncanny the way Cuauhtemoc knew just where to jab. I knew that it was within my power to have him flogged. Yet he had been the last *uei tlatoani*. He had defended his people with courage, and I was determined to treat him with respect. "My lord, I beg your permission to be excused," I said, biting my lip to keep the tears inside, tears that were less for what he'd said than for what he'd become.

I walked out of the compound with blurred eyes. Cuauhtemoc was right about me. I'd forsaken my beginnings and was no longer Indian. Yet I was not never would be a member of the conquering race. I was nothing; I belonged to no one. The camp pressed in on me like the walls of a prison. I fancied hostility in eyes of every color. I had to get away for some time to myself or I was sure I'd go mad.

A village lay within easy walking distance of the camp. Hernán, fearing any chance of conspiracy, had forbidden the Indians under his charge to enter it. But then, by my own definition, I was not included in that prohibition. For safety I would take two of my bearers along with me. They were in my charge, not Hernán's.

The grass of the high, hilly plain was still beaded with dew. I sucked the cold air into my lungs with relish. My eyes followed the flight of an eagle from the low branch of a tree, up and up to the dizzying heights above Orizaba's magnificent cone, where it disappeared into the blue. The snow-blanketed peak glittered in the morning sunlight. My feet and the feet of my bearers awakened sleeping insects as they brushed through the grass. A quail family bobbed across our path. Little by little, I felt my tightly clenched spirit unfolding like a new bud. I was outcast from all save this land—but the land was me and mine. As rough and weathered as a grandmother's hand, as cruel as the black blades of the *maquahuitl*, as beautiful as the smile of a bride—this land was my mother, my father; its rivers were my blood. Swiftly I bent down, pulled off my sandals and walked with my bare feet against the rocky ground. The soles of my feet were tender now, but the pain was sweet.

Now we passed villagers on their way to market, heads and backs piled with pottery, golden baskets, rolled-up mats, feathery bouquets of live turkeys with their legs tied together in bunches, cloth, corn, calabashes.

How long had it been since I'd stood by myself in an Indian town? I was a child again, walking through the market and holding my father's hand, tasting the biting scent of roasting chiles, smiling at the antics of grubby children as they played tag among the stalls. The two husky bearers moved unobtrusively at my heels, as silent as panthers.

My senses caught the frangrance of copal incense smoldering in hand-swung censers as a funeral procession wound its way through the crowd. The mourners, wild-eyed women with disheveled hair, followed the native priests and musicians.

After them trudged the friends and brothers of the dead man who, judging from the procession's meager trappings, had been old and poor. On a litter they carried the body, which had been wrapped in a squatting position, covered with cloth and festooned with paper flags. The widow walked behind them, a fragile figure in white whose face was partly hidden by a shawl.

I stepped aside to make room as the cortege passed. I was never quite sure of what happened next, but it seemed that the little widow suddenly raised her reddened eyes to stare at me and stopped in her tracks, letting her husband's body move on ahead without her. From her frail throat rose a shriek of the most incredulous delight. In the next moment, while the crowd pressed around us to stare, she was kneeling in the dirt, clinging to my legs and weeping with joy. "Malinalli . . . my little one!"

I raised her up by arms that felt as thin as a spider's limbs, so that I could look into her face. "Atototl!" I choked. I gathered the old woman into my arms, rocking her as I had been rocked as a child by the old slave.

The crowd stirred uneasily. Up ahead, the funeral procession had come to a confused halt. Atototl looked around awkwardly. "What a time for you to come," she said. "As you see, there are things I have to finish now." She straightened herself and moved back into line, drawing me along by the hand. "Walk beside me, child. Afterwards we'll talk."

The old man's funeral pyre had burned down to embers. A priest scooped the ashes of his body into an earthenware vase and dropped a little piece of jade in with them to represent his heart before handing the vase to Atototl. "He passed through Xicalango after they took you away," she said, gazing down into the neck of the vase. "The slave-dealer gave me to him for nothing." The old man had lost his wife, she explained, and needed a woman to care for him, but being poor, he could not afford a young one. "It's not been such a bad life. He was kind to me." She warmed her hands on the bottom of the vase. "I'll give these to his brother's family. They loved him. As for me, if you'll put up with an old woman, nothing could make me happier than being your slave again."

"My slave!" I shook my head emphatically. "My grandmother, I have enough servants to take care of us both."

The sun was climbing high in the sky, illuminating Orizaba

with a blinding whiteness as we began the trek back toward the Spanish camp. Atototl was glowing. I was pensive. Our meeting had opened doors that I thought had closed behind me forever. I'd felt an unexpected surge of feeling when Atototl told me that she'd been in touch with my mother. "The slave-dealer told her where to find me," the old woman said. Every month after that she sent food and clothing to us. When Itzcoatl died from the curse of the red spots, she sent messengers begging me to come back and live with her. But I had a husband. What could I do?" Atototl gripped my arm more tightly. The old black eyes squinted at me through the sun's rays. "She tried to find you too. The slaver told her you'd been taken to Tenochtitlan. She made the journey there herself to look for you."

As the old woman talked on, I walked beside her in silence, my emotions churning. "Imagine her astonishment," Atototl was saying, "when she learned from an Aztec messenger that you were the great Malintzin."

"Then why didn't she come to me?" I asked sullenly, my mind refusing to believe that my mother had cared.

"By then she was afraid. When she thought of what she'd done to you . . ." Atototl stopped walking and turned to face me. "Child, she fears for her life. You're the most powerful woman in Mexico." She linked her arm through mine and began to walk again. "But Oluta's not so far from here. It's been so long . . . surely you'll go and see her, won't you?"

I bit my lip and blinked away the tears. My mother had ceased to be my mother the night she let the slavers bind my hands and eyes and lead me away into the forest. I shook my head. "No," I whispered.

Our shadows were lengthening over the yellow grass by the time we reached the camp. Atototl was shaking. For all she'd heard about the white gods, they could be monsters who'd eat her alive.

"Don't be afraid, Grandmother," I squeezed her hand. "They won't hurt you. They laugh and cry and go to the bushes every morning just as you and I do." I remembered then that I'd left the camp that morning without telling Hernán where I was going. If he'd needed me during the day, he'd be angry. I left Atototl with Sancha. Then, apprehensively, I hurried to look for Hernán.

Outside his tent I paused to brace myself, hoping I wouldn't find him waiting inside. He could be vicious when he was displeased with me.

A gray stallion was standing alongside the tent, its reins looped around one of the supporting ropes. I stared at it. My unbelieving eyes traveled from the mottling on its flanks to the splash of white on its forehead, down to the tiny white spot behind the left hind foot. *"The Moors call that the mark of swiftness . . ."* a well-loved voice echoed out of my memory.

My first thought was that someone was playing a cruel joke. My second, more rational, was that someone had discovered the horse in Xilotepec and decided to make good use of it. My third . . . With my heart pounding like the death drum at Tlatelolco, I raised the flap of the tent and stepped inside.

He was seated alone at Hernán's table, with his eyes on the maps. I'd come into the tent so quietly that he hadn't heard me, and so I stood there for an instant, trembling as I devoured him with starving eyes, certain that at any moment I'd wake up and discover I'd been dreaming again. My voice, when I finally found the courage to use it, was no more than a whisper.

"Juan . . ."

He looked up. His eyes were even bluer than I'd remembered. "Don't move, Marina," he said softly, as he pulled back the chair and stood up. He walked toward me slowly. Of course it was a dream! But the tears streaming down my cheeks were real, as was his touch when he took my face between his two hands and looked deeply into my eyes. I saw that he'd aged. The creases at the corners of his eyes had deepened, and wherever he'd been the sun had bronzed his skin until it was as dark as my own.

It was so quite that we could hear each other's heartbeats. Juan tried to speak, but nothing came from his throat except a funny little choking sound. Then he caught me in his arms and crushed me tightly against him, his hands molding every curve of my body to his. "Marina," he murmured. "Marina, Thank God!" I found his mouth with my own and we stood there clinging together, laughing, crying, tasting each other's tears.

His story emerged between kisses. The ship had broken to pieces in the hurricane. Juan had saved himself by lashing his body to an empty barrel with a piece of the rigging and had floated on the sea for a day and a night before he was finally washed ashore, half dead, on a tiny deserted island. "Aguilar was shipwrecked for eight years," he said. "I was luckier. A ship stopped for water and found me after two years. They took me back to Cuba and from there I caught the first passage to Mexico again."

"What about your wife?" I asked.

He pulled me even closer. "There was no wife. Oh, I'll confess I did some looking around, but no girl deserves a man who's already given his heart to someone else. Do you still love me, *querida*?"

"Yes!" I whispered happily.

"Will you go back to Xilotepec with me? Now?"

"By the saints," I murmured firecely, "I'd go anywhere with you!"

He rubbed his face against my hair. "We'll have to tell Cortés," he said.

I remembered then that we were in Hernán's tent. I glanced around nervously.

"He'll be back," Juan said. "Before I came here I went to Coyoacan to find you. There was a letter for him there that had arrived after he left. I told the majordomo I'd deliver it to him."

"A letter from where?"

"From Spain. His father, perhaps. When I gave the letter to him, he opened it and read it at once. From the look on his face, I'd say it was good news, but he didn't tell me what it said. He just folded it again and told me to sit down and wait while he ran off to do some business." Juan bent down to kiss my forehead. "When he comes back we'll tell him."

"Juan . . ." I spoke timidly. ". . . I haven't really been his woman for a long time. I've only stayed because of Martín."

"It wouldn't have made any difference, love. Your being his woman is something I've had to live with for years."

"He's had others all along," I said. "But he's a strange man, Juan, and he's becoming stranger every day. He might not be willing to let me go." I remembered Hernán's possessiveness, his tenacious clinging to the past.

"I've thought of that," Juan said. "For two years I've had nothing to do but think. I promised myself and God that if I ever got off that accursed island, and if you still wanted me, nothing on earth would stop me from having you."

The determination in his voice made me shiver. "Then nothing can stop me from going with you," I whispered. "But I'm praying you won't have to fight Hernán to take me."

His arms tightened around me. "If I have to," he said, "I'll kill him!"

"My good Jaramillo," said a deep voice behind us. "You wouldn't really go that far, would you?"

Hernán Cortés, one hand resting casually on the hilt of his sword, stood in the entrance of the tent.

Chapter Twenty-Seven

Stepping boldly inside, Hernán looked into our stunned faces and chuckled. "Sit down, Jaramillo. Marina, what luck—I've just been out looking for you, and I come back to find you here. Take this seat, *vida mía*." He arranged two wooden stools on one side of the table. He himself sat down in the big armchair on the other side, leaned back and surveyed us with elaborate casualness, looking as though he enjoyed the suspense.

We stood awkwardly before him, not knowing what to expect. Juan had his right arm around my waist, his left hand on the hilt of his own sword.

"Sit down!" Hernán rumbled. "Orders of the Governor!"

We sat. I kept a frightened grip on Juan's hand.

Hernán pulled a folded letter from an inner pocket of his black jerkin. He balanced it between two fingers, then tapped one corner lightly on the table and cleared his throat. "As two of my dearest friends, I want you to be the first to hear some very happy tidings. It seems I'm about to be betrothed."

My heart leaped. I felt Juan's hand tighten around mine.

"This letter, as you may have guessed, is from my father, the honorable Don Martín Cortés de Monroy. He informs me that he's arranged a most auspicious marriage for his only son." He looked up at us with a flicker of a smile. "Well, aren't you going to congratulate me?"

"Of course." Juan found his tongue. "Congragulations," he said stiffly.

"Thank you." Hernán beamed, his eyes darting from Juan's face to mine and back. "Her name's Doña Juana de Zúniga, daughter of the Count of Aguilar and niece of the Duke of Bejar—royal to the very marrow! My father says she's quite a little beauty too. Golden hair . . . eyes like sapphires . . . skin like a rose petal . . ." As his gaze flickered over me I realized he was trying to hurt me. "A damsel of impeccable virtue." He was reading the letter now. " 'As pure a blossom as ever graced the—' Well, you have the idea." He folded the letter and tucked it into his jerkin. "Unfortunately for me, the wedding can't take place for another three or four years. You see, the young lady's only thirteen." His shoulders rose and fell in a sigh of mock impatience. "And those years, alas, will be a time of probation for me. One blot on my reputation and it will be goodbye, Doña Juana."

He took out the letter again, curled it into a hollow tube, and held the ends between his palms. "That's why I needed to talk with you, Marina *mía*. You see, in light of my coming marriage, you've become something . . . well, an encumbrance, my dear. I wish I knew of a more gentle way to say this . . . We've got to take care of things in a way that will be discreet and satisfactory to everyone involved."

I parted my lips to speak, then thought better of it. Hernán's pride would not allow anything to be taken from him. If he had to give me up, it would be on his own terms.

He stood up, went to a chest and took out a cask of wine and two silver goblets. Returning to the table, he placed one in front of Juan and the other near himself. From the cask he poured a few drops of the precious wine into each goblet.

"Jaramillo," he said, sitting down again and taking the stem of the goblet between his thumb and forefinger. "I have a fine block of land in Chapultepec. In exchange for it, would you be willing to marry this woman and take her off my hands? I'd consider it a great favor."

So that was the way it was to be. Juan knew as well as I did that Hernán would have his vanity. I marveled as he played out his own role in the little drama. He frowned, looked up at the top of the tent, then at Hernán and then down at his goblet. Slowly, as if signing away his soul, he picked up the goblet and brought the rim to meet that of its mate across the table in a silvery kiss.

Juan and I were married in the early dawn of the following morning by one of the chubby little Flemish priests, whose name I cannot remember to this day. Everyone involved had agreed on the wisdom of a small, private ceremony, and so there were only a few witnesses: Sandoval, two pages, Sancha, Atototl, the *ciuacoatl*, and the royal notary who had drawn up the marriage document. We gathered in a little clearing on a pine-covered knoll not far from the camp.

Hernán, dressed in black, was pale and silent as he helped me out of the litter to escort me to the altar, where the priest waited beside Juan. I took his arm. The grass was cold and wet under my sandals. Two magpies, unhappy at the morning's disturbance, scolded raucously from their perch in a gnarled pine tree. Through his velvet sleeve, I could feel the tension in Hernán's arm. His jaw was set, his eyes were hard as flints. I'd hoped for some private word from him, some little gesture of benediction, but there had been none. Five years at his side had taught me to recognize signs of pain in him, and he was in pain now. Despite the bravado with which he'd offered me to Juan, my eagerness to go had wounded him, I knew. I wondered if he'd ever been hurt by a woman before.

The previous evening had been disconcerting. All I'd really wanted was to be alone with Juan, but we'd been surrounded by old friends and well-wishers and besieged by secretaries with papers to sign. Even when we'd left the camp to choose the site for the ceremony, the rotund priest had gone with us, panting and muttering in his strange tongue.

Juan had read the frustration in my eyes as he bade me an unprivate goodnight at the entrance of my tent. "It's only for one more night, *querida*," he'd whispered. "After tomorrow we'll have the rest of our lives together." I'd gone to my mat alone and spent the night staring wide-eyed into the darkness while Juan bedded down with the soldiers.

Since I was to marry into a Spanish world, I elected to wear the one Spanish gown I owned, a pale blue silk with its own mantilla of matching lace, a gift from María de Estrada. Beads of dew from the wet grass clung to the hem of the long skirt. The priest, in white vestments, was shivering in the chilly morning air. Juan, glowing, stood before the altar, dressed simply in an open-necked white blouse under a jerkin of gray wool. Even the magpies were still as I took my place beside him. Hernán's arm drew away from me, and for a brief instant I experienced a feeling of suspension, of aloneness. Then Juan reached for my hand.

As our fingers met, the edge of the sun rose above the mountains, brushing the clouds, the icy slopes of Orizaba, and Juan's hair with warm golden light. I looked into the quiet depths of his eyes, felt his hand close over mine, and trembled at the reality of it. I was not dreaming this time. This was Juan kneeling beside me, and now the priest, in his funny little voice, was saying the words that would make me Juan's wife.

Afterwards, we took the gray stallion and another horse for me and rode south toward a mountain village where Bernal had built a hunting lodge. Juan knew a man in the town who kept a key for Bernal's friends. "Bernal would be insulted if we didn't use it," he said.

"I wish he could have been here." In Indian dress once more, narrow skirt hiked above my knees, I rode bareback along the winding trail. My hair hung loose to my waist, catching the light as I bounced along beside him. "Poor Bernal, to suffer with us all that time and then to miss our wedding!"

Juan's eyes twinkled. "How would it be if we staged the ceremony all over again in Coatzalcoalcos just for him, complete with the priest's teeth chattering?"

I reached over to touch his arm and felt a lump rising in my throat. In the course of this long, lovely day, with nothing to do except ride and talk, he'd revealed a new side of himself; clownish, tender, ironic, a bit outrageous. It had hit me with a sudden wrench that for the first time in all the years I'd known him, I was seeing Juan when he was happy.

"Once is enough," I laughed. "Especially for that poor little priest." We would have a few days to spend by ourselves while the army pushed on south to Coatzalcoalcos. Then we planned to circle down and meet them there, where we would visit Bernal, return the extra horse, collect my servants and baggage and depart for Xilotepec. It was an awkward plan, but we'd been unable to think of a better one.

Toward evening we descended into a narrow valley with a whitewashed village nestled at one end. In one of the houses a smiling man recognized Juan and gave him a massive iron key. Juan thanked him in passable Nahuatl.

"Listening to you speak my language does something to me here—" I touched my chest with the tips of my fingers as we wound our way back up the mountain slope.

"It's a beautiful language," said Juan, "but I only know how to give orders. There are other things I'd like to be able to say. Especially now." He gave me an affectionate glance over his shoulder.

"I'll teach you." I looked ahead through the pines and saw the walls of the lodge rising above a nest of boulders.

The hunting lodge was a small structure of logs, roughly made, but so richly hung with animal skins and native tapestries inside that its very walls exuded a feeling of luxury. We'd arrived at sundown, built a fire in the stone fireplace and sat down to a simple meal of tortillas and beans purchased in the village below. Then Juan had excused himself and gone outside to cut more wood and to wash, purposely giving me a little time alone.

Now, wrapped in a blanket, I sat on a jaguar skin before the fire, my head resting on my drawn-up knees. I remembered fleetingly how I had once sat that way in a tiny room in Centla and waited for Chilam to step through the doorway. There was no reason, certainly, to feel the same fluttering fear now. Yet it was there. I'd undressed slowly, studying my body with a critical eye, trying to see myself as Juan would see me. My breasts, especially since I'd stopped nursing Martín, had lost some of their youthful firmness. My skin, from navel to thigh, was interlaced with silvery stretch marks, the combat ribbons of childbearing. The ideal bride would be young, seventeen at the most, pure and innocent. I was twenty-four, and as to purity—Mother of God, what life hadn't given me! I'd covered my shame with a blanket from the big wooden bed that sat in one corner of the room and sunk down before the fire, staring morosely into the flames.

Juan, coming in through the door a few minutes later with a length of towel wrapped around his lithe, suntanned body, found me in tears. Quickly he sat down and put his arms around me, blanket and all, holding me like a little girl. "Tell me," he said.

I tried. "Juan, you deserve someone young, someone sweet. Instead, you've married . . . an old shoe—"

"And that's all that's bothering you?" He sounded relieved. "Look at me, *querida*. I'm going to be cruel for a moment and then I'll never mention this again." He lifted my chin with one hand, forcing me to look into his face. "What do you think you're getting?" he said. "Look at me. A man with ten years at sea behind him ! I left home at seventeen. When a wild young buck like I was steps off the gangplank in a strange port, I don't have to tell you what he looks for first. Don't you think I'd like to erase all that and come to you clean and new? Ten years at sea and a marriage, Marina! If you're an old shoe, we'll make a comfortable pair. Now, let's forget this nonsense!"

I dissolved in a torrent of fresh tears, feeling wretched for having wrung such a bitter confession out of him. He gathered me close, rocking me gently. "My poor little love. That's not what you wanted to hear, is it? I ought to be horsewhipped." He pressed his cheek against my hair. "How long have you known me, Marina?" Silently I calculated. Five years. "Add up the days in that time," he said. "Count the hours in each day, the minutes. Then you'll know how long I've loved you, but you won't know how much. I can't tell you that. Maybe I can't even show you, but I can try if you'll let me." He brushed my forehead, my eyes, the tip of my nose with his lips. "When I left Cuba I was coming back to you," he murmured. "After the shipwreck the only thing that kept me from dying was knowing that if I left this world I'd be leaving you. Now, after all that, if you think I'd change anything—" He drew me up against him and kissed me with an urgency that made me realize how much he had always restrained himself with me. The blood had begun to pound wildly in my ears.

"Juan," I whispered, "I think I'm afraid."

"Of me? I'll be gentle, love."

"No, it's not that." I buried my face against the hollow of his neck. "I've never been happy before. I've never been loved—not really. It's the first time."

"Then let it be, Marina," he said huskily. "The fear, the trembling, the love—feel it all! Let it be the first time, then! But no more words, *querida*, not now!" He lifted my face to his. My arms slipped hungrily around his neck and I gave myself up to joy.

I lay next to him on the morning of our third day, nestled against his side matching the rhythm of my breathing to his . One thing I had already learned in our brief time together was that Juan slept as lightly as a forest animal. Even the rustle of a leaf could startle him into wakefulness, so I kept very still, reluctant to begin the day that would take us away from these four walls I'd come to treasure.

The sunlight filtered through the curtains of the high window, casting dancing patterns on the opposite wall. Juan stretched like a drowsy cat and turned over on his back. I held my breath, but his eyes did not open. Cautiously I raised myself on one elbow and looked at him—this old friend, this lover, this stranger who was my husband. "I can read the story of the conquest in your scars," I'd teased him. It was true. There along the side of his face ran the thin white line that was a souvenir of Cholula. His wrist bore a small nick that he'd carried since Tlaxcala. My eyes traced the jagged slash along his shoulder, earned on the Tlacopan causeway, and caressed the small V-shaped scar on his right cheek, bestowed on him at Otumba. Blessed Lady, I thought, what did I do to deserve to be this happy?

He'd told me about his time on the island. Two other men from the ship had drifted there along with him. One of them had lived only a few days and the other, a sailor from Santiago, had died near the end of the first year. "It was awful," Juan had told me as we lay in each other's arms. "He was sick, yes, but not that sick. He just gave up living. I sat there by his side, begging him not to die. It was the worst day of my life."

'What did you do then?" I asked him.

"To keep from losing my mind? Luckily, just staying alive took most of my time. I had to fish, to set snares and check them every day, and then I had to cook what I caught. As for the rest of the time, I explored the island until I knew every rock and blade of grass. I kept adding to the hut I'd built until it was as complicated as a palace. When I tired of that, I found some rushes and tried my hand at weaving. Remind me to make you a lopsided basket some day. I even wrote poetry."

"About me?"

"Some of it. Most of it."

"I love poetry. Ixtlilxochitl's grandfather wrote some wonderful poems. But I want to hear yours."

"Then you'd better ask me some night when I'm drunk, *querida*." He'd laughed and pulled me close to him and I'd forgotten about poetry for the rest of the night.

His eyelids—the lashes, I'd noticed, were golden—fluttered and opened. He smiled at me. "You were dreaming again last night, love," he said. "Remember?"

I pressed my lips together hard. "They'll go away," I said. "It was finding Atototl again that brought them back."

"You were crying," he persisted. "You kept saying, 'Where's my mother? Don't let them take me, Mother!' It was all in Nahuatl, but I understood most of it." He pulled my head down onto his shoulder. "Two nights and two bad dreams, Marina," he stroked my hair. "We can go back by way of Oluta. It's not far from here."

"I don't want to see her," I said.

"The old woman told you she tried to find you. Haven't you punished her enough?" Juan took my hand and pressed the tips of my fingers to his lips. "I want you to go and find her, Marina."

"Why? She's not my mother anymore, Juan."

"She is, and I want those dreams to end. They will, I think, if you'll face her and get it over with. Besides, love, I want to know her myself." He tickled my neck with his beard. "Every man should have the chance to know his mother-in-law. Do it for me."

I gave a little moan of surrender. "All right. But let's not go today."

"We've got to. If we don't leave today we won't make it back to Coatzalcoalcos before the army heads on south. We'll miss Bernal and who knows what else."

I stretched out beside him. "When I die," I said, "I don't want to go to heaven. I want my spirit to come back and haunt this room because it's been heaven to me. We don't have to get up for a little while yet, do we?"

"No, not for a little while," he whispered, and the sun made dancing patterns on the wall above us.

We left the key with the man in the village and then rode for several days, southward and down out of the mountains and onto the warm coastal plain, spending our nights under the stars. The nearer we came to Oluta, the more my spirit cringed inside me.

"I should have sent messengers ahead," I said. We were riding along a narrow forest trail that somehow set my memory to stirring. "I'm scared, Juan. I don't know what I'll say to her."

"You'll know when you see her." He ducked his head as his horse passed under the moss-hung limb of a tree.

"You've seen her," I said. "What's she like?"

"Very much like you, *querida*. Older, though, with big, sorrowful eyes. A woman who's suffered."

"Maybe she won't want to see me. Atototl says she's afraid." I lapsed into silence for a time, trembling as the forest began to take on a heartbreaking familiarity. "Juan," I whispered suddenly, "there's my tree!" He followed my pointing finger to a spot where a gnarled old monarch of the forest, half dead, twisted its way out of the earth. One convoluted root rose up to form a perfect seat. My tree, the very spot where I had sat that morning when Miahuaxitl died! It was too late to turn back now.

My heart pounding against my eardrums, I rode forward with Juan at my side. "Stay close to me—" I gripped his hand convulsively. The forest opened up into *milpas*, where the blades of new corn shone like slivers of emerald in the sun. Beyond them rose the temples of Oluta.

At the sight of the two horses, men rose up from their labors in the fields to stare. Children ran shrieking out of our path to peer at us again from the doors of their huts.

We rode slowly into the square. On our left, the deserted pyramid of Huitzilopochtli, where my father had ended his life, towered above the rest of the town. Only brown stains remained on the steps where three seasons of rain had washed away the blood of a thousand sacrifices.

Had the market always been so small? For years it had been such a grand sight to me, but then I'd seen Tlatelolco at its grandest. The tribute house was still busy, for the new masters were as hungry for wealth as the old ones had been.

The crowds in the square kept a safe distance. White men and horses were no longer unheard of in Oluta, but still they were not to be trusted. I sensed many pairs of eyes looking at me, but there was no sign of recognition. It had been such a long time.

We rode toward the council hall. At the bottom of the steps a gang of boys was playing with a ball of *chicle*, bouncing it back and forth using only knees and hips in the manner of the *tlachtli* games that had once been played on the royal ball courts. Seeing the horses, the youths left their ball and scattered like a flock of quail, all except for one, a strikingly handsome boy of about twelve who stood on the bottom step and faced the newcomers haughtily. "Run!" hissed one of his companions. "Don't be a fool, Xochipilli!"

But the youngster stood his ground defiantly. "The *tlatoani* does not run like a scared rabbit," he announced in a piping voice.

I caught my breath. The name was right, as well as the age. And the face. My little brother had his mother's beauty and his father's arrogance. Despite his bravado, he was trembling like a butterfly.

"We won't harm you," I said softly, not yet daring to reveal myself. "Is your mother well, little prince?"

"She's well. She's at home weaving. Do you want to see her?"

Breathless, I nodded to the boy. "Will you take us to her?"

"Yes," he said after a pause for thought. "But you must get off your horses and lead them. They're frightening my people. Besides, I'm the *tlatoani* and it's not right that you should be so far above me."

We dismounted. When I glanced at Juan I saw that he was trying to hide a smile. Leading the horses, we followed the boy across the square and down one of the side streets to a handsome dwelling that I did not recognize.

"Have you always lived in this house?" I asked the boy.

"Only since my father died from the curse. My mother didn't want to go back to our old house after that. Why do you want to see her?"

"I knew her . . . once." We tied our horses in the outer courtyard.

"Don't let them eat the flowers or my mother will be angry," said Xochipilli. "This way. Come." He led us through the house to the inner garden where, under a willow tree, a woman sat with her back to us. She was busy at her weaving. One end of the loom was tied to the tree and the other, a body's length away, was fastened behind her waist. Even if the woman had been a stranger, I would have recognized my mother's weaving, for Cimatl was a master of the art. The robes of Moctezuma himself would have come away second best in any comparison with the exquisite pieces that took form under her hands. This one was blue and gold . . .

The woman turned her head. Her eyes, two great black pools of sorrow, met mine and held them. She gave a little gasp. Slowly, shakily, she unfastened the loom and rose to her feet. She was not as tall as I remembered her, but then I had always seen her through a child's eyes. Her braided hair was a tapestry of ebony and silver; her face was etched with little furrows of age and suffering. Yet she was beautiful, elegant in a green *huipilli* bordered with black, and jade earrings that dangled the length of her still-graceful neck.

As I stood looking at her, suddenly all the bitterness, all the hatred I'd felt for her washed away in one surge of love. "Mother!" I whispered weakly.

"Malintzin," Cimatl answered, kneeling. Not Malinalli, not her daughter's name, but Malintzin. "My prayers to the gods have been answered," she said. "I've seen you again. Now I'm ready to die like a *tlatoani*."

"To die?" I choked, bewildered.

Her voice was bitter. "And after what I did to you, why would you come except to kill me? Well, I'm ready. I ask you only to spare your little brother. He was just a baby." Her voice softened when she spoke of her son. "But as for me, death will mean no more than an end to my suffering. I see you've brought an executioner. Tell him to be swift . . ."

Shocked beyond words, I turned and followed my mother's gaze to where Juan stood in the doorway. Her eyes were fixed on the long sword that hung at his hip, part of the uniform of almost every Spaniard of the day.

Juan had understood her. "Good Lord!" he burst out, and stepped forward, ready to do his own explaining.

I ran to him and put my arms around his waist, partly to reassure my mother. "No—you'll only frighten her more," I whispered. "Leave me alone with her."

"I suppose you're right, *querida*." With a respectful nod he retreated from the garden, leaving me to try again.

Something in Cimatl's proud, frightened eyes made me keep my distance. "My poor mother," I said softly. "You look as if I'd already killed you twenty times. Don't you think you've suffered enough?"

A look of amazement passed over her pale face. "You mean," she said hoarsely, "you've come to forgive me?"

I stood in the garden facing my mother, transfixed by what was happening inside me. I closed my eyes with the sweet, painful ecstasy of it, for it was as though the turbulent waters of my spirit had suddenly become as calm and clear as the purest mountain lake. I felt a heavy black weight break loose from the depths of my being and float upward, leaving me as light, clean and transparent as the air itself.

"No, I haven't come to forgive you," I said very slowly. Was it really my own voice speaking? "Mother . . . I've come to *thank* you."

Cimatl stared at me, mystified.

"Don't you see?" My words spilled out in a torrent. "It was you who set my feet on the path that led me to the true God—and to my husband. It's true you didn't know what you were doing, but God did." My face flushed with the excitement of my own discovery. I felt myself reaching out, open, unashamed. "And now all I want is to be your daughter again." I held out my arms and Cimatl, with a little cry, stumbled into them.

"Malinalli! My little girl . . . my child!" Both of us were weeping.

"Forgive me, Mother," I sobbed.

"Forgive you! For what?"

"For all the years I've fed on my own bitterness and self-pity. For all the times I've drunk my own posion. For not having come back and found you long before this—" Achingly, I thought of what both of us had missed. "You have a grandson in Coyoacan, the son of Hernán Cortés. And I've brought my husband, Wait! I'll get him."

Juan was with the horses. I hugged him. "It's all right now. Come on, I want her to meet you." I pulled at his hand. "Oh, wait! Why didn't I think of it?" I frowned. "If only we'd brought a gift for her. It's the custom and it would please her . . . but we haven't a thing."

Juan wrinkled his forehead. "I have something," he said. "I'll show it to you and you can decide whether you want to give it to her." Eyes twinkling mysteriously, he reached into the depths of one of his saddlebags. His hand pulled out a heavy gold chain with something attached to it. I caught my breath as I recognized the *chalchihuitl*.

"I took it to Cuba with me because it reminded me of you," he said. "It was with me on the island. If only you knew how many hours I'd spent looking at it."

"And you'd part with it now?"

He smiled at me. "I have something better."

"In that case, I want you to be the one to give it to her."

I could never have worn the *chalchihuitl* myself. For me, it was weighted down with memories. Hernán, by his own admission, had not liked it because it was "too Indian." I could not picture Juan wearing it, with his simple tastes, but on Cimatl's regal breast the beautiful green stone in its setting of gold and pearls had come home at last. My mother was delighted with the gift and with the giver as well.

"You'll have to forgive this old woman for taking your bride away from you, my son," Cimatl said, wagging an affectionate finger at Juan. "You'll have her back in good time, but we've so much to say to each other."

Xochipilli stood at one side, fidgeting restlessly and glancing at Juan. He had given me a dutiful embrace, but I realized he had no memory of me. Any bond of love between us would have to grow from its beginnings now. Having a sister was well and good, his manner clearly said, but this golden-haired, bearded stranger who'd come with her—now here was someone interesting!

The stranger gave him a friendly wink. "Little brother," he said in the best Nahuatl he could manage, "since these two women seem to have forgotten us, why don't we go and see how fast you can learn to ride a horse?"

Xochipilli gave a most unseemly whoop for a *tlatoani*, grabbed Juan's hand, and raced him out of the garden.

The next morning we left for Coatzalcoalcos, an easy day's march from Oluta. My mother went with us, with her litter-bearers and a retinue of servants, for not only had she consented to talk with the priest about her baptism, but she was anxious to see the famous Hernán Cortés, who had reshaped her nation and her daughter's life so powerfully, Xochipilli, in his glory, rode alternately behind Juan and me on our horses.

It was a happy little procession that, toward evening, drew within sight of the banners and bonfires of the Spanish camp. Yet I had been silent much of the time. In the morning Juan and I would gather my possessions and my servants and begin the trip north to Xilotepec. Hernán and the rest of the company would march south into Mayan country toward the unknown land they called Las Hibueras, or sometimes Honduras. The journey would be full of danger, I knew. Most of the area was jungle, unmapped and without roads, full of hostile Indian tribes. It was said there were rivers so wide that the tallest tree could not bridge them and so turbulent that no boat could cross them. I'd heard tales of strange animals there, snakes that could swallow a man, ants that could reduce a body to clean bones in a day. Hernán and his men could vanish into that vast green hell like raindrops into the sea and never be seen again.

"It won't be easy to say goodbye to him tomorrow, will it *querida*?" Juan reached over and took my hand. There was no trace of jealousy in his voice. I raised his fingers and rubbed them against my cheek. Dear Juan! He gave me so much of himself and demanded so little in return. I belonged to him more completely than to any man who'd ever possessed me. Yet when Hernán Cortés rode off into the jungle at dawn, a part of me would go with him. Juan knew and understood.

The yellow glow from the campfires flared up ahead. It was dusk, just light enough to see the road without difficulty. The camp would lie just over the next little hill, beyond the enormous ceiba tree that loomed ahead of us in the twilight.

Then, all at the same time, we saw something hanging from one of the thick branches of the tree. Someone's killed two of the pigs, was my first thought. But the naked forms that dangled from ropes tied to their feet were long and slender. Not pigs. Then Cimatl screamed. "They have no heads!"

"Stay here!" Juan dismounted and walked over to the tree. He looked down at two objects in the grass and turned them over one at a time with the toe of his boot. "It's the king of Tlacopan," he said grimly, ". . . and Cuauhtemoc! No, stay there, Marina! There's nothing you can do now."

No, there was nothing I could do. Numbly, I waited for Juan to return. Then we rode on with the others behind us. The camp was quiet. The laughter and quarreling, the clatter of pots and pans—all the customary babble to which I'd grown so accustomed—was strangely subdued. Men walked cautiously, talking in twos and threes or lost in their own thoughts. Abruptly, a tall figure stepped in front of us.

"Juan Jaramillo! By the saints, I've been waiting for you all day."

"Bernal!" Juan was out of the saddle and in a flash the two were hugging each other like a pair of wrestling bears.

Bernal wiped his eyes. "When they told me you were alive I was afraid to believe it." He looked at me. "And when they told me you two were married . . . Damn it! All I can say is it's about time! Come here, Señora de Jaramillo. I think I'm entitled to kiss the bride." He lifted me right off the horse with his long arms and kissed my cheek resoundingly.

Sancha had spotted us and came running up. I gave her some quick instructions for seeing to the comfort of my mother. Xochipilli, fascinated by everything he saw and determined to see more before being put to bed, had already disappeared.

Bernal looped one arm around my shoulders and one around Juan's. "We used your hunting lodge," I told him.

"Used it for what?" Bernal rolled his eyes heavenward in a caricature of innocence. "Well, now it's yours—call it a wedding gift. I only ask that you let me borrow it whenever I want to." He drew us both closer to him. "By the devil, I'm glad to see you. You're the only good thing that's happened all week."

"We went past the tree," Juan said.

"He hanged the poor bastards this morning." Bernal grimaced. "Then he had somebody cut them down, chop off their heads and string them up again by the feet. Said he wanted them left there as a warning."

"Why?" My horror crept back over me. "What could have happened?"

"Nothing. A stupid rumor. One of the lesser chiefs—he was just jealous for all I know—told Cortés that Cuauhtemoc and the king of Tlacopan were plotting a rebellion with the local natives. He had them questioned. Told each of them the other had confessed and blamed him. Whatever they answered, it was enough to hang them."

"Bernal, what's happening to him?" I shivered.

"I don't know. Some of the men say he's going mad. This obsession with Olid . . . Hell, let Olid rot in Hibueras! Nobody else cares!" He looked around to see if anyone was listening. "That's not all he's done. Here in Coatzalcoalcos he's been recruiting men by force. He's announced that any man who refuses to march with him is liable to hang for treason. They can join Cuauhtemoc on the tree, he says. I tell you, this camp's buzzing like a hornets' nest."

"I want to see him," I said.

If anything flickered in Juan's eyes he masked it quickly. "I suppose Bernal can keep me out of mischief for a while," he said.

I took hold of his hand, loving him more than ever. "I can't face him without you," I said. "Bernal will have to keep himself out of mischief."

Hernán was seated alone at the table in his tent, staring into an empty goblet. The lantern at his elbow made black valleys of the lines in his face. He looked incredibly tired. "So you've come to say goodbye," he said, when Juan and I stood before him. "Sit down. Are you happy with him, Marina *mía*?"

"Yes," I said softly.

"I thought so. You look it. When are you leaving?"

"Tomorrow," said Juan.

"Good, then there's time to talk. As you've no doubt seen, things aren't going so well for me. They're saying I'm a fool. They're saying that this is a madman's venture and that none of us will come back alive. Do you agree, Marina?"

"Yes," I said. "I agree with them."

"My wise little Marina. I've never known you to be wrong." He leaned toward us. "But I'm going anyway. Nothing is going to stop me. And what's more, I'm asking you to go with me. Both of you, of course." One drop of wine remained in his goblet. He tilted it and watched the transparent red path flow around the rim. "I can't seem to manage without you, Marina. I think I've proved that to myself and everyone else these past few days."

Juan drummed one finger on the tabletop. I could see that he was perturbed by Hernán's words. "You've got Orteguilla and at least a half-dozen Indians who can translate," he said. "Why do you need Marina?"

"Oh, I know what you're thinking, Jaramillo." Hernán flicked drop of wine from his gray-streaked beard. "Have no fear! She's yours and she'll never be mine again. In a way, she's been yours all along." He glanced up at us sharply. "Don't look so shocked. Don't you think I haven't known? I'd have let her go to you long ago, only . . . only I just couldn't bear the thought of it. I needed her. Now I need you both." He put the silver goblet down, folded his hands on the table and looked squarely at us. "I've forced others. I'll never force you. Will you come with me?"

I reached for Juan's hand. "I'm a married woman now," I said. "I go where my husband goes."

"Then I suppose it's up to you, Jaramillo." Hernán leaned back in his chair and waited.

Cimatl and her son, newly baptized Doña Marta and Don Lázaro, stood by the side of the trail and watched the long column file into the forest. Atototl stood beside them, too frail to follow her Malinalli on the strenuous journey to the south. Many of the trappings that had encumbered the expedition until now—litters, furniture, finery and extra servants—had been sent back home again. Those who had traveled the country before knew that progress would be difficult enough without them. Still, it was a grand procession. The early morning sun illuminated the golden tassels on Hernán Cortés's black and red ensign and glittered on polished helmets, cuirasses, spear tips and bucklers. Pennons fluttered in the breeze as we moved along. Horses pranced and snorted with excitement.

Riding side by side just behind Hernán, Juan and I waved to them until they were lost from sight. What a beautiful morning it was! The trees, filled with chattering birds, closed in to form a canopy over our heads, with just enough sunlight filtering through to bring out the flowers. They grew in profusion, in clusters beside the trail, on hanging vines and even in the hollows of the tree limbs.

Soon we came to a twisted stump, rising at a bend in the trail. It was covered by a vine bearing hundreds of flame-colored blossoms. Juan touched my arm cautiously. "Look," he whispered. "I've never seen so many!"

There, filling the air about the vine, were nearly a score of hummingbirds, darting in and out among the flowers, catching the light like tiny, winged rainbows.

I reached over and pressed his hand. "Remember what I told you about them once? How when a warrior dies he lives with the sun for four years and then returns to earth as hummingbird? Think, Juan, how long has it been?"

He puckered his brows in thought. "Marina . . ."

I smiled at his consternation. "Haven't you noticed how many hummingbirds there are this year?"

Juan shook his head in disbelief, but I knew he was thinking of Cholula, of Otumba, of Tenochtitlan, and counting the years.

As we passed the stump I slowed my mount and turned to look back at it for as long as I could. Soon we would be riding into jungle so dense that the trees would block out the sun and there would be no more flowers and no more hummingbirds. How lovely they were!

"Goodbye, little warriors," I murmured tenderly. And then I pressed my horse to a trot and caught up with Juan.

Epilogue

Xilotepec—31 May 1550

To:
La Señora María Jaramillo de Quesada

My sweet daughter,

I am sending these pages of your mother's to you by trusted messenger with the heartfelt assurance that you will treasure them as I have. Beatriz found them at the bottom of an old trunk during one of her housecleaning forays. They'd been put there, I suppose, along with some of your mother's things after her death, and they'd lain there forgotten for the past twenty-one years. I'll confess that they were found some months ago and I've kept them to myself until now. I've read and reread them more times than I can count. Whenever I take these precious pages in my hands I become young again, and for a while I feel the presence of my beautiful Marina beside me once more. Please forgive a sentimental old man for wanting to hold onto the past.

Beatriz, I suppose, will be happy to be rid of them. She's a fine woman but I did her an injustice by marrying again when my grief was still such a raw wound. You needed a mother and I was desperate to fill that awful, aching void that had opened up inside me. But it was cruel thing I did. Poor Beatriz has done nothing to deserve what she has: a husband whose heart was already dead and buried when he married her. I always meant to make it up to her with kindness, with generosity—ah, but a woman knows. And with a woman, nothing can compensate for love.

But enough of my complaints! Now I wish to do one last service to your mother and finish for you, in my own poor way, the story she did not live to complete.

Much of it you already know. I've told you about our ordeal in the jungles of Honduras with Hernán Cortés, how most of his men were drowned or starved, or died of tropical sicknesses, among them your mother's great friend, the *ciuacoatl*. You know too how Cortés, after seven months in the jungle, arrived at the coast to find that Olid had been stabbed, tried and hanged by Las Casas, the man he'd sent to do the job in the first place, and how, still searching for glory, he spent another year slogging aimlessly through the swamps and forests of Central America. Finally, after twenty months of green hell and with your mother about to give birth, we emerged on the coast again and caught a ship to Cuba and then to Mexico. You, my María, were born aboard that ship at great peril to your mother's life.

Cortés returned to his capital, his health, resources and prestige all sadly depleted. Although he was able to oust Salazar, whose administration had been one long string of atrocities, he never again regained control of the country he'd conquered. In 1528 he departed for Spain where he married young Juana de Zúniga and subsequently fathered six children, including a second Martín who became his heir. With no higher title than Marquis of the Valley of Oaxaca, he returned to Mexico in 1530 and reluctantly settled down to a life of ease in Cuernavaca. In 1535, following a quarrel with the viceroy, he went back to Spain where he remained, neglected and heavily in debt, until his death in 1547 at the age of sixty-two.

Perhaps the greatest sorrow of your mother's life was that Cortés did not allow her to raise their son, Martín. The boy, as you know, was legitimatized by his father and has grown to be a fine young man. He writes me occasionally from Spain where he has been made a Knight of the Order of Santiago and is soon to marry the daughter of a count.

Gonzalo de Sandoval, one of the most valiant and able men I have ever known, accompanied his beloved commander to Spain in 1528, became ill during the voyage and died at an inn in the city of Palos just a few days after reaching port. Who knows what heights he might have achieved, had he lived to the fullness of his years.

Restless Alvarado extended his own conquest into Guatemala and later into Ecuador. After the death of his Luisa he married a young Spanish noblewoman who died within a few months of the wedding. He then married her sister. In 1541 at the age of fifty-six, he met a most unhappy death when the horse of a young subordinate reared and fell on him.

Only last month I attended the funeral of Doña Isabel, born Tecuichpo, daughter of Moctezuma, and long famed as the most beautiful woman in Mexico—although I always considered your mother far lovelier. I extended my condolences to Señor Juan Cano, her third Spanish husband. He and their children will be desolate without her. Her oldest daughter, Doña Leonor Cortés Moctezuma, the wife of Juan de Tolosa, is, as you know, the child of Hernán Cortés. She was conceived after the death of Doña Isabel's first Spanish husband, Alonzo Grado, and born about five months after her second marriage, to Pedro Gallego de Andrade. What a striking girl she is!

Prince Ixtlilxochitl of Texcoco, who would have been about the same age as your mother, sickened and died in 1531.

Bernal Diaz left for Guatemala yesterday, after a delightful week as a guest in our house. It was so good to see him again! The last time was eleven years ago, when I had the honor of signing as a witness to a testimony of merit and service on his behalf.

For a long time your mother and I wondered whether Bernal would ever find it in his heart to settle in one place. Then, on a visit to Guatemala City, he met and married Teresa Becerra, the daughter of one of that city's *regidores*, and stayed to become a *regidor* himself. He's hardly changed a whit since then. The way he looks, I'd suspect the old lion's going to outlive me by twenty years. Well, let him! I'm already beginning to feel a weakening in my bones, a sort of letting go, and I find myself looking forward to the day when I embrace that sweet spirit who has never been out of my thoughts.

Bernal was most indignant because he'd just read an account of the conquest written by Cortés's secretary, a silkpanted fop named Gómara. He says it's full of lies and half-truths and that he has a good mind to sit down and write his own version of the true history of the conquest of New Spain someday. I'm hoping he will, and that his telling of it will be as warm, as witty and as blunt as he is!

And now, María, your stepmother is getting impatient because I promised to escort her to mass tonight and it's growing late, so I'd best be done with this and commend these treasured pages to your hand. Cherish them as I have; read them in the spirit of love with which they were written. Kiss your children for their grandfather. I hope that you and Luis will come to visit soon and that you will bring the children along. You and they, along with my memories, are all that I have left of my Marina.

Your affectionate father,

Juan Jaramillo

Notes on Pronunciation

In both Spanish and Nahuatl, the vowels have approximately the following sounds:

a as in FATHER
e as the *ay* in BAY
i as the *ie* in FIELD
o as in NO
u as *oo* in MOON

Spanish consonants are similar to English, with the following exceptions:

b, which has a softer sound, similar to an English *v*
d, which is pronounced like *th* between vowels and at the end of a word
h, which is always silent
j, which approximates the sound of English *h*
ll, which is pronounced *ly* in Spain (as in MILLION) and *y* (as in LAYER) in Latin America
ñ, which is pronounced like *ny* in CANYON
qu, which is pronounced like *k* before *i* and *e* and like English *qu* before *a* and *o*
r, which is trilled slightly; *rr* is doubly trilled
x, which is pronounced like English *h* at the beginning of a word and like *s* elsewhere

STRESS: In Spanish the, stress is on any syllable that carries an accent mark. Without the mark, the stress is on the final syllable, or, if a word ends in a vowel or *n* or *s*, on the second-to-last syllable.

In Nahuatl, the vowels are pronounced as they are in Spanish.

The consonants are pronounced as they are in English, with the following exceptions:

x, pronounced like English *sh*
z, pronounced like English *s*
qu, pronounced like *k* before *i* and *e* and like English *qu* before *a*.

The stress is usually on the second-to-last syllable.

Glossary

AZTEC WORDS USED IN THIS BOOK

amatl: a type of paper made from bark
atolli: a porridge made from ground corn
auianime: a sort of legalized prostitute for unmarried warriors
axin: a cosmetic which gave the skin a yellow shine
calpixque: tribute-collectors, usually of noble rank
ce acatl: (lit., "one-reed") a year-date occurring once in each fifty-two-year cycle of the Aztec calendar
chalchihuitl: a piece of polished jade
chinampas: floating mats of earth on which gardens were planted
chocolatl: chocolate
copalxocotl: a tree whose crushed fruit was used for soap.
cumal: a clay griddle, slightly dish-shaped
huipilli: a square-cut blouse, reaching to the hips or sometimes to the knees
icpalli: chairs having backs and seats, but no legs
mamalhoatzli: the Pleiades star cluster, or Seven Sisters
maquahuitl: a wooden war club edged with sharp pieces of obsidian
masa: dough made from ground corn
metatl: a hollow stone dish used for grinding
milpa: cornfield
nemontemi: the five final days of the Aztec calendar year
octli: a liquor made from the fermented pulp of the maguey plant
pochteca: one of a class of traveling merchants
quachtli: a length of cloth used as a unit of money in large transactions
tamale: a sort of meat pie with corn dough on the outside
teocalli: (lit. "god-house") a temple atop a pyramid
teponatzli: a small, two-toned wooden drum played with beaters
tilmatli: a cloak consisting of a square cloth knotted at the shoulder

tlamemes: men trained and employed as carriers
tlatoani: (lit. "speaker") chief of ruler; *uei tlatoani*: the emperor
tlaxcalli: flat cakes of corn dough, tortillas
totoloque: a throwing game played with metal balls and a metal target
tzictli: chicle, a form of chewing gum
tzitzimitles: mythical monsters
tzompantli: skull rack

SPANISH WORDS AND EXPRESSIONS USED IN THIS BOOK

abrazo: embrace
alcalde: mayor or other high city official
alcaldia: town hall
alferez: ensign, standard-bearer
alguacil: constable
amor: love; *amorcita*: little love
asno: jackass
barragana: a sort of legalized concubine, less than a wife, more than a mistress
basura: trash
cabrón: he-goat
cacique: chief
calmecac: a school for young Aztec nobles
caspa: dandruff
chinches: bedbugs
chiquita: little girl
cómo no: of course
cucaracha: cockroach
Diós: God
Don, Doña: titles of respect
fiesta: celebration
hasta mañana: until tomorrow
hermano: brother
hidalgo: a wellborn gentleman
hijo; *hija*: son; daughter
hijo de puta: son of a whore
hombre: man
heuvos: (lit, "eggs") nerve, gall
jefe: boss
luto: mourning
madre: mother
maldito: damned

medianero: go-between
mía; mío: my or mine
niña: little girl
pase: pass, come in
preciosa: precious, darling
pulque: a drink made from the fermented pulp of the maguey plant
Qué bella: What a beauty!
querida: beloved, dear
Quién sabe?: Who knows?
ranchito: a little ranch
regidor: alderman
San; Santo; Santa: Saint
Santiago: Saint James, patron of the conquest
Señor; Señora; Señorita: Mr.; Mrs.; Miss
Válgame Diós: God defend me!
Vaya con Diós: (lit. "go with God") farewell
verdad: truth; *Verdad?*: Isn't it true?
vida mía: my life (an endearment)
viruelas: smallpox